LUX

CONSEQUENCES

LUX

CONSEQUENCES

(Opal and Origin)

BOOKS THREE AND FOUR

from #1 *NYT* bestselling author

JENNIFER L. ARMENTROUT

Entangled Publishing, LLC
2614 South Timberline Road
Suite 109
Fort Collins, C. 80525
Visit our website at www.entangledpublishing.com.

Edited by Liz Pelletier
Cover design by Liz Pelletier and Heather Howland
Text design by E. J. Strongin, Neuwirth & Associates, Inc.

Hardcover ISBN 978-1-62266-481-8
Paperback ISBN 978-1-62266-449-8

Manufactured in the United States of America

First Edition June 2014

OPAL

After everything, I'm no longer the same Katy. I'm different . . . and I'm not sure what that will mean in the end. When each step we take in discovering the truth puts us in the path of the secret organization responsible for torturing and testing alien hybrids, the more I realize there is no end to what I'm capable of. The death of someone close still lingers, help comes from the most unlikely source, and friends will become the deadliest of enemies, but we won't turn back. Even if the outcome will shatter our worlds forever.

ORIGIN

Daemon will do anything to get Katy back. After the successful but disastrous raid on Mount Weather, he's facing the impossible. Katy is gone. Taken. Everything becomes about finding her. But the most dangerous foe has been there all along, and when the truths are exposed and the lies come crumbling down, which side will Daemon and Katy be standing on? And will they even be together?

OPAL

A Lux Novel

BOOK THREE

JENNIFER L. ARMENTROUT

Entangled Publishing, LLC
2614 South Timberline Road,
Suite 109
Fort Collins, CO 80525
Visit our website at www.entangledpublishing.com

Edited by Liz Pelletier
Text design by E. J. Strongin, Neuwirth & Associates, Inc.

Print ISBN 978-1-62061-009-1
Ebook ISBN 978-1-62061-010-7

Manufactured in the United States of America

First edition December 2012

This book is dedicated to the winning Daemon Invasion team.
You ladies rock!

Janalou Cruz

Nikki

Ria

Beth

Jessica Baker

Beverley

Jessica Jillings

Shaaista G

Paulina Zimnoch

Rachel

1

I wasn't sure what woke me. The howling wind from the first hardcore blizzard of the year had calmed last night and my room was quiet. Peaceful. I rolled onto my side and blinked.

Eyes the color of dew-covered leaves stared into mine. Eyes eerily familiar but lackluster compared to the ones I loved.

Dawson.

Clenching the blanket to my chest, I sat up slowly and pushed the tangled hair out of my face. Maybe I was still asleep, because I really had no idea why Dawson, the twin brother of the boy I was madly, deeply, and quite possibly insanely in love with was perched on the edge of my bed.

"Um, is . . . is everything okay?" I cleared my throat, but the words came out raspy, like I was trying to sound sexy and, in my opinion, failing miserably. All the screaming I'd done while Mr. Michaels, my mom's psycho boyfriend, had me locked in the cage in the warehouse was still reflected in my voice a week later.

Dawson lowered his gaze. Thick, sooty lashes fanned the tips of high, angular cheeks that were paler than they should be. If I'd learned anything, Dawson was damaged goods.

I glanced at the clock. It was close to six in the morning. "How did you get in here?"

"I let myself in. Your mom's not home."

With anyone else, that would've creeped the hell out of me, but I wasn't afraid of Dawson. "She's snowed in at Winchester."

He nodded. "I couldn't sleep. I haven't slept."

"At all?"

"No. And Dee and Daemon are affected by it." He just stared at me, as if willing me to understand what he couldn't put into words.

The triplets—hell, *everyone*—was coiled tight, waiting for the Department of Defense to show up as the days ticked by since Dawson escaped their Lux prison. Dee was still trying to process her boyfriend Adam's death and her beloved brother's reappearance. Daemon was trying to be there for his brother and to keep an eye on them. And though storm troopers hadn't busted up in our houses yet, none of us were relaxed.

Everything was too easy, which usually didn't bode well.

Sometimes . . . sometimes I felt like a trap had been set, and we'd galloped right into it.

"What have you been doing?" I asked.

"Walking," he said, glancing out the window. "I never thought I'd be back here."

The stuff that Dawson had been put through and made to do was too horrific to even think about. A deep ache filled my chest. I tried not to think about it, because when I did, I thought of Daemon being in that same position, and I couldn't bear it.

But Dawson . . . He needed someone. I reached up, wrapping my fingers around the familiar weight of the obsidian necklace. "Do you want to talk about it?"

He shook his head again, shaggy wisps of hair partially obscuring his eyes. It was longer than Daemon's—curlier—and probably needed a trim. Dawson and Daemon were identical, but right now, they looked nothing alike, and it was more than the hair. "You remind me of her—Beth."

I had no idea what to say to that. If he loved her half as much as I loved Daemon . . . "You know she's alive. I've seen her."

Dawson's gaze met mine. A wealth of sadness and secrets were held in its depths. "I know, but she's not the same." He paused, lowering his head. The same section of hair that always fell on Daemon's forehead toppled onto his. "You . . . love my brother?"

My chest hurt at the desolation in his voice, as if he never expected to love again, couldn't really even believe in it anymore. "Yes."

"I'm sorry."

I jerked back, losing my grip on the blanket as it fell lower. "Why would you apologize?"

Dawson lifted his head, letting out a weary sigh. Then, moving faster than I thought he was capable of, his fingers brushed over my skin—over the faint pink marks that circled both wrists from fighting against the manacles.

I hated those blemishes, prayed for the day when they completely faded. Every time I saw them, I remembered the pain the onyx had caused as it pressed into my flesh. My ruined voice was hard enough to explain to my mom, not to mention Dawson's sudden reappearance. The look on her face when she'd seen Dawson with Daemon before the snowstorm was sort of comical, though she seemed happy that the "runaway brother" had returned home. But these babies I had to hide with long-sleeved shirts. That worked during the colder months, but I had no idea how I'd hide these in the summer.

"Beth had those kinds of marks when I saw her," Dawson said quietly, pulling his hand back. "She got really good at escaping, but they always caught her, and she always had these marks. Usually around her neck, though."

Nausea rose, and I swallowed. Around her neck? I couldn't . . . "Did . . . did you get to see Beth often?" I knew they'd allowed at least one visit between them while imprisoned in the DOD facility.

"I don't know. Time was messed up for me. I kept track in the beginning, using the humans they brought to me. I'd heal them and usually if they . . . lived, I could count the days until everything fell apart. Four days." He went back to staring out the window. Through curtains that had been drawn back, all I could see was the night sky and snow-covered branches. "They hated when everything fell apart."

I could imagine. The DOD—or Daedalus, a group supposedly within the DOD—had made it their mission to use Luxens to successfully mutate humans. Sometimes it worked.

Sometimes it didn't.

I watched Dawson, trying to remember what Daemon and Dee had said about him. Dawson was the nice one, funny and charming—the male equivalent of Dee and nothing like his brother.

But this Dawson was different: morose and distant. Besides not talking to his brother, from what I knew, he hadn't said a word to anyone about what had been done to him. Matthew, their unofficial guardian, thought it was best no one pushed for more.

Dawson hadn't even told anyone how he escaped. I suspected Dr. Michaels—that lying rat bastard—had led us on a wild goose chase to find Dawson to give himself time to get the hell out of Dodge and had then "released" Dawson. It was the only thing that made sense.

My other guess was much, much darker and more nefarious.

Dawson glanced down at his hands. "Daemon . . . He loves you, too?"

I blinked, brought back to the present. "Yes. I think so."

"He told you?"

Not in so many words. "He hasn't *said it*, said it. But I think he does."

"He should tell you. Every day." Dawson tipped back his head and closed his eyes. "I haven't seen the snow in so long," he said, almost wistfully.

Yawning, I glanced out the window. The nor'easter everyone predicted had hit this little speck of the world and had made Grant County its bitch over the weekend. School had been canceled on Monday and today, and the news last night said they'd still be digging everyone out by the end of the week. The snowstorm couldn't have come at a better time. At least we had an entire week to figure out what in the hell we were going to do with Dawson.

It wasn't like he could just pop back up in school.

"I haven't seen it snow like this ever," I said. I was originally from Northern Florida, and we'd gotten a couple of freak ice storms before but never the white, fluffy stuff.

A small, sad smile appeared on his lips. "When the sun comes up, it'll be beautiful. You'll see."

No doubt. Everything would be encased in white.

Dawson jumped up and suddenly appeared on the other side of the room. A second later I felt warmth tingle along my neck and my heart rate pick up. He looked away. "My brother is coming."

No more than ten seconds later, Daemon was standing in the doorway of my bedroom. Hair messy from sleep, flannel pajama bottoms rumpled. No shirt. Three feet plus of snow outside, and he was still half naked.

I almost rolled my eyes, but that would've required I take my eyes off his chest . . . and his stomach. He really needed to wear shirts more often.

Daemon's gaze slipped from his brother to me and then back to his brother. "Are we having a slumber party? And I'm not invited?"

His brother drifted past him silently and disappeared into the hallway. A few seconds later, I heard the front door close.

"Okay." Daemon sighed. "That's been my life for the last couple of days."

My heart ached for him. "I'm sorry."

He sauntered over to the bed, his head cocked to the side. "Do I even want to know why my brother was in your bedroom?"

"He couldn't sleep." I watched him bend down and tug the covers. Without realizing it, I'd grabbed them again. Daemon pulled once more, and I easily let them go. "He said it was bothering you guys."

Daemon slipped under the covers, easing onto his side and facing me. "He's not bothering us."

The bed was way too small with him in it. Seven months ago—heck, four months ago—I would've run laughing into the hills if someone said the hottest, *moodiest* boy in school would be in my bed. But a lot had changed. And seven months ago, I didn't believe in aliens.

"I know," I said, settling on my side, too. My gaze flickered over his broad cheekbones, full bottom lip, and those extraordinarily bright green eyes. Daemon was beautiful but prickly, like a Christmas cactus. It had taken a lot for us to get to this point, being in the same room with each other and not overcome by the urge to commit first-degree murder. Daemon had to prove his feelings for me were real and he did . . . finally. He hadn't been the nicest person when we first met, and he had to really make up for that. Momma didn't raise a pushover. "He said I remind him of Beth."

Daemon's brows slammed down. I rolled my eyes. "Not in the way you're thinking."

"Honestly, as much as I love my brother, I'm not sure how I feel about him hanging out in your bedroom." He reached out with a muscular arm and used his fingers to brush a few strands of hair off my cheek, tucking them behind my ear. I shivered, and he smiled. "I feel like I need to mark my territory."

"Shut up."

"Oh, I love it when you get all bossy-pants. It's sexy."

"You're incorrigible."

Daemon inched closer, pressing his thigh against mine. "I'm glad your mom is snowed in elsewhere."

I arched a brow. "Why?"

One broad shoulder shrugged. "I doubt she'd be cool with this right now."

"Oh, she wouldn't."

More shifting and our bodies were separated by a hair-breadth. The heat that always rolled off his body swamped mine. "Has your mom said anything about Will?"

Ice coated my insides. Back to reality—a scary, unpredict-able reality where nothing was what it seemed. Namely Mr. Michaels. "Just what she said last week, that he was going out of town on some kind of conference and visiting family, which we both know is a lie."

"He obviously planned ahead so no one would question his absence."

To disappear was what he needed, because if the forced mutation worked on any level, he'd need some time off. "Do you think he'll come back?"

Running the back of his knuckles down my cheek, he said, "He'd be crazy."

Not really, I thought, closing my eyes. Daemon hadn't wanted to heal Will but his hand had been forced. The heal-ing hadn't been on the level required to change a human at the cellular scale. And Will's wound hadn't been fatal, so either the mutation would stick or it would fade away. And if it faded, Will would be back. I would bet on it. Although he conspired against the DOD for his own gain, the fact he knew it had been Daemon who mutated me was valuable to the DOD, so they'd be forced to take him back. He was a problem—a huge one.

So we were waiting . . . Waiting for both shoes to drop at once.

I opened my eyes, finding Daemon hadn't taken his off me. "About Dawson . . ."

"I don't know what to do," he admitted, trailing the back of his knuckles down my throat, over the swell of my chest. My breath caught. "He won't talk to me, and he barely talks to Dee. Most of the time, he's locked up in his bedroom or out wandering in the woods. I follow him, and he knows." Daemon's hand found its way to my hip and stayed. "But he—"

"He needs time, right?" I kissed the tip of his nose and pulled back. "He's been through a lot, Daemon."

His fingers tightened. "I know. Anyway . . ." Daemon shifted so fast, I didn't realize what he was doing until he'd rolled me onto my back and hovered above me, hands braced on either side of my face. "I've been remiss in my duties."

And just like that, everything that was going on, all our worries, fears, and unanswered questions, simply faded into nothing. Daemon had that kind of effect. I stared up at him, finding it hard to breathe. I wasn't 100 percent on what his "duties" were, but I had a very vivid imagination.

"I haven't spent a lot of time with you." He pressed his lips against my right temple and then my left. "But that doesn't mean I haven't been thinking about you."

My heart leaped into my throat. "I know you've been occupied."

"Do you?" His lips drifted over the arch of my brow. When I nodded, he shifted, supporting most of his weight on one elbow. He caught my chin with his free hand, tipping my head back. His eyes searched mine. "How are you dealing?"

Using every ounce of self-control I had, I focused on what he was saying. "I'm dealing. You don't need to worry about me."

He looked doubtful. "Your voice . . ."

I winced and uselessly cleared my throat again. "It's getting much better."

His eyes darkened as he ran his thumb along my jaw. "Not enough, but it's growing on me."

I smiled. "It is?"

Daemon nodded and brought his lips to mine. The kiss was sweet and soft, and I felt it in every part of me. "It's kind of sexy." His mouth was on mine again, taking it deeper and longer. "The whole raspy thing, but I wish—"

"Don't." I placed my hands on his smooth cheeks. "I'm okay. And we have enough things to worry about without my vocal chords. In the big scheme of things, they're nowhere near the top of the list."

He arched a brow and wow, I did sound kind of uber-mature. I giggled at his expression, ruining my newly discovered maturity. "I have missed you," I admitted.

"I know. You can't live without me."

"I wouldn't go that far."

"Just admit it."

"There you go. That ego of yours getting in the way," I teased.

His lips found the underside of my jaw. "Of what?"

"The perfect package."

He snorted. "Let me tell you, I have the perfect—"

"Don't be gross." I shivered, though, because when he kissed the hollow of my throat, there was nothing flawed about that.

I would never tell him this, but beside the . . . *pricklier* side of him that reared its ugly head from time to time, he was the closest thing to perfect I'd ever met.

With a knowing chuckle that had me squirming, he slid his hand down my arm, over my waist, and caught my thigh, hooking my leg around his hip. "You have such a dirty mind. I was going to say I'm perfect in all the ways that count."

Laughing, I wrapped my arms around his neck. "Sure you were. Completely innocent, you are."

"Oh, I've never claimed to be *that* nice." The lower part of his body sank into mine, and I sucked in a sharp breath. "I'm more—"

"Naughty?" I pressed my face into his neck and inhaled deeply. He always had this outdoorsy scent, like fresh leaves and spice. "Yeah, I know, but you're nice under the naughty. That's why I love you."

A shudder rolled through him, and then Daemon froze. A stuttered heartbeat passed and he rolled onto his side, wrapping his arms around me tightly. So tightly I had to wiggle a little to lift my head.

"Daemon?"

"It's okay." Voice thick, he kissed my forehead. "I'm okay. It's . . . early still. No school or Mom coming home, yelling your full name. Just for a little while we can pretend that crazy doesn't wait for us. We can sleep in, like normal teenagers."

Like normal teenagers. "I like the sound of that."

"Me, too."

"Me, three," I murmured, snuggling against him until we were practically one. I could feel his heart beating in tandem with mine. Perfect. This was what we needed—quiet moments of being normal. Where it was just Daemon and me—

The window overlooking the front yard blew apart as something large and white crashed through it, sending chunks of glass and snow shooting onto the floor.

My startled scream was cut off as Daemon rolled, springing to his feet as he slipped into his true Luxen form, becoming a human shape of light that shone so brightly I could only stare at him for a few precious seconds.

Holy crap, Daemon's voice said, filtering through my own thoughts.

Since Daemon hadn't gone ape wild on someone, I scrambled to my knees and peered over the edge of the bed.

"Holy crap," I said out loud.

Our precious moment of being normal ended with a body lying on my bedroom floor.

2

I stared down at the dead man, dressed like he was prepared to join the rebel alliance on the Hoth system. My thoughts were a little hazy at first, which was why it took me a few seconds to realize, dressed like that, he'd really blend in with the snow. Except for all the red streaming from his head . . .

My already pounding heartbeat skyrocketed. "Daemon . . . ?"

He pivoted, slipping back into his human form as he wrapped an arm around my waist, pulling me back from the carnage.

"He's a-an Officer," I stuttered, smacking at his arms to get free. "He's with the—"

Dawson suddenly stood in the doorway, his eyes glowing much like Daemon's were. Two bright white lights, like polished diamonds. "He was sneaking around outside by the tree line."

Daemon's arm loosened. "You . . . you did this?"

His brother's gaze flickered to the body. *It*—because I couldn't really think of *it* as a human being—lay in a twisted, unnatural heap. "He was watching the house—taking pictures." Dawson held up what looked like a melted camera. "I stopped him."

Yeah, Dawson had stopped him right through my bedroom window.

Letting go of me, Daemon made his way over to it. He knelt and pulled back the insulated white down jacket. There was a charred spot on the chest that smoked. The smell of burned flesh wafted into the air.

I climbed off the bed, pressing my hand to my mouth just in case I started to hurl. I'd seen Daemon hit a human with the Source—their power based in light—before. Nothing but ashes had remained, but it had a hole burned through its chest.

"Your aim is off, brother." Daemon let go of the jacket, the thick cords of muscles in his back bunched with tension. "The window?"

Dawson's eyes drifted to the window. "I've been out of practice."

My mouth dropped open. Out of practice? Instead of incinerating it, he'd knocked it into the air and through my window. Not to mention he'd *killed* it. No, I wouldn't think of that.

"My mom's gonna kill me," I said, feeling numb. "She's really going to kill me."

A broken window—of all the things to focus on, but it was something, something other than *it* lying on my floor.

Daemon stood slowly, eyes sheltered and jaw set like stone. He didn't take his gaze off his brother, his expression a blank mask. I turned to Dawson, our gazes colliding, and for the first time, I was scared of him.

After a quick change and bathroom visit, I stood in the living room, surrounded by aliens for the first time in days. A perk of being made of light, I guessed—the ability to go just about anywhere in a blink of an eye.

Since Adam's death, everyone had pretty much given me a wide berth, so I was unsure what was about to go down. Probably a lynching. I knew I'd want one for whoever had been responsible for the death of someone I loved.

Hands shoved into his pockets, Dawson pressed his forehead against the window by where the Christmas tree had once stood, his back to the room. He'd said *nothing* since the bat signal had been sent out and the aliens had come a-running.

Dee sat perched on the couch, her eyes fixed on her brother's back. She looked wired, her cheeks flushed with anger. I think it bothered her being in this house. Or just being near me. We hadn't had a chance to really talk after . . . everything.

My gaze slid to the other occupants. The evil wonder twins, Ash and Andrew, were seated beside Dee, their gazes locked onto the spot where their brother, Adam, had last stood . . . and died.

Part of me hated being in the living room since it reminded me of what had happened when Blake finally fessed up to his true purpose. When I had to come in here, which wasn't often since I moved all my books out of the living room, I looked right at the spot to the left of the throw carpet under the coffee table. The pine floors were bare and shiny now, but I could still see the pool of bluish liquid that I'd mopped up along with Matthew on New Year's Eve.

I wrapped my arms around my waist to try to suppress the shudder.

Two sets of footfalls came down the steps, and I turned, finding Daemon and his guardian, Matthew. Earlier, they'd gotten rid of . . . *it*, incinerating it outside, deep in the woods, after doing a quick run of the area.

Walking to my side, Daemon tugged on the edge of my hoodie. "It's been taken care of."

Matthew and Daemon had gone upstairs no more than ten minutes ago with a tarp, a hammer, and a bunch of nails. "Thank you."

He nodded as his gaze slid to his brother. "Did anyone find a vehicle?"

"There was an Expedition near the access road," Andrew said, blinking. "I torched it."

Matthew sat on the edge of the recliner, looking like he needed some liquor. "That's good, but it's not good."

"No shit," Ash snapped. Upon a closer look, she wasn't the picture perfect ice princess today. Her hair hung limply around her face, and she wore sweats. I didn't think I'd ever seen her in sweats. "That's *another* dead DOD Officer. How many does that make it? Two?"

Well, actually, that made it number four, but they didn't need to know that.

She tucked her hair back, her chipped fingernails pressing into her cheeks. "They're going to wonder where they are, you know? People don't disappear."

"People disappear all the time," Dawson said quietly without turning around, his words sucking the oxygen from the air.

Ash's bright sapphire eyes slid to him. Well, everyone pretty much looked at Dawson, since that was the first time he'd spoken since we all gathered. She shook her head but wisely remained quiet.

"What about the camera?" Matthew asked.

I picked up the melted thing, turning it over. Warmth still radiated from it. "If there're pictures, they're gone now."

Dawson turned around. "He was watching this house."

"We know," Daemon said, moving closer to me.

His brother tilted his head to the side and when he spoke, his voice was empty. "Does it matter what was on the camera? They were watching you—*her*. All of us."

Another shudder rolled through me. It was his tone more than anything that got to me.

"But next time, we need to kind of . . . oh, I don't know, talk first and then throw people through windows later." Daemon crossed his arms. "Can we try that?"

"And we can just let killers go?" Dee said, voice shaking as her eyes darkened, flashing with fury. "Because that's apparently what should happen. I mean, that Officer could've killed one of us, and you would have just let him go."

Oh, no. My stomach sank.

"Dee," Daemon said, stepping forward. "I know—"

"Don't 'I know, Dee' me." Her lower lip trembled. "You let Blake go." Her gaze moved to me, and it felt like a kick in the stomach. "Both of you let Blake go."

Daemon shook his head as he unfolded his arms. "Dee, there was enough killing that night. Enough death."

Dee reacted as though Daemon had hit her with his words, wrapping her arms around her waist for protection.

"Adam wouldn't have wanted that," Ash said quietly, sitting back against the couch. "More deaths. He was such a pacifist."

"Too bad we can't ask him how he really feels about it, isn't it?" Dee's spine stiffened, as though she was forcing herself to bite out her next words. "He's dead."

Apologies bubbled up in my throat, but before they could break free, Andrew spoke. "Not only did you guys let Blake go, you lied to us. From her?" He gestured at me. "I don't expect loyalty. But you? Daemon, you kept everything from us. And Adam died."

I whipped around. "Adam's death isn't Daemon's fault. Don't put that on him."

"Kat—"

"Then whose is it?" Dee's gaze met mine. "Yours?"

I sucked in a sharp breath. "Yeah, it is."

Daemon's body went rigid beside me, and then, always the referee, Matthew jumped in. "All right, guys, that's enough. Fighting and casting blame isn't helping anyone."

"It makes us feel better," Ash muttered, closing her eyes.

I blinked back tears and sat on the edge of the table, frustrated that I was even close to crying because I didn't own the right to those tears. Not like they did. Squeezing my knees until my fingers dug in through the soft material, I let out a breath.

"Right now, we need to get along," Matthew went on. "All of us, because we have lost too much already."

There was a pause and then, "I'm going after Beth."

Everyone in the room turned to Dawson again. Not a single thing had changed in his expression. No emotion. Nothing. And then everyone started talking at once.

Daemon's voice boomed over the chaos. "Absolutely not, Dawson—no way."

"It's too dangerous." Dee stood, clasping her hands together. "You'll get captured, and I won't survive that. Not again."

Dawson's expression remained blank, like nothing his friends or family had said made any difference to him. "I have to get her back. Sorry."

It looked like a dumbfounded stick had smacked Ash in the face. I probably looked the same. "He's insane," she whispered. "Freaking insane."

Dawson shrugged.

Matthew leaned forward. "Dawson, I know, we all know, that Beth means a lot to you, but there's no way you can get her. Not until we know what we're dealing with."

Emotion flashed in Dawson's eyes, turning them forest green. Anger, I realized. The first emotion I'd seen from Dawson was anger. "I know what I'm dealing with. And I know what they are doing to her."

Prowling forward, Daemon stopped in front of his brother, legs spread wide, arms crossed again, ready for battle. Standing together like that, it was surreal seeing them. They were identical, with the exception of Dawson's thinner frame and shaggier hair.

"I cannot allow you to do that," Daemon said, voice so low I barely heard him. "I know you don't want to hear that, but no way."

Dawson didn't budge. "You don't have a say over it. You never did."

At least they were talking. That was a good thing, right? Somehow I knew that the two brothers going toe-to-toe was oddly comforting as much as it was distressing. Something Daemon and Dee thought they'd never experience again.

Out of the corner of my eye, I saw Dee moving toward them, but Andrew reached out, catching her hand and stopping her.

"I'm not trying to control you, Dawson. It's never been about that, but you just got back from hell. We just got *you* back."

"I'm still in hell," Dawson replied. "And if you get in my way, I will drag you down with me."

A look of pain shot across Daemon's face. "Dawson . . ."

I jumped to my feet, reacting to Daemon's response without thinking. An unknown urge propelled me to do so. I guess that urge was love, because I didn't like the pain flickering across his face. Now I understood why my mom got all Mama Bear sometimes when she thought I was threatened or upset.

A wind blew through the living room, stirring the curtains and flipping the pages of Mom's magazines. I felt the girls' eyes on me and their surprise, but I was focused.

"All right, the alien testosterone right now is a little too much, and I really don't want to have an alien brawl in my house on top of the broken window and the dead body that came through it." I took a breath. "But if you two don't knock it off, I'll kick both of your asses."

Now everyone was staring at me. "What?" I demanded, cheeks flushing.

A slow, wry smile teased Daemon's lips. "Simmer down, Kitten, before I have to get you a ball of yarn to play with."

Annoyance flared deep inside me. "Don't start with me, jerk-face."

He smirked as he focused on his brother.

Beside him, Dawson looked sort of . . . amused. Or in pain— one of the two, because he really wasn't smiling or frowning. But then, without saying a word, he stalked out of the living room, the front door slamming shut behind him.

Daemon glanced at me, and I nodded. Sighing deeply, he followed his brother, because there really was no telling what Dawson would do or where he would go.

The alien Kumbaya fell apart after that. I followed them to the door, my attention fixed on Dee. We so needed to talk. First off, I had to apologize for a lot of things, and then I had to try to explain myself. Forgiveness wasn't expected, but I needed to try to talk.

I clenched the door knob until my knuckles bleached. "Dee . . . ?"

She stopped on the porch, back straight. She didn't face me. "I'm not ready."

And with that, the front door tore free from my hand and swung shut.

3

Already treading on thin ice with my mom, I decided not to mention the whole window thing when she called later in the evening, checking in. I was hoping and praying the roads were cleared enough to get someone out here to fix the window before Mom could make her way home.

I hated lying to her, though. All I'd been doing lately was lying to her, and I knew I needed to tell her everything, especially about her supposed boyfriend, Will. But how would this kind of conversation go? *Hey, Mom, our neighbors are aliens. One of them accidentally mutated me, and Will is a psycho. Any questions?*

Yeah, that was so not going to happen.

Right before I hung up, she pushed the whole going-to-see-a-doctor-for-my-voice thing again. Telling her it was just a cold worked now, but what was I going to say in a week or two from now? God, I really hoped my voice healed by then, although a part of me knew this might be permanent. Another reminder of . . . everything.

I had to tell her the truth.

Grabbing a package of instant mac and cheese, I started to pop it in the microwave but then stared down at my hands, frowning. Did they have microwave powers like Dee and Daemon did? I turned over the bowl, shrugging. I was too hungry to risk it.

Heat wasn't my thing. When Blake was training me to handle the Source and tried to teach me how to create heat— i.e. fire—I'd caught my hands on fire instead of the candle.

As I waited for the mac, I stared out the window over the sink. Dawson had been right earlier. It really was beautiful now that the sun had risen. Snow blanketed the ground and covered the branches. Icicles hung from the elms. Even now, after the sun had set, it was a beautiful white world out there. I kind of wanted to go out and play.

The microwave dinged, and I ate my unhealthy dinner standing, figuring at least I would burn off calories that way. Ever since Daemon had mutated me into this human-alien-hybrid-mutant-freak, my appetite was out of this world. There was almost nothing left in the house.

When I finished, I quickly grabbed my laptop and sat at the kitchen table. My brain had been scattered the last week, and I wanted to look up something before I forgot. Again.

Pulling up Google, I typed in DAEDALUS and hit enter. Wikipedia served up the first link and since I wasn't expecting a "Welcome to Daedalus: Secret Government Organization" website, I clicked.

And I got all acquainted with Greek myths.

Daedalus was considered an innovator, creating the labyrinth the Minotaur resided in, among other things. And he was also the daddy of Icarus, the kid who flew too close to the sun on wings fashioned by Daedalus, and then drowned. Icarus got giddy from flying and, knowing the gods, it was probably a form of passive punishment, leading to Icarus losing his wings. That and a punishment for Daedalus, who'd outfitted Icarus with the contraption that gave the boy the godlike ability to fly.

Nice history lesson, but what was the point? Why would the DOD name an organization overseeing human mutation after some dude—?

Then it struck me.

Daedalus created all kinds of things that bettered man, and the whole godlike-abilities angle was kind of like humans who were mutated by the Luxen. It was a leap in logic, but come on, the government *would* be so full of themselves they'd name their organization after a Greek legend.

Closing the laptop, I stood and found myself grabbing my jacket and going outside. I really didn't know why. Who knew if there were more Officers sneaking around? My overactive imagination formed the image of a sniper hiding in the tree and a red dot appearing on my forehead. Nice.

Sighing, I dug out a pair of gloves from the pockets of my jacket and high-stepped it through the mounds of snow. Needing some form of physical exercise to keep my brain from going into overdrive, I started rolling a ball of snow across the front yard. Everything had changed in a matter of months and then again in a matter of seconds. Going from shy, book-nerd Katy to something impossible; someone who had changed on more than a cellular level. I no longer saw the world in black and white and deep down I knew I didn't operate on basic social norms anymore.

Like thy shalt not kill or whatever.

I hadn't killed Brian Vaughn, the Officer who had been paid off by Will to turn me over to him instead of the Daedalus as I could be used as leverage to ensure that Daemon mutated him instead of killing him outright, but I had *wanted* to and I would have if Daemon hadn't beaten me to it.

I'd been totally okay with the idea of killing someone.

For some reason, killing the two evil aliens, the Arum, hadn't affected me as much as the idea of being totally kosher with killing a human did. Not sure what that said about me, because like Daemon had said once before, a life was a life, but I didn't know how to process adding the words 'okay with killing' to the bio section on my book blog.

My cotton gloves were soaked by the time I finished with the first ball and moved on to rolling the second lump of snow. This whole physical-exertion thing wasn't doing anything other than causing my cheeks to burn in the frosty, snow-scented air. Fail.

When I was done, my snowman had three sections, but no arms or face. It kind of mirrored how I felt inside. I had most of the body parts but was missing vital pieces to make me real.

I really didn't know who I was anymore.

Stepping back, I ran the sleeve of my arm over my fore-head and let out a ragged breath. Muscles burned and skin ached, but I stood there until the moon peeked out behind thick clouds, sending a slice of silvery light over my incomplete creation.

There'd been a dead body in my bedroom this morning.

I sat down in the middle of my front yard, right in a pile of cold snow. A dead body—another dead body, just like Vaughn's dead body that had fallen near the driveway, just like Adam's dead body that had lain in the living room. Another thought I'd tried to ignore wormed its way through my defenses. Adam had died trying to protect me.

Wet, cold air stung my eyes.

If I had been honest with Dee, telling her from the start about what really happened in the clearing that night we fought Baruck and about everything thereafter, she and Adam would have been more cautious about bum-rushing my house. They would've known about Blake and how he was like me, capable of fighting back on a souped-up alien level.

Blake.

I should've listened to Daemon. Instead, I wanted to prove myself. I wanted to believe that Blake had good intentions when Daemon had sensed something off about the boy. I should've known when Blake had thrown a knife at my head and left me alone with an Arum that there was something very demented about him.

Except was Blake demented? I didn't think so. He'd been desperate. Frantic to keep his friend Chris alive and trapped by what he'd become. Blake would've done anything to protect Chris. Not because his life was joined with the Luxen, but because he cared for his friend. Maybe that's why I hadn't killed him, because even in those moments where everything was pure chaos, I saw a part of me in Blake.

I'd been okay with the idea of killing his uncle to protect my friends.

And Blake had killed my friend to protect his.

Who was right? Was anyone?

I was so caught up in my thoughts, I didn't pay much attention to the warmth skipping across my neck. I jumped when I heard Daemon's voice.

"Kitten, what are you doing?"

I twisted around and lifted my head. He stood behind me, dressed in a thin sweater and jeans. His eyes glimmered under thick lashes.

"I was making a snowman."

His gaze drifted beyond me. "I see. It's missing some stuff."

"Yeah," I said morosely.

Daemon frowned. "That doesn't tell me why you're sitting in the snow. Your jeans have to be soaked." There was a pause and damn if that frown didn't turn upside down. "Wait. That means I'd probably get a better look at your butt, then."

I laughed. Leave it to Daemon to always take things down a level or two.

He glided forward as if the snow moved out of the way for him and sat beside me, crossing his legs. Neither of us said anything for a moment, and then he leaned over, pushing me with his shoulder.

"What are you really doing out here?" he asked.

I'd never been able to hide anything from him, but I really wasn't ready to go *there* with him yet. "What's going on with Dawson? Has he run off yet?"

Daemon looked like he was going to push the subject for a moment but then just nodded. "Not yet, because I followed him around today like a babysitter. I'm thinking about putting a bell on him."

I laughed softly. "I doubt he'll appreciate that."

"I don't care." A little bit of anger flashed in his voice. "Running off after Beth isn't going to end well. We all know that."

No doubt. "Daemon, do you . . ."

"What?"

It was hard to put into words what I thought, because once I said them, they became real. "Why haven't they come after Dawson? They have to know he's here. It would be the first place he'd come back to if he had escaped. And they've obviously been watching." I gestured back at my house. "Why haven't they come for him? For us?"

Daemon glanced at the snowman, silent for several heartbeats. "I don't know. Well, I have my suspicions."

I swallowed past the lump of fear growing in my throat. "What are they?"

"You really want to hear them?" When I nodded, he went back to staring at the snowman. "I think the DOD was aware of Will's plans, knew he was going to arrange for Dawson to be released. And they let it happen."

I drew in a shallow breath as I picked up a handful of snow. "That's what I think."

He glanced at me, eyes hidden behind his lashes. "But the big question is why."

"It can't be good." I let most of the snow slip through my gloved fingers. "It's a trap. Has to be."

"We'll be ready," he said after a few seconds. "Don't worry, Kat."

"I'm not worried." Such a lie, but it seemed like the right thing to say. "We need to stay ahead of them somehow."

"True." Daemon stretched out his long legs. The underside of his jeans was a darker blue now. "You know how we stay under the humans' radar?"

"By pissing them off and alienating yourselves?" I gave him a cheeky grin.

"Ha. Ha. No. We pretend. We constantly pretend like we're not different, that nothing's happening."

"I'm not following."

He flopped onto his back, his dark hair splashing against the white. "If we pretend like we've gotten away with Dawson being released, that we don't think anything's suspicious or that we know they're aware of our abilities, then it may buy us time to figure out what they're doing."

I watched him throw his arms out to his sides. "You think they'll slip up then?"

"Don't know. I wouldn't put money on it, but it kind of gives us the edge. It's the best we have right now."

The best we had kind of sucked.

Grinning as if he didn't have a care in the world, he started sliding his arms through the snow, along with his legs, moving them like windshield wipers. Really nice-looking windshield wipers.

I started to laugh, but it got stuck in my throat as my heart swelled. Never in my life did I think Daemon would be into the snow-angel-making business. And for some reason, that made me all warm and fuzzy.

"You should try it," he coaxed, eyes closed. "It gives you perspective."

I doubted it could give me perspective on anything, but I lay down beside him and followed suit. "So I Googled Daedalus."

"Yeah? What did you find out?"

I told him about the myth and my suspicions, which Daemon smirked at. "It wouldn't surprise me—the ego behind that."

"You'd know," I said.

"Hardy har-har."

I grinned. "How is this giving me perspective, by the way?"

He chuckled. "Wait for a couple more seconds."

I did and when he stopped and sat, he reached over, grasping my hand, and pulled me up with him. We brushed the snow off of each other—Daemon taking a little longer than necessary on certain areas. Finished, we turned to our snow angels.

Mine was much smaller and less even than his, like I was top heavy. His was perfect—show-off. I folded my arms around me. "Waiting for the epiphany to happen."

"There isn't one." He dropped a heavy arm over my shoulder, leaned in, and pressed a kiss against my cheek. His lips were so, so warm. "But it was fun, wasn't it? Now . . ." He steered me back to the snowman. "Let's finish with your snowman. It can't be incomplete. Not with me here."

My heart tripped up. There were so many times I wondered if Daemon could read minds. He could be amazingly spot-on when he wanted. I tilted my head back against his shoulder, wondering how he'd gone from douchebag extraordinaire to this . . . this guy who still infuriated me but also constantly surprised and amazed me.

To this guy I'd fallen madly in love with.

4

When the plows came out, clearing a path through town and down the back roads, Matthew got a glass repair company here in the nick of time. They'd left minutes before Mom arrived home on Friday, looking like she'd ate, slept, and saved lives in her polka-dot scrubs.

She threw her arms around me, nearly taking me to the floor. "Baby, I've missed you!"

I hugged her back just as tightly. "Same here. I . . ." I let go, blinking back tears. Looking away, I cleared my throat. "Have you actually showered in the last week?"

"No." She tried to hug me again, but I jumped back. She laughed but I caught a flash of sadness in her eyes just before she turned toward the kitchen. "Just kidding.. There're showers at the hospital, honey. I'm clean. I swear!"

I followed behind her, wincing as she went straight to the raided fridge. Mom threw open the door and then stepped back, looking over her shoulder. Wisps of blond hair sneaked out of her bun.

Her delicately arched brows lowered and her perky little nose wrinkled. "Katy . . . ?"

"Sorry." I shrugged. "I was snowed in. And I got hungry. A lot."

"I can tell." She closed the door. "It's okay. I'll run to the store later. The roads aren't bad now." She paused, rubbing her brow. "Well, some look like you'd need a snowmobile to get down, but I can make it into town."

Which meant there'd be school on Monday. Boo. "I can go with."

"That would be nice, honey. As long as you plan not to put stuff in the cart and then throw a fit when I take it out."

I gave her a bland look. "I'm not two."

Her saucy smile was cut off by her yawn. "I've barely had any down time. Most of the nurses couldn't make it in. I covered the ER, prenatal ward, and my favorite," she said, grabbing a bottle of water, "the detox floor."

"That blows." I trailed behind her again, feeling incredibly Mommy needy.

"You have no idea." She took a sip, stopping at the base of the stairs. "I've been bled on, peed on, and thrown up on. In that order and sometimes not."

"Ew," I said. Mental note: nursing was now placed with school administration in the Not Going To Happen Possible Job list.

"Oh!" She started up the stairs, twisting halfway around and teetering on the edge of the step. Oh, dear. "Before I forget, I'm changing shifts next week. Instead of working at Grant on the weekends, it will be Winchester. Busier in the city and more action on the weekends than doing the shift around here, and Will works weekends anyway, so it works out better."

Which also meant more time away— *What*? My heart stuttered and there was this falling, spinning-down feeling. "What did you say?"

Mom frowned. "Honey, your voice . . . I really want to look at your throat. Okay? Or we can get Will to take a look. I'm sure he won't mind."

I was frozen. "Have . . . have you heard from Will?"

"Yes, we've talked while he's been out west attending an Internal Med conference." She smiled slowly. "Are you okay?"

No. I was not okay.

"Here," she said. "Come upstairs, and I'll take a look at your throat with the scope—"

"When . . . when did you talk to Will?"

Confusion flickered across my mom's pretty face. "A couple of days ago. Honey, your voice—"

"Nothing's wrong with my voice!" It cracked halfway through, of course, and Mom stared at me like I was telling her I was considering making her a grandma. This was my chance to tell her the truth.

I went up a step and stopped. All the words—the truth—got tangled up somewhere between my vocal chords and my lips. I hadn't cleared telling my mom the truth with anyone—or at least given any of them a heads-up. And would she believe me? Worst yet, Mom . . . She loved Will. I knew she did.

Stomach twisting into raw knots, I forced the panic out of my voice. "When is Will coming home?"

She watched me closely, her lips pressing into a pinched line. "Not for another week, but Katy . . . Are you sure that's what you wanted to say?"

Was he really coming back? And if he was talking to Mom, did that mean he'd gone through the mutation successfully and Daemon and I were now linked to him? Or had it faded?

I needed to talk to Daemon. Now.

My mouth was so dry I couldn't swallow. "Yes. Sorry. I have to go . . ."

"Go where?" she asked.

"See Daemon." I backpedaled, heading for my boots.

"Katy." She waited until I stopped. "Will told me."

Ice drenched my veins as I turned around slowly. "Told you what?"

"He told me about you and Daemon—that you two had decided to start seeing each other." She paused and got that *Mom* look. The one that said, *I'm so disappointed in you.* "He said you mentioned it and honey, I just wish you would've told me instead. Finding out through someone else about my daughter's boyfriend isn't how I wanted to learn."

My jaw hit the floor.

She said something else, and I think I nodded. Honestly, she could've been telling me that Thor and Loki had a battle royale down the street. I wasn't hearing her anymore. What was Will up to?

When Mom finally gave up on trying to hold a conversation with me, I hurried to my boots and hauled butt to Daemon's house. When the door swung open, I already knew it wasn't Daemon answering. I hadn't experienced the freaky alien connection thing, the warmth on the back of my neck whenever he was near.

But Andrew's blazing ocean-colored eyes weren't what I was expecting.

"You," he said, contempt lacing his tone.

I blinked. "Me?"

He folded his arms. "Yeah, you—as in Katy, the little human-alien-hybrid baby."

"Um, okay. I need to see Daemon." I started to step in, but he moved quickly, blocking me. "Andrew."

"Daemon's not here." He smiled, and there wasn't an ounce of warmth in it.

Folding my arms, I refused to back down. Andrew never liked me. I don't even think he liked people in general. Or puppies. Or bacon. "And where is he?"

Andrew stepped out, shutting the door behind him. He was so close that the toes of his boots touched mine. "Daemon took off this morning. I assume he's following Rain Man."

Fury flashed through me. "There's nothing wrong with Dawson."

"Is that so?" Andrew cocked an eyebrow. "I think he's said three coherent sentences a day and that's about it."

My hands curled into fists against my sides. A soft breeze picked up my hair, stirring the strands around my shoulders. I so wanted to hit him. "He's been going through God knows what. Have some compassion, ass. Anyway, I don't know why I'm talking to you. Where's Dee?"

The smirk faded from his face, replaced by cold, hard hatred. "Dee is here."

I waited for a little more detail. "Yeah, I figured that much." When there was still no response, I was two seconds from showing him what a little human-alien-hybrid baby could do. "Why are you here?"

"Because I was invited." He leaned down, close enough to kiss, and I had no other option but to take a step back. He followed. "And you're not."

Ouch. Okay, that stung. Before I knew it, my back hit the railing and I was trapped. There was nowhere for me to go, and Andrew wasn't budging. I felt the Source, the pure energy that the Luxen—and now I—could harness building inside me, spreading over my skin like static electricity.

I could make Andrew move.

Andrew must've seen something in my eyes because he sneered. "Don't even think about pulling that crap with me, because you push? I'll push right back. There won't be any lost sleep over it."

Fighting my body's response to lay it on him was the hardest thing. My human side and the other side, whatever it was, wanted to tap into that power and use it—exploit it. It was like an unused muscle flexing. I remembered the dizzying rush of power, and the release.

A part of me, a teeny, tiny part of me liked it, and that scared the crap out of me.

Good for Andrew, because the fear coiling tightly inside had knocked the wind right out from underneath me. "Why do you hate me?" I asked.

Andrew cocked his head to the side. "It's the same thing as it was with Beth. Everything was fine, and then she came around. We lost Dawson and you know damn well we haven't gotten him back, not really. And now it's happening with Daemon, except this time around, we lost Adam in the mess. He's gone."

For the first time, something other than arrogant disdain peered through his crystalized eyes. Pain—the kind of suffering I was well familiar with. The same shattered, hopeless look I'd worn after my dad passed away from cancer.

"He's not going to be the only one we lose," Andrew continued, voice hoarse. "You know that, but do you care? No. Humans are ultimately the most selfish life-form there is. And don't try to pretend you're any better. If you were, you would've stayed away from Dee in the beginning. You would've never gotten attacked, and Daemon would've never had to heal you. None of this would've happened. It's your fault. It's on your head."

Yeah, the rest of my day sort of sucked. I was worried about what Dawson had done that required Daemon to chase after him all day and feared the DOD was waiting to bring us all in. On top of that, I was freaking out over whatever Will had up his sleeve, and after that conversation with Andrew, I felt like I needed to crawl under my blankets.

And I did for about an hour. My self-pity always had a time limit because I usually got annoyed with myself.

Pulling my head out of my rear, I cracked open my laptop and started doing some reviews. Since I'd been snowed in and Daemon had mostly been busy with Dawson, I'd gotten four books read. Not my all-time high score, but pretty good considering I'd been slacking like a mofo on the reviews.

It always felt good typing up a review on a book I enjoyed and I went all out, finding bizarre pictures to emphasize the wow factor. I preferred ones with cute kittens and llamas. And Dean Winchester. Hitting 'publish post' cracked a smile.

One down, three more to go.

I spent the rest of the day spewing out reviews and then stalking a few of my favorite bloggers. One of them had a header on their blog I'd do terrible things for. I was never that good at web design, which explained my less than stellar background.

After a quick run to the grocery store with Mom and dinner, I was about to start a manhunt for Daemon when I felt a warm tingle along the back of my neck.

I shot from the kitchen, nearly barreling through a startled Mom. I whipped open the door an instant after Daemon knocked and then threw myself—literally—into his not-so-waiting arms.

Unprepared for my attack, he stumbled back a step. But then he laughed deeply against the top of my head and wrapped his arms around me. I held on, squeezing the hell out of his shoulders, and we were so tightly pressed against each other that I could feel his heart picking up as fast as mine.

"Kitten," he murmured. "You know how much I like it when you say hi this way."

Head buried in the space between his neck and shoulder, which smelled like spice and male, I murmured something unintelligible.

Daemon lifted me clear off my feet. "You've been worried, haven't you?"

"Mmm-hmm." Then I remembered how much I'd been worried all freaking day. I broke free and smacked his chest. Very, very hard.

"Ouch!" He grinned, though, as he rubbed his chest. "What was that for?"

I folded my arms and tried to keep my voice low. "Have you heard of a cell phone?"

He arched his brow. "Why, yes, it's this small thing that has all these cool apps on it—"

"Then why didn't you have it on you today?" I interrupted.

Leaning down, his lips grazed my cheek as he spoke, sending shivers through me. Not fair. "Going in and out of my true form all day kind of kills the electronics."

Oh. Well, I hadn't thought of that. "You should've checked in, though. I thought . . ."

"You thought what?"

I gave him a *Do I really need to explain it?* look.

The twinkling in Daemon's eyes faded. Placing his hands on my cheeks, he brought his lips to mine, kissing me sweetly. When he spoke, he kept his voice low. "Kitten, nothing's going to happen to me. I'm the last person you need to worry about."

I closed my eyes, breathing in his warmth. "See, that's possibly the stupidest thing you've ever said."

"For real? I say a lot of stupid things."

"I know. So that's saying something." I took a breath. "I'm not trying to act like one of those obsessive girlfriends, but things . . . things are different with us."

There was a pause, and then his lips stretched into a smile. "You're right."

Hell froze over. Pigs were flying. "Come again?"

"You're right. I should've checked in at some point. I'm sorry."

The world was flat. I didn't know what to say. According to Daemon, he was right about 99 percent of the time. Wow.

"You're speechless." He chuckled. "I like that. And I also like you all feisty. Want to hit me again?"

I laughed. "You're a—"

Opening the door behind me, Mom cleared her throat and said, "I don't know what it is with you two and porches, but come in; it's freezing out there."

Cheeks flaming an unholy red, I couldn't do anything to stop Daemon. He let go, sauntered inside, and immediately started charming my mom until she was nothing but a gooey puddle in the middle of the foyer.

He loved her new haircut. She got one? I guessed her hair did look different. Like she'd washed it or something. Daemon told her that her diamond earrings were beautiful. The rug below the steps was really nice. And that leftover scent of mystery dinner—'cause I still hadn't figured out what she fed me—smelled divine. He admired nurses worldwide, and by that point, I couldn't keep my eye rolls to a minimum.

Daemon was ridiculous.

I grabbed his arm and started pulling him to the steps. "Okay, well, this has been nice . . ."

Mom folded her arms. "Katy, what did I tell you about the bedroom?"

And here I thought my face couldn't get any redder. "Mom . . ." I tugged on Daemon's arm. He didn't move.

Her expression remained the same.

I sighed. "Mom, it's not like we're going to have sex with you home."

"Well, honey, it's good to know that you only have sex when I'm not home."

Daemon coughed as he fought a smile. "We can stay—"

Shooting him a death glare, I managed to get him to come up a step. *"Mo-om."* Whininess ensued.

Finally, she relented. "Keep the door open."

I beamed. "Thanks!" Then I pivoted around, dragging Daemon to my bedroom before he turned my mom into a fangirl. Pushing him inside, I shook my head at him. "You're terrible."

"And you're naughty." He backed up, grinning. "Thought she said leave the door open."

"It is." I gestured behind me. "It's cracked. That's open."

"Technicalities," he said, sitting down on the bed as he raised one arm, curling his fingers at me. A wicked gleam deepened the green hue of his eyes. "Come on . . . come closer."

I stood my ground. "I didn't get you up here to indulge in wild monkey lust."

"Crap." He dropped his hand to his lap.

Forcing myself not to laugh, because it only encouraged him, I decided to cut to the chase. "We need to talk." I crept closer to the bed, making sure my voice was low. "Will's been talking to my mom."

His eyes narrowed. "Details."

I sat beside him, tucking my legs against my chest. As I told him what my mom had said, the muscle in his jaw started ticking like a heartbeat. The news didn't sit well and there was no way for any of us to find out if the mutation had held or what he was up to, short of asking Will, and yeah right on that.

"He can't come back," I said, rubbing my temples, where a throbbing seemed to be in tune with the muscle in Daemon's jaw. "If the mutation didn't hold, he knows you'll kill him. And if it did . . ."

"He has the upper hand," Daemon admitted.

I flopped onto my back. "God, this is a mess—a freaking mess of epic proportions." It was like we were damned if we did from every corner. "If he comes back, I can't let him near my mom. I have to tell her the truth."

Daemon was silent as he shifted on the bed until he was leaning against the headboard. "I don't want you to tell her."

I frowned as I tipped my head to the side, meeting his stare. "I need to tell her. She's in danger."

"She's in danger if you tell her." He folded his arms. "I understand why you want to and need to, but if she knows the truth, she's in danger."

Part of me got that. Any human who knew the truth was at risk. "But keeping her in the dark is worse, Daemon." I sat up and twisted toward him, resting on my knees. "Will is a psycho. What if he comes back and picks up where he left off?" Bile rose in my throat. "I can't let that happen."

Daemon ran a hand through his hair, the gesture stretching the thin material of his long-sleeved shirt over his bicep. He exhaled long and hard. "First we need to find out if Will actually has intentions of coming back."

Irritation spiked. "And how do you propose we do that?"

"That I haven't figured out." Daemon flashed a weak grin. "But I will."

I sat up, frustrated. Logically, we had time. Not an endless supply—days or a week if we were lucky—but there was time. I just didn't like the idea of keeping her in the dark.

"What were you doing all day? Chasing Dawson?" I asked, letting the topic drop for now. When he nodded, I felt for him. "What was he doing?"

"He was just roaming around, but he was trying to shake me. I know he wanted to get back to that office building and if I hadn't followed him, he would've. The only reason I feel safe leaving him alone right now is because Dee has him cornered." He paused, looking away. His shoulders stiffened as if a terrible weight had settled on them. "Dawson . . . He's going to get himself captured again."

5

Color me surprised when Daemon swung by early Saturday evening and wanted to go out. Like, brave snow-slick roads and do something normal. A date. As if we had the luxury of doing such a thing. And I couldn't help but remember what he had said to me when I'd been in his bed and so ready to give him the go-ahead.

He'd wanted to do things right. Dates. Movies.

Dee was currently on Dawson-babysitting duty, and Daemon felt confident enough to leave her with him.

I dug out a pair of dark denim jeans and a red turtleneck. Taking a few extra minutes with my makeup, I then bounced down the stairs. It took me about a half an hour to weasel Daemon away from my mom.

Maybe I wouldn't have to worry about her and Will. Maybe I needed to worry about her and Daemon. Cougar.

Once inside the comfy interior of Dolly, his SUV, he kicked on the heat and slid me a grin. "Okay. There are some rules about our date."

My brows rose. "There are?"

"Yep." He eased Dolly around and started down the driveway, careful to avoid the thick patches of black ice. "Rule number one is we don't talk about anything DOD related."

"Okay." I bit down on my lip.

He glanced at me sideways, as if he knew I was fighting a stupid love-struck grin. "Rule number two is that we don't talk about Dawson or Will. And number three, we focus on my awesomeness."

Okay. No fighting my grin. It spread ear to ear. "I think I can deal with these rules."

"You better, because there is punishment for breaking the rules."

"And what kind of punishment would that be?"

He chuckled. "Probably the sort of punishment you'd enjoy."

Warmth infused my cheeks and veins. I chose not to respond to that statement. Instead, I reached for the radio station at the same time Daemon did. Our fingers brushed and static raced down my arm, spreading to his flesh. I jerked back, and he laughed again, but the sound was husky and made the roomy SUV seem way too small.

Daemon settled on a rock station but kept the volume low. The trip to town was uneventful but fun . . . because nothing crazy happened. He picked out an Italian restaurant, and we were seated at a small table lit by flickering candles. I glanced around. None of the other tables had candles. They were covered with cheesy red-and-white-checkered mats.

But our wooden table was bare except for those candles and two wineglasses filled with water. Even the napkins looked like real linen.

Considering the possibilities as we were seated, my heart did a flip-flop. "Did you . . . ?"

He propped his elbows on the table and leaned forward. Soft shadows danced over his face, highlighting the arch of his cheekbones and the curve of his lips. "Did I do what?"

"Arrange this?" I waved at the candles.

Daemon shrugged. "Maybe . . ."

I tucked my hair back, smiling. "Thank you. It's very . . ."

"Awesome?"

I laughed. "Romantic—it's very romantic. And awesome, too."

"As long as you think it is awesome, then it was worth it." He glanced up as the waitress arrived at our table. Her nametag read RHONDA.

When she turned to take Daemon's order, her eyes glazed over—a common side effect of being around Mr. Awesome, I was learning. "And what about you, sweetie?"

"Spaghetti with meat sauce," I said, closing the menu and handing it over.

Rhonda glanced at Daemon, and I think she might have sighed. "I'll bring your breadsticks out immediately."

After we were alone, I grinned at my date. "I think we're going to get extra meatballs."

He laughed. "Hey, I'm good for some things."

"You're good for a lot of things." The moment that left my mouth, I blushed. Whoa. That could be perceived in many ways.

Surprisingly, Daemon let it slide and started teasing me about a book he'd seen in my bedroom. It was a romance novel. Typical barrel-chested alpha male cover model with sixteen-pack abs. By the time our *heaping* pile of breadsticks arrived, I'd almost convinced him that he'd be a perfect cover model for one of those books.

"I don't wear leather pants," he said, biting into the garlicky and buttery goodness.

And that was a damn shame. "Still. You have the look."

He rolled his eyes. "You just like me for my body. Admit it."

"Well, yeah . . ."

His lashes lifted and his eyes glittered like jewels. "I feel like man-candy."

I busted out laughing. But then he asked a question I hadn't expected. "What are you going to do about college?"

I blinked. College? Sitting back, my gaze dropped to the small flame. "I don't know. I mean, it's not really possible unless I go to one near a buttload of quartz—"

"You just broke a rule," he reminded me, lips forming a half smile.

I rolled my eyes. "What about you? What are you doing for college?"

He shrugged. "Haven't decided yet."

"You're running out of time," I said, sounding like Carissa, who loved to remind me of that every time we talked.

"Actually, we've both run out of time, unless we do a late acceptance."

"Okay. Rule-breaking aside, how is it possible? Do online classes?" He shrugged again, and I sort of wanted to stab him in the eye with my fork. "Unless you know of a college that has . . . a suitable environment?"

Our meals arrived, staving off the conversation while the waitress grated cheese over Daemon's plate. She eventually offered me some. And the moment she left, I pounced. "So, do you?"

Knife and fork in hand, he started cutting into a piece of lasagna the size of a truck. "The Flatirons."

"The what-a-what?"

"The Flatirons is a mountain just outside of Boulder, Colorado." He cut his meal into tiny bites. Daemon had such delicate eating habits, while I was slopping my spaghetti around my plate. "They are full of quartzite. Not as well-known or as visible as some places, but they are there, under several feet of sediment."

"Okay." I tried to eat my spaghetti in daintier bites. "What does that have to do with anything?"

He peered up through sooty lashes. "University of Colorado is about two miles from the Flatirons."

"Oh." I chewed slowly and then suddenly my appetite vanished. "Is . . . is that where you want to go to school?"

There was another shrug. "Colorado isn't a bad place. I think you'd like it."

Staring at him, I forgot about the food. Was he getting at what I thought he was getting at? I didn't want to jump to conclusions, and I was too afraid to ask, because he could be suggesting that it was a place I'd like to visit versus living there . . . with him. And that would be super mortifying.

Hands cold, I set down my fork. What if Daemon did leave? For some reason I'd been operating on the assumption that he wouldn't leave here. Ever. And I'd accepted, on a subconscious level, being stuck here, mainly because I really hadn't considered finding another place that was protected from the Arum.

My gaze dropped to my plate. Had I accepted staying here because of Daemon? Was that right? *He's never said he loves you*, an insidious and annoying voice whispered. *Not even after you've said it.*

Ah, the stupid voice had a point.

Out of nowhere, a breadstick tapped the tip of my nose. My head jerked up. Sprinkles of garlic salt rained down.

Daemon held the stick between two fingers, brows arched. "What were you just thinking about?"

I brushed off the crumbs. A pitching sensation filled my stomach, and I forced a smile. "I . . . I think Colorado sounds nice."

Liar, said his expression, but he went back to his food. Strained silence descended between us, which was a first. I forced myself to enjoy the food, and the funniest thing happened. With Daemon's light teasing and the conversation turning to different subjects, like his obsession with all things ghost-related, I *was* having fun again.

"Do you believe in ghosts?" I asked, chasing after the last of my noodles.

He cleared his plate, sat back, and sipped from his glass. "I think they exist."

Surprise flickered through me. "Really? Huh. I thought you just watched those ghost shows for entertainment."

"Well, I do. I like the one where the guy yells, 'Dude! Bro!' every five seconds." He smiled when I laughed. "But in all seriousness, it can't be impossible. Too many people have witnessed things that can't be explained."

"Like too many people witnessing aliens and UFOs." I grinned.

"Exactly." He set down his glass. "Except the UFOs are total bunk. Government's responsible for all Unidentified Flying Objects."

My mouth dropped open. Why was I even surprised?

Rhonda appeared with our check, and I was reluctant to leave. The whole date thing was a way too brief moment of normalcy both of us had been sorely lacking. As we headed to the front of the restaurant, I wanted to grab his hand and wrap my fingers around his, but I refrained. Daemon did a lot of crazy things in public, but hand-holding?

So didn't seem up his alley.

There were a couple of kids from school seated by the door. Their eyes got all saucer-sized when they saw us. Considering Daemon and I had this hate-hate relationship for most of the year, I could understand their surprise.

It had started to flurry while we were inside and a thin coating of snow covered the parking lot and cars. The white stuff was still coming down. Stopping by the passenger side, I tipped my head back and opened my mouth, catching a tiny flake on the tip of my tongue.

Daemon's eyes narrowed on me and the intensity in his gaze caused a nervous fluttering low in my stomach. An urge to go forward, cross the distance between us, hit me hard, but I couldn't move. My feet were rooted to the ground and the air expelled from my lungs.

"What?" I whispered.

His lips parted. "I was thinking about a movie."

"Okay." I felt hot even though it snowed. "And?"

"But you've broken the rules, Kitten. Several times. You're owed some punishment."

My heart jumped. "I *am* a rule breaker."

His lips tilted up on one corner. "You are."

Moving lightning fast, Daemon was in front of me before I could say another word, cupping my cheeks, tilting my head back as he lowered his. Lips brushed against mine, sending a shiver down my spine. The initial touch was feather soft, heartbreakingly tender. Then the contact evolved with the second sweep of his lips and mine parted, welcoming him.

I really liked this form of punishment.

Daemon's hands slid down to my hips, and he pulled me against him at the same time we were moving backward, stopping when my back pressed against the cool, damp metal of his car—hopefully his car. I doubted someone would want a couple doing what we were doing on their vehicle.

Because we were kissing, really kissing, and there wasn't a centimeter of space between our bodies. My arms found their way around his neck, fingers sliding through silky locks covered in light snow. We fit everywhere it was important.

"Movie?" he murmured, kissing me again. "And then what, Kitten?"

I couldn't think around how he tasted and felt. How my heart was jackhammering as his fingers slid under my turtleneck, splaying along my bare skin. And I wanted to be bare—completely and only with him, always him. He knew what the "and then what" was. Doing things right . . . and dear God, I wanted to do those right things right now.

Since I couldn't get my mouth to work between his drugging kisses, I opted to do the show-not-tell thing, sliding my hands down to his jean-clad hips. Hooking my fingers in the belt hoop, I tugged him against me.

Daemon growled, and my pulse pounded. Yeah, he got it. His hand slid up, fingertips brushing against lace and—

His cell phone went off in his pocket, shrilling as loud as a fire alarm. I thought for a tiny instant he was going to ignore it, but he pulled back, panting. "One second."

He kissed me quickly, keeping one hand where it was while he dug out his phone. I burrowed my face against his chest, breathing rapidly. He left my senses spinning in a delicious mess that was out of control.

When Daemon spoke, his voice was rough. "This better be really important—"

I felt him stiffen, his heart rate picking up, and I knew instantly something bad had happened. Pulling back, I peered up at him. "What?"

"Okay," he said into the phone, his pupils becoming luminous. "Don't worry, Dee. I'll take care of it. I promise."

Fear cooled the heat inside me. As Daemon lowered the phone, sliding it back into his pocket, my stomach dropped. "What?" I asked again.

Every single muscle in his body locked up. "It's Dawson. He made a run for it."

6

I stared at Daemon, praying I'd misunderstood him, but the keen desperation and the hint of fury in his ultra-bright eyes told me I hadn't.

"I'm sorry," he said.

"No. I completely understand." I tucked my hair back. "What can I do?"

"I need to go," he said, grabbing his keys from his pocket and placing them in my hand. "And I mean I need to go really fast. You should go home and stay there." He then handed me his cell. "Keep that in the car. I'll be back as soon as possible."

Go home? "Daemon, I can help you. I can go—"

"Please." He grasped my face again—his hands warm against my now-cool cheeks. He kissed me, part longing and part angry. Then he backed away. "Go home."

And then he was gone, moving too fast for any human eye to track. I stood there for several moments. We'd had an hour, maybe two, before everything went to shit? My hands tightened around the keys. Sharp metal dug into my flesh.

A ruined date was the least of my problems.

"Dammit." I spun and jogged around the SUV. Climbing in, I readjusted the seat from Godzilla setting to Normal so my feet could reach the pedals.

Go home.

Dawson would've gone to one of two places. Yesterday, Daemon had said Dawson tried to go to the office building, which was the last place he'd been kept. That would logically be his first place to check.

Go home and stay there.

I pulled out of the parking lot, gripping the steering wheel. If I went home and waited like a good little girl, I could curl up on the couch and read a book. Write a review and make some popcorn. Then when Daemon came back, as long as nothing horrific happened, I'd throw myself in his arms again.

Making a right instead of a left, I laughed out loud. The sound was throaty and low, courtesy of my screwed-up vocal chords and anxiety.

Screw going home. This wasn't the 1950s. I wasn't a fragile human being. And I sure as hell wasn't the Katy Daemon had initially met. He was going to have to deal with it.

I gunned the engine, hoping the boys in blue were busy doing other things besides monitoring traffic tonight. There was no way I'd beat Daemon there, but if they ran into any trouble, I could run distraction or something. I could do *something*.

Halfway there, I caught a flash of white light out of the corner of my eye, deep within the wooden tree line crowding the highway. Then it came again—white tinged with red.

Slamming on the brakes, I swerved to the right as the back end of the SUV fishtailed until it came to an uneven stop along the shoulder. Pulse pounding, I flipped on the hazard lights and threw open the door. I bolted across the two-lane highway, half slipping until my feet hit the other shoulder and I gained traction. Tapping into the Source and whatever existed inside me, I picked up speed, running so fast that my feet barely touched the ground.

Low-hanging branches snagged at my hair. Sheets of snow fell as I dipped around a thick tree, disrupting once pristine land. To my left, there was a blur of brown racing away from me. Most likely a deer or, knowing my luck, a chupacabra.

A whitish-blue light flared up ahead, like a bolt of horizontal lightning. Definitely power of Luxen origin but not Daemon's—his was reddish. It had to be Dawson or . . .

I raced around a cluster of large rocks, kicking up snow as murderous icicles fell from elms, shattering into the ground around me. Flying through the maze of trees, I hung a sharp right—

There they were, two Luxen in full glowworm mode and they were . . . *What the hell*? I skidded to a stop, gulping in air.

One was taller, pure white with edges dipped in red. The other was a slender, slower form with a bluish glow. The bigger one, which I knew was Daemon, had the other in what looked like a headlock. A glowing, human-shaped headlock I may've seen used in the WWE before.

I'd officially seen everything.

Assuming the other one was Dawson, Daemon's brother was pretty scrappy, breaking loose and pushing Daemon back a foot. But Daemon wrapped his arms around the center of the light, raised it up in the air and *body slamming* it so hard that more icicles fell from the trees crowding us.

Dawson's light pulsed and streaks of blue light rebounded off the trees, shooting back at the two, narrowly avoiding them. He tried to roll Daemon—at least that's what it looked like—but Daemon had the upper hand.

I folded my arms, shivering. "You have got to be kidding me." The two alien hotheads froze, and I really wanted to walk up and kick them both. A second later, their lights flickered out. Daemon's still-incandescent eyes met mine.

"I thought I told you to go home and stay there," he said, voice thin with warning.

"And the last time I checked, you don't get to tell me to go home and stay." I took a step forward, ignoring the way his eyes brightened. "Look, I was worried. I thought I'd come and help."

His lips pulled back. "And how would you have helped?"

"I think I did. I got you two idiots to stop fighting."

He stared at me a moment longer and his look promised lots of trouble later. Maybe punishable trouble. Ah, scratch that. His look didn't promise anything of the fun kind.

"Let me up, brother."

Daemon looked down. "I don't know. You're probably going to run and make me chase you again."

"You can't stop me," Dawson said, voice creepily apathetic.

Muscles bulged under Daemon's sweater. "I can and I will. I'm not letting you do this to yourself. She—"

"She's what? Not worth it?"

"She wouldn't want you to do this," Daemon seethed. "If the situation were flipped, you wouldn't want her doing this."

Dawson reared up, managing to get enough space between them so he could stand. On their feet, they shared wary stances. "If they had Katy—"

"Don't go there." Daemon's hands curled into powerful fists.

His brother was unaffected. "If they had her, you'd be doing the same thing. Don't lie."

Daemon opened his mouth but said nothing. We all knew what he'd do and no one would stop him. And knowing that, how could we ever stop Dawson? We couldn't.

I knew the exact moment that Daemon realized this, because he stepped back and thrust both hands through his windblown hair. Torn between doing what was right and what needed to be done.

Stepping forward, I swore I could feel the weight Daemon carried as if it were my own. "We can't stop you. You're right."

Dawson jerked toward me, eyes a brilliant green. "Then let me go."

"But we can't do that, either." I dared a peek at Daemon. Nothing could be gained from his expression. "Dee and your brother have spent the last year believing you were dead. That killed them. You have no idea."

"You have no idea what I went through." He lowered his gaze. "Okay, maybe you do a little. What was done to you is being done a thousand times over to Beth. I can't just forget about her, even though I love my brother and sister."

I heard Daemon's sharp intake. It was the first time since Dawson's return that he admitted any feelings for his family. I took it and ran with it. "And they know that. I know that. No one expects you to forget about Beth, but running off and getting yourself captured isn't helping anyone."

Wow. When did I become the voice of reason?

"What are the alternatives?" Dawson asked. His head tilted to the side—a mannerism so like his brother.

Here was the problem. Dawson wouldn't stop. Deep down, Daemon knew and understood why and would do the same thing. It was hypocritical to the umpteenth degree to demand someone else do otherwise. There had to be a compromise.

And there was one. "Let us help you."

"What?" Daemon demanded.

I ignored him. "You know rushing the DOD isn't going to work. We need to find out where Beth is, if they are even keeping her here, and we need a plan to get to her. A really well-thought-out plan with low failure potential."

Both brothers stared at me. I held my breath. This was it. There was no way Daemon could keep watch over his brother forever. And it wasn't fair to assume that he could.

Dawson turned away, back straight. Several seconds passed as the wind whipped through the trees, spinning snow. "I can't stand the idea of them having her. It hurts to breathe just thinking about it."

"I know," I whispered.

Moonlight sliced through the branches, carving Daemon's face in a harsh light. He had gone quiet, but anger rolled off him. Did he really think he could keep going after Dawson? If so, then he was insane.

Finally Dawson nodded. "Okay."

Sweet relief flooded me, making my legs feel weak. "But you have to promise to give us time." Everything came down to time we had no ownership of. "You can't get impatient and run off. You have to swear."

He faced me and a shudder rolled through him, taking the fight out of him. As he stood there, tension uncoiled, and his arms fell to his sides limply. "I swear. Help me and I swear."

"It's a deal."

There was a moment of silence, like the wilderness was soaking up his promise and my deal, committing it to memory. And then the three of us headed back to the SUV, the atmosphere silent and strained. My fingers were like Popsicles as I handed the keys over to Daemon.

Dawson climbed into the back, resting his head against the seat, eyes closed. I kept glancing at Daemon, expecting him to say something, anything, but he was focused on the road, his silence a ticking time bomb.

I peeked over the back of the seat. Behind thin slits, he was watching Daemon. "Hey. Dawson . . . ?"

His gaze slid to mine. "Yeah?"

"Do you want to go back to school?" School would keep him busy while we figured out how in the hell to get to Beth. And it matched Daemon's plan of pretending like we'd pulled one on the DOD while enabling us to keep an eye on Dawson just in case he reneged on his promise. "I mean, I'm sure you can. You could tell everyone you ran away. It happens."

"People think he's dead," Daemon said.

"I'm sure some runaways all across the nation are believed to be dead and aren't," I reasoned.

Dawson appeared to consider that. "What do I tell them about Beth?"

"That's a good question." Challenge dripped from Daemon's voice.

I stopped chewing on my finger. "That you both ran away, and you decided to come home. She didn't."

Leaning forward, Dawson rested his chin in the palms of his hands. "Better than sitting around thinking about everything."

Damn straight. He'd go crazy if he did.

"He'd have to get registered for classes," Daemon said, fingers tapping off the steering wheel. "I'll talk to Matthew. See what we can do to get it taken care of."

Thrilled Daemon was finally getting behind this, I settled back and smiled. Crisis averted. Now only if I could fix everything else so easily.

Dee was waiting on the front porch when we pulled into the driveway, Andrew standing sentry beside her. Dawson slid out of the backseat and approached his sister. Words were exchanged, too low for me to hear, and then they embraced each other.

That was an amazing kind of love. Different from what my parents had shared but still strong and unbreakable. No matter what crazy hell they put each other through.

"I thought I told you to go home."

I hadn't realized I was smiling until it faded at the sound of Daemon's voice. I looked at him and felt my heart drop. Yeah, here was the trouble promised earlier. "I had to help."

He looked out the windshield. "What would you have done if it wasn't Dawson you came upon, but me fighting the DOD or whatever the hell the other group is?"

"Daedalus," I said. "And if it were them, I would've still helped."

"Yeah, and that's what I have a problem with." He got out of the SUV, leaving me staring at him.

Drawing in a frustrated breath, I climbed out. He was leaning against the bumper, arms folded over his chest. He didn't look at me when I stopped beside him. "I know you're upset because you worry about me, but I'm not going to be the girl who sits at home and waits for the hero to wipe out the villains."

"This isn't a book," he snapped.

"Well, duh—"

"No. You don't get it." He turned to me, furious. "This isn't a paranormal fantasy or whatever the hell it is you read. There is no set plot or clear idea of where any of this is going. The enemies aren't obvious. There are no guaranteed happy endings and you—" He lowered his head so we were eye level. "You are not a superhero, no matter what the hell you can do."

Wow. He'd really been stalking my blog. But not the point. "I know this isn't a book, Daemon. I'm not stupid."

"You're not?" He laughed without humor. "Because being smart isn't rushing off after me."

"The same could be said about you!" My anger now matched his. "You ran off after Dawson without knowing what you were getting into."

"No shit. But I can control the Source without trying. I know what I'm capable of. You don't."

"I know what I'm capable of."

"Really?" he questioned. The tips of his cheeks flushed with fury. "If I'd been surrounded by human officers, would you have been able to take them down? And live with yourself after that?"

Anxiety blossomed in my stomach, its smoky tendrils wrapping themselves around me. When I was alone and it was quiet, the fact I'd been so willing to take a human life was all I thought about. "I'm prepared to do that." My voice came out a whisper.

He took a step back, shaking his head. "Dammit, Kat, I don't want you to experience that." Raw emotion filled his expression. "Killing isn't hard. It's what comes afterward—the guilt. I don't want you to deal with that. Don't you understand? I don't want you to have this kind of life."

"But I already have this kind of life. All the hoping, wishing, and good intentions in the world aren't going to change that."

The truth appeared to infuriate him more. "That issue aside, what you promised Dawson was freaking unbelievable."

"What?" My arms dropped to my sides.

"Help him find Beth? How in the hell are we supposed to do that?"

I shifted from one foot to the other. "I don't know, but we'll figure something out."

"Oh, that's good, Kat. We don't know how to find her but we'll help. Awesome plan."

Heat rushed up my spine. Oh, this was grand. "You're such a hypocrite! You told me yesterday we'd find out what Will was up to, but you have no idea how. The same thing with Daedalus!" He opened his mouth, but I knew I had him. "And you couldn't lie to Dawson when he asked what you'd do if they had me. You're not the only one who gets to make brash and stupid decisions."

His mouth snapped shut. "That's not the point."

I cocked a brow. "Lame argument."

Daemon shot forward, his voice harsh. "You had no right to make those kinds of promises to *my* brother. He's not *your* family."

I flinched, taking a step back. Being smacked would've felt better. The way I saw it, at least I talked Dawson off the cliff. Sure, promising to help find Beth wasn't ideal, but it was better than him running off like a crackhead.

I tried to rein in my anger and disappointment, because I

understood where a lot of his fury was coming from. Daemon didn't want me to get hurt, and he was worried about his brother, but his inherent, near-obsessive need to be protective didn't excuse his douchebaggery.

"Dawson is my problem, because he's your problem," I said. "We're in this together."

Daemon's eyes met mine. "Not on everything, Kat. Sorry. That's just the way it is."

The back of my throat burned, and I blinked several times, refusing to shed tears even though my chest ached so badly. "If we're not together on everything, then how can we really be together?" My voice cracked. "Because I don't see how that's possible."

His eyes widened. "Kat—"

I shook my head, knowing where this conversation was heading. Unless he was willing to see me as something other than a fragile piece of china, we were doomed.

Walking away from Daemon was the hardest thing I'd done. Made worse by the fact he didn't try to stop me, because that wasn't his style, but deep down, in a place that spoke only the truth, I hadn't expected him to. But I wanted him to. I needed him to.

And he didn't.

7

As expected, school resumed on Monday, and there was nothing worse than returning after an unexpected break and having all the teachers buzzing to make up for lost time. Add in the fact that Daemon and I hadn't made up after our major blowout yet and, well, Mondays always sucked.

I dropped into my seat, pulling out my massive trig textbook.

Carissa eyed me over the rim of her burnt-orange glasses. New ones. Again. "You look absolutely thrilled to be back."

"Whee," I said unenthusiastically.

Sympathy marked her expression. "How . . . how is Dee? I've tried calling her a couple of times, but she hasn't returned any of my calls."

"Or mine," Lesa added, sitting down in front of Carissa.

Lesa and Carissa had no idea that Adam hadn't really died in a car accident, and we had to keep them in the dark. "She's really not talking to anyone right now." Well, besides Andrew, which was so bizarre I couldn't even think about it.

Carissa sighed. "I wish they had the funeral for him here. I would've loved to pay my respects, you know?"

Apparently Luxen didn't do funerals. So we'd made up some excuse about the funeral being out of town and only family could visit.

"It just sucks," she said, glancing at Lesa. "I thought maybe we could go to the movies after school this week. Take her mind off it."

I nodded. I liked the sound of that but doubted we'd get very far with her. It was also time to put Plan A into motion—which was reintroducing Dawson to society. Even though I was on his brother's poo-poo list, Dawson had stopped by yesterday and explained that Matthew was on board. Probably wouldn't happen until the middle of the week, but it was a go.

"She may not be able to do anything this week, though," I said.

"Why?" Curiosity sparkled in Lesa's dark eyes. Loved the girl, but she was such a gossip whore. Which was exactly what I needed.

If people expected Dawson's return, it wouldn't be such a surprise when it did happen. Lesa would make sure word got out.

"You guys are not going to believe this, but . . . Dawson's come home."

Carissa turned several degrees paler, and Lesa shouted something that sounded an awful lot like *what the duck*. I'd kept my voice low, but their reactions garnered a lot of attention. "Yeah, apparently he's alive. Ran away and finally decided to come home."

"No way," Carissa breathed, her eyes going wide behind her glasses. "I can't believe this. I mean, it's great news but everyone thought . . . well, you know."

Lesa was just as shell-shocked. "Everyone thought he was dead."

I forced a casual shrug. "Well, he's not."

"Wow." Lesa pushed a section of tight curls out of her face. "I can't even process this. My brain has just shut down. A first."

Carissa asked the one question that was probably going to be on everyone's mind. "Did Beth come back?"

Keeping my face blank, I shook my head. "Apparently they ran off together, but Dawson wanted to come home. She didn't. He doesn't know where she is."

Carissa stared at me while Lesa kept fiddling with her hair. "That's . . . so weird." She paused, turning her attention to her notebook. A strange look, one I couldn't decipher, crept across her face, but then again, this was really WTF news. "Maybe she went to Nevada. Wasn't that where she's from? Her parents moved back there, I think."

"Maybe," I murmured, wondering what the hell we were supposed to do if we did free Beth. Wasn't like we could keep her here. Sure, she was eighteen now and legally an adult, but her family was in a different time zone.

Warmth spread over my neck, and I looked to the front of the class. A few seconds later, Daemon strolled in. My stomach tightened, and I forced myself not to look down. If I was arguing that I was capable of handling bad things, I couldn't hide from my boyfriend when we had a fight.

Daemon arched a single brow as he passed by, taking his seat behind me. Before my friends could verbally attack Daemon with all their Dawson-related questions, I twisted in my seat.

"Hey," I said, and then I flushed, because there was nothing lamer than *hey*.

He seemed to think the same thing and showed it as one side of his lip curled up into a trademark Daemon smirk. Sexy? Yes. Infuriating? Oh, yes. I wondered what he would say. Would he yell at me for talking to Dawson yesterday? Apologize? Because if he apologized, I'd probably crawl into his lap right there in class. Or would he go with the ever-faithful "talk in private" comment? While Daemon loved an audience, I knew what he showed the world wasn't really him, and if he were going to open himself up, vulnerable to the core, he wouldn't want people watching.

"I like your hair like that," he said.

My brows rose. Okay. Not what I was expecting. Lifting my arms, I smoothed my hands down the sides of my hair. The only thing I'd done differently was part it down the middle. Nothing amazing. "Um, thanks . . . ?"

The smirk remained on his face as we continued to stare at each other, and as the seconds passed, the more irritated I grew. Seriously?

"Anything else you want to say?" I asked.

He leaned forward, sliding his elbows across the desk. Our faces were inches apart. "Is there anything you want me to say?"

I took a deep breath. "Lots of things . . ."

Thick lashes lowered, and his voice was rich as satin. "I bet."

He thought I was flirting? Then he spoke again. "There's something I'd like you to say. How about 'I'm sorry for Saturday'?"

I wanted to clock him. Of all the arrogant nerve, I swear. Instead of being snarky, I shot him an annoyed look and turned around. I ignored him for the rest of class and even left without saying a word to him.

Of course, he was two steps behind me in the hallway. My entire back tingled under his scrutiny, and if I didn't know better, I'd think he was amused by all of this.

Morning classes dragged. Bio was weird, since the seat beside me was now empty. Lesa noticed it with a frown. "I haven't seen Blake since Christmas break ended."

I shrugged, studiously staring at the projector screen Matthew was pulling down. "I have no clue."

"You guys were like BFFs forevah, and you have no idea where he's been?" Doubt clouded her tone.

Her suspicions were totally understandable. Petersburg was like the Bermuda Triangle for teenagers. Many came. Some were never seen again while others resurfaced from the rabbit hole. In that moment, I found myself wanting to spill the beans like I did every so often. Keeping so many secrets was killer.

"I don't know. He mentioned something about visiting fam back in California. Maybe he decided to stay." God, I was getting frighteningly good at lying. "Petersburg is kind of boring."

"No doubt." She paused. "But he didn't tell you if he was coming back or not?"

I bit my lip. "Well, since Daemon and I are kind of seeing each other now, Blake and I haven't really talked."

"Ha." Her face transformed with a knowing grin. "Daemon seems like the RAWR type. He so wouldn't be cool with another guy being super friendly."

A flush crept over my cheeks. "Ah, he's okay with guy friends . . ." Just not ones who kill his friends. I rubbed my brow, sighing. "Anyway, how's Chad?"

"My boy toy?" She giggled. "He's perfect."

I managed to keep the conversation on Chad and how close they'd come to doing it. Of course, Lesa wanted to know about Daemon and me, and I refused to go there, much to her dismay. She admitted to wanting to live vicariously through me.

After bio, I stopped by my locker as usual and took my sweet old time changing out books. I doubted Dee wanted to see my face. The seating arrangements in the cafeteria were going to be super awkward, and I was still annoyed with Daemon. By the time I'd finished grabbing books, the hall was empty and the hum of conversation was distant.

I closed the locker door and twisted halfway, closing the flap on the messenger bag my mom had gotten me for Christmas.

Something moved at the end of the once-empty corridor, coming out of what seemed like nowhere. A tall and slender form at the end of the hall, obviously male by the quick look, and he was wearing a baseball cap, which was odd, because that was in violation of the school dress code. It was one of those God-awful trucker hats that guys found cool once upon a time.

DRIFTER was written in bold black and behind the words was an oval shape . . . that looked a lot like a surfboard.

My pulse spiked and I blinked, taking a step back. The guy was gone, but the door to the left was slowly swinging closed.

No . . . no, it couldn't be. He'd be crazy insane to come back here, but . . . Holding my bag tightly to my side, I started walking and then I was jogging before I knew it. I hit the door, throwing it open. Rushing to the railing, I peered over it. Mystery Dude was on the bottom level, as if he were waiting at the door.

I could see the trucker hat more clearly. It was definitely a surfboard.

Blake had been an avid surfer when he lived in California.

Then a golden-toned hand, as if the person spent his life under the sun, wrapped around the silver doorknob, and a wave of familiarity raised the tiny hairs on my arms.

Oh, crap.

Part of my brain clicked off. I went down the steps three at a time, my breath locked in my chest. The hallway was more crowded on the first floor as people headed for the cafeteria. I heard Carissa call my name, but I was focused on the top of the trucker hat moving toward the gymnasium and the back entrance, leading to the parking lots.

I darted around a couple totally getting into hallway PDA, slipped between friends talking, and lost sight of the hat for a second. *Dammit.* Everyone and their mother were in my way. I bumped into someone, mumbling an apology, and kept going.

When I reached the end of the hall, the only place he could've gone was out the door. I didn't think twice. Pushing the heavy double doors open, I stepped outside. Overcast skies turned everything dreary and cold, and as my eyes scanned the common area and, beyond that, the parking lots, I realized he was gone.

Only two things in this world could move that fast: aliens and humans mutated by aliens.

And I had no doubt in my mind that I'd seen Blake, and he'd wanted me to see him.

8

Finding Daemon wasn't hard at all. He was lounging against the painted mural of the school mascot in the cafeteria, talking to Billy Crump, a boy from our trig class. A carton of milk was in one hand and a slice of pizza folded in the other. What a gross-as-hell combination.

"We need to talk," I said, interrupting boy time.

Daemon took a bite of his pizza while Billy glanced down at me. There must've been something in my stare, because his smile faded and he lifted his hands, backing up slowly.

"Okay, well, I'll talk to you later, Daemon."

He nodded, eyes trained on me. "What's up, Kitten? Come to apologize?"

My eyes narrowed, and for a brief moment, I entertained the idea of body slamming him in the middle of the cafeteria. "Uh, no, I'm not here to apologize. *You* owe *me* an apology."

"How do you see that?" He took a drink, appearing naively curious.

"Well, for starters, I'm not an ass. You are."

He chuckled as he glanced to the side. "That's a good start."

"And I got Dawson to heel." I smiled victoriously when his eyes narrowed. "And— Wait. This isn't even important. God, you always do this."

"Do what?" His intense gaze swung back to me without a trace of anger. More like amusement and something really inappropriate, given that we were standing in the lunchroom. Dear God . . .

"Distract me with the inane. And in case you don't know what that means, it's silly—you always distract me with something silly."

He finished off his pizza. "I know what *inane* means."

"Shocker," I retorted.

A slow, cat-got-the-canary grin pulled at his lips. "I must be really distracting you, because you still haven't told me what you need to talk to me about."

Dammit. He was right. Ugh. Taking a deep breath, I focused. "I saw—"

Daemon cupped my elbow, spun me around, and started down the aisle. "Let's go somewhere more private."

I tried to yank my elbow from his grasp. I really hated it when he went all He-Man on me and ordered me around. "Stop dragging me, Daemon. I can walk on my own, Doofus."

"Uh huh." He led me down the hall, stopping by the gym doors. He placed his hands on either side of my head, caging me in as he leaned down. His forehead brushed mine. "Can I tell you something?"

I nodded.

"I find it incredibly attractive when you're all feisty with me." His lips brushed against my temple. "That probably makes me disturbed. But I like it."

Yeah, it kind of was wrong, but there was something . . . hot about how quickly he defended me whenever something happened.

His nearness was tempting, especially when his breath was tantalizingly warm and so near my lips. Summoning my willpower, I placed my hands on his chest and pushed lightly. "Focus," I said, not sure who I was talking to, me or him. "I have something more important to tell you than what disturbing things get you hot."

His lips quirked into a grin. "Okay, back to what you saw. I'm focused. My head's in the game and all that."

I laughed under my breath but sobered up pretty quickly. In no way was Daemon going to respond well to this. "I'm pretty sure I saw Blake today."

Daemon cocked his head to the side. "Say what?"

"I think I saw Blake here, just a few minutes ago."

"How sure are you? Did you see him—his face?" He was all business now, eyes as sharp as a hawk's and his face set in grim lines.

"Yeah, I saw—" I hadn't seen his face. Biting down on my lip, I glanced down the hall. Students piled out of the cafeteria, pushing into one another, laughing. I swallowed. "I didn't see his face."

He let out a long breath. "Okay. What did you see?"

"A hat—a trucker hat." God, that sounded lame. "That had a surfboard on it. And I saw his hand . . ." And that sounded even worse.

His brows arched up. "So, let me get this right. You saw a hat and a hand?"

"Yeah." I sighed, shoulders slumping.

Daemon smoothed out his expression and placed a heavy arm around my shoulder. "Are you really sure it was him? Because if not, that's okay. You've been under a lot of stress."

I wrinkled my nose. "I remember you saying something like that to me before. You know, when you were trying to hide what you were from me. Yeah, I remember that."

"Now, Kitten, you know this is different." He squeezed my shoulders. "Are you sure, Kat? I don't want to get everyone freaking out if you're not sure."

What I'd experienced was more of a feeling than a true sighting of Blake. God knew that a ton of boys around here broke the dress code with atrocities such as trucker hats. The thing was, I hadn't seen his face and looking back, I couldn't be 100 percent sure it had been Blake.

I looked into Daemon's bright gaze and felt my cheeks burn. There wasn't judgment in his eyes. More like sympathy. He thought I was cracking under the pressure of everything. Maybe I was imagining stuff.

"I'm not sure," I said finally, casting my eyes down.

And those words soured in my stomach.

Later that night, Daemon and I did babysitting duty. Although Dawson had promised not to do his own search-and-rescue mission, I knew Daemon wasn't comfortable leaving him alone and Dee wanted to get out tonight, go to the movies or something.

I wasn't invited.

Instead, I was sitting in between Daemon and Dawson, four hours into a George Romero zombiethon, with a bowl of popcorn in my lap and a notebook resting against my chest. We'd been making plans to look for Beth, getting as far as listing the two places that we knew to check before deciding to do surveillance this weekend to see what kind of security they had going on now. By the start of *Land of the Dead*, the zombies got uglier and smarter.

And I was having fun.

"I had no idea you were a zombie fan." Daemon grabbed a handful of popcorn. "What is it—the blood and guts or the in-your-face social undertones?"

I laughed. "Mostly the blood and guts."

"That's so un-girlie of you," Daemon commented, brows knitting as a zombie started to use its meat cleaver to break through a wall. "I don't know about this. How many hours do we have left?"

Dawson raised his arm and two DVDs shot into his hand. "Uh, we have *Diary of the Dead* and *Survival of the Dead.*"

"Great," Daemon muttered.

I rolled my eyes. "Wussy."

"Whatever." He elbowed me, knocking a kernel of popcorn between my chest and notebook. I sighed. "Want me to get that for you?" he asked.

Shooting him a look, I dug it out and then tossed it in his face. "You're going to be grateful when the zombie apocalypse occurs and I know what to do because of my zombie fetish."

He looked doubtful. "There are better fetishes out there, Kitten. I could show you a few."

"Uh, no, thank you." But I did flush. And there were a lot of images that suddenly polluted my brain.

"Aren't you supposed to go to the nearest Costco or something?" Dawson asked, letting the DVDs float back to the coffee table.

Daemon turned to his twin slowly, face incredulous. "And how would you know that?"

He shrugged. "It's in the *Zombie Survival Guide.*"

"It is." I nodded eagerly. "Costco has everything—thick walls, food, and supplies. They even sell guns and ammunition. You could hole up there for years while the zombies are getting their nom nom on."

Daemon's mouth dropped open.

"What?" I grinned. "Zombies got to eat, too, you know."

"Very true about the Costco thing." Dawson picked up a single kernel and popped it in his mouth. "But we could just blast the zombies. We'd be fine."

"Ah, good point." I rooted around in the bowl for a half-popped kernel—my favorite.

"I'm surrounded by freaks," Daemon said, looking dumbfounded as he shook his head, but I knew he was secretly thrilled.

For one thing, his body was completely relaxed next to mine and this was one of the first times that Dawson was acting . . . normal. Yeah, talking about zombies probably wasn't the biggest step known to mankind, but it was something.

On the flat screen, a zombie took a chunk out of some dude's arm. "What the hell?" Daemon complained. "The guy just stood there. Hello. There're zombies everywhere. Try looking behind you, douche canoe."

I giggled.

"This is why zombie movies are unbelievable to me," he went on. "Okay. Say the world ends in a shit storm of zombies. The last thing anyone with two working brain cells would do is just stand along a building waiting for a zombie to creep up on him."

Dawson cracked a smile.

"Shut up and watch the movie," I said.

He ignored that. "So you really think you'd do well in a zombie apocalypse?"

"Yeppers," I said. "I'd totally save your butt."

"Oh, really?" He glanced at the screen. Then he faded out and something . . . something else replaced him.

Shrieking, I jerked into Dawson. "Oh my God . . ."

Daemon's skin was ghastly gray and hanging loose from his face. Patches of decaying brown skin covered his cheekbones. One of his eyes was just . . . a hole. The other was glazed over and milky white. Clumps of hair were missing.

Zombie Daemon gave a rotted, toothy grin. "Save my butt? Yeah, I don't think so."

I could only stare.

Dawson actually laughed. Not sure what was more shocking: that or the zombie sitting next to me.

His form faded out and then he was back—beautiful, carved cheekbones and head full of hair. Thank God. "I think you'd suck at the zombie apocalypse," he said.

"You . . . you are disturbed," I murmured, carefully settling down next to him.

With a smug grin, he reached for the bowl and came up empty. Some of it might have been on the floor. Feeling eyes on me, I glanced at Dawson.

He was staring at us, but I wasn't sure if he was even seeing us. There was a reminiscent expression in his eyes, tainted with sadness and something else. Determination? I didn't really know, but for a second, the green hue brightened, no longer dull and listless, and he looked so much like Daemon that I drew in a shallow breath.

Then he gave his head a little shake and looked away.

I glanced at Daemon and I knew he'd noticed. He shrugged. "Anyone want more popcorn?" he asked. "We have food coloring. I can make it red for you."

"More popcorn but minus the food coloring, please." When he grabbed the bowl and stood, I caught him sneaking a relieved glance at his brother. "Want me to pause the movie?"

His look told me no and I giggled again. Daemon sauntered out of the room, stopping at the door when the zombies crested the water. Then he shook his head again and left. He wasn't fooling me.

"I think he secretly enjoys zombie movies," Dawson said, glancing at me.

I smiled at him. "I was just thinking the same thing. He has to, since he's all into ghost stuff."

Dawson nodded. "We used to record those shows and spend all day Saturday watching them. Sounds kind of lame, but it was fun." There was a pause and his gaze flickered back to the TV. "I miss that."

My heart went out to him and Daemon. I glanced at the screen, chewing on my lower lip. "You know, you still can."

He didn't respond.

I wondered if the problem was that Dawson wasn't comfortable alone with Daemon. There was definitely a lot of baggage between the two. "I'd love to watch some of them this Saturday before we check out the buildings."

Dawson was silent as he crossed his legs at the ankles. I was pretty sure he wasn't going to answer, just ignore what I offered, and I was okay with that. Small steps and all.

But then he did speak. "Yeah, that would be kind of cool. I . . . I can do that."

Surprised, my head swung toward Dawson. "Really?"

"Yeah." He smiled. It was weak, but it was a smile.

Happy about this, I nodded and then turned my attention back to the gore. But I saw Daemon standing just outside the living room. My gaze was drawn to his, and I sucked in an unsteady breath.

He'd heard everything.

Relief and gratitude poured from him. He didn't need to say anything. The thank-you was in his stare, in the way his hands gave a little shake around the fresh bowl of popcorn. He came into the room and sat, placing the bowl in my lap. Then he reached over, took my hand in his, and it stayed that way the rest of the night.

Over the next couple of days, I came to accept that I probably did have a mini freak-out on Monday. There had been no more trucker hat sightings from hell, and then on Thursday, the whole Blake thing became a nonissue.

Dawson had returned to PHS.

"I saw him this morning," Lesa said in trig, her body practically humming like a tuning fork with excitement. "Or at least I think I did. It really could've been Daemon, but this guy was thinner."

To me, it was easy to tell the two brothers apart. "It was Dawson."

"That's the strange thing." Some of the enthusiasm faded. "Dawson and I were never best buds, but he was always friendly. I went up to him, but he kept on walking like he hadn't even seen me. And hey, I'm hard to miss. My bubbly personality is like its own screaming person."

I laughed. "So true."

Lesa grinned. "But seriously, something . . . something was off about him."

"Oh?" My pulse picked up. Was there something about Dawson that humans could sense? "What do you mean?"

"I don't know." She looked to the front of the classroom, her eyes traveling over the faded formulas scribbled on the chalkboard. Her curls spilled around her shoulder. "It's hard to explain."

There wasn't much time to dig into what she meant. Carissa arrived to class and then Daemon. He placed a cup of mocha latte on my desk. Cinnamon permeated the air.

"Thanks." I held the warm cup. "Where's yours?"

"Not thirsty this morning," he said, twirling his pen. He glanced over my shoulder. "Hi, Lesa."

Lesa sighed. "I need a Daemon."

I turned to her, unable to hide my grin. "You have a Chad."

She rolled her eyes. "He doesn't bring me lattes."

Daemon chuckled. "Not everyone can be as great as I am."

Now I rolled my eyes. "Ego check, Daemon, ego check."

From across the aisle, Carissa fiddled with her glasses, her eyes serious and somber as she glanced at Daemon. "I just wanted to say I'm glad Dawson's back and okay." Two red spots bloomed on her cheeks. "It must be a huge relief."

Daemon nodded. "It is."

Talk of his brother ended right there. Carissa turned around, and though Lesa rarely let awkward topics detour her, she didn't pick up our conversation. But after class, as Daemon and I navigated the hall, people were almost at a standstill.

Everyone was staring at Daemon and there were a lot of whispers. Some tried to keep it quiet. Others didn't seem to care.

"Did you see?"

"Two of them again . . ."

"So weird that he'd come back without Beth . . ."

"Where is Beth . . . ?"

"Maybe he came back because of Adam . . ."

Gossip mill at its finest, I realized.

I took a sip of my still-warm mocha and peeked at Daemon. The curve of his jaw was hard. "Uh, maybe this wasn't a good idea."

His hand rested on the small of my back as he held open the door to the stairwell. "Now what makes you think that?"

I ignored his sarcasm. "But if he didn't come back, what was he supposed to do?"

Daemon stayed by my side as we headed to the second floor, taking up most of the cramped space. Kids had to squeeze past him. And I really had no idea where he was going. His class was on the first floor.

He leaned down, keeping his voice low. "It was a bad and good idea. He needs to get back into the world. There's going to be fallout, but it's worth it."

I nodded. What he said was true. At the door to my English class, he took a sip of my mocha and handed it back.

"See you at lunch," he said, kissing me briefly before pivoting around.

My lips tingled as I watched the back of his dark head disappear, and then I headed into class. So much was going on that concentrating was pretty much out of the question. The teacher called on me at one point, and I didn't notice. The entire class did, though. Awkward.

Turned out Dawson was in my bio class, and boy did he have a lot of eyes on him. He was seated beside Kimmy when I walked past. He nodded and then returned to flipping through his textbook. His tablemate's eyes were like two moons.

Did he get any sort of education while he was gone? Not that it mattered. The Luxen developed mentally a lot faster than humans. Missing over a year of school probably meant nothing to him.

"See?" Lesa twisted around as soon as I sat behind her.

"See what?"

"Dawson," she whispered. "That's not the Dawson I remember. He was always talking and laughing. Never reading a *bio* textbook."

I shrugged. "He's probably been through some crazy stuff." Not a lie. "And it's probably uncomfortable for him to be back here with *everyone* staring at him." Also not a lie.

"I don't know." She tugged on her backpack as she glanced over at Dawson's table. "He's moodier than Daemon used to be."

"Daemon was moody?" I said a bit dryly.

"Well, just not that friendly, I guess. He kind of stuck to himself before." She shrugged. "Oh! By the way, what the hell is up with Dee hanging out with the Bitch Squad?"

Bitch Squad was a code name Lesa had given Ash and Andrew when I first started at PHS. Once upon a time, I bet Daemon was a part of that group.

"Ah," I said, suddenly wanting to read *my* bio textbook. Whenever I thought of Dee, I wanted to cry. Our friendship had taken a sharp detour to Breakupsville. "I don't know. She's been . . . different since Adam."

"No. Shit." Lesa shook her head. "Her grieving process is scary. I tried to talk to her yesterday at her locker, and she looked at me, said nothing, and then walked away."

"Ouch."

"Yeah, it actually hurt my feelings."

"Pretty much what I've—"

The door to the classroom opened as the bell rang and the first thing I noticed was the vintage Nintendo shirt worn over a gray thermal. I loved all those old-school screen T-shirts. Then the messy bronze hair and hazel eyes.

My heart stopped; a buzzing started in my ears and picked up to a roar. The air was sucked right out of the room. I'd expected Will to come back, but not . . . *him*.

"Oh. Look who's here," Lesa said, smoothing her hands over her notebook. "Blake."

9

had to be dreaming because this could not be real. No way. Absolutely not. It wasn't Blake strolling into the classroom like it was any other day. Nor did Matthew drop his stack of notes. I glanced at Dawson before realizing he wouldn't know any better. He'd never seen Blake.

"You okay, Katy? Looking a little wigged out," Lesa said.

My eyes darted to hers wildly. "I . . ."

A second later, Blake was taking his seat—his seat beside me. The rest of the class blurred out. I was struck stupid by his reappearance.

He placed his book on the table and leaned back in his chair, folding his arms. Casting me a sidelong glance, he winked.

What the holy hell . . . ?

Giving up on waiting for me to finish what I was saying, Lesa turned around, shaking her head. "I have weird friends," she muttered.

Blake said nothing as Matthew gathered up his scattered papers. My heart was now racing so fast I was sure I was going to stroke out any second.

People were staring, but I couldn't pull my eyes off Blake. Finally, I found my voice. "What . . . are you doing?"

He looked at me, a thousand secrets among the green flecks in his gaze. "Going to class."

"You . . ." There were no words. And then the shock wore off, replaced with a spike of anger so powerful and so hot I felt static rush over my skin.

"Your eyes," Blake whispered, a grin teasing his lips, "are starting to glow."

Closing my eyes, I struggled to control my swirling emotions. When I was about 40 percent sure I wasn't going to jump on him like a monkey and snap his neck, I reopened my eyes. "You shouldn't be here."

"But I am."

This wasn't the time for evasive comments. I glanced toward the front of the classroom and saw Matthew writing on the chalkboard, his face pale. He was talking, but I didn't hear anything.

I tucked my hair back behind one ear and kept my hand there. Anything to keep me from hitting Blake, because it was a real possibility that I would. "We gave you a chance." I kept my voice low. "We won't do it again."

"But I think you will." He leaned over the small space, coming too close and causing my muscles to lock up. "Once you hear what I have to offer."

A crazed laugh bubbled up my throat as I kept my eyes fixed on Matthew. "You are so, so dead."

Lesa glanced over her shoulder questioningly. I forced a smile.

"Speaking of dead," he murmured once Lesa had turned back around. "I see the long lost twin has returned." He picked up his pen and started writing. "I bet Daemon is so thrilled. Ah, which reminds me, I'm pretty sure he's the one who mutated you."

My hand closest to him curled. A faint white light danced

over my knuckles, flicking like the core of a flame. The knowledge of who mutated me was dangerous. Besides the ramifications Daemon would face if it got out in the Luxen community, the DOD could use it against us. Just like they had with Dawson and Bethany.

"Careful," he said. "I can see you still need to work on your anger."

I shot him a dark, promising look. "Why are you here? For real?"

He put his finger over his lips. "Shush. I need to learn about . . ." He glanced at the board, eyes narrowing in concentration. "Different types of organisms. Yawn."

It took every ounce of my self-control to sit through that class. Even Matthew looked like he was having trouble, forgetting where he was going with his lecture every couple of minutes. I caught Dawson's stare once and wished I could communicate to him . . .

Wait. Couldn't I communicate to Daemon? We'd done it before, but he'd always been in his Luxen form when it happened. Taking a shallow breath, I lowered my gaze to the blurred lines on my notebook and concentrated as hard as I could.

Daemon?

The space between my ears buzzed like a TV on mute. No discernible sound but a high-frequency hum. *Daemon?* I waited, but there was no response.

Frustrated, I blew out a breath. I needed to find a way to let him know that Blake was back, like, really back and in school. I figured Dawson could get word to him, but there was no telling how Dawson would act if I got up to use the restroom and told him that the douchebag beside me was Blake.

I glanced at said douchebag. No doubt about it, Blake was good-looking. He rocked the whole messy hair and golden skin surfer-boy look. But beneath that easy grin lurked a killer.

The moment the bell rang, I gathered my stuff and headed toward the door, shooting Matthew a look. Somehow he seemed to know, because he waylaid Dawson and—I hoped—would keep Dawson from throwing Blake through a window in front of everyone once Matthew shared who Blake was. Lunch period was next, but I dug my cell out of my messenger bag.

I made it about three steps before Blake stalked up behind me in the hall and cupped my elbow. "We need to talk," he said.

I tried to pull my arm free. "And you need to let go of me."

"Or what? Are you going to do something about it?" His head angled toward me and I caught the familiar scent of his aftershave. "No. Because you know what the risk of exposure is."

I gritted my teeth. "What do you want?"

"Only to talk." He steered me into an empty classroom. Once inside, I tore my arm free as he locked the door. "Look—"

Acting on instinct, I dropped my bag on the floor and let the Source soar through me. Whitish-red light spread over my arms, crackling in the air. A ball of white light the size of a softball built above my palm.

Blake rolled his eyes. "Katy, I just want to talk. You don't need—"

I released the energy. The light shot across the room in a bolt. Blake darted out of the way and the light smacked into the chalkboard. The intensity melted the middle of the green slate and the smell of burning ozone filled the air.

The Source built in me again, and this time I wasn't going to miss. It rushed down my arms to my fingertips. In that moment, I really didn't know if it was powerful enough to kill Blake or just do some serious damage. Or maybe I did and I just didn't want to admit it.

Rushing behind a huge oak desk, Blake raised his hand. All the chairs to the left of me flew to the right, smacking into my legs and crowding me. My aim was off and the energy ball skyrocketed over Blake's head, slamming into the circular clock above the board. It exploded in a hundred dazzling pieces of plastic and glass that rained down . . .

And then the pieces stopped in midair, hung there as if attached to invisible strings. Below them, Blake straightened, his eyes luminous.

"Crap," I whispered, my gaze darting to the door. There was no way I'd make it there and if he'd frozen those pieces, most likely everything was frozen. The door. People outside the room, I imagined.

"Are you done yet?" Blake's voice was harsh in my ears. "Because you're going to tire yourself out here in a few seconds."

He had a point. Mutated humans didn't have the energy stores like the Luxen did. So when they used their abilities, they wimped out pretty quickly. There was also the fact that even though I whipped up on Blake the night everything went down, Daemon had been there and we were feeding off each other.

But it didn't mean I was going to just stand there and let Blake do whatever he planned.

I took a step forward and the chairs reacted in defense. They launched into the air, forcing me back as they stacked atop one another, forming a circle around me that reached the ceiling.

Raising my hands, I pictured the chairs with little desk areas attached flying apart. Moving stuff was easy to me now, so in theory, those babies should've shot at Blake like bullets. They began to tremble and slid away from me.

Blake pushed back and the wall of chairs shook but didn't budge. I kept the image of them moving away from me, drawing on the static energy inside me until a fierce throbbing sliced through my temples. The pain increased until I dropped my arms. My heart tripped up as I whirled around. Trapped—encased in a tomb of freaking chairs.

"And I bet you haven't been practicing at all?" Through the gaps in chairs, I saw him come around the desk. "I don't want to hurt you."

I paced in a tiny circle, dragging in deep breaths. My legs felt like jelly, skin dry and brittle. "You killed Adam."

"I didn't mean to. You have to believe that the last thing I wanted was for anyone to get hurt."

My mouth dropped open. "You were going to turn me over! And someone did get hurt, Blake."

"I know. And you have no idea how terrible I feel about that." He followed me on the other side of the wall. "Adam was a nice guy—"

"Don't talk about him!" I stopped, hands balling into weak, useless fists. "You shouldn't have come back."

Blake cocked his head to the side. "Why? Because Daemon's going to kill me?"

I mirrored his movements. "Because I'm going to kill you."

A brow arched and curiosity marked his features. "You already had your chance, Katy. Killing isn't in your nature."

"But it's in yours, right?" I stepped back, checking the chairs. They shook a little. Blake may have more experience with this stuff, but he was tiring, too. "Anything to protect your friend?"

He drew in a long breath. "Yes."

"Well, I'll do anything to protect mine."

There was a pause. During those seconds, the shattered pieces of the clock fell. I did a little victory dance inside. "You have changed," he finally said.

Part of me wanted to laugh, but the action got stuck in my throat. "You have no idea."

Moving back from the chairs, he ran a hand through his messy hair. "This is good, because maybe you'll understand the importance of what I'm about to offer you."

My eyes narrowed. "There is nothing you could offer."

A wry smile appeared on his lips—lips that I had kissed once. Bile stung the back of my throat. "I've been watching you all for days. At first I wasn't the only one, but you know that. Or at least your bedroom window does."

He folded his arms when he realized he had my full attention. "I know Dawson has been trying to find Beth, but he doesn't know where to look. I do. She's being kept with Chris."

I stopped pacing. "Where's that?"

Blake laughed. "Like I'm going to tell you when it's the only thing that might keep me alive. Agree to help me get Chris free, and I'll make sure Dawson gets to Beth. That's all I want."

Rendered speechless, I blinked. He was asking for our help after everything? That crazy laugh was building again and it came out this time, throaty and low. "You're freaking nuts."

His expression slipped into a scowl. "The DOD thinks I'm their perfect little hybrid. I asked to stay here because of the community of Luxen and the likelihood of another being mutated. I'm their implant. And I can get you into the facility where they're being held. I know where they are, what floor they're on, and what cell. And more importantly, I know their weaknesses."

He couldn't be serious. The chairs at the top wobbled, and I knew I was seconds away from being buried under the damn things.

"Without me, you'll never find her and all you'll do is walk right into Daedalus's hands." He took another step back. Over his shoulder, the air was distorted in waves. The kind of power he was throwing off . . .

"You need me," he said. "And yeah, I need you guys. I can't get to Chris alone."

Okay, he was being for real. "Why in the world would we trust you?"

"You don't have a choice." He cleared his throat and the chairs rattled. My gaze dropped. The legs of those on the bottom bent toward him. "You'll never find her, and Dawson will end up doing something crazy."

"We'll take our chances."

"I was afraid you'd say that." Blake picked up my bag and placed it on the teacher's desk. "Either you all help me or I go to Nancy Husher and tell her just how powerful you are." At the sound of her name, I sucked in a sharp breath. Nancy worked for the DOD and most likely Daedalus. "I never reported back to her and since Vaughn was working with Will Michaels, neither did he," he continued. "She thinks your mutation wore off. And handing over that kind of information might save my ass. It might not, but either way, they will come for you now. And before you think getting rid of me fixes this, you're wrong. I have a message that will be delivered to her if anything happens to me, which tells what you're capable of and exposes Daemon as the one who mutated you. Yeah, I've thought of everything."

Anger raged inside me and the chairs really started to shake. In seconds, he'd stripped away whatever power I truly gained, leaving me helpless. "You rat bastard . . ."

"I'm sorry." He was at the door now, and dear God, I was an idiot, because he looked and sounded sincere. "I didn't want it to come to this, but you understand, right? You even said it yourself. You'll do anything to protect your friends. We really aren't that different, Katy."

Then he opened the door and slipped out. The wall of chairs crumbled, spilling out across the floor. Kind of ironic how they fell upon themselves, just like my whole life was collapsing onto itself.

10

In a daze, I stepped out of the demolished classroom and made it halfway through the hall before the stairwell door swung open and Daemon burst through.

His eyes were an incredibly bright green when his gaze landed on me, and he took about four ground-eating steps before he was in front of me, grasping my shoulders. Behind him were Matthew and a slightly-confused-looking Dawson, but Daemon . . . I'd never seen him so furious, and that was saying something.

"We've been looking everywhere for you," he said, jaw clenched.

Matthew appeared at our sides. "Did you see where he went? Blake?"

Like I needed the clarification. Then I realized they didn't know I'd been with him. How much time had passed in that room? It felt like hours but could've only been minutes. And if Blake had frozen everyone outside the room, the other Luxen would've known, because it wouldn't have affected them. So Blake must not have affected anything out of the room.

I swallowed, knowing Daemon's reaction was going to be epic. "Yeah, he . . . wanted to talk."

Daemon went rigid. "What?"

I glanced nervously at Matthew. His expression was serene compared to the rage boiling from Daemon's gaze. "He's been watching us. I don't think he ever left."

Daemon dropped his hands and backed off, thrusting his fingers through his hair. "I cannot believe he's here. He has a death wish."

Confusion slipped from Dawson's expression, replaced by curiosity as he inched around his twin. "Why was he watching us?"

And here comes the kicker, I thought. "He wants us to help get Chris."

Daemon whipped around so fast he would've pulled a muscle if he were human. "Come again?"

As quickly as I could, I told them what Blake had said, leaving out the part about turning Daemon and me over to Nancy. I figured that was something best communicated in private. Good call, because Daemon almost went full Luxen mode right there.

Matthew shook his head. "He . . . he can't think we would trust him."

"I don't think he cares if we do," I said, tucking my hair back. All I wanted to do was sit down and eat a box of sugar cookies, my hands beginning to shake from exhaustion.

"But does he really know where they are keeping Beth?" Dawson's eyes were feverish.

"I don't know." I leaned against a locker. "There's no telling with him."

Dawson shot forward, suddenly in my face. "Did he say anything—anything we can use to find her?"

I blinked, surprised by his sudden animation. "No. Not really. I—"

"Think," Dawson ordered, head lowered. "He had to have said something, Katy."

Daemon clasped his brother's shoulder, wheeling him away. "Back off, Dawson. I mean it."

He shrugged Daemon's hand away, body coiled tight. "If he knows—"

"Don't go there," Daemon interrupted him. "He was sent here by the DOD to determine if Kat was a viable subject. To do to her what they are doing to Beth. He killed Adam, Dawson. We are not working with—"

My legs had started to wobble, and I swayed a little to the left. I really couldn't even begin to figure out how Daemon knew, but he spun toward me before I could straighten. Strong arms went around my waist, tucking me to his side.

Daemon's brows were dark slashes above his eyes. "What's wrong?"

My cheeks burned. "I'm okay. Really, I am."

"You're lying." His voice dropped low, dangerous. "Did you fight him?" And then his voice went even lower and a chill ran down my spine. "Did he try to hurt you? Because I swear right now, I will tear through this state—"

"I'm okay." I tried to wiggle free, but his arm was like a vise grip. "I used more of the attack first, ask questions later approach. I tired myself out, but he didn't hurt me."

Daemon didn't look convinced, but he turned his attention back to his brother. "I know you want to believe that Blake can help us somehow, but he can't be trusted."

Dawson looked away, a muscle ticking in his jaw. Frustration rolled off him in waves.

"Daemon's right." Matthew planted his hands on his hips. At the end of the hall, the door opened and two teachers entered, carrying steaming cups and papers. "But this is not the place to discuss any of this. After school, your house."

And with that, he spun in the other direction and stalked off.

"I know what you're going to say," Dawson said sharply. "I'm not going to do anything reckless. I promised both of you I wouldn't and I'm keeping my end of the deal. You better keep yours."

Daemon wasn't relieved as he watched Dawson head in the opposite direction. "This isn't good," he said.

"You have no idea." I glanced up at him and waited for the teachers to disappear into their classrooms. "Trusting Blake may be a moot point."

His eyes narrowed as he turned, angling his body as if he was shielding me. "What are you saying?"

I prayed he didn't lose it. "Blake confirmed what Will had said. The DOD and Daedalus believe my mutation wore off. Good news, right? But he's desperate—more so than we realized. If we don't agree to help him, he plans to turn us over."

Daemon's reaction was as expected. There was now a fist-sized indent in the locker beside us, and I grabbed his arm, dragging him into the nearby stairwell before teachers started inspecting the source of the noise.

Helpless anger seeped into the air and settled over him like a blanket. He knew what I wasn't willing to say yet. Like with Will, we'd been blackmailed—trapped again, and what could we do? Refuse to go along with Blake and be turned over? Or trust someone who had already proven he wasn't worthy of such a thing?

God, we were screwed to the tenth degree.

I could tell Daemon wanted to ditch school and search the entire county, but he also didn't want to leave me alone . . . no matter how hard I worked to convince him that, of all places, I was the safest at school. Because apparently I wasn't, not when Blake was back, acting like a normal student. And Blake knew that as long as he stayed around people, there was nothing we could do.

Throughout the rest of the day, I expected to see Blake again, but I didn't. When the final bell rang, I wasn't surprised when Daemon met me at my locker. "I'm riding home with you," he said.

"Sure." No point in arguing over this. "But how is Dolly getting home?"

He cracked a grin, loving it when I called his car by its stupid name. "I rode in with Dee this morning. Andrew and Ash are riding with her home."

I let that sink in, wondering when Dee had become so close with them. She had never been a big fan of theirs and their human-hating tendencies. So much had changed, and I knew I hadn't even seen the full spectrum yet.

"Do you think he'd really turn us over?" I asked once we were inside my little sedan. Outside, the bare trees surrounding the parking lot rattled like a thousand dry bones.

"He's obviously desperate." Daemon tried to stretch out his long legs, grumbling. "Blake killed already to protect his friend, and the only way for Blake to keep him safe is either by turning you over, as he was originally sent to do, or for us to help him. So, yeah, I believe he'd still do it."

I gripped the steering wheel, welcoming the lava-like anger suffusing my skin. We'd let Blake go, giving him a chance to get as far away as he could, and he came back to manipulate us. How ungrateful was that?

I glanced at Daemon. "What are we going to do?"

His jaw worked. "We have two options: work with him or kill him."

My eyes popped. "And you'd be the one to do that? Not right. It shouldn't always be you. You're not the only Luxen who can fight."

"I know, but I can't expect someone else to carry that burden." He looked at me.

"And I'm not trying to start another argument over whether

or not you'd make a good Wonder Woman, but I'd never expect you or my siblings to do that, either. I know you would have done it to . . . defend yourself and us, Kat, but I don't want that kind of guilt on your shoulders. Okay?"

I nodded. Imagining what I felt already, just magnified, twisted my insides. "I could handle it . . . if I had to."

A heartbeat passed, and I felt his hand on my cheek. I took my eyes off the road for a second. He smiled a little. "You burn bright, to me at least, and I know you could handle it, but the last thing I want is your light to be tainted by something so dark."

Stupid girlie tears burned my eyes and the road became a bit blurry. I couldn't let them fall, because crying over him saying something sweet really didn't help the "I'm A Badass" case. But I gave him a watery smile, and I think he understood.

I pulled into my driveway before the rest of the crew got there. Filled with nervous energy, I followed Daemon into his house and grabbed a bottle of water, then returned to the living room. Before I could begin the agitated wearing of the carpet, Daemon caught my hand and tugged me toward him as he sat, pulling me onto his lap.

Arms wrapped around me, he buried his face in my neck. "You know what we have to do," he said softly.

Dropping the bottle next to us, I wrapped my arms around his neck. "Kill Blake."

He choked on his laugh. "No, Kitten. We're not going to kill him."

I was surprised. "We're not?"

He pulled back, meeting my questioning stare. "We're going to have to do what he wants."

Okay, I was more than surprised. More like dumbstruck. "But . . . but . . . but . . ."

A grin teased his lips. "Use your words, Kitten."

I snapped out of my stupor. "But we can't trust him. This is most likely a trap!"

"We're kind of damned if we do and damned if we don't." He shifted, sliding his hands along my lower back. "But I've given it some thought."

"What? The whole ten minutes it took us to get home?"

"I think it's cute that you call my house *home*." His grin spread to his eyes, deepening their lustrous hue. "By the way, it *is* my house. My name is on the deed."

"Daemon," I said, sighing. "Nice to know, but it's not important right now."

"True, but it's good knowledge to have. Anyway, since you went totally off topic there—"

"What?" How did he figure that? "You're the one—"

"I know my brother. Dawson's going to go to Blake if we don't agree." All his humor was gone in an instant. "It's what I would do if our positions were reversed. And we know Blake better than he does."

"I don't know about this, Daemon."

He shrugged. "I'm not going to let him turn you over."

I frowned. "He'll turn you over, too, and what about your family? Bringing Blake into the fold is going to be dangerous . . . and stupid."

"The risk outweighs the possible consequences."

"I'm shocked," I admitted, disentangling my arms. "You didn't want me training with Blake because you didn't trust him and that was *before* we knew he was a killer."

"But now we're both going into this knowing what he's capable of. Our eyes are open."

"That makes no sense." At the sound of car doors shutting, I glanced out the window. "The only reason you're going to work with him is for Dawson and me. That's probably not the wisest decision you've made."

"Maybe not." He shifted quickly, clasping my cheeks and laying a deep one on me, and then he unceremoniously dumped me on the cushion beside him. "But my mind's made up. Be prepared. This meeting isn't going to go well."

Half sprawled across the couch, I gaped at him. Damn straight this wasn't going to go well. I dug the water bottle out from underneath my thigh and sat up as the alien pit crew made their way in.

Dee immediately took up pacing in front of the TV. Her long, wavy black hair streamed behind her. An unfamiliar, feverish glint lit her green eyes. "So Blake is back?"

"Yes." Daemon leaned forward, resting his elbows on his knees, watching his sister.

She glanced at me and then quickly looked away. "Of course he would talk to her like nothing happened. They were BFFs."

What the hell was up with the BFF statement? Anger stirred inside me, but I pushed it down. "It wasn't a particularly friendly conversation."

"Then what do we do?" Ash asked. Her cap of blond hair was slicked back into a tiny ponytail. On anyone else it would've looked too severe, but she pulled it off like a model going on a go-see.

"Kill him," Dee said, stopping in front of the coffee table.

At first, I thought she was kidding, because this was *Dee*. Over the summer, I'd once seen her scoop up a pile of dirt full of ants and move them out of the flowerbed so they wouldn't be suffocated under the mulch. But as I stared at her—as the *whole room* stared at her—I came to realize she was serious.

My mouth dropped open. "Dee . . . ?"

Her shoulders squared. "Don't tell me. You're against killing him? I already know that. You convinced my brother to let him live."

"She didn't convince me," Daemon said, fingers curling under his chin.

I jumped in before he could continue. It wasn't his job to

always rush to my defense. "I didn't convince him to do anything, Dee. We both agreed that enough people had died that night. We didn't think he'd come back."

"It's more than that," Matthew said. "He's also connected to another Luxen. He dies, his friend dies. We aren't just killing him. We're killing an innocent person."

"Like Katy and Daemon?" Ash asked, her voice lacking the usual venom. Her bitchiness must've transferred to Dee at some point.

Guilt dug in with barb-tipped fingers the second that thought finished and I squirmed, picking at a worn section on my jeans. That wasn't fair. Dee and Adam had a long history—a history spent ignoring what had probably always existed between them. Love and affection. And they'd only gotten to know each other on that level right before he was snatched away from her.

Ash glanced at Dawson. "And like you and Beth?" When the two boys nodded, Ash sat back and glanced at a silent Matthew. "We can't kill Blake knowing it's going to kill an innocent Luxen. That's like killing Katy and it taking out Daemon."

I arched a brow, which earned me a knee nudge from Daemon.

"I'm not suggesting we kill Katy or Beth," Dee reminded everyone. "We don't know who this other Luxen is. For all we know, he could be working with the DOD or whatever that other group is. Blake . . . He killed Adam, Ash."

"I know that," she snapped, eyes flashing a brilliant blue. "I was his sister."

Dee's spine straightened as she drew herself up. "And I was his girlfriend."

Holy smokes . . . It was like opposite day or something. I shook my head, stunned. "The group is called Daedalus."

Yeah, Dee couldn't care less what the group was called. She turned to Matthew. "We have to do something before someone else gets hurt."

Matthew looked just as shocked. "Dee, we're not—"

"Killers?" Her face flushed red and then paled. "We have killed before to protect ourselves! We kill Arum all the time. Daemon has killed DOD officers!"

Daemon flinched, and I immediately took offense to this. He may not show how much killing bothered him, but I knew it did. "Dee," I said, and surprisingly, she looked at me. "I know you're hurting right now, but this . . . This isn't you."

She sucked in a sharp breath and behind her the TV flickered on and off. "You don't know me. And you don't know shit. That . . . that human freak—whatever he is—was here because of what my brother did to you. In theory, if you never came here, none of this would've happened. Adam . . ." Her voice caught. "Adam would still be alive."

Daemon stiffened beside me. "That's enough, Dee. It wasn't her fault."

"It's okay." I sat back against the cushion, feeling as if the walls had shifted closer. Andrew had said the same thing days before and even though hearing him say it sucked, coming from Dee's mouth gave it a wasp-sting-like quality. Part of me almost couldn't believe Dee had said it. Not hyper and cute like Tinker Bell Dee. Not the girl who whipped into my life during the summer, feeling just as lonely as I had. This wasn't my best friend.

And then it hit me.

Dee wasn't my best friend anymore.

God, realizing that seemed more important than anything else that was going on. Yeah, that was stupid when the big picture was called into play, but Dee was important to me, and I had failed her.

Beside me, Dawson shifted forward. "If Katy hadn't come here, I would never have been freed. The world works in messed-up ways."

Dee looked like she hadn't even considered that. She pivoted around, playing with a strand of her hair—a nervous habit of hers. Her arm faded out for a few seconds, and then she sat on the coffee table, her back to us.

From the arm of the recliner, Andrew sighed. Every time I looked at him, he'd had his gaze fixed on Dee. "Guys, whether we like the idea of killing someone or not, we have to do something."

"We do," Daemon agreed. He glanced at me quickly before facing the group. "Arguing about what to do with Blake is a waste of time. If we don't help him free Chris and in turn get Beth back, he's going to turn Kat and me over."

"Wow," Matthew muttered, thrusting his fingers through his hair. And then he did something unheard of, for him at least. He swore.

Dee stood again, her movement abrupt and jerky. "He said that?"

"I don't doubt he's serious," I said, hating that all of them were put in this position because of me. If I had only listened to Daemon in the beginning . . . So many would've, could've moments. "He's incredibly desperate to free Chris."

"Then it's done," Dawson said, seeming relieved. "We help him, and he helps us."

Dee whirled. "You guys are freaking insane! We cannot help Adam's murderer!"

"Then what do you suggest we do?" Matthew asked. "Let him turn your brother and Katy over?"

Her eyes rolled. "No. Like I said, we kill him. That will stop him from doing anything."

I shook my head, stunned by the ferocity in her voice. I also believed Blake probably had to die, because why should he live when Adam hadn't, but hearing Dee like this cut through me with a dull knife.

Daemon stood, drawing in a long breath. "We are not going to kill Blake."

His sister's hands balled into fists. "Your call. Not mine."

"We are going to help him and we're going to keep an eye on him," Daemon continued sternly. "And none of us are going to kill him."

"Bullshit," she hissed.

On his feet, Andrew took a step forward. "Dee, I think you need to sit down and think about this. You've never killed before. Not even an Arum."

She folded her slender arms and her chin went up a notch. "There's always a first time."

Ash's eyes widened as she slid a look at me that said, *Holy crap*. I wished I knew what to do or say, but there was nothing.

Quickly losing patience, Daemon mirrored his sister's stance. "This isn't up for discussion, Dee."

A faint glimmer of white light shaded the outline of her trembling body. "You're right. There's nothing you can say that will convince me that his life should be spared."

"We don't have a choice. Blake has it set up that if anything happens to him, Nancy will be notified about Katy and me. We can't kill him."

She was undeterred. "Then we find out who he's talked to or working with and take care of them!"

Daemon's jaw dropped. "Are you serious?"

"Yes!"

He turned away, seconds from losing it. My stomach rolled. This whole situation was all wrong.

Beside me, Dawson leaned forward, taking on the same position that Daemon had earlier. "Is your need for vengeance more important than finding and stopping what they're doing to Beth?"

She didn't look away, but her lips pressed into a grim line.

All eyes were on Dawson. "Because, little sister, let me tell you that what Adam went through pales in comparison to what she's experiencing. The things I've seen . . ." He trailed off and his gaze lowered. "If you doubt what I say, then ask Katy. She's had a taste of some of their methods and she can still barely talk from screaming."

Dee blanched. We hadn't spoken, not really, since New Year's Eve. I had no idea what she knew about my brief capture or the methods Will had used to subdue me. Her gaze flickered to mine, and she looked away all too quickly.

"You ask a lot," she said hoarsely, lower lip trembling. But then her shoulders slumped, and she turned, walking to the front door. Without saying a word, she left.

Andrew was already behind her, shooting Daemon a look. "I'll keep an eye on her."

"Thank you," he said, rubbing his palm along his jaw. "Well, that went wonderfully."

"Did you really expect her or any of us to be okay with it?" Ash asked.

Daemon snorted. "No, but I have a problem with my sister so willing to kill."

"I can't . . ." I couldn't even finish. Going into this, I knew it wasn't going to be good, but Ash and Andrew were the ones I expected to want to go all serial killer—never Dee.

Matthew directed the conversation back to the present. "How do we contact Blake? It's not something I can or wish to discuss with him in class."

Everyone looked at me . . . everyone except Daemon. "What?"

"You have his number, don't you?" Ash said, glancing at her naked nails. "Text. Call him. Whatever. And tell him we're ridiculously stupid and plan to help him."

I made a face but reached for my bag and dug out my cell. Sending Blake a quick text, I sighed. A second later he responded. Knots formed in my stomach. "Tomorrow eve-ning—Saturday." My voice sounded weak. "He wants to meet tomorrow evening in a public spot—Smoke Hole."

Daemon gave a quick jerk of his chin.

My fingers wanted to rebel, but I typed out a quick *okay* and then tossed my phone back in the pack like it was a bomb about to go off in my hands. "It's done."

No one looked relieved. Not even Dawson. There was a very good chance that this was going to blow up in our faces like there was no tomorrow. But our choices were limited. Like Daemon had said, Dawson would go to Blake whether or not we did. And working with the enemy we knew was better than the one we didn't.

But something cold and icky opened up in my chest.

Not because we were going to go down this road with Blake and not because Dee wanted Blake to die. But because deep down, underneath the layers of skin, muscle, and bone, hidden away from everyone, even Daemon, I also wanted Blake dead. Innocent Luxen or not . . . My moral code wasn't at all offended by it. And there was something very, very wrong with that.

11

I hung around their house, hoping Dee would come back and I could chat with her, but everyone was leaving and she and Andrew hadn't returned.

Standing on the front porch, I watched Ash and Matthew drive off, my heart heavy with regret and a billion other things. I didn't need to look behind me to know that Daemon had joined me. I welcomed the warmth and strength his arms offered as they circled me from behind.

I leaned back against his chest, letting my eyes fall shut. He placed his chin atop my head and minutes passed with only the sound of a lonesome birdcall and a horn blowing off in the distance. Against my back, his heart beat steady and strong.

"I'm sorry," he said, surprising me.

"For what?"

He drew in a deep breath. "I shouldn't have flipped out over the whole Dawson thing last weekend. You did the right thing by telling him we'd help. If not, God knows what he would've done by now." He paused long enough to kiss the top of my head, and I grinned. He was so forgiven. "And thank you for everything with Dawson. Even though our Saturday will take a turn into crapsville, Dawson . . . He's been different since zombie night. Not the old Dawson, but close."

I bit my lip. "You don't need to thank me for that. Seriously."

"I do. And I meant it."

"Okay." Several seconds passed. "Do you think we made a mistake? Letting Blake go that night?"

His arms tightened. "I don't know. I really don't."

"We had good intentions, right? We wanted to give him a chance, I guess." Then I laughed.

"What?"

My eyes opened. "The road to hell is paved with good intentions. We should've blasted his ass."

Daemon lowered his head, his chin now on my shoulder. "Maybe I would've done something like that before you."

I turned my head toward his. "What do you mean?"

"Before you came along, I would've killed Blake for what he did and felt like crap afterward, but I would've done it." He pressed a kiss against my fluttering pulse. "And in a way, you did convince me. Not the way Dee thinks, but you could've taken out Blake, and you didn't."

Everything about that night seemed chaotic and surreal now. Adam's lifeless body and then the Arum that had attacked . . . Vaughn and the gun . . . Blake running . . . "I don't know."

"I do," he said, and his lips spread into a smile against my cheek. "You make me think before I act. You make me want to be a better person—Luxen—whatever."

I faced him completely, peering up at him. "You *are* a good person."

Daemon grinned, his eyes twinkling. "Kitten, you and I both know that's incredibly rare."

"No—"

He placed a finger over my lips. "I make terrible decisions. I can be a dickhead and I do it on purpose. I tend to bully people into doing what I want. And I let everything that had happened with Dawson amplify those . . . uh, personality traits. But—" He removed his finger, and his grin spread into a smile. "But you . . . you make me want to be different. That's why I didn't kill Blake. It's why I don't want you making those decisions or for you to be around me if I am choosing those things."

Overwhelmed by what he'd admitted, I didn't know what to say. But he lowered his head and kissed me, and I learned that sometimes when someone says something so devastatingly perfect, there isn't a need for a response. The words said it all.

I spent Saturday morning with my mom. We had a greasy, artery-killing breakfast at IHOP and then wasted a couple of hours dollar-store shopping. Usually I'd rather pluck my eyelashes out than meander those aisles, but I wanted to spend time with her.

Tonight, Daemon and I were meeting Blake—only us, per his request. Matthew and Andrew were going to play parking-lot spies as backup, since Dee and Dawson, for very different reasons, had been banned from coming within a mile of the place.

There was no telling what was going to happen, though. This could be my last Saturday, my last *anything* with my mom. And that made the whole experience bittersweet and scary. So many times over breakfast and while in the car I wanted to tell her what was going on, but I couldn't. And even if I could, the words probably wouldn't have come out. She was having fun—thrilled to spend time with me—and I couldn't bring myself to ruin it.

But the what-ifs haunted me. What if this were a trap? What if the DOD or Daedalus took us in? What if I became Beth and my mom never heard from me again? What if she moved back to Gainesville to escape the memory of me?

By the time we got home, I was pretty sure I was going to hurl. My stomach twisted and turned around the food. It was so bad that I went to lie down while Mom got some sleep before her shift started.

About an hour of staring at the wall later, Daemon texted and I responded, telling him to let himself in. No sooner had I hit send than I felt warmth shooting across the back of my neck and I rolled toward the door.

Daemon made no sound as he eased my door open and slid though, a wicked glint in his eyes. "Your mom's asleep?"

I nodded.

His gaze searched my face, and then he shut the door behind him. A heartbeat later, he was sitting beside me, brows drawn tight. "You're worried."

How he knew was beyond me. I started to tell him that I wasn't worried, because I hated the idea of him stressing out over me or thinking I was weak, but I didn't want to be strong right now. I needed comfort—I wanted *him*. "Yeah, a little."

He smiled. "It's going to be okay. No matter what, I'm not going to let anything happen to you."

Daemon ran the tips of his fingers down my cheek, and I realized then that I could have both. I could freak out a little on the inside and need him, but I could still be strong enough to get up at six and meet our fate head-on. I could be both.

God, I needed a little of both.

Wordlessly, I scooted over, giving him room. Daemon slid under the covers, throwing a heavy arm over my waist. I curled against him, resting my head under his chin, my hands folded on his chest. Using my fingers, I drew a heart above his, and he chuckled.

We lay there for a couple of hours. Sometimes talking and laughing quietly, making sure we didn't wake my mom. For a while, we dozed together and then I'd wake, tangled in his arms and legs. Other times, we kissed and the kissing . . . well, it took up most of the time.

He was just so damn good at it.

My lips felt swollen as he grinned at me, his lids heavily hooded, but behind those lashes, his eyes were like the color of dewy spring grass. Along the nape of his neck, his hair curled. I loved running my fingers through it, straightening the strands out and watching them spring back into place. And he liked when I played with it. Closing his eyes, he tilted his head to the side so I got better access, much like a cat stretching to be petted.

Ah, the little things in life.

Daemon caught my hand as I slid it around, over the thick muscles in his neck. He brought my palm to his lips. My heart did the flutter thing, and then he kissed me again . . . and again. His hand moved to my hip, his fingers curling into the denim before slipping under the hem of my shirt, causing my pulse to pound through me. He rolled over me, his weight doing crazy things to my stomach.

As his hand crept up, my back arched. "Daemon—"

His mouth silenced whatever it was that I was going to say, and my brain emptied. There was just him and me. What we had to do later simply disappeared off my worry radar. I moved, throwing a leg over his and my—

Footsteps trotted down the hall.

Daemon faded out above me, reappearing at my desk chair. Grinning shamelessly, he picked up a book as I fixed myself.

"Book's upside down," I taunted, smoothing my hand over my hair.

Laughing under his breath, he turned it over and cracked it open. With seconds to spare, Mom knocked on the door and then opened it. Her eyes shot from the bed to the chair.

"Hello, Ms. Swartz," Daemon said. "You look well-rested."

I shot him a look and then clamped my hand over my mouth, stifling my giggles. He'd picked up one of the historical romance novels with the bodice-ripping, barrel-chested covers.

Mom arched a brow. Her expression basically read WTF, and I almost lost it. "Good evening, Daemon." She turned to me, eyes narrowing.

Codpiece? Daemon mouthed, rolling his eyes.

"Bedroom door, Katy." Mom headed back to the door. "You know the rules."

"Sorry. We didn't want to wake you."

"How considerate, but it stays open."

When her footsteps receded, Daemon chucked the book at my head. I raised my hand, stopping it so that it hovered, and snatched it out of the air. "Nice reading material."

His eyes narrowed. "Shut up."

I giggled.

There was no laughter as we pulled into Smoke Hole Diner's parking lot a little before six. Looking over my shoulder, I saw Matthew's SUV parked in the back. I seriously hoped he and Andrew paid attention.

"The DOD isn't going to bust up in here," Daemon said, pulling out the keys. "Not in public."

"But Blake could freeze the entire place."

"So can I."

"Oh. I've never seen you do that."

He rolled his eyes. "Yes, you have. I froze the truck. Remember? Saved your life and all?"

"Ah, yes." I fought a grin. "You did do that."

He reached over, flicking me gently under the chin. "Yeah, you better remember that. Plus, I'm not a show-off."

Opening the door, I laughed. "You? Not a show-off? Okay."

"What?" Fake outrage crossed his face as he shut the door and loped around the front of the SUV. "I'm very modest."

"If I remember correctly, you said modesty was for saints and losers." The bantering helped ease my nerves. "*Modest* is not a word I'd use to describe you."

He dropped his arm over my shoulder. "I never said such a thing."

"Liar."

Daemon shot me a roguish grin as we headed in. I scanned the restaurant for Blake, my gaze dipping over the natural rock clusters jutting out of the floors and beside the booths, but he wasn't here yet. The server seated us in a booth near the back, cozied up to the roaring fireplace. I tried to keep myself busy by ripping the napkin into tiny pieces.

"Going to eat that or are you making homemade hamster bedding?" he asked.

I laughed. "Organic kitty litter, actually."

"Nice."

A redheaded waitress appeared, wearing a bright smile. "Daemon, how are you doing? Haven't seen you in ages."

"Good. How about you, Jocelyn?"

Of course I had to give her more than a passing look, since the two were on a first-name basis. Not out of jealousy or anything. Yeah, right. Jocelyn was older than us but not by much. Maybe early twenties, but she was really, really pretty with all that red hair piled up in thick curls, surrounding a porcelain complexion.

Okay, she was beautiful . . . as in, Luxen beautiful.

I sat straighter.

"I've been real good," she said. "I stepped down from managing since the babies. Working part-time instead, since they're a handful, but you and your family should visit soon, especially since . . ." She looked at me for the first time, and her smile drooped. "Since Dawson has come back. Roland would love to see both of you."

Total alien, I thought.

"We'd love to do that." Daemon glanced at me and winked slyly. "By the way, Jocelyn, this is my girlfriend, Katy."

I felt a ridiculous surge of pleasure as I extended my hand. "Hi."

Jocelyn blinked, and I'd swear her face got even whiter. "Girlfriend?"

"Girlfriend," Daemon repeated.

She recovered fast and shook my hand. A faint spark jumped from her skin to mine, and I pretended not to notice. "Nice . . . nice to meet you," she said, quickly releasing my hand. "Uh, what can I get you two?"

"Two Cokes," he ordered.

Jocelyn skedaddled off after that, and I raised my brows at Daemon. "Jocelyn . . . ?"

He slid over another napkin for my pile. "Are you jealous, Kitten?"

"Pfft. Whatever." I stopped tearing. "Okay, maybe a little until I realized she was in the ARP."

"ARP?" He stood, coming to my side while saying, "Scoot."

I scooted over. "Alien Relocation Program."

"Ha." He dropped his arm over the back of the booth and stretched out his legs. "Yeah, she's good people."

Jocelyn returned with our drinks and asked if we wanted to wait until our friend joined us to place our orders. That was a big fat no. Daemon ordered a meatloaf sandwich while I decided to eat half his order. I wasn't sure I could stomach anything more.

He angled his body toward mine as soon as he finished deciding between fries and mashed potatoes—fries won. "Nothing's going to happen," he said, voice low. "Okay?"

Putting on a brave face, I nodded as I looked around the diner. "I just want to get this over with."

Not even a minute later, the bells above the door jingled and before I could glance up, Daemon stiffened beside me. And I knew—I knew right then. My stomach lurched into my throat.

Spiky, bronze-tipped hair—styled messily with a ton of gel—came into view, and then hazel eyes locked on our table from the door.

Blake was here.

12

Blake had a confident air about him as he walked up to our table, but it had nothing on Daemon's deadly swagger or the cool and arrogant smile he was wearing that instant. It was a purely predatory look.

Suddenly, I wasn't sure a public place was a good idea.

"Bart," Daemon drawled, his fingers tapping along the booth behind me. "It's been so long."

"I see you still haven't figured out my name." Blake slid into the seat across from us. His gaze dropped to the pile of torn napkins, then to me. "Hey, Katy."

Daemon leaned forward. The smile was still on his face, but his words were like the arctic winds. "You don't talk to her. At all."

There was no stopping He-Man when he came out to play, but I pinched him under the table. Daemon ignored me.

"Well, only talking to you is going to make this conversation real rough."

"Like I care?" Daemon said, placing his other hand on the table.

I exhaled slowly. "Okay. Let's get to the point. Where are Beth and Chris, Blake?"

Blake's gaze slid to mine again. "I—"

A current of electricity coursed from Daemon's hand and shot across the table, shocking Blake. He jerked back with a hiss, his eyes narrowing on Daemon.

Daemon smiled.

"Look, you tool, you can't intimidate me this time." Blake's voice dripped contempt. "So you're just wasting time and pissing me off."

"We'll see about that."

Jocelyn returned with Daemon's massive meal and took Blake's order. Like me, he only requested a soda. When we were alone once more, I focused on Blake.

"Where are they?"

"If I tell you, I'd have to trust that you two, plus anyone else, aren't going to give me a cement swim."

I rolled my eyes at the mafia reference. "Trust is a two-way street."

"And we don't trust you," Daemon threw out.

Blake drew in a long breath. "I don't blame you. I've given you no reason to trust me other than the fact I didn't tell Daedalus about how well the mutation held."

"And I bet either your uncle—Vaughn—stopped you from turning me over, or you thought he was doing his job," I countered, trying not to remember the look of horror that had settled on Blake's face when his uncle betrayed him. He didn't deserve my sympathy. "But he screwed you over for money."

Blake's jaw worked. "He did. And he put Chris in danger. But it's not like I haven't had to convince them otherwise after the fact. They think I'm happy to be an implant. That I've drunk the Kool-Aid and asked for seconds."

Daemon snickered. "To save your own ass, I'm sure."

He ignored that comment. "The fact is, Daedalus doesn't believe you're a viable subject."

"How do you know?" Daemon's fingers tightened on his fork.

Blake shot him a *duh* look. "The only real wild card here is Will. Obviously he knew and used that knowledge."

"Will isn't our biggest or most annoying problem right now." Daemon took a bite, chewing slowly. "You either have a lot of courage or are incredibly stupid. I'm going to go with the incredibly stupid part."

Blake snorted. "Yeah. Okay."

A dangerous look shadowed Daemon's face, and for a moment, no one moved as Jocelyn returned with Blake's drink. The second she was gone, Daemon leaned forward, his eyes starting to shine behind his lashes. "We gave you a chance and you came back here after you killed one of our own. You think I'm the only person you have to look over your shoulder and watch out for? You're so wrong."

A thread of fear finally showed in Blake's churning eyes, but his voice was even. "The same goes for you, buddy."

Daemon sat back, eyes hooded. "As long as we're on the same page."

"Back to Daedalus," I said. "How do you know they're watching Dawson?"

"I've been watching you guys, and I've seen them hanging around." He leaned against the booth, folding his arms. "I don't know how much work Will did to get him free, but I doubt he pulled the wool over anyone's eyes. Dawson is free because they wanted him to be free."

I glanced at Daemon. Blake's suspicions mirrored our own, but that was another problem for another day, it seemed.

Blake's gaze fell to his glass. "Here's the deal. I know where they're keeping Beth and Chris. I've never been there, but I know someone who has and can give us the security codes to get into the facility."

"Hold up," I said, shaking my head. "So you can't really get us in. Someone else can?"

"Go figure." Daemon chuckled. "Biff is virtually useless."

Blake's lips thinned. "I know what level and cell they're being kept in, so without me, you'd just be running around the compound begging to be captured."

"And my fist is begging to be in your face," Daemon shot back.

I rolled my eyes. "Not only are you asking us to trust you but to trust someone else?"

"*That* someone else is just like us, Katy." Blake dropped his elbows on the table, rocking his glass. "He's a hybrid but has gotten out from under Daedalus. And as expected, he hates them and would love nothing more than to screw with them. He's not going to lead us astray."

Yeah, I wasn't liking any of this. "And how does anyone get 'out from under' Daedalus?"

Blake's smile lacked warmth. "They . . . disappear."

Oh, well that sounded reassuring. I tucked my hair back on both sides, feeling cagey. "Okay, say we do this; how do you get in contact with him?"

"You won't believe anything unless you're there to witness it for yourselves." And he was right about that. "I know where to find Luc."

Daemon's mouth curled. "His name is *Luc*?"

Blake nodded. "He's not going to be reachable by cell or e-mail. He's kind of paranoid about the government tapping cells and computers. We'll have to go to him."

"And where is that?" Daemon asked.

"Every Wednesday night he hangs at a club a few miles outside of Martinsburg," Blake explained. "He'll be there this Wednesday."

Daemon laughed, and I wondered what the hell he found

so funny. "The only clubs in that part of West Virginia are strip clubs."

"You would think that." Smugness crept over Blake's expression. "But this is a different kind of club." He glanced at me. "Females don't show up in jeans and sweaters."

I gave him a bland look as I plucked a fry from Daemon's plate. "What do they show up in? Nothing?"

"The closest thing to nothing." His smile was real now, causing the green in his eyes to sparkle, reminding me of the Blake I first met. "Bad for you. Yay for me."

"You really want to die, don't you?" Daemon said.

"Sometimes, I think so." There was a pause, and his shoulders rolled. "Anyway, we go to him, he'll get the codes, and then it's on. We go in, you get what you want, and I get what I want. You guys will never see me again."

"That's pretty much the only thing you've said so far that I like." Daemon's sharp gaze landed on Blake. "The thing is, I'm having a hard time believing you. You say this hybrid is in Martinsburg, right? There isn't any beta quartz near that place. How come he hasn't become some Arum's afternoon snack yet?"

A mysterious glimmer filled Blake's eyes. "Luc can take care of himself."

Something wasn't right here. "And where's the Luxen he's tied to?"

"With him," Blake said.

Well, that answered that question, but still, none of this sat well with me. Crap, this whole situation was looking dicey, but what choice did we have? We were already in deep. Might as well go in over our heads—sink or swim, as my dad would say.

"Look," Blake said, fixing a steady stare on Daemon. "What happened with Adam—I never wanted that. And I'm sorry, but you of all people have to understand. You'd do anything for Katy."

"I would." A faint tremor coursed through Daemon. Static built, raising the tiny hairs on my body. "So, if for one moment I think you're about to screw us, I won't hesitate. You won't get a third chance. And you haven't seen what I'm fully capable of, boy."

"Understood," Blake murmured, his eyes downcast. "Are we on?"

The million-dollar question—were we really going to do this? Daemon's heartbeat calmed, and I felt it in my own chest. His mind was made up. Not only would he do anything to keep me safe, he'd do anything for his brother.

Sink or swim.

I lifted my lashes and met Blake's eyes. "We're on."

I spent the bulk of Sunday at Daemon's house, watching a marathon of *Ghost Investigators* with the brothers while I waited for—er, stalked—Dee. She had to come home sometime. That's what Daemon said.

It was almost dusk when she returned. I hopped up from the couch, startling Dawson, who had dozed off around hour four of things that go bump in the night.

"Is everything okay?" He was wide awake now.

Daemon scooted over, taking my spot. "Everything's fine."

His brother stared back for a long second and then refocused on the TV. Knowing what I wanted to do without even telling him, Daemon nodded.

Dee started for the stairs without saying a word. "Do you have a couple of minutes?" I asked.

"Not really," she threw over her shoulder as she continued up the stairs.

I squared my shoulders and followed. "Well, if you only have a minute, then I'm taking up that minute."

Stopping at the top of the stairs, she turned around. For a moment, I thought she might push me down the steps, which would totally derail my make-up plans. "All right," she said, and then sighed as if she'd been asked to recite trig formulas. "We might as well get this over with."

Not the way I wanted to start this conversation, but at least she was talking to me. I followed her into her bedroom. Like every time before, I was overwhelmed by the amount of *pink*. Pink walls. Pink bed coverings. Pink laptop. Pink throw carpet. Pink lampshades.

Dee moved to the window seat and sat, crossing her slender ankles. "What do you want, Katy?"

Mustering courage, I took up residency on the edge of her bed. All day, I had planned out this long speech, but suddenly, I just wanted to grovel at her feet. I wanted my best friend back. A look of impatience pinched her delicate features, and my stomach fell.

"I don't know where to start," I admitted quietly.

She drew in a heavy breath. "Maybe start with why you lied to me for months?"

I flinched, but I deserved that question. "The night in the clearing, when we fought Baruck, I don't know what happened, but Daemon didn't kill him."

"You did?" She stared out the window, idly playing with a dark curl.

"Yeah . . . I connected with him—with you. We . . . we think it was because Daemon had healed me before. Somehow those healings had already blended us together." Leftover fear from that night surfaced, coiling my insides tightly. "But I was hurt—really badly, I guess, and Daemon healed me after you left."

Her shoulders tensed. "The first lie, right? He told me you were fine, and I was stupid for believing him. You looked . . . really bad. And afterward, when Daemon was gone, you didn't act right. I should've known something was up." She gave a little shake of her head. "Anyway, you could've told me the truth. I wouldn't have flipped out or anything."

"I know." I rushed to agree. "But we weren't sure what really happened. We thought it would be best not to say anything until we found out. And by the time we realized we were connected somehow, everything . . . everything else was going on."

"Blake?" She spat out the name, dropping the piece of her hair.

"Him . . . and other things." I wanted to sit beside her, but I knew not to push it. "Things started happening to me. I would want a glass of tea, and the glass would fly out of the cupboard. I couldn't control it, and I was so afraid of exposing you guys somehow."

She looked at me then, lashes lowered. "You told Daemon, though."

I nodded. "Only because I thought maybe he knew what was happening, since he healed me. It wasn't because I trusted him more than you."

Dee's lashes lifted. "But you stopped hanging out with me."

My cheeks flushed with shame. I had made so, so many poor decisions. "I thought it was the right thing to do. That if I ended up moving something without meaning to around you, I didn't want you to get caught up in it."

She barked a short laugh. "You're so like Daemon. Always thinking you know better than everyone else." I started to respond, but she went on. "The funny thing is, I could've helped you. Water under the bridge now, though."

"I'm sorry." I wished those two words could take back everything I had done wrong. "I'm really—"

"What about Blake?" Her hard stare met mine.

My gaze went to my hands. "I didn't know what he was at first. Honestly, I liked him because he was normal. He wasn't like Daemon and I thought . . . I thought I didn't have to question why Blake seemed to like me." I laughed, the sound just as harsh as Dee's. "I was an idiot. Right off, Daemon didn't trust Blake. I thought he was jealous or just being Daemon. But then there was this Arum that came into the diner when I was with Blake, and I found out what he was."

Dee faded out and reappeared by her dresser, hands on her hips. "So, let me get this right. There was an Arum, and never once did you think about telling me or any of the others?"

I twisted toward her. "I did, but Blake killed that one and Daemon knew. And we were watching for them—"

"Sounds like a lame excuse to me." Was it an excuse? It was, because I should've told them. I swallowed the sudden lump in my throat. Her eyes flashed bright. "You have no idea how hard it was to keep everything from you in the beginning! How worried I was that you'd get hurt just being around us and . . ." Dee stopped, closing her eyes. "I can't believe Daemon kept this from me."

"You shouldn't be upset with Daemon. He did everything to stop this. He didn't trust that Blake just wanted to help control my abilities. It was my fault." And the guilt gnawed away at me, bit by bit. "I thought that Blake could help me. That if I knew how to control my abilities, I could fight—I could help you guys. You would no longer need to protect me or be worried about me. I wouldn't be your problem."

Her eyes snapped open. "You were never a problem to me, Katy! You were my best friend—my first, only real friend. And yeah, I'm a little slow on how the whole friendship thing works, but I do know that friends are supposed to trust each other. And you should've known that I never saw you as being weak or a problem."

"I . . ." I puttered out, not knowing what to say.

"You never believed in our friendship." Wetness gathered in her eyes, and I felt like the biggest tool ever. "That's the part that kills me. From the beginning, you didn't believe in me."

"I did!" I started to stand, but I froze. "I made stupid decisions, Dee. I made mistakes. And by the time I realized how bad my mistakes were, it was . . ."

"Too late," she whispered. "It was too late, wasn't it?"

"Yeah." I took a breath, but it got stuck. "Blake was who he was, and everything that happened was because of me. I know that."

Dee came forward, her steps measured and slow. "How long did you know about Beth and Dawson?"

I lifted my gaze, meeting hers. A huge part of me wanted to lie—wanted to say it wasn't until Will confirmed it, but I couldn't. "Before Christmas break, I saw Beth. And then Matthew confirmed that if Beth was alive, Dawson had to be."

She sucked in a cry and her fingers curled in. "How . . . how dare you?"

I could tell she wanted to slap me, and my cheek stung even though she hadn't. I kind of wished she would. "We didn't know if we could find him or get him back. We didn't want to get your hopes up only for you to lose him again."

Dee stared at me like she didn't even know me. "That is the stupidest thing I've ever heard. Let me guess, it was Daemon's idea? Because it sounds like him. He'd want to protect me at the same time as he was holding me back—hurting me."

"Daemon—"

"Don't," she said, turning away. Her voice shook. "Don't defend him. I know my brother. I know he has good intentions that usually just suck. But you—you know how much losing Dawson hurt. It wasn't just Daemon who lost his shit. I may not have moved the house off the foundation, but a part of me died the day I was told he was dead. I *deserved* to know the moment you thought he was alive."

"You're right."

Her body shimmered for a second. "Okay. Okay . . . all of that aside. If you had told me about what was going on with Blake, Adam and I would've known what we were walking into. We still would've done it—believe me, we would've gone into that house to help you—but we wouldn't have been blindsided."

My throat seized up. There was a stain on my soul, dark and cold. I hadn't murdered Adam, but I had a hand in his death. Like an accessory after the fact. People made mistakes all the time, but most of them didn't cause someone's death.

Mine did.

My shoulders sagged under the weight. Saying sorry wasn't going to smooth that over, not for her or me. I couldn't change the hand of time. All I could do now was move forward and try to make up for it.

The anger seeped out of Dee as she watched me. Walking back to the window seat, she sat, tucking her legs against her chest. She rested her cheek on her knees. "And now you guys are making another mistake."

"We don't have a choice," I said. "We really don't."

"Yes, you do. We could take care of Blake and whoever he's told."

"What about Dawson?" I asked quietly.

She didn't answer for a long time. "I know I should be able to put aside how I feel about Blake for him, but I can't. It's wrong. I know. But I can't."

I nodded. "I don't expect you to, but I don't want things to be like this between us. There's got to be a way . . ." Pride went out the window. "I miss you, Dee, and I hate that we haven't been talking and that you're upset with me. I want to get past this."

"I'm sorry," she whispered.

Tears burned the back of my throat. "What can I do to fix this?"

"You can't. And I can't, either." Dee shook her head sadly. "I can't fix Adam's death. I can't fix why you and Daemon think working with Blake is a good thing. And I can't fix our friendship. Some things are just broken."

13

Lesa came over after school on Tuesday to help study for our bio exam the next day, which sucked, because the last thing I could concentrate on was schoolwork. Part of me expected Matthew to reschedule, since he knew what I had to do tomorrow night. I even suggested it on Monday after class, but oh no, no can do.

I rocked back in my computer chair, my barely read bio textbook in my lap. Lesa was reading her notes, and I was supposed to be listening, but I cracked open my advanced copy of a new young adult novel for my Teaser Tuesday post.

Typing up a quick post, I picked a couple of quick lines with an evil grin. *'I was his power-up—the ace up his sleeve. I was the beginning and he was the end. And together, we were everything.'* I hit post and then closed the pretty amber cover of the book.

"You are so not paying attention," Lesa said, sitting up.

"Yeah, I am." I wheeled around, fighting a grin. "You were saying something about cells and organisms."

She arched a brow. "Wow. You got this in the bag."

"I'm gonna fail." I dropped my head back, closed my eyes, and let out a long-suffering sigh. "I just can't concentrate. I'd rather read something interesting—like this." I waved toward the book I'd just posted about and then to where I knew a whole stack of other books sat. "And there's this thing I have to do tomorrow night."

"Oh! What thing? A thing with Daemon, and if you say yes, please tell me that thing starts with an *s* and ends with an *x*."

I opened my eyes and frowned. "Geez, you're worse than a dude."

Her curls bounced as she nodded. "You know it."

I threw my pen at her.

Laughing, she closed her notebook. "So, what are you doing tomorrow that has you so distracted?"

There wasn't much I could tell her, but I was full of nervous energy, and the need to talk about it snaked past my lips. "Daemon and I are going to this . . . club or something in Martinsburg to visit some of his friends."

"Well, that sounds like fun."

I shrugged. I'd already told my mom that I was going to the movies and, since she worked tomorrow night, curfew wasn't an issue. What was an issue was the fact that I had no idea what to wear and the stuff with Dee had put me in a huge funk.

I popped up from my seat and stalked over to my closet. "I'm supposed to wear something sexy. I don't have anything sexy."

Lesa followed. "I'm sure you have something in here."

There was a sea of jeans and sweaters, nothing like what Blake hinted at. Anger crept up my throat. With Blake being back in school, it was just messed up. He was a murderer—my lab partner was a murderer.

Queasy, I pushed a stack of jeans to the side. "Yeah, I don't know about any of this."

Lesa brushed me aside. "Let me take a look. I am the queen of smexy stuff. At least that's what Chad thinks and, well, I kinda got to give it to the boy." She flashed me a quick, saucy grin. "He's got good taste."

I leaned against the wall. "Do your magic."

Five minutes later, Lesa and I stared at the items placed on my bed as if an invisible hooker was wearing them. My cheeks were already beet red. "Uh . . ."

Lesa giggled. "You should see your face."

I shook my head helplessly. "Do you see what I normally wear? This—this isn't me."

"That's the fun thing about going to clubs, especially ones out of town." Her nose wrinkled. "Well, there ain't any clubs here, so everything is out of town, but anyway, you get to be someone else. Let your inner stripper come out and play."

I busted out laughing. "My inner stripper?"

She nodded. "Haven't you ever snuck into a bar or a club?"

"Yeah, but they were on beaches and everyone was dressed for summer. It's not summer."

"So?"

I rolled my eyes as I turned back to the bed. Lesa had found a denim skirt I'd ordered online last year for summer, but it had ended up being way too short. Like barely-covering-the-butt short, and I'd been too lazy to return it. Spaced above the scrap of denim was a cropped black sweater I'd usually wear over a shirt or tank. It was long sleeved, so it would cover the scars on my wrists but barely anything else. On the floor was a pair of knee-high boots I'd gotten on sale last winter.

And that was all.

Yep, that was it.

"My butt and my boobs are going to be showing."

Lesa scuffed. "Your boobs will be covered."

"Not my entire stomach!"

"You have a nice stomach; show it off." She picked up the skirt, holding it to her waist. "When you're done with this, I so want to borrow it."

"Sure." And then I frowned. "Where are you going to wear it?"

"School." She laughed at the look on my face. "I'll put some tights on underneath it, you priss."

An idea struck. "Tights!" I spun toward my dresser and started rummaging through my socks. I pulled out a pair of black opaque tights. "A-ha! I can wear these." And a jacket . . . maybe a mask, too.

She snatched the tights from me, tossing them across the room. "You can't wear tights."

My face fell. "No?"

"No." She peered over my shoulder and then grinned as she reached around me and pulled something else out. "But these you could wear."

My mouth dropped open. A pair of ripped tights dangled from her fingers. "That was, like, a part of a Halloween costume."

"Perfect." She placed them on the bed.

Oh, dear Mary, mother of God . . . I sat cross-legged on the floor. "Well, I think Daemon will approve, at least."

"Damn straight." She flopped on the bed, her grin fading. "Can I ask you something and you answer it honestly?" Warning bells went off, but I nodded. She took a deep breath. "Seriously, how good of a kisser is Daemon? Because I imagine he just makes you—"

"Lesa!"

"What? A girl's gotta know these kinds of things."

I bit my lip, flushing.

"Come on, it's sharing and caring time."

"He . . . he kisses like he's dying of thirst, and I'm water." I smacked my hands over my hot face. "I can't believe I just said that out loud."

Lesa giggled. "Sounds like one of those romance books you read."

"It does." I started giggling. "But, oh Lordie Lord, it's true.

I'm like a puddle of mush when he kisses me. It's embarrassing. I'm so, like, 'Thank you, can I have another?' Sad."

We both broke into giggles. It was weird, because a lot of tension seeped out of my body. Giggling over boys was so amazingly normal.

"You love him, don't you?" she asked when she took a breath.

"I do." I stretched out my legs on a sigh. "I really do. What about Chad?"

She slipped off the bed and leaned against it. "I like him—a lot. But we're going to different colleges. So I'm being realistic about it."

"I'm sorry."

"Don't be. Chad and I are having fun and seriously, what's the point in anything if you ain't having fun? That's my motto in life." She paused, pushing her springy curls off her face. "I think I need to teach Dee that motto. What the hell is up with her? She still hasn't talked to me or Carissa."

All my humor vanished and I tensed up. *I can't fix our friendship.* I had tried—really tried—but the damages I inflicted on our friendship had been irreparable.

I sighed. "A lot of stuff has gone on with her—Adam and with Dawson coming home."

Lesa jumped on that. "Isn't that the strangest thing, though?"

"What do you mean?"

"Don't you think it's weird? You didn't live here then, but Beth and Dawson were like the Romeo and Juliet of West Virginia. I can't believe he hasn't heard from her."

Unease slid down my spine. "I don't know. What do you think?"

Lesa looked away, chewing on her bottom lip. "It's just weird. Like Dawson is way different now. He's all sullen and broody."

I struggled for something to say. "Well, he probably still cares for her and is upset about things not working out, and he misses Adam. You know, there's a lot going on there."

"I guess." She looked at me sideways. "Some people have been talking."

Instincts flared. "Talking about what?"

"Well, it's mostly been the usual suspects—Kimmy and them. But so many strange things have happened around here." She pushed to her feet and yanked her curls into a messy ponytail. "First, Beth and Dawson just drop off the face of the Earth. Then Sarah Butler dropped dead last summer."

Ice coated my skin. Sarah Butler had been in the wrong place at the wrong time. The night I'd been attacked by the Arum, Daemon had showed up and chased him off. Out of anger, the Arum had killed the girl.

Lesa started to pace. "And then Simon Cutters disappeared. No one has heard from him. Adam dies in a freak car accident, and then Dawson pops up out of nowhere, minus the supposed love of his life."

"It's weird," I said slowly, "but totally coincidental."

"Is it?" Her dark eyes gleamed. She shook her head. "Some of the kids—Simon's friends—think something's happened to him."

Oh, no. "Like what?"

"That he was killed." She sat beside me, her voice low as if people were listening. "And that Adam had something to do with it."

"What?" Okay, I was so not expecting that.

She nodded. "They don't think Adam's really dead. No funeral that anyone could go to and all. They think he ran off before the police could figure out he did something to Simon."

I stared. "Trust me, Adam's dead. He's really dead."

Lesa's lips pursed. "I believe you."

I didn't think she did. "Why do they think Adam had something to do with Simon?"

"Well . . . some people know that Simon tried something on you. And Daemon beat the crap out of him. Maybe he tried something on Dee and Adam snapped."

I laughed, more out of shock. "Adam wouldn't have snapped. He wasn't like that."

"That's what I think, but others . . ." She leaned back. "Anyway, enough about this crap—you're going to look hot tomorrow night."

The conversation eventually went back to studying, but I had this icy feeling in the pit of my stomach, a piercing sensation. Like when you did something bad and knew you were about to get caught.

If people were starting to pay attention to all the weird stuff around here, how long would it take them to follow the clues back to the source of everything? Back to Daemon, his family, his kind, and to me?

14

Martinsburg wasn't really a town, but it couldn't be called a city, either, at least not by Gainesville standards. It was on the cusp of growth, about an hour from the nation's capital. It rested right off the interstate, nestled between two mountains—a gateway to larger cities like Hagerstown and Baltimore. The south side of the town was heavily developed—shopping centers, restaurants I'd give my favorite book for Petersburg to have, and office buildings. There was even a Starbucks, and dammit if it didn't suck to have to drive past that. We were running late.

The whole trip started off badly, which didn't speak well for how the night would progress.

First off, Blake and Daemon had gotten into it before we even made it out of Petersburg. Something about the quickest way to get to the eastern panhandle of the state. Blake said to go south. Daemon said to go north. Epic argument ensued.

Daemon ended up winning, because he was driving, which made Blake pout in the backseat. Then we hit a snow squall around Deep Creek, slowing us down, and Blake had felt the need to point out that the southern roads were probably clear.

Also, the amount of obsidian I was decked out in and the lack of clothing had me all kinds of twitchy. I went with Lesa's choice in attire, much to Daemon's happiness. If he made one more comment about the length of my skirt, I was going to hurt him.

And if Blake did, Daemon was going to maim him.

I kept expecting a fleet of Arum to arrive out of the middle of nowhere and knock our vehicle off the road, but so far, the obsidian necklace, bracelet, and knife strapped inside my boot—*for crying out loud*—had stayed cool.

By the time we arrived in Martinsburg, I wanted to jump from the moving vehicle. As we neared the Falling Waters exit, Daemon asked, "Which one?"

Blake popped forward, dropping his elbows on the backs of our seats. "One more exit—Spring Mills. You're going to take a left off the exit, like you're heading back to Hedgesville or Back Creek."

Back Creek? I shook my head. We'd gone farther into civilization, but the names of some of these towns begged to differ.

About two miles off the exit, Blake said, "See the old gas station up ahead—the pumps?"

Daemon's eyes narrowed. "Yeah."

"Turn there."

I leaned forward to get a better view. Tall weeds surrounded old, worn-out pumps. There was a building—mostly a shack—behind them. "The club is in a gas station?"

Blake laughed. "No. Just drive around the building. Stay on the dirt road."

Muttering about getting Dolly dirty, Daemon followed Blake's sketchy directions. The dirt road was more like a path cleared by thousands of tires. This was so shady I wanted to demand we turn around.

The farther we went, the scarier the scenery got. Thick trees crowded the path, broken up by rundown buildings with boarded-up windows and empty black spaces where doors once stood.

"I don't know about this," I admitted. "I think I've seen all of this in *Texas Chainsaw Massacre*."

Daemon snorted. The SUV bumped over the uneven terrain, and then there were cars. Everywhere. Cars parked in haphazard lines, beside trees, crammed across a field. Beyond the endless rows of vehicles was a squat, square-shaped building with no outdoor lighting.

"Okay. I think I actually saw this in *Hostel*—One *and* Two."

"You'll be fine," Blake said. "The place is hidden so it stays off the grid, not because they kidnap and kill unsuspecting tourists."

I totally reserved the right to disagree on that.

Daemon parked as far away as he could, obviously more afraid of getting dings in Dolly's sides than us being eaten by Bigfoot.

A guy stumbled out from among a pack of cars. Moonlight glinted off his spiked collar and green Mohawk.

Or getting eaten by a goth kid.

I opened the door and climbed out, hugging my peacoat close. "What kind of place is this?"

"A very different kind of place," was Blake's answer. He slammed his door shut, and Daemon about snapped off his head. Rolling his eyes, Blake stepped around me. "You'll have to lose the jacket."

"What?" I glared at him. "It's freezing out. See my breath?"

"You're not going to freeze in the seconds it takes us to walk to the door. They're not going to let you in."

I felt like stomping my feet as I looked at Daemon helplessly. Like Blake, he was dressed in dark jeans and a shirt. Yep. That's all. Apparently, these people didn't care about the *male* dress code.

"I don't get it," I whined. My jacket was my saving grace. It was bad enough that the torn tights did nothing to hide my legs. "So not fair."

Daemon sauntered up to me, placing his hands on mine. A lock of wavy hair fell into his eyes. "We don't have to do this if you don't want to. I mean it."

"If she doesn't, then this was one huge time waster."

"Shut up," Daemon growled over his shoulder and then to me, "I'm serious. Tell me now, and we'll go home. There's got to be another way."

But there wasn't another way. Blake, God forgive me, was right. I was wasting time. Shaking my head, I stepped back and started unbuttoning my jacket. "I'm fine. Pulling on big girl undies and all that jazz."

Daemon watched quietly as I stripped away what felt like armor. My jacket off, he sucked in a low breath as I tossed it on the passenger seat. As cold as it was, my entire body somehow managed to feel like it was on fire.

"Yeah," he muttered, stepping in front of me like a shield. "I'm not so sure about this."

Over his shoulder, Blake's brows shut up. "Wow."

Daemon whipped around, arm flying out, but Blake darted to the left, narrowly missing Daemon's hand. Whitish-red sparks flew, lighting up the dark lot like firecrackers.

I crossed my arms over my bare midsection, exposed by the cropped sweater and the low-rise skirt. I felt naked, which was stupid, because I wore bathing suits. Shaking my head, I stepped around Daemon. "Let's get in there."

Blake's eyes drifted over me quickly enough to avoid certain death from the irritated alien behind me. My hand itched to smack his eyeballs out of the back of his head.

Our walk to the steel door at the corner of the building was quick. There were no windows or anything, but as we drew closer, the heavy beat of music could be felt outside.

"So do we knock—?"

Out of the shadows, a huge mother of a dude appeared. Arms like tree trunks were shown off by the torn overalls he wore. No shirt, because it was, like, a hundred degrees out here or something. The guy's hair was spiked into three sections across the center of his otherwise shaved skull. They were purple.

I liked purple.

I swallowed nervously.

Studs glinted all over his face: nose, lips, and eyebrows. Two thick bolts pierced his earlobes. He said nothing as he stopped in front of us, his dark eyes roaming over the guys and then stopping on me.

I took a step back, bumping into Daemon, who placed a hand on my shoulder.

"See something you like?" Daemon asked.

The dude was big—pro wrestler big—and he smirked like he was sizing Daemon up for dinner. And I knew Daemon was probably doing the same thing. The likelihood of us getting out of here without a massive brawl was slim.

Blake intervened. "We're here to party. That's all."

Pro Wrestler said nothing for a second and then reached for the door. Eyes fastened on Daemon, he opened the door and music blared. He gave a mocking bow. "Welcome to The Harbinger. Have fun."

The Harbinger? What a . . . lovely, reassuring name for a club.

Blake glanced over his shoulder and said, "I think he liked you, Daemon."

"*Shut up,*" Daemon said.

Blake let out a low laugh and went in, and my legs carried me through a tight hallway that suddenly spilled into a different world. One full of shadowed enclaves and flashing strobe lights, and the smell alone was almost overwhelming. Not bad, but a potent mixture of sweat, perfume, and other questionable aromas. The bitter taste of alcohol was thick in the air.

Blue, red, and white lights streamed and dazzled over the

teeming throng of undulating bodies in dizzying intervals. If I were prone to seizures, I'd be on the floor in a heartbeat. All the bare skin—mostly female—shimmered like the girls had been dusted with glitter. The dance floor was packed, bodies moving, some in rhythm, others just thrusting. Beyond it was a raised dance stage. A girl with long, blonde hair whirled in the center of the chaos; her slender body was short but she moved like a dancer, all graceful and fluid motions as she spun.

I couldn't take my eyes off her. She stopped spinning; her lower half still swayed in tune to the beat as she shoved the damp hair back. Her face was radiant with innocence, her smile beautiful and wide. She was young—too young to be in a place like this.

Then again, as my eyes scanned the crowd, a lot of the kids were definitely not of drinking age. Some were, but the vast majority looked like they were our age.

But the most interesting part was what was above the stage. Cages hung from the ceiling, occupied by scantily clad girls. *Go-go dancers* was what my mom would've called them. I wasn't sure what the name was now, but the chicks had on some kick-ass boots. The top halves of their faces were covered with glittery masks. All of them had hair that was all the colors of the rainbow.

I glanced down at the skin between my denim skirt and cropped sweater. Yeah, I really could've gone crazier.

Even stranger, there wasn't a table or set of chairs anywhere I could see. There were couches peeking out of the shadowed sidelines, but there was no way in hell I'd sit on those things.

Daemon's hand was firmly on my back as he bent over, speaking into my ear. "A little out of your element, Kitten?"

Funny thing was, Daemon still stood out in this crowd. He was a good head taller than most, and none of them moved like him or looked like him. "I think you should've gone with the eyeliner."

His lips quirked up. "Not ever going to happen."

Blake moved in front of us as we followed him around the dance floor, the fast techno beat easing off and another picking up, heavy on the drums.

Everyone stopped.

Fists suddenly shot into the air, followed by shouts, and my eyes widened. Was there going to be a mosh pit? A part of me kind of wanted to try that out. The angry beat may have had something to do with it. The cage girls slammed their hands against the bars. The pretty girl on the stage with all that blond hair had disappeared.

Daemon's hand slid to mine and squeezed. My ears strained to pick up the lyrics over the screams. *Safe from pain and truth and choice and other poison devils . . .* The yells picked up, drowning out everything except the drums.

The hair rose on the back of my neck.

There was definitely something up with this club. Not right . . . Not right at all.

We rounded the bar and entered a narrow hallway. People were against the walls, so close to one another I couldn't tell where one body began and another ended. A guy peered up from the neck he was busy with, and his heavily kohl-outlined eyes met mine.

He winked.

I quickly looked away. Note to self: do not make eye contact.

Before I knew it, we'd stopped at a door that read Person-nel Only, but the Personnel part had been scratched out and someone had written Freaks in permanent marker.

Nice.

Blake went to rap his knuckles on the door, but it cracked open first. I couldn't see who was behind it. I glanced over my shoulder. Kohl Eyes was still watching. Skeevy.

"We're here to see Luc," Blake said.

Whatever the mystery person behind the door said didn't look good, because Blake's spine went rigid. "Tell him it's Blake, and he owes me." There was a pause and the back of his neck flushed red. "I don't care what he's doing; I *need* to see him."

"Great," Daemon muttered, his body tensing and relaxing in intervals. "He's friendless as usual."

Another garbled response and the door opened a little more. Then Blake growled, "Dammit, he owes me. These people are cool. Trust me. No bugs here."

Bugs? Oh, another word for implants.

Finally Blake turned to us, his brows drawn tightly. "He wants to talk to me first. Alone."

Daemon drew up to his full height. "Yeah, not gonna happen."

Blake didn't back down. "Then nothing's going to happen. Either you do as he wants and someone will come for you, or we made this trip for nothing."

I could tell Daemon wasn't cool with this, and I hadn't sat through the car ride from hell and brought out my inner stripper for nothing. Rising onto my toes, I pressed against his back. "Let's dance." Daemon turned halfway, eyes flashing. I tugged on his hand. "Come on."

He relented and as he turned completely, over his shoulder I saw the door open and Blake slid through. A bad feeling settled in my stomach, but there wasn't anything we could do now that we were here.

The drums had faded off, and a somewhat familiar song had started. Taking a deep breath, I pulled Daemon out to the floor, slipping around bodies as I searched out a spot. Finding one, I pivoted around.

He watched me curiously, almost like he was saying, *Are we really doing this?* We were. Dancing seemed crazy when so much rested on the information we'd come for, but I pushed away our reasons for coming here. Closing my eyes and drawing on courage, I stepped up to him, draped an arm around his neck, and placed my other hand on his waist.

I started to move against him, like the other dancers were, because in reality, when guys danced, they sort of just stood there and let the girls do all the work. If I remembered correctly from the few times I'd snuck off to clubs with friends in Gainesville, the girls made the guys look good.

It took a few seconds of stiffness to find the beat to the song and loosen up muscles that hadn't really seen any action recently, but when I did, the rhythm of the music resonated in my head and then through my body, my limbs. Swaying to the music, I whirled around and my shoulders moved with my hips. Daemon's arm crept around my waist, and I felt his chin graze my neck.

"Okay. I might have to thank Blake for being friendless," he said into my ear.

I smiled.

His arm tightened as the beat picked up and so did my movements. "I think I like this."

All around us, bodies were slick and shiny with sweat, as if they'd been dancing for years. That was the thing about places like this—you get caught up and hours go by but it only feels like long minutes.

Daemon spun me back to him, and I was on the tips of my boots, facing him. His head lowered, forehead pressing against mine, our lips brushing. A rush of power went through Daemon, transferring to my skin, and in the flashing lights, we were lost in this world. Our bodies surged with the beat, fitting together fluidly while others seemed to thrash beside us, never able to find the right sync.

When Daemon's lips pressed more firmly against mine, I

opened up, not losing the rhythm even though he was stealing my breath. My—*our* hearts were pounding, hands grabbing, clutching, his slipping over the curve of my back, and behind my lids, I saw a pinprick of white light.

Sliding my hands across his cheeks, I kissed him back. Static flowed, cascading off our bodies in streams of reddish-white light that was hidden under the flickering strobe lights, flowing over the floor like a wave of electricity. And all around us, people danced, either oblivious to the shocks or fueled by them, but I didn't care. Daemon's hands were on my hips, tugging me closer, and we were so gonna end up like one of those ambiguous couples in the hallway.

The music may've stopped or changed or whatever, but we were still pressed together, practically devouring each other. And maybe later, tomorrow or next week, I might be embarrassed by the PDA, but not now.

A hand landed on Daemon's shoulder, and he whirled away. With a second to spare, I grabbed his arm, stopping his fist from saying hello to Blake's jaw.

Blake smiled and yelled over the blaring music, "Are you guys having sex or dancing?"

My cheeks flared. Okay, maybe right now I'd be embarrassed.

Daemon growled something and Blake took a step back, hands going up. "Sorry," he shouted. "Geez. He's ready to see us if you're done eating each other's faces."

Blake was going to get punched at some point.

Taking my hand again, I followed Daemon and Blake back through the snake-like bodies and down the hallway. My heart was still racing, my chest rising and falling too fast. That dance . . .

Kohl Eyes was gone and this time when Blake went to knock, the door opened all the way. I followed, hoping my face wasn't burning.

I'm not sure what I was expecting to find behind the door. Maybe a smoky, dark room with men wearing sunglasses, cracking their knuckles, or another big guy in overalls, but I wasn't expecting what I found.

The room was large and the air clean, vanilla-scented. There were several couches, one occupied by a boy with shoulder-length brown hair tucked back behind his ears. Like the girl I'd seen dancing earlier, he was young. Maybe fifteen, if that, and he had holes in his jeans the size of Mars. Around his wrist was a silver cuff that circled a strange stone. It was black, but not obsidian. In the center of the stone, there was a reddish-orange flame and below it, speckles of blue and green.

Whatever stone it was, it was beautiful and *expensive* looking.

The kid glanced up from the DS he was playing on, and I was kind of dumbstruck by his boyish beauty. Eyes the color of amethyst locked with mine briefly and then went back to the game. That kid was going to be a looker one day.

Then I realized Daemon had stiffened and was staring at a guy in a leather chair. Stacks of hundreds were splayed across the desk in front of an icy-blond guy who was staring back at Daemon, brilliant silver eyes wide with shock.

The guy was probably in his early thirties, and my God, he was gorgeous.

Daemon stepped forward. The guy stood. And my heart sped up. My worst fears spread through me like wildfire. "What's going on?" I asked. Even Blake seemed nervous.

The kid on the couch coughed out a laugh, closing his DS. "Aliens. They have this wacky internal system that lets them sniff each other out. Guess neither of them was expecting to see the other."

I turned to the kid slowly.

He sat up, swinging his legs off the couch. He would've had a baby face if it wasn't for the keen intelligence in his eyes or the experience set in the hard lines of his mouth. "So, you crazy kids want to break into the Daedalus stronghold and you want my help?"

I gaped. Luc was a mother-freaking *kid*.

15

I waited for the kid to yell, "Psyche!" and scamper off to the nearest playground, but as the seconds stretched out, I came to accept that our messiah of information was barely a teen.

Luc smiled as if he knew what I was thinking. "Surprised? You shouldn't be. Surprised about anything, that is."

He stood, and I was shocked to discover that he was almost as tall as Daemon. "I was six when I decided to play chicken with a speeding cab. It won. Lost the coolest bike evah and a lot of blood, but lucky me, my childhood friend was an alien."

"How . . . how did you get away from Daedalus?" And so young, I wanted to add.

Luc moved over to the table, his steps smooth and effortless. "I was their star pupil." His grin was wicked, almost disturbing. "Never trust the one who excels. Isn't that right, Blake?"

Leaning against the wall, Blake gave a lopsided shrug. "Sounds about right."

"Why?" Luc sat on the edge of the desk. "Because eventually the pupil becomes smarter than the teacher, and I had some really, really intelligent teachers. So." He clapped his hands together. "You must be Daemon Black."

If Daemon was surprised Luc knew his name, he didn't show it. "That would be me."

The kid's ridiculously long lashes lowered. "I've heard of you. Blake's a big fan."

Blake raised a middle finger.

Daemon said drily, "Glad to know my fan club is far reaching."

Luc cocked his head to the side. "And what a fan club—oh, my bad, I didn't introduce you to your fellow Luxen all-star. This guy goes by Paris. Why? I don't know."

Paris smiled tightly as he extended his hand toward Daemon. "Always nice to meet another not bound by old beliefs and unnecessary rules."

Daemon shook his hand. "Same. How did you fall in with him?"

Luc laughed. "Long story for a different day—if there is a different day." Those extraordinary peepers slid back to me. "Do you have any idea what they will do to you if they realize you're a fully functional hybrid?" He tipped his head down, grinning. "We are so very rare. Three of us together is actually quite amazing."

"I have a good imagination," I said.

"Do you?" Luc's brows rose. "I doubt Blake has even told you the half of it—the worst of it."

I glanced at Blake. His expression went on lockdown. An icy wind ran up my spine that had nothing to do with my lack of clothing.

"But you know that." Luc stood and stretched, like a cat after a nap. "And still you are willing to take the huge risk of going into the hornet's nest."

"We really don't have a choice." Daemon shot the quiet Blake a dark look. "So are you going to give us the codes or not?"

Luc shrugged, running his fingers over the stacks of money. "What's in it for me?"

I exhaled roughly. "Other than pissing off Daedalus, we

really don't have much to offer."

"Hmm, I don't know about that." He picked up a cluster of hundreds secured with a rubber band. A second later, the edges of the bills curled inward, paper melting until the scorched scent filled the air and nothing remained.

I was envious, considering the whole using-light-for-heat-and-fire thing completely passed me over. "What can we do for you?"

"Obviously money's not an issue," Daemon added.

Luc's lips twitched. "Money isn't needed." He brushed his fingers off on his jeans. "Power isn't, either. Honestly, the only thing I need is a favor."

Blake snapped off the wall. "Luc—"

His eyes narrowed. "A favor is all I want—one that I can collect at any time. That's what I want in return, and I'll give you all you need to know."

Well, that sounded easy. "O—"

"Wait," Daemon cut me off. "You want us to agree to a favor without knowing what that favor is?"

Luc nodded. "Where's the risk if you know everything?"

"Where's the intelligence if we don't?" Daemon shot back.

The kid laughed. "I like you. A lot. But my help doesn't come without its own peril in exchange."

"God, you're like the preteen mafia," I muttered.

"Something like that." He flashed a beatific smile. "What you—all of you—don't understand is there are things much, much bigger than a brother's girlfriend or a friend . . . or even ending up under the man's thumb. There's change brewing behind the winds, and the winds are going to be fierce." He looked at Daemon. "The government fears the Luxen, because they represent mankind's fall from the top of the food chain. To fix that, they've created something much stronger than a Luxen. And I'm not talking about ordinary little baby hybrids."

I shivered. "What are you talking about?"

His purplish eyes met mine, but he said nothing.

Paris folded his arms. "Not to be rude, but if you're not willing to deal, there's the door."

Daemon and I exchanged looks. I honestly didn't know what to say. It seriously was like making a deal with the mafia—with a creepy kid-mafia boss.

"Guys," Blake said. "He's our only chance."

"Christ," Daemon muttered. "Fine. We owe you a favor."

Luc's eyes gleamed. "And you?"

I sighed. "Sure. Why not."

"Awesome! Paris?" He held out his hand. Paris bent down, grabbed a small MacBook Air, and handed it over. "Give me a sec."

We watched him punch away at the keyboard, brows drawn in concentration. While we waited, a door at the back of the room opened and the young girl from the stage peeked her head into the room.

Luc's head jerked up. "Not now."

The girl's frown was epic, but she closed the door. "She's the girl on—"

"Don't finish that sentence if you want me to continue. Don't even talk about her. Frankly, you've never even seen her," Luc said, eyes fastened on the screen again. "All deals will be off."

I clamped my mouth shut even though I had a thousand questions about how the two of them got away and how they were surviving virtually unprotected.

Finally, Luc placed the laptop on the desk. The screen was split into four sections, black and white, also grainy, like security film. One image contained woods. Another was of a tall fence and gate, the other a security booth, and the final one showed a man in uniform patrolling another section of fence.

"Say hello to Mount Weather—owned by FEMA, secured by

Homeland Security. Nestled away in the majestic Blue Ridge Mountains, it's used as a training facility and a stowaway for all the pretty officials in case someone bombs us," Luc said, snickering. "Also known as a complete front for the DOD and Daedalus, because underground, there are six-hundred thousand mother-effin' square feet for training and torture."

Blake stared at the screen. "You hacked into their security systems?"

He shrugged. "Like I said, star pupil and all. See this section here." He pointed to the screen where a guard patrolled the fence, almost blending into the grainy background. "This is the 'secret' entrance that doesn't exist. Very few people are aware of it—Blakey-boy is."

Luc tapped the space bar, and the camera moved to the right. A gate came into view. "Here's the dealio: Sunday evening at nine p.m. is going to be your best bet. It's a shift change and staffing is at a minimum—only two guards will be patrolling this gate. 'Cause, you know, Sunday is kind of a down day."

Paris whipped out a pad and a pen.

"This gate is your first obstacle of choice. You'll need to take out the guards, but that's a duh. I'll make sure the cameras are down between nine and nine fifteen—you know, pull a *Jurassic Park* moment. You'll have fifteen minutes to get in, get your buddies, and get the hell out. So don't let a spitting dragon take you down."

Daemon choked on a laugh.

"Fifteen minutes," Blake murmured, nodding. "Doable. Once inside the compound, the entrance leads to elevators. We can take them down to the tenth floor and go right up to the cell."

"Great." Luc tapped his finger on the gate. "The code to this gate is *Icarus*. See a trend?" He laughed. "You get inside the compound, you'll see three doors side by side."

Blake nodded again. "The middle door—I know. The code?"

"Wait. Where do the other doors take you?" I asked.

"To the great Oz," Luc said, tapping the space bar until the camera was now focused on the doors. "Actually, nowhere interesting. Just offices and actual FEMA stuff. Anyone want to guess what the code to this door is?"

"Daedalus?" I threw out.

He grinned. "Close. The code to this door is *Labyrinth*. It's a hard word to spell, I know, but make sure you do it correctly. You get one chance. Enter the wrong code and it'll get ugly. Take the elevator to the sixth floor like Blake said and then you enter the code *DAEDALUS*—all caps. *Voilà*!"

Daemon shook his head, doubtful. "There're only codes to enter? That's their security?"

"Ha!" Luc hit a few buttons and the screen went black. "I'm doing more than giving you codes and taking down cameras, my new BFF. I'm going to take down their eye recognition software. It can go down for about ten to fifteen minutes a day without raising an eyebrow."

"What happens if we're still in there and it goes back up?" I asked.

Luc raised his hands. "Uh, kind of like being on a plane that's about to crash. Stick your head between your knees and kiss 'em good-bye."

"Oh, that sounds great," I said. "So you're like a mutant hacker, too?"

He winked. "But be careful. I'm not taking down any other security precautions they may've decided to put up. *That* will raise concerns."

"Whoa." Daemon frowned. "What other security precautions could they have?"

"They rotate the codes every other day, I've discovered. Other than that, nothing but guards, but it's a shift change." Blake grinned. "We'll be fine. We got this."

Paris handed over a sheet with the codes scribbled down. Daemon snatched it before Blake could and slipped it into his pocket. "Thank you," he said.

Returning to the couch and his DS, Luc dropped down, his smile fading. "Don't thank me yet. Actually, don't thank me at all. I don't exist, you know, not until I need my favor." He flipped open his DS. "Just remember, this Sunday at nine p.m. You have fifteen minutes and that is all."

"Okay." I drew out the word, glancing at Blake. I would love to know how these two met. "Well, I guess . . ."

"We'll be going," Daemon supplied, taking my hand. "It was nice, kind of, meeting you all."

"Whatevs," he said, thumbs flying over the game board. Luc's voice stopped us at the door. "You have no idea what waits for you. Be careful. I would hate for my dealing to be one-sided if you all get yourselves killed . . . or worse."

I shuddered. Nice way to close the conversation with a healthy dose of freak-us-out.

Daemon nodded at the other Luxen, and we headed out, Blake closing the door behind him. Only then did I realize the room was soundproof.

"Well," Blake said, smiling. "That wasn't too bad, was it?"

I rolled my eyes. "I have the feeling we just made a deal with the devil, and he's going to come back and want our first-born child or something."

Daemon waggled his brows. "You want kids? Because you know, practice makes—"

"Shut up." I shook my head and started walking.

We hurried through the club, around the still-packed dance floor. I think all of us were ready to get out of there. As we neared the exit, I looked around Daemon and Blake, my eyes drifting over the dance floor.

Part of me wondered how many, if any, were hybrids. We were rare, but like I sensed at first, there was something different about this place. Something really different about the kid called Luc, too.

Pro Wrestler greeted us at the door. He stepped aside, massive arms folded across his chest. "Remember," he said. "You were never here."

16

We got home late from Martinsburg, and I went straight to bed. Daemon followed, but all we did was curl up and sleep. Both of us were exhausted from everything, and it was nice with him there, a steady presence that relaxed and soothed my frazzled nerves.

I was a zombie on Thursday, and Blake's disgustingly chipper attitude in bio made me want to hurl.

"You should be happier," he whispered as I hastily scribbled down notes. No doubt I'd failed the exam yesterday. "After Sunday, everything will be over."

Everything will be over. My pen stopped. A muscle in my neck tensed. "It won't be easy."

"Yes, it will be. You just need faith."

I almost laughed. Faith in who? Blake? Or the mafia kid? I didn't trust either of them. "After Sunday, you'll be gone."

"Like the last decade," he replied.

After class, I packed up my stuff, smiled at something Lesa said, and then waited for Dawson. I didn't like to leave him alone with Blake. Not when Dawson was eyeballing the dude like he wanted to pummel information out of him.

Blake brushed past us, grinning as he switched his books to

his other hand. He swaggered on down the hall, waving at a group of kids that called out his name.

"I don't like him," Dawson grumbled.

"Get in line." We headed down the hall. "But we need him until Sunday."

Dawson stared ahead. "Still don't like him." And then he asked, "He had a thing for you, didn't he?"

My cheeks burned. "What makes you think that?"

A small smile appeared. "My brother's hate for him knows no bounds."

"Well, he did kill Adam," I said in a low voice.

"Yeah, I know, but it's personal."

I frowned. "How is it more personal than that?"

"It is." Dawson pushed open the door, and we were attacked by the giggle squad on the landing.

Kimmy was captain. "Wow. Why aren't I surprised?"

I found myself moving in front of Dawson. "And why do I have no clue what you're talking about?"

Behind me, Dawson shifted his weight from one foot to the other.

"Well, it's pretty obvious." She leaned against the rail, her backpack resting on the top. Around her, the girls tittered. "One brother isn't enough for you."

Before I could react, Dawson stepped around me and spat, "You're sad and revolting."

Kimmy's smile froze, and maybe the old Dawson would've never said anything like that, because she and all her friends looked like someone just walked over their graves. Somewhere, in the back of my mind, I wanted to laugh, but I was so angry—so repulsed by the suggestion I'd be seeing two twin brothers.

I honestly don't know what happened next. A pulse of energy left me, and the pretty pink backpack shook and then tipped over the railing. The weight jerked Kimmy. Her heeled shoes came off the floor, and in a flash I saw what was going to happen.

She was going to go right over the railing, headfirst.

A scream started in my throat and came out of Kimmy. Her friends' horrified looks were permanently etched in my memory, and my heartbeat skyrocketed.

Dawson shot forward, catching one of her flailing arms. He had her on her feet before her scream had faded from my ears. "I got you," he said, surprisingly gentle. Kimmy gulped in air, clutching Dawson's hand. "It's okay. You're okay."

He carefully pried her fingers off his and stepped back. Her friends immediately surrounded her. Then he turned to me, his eyes clouded. Cupping my elbow, he quickly steered me down the stairwell.

As soon as we were out of hearing distance, he stopped and faced me. "What was that?"

My breath caught and I looked away, confused and full of shame. Everything had happened so fast, and I'd been so furious. But it had been me—a part of me that had acted without thought or knowledge. A part of me that had known the weight of her bag would've toppled her right over the edge.

At lunch, I didn't tell Daemon about what happened with Kimmy in the stairwell, convincing myself that since Carissa and Lesa were with us, it was so not the conversation to have. It was nothing more than an excuse, but I felt as revolting as Kimmy's words. Later that day, when we were at Daemon's house, going over plans for Sunday with the crew, I told myself it still wasn't the time.

Especially when Dee was demanding to go and Daemon was having none of that.

"I need you and Ash to hang back, along with Matthew, just in case something goes wrong."

Dee folded her arms. "What, you don't think I can handle myself with you guys? That I might trip and stab Blake to death?"

Her brother shot her a bland look. "Well, now that you say it . . ."

She rolled her eyes. "Is Katy going in with you?"

My shoulders slumped. *Here we go.*

Daemon's body tensed. "I don't want—"

"Yes." I cut him off with a deadly look. "Only because I got most of us into this mess, and Blake won't do any of this without Daemon and me."

Ash smirked from the settee. Other than staring at Daemon like she wanted to rekindle their romance, she wasn't doing or saying much. "How valiant of you, Katy."

I ignored her. "But we do need people on the outside in case something goes wrong."

"What?" Andrew asked. "You don't trust Blake? Go figure."

Daemon sat back, running both his hands through his hair. "Anyway, we'll be in and out. Then everything . . . everything will be over."

His brother blinked slowly, and I knew he was thinking about Beth. Maybe even picturing her, and I wondered how long it had been since he last saw her. So I asked and surprisingly, he answered.

"I don't know. Time there was different. Weeks? Months?" He stood, shoulders rolling. "I don't think I was at that Mount place. The place was always warm and dry whenever I was taken outside."

Taken outside, like a pet or something. Wrong on so many levels.

Dawson let out a ragged breath. "I need to walk or move."

I looked around quickly. The sun had set a while ago. Not like he needed it, though. He was already out the door before anyone could say a thing.

"I'll go." It was Dee this time.

Andrew stood. "I'll follow."

"I guess I'm out of here." This from Ash.

Matthew sighed. "One of these days, we will get through everything without any drama."

Daemon laughed tiredly. "Good luck with that."

In about five minutes, everyone except Daemon was cleared out of the house. Perfect time to 'fess up to almost breaking Kimmy's neck, except there was a glint in Daemon's jade-colored eyes.

My mouth dried. "What?"

Daemon stood and stretched, flashing a slice of taut skin. "It's quiet." He offered his hand and I took it in mine. "It's never quiet around here. Not anymore."

He did have a point. I let him tug me to my feet. "It's not going to last long."

"Nope." He pulled me to him and a second later, I was in his arms and we were zooming up the stairs. He placed me on my feet in his bedroom. "Admit it. You like my method of travel."

Feeling a little dizzy, I laughed. "One of these days I'm going to be faster than you."

"Keep dreaming."

"Tool," I threw back.

Daemon's lips curved up on one side. "Trouble."

"Oh." I widened my eyes. "Harsh."

"We should make use of this quiet time." He advanced toward me, like a predator with its prey in its sight.

"Really?" Suddenly feeling way too hot, I backed up until I hit his bed.

"Really." He kicked off his shoes. "I say we have about thirty minutes before someone interrupts us."

My gaze dropped as he pulled off his shirt and tossed it. I sucked in a sharp breath. "Probably not that long."

His lips formed a wicked smile. "True. So let's say we have twenty minutes, give or take five." He stopped in front of me, his eyes hooded. "Not nearly enough time for what I'd like to do, but we can work around that."

Heat swept through my veins, and I felt dizzy again. "We can?"

"Mmm-hmm." He placed his hands on my shoulders and pressed down until I was sitting on the very edge of the bed. Running his hands to my cheeks, he knelt between my boneless legs so that we were eye level with each other.

Daemon's lashes lowered, fanning his cheeks. "I've missed you."

I wrapped my fingers around his wrists. "You've seen me every day."

"Not enough," he murmured and pressed his lips where my pulse pounded along my neck. "And we're always with someone."

God, wasn't that the truth. Last time we were alone for any considerable amount of time, we'd both slept. So these moments were precious, brief, and stolen.

I smiled as he trailed a line of kisses up my chin, stopping short of my lips. "We probably shouldn't spend it talking, then."

"Uh-huh." He kissed a corner of my lips. "Talking is such a time waster." And then he kissed the other corner. "And when we talk, we usually end up arguing."

I laughed. "Not always."

Daemon pulled back, brows raised. "Kitten . . ."

"Okay." I scooted back and he followed, climbing over me,

his arms huge and powerful. God, I was in way over my head with him sometimes. "You might be right, but you're wasting time."

"I'm always right."

I opened my mouth to disagree, but his lips took control of mine, and his kiss reached deep down inside me, melted muscle and bone. His tongue swept over mine, and at that moment, he could have been right all he wanted as long as he kept kissing me like that.

I slid my fingers through his hair, tugging when he lifted his head. I started to protest, but he was kissing his way down my throat, over the edge of my cardigan, down the little buttons shaped like flowers, and lower still, until I couldn't keep ahold of his head. Or really keep track of where he was heading.

Daemon sat back on his haunches, going for my boots. He tugged one off, pitching it over his shoulder. It bounced off the wall with a soft *thud*. "What are these made of? Rabbit skin?"

"What?" I giggled. "No. They're faux sheepskin."

"They're so soft." He got the other one off and that too hit the wall. My socks were next. He kissed the top of my foot, and I jerked. "Not as soft as this, though." Grinning, he lifted his head. "Love the tights, by the way."

"Yeah?" My gaze fixed on the ceiling, but I really wasn't seeing a damn thing. Not when his hands moved up my calves. "Is it . . . because they're red?"

"That." I felt his cheek on my knee, and my hands fluttered to the bed. "And because they're so thin. And hot, but you already know that."

Hot? I felt hot. His hands traveled up my outer thighs, under the denim skirt, pushing the material up and up. I bit down on my lip, hard enough that a metallic taste sprung into my mouth. The material really was thin, a fragile almost nonexistent barrier between his skin and mine. I could feel every touch, and even the slightest was like a thousand volts of electricity.

"Kitten . . ."

"Hmm?" I fisted the covers.

"Just making sure you're still with me." He kissed the side of my leg, right above my knee. "Don't want you falling asleep or anything."

Like sleep was possible. Ever.

His eyes flared. "You know what. Give me two minutes. That's all I need."

"Whatever," I said. "What are you going to do with the left-over eighteen minutes?"

"Snuggle."

I started to laugh, but his fingers found the band along the top of my tights, and he pulled them down, cursing when they got tangled at my feet.

"Need help?" I offered, voice shaking.

"Got it," he muttered, balling them up. They too went flying somewhere.

Things were going further than they had before. I was nervous, but I didn't want to stop. I was too curious, and I trusted him irrevocably. And then there was nothing separating his hands from my skin or his lips and I stopped thinking, wasn't capable of forming any coherent thought. There was just him and the crazy rush of sensations he pulled forth, drew from me like an artist rendering some kind of masterpiece. Then I wasn't even me anymore, because my body couldn't shake that much. Like a balloon being pulled down and then released, I was floating and there was a soft whitish glow slipping over the walls that wasn't coming off Daemon.

When I came back down, Daemon's eyes were brilliant diamonds. He looked sort of awed, which I found strange, because he awed me.

"You glowed a little," he said, rising up. "I've only seen you do that once."

I knew the night, but I didn't want to think about that right now. I was happy where I was floating. It was good—great, even, and I really couldn't talk. My brain was mush. I had no idea *that* could be like that. Heck, I was shocked it even happened. I felt like I needed to say thank you or something.

The smile he gave me was part male pride and arrogance, like he knew he'd scrambled my brain. He stretched out beside me, tugging me close to him. He lowered his head, kissing me softly, deeply.

"Wasn't even two minutes," he said. "Told you."

My heart was somewhere in my throat. "You were right."

"Always."

17

Sometime later, I tried to stretch and when I spoke, my voice was muffled against his chest. "I can't move."

His laugh rumbled through me as he loosened his embrace. "This is how we snuggle."

"I really should head next door soon." I yawned, not wanting to leave. I was so relaxed I couldn't feel my toes. "Mom will be home soon."

"Do you have to leave now?"

I shook my head. We had maybe an hour. I wanted to make her dinner, so another thirty or forty minutes tops. Daemon placed a finger on my chin and lifted it. "What?" I asked.

His eyes searched mine. "I wanted to talk before you leave."

Anxiety blossomed low. "About what?"

"Sunday," he said, and my anxiety turned darker. "I know you feel like you got us into this, but you know you didn't, right?"

"Daemon . . ." I so knew where this conversation was heading. "We are at this point because of the decisions I—"

"We," he corrected gently. "Decisions *we* made."

"If I hadn't trained with Blake and had listened to you, we wouldn't be here. Adam would be alive. Dee wouldn't hate my guts. Will wouldn't be running around doing God knows what." I squeezed my eyes shut. "I could go on and on. You get my drift."

"And if you hadn't made any of those decisions, we wouldn't have Dawson back. It was kind of a stupid-smart move."

I laughed drily. "There's that."

"You can't carry this guilt with you, Kat." The bed moved as he rose up on one elbow. "You'll end up like me."

I peeked at him. "What? An extremely tall and douchey alien?"

He smiled. "The jerky part, yes. I blamed myself for what happened to Dawson. It changed me. I'm still not back to where I was before everything happened. Don't do that to yourself."

Harder said than done, but I nodded. Last thing I wanted was for Daemon to worry about the possibility of my future therapy bills. And it was time to get to what I knew he wanted. "You don't want me going Sunday."

Daemon took a deep breath. "Hear me out, okay?" When I nodded, he continued. "I know you want to help, and I know you can. I've seen what you're capable of. You can be pretty scary when mad."

He has no idea, I thought wryly.

"But . . . if things go south, I don't want you involved." His gaze held mine. "I want you to be somewhere safe."

I knew where he was coming from and I wanted to reassure him, but staying behind wasn't something I could do. "I don't want *you* involved, Daemon. I want *you* somewhere safe, but I'm not asking you to stay out of it."

His brows knitted. "That's different."

I sat up, smoothing out my sweater. "How's that different? And if you say it's because you're a guy, I'm going to hurt you."

"Come on, Kitten."

My eyes narrowed.

He sighed. "It's more than that. It's because I have experi-ence. That simple. You don't."

"Okay, you have a point, but I've also been *inside* a cage. With that intimate knowledge, I have more reason than you not to get caught."

"And that's more of a reason why I don't want you doing this." His eyes flared an intense green. A sure sign he was seconds from tapping into his protective-fueled temper. "You have no idea what went through my head when I saw you in that cage—when I hear how your voice *still* rasps when you get excited or upset. You screamed until there—"

"I don't need a reminder," I snapped, and then cursed under my breath. I tried to rein in my own temper. I put my hand on his arm. "One of the things I love about you is how protective you are, but it also drives me crazy. You can't pro-tect me forever."

His look said he could and would try.

I exhaled roughly. "I need to do this—I need to help Dawson and Beth."

"And Blake?" he asked.

"What?" I stared at him. "Where did that come from?"

"I don't know." He moved his arm away from me. "It doesn't matter. Can—"

"Wait. It does matter. Why would I want to help Blake after what he pulled? He killed Adam! I wanted him dead. You were the one who was, like, turning over a new leaf or something."

The moment those words left my mouth, I regretted them. His expression went on lockdown.

"I'm sorry," I said, meaning it. "I know why you didn't want to . . . do away with Blake, but I have to do this. It'll help me get past what I caused. Like making amends or something."

"You don't—"

"I do."

Daemon turned his cheek, jaw clenching. "Can you do this for me? Please?"

My chest ached, because when Daemon said please, which was rare, I knew how much something bothered him. "I can't."

Seconds passed and his shoulders tensed. "This is stupid. You shouldn't be doing this. All I'm going to worry about is you getting hurt."

"See? That's the problem! You can't always be worried about my getting hurt."

His brow arched. "You're *always* getting hurt."

My mouth dropped open. "I am not!"

He laughed. "Yeah, try that again."

I pushed at him, but he was a wall of immovable muscle. Infuriated, I scrambled over him, even more furious when I saw the humored glint in his eyes. "God, you tick me off."

"Well, at least I got you—"

"Don't even finish that statement!" I snatched up my socks and tights. Rolling them on, I hobbled on one foot. "Ugh, I hate you sometimes."

He sat up in one fluid motion. "Not too long ago, you were really, *really* loving me."

"Shut up." I moved on to the other leg. "I'm going with you guys on Sunday. That's it. End of discussion."

Daemon stood. "I don't want you going."

I wiggled up my tights, glaring at him. "You don't get to say what I can and can't do, Daemon." I grabbed one of my boots, wondering how it got all the way over there. "I'm not a frail, helpless heroine in need of your rescue."

"This isn't a book, Kat."

I yanked on my other boot. "No, really? Crap. I was hoping you skipped to the end and would tell me what happens. I actually love spoilers."

Spinning around, I left and went downstairs. Of course, he was a step behind me, one giant shadow. We made it outside when he stopped me.

"After everything that went down with Blake, you said you wouldn't doubt me," he said. "That you would trust my decisions, but you're doing it again. Not listening to me or common sense. And when this blows up in your face *again*, what am I supposed to do then?"

I gasped, backing up. "That's . . . That was a low blow."

He placed his hands on his hips. "It's the truth."

Tears stung my eyes, and it took a couple of seconds to get the next words out. "I know all of this is coming from a good place, but I don't need a friendly reminder of how badly I screwed up. I totally know. And I'm trying to fix that."

"Kat, I'm not trying to be a dick."

"I know, it just comes easily to you." Headlights peeked through the fog, coming up the road. My voice was hoarse when I spoke next. "I've got to go. Mom's home."

I hurried down the steps and across the gravel and hard, frozen ground. Before I reached my own porch, Daemon appeared. Stopping short, I sputtered, "I hate when you do that."

"Think about what I said, Kat." His gaze flickered over my shoulder. Mom's car was almost here. "You have nothing to prove."

"I don't?"

Daemon said no, but it didn't seem like it when he said he expected everything to blow up in my face again.

Tossing and turning, my brain wouldn't shut down. I replayed everything that had gone down from the point I'd stopped the branch in front of Blake to the moment I found Simon's bloodied watch in his truck. How many times had there been signs that he was more than what he said he was? Too many. And how many times had Daemon stepped in and tried to talk me out of training with Blake? Too many.

I flipped onto my back, squeezing my eyes shut.

And what had he meant about Blake? Did he really think I wanted to help him and for what purpose? The last thing I wanted to do was breathe the same air as Blake. There was no way Daemon could be jealous. No. No. No. I'd have to spin kick him in the face if that was the case. And then cry, because if he doubted me . . .

I couldn't even think about that.

Only one good thing had come from the mess—Dawson. But everything else was . . . Well, it was the reason I couldn't sit back and twiddle my thumbs.

I turned onto my side, punched my pillow, and forced my eyes to stay closed.

At the crack of dawn, I drifted off for what felt like seconds to only face the sun creeping through my bedroom window a minute later. Pulling myself out of bed, I showered and changed.

A dull ache had taken up residency behind my eyes. By the time I got to school and grabbed my books out of my locker, it hadn't faded like I'd hoped. I shuffled into trig and checked my phone for the first time since last night.

No messages.

I dropped the phone back into my bag and rested my chin in my hands. Lesa was the first one in.

Her nose wrinkled when she spotted me. "Ew. You look terrible."

"Thanks," I muttered.

"You're welcome. Carissa has the bird flu or something. Hope you don't have it."

I almost laughed. Since Daemon had healed me, I hadn't even sneezed once. And according to Will, once mutated, you couldn't get sick, which was why he had tried to force Daemon to mutate him.

"Maybe," I said.

"Probably that club you went to." She shivered.

Warmth danced along my neck, and I averted my eyes like a wuss as Daemon took his seat behind me. I knew he was staring at me. He didn't say anything for about sixty-two seconds. I counted them.

He poked me in the back with his trusty pen.

I twisted around, keeping my face blank. "Hey."

A single brow arched. "You look well-rested."

He, on the other hand, looked like he normally did. Freaking perfect. "Got tons of sleep last night. You?"

Daemon popped the pen behind his ear and leaned forward. "I slept for about an hour. I think."

I lowered my gaze. I wasn't happy that last night sucked for him, too, but at least it meant he was thinking about it. I started to ask, but he shook his head. "What?" I said.

"I haven't changed my mind, Kitten. I was hoping you had."

"No," I said, and the bell rang. One last meaningful look, and I turned around. Lesa shot me a weird expression, and I shrugged. Wasn't like I could explain why we were only exchanging a few syllables today. That would be an entertaining conversation.

When the bell rang, I debated on making a run for the door but reconsidered when two denim-clad legs filled my peripheral vision. I couldn't stop the tumbling my stomach did, even when I was angry with him.

I was such a loser.

Daemon didn't say anything as we left or when we parted ways, and after each class he appeared out of freaking nowhere. The same happened before bio, and he walked with me up the stairs, eyes scanning over the heads of the students.

"What are you doing?" I asked, finally tired of the silence.

He shrugged his broad shoulders. "Just thought I'd do the gentlemanly thing and walk you to your classes."

"Uh-huh."

There was no response, so I peeked at him. His eyes were narrowed and his lips pinched like he'd just eaten something sour. I went up on my tiptoes and bit back a curse. Blake was leaning against the wall next to the door, head tilted toward us, a cocky smile on his face.

"I dislike him so very much," Daemon muttered.

Blake pushed off the wall and swaggered over to us. "You guys look chipper for a Friday."

Daemon tapped a textbook on his thigh. "Do you have a reason to be standing here?"

"This is my class." He jerked his chin toward the open door. "With Katy."

Heat blew off Daemon as he took a step forward, staring down his nose at Blake. "You just love to push it, don't you?"

Blake swallowed nervously. "I don't know what you're talking about."

Daemon laughed, and it sent shivers down my spine. Sometimes I forgot how dangerous he could be. "Please. I may be a lot of things—a lot of really bad things, Biff, but stupid and blind aren't two of them."

"All right," I said, keeping my voice low. People were staring. "Time to play nice."

"I have to agree." Blake glanced around. "But this isn't a playground."

Daemon arched a brow. "You don't wanna play, Barf, because we can do that nifty freeze thing and play, right here and now."

Oh, for the love of backwoods babies everywhere, this wasn't necessary. I wrapped my fingers around Daemon's tense arm. "Come on," I whispered.

A second stretched out and static jumped from his arm to

mine. Slowly, he looked at me and then he bent down, planting his lips on mine. The kiss was unexpected—deep and forceful. Stunned, I just stood there as he pulled back, nipping at my bottom lip.

"Tasty, Kitten." Then he spun, planted his right hand on Blake's shoulder, knocking him back into a locker. "See you around," he said, smirking.

"Jesus," Blake muttered, straightening. "He has anger management problems."

The faces gaping at us blurred.

Clearing his throat, Blake slid past me. "You should really head in."

I nodded, but when the warning bell rang, I was still standing there, my fingers placed against my lips.

18

By lunch, Daemon's mood was somewhere between brooding and evil. He had half the student body frightened to death of crossing his path or breathing in the same air as him. I couldn't fathom what had his undies in a bunch. It couldn't be our argument carrying over this badly.

When he got up to grab his third helping of milk, Lesa sat back and let out a low whistle. "What is his deal?"

"I don't know," I said, pushing a lump of meat around my plate. "It must be his time of the month."

Chad barked out a laugh. "Yeah, not going there."

Lesa grinned at her boyfriend. "If you know what's wise for you, you won't."

"What's wise?" Daemon asked as he sat down.

"Nothing," the three of us said at the same time.

He frowned.

The rest of the afternoon went by way too fast and every so often the bottom of my stomach would drop. One more day—Saturday—and we were going to try the impossible. Break into Mount Weather and rescue Beth and Chris. What were we going to do with them if we succeeded? Not *if*—*when* we did, I quickly corrected myself.

On the way out, my cell vibrated. A quick check left a bitter taste in my mouth. I wished Blake would lose my phone number.

We need to talk.

Gritting my teeth, I texted back:

Y

The response was immediate:

Abt Sunday.

"Who put that scary look on your face?" Daemon asked, out of the blue.

Squealing, I jumped. "Good God, where did you come from?"

He grinned, which would've been a good thing considering his mood all day, but it only made me wary. "I'm quiet like a cat."

I sighed, showing him my phone. "Blake. He wants to talk about Sunday."

Daemon growled. "Why is he texting you?"

"Probably because he knows you want to do him bodily harm."

"And you don't?"

I shook my head. "He's obviously less afraid of me."

"Maybe we need to change that?" He dropped an arm over my shoulders, tucking me against his side as we headed out into the bitter February wind. "Tell him we'll talk tomorrow."

My body warmed against his. "Where?"

"My house," he replied with that evil smile. "If he has balls, he'll be there."

I made a yuck face but texted it back to Blake. "Why not tonight?"

Daemon's lips pursed. "We need some quality time alone." Quality time like yesterday's quality time? Because I could so get behind that, but we really needed to talk a few things through. Before I could broach that topic, Blake responded and tomorrow evening was a go.

"Did you drive by yourself today?" I asked.

He shook his head, eyes fixed on a stand of trees. "Came in with Dee. Was hoping we could do something normal. Like an afternoon matinee."

Half of me did a happy dance. The other more responsible part put on the schoolteacher's glasses and broke out the ruler. Annoying adult Katy won. "That sounds great, but don't you think we need to talk about last night?"

"About my giving nature?"

My cheeks flamed. "Um, no . . . After that."

There was a flicker of a smile. "Yeah, I kind of knew that. Make you a deal. We'll do the movies, and then we'll talk, okay?"

It was a good deal, so I agreed. And honestly, I loved getting to do normal things with Daemon—like going out. It was a rarity. He let me pick the movie, and I went with a rom-com. Surprisingly, he didn't complain. Might've had something to do with the huge bucket of popcorn we were stuffing our faces with in between the buttery kisses.

It was all so divinely normal.

Divinely normal ended the moment we got to his house and he stepped out of his car, eyes narrowing. All the lights were on. Dee wasn't about conserving energy, it appeared.

"Kat, I think you should go home."

"Huh?" I closed the car door, frowning. "I thought we were going to talk? And eat ice cream—you promised ice cream."

He chuckled under his breath. "I know, but I have company."

I planted myself in front of the porch steps. "What kind of company?"

"The Luxen kind," he said, placing his hands on my shoulders. His eerily bright green eyes met mine. "Elders."

Must be nice to have a wacky internal sensing system like that.

"And I can't come in?"

"I don't think that's a good idea." He glanced as I heard a door open. "And I don't think that's an option."

I looked over my shoulder. A man stood at the door—a distinguished-looking man. Three-piece suit and all, with midnight black hair that was silver at the temples. I didn't know what I was expecting from an Elder Luxen. Maybe a guy with a white gown and bald head—they did live in a colony at the foot of Seneca.

This was totally unexpected.

Even more so was the fact that Daemon didn't drop his hands and put appropriate alien-human distance between us. Instead, he whispered in his own language and slid a hand down my back as he stepped beside me.

"Ethan," Daemon said. "I wasn't expecting you."

The man's startling violet eyes slid toward me. "I can see. Is this the *girl* that your brother and sister kindly informed me about?"

Tension tightened Daemon's frame. "Depends on what they kindly informed you of."

Air stalled in my lungs. I didn't know what to do with myself, so I stood there, trying to look as unaware as possible. The fact that I knew the guy in a suit wasn't human was a big deal. Other Luxen couldn't know I was in on the secret or that I was a hybrid.

Ethan smiled. "That you've been seeing her. I was surprised. We're practically family."

Somehow I thought it might have had more to do with the fact that they wanted him to make little alien Daemon babies with Ash than him not sending out a mass text notifying everyone that he was no longer on the market.

"You know me, Ethan; I don't like to kiss and tell the world." His thumb trailed a lazy, soothing circle along the small of my back. "Kat, this is Ethan Smith. He's like a . . ."

"Godfather," I said, and then I flushed, because that was the stupidest thing I could say.

But Ethan's expression said he liked the sound of it. "Yes, like a godfather." Those odd eyes settled on me, and I forced my chin up a notch. "You're not from around here, are you, Kat?"

"No, sir, I'm from Florida."

"Oh." Dark brows rose. "Is West Virginia to your agreement?"

I glanced at Daemon. "Yeah, it's nice."

"That's lovely." Ethan came down a step. "It's a pleasure to meet you." He extended a hand.

Out of habit, I reached for it, but Daemon interceded, wrapping his fingers around mine. He brought my hand to his lips and kissed my palm. Ethan noted the action with a flicker of curiosity and something I couldn't place.

"Kat, I'll come over in a little while." He let go of my hand, placing his body in between us. "I have some catching up to do, okay?"

I nodded and forced a smile for Ethan. "It was nice to meet you."

"Likewise," the man said. "I'm sure we'll meet again."

For some reason, the words settled over me with a frost-like bite. I gave Daemon a little wave and then hurried back to my car and grabbed my bag. They'd already headed inside, and I'd give my left thumb to know what they were talking about. As long as I'd known Daemon and Dee, I'd never seen another Luxen from the colony come to their home.

Kind of wigged out by Ethan's appearance, I dropped my backpack inside the hall and grabbed a glass of orange juice. Mom was asleep, so I tiptoed down the hall and shut my bedroom door. I sat on the bed, placed the glass on the table. Concentrating on my laptop, I raised my hand.

It came off the desk and moved straight to my hand. I tried not to use the alien abilities too often—maybe once or twice a day to keep the . . . uh, *whatever* well oiled. There was always this weird rush when I used it, like being on a roller coaster as it crests a hill, ready to fly down at eighty miles an hour—the moment when the stomach jumps and the skin tingles with awareness. It was a different feeling—not bad, kind of fun, and maybe even a little addictive.

And when I'd tapped into whatever it was the night Adam died, I'd never felt more powerful in my life. So, yeah, I could see how that power would go straight to the head. If the mutation had stuck with Will, God knew what crazy things he was doing.

I couldn't afford to think about him now, so I powered up my laptop and trolled the Internet for a half an hour, reading reviews until I shut off my computer and sent it back to my desk. Grabbing a book, I curled up, hoping to get some chapters in before Daemon swung over, but I ended up drifting off to sleep three pages in.

When I woke up, it was dark in my bedroom and upon further investigation, I discovered it was already past nine and Mom had left for work. Surprised that Daemon hadn't stopped over, I slipped on my boots and headed next door.

Dawson answered, a can of soda in one hand and a Pop-Tart in the other. "Nice sugar rush you got going on there," I said, grinning.

He glanced down. "Yeah, I guess I'm not sleeping anytime soon."

I remembered what he'd said about not sleeping at all, and

I hoped that had changed. Before I could ask, though, he said, "Daemon's not here."

"Oh." I tried to hide my disappointment. "Is he still with the Elder guy?"

"God, no, Ethan was only here for about an hour. He wasn't happy. But Daemon went out with Andrew."

"Andrew?" Unexpected.

He nodded. "Yeah, Andrew and Dee and Ash wanted to grab something to eat. I didn't want to go."

"Ash?" I whispered. Okay, really unexpected. And what was totally expected was the wave of irrational jealousy that swept through me, determined to carry me into crazy-girl land.

"Yeah," he said, and then he winced. "You want to come in?"

I didn't realize I'd followed him inside until I was sitting on the couch, my knees pressed together. Daemon really went out to dinner with Ash and the others? "When did they leave?"

Dawson took a bite of his Pop-Tart. "Uh, not that long ago."

"It's almost ten at night." The Luxen had huge appetites, but come on; they didn't do dinner at night. I knew better than that.

He sat in the armchair and glanced down at his pastry. "Ethan left around five. And then Andrew, he came over around . . ." Dawson glanced at the wall clock, expression pinched. "He and Ash came over around six."

My stomach tumbled over itself. "And the four of them left after that to go get something to eat?"

Dawson nodded, as if speaking was too painfully awkward.

Four hours for dinner. I suddenly couldn't sit any longer. I wanted to know what restaurant they went to. I wanted to find him. I started to stand, but I tried to swallow down that god-awful burning lump in the back of my throat.

"It's not what you think," Dawson said quietly.

My head jerked toward him, and I was horrified to find

tears in my eyes. The irony of it all bitch-slapped me in the face. Was this how Daemon had felt when he knew I went to dinner and then lunch with Blake? But we weren't together then. Wasn't like I'd owed him a ton of obligations at that moment.

"It isn't?" I croaked.

Dawson finished off his Pop-Tart. "No. I think he just needed to get out for a little while."

"Without me?"

He brushed a few sugary crumbs off his jeans "Maybe without you or maybe not. He's not the same brother I knew. I would've never thought he'd be with a human. No offense."

"None taken," I whispered. *Without me. Without me.* Those words were on repeat. I wasn't one of those needy girls who had to be around her boyfriend all the time, but damn if it didn't sting.

And that sting was turned into a hot, angry knife when I pictured Dee and Andrew sitting on one side of a booth and Daemon and Ash on the other, because that's how they had to have sat when they went out to eat. It would be like old times—when Daemon and Ash were together.

Blake and I may've kissed once, but we didn't have a long-standing relationship. God, they'd probably had—

I checked myself right there.

Dawson stood, made his way around the coffee table, and sat beside me. "Ethan pissed him off. He wanted to know that Daemon's relationship with you wouldn't interfere with his loyalties to his kind." Dawson leaned forward, rubbing his palms over his bent knees. "And, well, you can imagine Daemon's response."

I wasn't so sure that I could. "What did he say?"

Dawson laughed, eyes squinting like Daemon's did. "Let's just say Daemon explained that who he was with didn't affect his loyalties, but he used different words."

I grinned a little. "Bad words?"

"Very bad words," he said, glancing at me. "They didn't expect this from him. No one did. Me? Yeah, well, they never expected much from me. Mainly because I didn't care what they thought—not that Daemon does, but . . ."

"I know. He's always been the one to take care of everything, right? Not the one to cause problems like this."

He nodded. "They don't know what you are, but I doubt Ethan's going to let this drop."

"They'll outcast him?" When he nodded, I shook my head. If a Luxen was outcasted, he wasn't allowed in or near Luxen communities, which meant he couldn't be near the protective cluster of beta quartz. He'd be virtually on his own against the Arum. "What is Ethan? I get he's an Elder, but so what?"

Dawson's brows pinched. "Elders are like the mayors and presidents of our communities. Ethan is our president."

My brows rose. "Sounds important."

"All those who live in the colony will listen to him. Those who don't risk the same social fallout." He leaned back, closing his eyes. "Even those who mingle with humans, like the ones who work outside the colony and whatever, are afraid of ticking off the Elders. None of us can just leave without the DOD's permission, but damn, if they wanted us out, they'd find a way to do so."

"Did they do that to you because of Beth?"

His face tensed. "They would've, but there hadn't been enough time. Not enough time for anything."

Pain sliced my chest and I placed my hand on his arm. "We're going to get Beth back."

A small smile appeared. "I know. This Sunday . . . Everything comes down to this Sunday."

My stomach did a topsy-turvy thing, and my pulse picked up. "What was it like in there?"

His eyes opened into thin slits. Several moments passed

before he answered. "At first, it wasn't too bad. They let Beth and me see each other. They told us they were keeping us for our safety. You know, the whole 'if people find out what I did to Beth, it would get bad and we needed to be protected' bit. Daedalus was on our side. It really seemed that way for a while. I . . . I almost believed we'd walk out of it together."

It was the first time I heard him say *Daedalus*. The word sounded strange on his lips.

"Believing in that led to nothing but misery and eventually madness when the hope faded." His lips tipped up at the corners. "Daedalus wanted me to recreate what I had with Beth. They wanted me to *create* more like her. To help better mankind and all that BS, and when it didn't work, things . . . things changed."

I shifted. "How did they change?"

The line of his jaw tightened. "At first, they wouldn't let me see Beth—my punishment for failing when it seemed all too easy to them. They didn't get I didn't know how I healed and changed her. They'd bring these dying humans to me and I tried, Katy, I really tried. They just died no matter what I did."

Nausea welled up inside me, and I wished I knew what to say, but it seemed like this was one of those moments when saying nothing meant everything.

"Then they started bringing in healthy humans and doing things to them—hurting them—and I healed them. Some . . . some of them got better. At least they did for a little while, and it was like whatever wounds were inflicted on them came back with a vengeance. Others . . . others destabilized."

"Destabilized?"

Dawson's hands opened and closed on his thighs. "They'd develop some of our abilities, but something . . . something went wrong. This one girl—she wasn't much older than us and she was nice, very nice. They gave her some kind of pill and she was dying. I healed her. I really wanted to heal her, because she was so scared." Emerald eyes met mine. "And we thought it worked. She got sick like Beth was when they first brought us in. And then she could move just as fast as us. About a day after the sickness faded, she ran into a wall."

I frowned. "How is that so bad?"

His gaze slipped away. "We can move faster than bullets, Katy. She crashed into the wall. It was like hitting it at supersonic speed."

"Oh my God . . ."

"And it was like she couldn't stop herself. Sometimes I wonder if she did it on purpose. There were many, many more after her. Humans who died with my hands on them. Humans who died after I healed them. Humans who lived with no mutations but were never seen again." He looked down. "There's so much blood on my hands."

"No." I shook my head vigorously. "None of that was your fault."

"It wasn't?" Anger deepened his voice. "I have this ability to heal, but I couldn't get it right."

"But you had to want to heal them—like on a cellular level. You were being forced to do it."

"It doesn't change that so many people died." He sat forward again, antsy. "There was a period of time that I believed I deserved what they were doing to me, but never . . . never to Beth. She didn't deserve that."

"You didn't either, Dawson."

He stared at me a moment, then looked away. "They withheld Beth, then food, then water, and when that still didn't work, they got creative." He let out a long breath. "I guess they did the same to Beth, but I really didn't know. All I saw was what they did in front of me."

My stomach sank to the couch cushion. I had a really bad feeling about this.

"They'd hurt her just so I could heal her, and they could study the process." Dawson's jaw worked. "Each time I felt the worst kind of fear. What if it didn't work? What if I failed Beth? I'd . . ." He moved his neck, as if working out a kink.

He'd never be the same. Tears climbed up my throat again. I wanted to cry for him, for Beth, but most of all, for the people they once were but never would be again.

19

After that, Dawson shut down. He talked about anything—weather, football, the Smurfs—but nothing about Daedalus or what they did to him and Beth. Part of me was grateful. I wasn't sure how much more I could handle knowing, as selfish as that sounded.

But the bad part was that once we stopped talking about serious stuff, my brain ran right back to where Daemon was and what he was doing. When it neared midnight and he still hadn't come home, I couldn't sit there any longer.

I couldn't sit anywhere.

Saying good night, I made the quick and chilly trek across the lawn. The first thing I did was check my cell. There was a text waiting and my heart stuttered.

        Srry abt tnght. Tlk tmrw.

It had come in about an hour ago. Meaning he was still with Ash—er, Andrew, Dee, *and* Ash.

I glanced at the clock, like that would somehow change the time. My heart was pounding in my chest, as though I'd run from next door. Looking down at my cell, I fought the urge to throw it against the wall. I knew I was being ridiculous.

Daemon was friends with them, including Ash. He could hang out with them without me. And with the fallout between Dee and me, he hadn't been spending a lot of time with her.

Ridiculous or not, my feelings were hurt. And I hated that—hated that something as stupid as this would upset me.

Taking my phone upstairs, I washed my face, brushed my teeth, and changed into my jammies, still debating on texting him back. I wanted the willpower not to, kind of like my *in your face*, but damn if that wasn't stupid considering everything that was going on.

On the flip side, I was butt sore about this. So I placed the cell on my stand and I climbed under the covers, pulling them to my chin. I stayed that way, beating myself up for not texting him back, for going out with Blake the first time, for kissing him, and for lying awake beating myself up. Finally, my brain had enough and it closed shop for the night.

Sometime later, I wasn't sure if I was dreaming or not. I was in that hazy stage where reality mixed with the subconscious. Part of it was a dream, I knew that much, because I could see Daemon in this building. I'd catch sight of his dark hair and then he drifted away. He was in one room and before I could get to him, he went to another. It was an endless maze and he kept moving around, never responding to me as I yelled his name.

Frustration swelled inside me and my chest ached. Chasing him, never reaching him in time, losing him . . . It wouldn't end.

And then the bed shifted and the building faded, evaporated into wisps of smoke and darkness. A heavy weight settled beside me. A hand brushed the hair back from my face, and I think I smiled, because he was here and that soothed me. I slipped back into deep sleep, where I wasn't chasing Daemon in my dreams.

When morning came, I rolled over, expecting to find Daemon. Mom worked until late morning on Saturdays and Daemon had taken to staying as long as he could, but my bed was empty.

Smoothing my hand along the extra pillow, I inhaled, expecting the outdoorsy clean scent that was uniquely his, but all I smelled was a faint trace of citrus. Had I dreamt Daemon's presence?

Geez, I was so lame if so.

Frowning, I sat up and grabbed my cell. There was a missed text that had come in around two in the morning from Daemon.

```
    Bacon & eggs 4 breakfast. Cme over when
                    u wake.
```

"Two in the morning?" I stared at the phone. Had he been out with them till then?

My heart was racing again and I flopped onto my back, groaning. Apparently I was lame and Daemon had a really late night but not with me.

Dragging myself out of bed, I showered and threw on a pair of jeans and a sweater. Numbness had settled over me as I dried my hair halfway and twisted it up into a messy bun. I headed next door and found that the door was locked.

I placed my hand on the handle and waited until I heard the locks turning over. As I opened the door, unease blossomed. It was way too easy to get in and out of people's houses, including mine.

Shaking my head, I eased the door shut and took a deep breath. The house was tomb silent. Everyone was still asleep. I went upstairs, careful of the two steps at the top that creaked.

Dawson's and Dee's bedroom doors were shut, but I could hear the soft hum of music coming from Daemon's.

I cracked open Daemon's bedroom door and slipped through. My gaze went straight to the bed and I couldn't have stopped the flutter in my chest if I wanted to.

Daemon was sprawled on his back, one arm stretched across the space beside him and the other rested across his bare stomach. Sheets were twisted around his narrow hips. His face was almost angelic in sleep, chiseled lines softened and lips relaxed. Thick lashes fanned the top of his cheeks.

He looked so much younger at rest but, in a weird way, he was even more out of my league. His kind of masculine beauty was otherworldly and intimidating. Something that existed in between the pages of the books I read.

Sometimes I had a hard time convincing myself he was real.

I tiptoed over to him and sat on the edge of the bed, unable to pull my eyes away. I didn't want to wake him. So I sat there like a total creeper, watching the steady rise and fall of his chest. I wondered if I had dreamt him last night or if he had stopped in to check on me. The fluttering was back and I could almost forget the punch of anxiety of last night. Almost but not—

Daemon rolled suddenly, snaking an arm around my waist and pulling me down beside him. He kept moving, burying his face in my neck. "Good morning," he murmured.

A smile swept across my face as I placed a hand on his shoulder. His skin was hot. "Morning."

He threw a leg over mine and snuggled closer. "Where's my bacon and eggs?"

"I thought you were offering to make them."

"You mistook what I said. Get to the kitchen, woman."

"Whatever." I rolled onto my side, facing him. He lifted his head, kissed my nose, and then buried his face in the pillow. I laughed.

"It's too early," he grumbled.

"It's almost ten o'clock."

"Too early."

A stone settled in my stomach. I bit down on my lip, unsure of what I should say.

He lazily dropped an arm over my hip and turned his head so I could see his face. "You didn't respond last night."

So we *were* going to go there. "I fell asleep and I . . . figured you were busy."

A brow arched. "I wasn't busy."

"I stopped over last night to see you, and I waited for a little while." I fiddled with the edge of the sheet, twisting it around my fingers. "You stayed out late."

One eye opened. "So you did get my text and had time to respond."

I'd walked right into that one.

Daemon sighed. "Why did you ignore me, Kitten? My feelings are hurt."

"I'm sure Ash soothed them for you." The moment those words left my mouth, I wanted to smack myself.

Both eyes were open now, and then he did something that surprised and ticked me off: he smiled that really big one. "You're jealous."

To me, the way he said it made it sound like a good thing. I started to sit up, but his arm kept me down. "I'm not jealous."

"Kitten . . ."

I rolled my eyes and then a bad, bad case of verbal diarrhea occurred. "I was worried about the Elder being here, and we were supposed to talk last night. You never showed up. Instead you went out with Andrew, Dee, and *Ash*. Ash, as in the ex-girlfriend Ash, and how do I find out? Your brother. And how did those seating arrangements work out? Did Dee and Andrew sit on one side and you and Ash on the other? I bet that was real comfy."

"Kitten . . ."

"Don't Kitten me." I scowled, on a roll now. "You left around five or so and didn't get back till when? Past two in the morning? What were you guys doing? And get that stupid smile off your face. This isn't funny."

Daemon tried to get rid of the smile but failed. "I love when your claws come out."

"Oh, shut up." Disgusted, I pushed at his arm. "Let me go. You can call up Ash and see if she'll make you some eggs and bacon. I'm out of here."

Instead of letting me go, he shifted atop me, holding himself up with his hands planted on either side of my shoulders. Now he was grinning—that infuriating, cocky grin of his. "I just want to hear you say it: I'm jealous."

"I already said it, butt-face. I'm jealous. Why wouldn't I be?"

He cocked his head to the side. "Oh, I don't know. Maybe because I never wanted Ash, and I wanted you from the first moment I saw you—and before you get started, I know I had a bad way of showing it, but you know I wanted you. Only you. You're insane to be jealous."

"I am?" I fought back angry tears. "You guys were together."

"*Were* together."

"She probably still wants you."

"I don't want her, so it doesn't matter."

It mattered to me. "She's model beautiful."

"And you're more beautiful."

"Don't try to sweet-talk me."

"I'm not," he said.

Staring over his shoulder, I bit my lip. "You know, at first I thought I kind of deserved last night. Now I know how you felt when I went out with Blake. Like karma was schooling me, but it's not the same. You and I weren't together then and Blake and I didn't have that kind of history."

He took a deep breath. "You're right; it's not the same thing. I didn't go out with Ash on a date. Andrew stopped by and we got to talking about Ethan. Andrew was hungry, so we decided to get something to eat. Dee tagged along and Ash was there, because you know, she's his sister."

I gave a lopsided shrug. Okay, he had a point.

"And we didn't go out to eat. We ended up ordering pizza, went back to Andrew's house, and we talked about Sunday. Ash is scared to death that she's going to lose Andrew, too. Dee still wants to murder Blake. I spent *hours* talking them through this. It wasn't a party you weren't invited to."

But I wasn't invited at all, I wanted to say, but I knew that was stupid. "Why didn't you tell me, at least? You could've said something. Then my imagination wouldn't have run circles around me."

He stared at me a moment, then pushed up, sitting beside me. "I meant to stop by when I got home, but it was late."

So last night *was* a dream. Lameness officially confirmed.

"Look, I didn't think about it."

"Apparently," I muttered.

Daemon rubbed the spot above his heart. "I honestly didn't think you'd get this upset. I figured you'd know better."

I was still flat on my back, too weary to move. "Know better?"

"Yeah, that you'd know if Ash pranced naked into my bedroom right now, I'd still send her packing. That you didn't have anything to worry about."

"Thanks for that image you implanted into my brain forever."

He shook his head, huffing out a dry laugh. "This insecurity thing ticks me off, Kat."

My mouth dropped open and I flew up, coming to rest on my knees. "Excuse me? Are you the only one who's allowed to be insecure?"

"What?" He smirked. "Why would I be insecure?"

"Good question, but what do you call your little episode with Blake yesterday in the hallway? And that stupid question about me wanting to help Blake?"

He snapped his mouth shut.

"Ha! Exactly. It's even more ridiculous for you to be insecure. Let me spell it out for you." When my anger rose, the Source did, too. It skated over my skin. "I loathe Blake. He used me and was ready to turn me over to Daedalus. He killed Adam. There's only a teeny tiny bit of me that can actually tolerate him. How can you even be any bit jealous of him?"

Daemon's jaw popped. "He wants you."

"Oh, dear God, he does not."

"Whatever. I'm a guy. I know what other guys are thinking."

I threw my hands up. "It doesn't matter if he did. I. Hate. Him."

He looked away. "Okay."

"And you don't hate Ash. There's a part of you that loves her. I know you do and maybe not in the way you feel about me, but there's affection there—there's history. Sue me if I'm a little bit intimidated by that."

I pushed off the bed, wanting to stomp across the room like a toddler. Maybe even throw myself on the floor. I'd work off some energy that way.

Daemon appeared in front of me and stepped forward, cradling my cheeks. "Okay. I see your point. I should've said something. And the stuff with Blake—yeah, it's stupid, too."

"Good." I folded my arms.

His lips twitched. "But you've got to understand that you are who I want. Not Ash. Not anyone else."

"Even if the Elders want you to be with someone like her?"

He lowered his head, brushing his lips along my cheekbone. "I don't care what they want. I'm incredibly selfish like that." He kissed my temple. "Okay?"

My eyes drifted shut. "Okay."

"We're good then?"

"If you promise not to give me any crap about going with you tomorrow."

He pressed his forehead against mine. "You drive a hard bargain."

"I do."

"I don't want you going, Kitten." He sighed, wrapping his arms around me. "But I can't stop you. Promise you'll stay close to me."

My smile was hidden against his chest. "I promise."

Daemon kissed the top of my head. "You always get your way, don't you?"

"Not always." I placed my hands on his sides, drawing in his warmth. If I had my way, none of this would be happening. But that was the thing about all of this. I wondered if any of us would get our way.

His arms tightened, and I felt a sigh shudder through him. "Come on. Let's get the bacon and eggs going. I need all my strength for today."

"What, for . . ." I trailed off, realizing what he was saying. "Oh, yeah . . . Blake."

"Yeah." He kissed me softly. "It's going to take a lot for me not to commit bodily harm. You know that, right? So extra bacon for me."

20

Dee was perched on the bottom step like a demented pixie about to unleash holy hell. Her hair was pulled back sharply, her eyes a bright and feverish green. A thin slash formed on her lips. Her fingers curled over her knees like razor-sharp claws ready to dig in.

"He's here," she said, gaze focused on the window beside the door.

I glanced at Daemon. A wolfish smile spread across his face. He wasn't at all concerned about his sister's murderous desires. Perhaps having Blake come here wasn't a good idea.

She sprung from the step, throwing open the door before Blake even knocked. No one stopped her or even moved forward.

Surprised, Blake lowered his hand. "Uh, hi—"

Dee cocked back a slender arm and slammed her fist right into Blake's jaw. The impact knocked him back a good three feet.

My mouth dropped open.

Andrew laughed.

Spinning around, she let out a long breath. "Okay. I'm done."

I watched her move toward the armchair and sit, shaking her hand.

"I promised her one good hit," Daemon said, chuckling. "She'll behave now."

I stared at him.

Blake staggered through the door, rubbing his jaw. "Okay," he said, wincing. "I deserved that."

"You deserve far worse than that," Andrew said. "Keep that in mind."

He nodded and looked around the room. Six Luxen and a baby hybrid stared back at him. He had the sense to look nervous, even afraid. The animosity in the room was palpable.

Blake moved so that his back was against the wall. Smart guy. Slowly, he reached into his back pocket and pulled out a rolled-up paper. "I guess we should get this over with quickly."

"I guess so," Daemon said, snatching the paper from him. "What's this?"

"A map," he answered. "The route we need to take is outlined in red. It's a fire access road and will lead up to the back entrance of Mount Weather."

Daemon unrolled the map on the coffee table. Dawson peered over his brother's shoulder, running his finger along the wiggling red line. "How long will it take to get up this road?"

"About twenty minutes by car, but there's no way we're going to get a car up there unnoticed." He took a timid step forward, eyeing Dee, who was eyeballing him back. A red mark marred his right cheek. That was gonna bruise. "We're going to do it by foot and fast."

"How fast are we talking?" Matthew asked from his post by the dining room door.

"As fast as inhumanly possible," Blake responded. "We need to move at the light-speed thing. Luc's giving us fifteen minutes and we can't hang around Mount Weather, waiting for nine. We need to get there about five minutes before and hit this road as fast as possible."

I sat back. Only once did I hit the speeds necessary for what they were talking about. That's when I'd been chasing Blake's ass down.

Daemon glanced up. "Can you do this?"

"Yes." Given the reasons, I was sure I could do it. Hopefully.

Shaking her head, Dee stood. "How fast can they really run?"

"Damn fast when need be," Blake said. "Come at me again, and I'll show you how fast I can run."

Dee snickered. "I bet I'll still catch you."

"Perhaps," he murmured and then said, "You need to practice all day tomorrow. Maybe even tonight. We can't have anyone slowing us down."

It took me a second to realize he was talking to me. "I'm not going to slow anyone down."

"Just making sure." His eyes churned as they met mine.

I looked away quickly. The fact that I was obviously the weakest link burned me. Dee or Ash would probably be a better choice for this, but I knew I could do it.

"She's not your problem to worry about," Daemon snapped.

Matthew came forward, fitting in between Daemon and Blake. "Okay. We know we have this road to go up, but you want us to remain back where?"

Daemon folded his arms, eyes narrowed. "At the bottom of the access road, this should give you a running chance to get out if something goes wrong."

"Nothing's going to go wrong," Ash said, watching Daemon. "We'll wait there for you."

"Of course," Daemon said, smiling reassuringly. "We'll be fine, Ash."

I pinched my thigh. *He doesn't want her. He doesn't want her. He doesn't want her.* That helped.

"I trust you," Ash said, eyes latched to his adoringly. Like Daemon was a saint or something.

I pinched my thigh harder. *I'm going to hit her. I'm going to hit her. I'm going to hit her.* That didn't help.

Blake cleared his throat. "Anyway, Luc said there's an old farm at the bottom of the access road. We should be able to park the cars there."

"Sounds good." Dawson stepped back, placing his hands on his hips. A lock of hair fell forward. "Once we're there, we have fifteen minutes, right?"

Daemon nodded. "According to the tween mafia leader, Luc, that's what we have."

"And this kid is trustworthy?" Matthew asked.

"I can speak for him."

I looked at Blake. "That's a ringing endorsement."

His cheeks flushed. "He's trustworthy."

"Do you think it's enough time?" Dawson asked his brother. "To get in there, get to Beth and Chris, and get out?"

"It should be." Daemon folded up the map and slid it into his back pocket. "You'll get Beth and dipshit here will get Chris."

Blake rolled his eyes.

"Andrew, Kat, and I are going to cover them. This shouldn't even take fifteen minutes." Daemon sat beside me and leveled a pointed glare at Blake. "And then you will take Chris and get the hell out of here. You have no reason to come back."

"And what if he does?" Dee asked. "What if he finds another excuse to blackmail you into helping him?"

"I won't," Blake said, and I felt his stare. "I don't have a reason to come back."

Daemon went taut. "If you do, you're going to make me do something I don't want to do—I'll probably enjoy it, but I don't want to."

Blake jerked his chin. "I got you."

"Okay then," Matthew said, addressing the room. "We meet here at six thirty tomorrow. Do you have things covered, Katy?"

I nodded. "Mom thinks I'm doing a sleepover with Lesa. She works anyway."

"She always works," Ash said, staring at her nails. "Does she even like to be home?"

Unsure if that was a dig or not, I kept my temper in check. "She's paying for a mortgage, food, bills, and all my expenses by herself. She has to work a lot."

"Maybe you should get a job," she suggested, her eyes flicking up. "Like something after school that takes about twenty hours or so of your life."

I folded my arms, lips pursed. "Why are you suggesting that, pray tell?"

A catlike smile appeared as her attention slid to beside me. "I just think if you were concerned about your mom making ends meet, you would help out."

"I'm sure that's why." I relaxed when Daemon slid a hand across my back.

Ash noticed the gesture and got a sour pinch to her lips.

Take that.

"There's only one thing we have to worry about," Blake said, as if it really was only *one thing* that could go wrong. "They have emergency doors that shut every so many feet when alarms are sounded. Those doors also have a defensive weapon. Don't go near the blue lights. They're lasers. Rip you right apart."

All of us stared. Wow, yeah, that was a big problem.

Blake smiled. "But they shouldn't be a problem. We should be in and out without being seen."

"Okay," Andrew said slowly. "Anything else? Like an onyx net we have to worry about?"

Blake laughed. "No, that should cover it."

Dee wanted Blake out once the plans were underway. Without protest, he headed to the door and stopped as if he were going to say something. I felt his gaze once more, but then he left. Our group disbanded, leaving the siblings behind.

I clasped my hands together. "I want to practice the speed thing. I mean, I know I can do it as fast as you guys, but I just want to practice."

Dee focused on the arm of the couch, drawing in a deep breath.

"We can do that." Dawson smiled crookedly. "I could use the practice myself."

Daemon stretched back, wrapping an arm around my waist. "It's a little dark right now. You'll probably end up breaking your neck, but we can do it tomorrow."

"Thanks for the vote of confidence."

"You got it."

I elbowed him as I turned to Dee. She was still staring at the furniture like it held the answer to something. Here goes nothing. "Will . . . will you help?"

She opened her mouth and then closed it, shaking her head. Then, without saying a word, she pivoted around and headed upstairs. I deflated.

"She'll come around," Daemon said, giving me a little squeeze. "I know she will."

Doubted that, but I nodded. Dee was never going to *come around*. I don't know why I even bothered.

Dawson sat on my other side, confusion marking his expression. "I don't know what happened to her while I was gone. I don't understand."

I pressed my lips together. *I* happened.

"We all changed, brother." Daemon tugged me back so I was against his side. "But things . . . Things are going to get back to normal soon."

He watched us, brows drawn tight. Sorrow crept into his

eyes, dulling their vibrant color. I wondered what he thought when he saw us together. Memories of him and Beth cuddled together on the couch? Then he blinked and a wan smile appeared. "*Ghost Investigators* marathon?"

"You do not have to ask me twice." Daemon raised his hand and the remote control shot toward him. "I have, like, six hours saved up. Popcorn? We need popcorn."

"And ice cream." Dawson stood. "I get the munchies."

The wall clock read seven thirty. It was going to be a long night, but as I settled in next to Daemon, I realized I didn't want to be any place else.

Daemon brushed his lips along my cheek as he reached behind us, tugging a blanket off the back of the couch. He draped it over both of us, allowing most of the blanket to swallow me. "He's coming around, isn't he?"

I turned to him, smiling. "Yeah, he is."

His eyes met mine. "Let's just make sure tomorrow doesn't make it all for nothing."

By one o'clock the following day, I was covered in mud and sweating like a pig in hell. I'd done better than I feared, able to keep up easily with Dawson and I only fell, like . . . four times. The terrain was unforgiving.

I walked past Daemon, and he made a swipe for me. I shot him a level look, which he returned with a mischievous grin.

"You have dirt on your cheek," he said. "Cute."

As usual, he looked perfect. Hadn't even broken a sweat for crying out loud. "Is he always this annoyingly good?"

Dawson, who looked as rough as I did, nodded. "Yeah, he's the best at this kind of stuff—fighting, running, physical stuff."

His brother beamed as I knocked the mud off my sneakers and said, "You suck."

Daemon laughed.

I stuck my tongue out and returned to stand next to the brothers. We were at the edge of the woods that ran up to my front yard. I took a couple of deep breaths and welcomed the Source rushing through me. That roller-coaster feeling was back and my muscles locked up.

"Get ready," Daemon said, hands curling at his sides. "Go!"

Pushing off, I dug my feet into the ground, then raced against the brothers. Air whipped around me as I picked up speed. Now that I knew to watch out for rotted branches and stones, I kept my eyes trained on the ground and my surroundings. The wind bit at my cheeks, but it was a good kind of sting. It meant I was fast.

Trees blurred as I darted around them and under low-hanging branches. Jumping over bushes and boulders, I moved ahead of Dawson. The speed tore at my hair, pulling it free from my ponytail. A laugh escaped my throat. As I ran, I forgot about the stupid jealousy, the lingering issue of Will, and even what we had to do later that night.

Running like this, as fast as the wind, was freeing.

Daemon blew past us, reaching the stream a good ten seconds before we did. Slowing down was an issue. You couldn't just stop, not at this speed. You'd face-plant into the ground in seconds. So I dug my feet in, kicking up sediment and loose rock as I slid the last few inches.

Daemon's arm shot out, wrapping around my waist so I didn't end up in the lake. Laughing, I spun around and reached up, kissing his cheek.

He grinned. "Your eyes are glowing."

"Really—like yours do? The whole diamond shining thing?"

Dawson stopped, knocking the mop of hair off his forehead. "Nah, just the color's luminous. It's pretty."

"It's beautiful," Daemon corrected. "But you better be careful not to do that in front of people." When I nodded, he walked over to his brother, clapping him on his back. "Why don't we call it quits? Both of you are good to go, and I'm starving."

A thrill of pride sparked inside me until I remembered how important tonight would be. I couldn't be the weakest link. "You guys go ahead and head back. I'm going to do some more runs."

"You sure?"

"Yep. I want to run circles around you."

"Never going to happen, Kitten." He swaggered up to me and kissed my cheek. "You might as well give it up."

I pushed at his chest playfully. "One of these days you're going to eat crow."

"I doubt any of us will be around to see that." Dawson grinned at his brother.

My heart stopped when I saw the two of them joking, and I forced my expression to remain the same, although I saw Daemon falter a little. Unaware of the importance of the exchange, Dawson knocked his hair back again and started toward the house.

"Race you, brother," Dawson called.

Go, I mouthed at Daemon.

He sent me a quick smile and then trotted up to his brother. "You know you're going to lose."

"Probably, but hey, it's good for your ego, right?"

Like he needed help with that, but I smiled and felt all warm and fuzzy as they joked and then took off. I waited a few minutes, cleared my thoughts, and then jogged back toward the house. At normal speed, it took about five minutes if I was adding correctly. Once at the tree line, I spun around and got ready. Feeling the Source snap loose, I launched forward.

Two minutes.

I did it again and timed it.

A minute and thirty seconds the second trip back. I did it again and again, until my muscles burned along with my lungs and the five-minute jog took me fifty seconds. I didn't think I could get any better than that.

And the funny thing was that even though my muscles were shaky, they didn't hurt. Like I'd been running this way for years, and I pretty much ran from the front of the bookstore to the new release section and that was all.

Stretching, I watched the sun filter through the trees and bounce off the partially frozen creek. Spring wasn't too far away. I pushed at my hair, tucked it over one shoulder. That was, if we all made it out of Mount Weather tonight.

"I was wrong. You really don't need practice."

I whirled at the sound of Blake's voice. Standing several feet away, he leaned against a thick tree, hands in his pockets. Unease and discord balled in my stomach.

"What are you doing here?" I demanded, keeping my voice even.

Blake shrugged. "Watching."

"Yeah, that's not creepy or anything."

He smiled tightly. "I probably should have thought of a better way of phrasing that. I was watching you all run. You guys are good—you're great. Daedalus would love to have you on board."

The ball in my stomach grew. "Is that a threat?"

"No." He blinked, cheeks flushing. "God, no, I just meant that you're that good. You're what they want in a hybrid."

"Like you?"

His gaze dropped to the ground. "Yeah, like me."

This was awkward and breathing the same air as Blake irritated me. Normally, I didn't hold grudges, but I made an exception with him. I started heading back to the house.

"Are you worried about tonight?"

"I don't want to talk to you."

He was beside me quickly. "Why not?"

Why not? Seriously? *Why not?* That question enraged me. Without thinking, I snapped around and slammed my fist into his solar plexus. Air expelled from him in a rush and giddy satisfaction planted a smile on my face.

"God!" he grunted, doubling over. "What is up with you chicks hitting me?"

"You deserve much worse than that." I pivoted around before I hit him again and restarted my trek back. "Why don't I want to talk to you? Why don't we ask Adam?"

"Okay." He caught up with me, rubbing his stomach. "You're right. But I've said I'm sorry."

"Sorry doesn't fix things like this." I took a breath, squinting at the harsh glare of the sun cutting through the branches. I couldn't believe I was having this conversation.

"I'm trying to make up for it."

I laughed at the ridiculous notion that he could make up for all that he had done. Ever since the night Adam died, a part of me understood capital punishment and why it was created. Maybe not a life for a life, but I got the whole life-in-prison thing.

I stopped. "Why are you really here right now? You know Daemon is probably going to be ticked off, and he hits harder than Dee or me."

"I wanted to talk to you." His gaze tipped upward. "And there was a time that you used to like talking to me."

Yeah, before he turned out to be the devil incarnate, he was a pretty cool guy. "I hate you," I said, and I meant it. The level of animosity that I felt for this boy was a chart topper.

Blake flinched but didn't look away. Wind roared through the trees, whipping my hair around my face and causing his to stand straight up. "I never wanted you to hate me."

I barked out a short laugh and started walking again. "You suck at the whole not-making-me-hate-you part."

"I know." He fell in step beside me. "And I know I can't change that. I'm not even sure I would if I had a chance to do it again."

I cut him a hateful glare. "At least you're honest, right? Whatever."

He shoved his hands into his jeans. "You would do the same if you were in my shoes—if that was Daemon you needed to protect."

A shiver tiptoed down my spine as my jaw locked into place.

"You would," he insisted quietly. "You would do just as I did. And that's what bothers you more than anything. We're more alike than you want to admit."

"We're nothing alike!" My stomach seized up, though, because deep down, like I'd told Daemon before, I was a lot like Blake. Knowing that didn't mean I was going to give him the pleasure of admitting it, especially since what he'd done had changed me.

My hands curled into fists as I stomped over branches and shrubs. "You're a monster, Blake. A real live, breathing monster—I don't want to be that."

He didn't say anything for a moment. "You're not a monster."

My jaw ached from how hard I was grinding my teeth.

"You're like me, Katy, you really are, but you're better than me." There was a pause and then he said, "I've liked you from the moment we met. Even though I knew it was stupid to like you, I do."

Dumbstruck, I stopped and looked at him. "What?"

The tips of his cheeks burned red. "I like you, Katy. A lot. And I know you hate me, and you love Daemon. I get that, but I just wanted to get that out there in case the shit hits the fan tonight. Not that it will, but you know . . . Whatever."

I couldn't even process what he was saying. There was no way. I turned and started back to the house that was now in sight, shaking my head. He liked me. *A lot.* That's why he betrayed my friends and me. Killed Adam and then returned to blackmail us. A hysterical laugh formed in my throat and once I started laughing, I couldn't stop.

"Thanks," he muttered. "I put it out there, and you laugh at me."

"You should be glad I'm laughing. Because the other option is hitting you again, which is still up—"

Blake slammed into my back, throwing me to the ground. Air flew from my lungs in a rush and his weight immediately primed my body for a fight.

"Don't," he whispered in my ear, his hands wrapping around my upper arms. "We have company—and not the good kind."

21

My heart leaped into my throat. As I managed to lift my head, I expected to see a fleet of DOD officers converging on us.

I saw nothing.

"What are you talking about?" I asked in a hushed voice. "I don't see—"

"Quiet."

I bristled but remained quiet. After a few seconds, though, I was convinced he was just getting a cheap thrill or something. "If you don't get off me, I'm going to really hurt—"

And then I saw what he was talking about. Creeping along the side of my house was a man in a black suit. Something about his appearance looked familiar, and then I remembered where I'd seen him before.

He had been with Nancy Husher the day the DOD showed up, while Daemon and I had been at the field where we'd fought Baruck.

Officer Lane.

Then I saw his Expedition parked farther down the street.

I swallowed thickly. "What is he doing here?"

"I don't know." Blake's breath was warm against my

cheek, and I gritted my teeth. "But he's obviously looking for something."

A second or so later, movement at Daemon's house caught my eyes. The front door opened, and Daemon stepped outside. To the human eye, he vanished from the front porch and reappeared in my driveway, a few feet from Officer Lane. But he just moved so quickly that he couldn't be tracked.

"Is there something I can help you with, Lane?" His voice carried over the distance, even and without emotion.

Surprised by his sudden appearance, Lane took a step back and pressed his hand to his chest. "Daemon, God, I hate when you do that."

Daemon didn't smile and whatever the Officer saw in Daemon's eyes got him straight down to business. "I'm doing an investigation."

"Okay."

Lane reached into the breast pocket of his suit and pulled out a small notebook, flipping it open. His jacket got stuck on his gun holster. I wasn't sure if it was on purpose or not. "Officer Brian Vaughn has been missing since before New Year's. I'm checking all possible leads."

"Crap," I muttered.

Daemon folded his arms. "Why would I know what happened to him or care?"

"When was the last time you saw him?"

"I haven't seen him since the day you guys showed up to do your check-in and you all wanted to eat at the disgusting Chinese buffet," Daemon responded, his voice so convincing that I almost believed him. "I still haven't recovered from that."

Lane gave a reluctant grin. "Yes, the food was terrible." He scribbled something down and then slid his notebook back into his pocket. "So you haven't seen Vaughn at all?"

"Nope," he said.

The other man nodded. "I know you two weren't big fans of

each other. I didn't figure he'd make any unauthorized visits, but we have to check every avenue at this point."

"Understandable." Daemon's gaze landed on the trees we were hidden behind. "Why were you checking out the neighbor's house?"

"I was checking out all the houses," he replied. "You still friends with the girl we saw you with?"

Oh, no.

Daemon said nothing, but even from my prone position, I could see the way his eyes narrowed on the Officer.

Lane laughed. "Daemon, when are you ever going to loosen up?" He clapped him on the shoulder as he headed past him. "I don't care who you . . . spend your time with. I'm just doing my job."

Daemon followed the Officer's movements, twisting toward him. "So, if I decided to exclusively date humans and settle down with one, you wouldn't report me?"

"As long as I don't see undeniable evidence, I don't care. This is just a job with a good retirement, and I hope to make it to that point." He started for his vehicle but stopped, facing Daemon. "There's a difference between evidence and my gut. For example, my gut told me that your brother was in a serious relationship with the human he disappeared with, but there wasn't any evidence."

And of course, we knew how the DOD found out about Beth and Dawson: Will. But was this guy insinuating that he knew nothing about Dawson?

Daemon leaned against Lane's SUV. "Did you see my brother's body when they found him?"

A tense moment followed, and Lane lowered his chin. "I wasn't there when they said they found his body along with the girl's. I was only told what happened. I'm just an Officer." He raised his head. "And I haven't been told any differently. I'm nothing in the big scheme of things, but I'm not blind."

I held my breath. I felt Blake do the same.

"What are you saying?" Daemon asked.

Lane smiled tightly. "I know who's in your house, Daemon. I know that I was lied to—a lot of us have been lied to and have no idea what's really going on. We just have jobs. We do them, and we keep our heads down."

Daemon nodded. "And you're keeping your head down now?"

"I was told to check on Vaughn's possible whereabouts and that was about it." He motioned at his car door, and Daemon stepped away from it. "I know not to address anything unless told so. I really want that retirement plan." He climbed in, closing the car door. "You take care."

Daemon moved back. "See you around, Lane."

Tires wheeled and kicked up gravel as the Expedition pulled back onto the road, puffing out exhaust.

What the heck just happened? Better yet, why was Blake still on top of me?

Throwing my elbow back, it connected with his stomach and a grunt followed. "Get off me."

He rolled to his feet, eyes sparkling. "You like to hit."

I scrambled up, glaring. "You need to get out of here. Right now, we don't need to deal with you."

"Good point." He backed off, his grin fading. "See you later tonight."

"Whatever," I muttered, turning back to where Daemon was walking up the driveway. I trotted out of the woods and over to his side. "Is everything okay?"

Daemon nodded. "Did you hear any of that?"

"Yeah, I was heading back when I saw him." I figured if Daemon didn't know about Blake being all Creepy

McCreepsters before we raided Mount Weather, it was a good thing. "Do you believe him?"

"I don't know." He dropped his arm over my shoulders, steering me toward his house. "Lane has always been a decent guy, but this doesn't sit well with me."

I wrapped an arm around his waist and leaned into him. "Which part?"

"All of it—this whole scenario," he said, sitting down on the step one from the top. He tugged me into his lap, keeping his arms around me. "The fact that the DOD—even Lane— knows damn well that Dawson's back, and that they have to realize we know they lied. And they're doing nothing." He closed his eyes as I pressed my cheek to his. "And what we're doing tonight—it can work, but it's so insane. Part of me wonders if they already know we're coming."

Smoothing my thumb along his jaw, I pressed a kiss against his cheek, wishing there was something I could do. "Do you think we're walking into a trap?"

"I think we've been inside the trap the entire time and we're just waiting for it to spring closed." He captured my dirty hand in his and held on.

A breath shuddered through me. "And we're going to still do this?"

The determined set of his shoulders was answer enough. "You don't have to."

"Neither do you," I reasoned softly. "But we both are."

Daemon tilted his head back, eyes meeting mine. "That we are."

We weren't doing this because we had a death wish or that we were stupid, but because there were two lives at stake, probably more, that were worth as much as ours. Perhaps this whole endeavor was sacrificial, but if we didn't go through with it, we'd lose Beth, Chris, and Dawson. Blake was an acceptable loss.

A tendril of panic seized my chest, though. I was scared—
frightened out of my mind. Who wouldn't be? But I'd gotten
us to this point and now it was bigger than me, bigger than
my fear.

Drawing in a shaky breath, I dipped my head and kissed
his lips. "I think I'm going to spend some time with my mom
before we leave." My throat felt thick. "She should be awake
soon."

He kissed me back, his lips lingering. The touch was part
yearning with a hint of desperation and acceptance. If things
went badly tonight, there really hadn't been enough time for
us. Maybe there'd never be enough time, though.

Finally, he said in a rough, raw voice, "That's a good idea,
Kitten."

When the time came to pile into Daemon's SUV and start the
drive to the Blue Ridge Mountains, the mood was strained.
And for once, it really had nothing to do with Blake's presence.

There were outbursts of laughter and curses, but everyone
was on pins and needles.

Ash was getting into the passenger seat of Matthew's vehicle. She was decked out in all black—black tights, black sneakers, and a skintight black turtleneck. She looked like a ninja.
Next to her, Dee was in pink. Apparently Dee had gotten the
memo about staying in the vehicle. Unless Ash planned to
blend in with the seat cushions, I wasn't sure why she was
dressed that way.

Other than the fact she looked insanely hot.

On the other hand, I wore dark sweats and a black thermal
that no longer fit Daemon. It must've been from his preteen
years, because it wouldn't even fit over his head now, and I
looked like I was going to the gym.

I was a total fail next to Ash, but Daemon said something

about me wearing his clothes that sent blood rushing to every part of my body and I didn't care if I looked like a hunchback next to her.

Dawson and Blake were riding with us, the rest with Matthew. As we pulled out of the driveway, my eyes were glued to my house until it faded out of sight. The few hours I had spent with Mom had been great . . . really great.

The first thirty minutes of the trip wasn't bad. Blake stayed quiet, but when he started talking, things went downhill from there. A few times I thought Daemon was going to stop the vehicle and throttle him.

I didn't think Dawson or I would've stopped him.

Dawson shifted, dropping his head into his hand. "Do you ever stop talking?"

"When I'm sleeping," Blake replied.

"And when you're dead," Daemon threw back. "You'll stop talking when you're dead."

Blake's lips thinned. "Point taken."

"Good." Daemon focused on the road. "Try shutting up for a while."

I hid my smile as I twisted around. "What are you going to do when you see Beth?"

Awe crept across Dawson's features, and he shook his head slowly. "Oh, man, I don't know. Breathe—I'll finally be able to breathe."

Moved to tears, I gave him a watery smile. "I'm sure she'll feel the same way." At least, I hoped so. The last time I had seen Beth, she wasn't all there in the head. But if I knew anything about Dawson, I knew he could handle it, because he loved her—he had my mom and dad's kind of love.

Out of the corner of my eyes, I saw Daemon's lips tip up at the corners. Something deep in my chest fluttered.

Sucking in a soft breath, I focused on Blake. The side of his head was against the window as he stared out into the dark night. "What about you?"

His gaze slid to mine. For several seconds, he didn't answer. "We'll leave here and head west. And the first thing we're going to do is go surfing. He really used to dig the sea."

I turned around, staring at my hands. Sometimes it was hard to hate without feeling sorry. And I did feel sorry for his friend. I even felt sorry for Blake. "That's . . . that's good."

None of us spoke after that, and at first, the mood was somber and heavy with memories and probably a thousand what ifs and a dozen scenarios of what tonight would be like for Dawson and Blake, but as we passed Winchester and crossed over the river and could see the darker shades of the Blue Ridge up ahead, the mood shifted.

The boys were tense, throwing off testosterone in buckets. Antsy and ready to just do this, I glanced at the time. Twenty till nine.

"How much longer?" Dawson asked.

"We've got time."

The SUV slipped into a lower gear as we started up the mountain. Behind us, Matthew followed closely. He knew the directions. The access road was supposedly about a half a mile before the main entrance. Daemon had typed it into his GPS, but it pretty much spewed the request back out.

A cell phone dinged and Blake pulled out his cell. "It's from Luc. He wants to make sure we're on schedule."

"We are," Daemon answered.

His brother popped between the front seats. "Are we sure?"

Daemon rolled his eyes. "Yes. I'm sure."

"Just checking," Dawson grumbled, sitting back.

Now Blake was between the seats. "All right, Luc's ready to do this. He wanted to remind us we've only got fifteen minutes. Anything goes wrong, we get out and try again later."

"I don't want to try again later," Dawson protested. "Once we get in, we've got to keep going."

Blake frowned. "I want to get them out just as badly as you, man, but we have a limited gap of time. That's all."

"We stick to the plan." Daemon's gaze met his brother's in the window. "That's it, Dawson. I'm not losing you again."

"Nothing's going to go wrong, anyway," I interjected before it turned into a royal rumble in the car. "Everything will go as planned."

I focused on the road. The highway was four lanes and heavy trees crowded the roads on the south and north lanes. It was a blur of shadows. I had no idea how Daemon would find this road, but he started to slow down and merged into the left lane.

Pressure settled on my chest as he turned onto a barely visible road. There were no markings—nothing signaling that there was even a road there. Two headlights followed us up the narrow opening that was more dirt and gravel than pavement. About two hundred feet in, under the pale moonlight, an old farmhouse sat to the right. Half the roof was missing. Weeds choked the front and sides.

"Creepy," I murmured. "I bet your ghost guys would say this place is haunted."

Daemon chuckled. "They say every place is haunted. That's why I love them."

"Ain't that the truth," Dawson said as we parked and Matthew pulled in beside us.

Both cars killed the lights and engines and with no other source of light, it was black as oil. My stomach pitched. Five till nine. There was no backing out now.

Blake's cell went off again. "He's just making sure we're ready."

"God, he's an annoying little kid," Daemon muttered, facing where Matthew parked. "We're getting ready to do this. Andrew?"

He slipped out, murmuring something to Dee and his sister. Then he turned, throwing up what I'd swear were gang signals. "I'm ready steady."

"Geez," Blake muttered.

"We stick to the plan. At no time do *any* of us"—Daemon directed this at his brother—"deviate from the plan. All of us are coming back tonight."

There were murmurs of agreement. With my pulse racing into cardiac arrest territory, I opened the door.

Daemon placed his hand on my arm. "Stick close to me."

My vocal chords seemed to have stopped working, so I nodded. Then the four of us were out of the car, breathing in the chilled mountain air. Everything was dark—with slices of moonlight cutting across the access road. I was probably standing next to a bear and had no idea.

I moved around the front of the vehicle and stood next to Daemon. Another moved beside me and I realized it was Blake.

"Time," Daemon said.

There was a quick flash of cell phone light, and Blake said, "One minute."

I drew in a shallow gasp, but it got stuck. I could feel my heartbeat in every part of my body. Out of the darkness, Daemon found my hand and squeezed.

We can do this, I told myself. *We can do this. We will do this*.

"Thirty seconds," Blake said.

I worked on my mantra, because I remembered reading something about the laws of the universe and believing in something will make it happen. God, I hoped they were right.

"Ten seconds."

Daemon gave one more squeeze, and I realized he wasn't going to let go. I would slow him down, but there was no time to protest it. A shudder rolled through my arms. I felt the Source rattle and wake up. My weight shifted back and forth.

Beside me, Blake bent forward. "Three, two, go!"

I kicked off, letting the Source rush through, expanding each cell with light. None of the guys were glowing, but we all were running, practically flying. My sneakers skidded over the road. Up we climbed, sticking to the side of the road, avoiding the streams of light. In the back of my head, I realized that keeping up with them had never been the issue.

It was seeing where to go.

But Daemon's hand remained in mine and he wasn't pulling me, more like guiding me through the night, around potholes the size of craters, and up the twisting mountain road.

Seventy-five seconds later, because I counted, a twenty-foot-tall fence came into view under spotlights. We slowed down, coming to a complete stop behind the last stand of trees.

I dragged in air, eyes wide. Red and white signs marked the fence as being electrical. Beyond them was a football-field length of open space and then a massive structure.

"Time?" Daemon asked.

"One minute after nine." Blake ran a hand through his spiky hair. "Okay, I got one guard at the gate. Do you see any others?"

We waited for about another minute to see if any were patrolling, but as Luc had said, it was shift change. Only the gate was covered. We couldn't wait any longer.

"Give me a second," Andrew said, slipping away from the trees, creeping toward the guard dressed in black.

I was just about to ask what the hell he was doing when I saw him dip and place his hand on the ground. Blue sparks flew and the guard started to twist toward him, but the surge of electricity reached him.

A violent tremor ran up the man's body, and he dropped the gun. A second later, he was lying beside it. The boys headed forward and I followed, sneaking a glance at the guard. His chest moved and fell, but he was out cold.

"He doesn't know what hit him." Andrew grinned as he blew a breath over his fingers. "He'll be out for about twenty or so minutes."

"Nice," Dawson said. "I'd have fried his brain if I tried that."

My eyes widened.

Daemon was on the move, approaching the gate. The white keypad looked unassuming, but it was the first test. We could only hope Luc took the cameras down and had given us the right codes.

"Icarus," Blake said quietly.

Nodding, Daemon's shoulders tensed as he quickly typed in the code. There was a mechanical clicking, a low hum followed, and then the gate shuddered. It swung open, beckoning us like a rolled-out red carpet.

Daemon motioned us forward. We sped across the field, taking a couple of heartbeats to reach the doors Luc and Blake had confirmed. I came up behind Daemon as they searched the wall.

"Where's the damn keypad?" Dawson demanded, pacing between the doors.

I stepped back and forced my gaze to move left to right slowly. "There." I pointed toward the right. The pad was small, stuck back behind the overlay.

Andrew jogged to it, glancing over his shoulder. "Ready?"

Dawson glanced down at me and then at the middle door in front of us. "Yes."

"Labyrinth," Daemon murmured from behind us. "And please, God, spell it correctly."

Andrew snickered and keyed in the code. I wanted to squeeze my eyes shut just in case we ended up with a dozen guns leveled at our faces. The door before us slid open, revealing the space beyond inch by inch.

No guns. No people.

I let out the breath I was holding.

Beyond the door was a wide orange tunnel and at the end were the elevators. Not even a hundred feet and all we had to do was get to those elevators and go down six floors. Blake knew the cells.

We were seriously going to do this.

The door was wide enough for two people to move through at once, but Dawson stepped forward first. Understandable, considering what he had to gain by night's end. I followed behind. As he moved under the doorframe, there was a sound of air releasing, a small puffing noise.

Dawson dropped like he'd been shot, but there'd been no blast. One second he was standing in the doorway and the next he was on the other side, withering on the floor, his mouth opened in a silent scream.

"No one moves," Andrew ordered.

Time stopped. The hair on the back of my neck rose. I looked up. A row of tiny nozzles, barely even noticeable, faced down. Too late, I realized in horror. The puffing sound came again.

Red-hot pain seared through my skin, as if a thousand tiny knives were slicing me apart from the inside, attacking every cell. Every part of my body erupted as I dragged in a scorching breath. My legs crumbled and I went down, unable to even ease the fall. My cheek smacked off the concrete, that flash of pain nothing compared to the fire ravaging my body.

Brain cells were scrambled and twisted. Muscles locked up in panic and pain. My eyelids were peeled open. Lungs tried to expand, to drag in air, but there was something wrong with the air—it scalded my mouth and throat. Somewhere, in the distant part of me that could still function, I knew what this was.

Onyx—airborne, weaponized onyx.

22

My body spasmed uncontrollably as waves of pain rocked through me. Distantly, I could hear panicked voices, and I tried to process what they were saying. Nothing made sense but the deep, slicing agony of the onyx.

Strong hands gripped my arms and the anguish skyrocketed. My mouth opened and a hoarse gasp escaped. Then I was lifted up, my face pressed against something warm and solid. I recognized the fresh scent.

Then we were flying.

We had to be, because we were moving so fast that the wind howled and roared in my ears. My eyes were open, but everything was dark as my skin felt like it was being flayed open with tiny razors.

When we slowed down, I thought I heard Dee's shocked cry and then someone said *river*. We were flying again, and I didn't know where Dawson was or if they had gotten to him on the other side of the door.

All I knew was the pain pumping through my body, the racing of my pulse and thundering heart.

It felt like hours before we stopped again, but I knew it had to be only minutes. Damp, cold air that smelled musky blew over us.

"Hold on to me." Daemon's voice was harsh in my ears. "It's going to be cold, but the onyx is all over your clothes and hair. Just hold on, okay?"

I couldn't answer, and I thought that if it was all over me, it had to be on Daemon. It had to be on him the whole way from Mount Weather to the river, which was miles. He had to be hurting.

Daemon stepped forward, slid a few feet down, and then let out a muttered curse. Moments later, the shock of icy water hit my legs and even through the pain, I tried to scramble up Daemon's body to escape, but he kept going out farther and the ice lapped up my waist.

"Hold on," he said again. "Just hold on for me."

Then we slipped under and my breath was stolen again. Shaking my head vigorously, sediment was stirred in the murky water and my hair floated around my face, blinding me. But the fire of the onyx . . . It was fading.

Arms tightened around me, and then we were propelled up. As my head broke the surface, I dragged in air by the lungful. Stars cartwheeled and blurred, and Daemon moved us out of the water to the bank.

Water splashed a few feet away and as my vision cleared, Blake and Andrew dragged Dawson out of the water, laying him on the bank. Blake sat down next to him, thrusting his hands through his soaked hair.

My heart dropped. Was he . . . ?

Dawson flung an arm over his face as he bent one leg. "Crap."

Relief made my knees weak. I felt Daemon's hands on my cheeks and then he turned my face to his. Bright green eyes met mine.

"Are you okay?" he asked. "Say something, Kitten. Please."

I forced my chilled lips to move. "Wow."

His brows lowered as he shook his head, confounded, and then he threw his arms around me, squeezing me so tightly I squealed.

"God, I don't even know . . ." He cupped the back of my head as he twisted away from the group, lowering his voice. "I was scared to death."

"I'm okay." My voice was muffled. "What about you? You had to have—"

"It's all off me. Don't even worry about that." A shudder rocked him. "Damn, Kitten . . ."

I kept quiet as he squeezed me again, patted me down like he was checking to make sure I still had arms and fingers. When he kissed my eyelids, though, I thought I would cry, because his hands were trembling.

Four sets of headlights bore down on us and then there was a stream of voices and questions. Dee was the first on the scene. She dropped beside Dawson, grabbing his hand.

"What happened?" she demanded. "Someone tell us what happened."

Matthew and Ash appeared, curious and concerned. It was Andrew who spoke up. "I don't know. They had something that came out of the doors when they opened. It was some kind of spray, but it had no smell and we couldn't see it."

"It hurt like a bitch." Dawson sat up, rubbing his arms. "And there's only one thing that feels like that. Onyx."

Of course he'd also know what it was. I shuddered. God knows how many times it had been used against him.

"But I've never seen it like that before," he continued, slowly climbing to his feet with Ash's and Dee's help. "It was airborne. Insane. I think I swallowed some."

"Are you okay? Katy?" Matthew asked.

We both nodded. My skin ached a little, but the worst of it had passed. "How did you know to get us to the river?"

Daemon brushed wet curls off his forehead. "I guessed it was onyx when I didn't see any visible wounds, figured it was on your clothes and skin. I remembered passing the river. Thought it was the best place to go."

"Good thinking," Matthew said. "Hell . . ."

"We didn't even make it past the first set of doors." Andrew barked out a laugh. "What the hell were we thinking? They have that place wired against Luxen and, apparently, hybrids."

Daemon disentangled his arms from me and stalked over to where the rest stood. He stopped behind Blake. "You've been to Mount Weather before, right?"

Slowly, Blake pushed to his feet. His cheeks were pale in the silvery moonlight. "Yeah, but nothing—"

Daemon was like a cobra striking. His fist came out, slamming into Blake's jaw. Blake stumbled back and fell, hitting the ground on his butt. Leaning over, he spit out a mouthful of blood. "I didn't know—I didn't know they had something like that!"

"I'm finding that hard to believe." Daemon stalked the boy's movements.

Blake lifted his head. "You have to believe me! Nothing like that ever happened before. I don't understand."

"Bullshit," Andrew said. "You set us up."

"No. No way." Blake stood with his back to the calm river. He placed a hand to his jaw. "Why would I set you guys up? My friend is—"

"I don't care about your friend!" Andrew shouted. "You've been there! How could you not know they had the doors rigged with that stuff?"

Blake turned to me. "You have got to believe me. I had no idea that was going to happen. I wouldn't lead you guys into a trap."

I stared at the river, unsure of what to believe. It seemed stupid for him to set us up this way and if he had, wouldn't the DOD be surrounding us now? Something wasn't right. "And Luc didn't know?"

"If he did, he would've told us. Katy—"

"Don't," Daemon warned and his voice was so low it caught my attention. The lines of his body shimmered. "Don't talk to her. Don't even talk to any of us right now."

Blake opened his mouth but nothing came out. He shook his head as he stalked back to the cars.

There was a gap of silence and then Ash asked, "What do we do now?"

"I don't know." Half of Daemon's face was shadowed as he watched his brother pace. "I really don't know."

Dee rose. "This sucks. This *sucks* donkey butt."

"We're back at square one," Andrew said. "Hell, we're at negative one."

Dawson whipped toward his brother. "We can't give up. Promise me we won't give up."

"We won't." Daemon was quick to reassure him. "We're not giving up."

I didn't even realize I was shaking until Matthew draped a blanket over my shoulders. He met my eyes and then focused on the headlight beams. "I always carry a blanket just in case."

Teeth chattering, I hunkered down in the blanket. "Thank you."

He nodded as he placed a hand on my shoulder. "Come on. Let's get you in the car where it's warm. We're done for the night."

I let him steer me toward Daemon's SUV and the welcoming blast of heat felt wonderful, but there wasn't anything to rejoice in. Disappointment swelled. Unless we figured out a way around the onyx, we weren't just done for the night.

We were circling the drain. We were done period.

In Dee's words, the ride home sucked donkey butt. It was near midnight when we pulled into the driveway. Blake said nothing as he slipped out of the SUV and headed toward his truck. The engine roared and tires peeled as he pulled out of the driveway.

I started toward my own house, but Daemon cut me off and guided me toward his. "You're not leaving yet," he said.

My brows rose at that and the glint in his eyes, but I wasn't in the mood to argue. It was late, school was tomorrow, and tonight had been one giant fail boat.

I went into their house, still shrouded in Matthew's blanket. My skin was so chilled underneath my damp clothes that I was numb. Exhausted, my legs shook to keep me standing, but everyone was talking—Dee, Andrew, Ash, and Dawson. Matthew was trying to keep them calm, but that wasn't happening. Everyone was hyped up on anger and residual adrenaline, and I think Dawson kept talking because if he stopped then he had to deal with what happened tonight.

Beth was still with Daedalus.

"Let's get you into some dry clothes," Daemon said quietly, taking my hand.

At the bottom of the stairs, Daemon went to pick me up, but I waved him off. "I'm fine."

He made a sound in the back of his throat that reminded me of a disgruntled lion, but he followed my slow ascension. Once inside his bedroom, he closed his door. Determination seeped from his pores.

I sighed. Tonight had been a tragedy. "We kind of deserved this."

He prowled over to me, catching the edges of the blanket, pulling it off. Then he took ahold of my borrowed thermal. "How so?"

It seemed obvious to me. "We're a bunch of teenagers, and

we thought we could break into a facility run by Homeland Security and the DOD? I mean, come on. This was bound to go wrong— Wait!" The thermal was halfway up my stomach. My chilled fingers circled his wrists. "What are you doing?"

"Getting you naked."

My mouth dropped open at the same time my heart did a backflip. A heady warmth cascaded through my veins. "Uh, wow. Way to cut to the point."

A lopsided grin teased his lips. "Your shirt and pants are soaked and cold. And there are probably traces of onyx still on them. You need to get out of your clothes."

I smacked his hands away. "I can do that myself."

Daemon leaned in, speaking into my ear. "Where's the fun in that?" He let go, though, and headed for his dresser. "You really think we were doomed to fail?"

Since he'd turned his back, I made haste with removing my clothes. *Everything* beside the cold piece of obsidian hanging around my neck was ruined and had to come off. The clothing smelled like musky river water. Shivering, I folded my arms across my chest. "Don't . . . don't turn around."

His shoulders shook with silent laughter as he rummaged around for something for me to wear. Hopefully.

"I don't know," I said, finally answering his question. "It was a huge undertaking for trained spies. We're in over our heads."

"But we were fine until we hit those doors." He pulled out a shirt. "I hate to say this, but I really don't think Blake knew about them. The look on his face when you and Dawson went down—it was too real."

"Then why did you punch him in the face?"

"I wanted to." He turned around, one hand over his eyes as he offered me a shirt. "Here you go."

I snatched it away and quickly tugged it over my head. The soft, worn material billowed around me, ending at my thighs.

When I glanced up, I saw his fingers split over his eyes. "You were peeking."

"Maybe." He took my hand, pulling me toward his bed. "Get in. I'm going to check on Dawson and I'll be back."

I really should have headed next door to my own bed, but I reasoned that tonight was different. Besides, Mom wouldn't be home before school started and I didn't want to be alone. Doing as he requested, I climbed in and yanked the comforter up to my chin. It smelled of fresh linen and Daemon. He wasn't gone long, but in that short time, my lids fluttered shut. The onyx had zapped most of my energy, as it was meant to. We'd been so damn lucky to even make it out of there before the guard came to.

Daemon returned, moving around the room silently, and I was feeling way too lazy to open my eyes and see what he was up to. Clothing rustled to the floor and my temperature went up a degree. Another drawer opened and then he was tugging back the covers, sliding in.

Lying on his side, he wrapped an arm around my waist and tucked me against his bare chest. The flannel of his pajama bottoms teased my legs, and I let out a contented sigh.

"How's Dawson?" I asked, wiggling closer so I was pretty much plastered to him.

"He's doing okay." Daemon brushed the hair back from my cheek, his hand lingering. "He's not a happy camper, though."

I could imagine. We'd come so close to Beth only to have to turn around. That is, if Beth had really been there. Blake may've not known about the onyx defense system from hell, but I didn't trust him. None of us did.

"Thank you for getting us out of there." I tilted my head back, searching out his face in the darkness. His eyes glowed softly.

"I had help." He pressed his lips against my forehead and his arm tightened around me. "You feeling okay?"

"I feel fine. Stop worrying about me."

His eyes met mine. "Don't ever walk through a door first again, okay? And don't argue with me about it or accuse me of being chauvinistic. I don't ever want to see you in that kind of pain again."

Instead of arguing, I twisted in his embrace and placed my lips on his, kissing him softly. His lashes lowered, shielding his eyes. He returned the kiss and it was sweet and tender and so perfect that there was a good chance I'd start bawling like a baby.

But then the kisses, well, they changed. They deepened as I rolled onto my back and he followed, his weight a delicious feeling against my legs, and these kisses were anything but sweet. They scorched deep inside me, washing away the events of the last couple of hours like the river had taken away the unholy burn of the onyx. When he kissed like this, every muscle in his body coiling into a tight spring, he undid me.

His hand smoothed the shirt down, baring a shoulder, and his mouth followed. Static built in the air and a tremble coursed through his body. In that moment, after everything that happened, I wanted the feel of him against me with no barriers, nothing getting in the way. Lifting up, I raised my arms and Daemon didn't hesitate. He took what was offered. With nothing there, his hands were everywhere, tracing the slender piece of obsidian, smoothing down the curve of my stomach, over my hips, and I was pretty sure there would be no other moment as perfect as this.

Or maybe it was how close we came to losing it all tonight that propelled us both? I didn't know, nor was I sure how we'd come to this point, but all that mattered was we were both here and ready. Really ready. And when his clothing joined mine on the floor, there was no going back.

"Don't stop," I said, just in case he had any doubts about what I wanted.

There was a flash of a grin, and then he kissed me again and I was drowning in the rawness of what was building between us. Electricity coursed over our skin, throwing dancing shadows over the walls as he reared up, reaching for the small bedside table beside us.

I flushed, realizing what he was going for. When he sat up and our eyes met, I started to giggle. A wide, beautiful smile broke out across his face, softening lines that held a harsh beauty.

Daemon spoke in his language. The lyrical quality of his words made no sense to me, but they were beautiful, like spoken music that the alien part of me danced to.

"What did you say?" I asked.

He peered up through thick lashes, the foil package in his fist. "There's really no translation for it," he said, "but the closest human words would be, you are beautiful to me."

I sucked in a sharp breath and our gazes locked. Tears built in my eyes. I reached for him, sinking my fingers into his silky hair. My heart was pounding fast, and I knew his was, too.

This was it. And it was right. Perfect without the dinner, movies, and flowers, because how could you really plan something like this? You couldn't.

Daemon sat back—

A fist pounded on the door, and Andrew's voice intruded. "Daemon, are you awake?"

We stared at each other in disbelief. "If I ignore him," he whispered, "do you think he'll go away?"

My hands dropped to my sides. "Maybe."

The pounding came again. "Daemon, I really need you downstairs. Dawson is ready to go back to Mount Weather. Nothing Dee or I are saying to him is making a bit of difference. He's like a suicidal Energizer bunny."

Daemon squeezed his eyes shut. "Son of a bitch . . ."

"It's okay." I started to sit up. "He needs you."

He let out a ragged sigh. "Stay here and get some rest. I'll talk—or beat some sense into him." He kissed me briefly and then gently pushed me back down. "I'll be back."

Settling in, I smiled. "Try not to kill him."

"No promises." He stood, pulled on his pajama bottoms, and headed for the door. Stopping short, he looked over his shoulder, his intense gaze melting my bones. "Dammit."

A few seconds after he stepped out into the hallway and closed the door behind him, there was a fleshly smack and then Andrew yelling, "Ouch. What in the hell was that for?"

"Your timing sucks on an epic level," Daemon shot back.

Smiling sleepily, I rolled onto my side and ordered myself to stay awake, but as my breathing returned to normal, sleep dragged me under. Sometime later, I heard the door open and then Daemon was beside me, pulling me back against him. It wasn't long before the steady rise and fall of his chest lulled me back into the rhythm of sleep. Every so often I'd wake up when his arms clenched around me, his embrace so tight I thought he'd cut off my circulation, holding me as if even in his sleep he was haunted by the fear of losing me.

23

Daemon and I rode together to school on Monday. The car still carried a musty, wet scent to it, a painful reminder of where our mission had ended—in a river. On the way, Daemon was convinced that his brother had been talked down from bum-rushing Mount Weather, but I knew we needed to come up with another way to get to Beth and Chris. Dawson couldn't wait forever, and I could understand that. If it were Daemon locked up, I don't think anyone would be able to stop me.

As soon as we stepped out, I saw Blake leaning against his truck a few spaces down. He pushed off and trotted over the moment he spotted us.

Daemon groaned. "He is not who I want to see as soon as I get to school."

"Agreed," I said, wrapping my hand around Daemon's. "Just remember we are in public."

"No fun."

Blake slowed as he reached us, his gaze dipping to our joined hands and then quickly sweeping up. "We all need to talk."

We kept walking—or Daemon kept walking. "Talking to you is the last thing I want to do."

"I can understand that." He caught up to us. "But I seriously didn't know about the onyx shields in the doors. I had no idea."

"I believe you," Daemon said.

Blake's step faltered. "You punched me."

"That's because he wanted to," I answered for Daemon, earning a wink from him. "Look, I don't trust you, but maybe you didn't know about the shields. It doesn't change the fact that we're not going to be able to get in there."

"I talked to Luc last night. He didn't know about the shields, either." Blake shoved his hands into his pockets and stopped in front of us. He was lucky Daemon didn't lay him out right there. "He's willing to do it again—take down the cameras and stuff."

Daemon blew out a long breath. "And what good does that do us? We can't get past those doors."

"Or if every door is set up like that," I added, shivering. I couldn't imagine going through that three or four times. Sure, I'd been in that cage longer, but the airborne onyx had covered everything.

The three of us were huddled along the fence surrounding the track, careful of keeping our voices low so other students didn't overhear us and wonder what the heck.

"Well, I was thinking about that," Blake said, shifting from one foot to the other. "While I was with Daedalus, they used to expose us to this stone each day. Our forks and silverware were encased in it. A lot of stuff was, almost everything we came into contact with. Burned like holy hell to touch, but we didn't have any other choice. I've walked through the doors before and recently. Nothing happened."

Daemon laughed as he looked away from Blake. "And you now just thought this was a good thing to tell us?"

"I didn't know what it was. None of us did." Blake's gaze pleaded with mine. "I didn't think much about it."

Dumbfounded, I realized they'd been conditioning Blake. Probably exposing him and others to the onyx over and over but like last night, something wasn't right. Why would they expose them to it? Sick and twisted punishment or for tolerance? And why would they want Luxen or hybrids to develop a tolerance to the one weapon that could be used against them?

"You can't tell me you never knew about the onyx and what it could do," I said.

He met me dead-on. "I didn't know that it could incapacitate us."

I pressed my lips together. "You know, there's so much we have to just trust you with. That you really are working against Daedalus and not for them. That Beth and Chris are where you're saying they are, and now, that you didn't really know about onyx."

"I know how this looks."

"I don't think you do," Daemon said, letting go of my hand as he propped his hip against the fence. "We have no reason to trust you."

"And you've blackmailed us into helping you," I added.

Blake exhaled roughly. "Okay. I don't have a glowing history, but I want nothing more than to get my friend away from them. That's why I'm here."

"And why are you here right this instant?" Daemon asked, obviously at his patience threshold.

"I think we can get around the onyx," he said, pulling his hands out of his pockets and holding them in front of him. "Now, hear me out. This is going to sound crazy."

"Oh, goodie," Daemon muttered.

"I think we need to build up a tolerance. If that was what Daedalus was doing, then that makes sense. Hybrids have to go in and out of those doors. If we expose ourselves to it—"

"Are you insane?" Daemon turned around, running his

hand through his hair, clasping the back of his neck. "You want us to expose ourselves to onyx?"

"Do you see any other option?"

Yeah, there was one—we didn't go back. But was it really an option? Daemon was starting to pace. Not a good sign. "Can we do this later? We're going to be late."

"Sure." He sidestepped Daemon. "After school?"

"Maybe," I said, focusing on Daemon. "We'll talk later."

Taking the hint, Blake skedaddled out of there. I had no idea what to say to any of this. "Expose ourselves to onyx?"

Daemon huffed. "He's insane."

He was. "Do you think it would work?"

"You're not . . . ?"

"I don't know." I switched my backpack to the other shoulder and we started toward the school. "I really don't know. We can't give up, but what other options do we have?"

"We don't even know if it will work."

"But if Blake really is sort of immune to it, then we can test it out on him."

A wide grin spread across his face. "I like the sound of that."

I laughed. "Why doesn't that surprise me? But seriously, if he has a tolerance to it, then shouldn't we be able to? It's something. We'd just need to figure out how to get some." Daemon was quiet for a few seconds "What?" I asked.

He squinted. "I think I have the onyx part covered."

"What do you mean?" I stopped again, ignoring the faint warning bell.

"After Will got you and a couple of days after Dawson came back, I returned to the warehouse and stripped most of the onyx from the outside."

My jaw hit the ground. "What?"

"Yeah, I don't know why I did it. Kind of like my big FU to the establishment." He laughed. "Imagine their faces when they went back and saw it was all gone."

I was speechless.

He tweaked my nose. I smacked his hand away. "You're insane. You could've gotten caught!"

"But I didn't."

I smacked him again, this time harder. "You're crazy."

"But you love my craziness." He leaned down, kissing the corner of my lip. "Come on, we're late. The last thing we need is detention."

I snorted. "Yeah, like *that* would be the biggest of our problems."

Carissa still hadn't returned to school on Monday. The flu must've been kicking her butt. Lesa seemed a bit jealous over the whole thing. "I'm, like, five pounds from my goal weight," she said before trig started. "Why can't I come down with something? Geesh."

I giggled and we moved on to some gossip. For a little while, I forgot about everything. It was nice and much needed downtime even though we were in school. The morning blew by and when Blake entered bio, I refused to let him ruin my mood.

But then he opened his mouth and the big "what the hell" statement came out. "You didn't tell Daemon about what I said to you in the woods? About me liking you?"

Ah, what the frig, man? "Um, no. He'd kill you."

Blake laughed.

I frowned. "I'm being serious."

"Oh." His smile faded and he paled. I imagined that he was playing that scenario out in his head: me telling Daemon about his dirty little secret and Daemon going ape poo poo over it. He came to the same conclusion as me. "Yeah, good call.

"Anyway," he continued. "About what I said this morning—"

"Not now." I opened my notebook. "I really don't want to talk about that right now."

I smiled when Lesa sat down and luckily, Blake respected my request. He chatted it up with Lesa like a normal person would. He was good at that—pretending.

A knot formed in my stomach as I looked at him sharply. He was telling Lesa about different kinds of surfing techniques. I was pretty sure she wasn't even listening, considering her gaze was trained on how his shirt strained over his biceps.

He laughed easily, blending in perfectly. Like a good implant would, and I knew from previous experience that Blake was skilled at faking it. There really was no way of telling what side Blake was truly on, and it was stupid to even guess.

At the front of the class, Matthew pulled out his roll book. His eyes met mine briefly and then shifted to the boy beside me. I wondered how Matthew did it—kept calm all the time. How he stayed the glue that kept everyone together.

I stopped at my locker and grabbed my US history text at the end of the day. The chances of a pop quiz tomorrow were high. Mrs. Kerns had a schedule, which really didn't make the quiz a big surprise. I closed my locker door and turned, shoving my book into the bag. The crowd was thinning out as everyone rushed to get out of the school. I wasn't sure if I wanted to rush or not. Blake had already texted me during gym about getting everyone together to talk about the onyx situation, and I really didn't want to.

I wanted one day to go home and do nothing—no plotting or dealing with alien shenanigans. Books needed reading and reviewing and my poor blog could really use a makeover. I couldn't think of a better way to finish out a Monday.

But it was probably not going to happen.

Stepping outside, I trailed behind the last group of students heading to the parking lot. From my vantage point, I could hear Kimmy's high-pitched voice from the front.

"My daddy said that Simon's father has been talking to the FBI. He's demanding a full investigation and won't stop until Simon comes home."

I wondered if the FBI knew about the aliens. Images of *The X-Files* flew through my head.

"I heard on TV that the longer a person is missing, the less likely it is for them to turn up alive," one of her friends said.

"But look at Dawson. He was gone for over a year, and he's back," another said.

Tommy Cruz rubbed a beefy hand along the back of his neck. "And isn't that strange? He's gone forever. The one Thompson kid bites it and then Dawson shows up? Something insane with that."

I'd heard enough. Going between cars, I put distance between the group and me. I doubted their suspicious would go anywhere, but I wasn't trolling for new things to worry about. We had enough.

Daemon waited by his car. Long legs crossed at the ankles. He smiled when he saw me and pushed off the side of the vehicle. "I was beginning to wonder if you were going to stay here."

"Sorry." He opened the passenger door and bowed. Grinning, I jumped in. I waited until he was behind the wheel. "Blake wants to talk tonight."

"Yeah, I know. He apparently got ahold of Dawson and already told him about the whole onyx tolerance thing." He backed out, hand on the gear shifter. Anger lit up his eyes. "And of course, Dawson is all about that. It was like handing him a winning lottery ticket."

"Great." I tilted my head back against the seat. Dawson really was a suicidal Energizer bunny.

And suddenly it struck me. This was my life—all of this craziness. The ups and downs, the near-death moments and those far worse, the lies and the fact I probably wouldn't be able to trust anyone who befriended me without worrying if they were an implant. And hell, how could I really befriend anyone normal? Like Daemon in the beginning—he'd stayed away and wanted Dee to do the same so I wouldn't be caught in their world.

It would be the same with anyone I met.

My life wasn't my own. Every moment was like waiting for the other shoe to drop. I sank back against the seat, weighted down, and sighed. "There go my reviewing and reading plans."

"Shouldn't it be reading and then reviewing?"

"Whatever," I muttered.

Daemon coasted the SUV out onto the road. "Why can't you still do that?"

"If Blake wants to talk tonight, then that's going to soak up all my time." I really wanted to pout. Maybe even kick my feet.

With one hand on the wheel and the other arm thrown over the back of my seat, he cast me a half smile. "You don't need to be there, Kitten. We can talk to him without you."

"Yeah right." I laughed. "There's a good chance someone will kill Blake without me there."

"And would you really be torn up about that?"

I made a face. "Well . . ."

Daemon laughed.

"And the fact that upon his untimely death, there's a letter delivered to Nancy Husher. So, we kind of need him alive."

"True," he said, catching a strand of my hair between his fingers. "But we can keep it short. You'll have a normal Monday evening full of normal suck and not extraterrestrial suckage."

Shame burned my cheeks as I bit down on my lip. As crazy as everything had turned out, I could admit that things could be worse. "That's really selfish of me."

"What?" He tugged on my hair gently. "It's not selfish, Kitten. Your whole life can't revolve around this crap. It won't."

Straightening my fingers, I smiled. "You sound so determined."

"And you know what happens when I get determined."

"You get your way." He raised his brows at me, and I laughed. "But what about you—your life can't revolve around this crap."

He pulled his hand back, resting it on his thigh. "I was born into this. I'm used to it, and besides, it's all about time management. Say, like time management last night. We did our mission thing—"

"And failed."

"There's that, but the rest of last night?" One side of his lips curled up and I felt my cheeks heat for a totally different reason. "We had the bad—the not-normal. And then we had the good—the normal. Granted, the good was interrupted by the bad, but there was time management there."

"You make it sound so easy." I stretched out my legs, relaxing.

"It is that easy, Kat. You just need to know when to draw the line, when you've had enough." There was a pause as he slowed and turned onto the lonely road leading up to our houses. "And if you've had enough for today, you have. Nothing to feel guilty about or to worry about."

Daemon coasted to a stop in his driveway and killed the engine. "And no one will kill Bill."

I laughed softly as I unbuckled the seat belt. "Blake. His name is Blake."

Daemon pulled the keys out and leaned back, his eyes glimmering with amusement. "He's whatever I decide to call him."

"You're terrible." Crossing the distance between us, I kissed him. As I pulled away, he reached for me and I giggled, opening the door. "And by the way, I haven't had enough today. I just needed a kick in the pants. But I do need to be home by seven."

I shut the door and turned. Daemon stood before me. He stepped forward and there was nowhere for me to go if I wanted to. And I didn't.

"You haven't had enough?" he asked.

Recognizing the tone of his voice, my bones melted in response. "No, not nearly enough."

"Good." His hands were on my hips, tugging me forward. "That's what I like to hear."

Placing my hands on his chest, I tilted my head back. This was totally an exercise in time management. Our lips brushed and warmth cascaded through me. It was a really fun exercise. I rose onto the tips of my toes and slid my hands up the hard plane of his chest, marveled at the way it rose unsteadily.

Daemon whispered something and then the soft kiss, which wasn't much more than a butterfly touch, strengthened me and unraveled him. His arms swept around me, and I could feel his heart pounding in tandem with mine.

"Hey!" Dawson yelled from the front door. "I think Dee caught the microwave on fire. Again. And I tried popping some popcorn with my hands and it kind of went wrong. Like really, really wrong."

Daemon pressed his forehead against mine and growled. *"Dammit."*

I couldn't help but laugh. "Time management, right?"

"Time management," he muttered.

Surprisingly, pretty much everyone was on board with the onyx thing. I was convinced we had an invasion of the body snatchers or something, because even Matthew was nodding like exposing yourself to the hellishly painful onyx was a good thing.

I had a feeling that would change the first time he came in contact with it.

"This is so insane," Dee said, and I had to agree. "This is tantamount to self-mutilation."

Ah, she kind of had a point.

Dawson's head dropped back, and he sighed. "That's a little extreme."

"I remember what you looked like when they brought you back down the mountain." She twisted her hair around her hand. "And Katy lost her voice for a while from screaming. Who signs up for that?"

"Crazy people." Daemon sighed. "Dee, I don't want you doing this."

Her expression was clearly a *no duh* one. "No offense, Dawson, I love you and want you to see Beth and to hold her, because I wish . . ." Her voice cracked, but her spine straightened. "But I don't want to do this."

Dawson shot forward, placing a hand on her arm. "It's okay. I don't expect you to do this."

"I want to help." Her voice was wobbly. "But I can't . . ."

"It's fine." Dawson smiled and there was a moment between the siblings, as if he were saying more with just that gesture alone. Whatever it was, it worked, because Dee relaxed. "Not all of us need to do this."

"Then who's in?" Blake's eyes touched on all of us. "If we are going to do this, we need to start, like, yesterday, because I don't know how long it'll take to build a tolerance."

Antsy, Dawson stood. "It can't take that long."

Blake let out a surprised laugh. "I've been with Daedalus for years, so there's no telling at what point I built a tolerance . . . or if I really even have one."

"We've got to test that out, then." I grinned.

He frowned. "Wow. Kind of excited about that?"

I nodded.

Dee twisted around, eyeing Blake. "Can I test it out, too?"

"I'm pretty sure everyone will get a round." Daemon's

sinister twist of the lips was actually kind of frightening. "Anyway, back to the basics. Who's in?"

Matthew raised his hand. "I want to be in on this. No offense, Andrew, but I prefer to take your place this time."

Andrew nodded his head. "No problem. I can wait with Dee and Ash."

Ash, who hadn't said more than two words, just nodded. I realized that half of the room was staring at me. "Oh," I said. "Yeah, I'm in." Beside me, Daemon gave me a look that said, *You are so out of your mind.* I folded my arms. "Don't start with me. I'm in. Nothing you can say will change that."

The next look translated into, *This is going to turn into a conversation—argument—in private.* Blake watched with approval—a ringing endorsement I didn't want or need. Frankly, it made my skin crawl, since it reminded me of when I had killed the Arum he'd practically thrown at me.

God, I wanted to hit him again.

Plans were made to meet after school and, weather permitting, we'd head out to the lake to basically start causing ourselves an obscene amount of pain. Whee.

Since there were some hours left before bedtime, I said my good-byes and left to get some studying in and hopefully a dang review.

Daemon walked me over and I knew it wasn't a gentlemanly act, but I let him in and offered him his favorite: milk.

He downed the drink in five seconds flat. "Can we talk about this?"

I hopped up on the counter and opened my bag, pulling out my history book. "Nope."

"Kat."

"Hmm?" I flipped open to the chapter we'd been reading in class.

He stalked over, placing his hands on either side of my crossed legs. "I can't watch you get hurt over and over again."

I dug out a Highlighter.

"Seeing what happened last night and when Will had you handcuffed in that stuff? And I'm supposed to just stand there— Are you listening to me?"

Halfway through the sentence I'd highlighted, I stopped. "I'm listening."

"Then look at me."

I lifted my lashes. "I'm looking at you."

Daemon scowled.

Sighing, I put the cap back on the Highlighter. "Okay. I don't want to see you in pain."

"Kat—"

"No. Don't interrupt. I don't want to see you in pain and just thinking about you going through what that feels like makes me want to hurl."

"I can handle it."

Our eyes locked. "I know you can, but that doesn't change how horrible it's going to be to see you go through that, but I'm not asking you not to do it."

He pushed off and pivoted around, thrusting his fingers through his hair. Tension and frustration settled over the kitchen like a well-worn blanket.

Setting my stuff aside, I hopped down. "I don't want to argue with you, Daemon, but you can't say it's okay for me to watch you go through this and not you."

I made my way over to him and wrapped my arms around his waist. He stiffened. "I know this is coming from a good place, but just because it's getting ugly, I can't back out. And you know you're not going to. It's only fair."

"I hate your logic." He placed his hands on mine, though, and I pressed against his back, smiling. "And I'm really going to hate this."

Squeezing him like my favorite teddy bear, I knew how hard this was for him to give on. This was monumental, actually. He twisted in my arms, lowered his head, and I thought, *Wow, this is how adults do things.* They may not agree on stuff all the time, they may argue, but in the end, they work it out and they love.

Like my mom and dad.

A lump formed in my throat. Crying so wouldn't be the right thing to do, but it was hard to keep those tears back.

"The only good thing is that I'm going to hold Buff down and make him kiss onyx over and over again," he said.

I choked out a laugh. "You're sadistic."

"And you need to study, right? It's school time management—not Daemon time management, which blows, because we're alone and it requires more effort for them to interrupt us over here."

Disappointed, I pulled free. "Yeah, I need to study."

He pouted and it was incredibly sexy on him. Wrong. "All right, I'm leaving."

I followed him to the door. "I'll text when I'm done and you can come over and tuck me in."

"'Kay," he said, kissing the top of my head. "I'll be waiting."

And knowing that had me all warm and fuzzy. Wiggling my fingers at him, I closed the door and went back to the kitchen, grabbed my stuff and a glass of OJ. Happy that an all-out brouhaha was avoided with Daemon, I went upstairs and bumped open my door.

I came to a complete stop.

A girl sat on my bed, hands folded primly in her lap. It took me a moment to recognize her, because her hair hung in limp strands around her pale face and her almond-shaped eyes weren't hidden behind purple or pink glasses.

"Carissa," I said, stunned. "How . . . how did you get in here?"

She stood wordlessly. Her hands extended out. The overhead light reflected off a bracelet I also recognized—black stone with fire inside.

What the hell . . . ? Luc had that stone. Why would—?

Static crackled in the air and there was a smell of burned ozone a second before whitish-blue light radiated from Carissa's hands. The bracelet was no longer a concern.

Shocked into a stupor, I stared at my friend in disbelief. "Crap."

Carissa attacked.

24

The bolt of energy slammed into my history textbook, burning a hole right through. It fizzled out before it could touch me, but the book casualty told me what I needed to know.

Carissa was not a friendly.

And that little display of the Source was not a warning.

I dropped the book and darted to the left as she lunged at me. OJ sloshed over the side of my glass, covering my fingers. Why was I still holding it? My brain was so not catching up to this turn of events.

She shot toward me, and I did the only thing I could think of in that moment. I threw the glass at her face. Glass shattered as she stumbled back, raising her hands to her eyes. Sticky liquid and glass coursed down her cheeks, mixing with tiny flecks of blood.

I bet that stung like a bitch.

"Carissa," I said, backing up. "I have no idea how this happened, but I'm a friend—I can help you! Just calm down. Okay?"

She wiped at her eyes, flinging liquid against the walls. When her gaze met mine, there wasn't an ounce of recognition in it. Her eyes were frighteningly empty and vast. Like months had been washed away, and I was nothing to her. There was zilch going on behind those eyes.

My eyes had to be deceiving me or I was dreaming, because she was definitely a hybrid and that didn't make sense. Carissa didn't know about aliens. She was just a normal girl. Quiet and maybe a little bit shy.

But she'd been out with the *flu* . . .

Oh, dear baby kittens . . . She'd been mutated.

Her head cocked to the side, eyes narrowing.

"Carissa, please, it's me. Katy. You know me," I pleaded. My back hit the desk as I eyed the open door behind her. "We're friends. You don't want to do this."

She stalked toward me, like that freaky female terminator after John Connor.

And I was so John Connor.

I drew in a breath, but it got stuck. "We go to school together—we have trig and we eat lunch together. You wear glasses—really funky glasses." I didn't know what to say, but I kept babbling, hoping to somehow reach her, because the last thing I wanted to do was hurt her. "Carissa, *please*."

But she apparently had no qualms over doing some damage to me.

The air charged with static again. I lurched to the side as she let go of the Source again. The tail end of it singed my sweater. A smell of burned hair and cotton wafted into the air as I spun toward my desk. There was a low whine from the desk and then smoke billowed out of my closed laptop.

I gaped.

My precious, perfectly brand new laptop I cherished like one would a small child.

Son of a mother . . .

Friend or not, it was so on.

I lunged at Carissa, taking her down to my bedroom floor. My hands went around her hair and lifted. A stream of dark strands billowed, and then I slammed her head down. There was a satisfactory *thud* and she let out a low squeal of pain.

"You stupid—" Carissa tilted her pelvis up, wrapped her legs around my hips and rolled, gaining the upper hand in seconds. She was like a damn ninja—who knew? She slammed my head back much harder and damn, did paybacks suck. Starbursts clouded my vision. Sharp pain exploded along my jaw, momentarily startling me.

And then something inside me snapped.

Blistering rage welled up, coating my skin, setting a fire to every cell in my body. There was a heady rush of power centered in my chest. It flowed like lava through my veins, reaching the tips of my fingers. A veil of whitish-red fell over my eyes.

Time was slowing down again to an infinite crawl. Heat from the vents blew the curtains out, and the flimsy material reached toward us and then stopped, suspending in air. The small puffs of gray and white smoke froze. And in the back of my mind, I realized that they weren't really frozen, but I was moving so fast that everything appeared to have been stopped.

I didn't want to hurt her but I *was* going to stop her.

Arching back, I slammed both hands into her chest. Carissa flew into my dresser. Bottles of lotion rattled and fell over, clunking off her head.

I leaped to my feet, breathing heavily. The Source raged in me, demanded to be tapped into, to be used again. Holding back was like daring not to breathe.

"Okay," I gasped. "Let's just take a moment and calm down. We can talk this out, figure out what's going on."

Slowly, painfully, Carissa climbed to her feet. Our eyes locked and the absent look in hers sent shivers to my very core.

"Don't," I warned. "I don't want to hurt—"

Her hand snaked out, lightning quick, caught my cheek, and spun me around. I hit the bed on my hip and slid to the floor. A metallic taste burst into my mouth. My lip stung and ears rang.

Carissa grabbed a handful of my hair and yanked me to my feet. Fire burned my scalp, and I let out a hoarse scream. She forced me on my back, wrapping her hands around my neck. Slender fingers dug into my windpipe, cutting off air. The moment I couldn't breathe brought me back to my very first run-in with the Arum, reviving the sense of desperation and helplessness as my lungs were starved for oxygen.

I wasn't the same girl as then, too afraid to put up a fight.

Screw that.

Letting the Source build inside me, I let it go. Stars exploded in my room, dazzling in their effect as the blast knocked Carissa back into the wall. Plaster cracked but she remained on her feet. Wisps of smoke streamed from her charred sweater.

Good God, the chick wouldn't go down.

I rolled onto my feet, trying one more time to reach her. "Carissa, we are friends. You don't want to do this. Please listen to me. *Please*."

Energy crackled over her knuckles, forming a ball, and in any other situation, I'd be jealous of how easily she'd mastered the ability in what seemed like a nanosecond, because last week . . . last week she'd been normal.

And now I didn't know what or who stood in front of me.

Ice filled the pit of my stomach, forming shards around my insides. There was no reasoning with her. No chance whatsoever, and the realization cost me. Distracted, I didn't move fast enough when she released the ball of energy.

I raised my hands and screamed, "Stop!" Throwing everything I had into the single word, picturing the tiny light particles in the air responding to my call, forming a barrier.

Air shimmered around me as if a tub of glitter had been

dumped in a perfect line. Each speck glowed with the power of a thousand suns. And in the back of my mind, I knew that whatever was going on should've been able to stop the ball.

But it broke through, shattering the glimmering wall, slowing it down but not stopping it.

The energy smacked into my shoulder and pain exploded, momentarily robbing me of sight and sound as it knocked me down, my legs over my head. I landed on my stomach on the bed with a loud *oomph*. Air rushed from my lungs, but I knew I didn't have time to let the pain sink through.

I lifted my head, peering through strands of tangled hair.

Carissa stalked forward; her movements were fluid and then . . . not so much. Her left leg started to tremble and then quake violently. The shudder rolled up the left side of her body and *only* the left side of her body. Her arm flailed and half her face spasmed.

I pushed up on weak arms, scooting across my bed until I toppled off the side. "Carissa?"

Her entire body began to quiver like the earth shook only for her. I thought maybe she was having a seizure, and I stood.

Sparks flew from her skin. The stink of burning cloth and skin singed my nostrils. She kept shaking, her head flopping on her boneless neck.

I clamped my hand over my mouth as I took a step toward her. I needed to help her, but I didn't know how.

"Carissa, I—"

The air around her imploded.

A shock wave tore through my room. The computer chair overturned; the bed lifted up on one side, suspended; and the wave kept coming. Clothing flew from my closet. Papers swirled and fell like sheets of snow.

When the wave reached me, it lifted me off my feet and flung me back like I weighed nothing more than one of the floating papers. I hit the wall beside the little stand next to my bed, and I hung there as the shock wave surged.

I couldn't move or breathe.

And Carissa . . . Oh my God, Carissa . . .

Her skin and bones sunk in as if someone had hooked up a vacuum to the back of her and kicked it on. Inch by inch she shrank until a burst of light with the power of a solar storm lit the room—lit the entire house and probably the entire street, blinding me.

A loud, deafening *pop* sounded and as the light receded, so did the shock wave. I slipped to the floor, a heap among piles of clothing and papers, dragging in air. I couldn't get enough oxygen, because the room was empty.

I stared at the area where Carissa had once stood. There was nothing but a darkened spot on the floor, like what Baruck had left behind when he was killed.

There was nothing, absolutely nothing of the girl—of my friend.

Nothing.

25

I felt the warm tingle on the back of my neck numbly, and then Daemon stood in the doorway, brows lifted and his mouth hanging open.

"I can't leave you alone for two seconds, Kitten."

I sprung from the mess of clothing and threw myself in his arms. All of it came out in an incoherent babble of words and run-on sentences. Several times he slowed me down and asked me to repeat myself before he got the general gist of what went down.

He took me downstairs and sat beside me on the couch, his fingers moving over my bottom lip as his eyes narrowed in concentration. Healing warmth spread along my lips and across my aching cheeks.

"I don't understand what happened," I said, tracking his movements. "She was normal last week. Daemon, you saw her. How did we not know this?"

His jaw tightened. "I think the better question is, why did she come after you?"

The knot that had been in my stomach moved upward, settling on my chest and making it hard to breathe. "I don't know."

I didn't know anything anymore. I kept rewinding every conversation with Carissa, from the first time I met her up until she was out of school with the "flu." Where were the clues, the red herring? I couldn't find one that stood out.

Daemon frowned. "She could've known a Luxen—known the truth and knew not to tell anyone. I mean, no one inside of the colony knows that you're aware of the truth."

"But there's no other Luxen around our age," I said.

His gaze flicked up. "None outside the colony, but there are a few who are only a couple years older or younger than us *in* the colony."

It was possible that Carissa had always known and we didn't. I'd never told her or Lesa, so it took no leap of the imagination to think that Carissa knew but never told anyone. But why did she try and kill me?

Entirely possible that I wasn't the only person around here who knew what lived among us, but dear God, what went wrong? Had she been hurt and a Luxen tried to heal her? "You don't think . . ." I couldn't finish the question. It was too sickening, but Daemon knew where I was going with it.

"That Daedalus took her and forced a Luxen to heal her like with Dawson?" Anger darkened the green hue. "I seriously pray that's not the case. If so, it's just . . ."

"Revolting," I said hoarsely. My hands shook so I shoved them between my knees. "She wasn't there. Not even a flicker of her personality. She was like a zombie, you know? Just freaking crazed. Is that what instability does?"

Daemon moved his hands away and the healing warmth ebbed off. When it did, so did the barrier that had kept the truth of everything from really breaking free and consuming me. "God, she . . . she died. Does that mean . . . ?" I swallowed, but the lump was pushing its way up my throat.

Daemon's arms tightened. "If it were one of the Luxen here, then I'll hear about it, but we don't know if the mutation held.

Blake has said that sometimes the mutation is unstable and that sounded pretty damn unstable. The bonding only happens if it's a stable mutation, I believe."

"We need to talk to Blake," I said, and a shudder rolled through me. I blinked, but my vision blurred even more. I took a breath and choked. "Oh . . . oh, God, Daemon . . . that was Carissa. That was Carissa and that wasn't right."

Another shudder racked my shoulders and before I knew what was happening, I was crying—those big, breath-stealing sobs. Vaguely, I realized that Daemon had pulled me over to him and cradled my head to his chest.

I'm not sure how long the tears came, but every part of me ached in a way that couldn't by repaired by Daemon. Carissa was wholly innocent in all of this, or at least I believed her to be, and maybe that's what made this whole thing worse. I didn't know how deep Carissa was involved, and how would I ever find out?

The tears . . . they flowed, practically soaking Daemon's shirt, but he didn't pull away. If anything, he held me tighter and he whispered in that lyrical voice of his in a language I could never understand but felt drawn to nonetheless. The unknown words soothed me and I wondered if long ago someone, a parent maybe, had held him and whispered the same words to him. And how many times had he done it for his siblings? Even with all the bark *and* bite he carried, he was a natural at this.

It calmed the dark abyss, dulled the edges of the sharp blow.

Carissa . . . Carissa was gone, and I didn't know how to deal with that. Or with the fact that her last act had been to try to take me out, which was so, so unlike her.

When the tears finally subsided, I sniffled and wiped at my face with my sleeves. The one on my right was charred from the energy blast and was rough against my cheek. The scratchy feeling poked a memory free.

I lifted my head. "She had a bracelet I'd never seen her wear before. The same kind of bracelet that Luc had on."

"Are you sure?" When I nodded, he leaned back against the couch, keeping me in his embrace. "This is even more suspicious."

"Yeah."

"We need to talk to Luc without our unwanted sidekick first." He tipped his chin up, letting out a long sigh. Worry touched his face, roughened his voice. "I'll let the others know." I started to speak, but he shook his head. "I don't want you to have to go through telling them what happened."

I lowered my cheek to his shoulder. "Thank you."

"And I'll take care of your bedroom. We'll get it cleaned up."

Relief coursed through me. Cleaning up that room, seeing the spot on the floor, was the last thing I wanted to do. "You're perfect, you know."

"Sometimes," he murmured, brushing his chin along my cheek. "I'm sorry, Kat. I'm sorry about Carissa. She was a good girl and didn't deserve this."

My lips trembled. "No, she didn't."

"And you didn't deserve to have to go through that with her."

I didn't say anything to that, because I wasn't so sure what I deserved anymore. Sometimes I didn't think I even deserved Daemon.

We made plans to go to Martinsburg on Wednesday, which meant we'd be missing our second day of onyx training, but I couldn't think about that right now. Finding out how Carissa ended up a hybrid and in possession of the same kind of bracelet Luc wore was paramount. If I could figure out what happened to her, then there would be some kind of justice.

I had no idea what I was supposed to say at school when Carissa never came back and the inevitable questions began.

I didn't think I had it in me to pretend to be clueless and tell more lies. Another kid missing . . .

Oh, God, Lesa . . . What would Lesa do? They'd been best friends since grade school.

I squeezed my eyes tight and curled up against Daemon. The aches of the fight had long faded, but I was weary to the core, mentally and physically drained. It was ironic that I'd spent the last month avoiding the living room and now it would be my bedroom. I was running out of rooms to hide from.

Daemon kept up talking in his beautiful language, a streaming melody, until I drifted off in his arms. I was only a little aware of him placing me on the couch and drawing the afghan over me.

Hours later, I opened my eyes and saw Dee sitting in the recliner, legs tucked against her chest, reading one of my books. A favorite YA paranormal of mine—about a demon-hunting girl living in Atlanta.

But what was Dee doing here?

I sat up, pushing my hair out of my face. The clock below the TV, an old-fashioned windup one that my mom loved, read a quarter till midnight.

Dee closed the book. "Daemon went to Walmart in Moorefield. So that will take an absurd amount of time, but it's the only place open that has throw rugs."

"Throw rugs?"

Her features tightened. "For your bedroom . . . There weren't any extra ones in the house and he didn't want your mom looking for one and finding the spot, thinking you were trying to burn down the house."

The spot . . . ? Sleep faded away completely as the last couple of hours resurfaced. The spot on my bedroom floor where Carissa had basically self-destructed.

"Oh, God . . ." I threw my legs off the couch, but they shook too much to stand. Tears welled behind my eyes. "I didn't . . . I didn't kill her."

I don't know why I said that. Maybe it was because deep down I wondered if Dee would automatically assume I was responsible for what happened to Carissa.

"I know. Daemon told me everything." She unfurled her legs, lashes lowered, fanning her cheeks. "I can't . . ."

"You can't believe this happened?" She nodded, and I tucked my legs up, wrapping my arms around them. "I can't, either. I just can't even wrap my brain around it."

Dee was silent for a moment. "I haven't talked to her since . . . well, since everything." She tipped her head down and her hair slipped over her shoulders, shielding her face. "I liked her and I was a complete bitch to her."

I started to tell her that she hadn't been, but Dee looked up, a wry smile on her lips. "Don't lie to make me feel better. I appreciate it, but it doesn't change the fact. I don't think I even said two words to her since Adam . . . died, and now . . ."

And now she was dead, too.

I wanted to comfort her, but there was a gulf and a ten-foot wall topped with barbed wire between Dee and me. The electrical fence surrounding the wall had disappeared, but there wasn't any level of ease between us, and right now, that hurt more than anything.

Rubbing a kink in my neck, I closed my eyes. My brain was sluggish and I wasn't sure what I should be doing right now. All I wanted to do was mourn my friend, but how was I supposed to grieve someone who no one in the outside would knew had passed?

Dee cleared her throat. "Daemon and I cleaned up your bedroom. Um, there are a few things that weren't salvageable. Some clothing that was burned or torn I threw away. I . . . I hung a picture over the crack in the wall." She peeked up as if gauging my reaction. "Your laptop . . . It's not . . . in functioning shape."

My shoulders slumped. The laptop was the least of tonight's causalities, but I had no idea how I was going to explain that to my mom.

"Thank you," I said finally, voice thick. "I don't think I could've done that."

Dee twisted a strand of hair around her finger. Minutes passed in silence and then, "Are you okay, Katy? Like, really okay?"

Shock caused me to take a few seconds to respond. "No, I'm not," I said truthfully.

"I didn't think so." She paused, wiping under her eyes with the palm of her hand. "I really liked Carissa."

"Me, too," I whispered, and there was nothing else to be said.

Everything that came before tonight and everything we'd been so focused on seemed almost unimportant, which those issues weren't, but a friend was dead—another friend. Her death and her life was a mystery. I'd known her for six months, but I hadn't known her at all.

26

Playing sick on Tuesday, I stayed home and vegetated on the couch. I couldn't do the school thing. See Lesa and know her best friend was dead and pretend I didn't know a thing. I just couldn't do it yet.

Every so often, I saw Carissa's face. There were two versions: before last night and afterward. When I saw her and her funky glasses in my memories, my chest ached, and when I saw those vastly empty eyes, I wanted to cry all over again.

And I did.

Mom didn't push it. For one thing, I rarely skipped school. And secondly, I looked like crap. Being sick didn't take a leap of faith. She spent the better part of the morning coddling me and I soaked it up, needing my mom more than she could ever know.

Later, after she went upstairs to get some sleep, Daemon showed up unexpectedly. Wearing a black cap pulled down low, he came in and closed the door behind him.

"What are you doing here?" It was only one in the afternoon.

He took my hand, pulling me into the living room. "Nice jammies."

I ignored that. "Shouldn't you be in school?"

"You shouldn't be alone right now." He twisted his cap around.

"I'm all right."

Daemon shot me a knowing look. Admittedly, I was happy that he was here, because I did need someone who knew what was really going on. All day I'd been ripped apart, caught by guilt and confusion, tossed around by sorrow I couldn't really even grasp.

Wordlessly, he led me to the couch and stretched out, tucking me against his side. His heavy arm around my waist had a soothing weight. Keeping our voices low, we talked about normal things—safe things that didn't slice through him or me.

After a while, I twisted in his arms so that our noses brushed. We didn't kiss. There wasn't one shenanigan going on between us. We held each other, though, and that was more intimate than anything else we could've done. Daemon's presence eased me. At some point, we dozed off, our breaths mixing.

My mom had to have come downstairs at some point and seen us together on the couch, just the way we were when I woke: Daemon's head resting atop mine, my hand balled around his shirt. It was the scent of the coffee that roused me just around five.

Reluctantly, I pulled out of his embrace and smoothed my hands through my hair. Mom stood in the doorway, one leg crossed over her ankle as she leaned against the frame. A steaming cup of coffee was in her hands.

Mom was wearing Lucky Charms pajamas.

Oh, holy Houdini. "Where did you get them?" I asked.

"What?" She took a sip.

"Those . . . hideous pajamas," I said.

She shrugged. "I like them."

"They're cute," Daemon said, taking off his hat and running

his hand through his messy hair. I elbowed him, and he gave me a cheeky grin. "I'm sorry, Miss Swartz, I didn't mean to fall asleep with—"

"It's okay." She waved him off. "Katy hasn't been feeling well, and I'm glad you wanted to be here for her, but I hope you don't get what she has."

He cast me a sideways look. "I hope you didn't give me cooties."

I huffed. If anyone was spreading alien cooties, it was Daemon.

Mom's cell went off, and she dug it out of her pajama pocket, sloshing coffee onto the floor. Her face lit up, the way it always did when Will called her. My heart dropped as she turned and headed into the kitchen.

"Will," I whispered, standing before I realized it.

Daemon was right behind me. "You don't know that for sure."

"I do. It's in her eyes—he makes her glow." I wanted to barf, like, seriously. Suddenly, I saw Mom on the bedroom floor, lifeless, gone like Carissa. Panic blossomed and took root. "I need to tell her why Will got close to her."

"Tell her what?" He blocked me. "That he was here to get close to you—that he used her? I don't think that's going to lessen any blows."

I opened my mouth, but he had a point.

He placed his hands on my shoulders. "We don't know if it was him calling or what's happened to him. Look at Carissa," he said, keeping his voice low. "Her mutation was unstable. It didn't take long for it . . . to do what it did."

"Then that means it held." He wasn't making me feel better about anything right now.

"Or it means it faded off." He tried again. "We can't do anything until we know what we're dealing with."

I shifted my weight restlessly, watching over his shoulder.

Stress built in me like a seven-ton ball that settled on my shoulders. There was so much to deal with.

"One at a time," Daemon said, as if he read my thoughts. "We're going to deal with things one at a time. That's all we can do."

Nodding, I took a deep breath and let it out slowly. My heart still raced. "I'm going to see if it was him."

He let go and stepped aside, and I hurried to the door.

"I like your pajamas better," he said, and I turned. Daemon grinned at me, that lopsided one that hinted at laughter.

My jammies weren't much better than Mom's. They had, like, a thousand pink and purple polka dots on them. "Shut up," I said.

Daemon returned to the couch. "I'll be waiting."

I went to the kitchen just as Mom was getting off the phone, her features pinched. The weight on my shoulders increased. "What's wrong?"

She blinked and forced a smile. "Oh, nothing, honey."

Grabbing a towel, I wiped up the spilled sugar. "Doesn't look like nothing." In fact, it looked like a whole lot of something.

Mom grimaced. "It was Will. He's still out west. He thinks he came down with something traveling. He's going to stay out there until he feels better."

I froze. *Liar*, I wanted to scream.

She dumped her coffee and rinsed out her cup. "I didn't tell you this, honey, because I didn't want to drag up bad memories, but Will . . . well, he was sick once, like your father."

My mouth dropped open.

Mistaking my surprise, she said, "I know. It seems cosmically unfair, doesn't it? But Will has been in remission. His cancer was completely curable."

I had nothing to say. Nothing. Will had told her he'd been sick.

"But of course, I worry." She placed the cup in the dishwasher, but she didn't close the door all the way. I shut it out of habit. "Useless to worry over something like that, I know." She stopped in front of me, placing her hand on my forehead. "You don't feel warm. Are you feeling better?"

The change in conversation threw me. "Yeah, I feel fine."

"Good." Mom smiled then and it wasn't forced. "Don't worry about Will, honey. He'll be fine and back before we know it. Everything will be okay."

My heart tripped up. "Mom?"

"Yes?"

I came so close to telling her everything, but I froze. Daemon was right. What could I say? I shook my head. "I'm sure . . . Will's okay."

She bent quickly, kissing my cheek. "He'd be happy to know you were concerned."

A hysterical laugh crept up my throat. I was sure he would be.

Later that day, after Mom had left for work, I stood beside the lake, staring at a pile of glittering onyx.

Matthew and Daemon hadn't said much since we arrived, and even Blake was abnormally quiet. They all knew what had happened last night with Carissa. Daemon had spoken to Blake earlier in the day; the entire conversation had gone down between the two without fists being thrown and I'd missed it. Apparently Blake had never witnessed an unstable hybrid with his own eyes. He'd only heard about them.

But Dawson had.

He'd seen people who'd been brought to him, had been normal Joes before the mutation and then snapped days later. Violent outbursts were common right before they went into self-destruction mode. All of them had been given the serum

I'd been given. Without it, according to Blake, the mutation could hold, but it was rare and in most cases, the mutations faded.

Since I arrived at the lake, Dawson had stayed close to my side while Daemon and Matthew handled the onyx carefully.

"I had to do it once," Dawson said quietly, focused on the overcast sky.

"Do what?"

"Watch a hybrid die like that." He took a breath, squinting. "The guy just went crazy, and no one could stop him. He took out one of the officers and then there was a flash of light. Sort of like spontaneous combustion, because when the light faded, he was gone. Nothing was left. It happened so fast, he couldn't have felt a thing."

I remembered how Carissa was shaking, and I knew she *had* to feel that. Feeling nauseous, I focused on Daemon. The onyx was in a hole, and he knelt in front of it, talking quietly to Matthew. I was glad the rest of the group wasn't there.

"Did the people they brought to you know why they were there?" I asked.

"Some did, like they signed up for it. Others were sedated. They didn't have a clue. I think they were homeless people."

That was sickening. Unable to stay still, I headed toward the bank of the lake. The water wasn't frozen over anymore, but it was still and calm. Completely at odds with how I felt inside.

Dawson followed. "Carissa was a good person. She didn't deserve this. Do we even know why they chose her?"

I shook my head. I'd spent a good part of the day thinking about everything. Even if Carissa had known about the Luxen and had been healed by one, Daedalus was involved. I knew it. But the hows and whys were the mysteries. As was the stone I'd seen around her wrist.

"Did you ever see anything on the hybrids there? Like a weird black stone that looked like it had fire inside it?"

His brows knitted. "None of mine made it except Beth. They didn't have anything like that on them. I never saw the others."

Terrible . . . It was just terrible.

I swallowed thickly, but my throat felt tight. A soft breeze stirred the lake, and a wave rippled from one bank to the next. Like a shock wave . . .

"Guys?" Daemon called, and we turned. "Are you ready?"

Were we ready to step into the house of pain? Uh, no. But we walked over to them. Daemon stood, holding a circular piece of onyx in his gloved hand.

He turned to Blake. "This is your show."

Blake took a deep breath and nodded. "I think the first thing to test out is if I do have a tolerance to onyx. If I do, then that gives us a starting point, right? At least then we know that we can build up a tolerance."

Across from him, Daemon glanced down at the onyx he held and shrugged. Without preamble, he shot forward, placing the onyx against Blake's cheek.

My jaw hit the ground.

Matthew stepped back. "God."

Beside me, Dawson laughed under his breath.

But nothing happened for several moments. Finally, Blake knocked the onyx away, his nostrils flaring. "What the hell?"

Disappointed, Daemon tossed the rock in the pile. "Well, apparently you have a tolerance to onyx and here I was hoping you didn't."

I clamped my hand over my mouth, stifling a giggle. He was such an asshole, and I loved him.

Blake stared. "What if I didn't have a tolerance to it? Good God, I kind of wanted to prepare myself for that."

"I know." Daemon smirked.

Matthew shook his head. "Okay, back on track, boys. How do you suggest doing this?"

Stalking over to the pile of onyx, Blake picked one up. There was a slight ripple of unease this time, but he held on. "I suggest Daemon goes first. We hold it to the skin until you drop. No longer."

"Oh, dear Lord," I muttered.

Daemon took off his gloves and held out his arms. "Bring it."

There wasn't a moment of hesitation. Blake stepped forward and pressed that onyx against Daemon's palm. Immediately, his face contorted and he appeared to try to step back, but the onyx held him in place. A tremor started in his arm and traveled through his body.

Dawson and I both stepped forward. Neither of us could help it. Standing here, watching the pain harshen his beautiful face, was too much. Panic shot through me.

But then Blake pulled back and Daemon dropped to his knees, slamming his hands onto the ground before him. "Crap . . ."

I rushed forward, touching his shoulders. "Are you okay?"

"He's fine," Blake said, placing the onyx on the ground. His right hand shook as our eyes met. "It started to burn. There must be a limit to my tolerance . . ."

Daemon stood unsteadily, and I followed. "I'm okay." Then he said to his brother, who was eyeballing Blake like he wanted to toss him through a window, "I'm fine, Dawson."

"How do we know this will work?" Matthew demanded. "Touching onyx is completely different than being sprayed all over with it."

"I've walked out of those doors before and nothing happened. And it's not like they've sprayed onyx in my face before. This has to be it."

I remembered how he said everything he touched had been encased in the shiny jewel. "Okay. Let's do this."

Daemon opened his mouth, but I cut him off with a glare. He wasn't going to talk me out of this.

Picking up a glove, Blake handled the onyx differently now. He didn't come to me but to Matthew. The same thing happened with the older Luxen. He was on his knees, gasping for air, and then it was Dawson's turn.

It took a little longer for him, which made sense. He'd been exposed to the spray like me and had been tortured by the stuff off and on. But after about ten seconds, he went down and his brother massacred the English language.

Then it was my turn.

Squaring my shoulders, I nodded. I was ready for this, wasn't I? Heck no. Who was I fooling? This was going to *hurt*.

Blake winced and moved forward, but Daemon stopped him. Using the glove, he took the onyx from him and stood in front of me.

"No," I said. "I don't want you to do this."

The determined set to his jaw infuriated me. "I'm not letting him do it."

"Then let someone else do it." There was no way he could be the one who placed the onyx on me. "Please." Daemon shook his head, and I wanted to punch him. "This isn't right."

"It's either me or no one."

And then I understood. He was trying to get his way. Taking a breath, I met him head-on. "Do it."

Surprise flickered in his bottle-green eyes and then anger deepened them. "I hate this," he said, loudly enough for only me to hear.

"I do, too." Anxiety climbed up my throat. "Just do it."

He didn't look away, but I could tell he wanted to. Whatever pain I knew I was about to feel would be symbiotic. He would feel it—not the physical, but the anguish would travel to him, as if it were his own. It was the same when Daemon was in pain.

I closed my eyes, thinking that would help him. It seemed to, because maybe ten seconds later, I felt the coolness of the onyx against my hand and the roughness of his glove. Nothing happened immediately, but then it did.

A rapidly growing burn traveled across my hand and then shot up my arm. A thousand tiny pricks of pain radiated across my body. I bit down on my lip, stifling my scream. It didn't take long after that before I hit the ground, gulping in air as I waited for the burn to ease off.

My body shuddered. "All right . . . Okay . . . Not too bad."

"Bull," Daemon said, hauling me onto my feet. "Kat—"

I tugged free, taking more deep breaths. "Really, I'm okay. We need to keep going."

Daemon looked like he wanted to toss me over his shoulder and run off like a caveman, but we moved on. Over and over again, each of us touched the onyx, holding on until our body refused to cooperate. None of us increased in time, but we were just getting started.

"It's like getting hit with a Taser," Matthew said as he dropped a sheet of plywood over the onyx, then placed two heavy rocks on the board. It was late and all of us were twitchy. Even Blake. "Not that I've ever been Tased, but I image that's how it feels."

I wondered if there'd be any long-term effects from this. Like messed-up heart rhythms or post-traumatic stress. The one good thing that came out of this was that between the mind-blowing pain and watching other people succumb to it, I really hadn't been capable of thinking about anything else.

As we finished up and began to limp back to the house, Blake slowed down until he was beside me. "I'm sorry," he said.

I said nothing.

He shoved his hands into his jeans. "I liked Carissa. I wish . . ."

"If wishes were fishes, we'd all throw nets, right? Isn't that what they say?" Bitterness sharpened my tone.

"Yeah, that's what they say." He paused. "Things are gonna get crazy at school."

"Why do you care? You're going to leave as soon as you get Chris. You'll just be another one of those kids who vanished into thin air."

He stopped, head cocked to the side. "I would stay if I could. I can't, though."

Frowning, I glanced ahead. Daemon had slowed down, no doubt doing his best not to physically put more distance between Blake and me. For a second, I considered asking Blake about the stone. He'd have to know, since he worked for Daedalus—still did. But it was too tricky. Blake claimed to be playing double agent. Key word: *claimed*.

I wrapped my arms around my waist. Overhead, the branches cracked against one another like a low, steady drum.

"I would stay," he said again, placing a hand on my shoulder. "I—"

Daemon was there in an instant, prying Blake's fingers off my shoulder. "Don't touch her."

Blake paled as he pulled his hand free and stepped back. "Dude, I wasn't doing anything. Overprotective much?"

Implanting himself in between us, Daemon said, "I thought we had an understanding. You're here because we don't have a choice. You're still alive because she is better than me. You're not here to comfort her. Got that?"

Blake's jaw popped. "Whatever. I'll see you guys later."

I watched Blake stalk past Matthew and Dawson. "That was a little overprotective."

"I don't like him touching you," he growled. His eyes started doing that glowing-orb thing. "I don't like him even being in the same time zone as you. I don't trust him."

Rising up, I kissed Daemon's cheek. "No one trusts him, but you can't threaten him every five seconds."

"Yes, I can."

I laughed and stepped in, wrapping my arms around his waist. Under my cheek, his heart beat steadily. His hands slid down my back as his head bent close to mine. "Do you really want to do more days like this?" he asked. "An endless stretch of days filled with pain?"

It wasn't on the top of my to-do list. "It serves a pretty good distraction, and I need that right now."

I expected him to argue, but he didn't. Instead, he kissed the top of my head. We stood like that for a little while. When we pulled apart, Dawson and Matthew were gone. Moonlight started to peek through the branches. Holding hands, we walked back to our houses, and he went to his to clean up.

My house was dark and silent, and as I stood at the base of the stairs, I struggled to breathe. I couldn't be afraid of my bedroom. That was just stupid. I placed my hand on the banister and took one step.

Muscles locked up.

It was just a bedroom. I couldn't sleep on the couch forever, and I couldn't run in and out of my bedroom as if an Arum were chasing me.

Each step up was a fight when my natural response was to turn and run in the opposite direction, but I continued until I stood in the doorway, my hands clasped under my chin.

Daemon and Dee had cleaned up everything like they said. My bed was made. Clothing put away and all the papers were stacked on my desk. My destroyed laptop was gone. And there was a neat little circular rug over the spot Carissa had stood. It was a muted, soft brown. Daemon knew I wasn't big on flashy color, not like Dee. Other than that, the room looked normal.

Holding my breath, I forced myself to go in. I moved around, picking up books and placing them back in the order I had them in, keeping my mind blank. Sometime later, I changed into an old shirt and knee-high socks, then I tunneled under the blankets and rolled onto my side.

Beyond my bedroom window, scattered stars broke up the dark blue of the sky. One fell, leaving a short stream of light behind as it crashed to Earth. Curling my fingers around the blanket, I wondered if it were a falling star or something else. All the Luxen were here, weren't they?

I forced my eyes closed and focused on tomorrow. After school, Daemon and I were heading to Martinsburg in an attempt to find Luc. The group thought we were just getting away for the night. Hopefully after our visit, we'd know a little more about what happened to Carissa.

I slept fitfully that night. It had to be late when I felt Daemon settle in beside me, his arm firmly around my waist. Half asleep, I decided he needed to be more careful. If my mom caught him in my bed again, things would get ugly. But I was content in his arms and settled back against him, lulled to sleep by his warm breath along the back of my neck.

"I love you," I think I said. It may have been a dream, but his arm tightened and his leg slid around mine. Maybe this was just a dream, because there was a surreal quality to it. Even if it was, it was enough.

27

Lesa practically tackled me the moment I stepped into school the following day. I hadn't even made it to my locker. Grabbing my arm, she tugged me into the alcove near the trophy case.

I knew from the moment I saw her that somehow she knew something bad had happened. Her face was pale, eyes shadowed, and her lower lip trembled. I'd never seen her so upset.

"What's wrong?" I forced my voice even.

Her fingers bit into my arm. "Carissa's missing."

I felt the blood drain from my face and croaked out a, "What?"

Eyes shiny, she nodded. "She had the flu, right? And apparently she got really sick in the last couple of days, running a high temperature. Her mom and dad took her to the hospital. They thought she had meningitis or something."

She let out a shuddering breath. "I didn't know anything until her parents called me this morning asking if I'd seen or talked to her. And I was like, 'No. Why? She's been too sick to get on the phone and all.' And they told me she disappeared a couple of nights ago from the hospital room. Her parents have been looking for her and the police wouldn't file a missing person's report until she was gone for forty-eight hours."

The horror that whiplashed through me wasn't faked. I said a few things and I really didn't know what. Lesa wasn't processing anything anyway.

"They think she walked out of the hospital—that she was that sick and she's probably out there somewhere, lost and confused." Her voice trembled. "How could no one see and stop her?"

"I don't know," I whispered.

Lesa circled her arms around herself. "This isn't happening, is it? It can't be. Not Carissa."

My heart felt like it was cracking. Most times I wanted to tell the truth and confide in Lesa, but this was one of those moments when nothing in this world could have made me want to be the bearer of this news.

There wasn't anything I could say, but I wrapped my arms around her and held on until the first bell rang. We headed straight to class without our textbooks. It didn't matter. News of Carissa's disappearance had begun to spread, and no one was paying attention in class.

Kimmy announced at the end of class that the police were organizing a search party after school. She and Carissa hadn't been friends, but that wasn't important, I realized. Too many kids had disappeared, and it was touching everyone's lives. I glanced over my shoulder at Daemon and he gave me a reassuring smile. It did little to soothe me. I was a bundle of nerves. When class ended, Lesa waited for me.

"I think I'm going home," she said, blinking rapidly. "I don't . . . I just can't be here right now."

"Do you want me to go with you?" I asked, not wanting to leave her alone if she felt she needed someone.

Lesa shook her head. "No. But thank you."

I gave her a quick hug and then watched her hurry from class, my heart heavy.

Daemon said nothing as he pressed a kiss to my temple. He knew there wasn't anything to say. "Do you think we have time to join the search party before we leave?" I asked.

Both of us knew it was pointless, but it seemed a dishonor to her memory to not give her this respect. Or was it wrong to do it knowing what really happened? I didn't know.

Daemon didn't seem to know, either, but he agreed. "Of course."

I wanted to leave the school, too. Especially since everyone was talking about Carissa and finding her. People were in high hopes that she *would* be found, because it seemed impossible that she'd end up like Simon.

Guilt and anger warred inside me, and throughout the day, I tipped into each side. Sitting in class seemed pointless when so many things hung in the balance. These people—these kids—had no idea what was going on around them. They lived in this blissful bubble of ignorance and not even the disappearances burst it. Only tiny holes were pricked by each disappearance and I was waiting for everyone to finally pop.

At lunch, for the first time, we all sat together. Even Blake joined us. My lack of appetite had nothing to do with the mystery food occupying my plate.

"Are you guys going to the search party?" Andrew asked.

I nodded. "But we're still doing our own thing afterward."

Blake scowled. "I really think you guys should wait."

"Why?" I asked before Daemon could snap his head off his shoulders.

"You need to be working on building up a tolerance, not date night." Across from him, Ash nodded in agreement. "That's not what's important right now."

Daemon looked at him. "Shut up."

Cheeks flushing, Blake leaned on the table. "We need every day that we can get if we have any hopes of doing this soon."

A muscle flexed in Daemon's jaw. "One day isn't going to change anything. You guys can still practice or not. I don't care."

Blake started to protest, but Dawson stepped in. "Let them go. They need this. We'll be fine."

I picked up my fork, feeling my cheeks flame. Everyone thought I needed to get away, take some downtime, and I didn't want them feeling sorry for or worrying about me. But tonight wasn't date night. What Daemon and I had to do was going to be as tricky as playing with onyx.

As if he sensed my dark thoughts, he twisted beside me and his hand found mine under the table. He squeezed and for some reason I felt like crying. I was turning into such a wuss and it was all his fault.

I might have dreamed him up last night, because in the light of morning, he'd been gone and the pillow beside me didn't carry that scent I could place anywhere. But I liked to think it was real. That I hadn't dreamt him holding me close, his warm hands on my hips or his lips trailing down my neck.

If I had imagined that . . . Oh boy, my dreams were realistic. I couldn't ask him, because that would be way too embarrassing, not to mention Daemon's ego did not need to be stroked by the knowledge I was dreaming about him.

Thinking about his reaction to that, which would bring a whole lot of smugness to the table, I grinned a little. Daemon caught sight of it and my heart skipped a beat, because his heart had jumped first.

Sometimes the whole bizarro alien connection thing had its perks. Like it told me that I affected Daemon just as much as he affected me, and on days like this, I needed whatever pick-me-upper there was.

28

The search party was just like the ones I'd seen on TV and in movies. People milled through fields in a direct, horizontal line behind the policemen and their search dogs. Everything was a clue to the inexperienced—a disturbed pile of leaves; a torn, old piece of clothing; faded footprints.

It was a sad affair.

Mainly because there was so much hope—hope that Carissa would be found, that she would be okay if not a little worse for wear, and everything would go back to normal. She wouldn't be the latest missing person's case, because her situation was different. She seemingly walked out of a hospital.

However, I had a hard time believing that.

Will had been an implant in the local medical center, and I didn't have to be an investigator to figure out that he wasn't the only one. My guess was Carissa had *help* leaving that hospital.

Daemon and I left after five, heading back to our houses. I went inside to get changed for our "date night." I wasn't going all out like I did last time. I settled on a pair of skinny jeans, heels, and an Lesa-approved skintight sweater that flashed a little bit of stomach.

Mom was in the kitchen making an omelet. My eyes bugged as I tugged the hem of my sweater down. She glanced over her shoulder, tossing the eggs and missing most of the frying pan.

She took Hell's Kitchen to a new extreme.

"Are you going out tonight with Daemon?"

"Yeah," I said, grabbing a paper towel. I scooped up the eggs before the burnt smell could reach my gag reflex. "We're going to do dinner and then a movie."

"Remember your curfew. It's a school night."

"I know." I threw the towel away and held onto my sweater with one hand. "Did you hear about Carissa?"

Mom nodded. "I wasn't working at Grant when she was admitted or for the last two days, but the hospital is crawling with police and the heads are doing their own investigations."

She'd been pulling her shifts in Winchester. "So, they think she really just walked out of there?"

"From what I hear, she was being treated for meningitis and that can come along with a high fever. People do strange things when they are that sick. It's why I was so worried about you when you got sick in November." She turned off the stove. "But there is no excuse for what happened. Someone should've stopped the poor girl. Those night-shift nurses will have a lot of explaining to do. Without meds, Carissa . . ." She clamped up, focusing on dumping the eggs onto her plate. A few pieces splattered across the floor. I sighed. "Honey, they'll find Carissa."

No, they won't, I wanted to rage.

"She couldn't have gone far," Mom continued as I picked up the yellow clumps stuffed with peppers and onions. "And those nurses won't allow something as careless as this to happen again."

I doubted it was an act of carelessness. They probably turned their cheek or helped. The desire to get even or at least walk into that hospital and smack a bunch of people in their faces was almost too hard to ignore.

Saying good-bye to Mom and promising not to stay out past curfew, I kissed her cheek and then grabbed my sweater jacket and purse. Daemon was alone next door. Everyone was down by the lake, either putting themselves through untold pain or watching it.

He swaggered up to me, his eyes dropping right to the tiny flash of skin . . . and something moved over his face. "I like this better than the other outfit."

"Really?" I felt exposed when he looked at me like he was staring at a piece of art commissioned just for him. "I thought you liked the skirt."

"I do, but this . . . ?" He tugged on my belt loop and made a deep sound in the back of his throat. "I really like this."

A dizzying warmth swept through me, making my knees weak.

Shaking his head, he dropped his hand and pulled his keys out of his pocket. "We need to get going. You hungry? You didn't eat any lunch."

It took me a moment to collect myself. "I could do a Happy Meal."

He laughed as we headed outside. "A Happy Meal?"

"What's wrong with that?" I tugged my sweater coat on. "It's perfect."

"It's the toy, isn't it?"

I grinned as I stopped at the passenger side. "The boys get better toys."

Daemon turned suddenly, placing his hands on my hips and lifting me against him. Startled, I dropped my purse as I groped his arms.

"What—?"

He silenced me with a kiss that reached a deep place inside

that both thrilled and frightened me. When he kissed me, it was like he was reaching for my soul.

Funny thing was, he already had that and my heart in his hands.

Slowly, he let me slide down him and placed me on my feet. Dazed, I stared up at him. "What was that for?"

"You smiled." His fingers trailed along my cheek, then down my throat. He buttoned up my sweater quickly. "You haven't been smiling much. I missed it, so I decided to reward you for doing it."

"Reward me?" I laughed. "God, only you would think kissing someone is a reward."

"You know it is. My lips change lives, baby." Daemon bent, grabbing my purse off the ground. "Ready?"

Taking the purse, I hopped into his car on wobbly knees. Once beside me, he revved the engine, and we were heading into town, stopping by the local fast-food joint so I could get my Happy Meal.

He got me a boy one, too.

His dinner included three hamburgers and two orders of fries. I had no idea where those calories went. To his ego, maybe? It seemed likely after that last comment about his lips. I was hungry more often after the mutation, but not like Daemon.

On the way to Martinsburg, we started out with a game of I Spy, but Daemon cheated and I didn't want to play anymore.

He laughed deeply, the sound pleasing. "How can I cheat at I Spy?"

"You keep picking things that no human in this world can see!" I fought back a grin at his offended expression. "Or you pick *c*—you keep picking *c*. I spy with my little eye, something that starts with a *c*!"

"Car," he said, smiling. "Cat. Coat. Church." He paused, casting me a wicked sidelong glance. "Chest."

"Shut up." I smacked him on the arm. A few moments of silence later, and I was desperate to find another game. This nonsense was keeping my mind blank. We moved onto the license plate game, and I swear he pulled up on cars so I couldn't see the plates. He had a mean competitive streak.

Before we knew it, we were heading off the exit and neither of us was in the playing mood anymore. "Do you think we'll get in?"

"Yes."

I shot him a look. "That bouncer was really big."

His lips quirked. "Oh, Kitten, see, I try to not say bad things."

"What?"

The grin spread. "I would say size doesn't matter, but it does. I would know." He winked, and I let out a disgusted groan. He laughed. "Sorry, you walked into that one. Seriously, though, the bouncer won't be a problem. I think he liked me."

"W-w-what?"

He eased the SUV around the curves. "I think he liked me, like, really liked me."

"Your ego knows no limit, you know that?"

"You'll see. I know these kinds of things."

From what I recalled, the bouncer looked like he wanted to kill Daemon. Shaking my head, I sat back and started nibbling on my thumbnail. Gross habit, but nerves were getting the best of me.

The abandoned gas station loomed up ahead. The SUV bumped over the uneven road and I gripped the door handle. Cars lined the field in front of the club, as expected. Once again, Daemon parked Dolly far away from other cars.

I knew to get rid of my sweater this time around. I wrapped it around my purse and sat it on the floorboard. We made our way around the cars. Stopping at the first row, I bent over and tossed my hair over my head, shaking it out.

"This reminds me of a Whitesnake video," Daemon said.

"Huh?" I ran my hands through my hair, hoping for the sexy look and not the "I had my head out of the car" look.

"If you start climbing on car hoods, I think I might marry you."

I rolled my eyes and straightened, giving my head one more shake. "Done."

He stared at me. "You're cute."

"You're weird." I rose up and gave him a quick kiss on the cheek before I teetered through the knee-high grass. Heels—so not a good idea.

The lumberjack bouncer appeared out of nowhere, still in those overalls. Barrel-sized arms folded across his chest. "I thought I told ya two to forget this place?"

Daemon moved in front of me. "We need to see Luc."

"I need a lot of things in life. Like I wish I could find a decent stock trader who wouldn't lose half of my money."

Oookay. I cleared my throat. "We won't be here long, but please, we really need to see him."

"Sorry," the bouncer said.

Daemon tipped his head to the side. "There's got to be something we can do to convince you."

Oh, man, please tell me he wasn't . . .

The bouncer raised a brow and waited.

Daemon smiled—that sexy quirk of his lips that had every girl at school stumbling over themselves, and I . . . I wanted to crawl under a car.

Before I could die from embarrassment, the bouncer's cell went off, and he pulled it out of his front pocket. "What's up?"

I took the moment to elbow Daemon.

"What?" he said. "It was working."

The bouncer laughed. "I ain't doin' much. Just talkin' to a douche and a pretty lady."

"Excuse me?" Daemon said, surprised.

I choked on my laugh.

There was a toothy grin, and then the bouncer sighed. "Yep, they're here for ya." There was a pause. "Sure."

He clicked the phone shut. "Luc will see you. Go in and head straight to him. No dancing tonight, or whatever it was the two of ya did last time."

Awkward. I lowered my head and slipped past the bouncer. At the door, he stopped Daemon. I looked over my shoulder.

The bouncer winked at Daemon as he handed him what looked like a business card. "Ya not normally my type, but I can make an exception."

My mouth dropped open.

Daemon took the card with a smile and then opened the door. "Told you," he said to me.

I refused to give him the benefit of a response, instead focusing on the club. Nothing had changed from the last time. The dance floor was packed. Accompanied cages hung from the ceiling, swaying from the movements inside. People grinded to the heavy beat. A different, strange world tucked away in the epicenter of normalcy.

And the place was still alluring to me in a weird way.

Down the shadowy hallway, a tall man waited at the door for us. Paris—the blond Luxen we'd met last time. He nodded at Daemon, opened the door, and then stepped aside.

I expected to see Luc sprawled on the couch, playing DS like last time, so I was shocked when I discovered him at the desk, pecking away at a laptop, his face screwed in concentration.

The stacks of hundreds were gone.

Luc didn't look up. "Please sit." He waved at the nearby couch, all businesslike.

Glancing at Daemon, I moved with him to the couch and sat. In the corner, a tall yellow candle spread a peaches scent throughout the room. That was all the decoration. Did the door behind the desk lead to another room? Did Luc live here?

"Heard you guys didn't get very far at Mount Weather last time." He closed the laptop and folded his hands under his chin.

"About that," Daemon said, leaning forward. "You didn't know about the onyx shields?"

The boy, the little mini mogul/mafia kingpin/whatever he was became very still. Tension filled the room. I waited for something to blow up. Hopefully not one of us.

"I warned you that there may be things I'm unaware of," he said. "Even I don't know everything about Daedalus. But I think Blake's on the right track. He is right about everything being encased in a shiny blackish-red material. Perhaps we did build a tolerance so we were not affected by the onyx shields."

"And what if that's not it?" I asked, hating the icy feeling slushing through my veins.

Luc's amethyst gaze was concentrated. "What if it's not? I have a feeling that's not going to stop you from trying again. It's a risk and everything has risks. You're lucky you got out of there last time before anyone realized what happened. You get another chance. Most people don't."

Talking to this kid was weird, because he had the mannerisms and speech patterns of a well-educated adult. "You're right," I said. "We're still going to try."

"But knowing all the perils ahead seems unfair?" He tucked back a strand of brown hair, his angelic face impassive. "Life's not fair, babe."

Daemon stiffened beside me. "Why do I have a feeling there's a lot you're not telling us?"

Luc's lips formed a half smile. "Anyway, you came here for a reason other than those onyx shields? Let's get to the point."

Annoyance flashed across Daemon's face. "An unstable hybrid attacked Kat."

"That's what unstable people do, hybrid or not."

I bit back a snappy retort. "Yeah, we figured that much, but she was my friend. She gave no indication that she knew anything about the Luxen. She was fine, got sick, and then came to my house and went nuts."

"You didn't give any indication you know ET didn't phone home."

What a little brat. I took a deep breath. "I get that, but this was out of the blue."

Luc leaned back in his chair, kicking his legs onto the desk. He crossed them at the ankles. "I don't know what to tell you about that. She may've known about the Luxen, gotten hurt, and some poor sap tried and failed to heal her. Or the Man pulled her off the street like they do at times. And unless you know some darn good torture techniques and are willing to employ them on an Officer of Daedalus, I don't see how you'll ever know."

"I refuse to accept that," I whispered. Knowing would bring some kind of closure and justice.

He shrugged. "What happened to her?" Curiosity colored his tone.

My breath caught in my throat as I balled my hands into fists. "She's no longer . . ."

"Ah," Luc murmured. "She did the whole spontaneous combustion thing?" The look on my face must've been answer enough because he sighed sadly. "Sick. Sorry about that. A twisted history lesson for you—you know all those unexplained cases of spontaneous combustion throughout history?"

Daemon grimaced. "I'm afraid to ask."

"Funny how there's not many cases known, but they do happen out in the noob world." He spread his arms wide to indicate the world outside this office. "Hybrids—my theory at least, and it makes sense if you think about it—most do the self-destruction thing in the facilities, but a few do it outside. That's why the occurrence is rare to humans."

All of this was good and a little disturbing to think about, but it wasn't why we were here. "My friend was wearing a bracelet—"

"Tiffany's?" he asked and smirked.

"No." I smiled tightly. "It was just like the one you're wearing."

Surprise rolled over Luc's face like a wave. The little punk dropped his legs onto the floor and sat straight. "Not good."

Foreboding chills skated over my skin as Daemon zeroed in on Luc. "Why is that not good?"

He seemed to debate whether he should talk about it and then went with a, "Oh, what the hell. You'll owe me, hope you realize. But what you see here?" Luc flicked a finger along the stone. "It's a black opal—so rare that only a few mines can even unearth these babies. And it's only *these* kinds."

"The ones that look like they have fire in them?" I asked, leaning forward to get a better look. It really did look like a black orb with a flame inside. "Where are they mined?"

"Australia, usually. There's something in the composition of a black opal that's like a power booster. You know, like Mario gets when he hits a mushroom. Imagine that sound. That's what a black opal does."

"What kind of composition?" Daemon asked, eyes sharp with interest.

Luc unhooked the bracelet and held it up in the dim light. "Opals have this remarkable ability to refract and reflect specific wavelengths of light."

"No way," Daemon breathed, and apparently that was super cool. I was still lost on the whole stone and light thing.

"Yes." Luc smiled at the stone, like a father smiles at his prodigal son. "I don't know who discovered it. Someone in

Daedalus, I'm sure. Once they figured out what it could do, they kept it away from the Luxen and ones like us."

"Why?" I felt stupid for asking, mainly because both of them looked at me like I was. "What? I don't have a degree in alien mineralogy. Geez."

Daemon patted my thigh. "It's okay. Refracting and reflecting wavelengths of lights affects us, like the obsidian affects Arum and onyx affects us."

"Okay," I said slowly.

Luc's purple eyes glimmered. "Refracting light changes the direction and speed. Our friendly neighborhood aliens are made of light—well, made of more than that, but let me explain it this way: let's say their DNA is light. And let's say that once a human is mutated, their DNA is now encased in wavelengths of light."

I remembered Daemon trying to explain this before. "And onyx disrupts those wavelengths of light, right? Kind of makes them bounce around and go crazy."

Luc nodded. "Opal's ability to refract allows a Luxen or a hybrid to be more powerful—it enhances our ability to refract light."

"And the reflection part—wow." Awed, Daemon grinned.

I got the whole refraction thing. Sure, super speed, ability to pull on the Source more easily, and probably a slew of other benefits, but reflection? I waited.

Daemon nudged me with his elbow. "We flicker or fade sometimes because we move fast. And sometimes you see us fade in and out—it's just reflection. Something all of us have to work at to control when we're younger."

"And it's hard when you're excited or upset?"

He nodded. "Among other things, but to control reflection?" He fixed on Luc. "Are you saying you can do what I think you can?"

Laughing, Luc hooked the bracelet around his wrist and sat back, dropping his legs on the desk again. "Hybrids are good. We can move faster than humans, but with the obesity rates nowadays, turtles can move faster than most humans. Sometimes we're even stronger than the average Luxen when it comes to the Source—it's the mixture of human and alien DNA that can create something powerful, but that's not standard." A self-fulfilled smile stretched Luc's lips. "But give a Luxen one of these, and they can completely reflect light."

My heart skipped a beat. "You mean . . . like, invisible?"

"So cool," Daemon said, staring at the stone. "We can change the way we look, but become invisible? Yeah, that's new."

Confounded, I shook my head. "Can we be invisible?"

"No. Our human DNA gets in the way of that, but it makes us just as powerful as the strongest Luxen and then some." He wiggled a little in his seat. "So you can imagine that they wouldn't want any of us having these . . . especially one that hasn't been proven to be stable, unless . . ."

A cold breath of air shot over my neck. "Unless what?"

Some of the enthusiasm faded from his face. "Unless they didn't care what kind of damage the hybrid caused. Maybe your friend was a test run for a bigger incident."

"What?" Daemon tensed. "You think they did this on purpose? Hooked up an unstable hybrid and sent her out into the wild to see what happens?"

"Paris thinks I'm a conspiracy theorist with a hint of schizophrenic paranoia." He shrugged. "But you can't tell me that Daedalus doesn't have a master plan up their sleeves. I wouldn't put a single thing past them."

"But why would she come after me? Blake says they don't know the mutation held. So it wasn't like they'd send her after me." I paused. "And, well, that's if Blake's telling the truth."

"I'm sure he is about the mutation," Luc responded. "If he wasn't, you wouldn't be sitting here. See, I'm not sure even Daedalus knows everything that this stone is capable of and how it affects us. I'm still learning."

"And what have you learned?" Daemon asked.

"For starters, before I got my grubby paws on one of these, I couldn't pick out another hybrid if one did a jig in front of me. I knew the moment you and Blake arrived in Martinsburg, Katy. It was weird, like a breath washing over my entire body. Your friend probably sensed you. That's the least terrible probability."

Daemon blew out a long breath and then looked away for a moment. "Do you know if it can enhance the Arum's abilities?"

"I imagine it could if they were bloated on a Luxen's powers."

Overwhelmed, I sat back and then shot forward. "Do you think the opal can, like, counteract the onyx?"

"It's possible, but I don't know. Haven't hugged any onyx recently."

I ignored the sarcastic tone. "Where can we get some of the opal?"

Luc laughed and I wanted to kick his legs off the desk. "Unless you have about thirty thousand dollars lying around and know someone who mines opals, or you want to ask Daedalus for some, you're out of luck. And I'm not giving you mine."

My shoulders slumped. Yippee, another dead end. We couldn't catch a break if it slapped us upside the face.

"Anyway, it's about time for you guys to hit the road." He tipped his head back, closing his eyes. "I'm assuming I won't hear from you two again until you're ready to go to Mount Weather?"

Ah, we'd been dismissed. As I stood, I debated on bum-rushing Luc and grabbing his bracelet. The way his eyes opened into thin slits warned me to forget that idea.

"Is there anything else you can tell me?" Daemon prodded.

"Sure, I have something else." Luc lifted those long lashes. "You really shouldn't trust a soul in this game. Not when everyone has something to gain or lose."

29

Over the course of several weeks, interviews given by local law enforcement and tearful pleas from Carissa's parents appeared on the nightly news, candlelight vigils were held, and reporters from all around came, drawn in by morbid curiosity. How could such a little town have so many children who just disappeared? Some even speculated that a serial killer had targeted the sleepy town in West Virginia.

Being at school, listening to everyone talk about Carissa, Simon, and even Adam and Beth was hard to do. Not just for me, but for all of us who knew the truth.

These kids didn't disappear.

Adam and Carissa were dead, most likely Simon, too. Beth was being held against her will in a government facility.

A dark, somber mood settled, creeping into every part of us, and there was no shaking it. Of course suspicion blossomed along with the spring grass and tiny buds at school, because only one of the kids had reappeared and that had been Dawson. But his reappearance had signaled the disappearance of others.

There were whispers in the hall and long looks passed among students whenever Dawson or Daemon was around. Possibly because very few could tell them apart, but both brothers acted like they didn't hear it. Or maybe they just didn't care.

Even Lesa had changed. Losing a friend would do that, as would the inability to find any closure. There was never a reason for why Carissa had disappeared, at least not for Lesa. She, like so many others, would spend a lifetime wondering why and how it happened. And not knowing created this powerlessness to move on. Even though the seasons were changing and spring was well on its way, Lesa was stuck on the day before she found out her best friend had vanished and the day after. She was the same girl in some ways: moments where she'd say something wholly inappropriate and she would laugh, and then others when she didn't think I was looking, her eyes would cloud with misgiving.

Carissa wasn't the only newsworthy case, though.

Dr. William Michaels, aka Mom's boyfriend and all-around douche canoe, was reported missing by his sister about three weeks after Carissa dropped off the radar. A frenzied storm descended once again. Mom had been questioned and she . . . She had been a wreck. Especially when she learned that Will had never signed in at any conference in the west, and no one had seen or heard from him since he left Petersburg.

Officials suspected that foul play might have been involved. Others whispered that he had to have something to do with what happened to Carissa and Simon. A prominent doctor just didn't simply cease to exist.

But Daemon and I were still alive, so all we could assume was that the mutation had held and since he had gotten what he wanted, he was in hiding. Worst-case scenario, Daedalus had picked him up somewhere. Didn't bode well for us if that happened, but hey, it served him right if *he* was locked in a cage somewhere.

All in all I wasn't torn up over the fact that for right now, Will was a nonissue, but I hated seeing Mom go through this again. And I hated Will even more for putting her through it. She hit every stage of the grieving process: disbelief; sorrow; that horrible, lingering lost feeling; and then anger.

I had no idea what to do for her. The best I could was spend the evenings with her on her days off, after I finished with the onyx stuff. Keeping her company and distracted seemed to help.

As weeks passed and there was no sign of Carissa or anyone else who had held the little town captive, the inevitable happened. People didn't forget, but the reporters went away and then other things occupied the nightly news. By mid-April, everyone for the most part was back to doing their own thing.

I'd asked Daemon one evening as we walked back from the lake, enjoying the warmer temperatures, how could people forget so easily? A bitter sensation had taken up residence in my tummy. Would that happen to me one day if we didn't come back from Mount Weather? People would just get over it?

Daemon had squeezed my hand and said, "It's the human condition, Kitten. The unknown isn't something that sits well. They'd rather push it away—not completely, but just enough that it's not always shadowing their every thought and action."

"And that's okay?"

"Not saying that it is." He'd stopped, placing his hands on my upper arms. "But not having the answers to something can be scary. People can't focus on that forever. Just like you couldn't focus on why it was your dad who had to get sick and pass away. That's the big unknown. You had to let it go eventually."

I'd stared up at him, his striking features highlighted in the waning light. "I can't believe you can sound so wise."

Daemon had chuckled, running his hands up and down my arms. Promising chills followed. "I'm more than looks, Kitten. You should know that."

And I did. Daemon was ridiculously supportive most of the time. He still hated that I was taking part in the onyx training, but he wasn't pushing it and I appreciated that.

I threw myself into training with the onyx, which left little time for anything other than going to school. Onyx stripped away energy and after every session, all of us were quick to pass out. And we were so wrapped up in building our tolerance, watching out for officers and implants that we hadn't even celebrated Valentine's Day besides the flowers he'd bought me and the card I'd given him.

We kept planning to make up for it, to do the dinner thing, but time got away from us or someone got in between us. Either it was Dawson impatient to save Beth and a hairbreadth from storming Mount Weather, Dee wanting to murder someone, or Blake demanding that we do the onyx thing every day. I'd forgotten what it felt like when it was just Daemon and me.

I really began to think his sporadic late-night visits really were a product of my overactive imagination, because at the end of the night, he was just as whipped as I was. Every morning it seemed like a vivid dream and since Daemon never mentioned it, I let it go while looking forward to it. Dream Daemon was better than no Daemon, I guessed.

But by the beginning of May, the five of us could handle the onyx for about fifty seconds without losing control of our muscle functions. Didn't seem like a lot of time to the others, but it was progress to us.

Halfway through today's practice, we gained an audience that included Ash and Dee. Those two were becoming real bosom buddies of late, while I was basically friendless with the exception of Lesa on good days.

Bad days were when she missed Carissa and no one could replace that lost friendship.

Watching Ash teeter around on her ridiculous heels, I had

to wonder how Ash and Dee were even getting along. Besides their obsession with fashion, they had little in common.

Then I realized what probably had bonded them together: their grief. And here I was, begrudging them of that. I could be such a tool.

Matthew was in the process of picking himself off the ground as Ash tottered over to the onyx, frowning. "It can't be that bad. I have to try it."

I bit back a mad grin. I was *so* not going to stop her.

"Uh, Ash, I really wouldn't suggest doing that," Daemon began.

Party pooper, I thought, but Ash was a determined little alien. So I sat down, stretched out my legs, and waited for the show to begin.

I didn't have to wait long.

Bending over gracefully, she picked up one of the shiny blackish-red jewels while I held my breath. Not even a second later, she shrieked, dropped the onyx as if it were a snake, and stumbled backward, falling flat on her butt.

"Yep, not bad at all," Dawson commented drily.

Ash's eyes were wide, mouth gulping like a fish's. "What . . . what was that?"

"Onyx," I responded, lying on my back. Bright blue skies and a touch of sun warmed the air. I'd already had three rounds with it today. I couldn't feel my fingers. "It sucks."

"It felt . . . It felt like my skin was ripping apart," she said. Shock roughened her voice. "Why would you guys put yourselves through this for months?"

Dawson cleared his throat. "You know why, Ash."

"But she's . . ."

Oh, no.

"She's what?" Dawson was on his feet. "She's my girlfriend."

"I didn't mean anything." Ash looked around for help, but she was alone on this one. Standing carefully, she took an unsteady step toward Dawson. "I'm sorry. It's just . . . that hurt."

Dawson said nothing as he brushed past Daemon, disappearing into the thicket. Daemon's eyes met mine, then he sighed and trotted off after his brother.

"Ash, you need to learn a tad bit more sensitivity," Matthew said, brushing loose dirt off his jeans.

Her face fell and then crumbled. "I'm sorry. I didn't mean anything by it."

I couldn't believe it. A rarity was to see Ash show any emotion other than bitchiness. Dee went to her side and the two walked off, Matthew following after them, looking like he needed a vacation or a bottle of whiskey.

Which left me alone with Blake.

Groaning, I closed my eyes and lay back down. My body felt heavy, like I could sink through the ground. In a couple of weeks, I'd sprout flowers.

"Are you feeling okay?" Blake asked.

Several snarky responses lined up on my tongue like little soldiers, but all I said was, "I'm just tired."

There was a pregnant pause, and then I heard his footsteps move closer. Blake sat down beside me. "Onyx is killer, isn't it? I never really thought about it, but when I was first *inducted* into Daedalus, I was always tired."

I didn't know what to say so I kept quiet and for a while, so did he. Blake was probably the hardest person to be around. Because deep down, he wasn't a horrible person, maybe not even a monster. He was a desperate person and desperation can make people do crazy things.

He brought forth conflicted feelings. Over the last couple of months, I had grown, like the others, to tolerate him but not trust him, because I remembered Luc's parting words— *You really shouldn't trust a soul in this game. Not when everyone has something to gain or lose.* I couldn't help but wonder if he'd meant Blake. I didn't want to go easy on him because of what he did to Adam, and I didn't want to feel sorry for him, but I did at times. He was a product of his environment. Wasn't a justification of any sorts, but Blake didn't do what he did all by himself. There had been several factors. The strangest thing of all had been at lunch, seeing him sitting at the same table with the siblings of the boy he'd killed.

I honestly didn't think anyone knew how to handle Blake.

Finally, he said, "I know what you're thinking."

"I thought you couldn't read other hybrids' minds."

He laughed. "I can't, but it's obvious. You're uncomfortable with my being here with you, but you're too tired and it's too nice to get up."

Blake was right on all accounts. "And yet you're still here."

"Yeah, about that . . . I don't think sleeping out here is the safest thing to do. Besides the bears and coyotes, the DOD or Daedalus could always come around."

I opened my eyes, sighing. "And what would be suspicious about my being out here?"

"Well, besides that it's a little early in May and late in the day for sunbathing . . . They know I still talk to you. Keeping up appearances and all."

I tilted my head toward him. Each of the Luxen took turns scouting the area while we practiced, making sure no one was watching. Seemed odd Blake would be concerned about that now. "Really," I said.

He bent his knees, resting his arms over them as he stared out over the peaceful lake. There was another gap of silence and then, "I know you and Daemon went to see Luc back in February."

I opened my mouth but then shook my head. I sure as hell didn't need to explain why to him.

Blake sighed. "I know you don't and won't ever trust me, but I could've saved you a trip. I knew what the black opal does. Seen Luc pull off some crazy-insane stuff because of it."

Irritation flared. "And you didn't think to tell us about it?"

"I didn't think it would be an issue," he said. "That kind of opal is damn near impossible to get ahold of and the last thing I expected was for Daedalus to be outfitting hybrids with it. Hell, I haven't even thought of it."

Here I was, in the same position with Blake as usual: to believe or to not believe him. I crossed my legs at the ankles and watched a thick, fluffy cloud shuttle across the sky.

"Okay," I said, because honestly, there was no way to prove if he was lying or not. I bet if we hooked him up to a lie detector the results would be inconclusive.

Blake seemed surprised. "I wish things were different, Katy."

I snorted. "Me, too, and probably a hundred other people."

"I know." He dug through the soil, finding a pebble. He turned it over in his hand slowly. "I've been thinking lately, about what I'm going to do when this is all over. There's a good chance that Chris . . . He won't be right, you know? We have to go somewhere and disappear, but what if he can't blend in? If he's . . . different?"

Not right, like Beth had been when I'd seen her. "You've said he likes the beach. So do you. That's where you should go."

"Sounds like a plan . . ." He glanced at me. "What are you guys going to do with Beth? Hell, what are you going to do after you get her back? Daedalus is going to be looking for her."

"I know." I sighed, wanting to sink through the ground. "We're going to have to hide her, I guess. See how she is. Cross that bridge when we get there, that kind of thing, but as long as everyone is together, we'll figure something out."

"Yeah . . ." He stopped, lips thinning. Swinging his arm

to the side, he tossed the pebble out into the lake. It skipped three times before sinking under. Then he stood. "I'll leave you alone, but I'll be nearby."

Before I could respond, he stood and jogged off. Frowning, I arched my back so I could see him The bank around the lake was empty, with the exception of a few robins hopping on the ground near a tree.

Now that was an odd conversation.

Settling back down, I closed my eyes and forced my mind blank. The moment I was alone and it was silent, a thousand things came from every direction inside me. Falling asleep was difficult, so I had this habit of picturing this beach in Florida that Dad liked to go to. Creating the image of frothy waves lapping blue-green foam against the shore as they crested and receded, I kept that scene going on a loop. Nothing else but that image snuck into the recesses of my thoughts. I hadn't really been planning on dozing off out here, but as exhausted as I was, I fell asleep pretty fast.

I'm not sure what woke me, but as I blinked my eyes open I found myself staring into a pair of bright green eyes. I smiled. "Hey," I murmured.

One side of his full lips tipped up. "Hey there, sleeping beauty . . ."

Over his shoulder, the sky had deepened to a denim blue. "Did you kiss me awake?"

"I did." Daemon was propped on his side, using his arm to support his head. He placed his hand on my stomach and my chest fluttered in response. "Told you, my lips have mystical powers."

My shoulders moved in a silent laugh. "How long have you been here?"

"Not long." His eyes searched mine. "I found Blake sulking around the woods. He didn't want to leave while you were out here."

I rolled my eyes.

"As much as it bothers me, I'm glad he didn't."

"Wow. Pigs are flying." When he narrowed his eyes, I lifted my hand, running my fingers through the soft waves that fell over his forehead. His eyes drifted shut and my breath caught. "How's Dawson?"

"Calmed down. How's Kitten?"

"Sleepy."

"And?"

Slowly, I trailed my fingers down the side of his face, along his broad cheek and down the hard line of his jaw. He turned into my palm, pressing his lips to it. "Happy you're here."

His fingers made quick work of the light cardigan I was wearing, separating the thin flaps of material. His knuckles brushed against the tank top I had on underneath. "And?"

"And glad I didn't get eaten by a bear or coyote."

He arched a brow. "What?"

I grinned. "Apparently they're a problem around here."

Daemon shook his head. "Back to talking about me."

Instead of telling him, I showed. As Daemon would say, it was the book lover in me. Showing was so much better than telling. My fingers smoothed over his bottom lip and then I moved my hand to his chest. I lifted my head and he met me halfway.

The kiss started off tentative and smooth. Silky kisses created a yearning that was becoming all too familiar. The sensation of his lips against mine, the knowledge of what I wanted, sparked deep inside us and our hearts picked up together, beating heavily and fast. I let myself fall into that kiss, drown in it, become it. The swelling wave of feelings was hard to process. At once both exhilarating and frightening. I was ready, had been ready, and yet I knew I was scared, because like Daemon had said before: humans were afraid of the unknown. And Daemon and I had been hovering on the verge of the unknown for a while.

He pressed down until I was flat on my back, and he was above me, his weight perfect and crazy. His hand slid up, bunching the material, his fingers grazing. The touch was too much and not enough. My chest rose and fell rapidly as his leg moved over mine, between mine. When he broke away, I gasped for air, for control I was quickly losing.

"I need to stop," he said roughly, eyes closing tightly, lashes fanning the tips of his cheeks. "Like, right now."

I threaded my fingers through the curls at the back of his neck, hoping he didn't notice how badly my hand shook. "Yeah, we should."

He nodded, but then he lowered his head and kissed me again. Good to see he had the same amount of willpower as I did, which was zilch. My hands slid down his back, digging into the shirt he wore, finding their way under it, splaying across his warm skin. I curled my leg around his. We were close, so close that even if our hearts hadn't beat in tandem before, it wouldn't have mattered, because they would've found each other and joined now.

Our breaths were coming fast. This was insane. Perfect. His hand crept under my shirt, moving up and up, and every part of me wanted to press the stop button on the world and then hit repeat so I could feel this way over and over again.

Daemon stiffened.

"Oh, dear God and baby Jesus in the manger, my eyes!" Dee shrieked. "My eyes!"

My own eyes snapped open. Daemon lifted his head, eyes luminous. Then I realized my hands were still up his shirt. I yanked them out.

"Oh my God," I whispered, mortified.

Daemon said something that burned my ears. "Dee, you didn't see anything." And then he added much lower, "Because you have impeccable timing."

"You were on . . . her and your mouths were doing this." I

could just imagine her hand signals at that point. She went on. "And that's more than I want to see. Like, ever."

I pushed at Daemon's chest, and he rolled off. I sat up and twisted around, keeping my head low so my hair could hide my burning cheeks. I caught sight of Dee and even though you'd think she'd caught us buck naked in the act, instead of making out, she was grinning.

"What do you want, Dee?" Daemon said.

She huffed, pressing her hands on her hips. "Well, I don't want anything from *you*. I wanted to talk to Katy."

My head jerked up, embarrassment be damned. "You do?"

"Ash and I were going to this new little shop in Moorefield Saturday afternoon. They sell vintage dresses. For prom," she added as I continued to stare at her.

"Prom?" I didn't get it.

"Yeah, prom's at the end of the month." She glanced at her brother, her cheeks turning rosy. "Most of the dresses are going to be gone. And I don't know if the place has anything, but Ash heard about it and you know how she is with clothes, so she's in the know. Like, a couple of days ago, she found this really cute cropped sweater that—"

"Dee," Daemon said, a small grin tugging his lips.

"What? I'm not talking to you." She faced me, exasperated. "Anyway, would you like to go with us? Or have you already gotten a dress? Because if you have gotten a dress, then I guess the trip is pointless, but you could still—"

"No. I haven't gotten a dress." I couldn't believe she was asking me to do something with her. I was stunned and hopeful and stunned some more.

"Good!" She grinned. "Then we can go on Saturday. I thought about asking Lesa if she wanted to go . . ."

I had to be dreaming. She wanted to ask Lesa, too? What did I miss? I glanced at Daemon as his sister chattered on and he grinned. "Wait," I said. "I wasn't planning on prom."

"What?" Dee's mouth dropped open. "It's senior prom."

"I know, but with everything going on . . . I haven't really thought about it." A lie, because you couldn't step anywhere at school and not see flyers and banners about it.

Dee's incredulous expression grew. "It's *senior* prom."

"But . . ." I tucked my hair back and glanced at Daemon. "You haven't even asked me to go."

He smiled. "I didn't think I needed to ask. I assumed we would go."

"Well, you know what they say about people who assume," Dee said, rocking back on the balls of her feet.

He ignored her, his grin fading. "What, Kitten?"

I blinked. "How can we go to prom with everything going on? We're so close to having enough tolerance to go back to Mount Weather and—"

"And prom is on a Saturday," he said, pulling my hand away from my hair. "So let's say that in two weeks when we're ready to go, it will be Sunday."

Dee shot forward, hobbling from one foot to the other like her feet were playing hot potato. "And it's only a few hours. You guys can halt the self-mutilation for a few hours."

The problem wasn't the time or really even the onyx. It didn't seem right to go to prom after everything, after Carissa . . .

Daemon slipped his arm around me as he leaned, his voice low as he spoke. "It's not wrong, Kat. You deserve this."

I closed my eyes. "Why should we get to celebrate when she can't?"

He rested his cheek against mine. "We're still here and we deserve to be, to do normal things every once in a while."

Did we?

"It's not your fault," he whispered, and then kissed my temple. He pulled back, eyes searching mine. "Will you go to prom with me, Kat?"

Dee shifted some more. "You should really say yes, so we can go dress shopping and so I don't have to witness a really awkward moment of you turning down my brother. Even though he deserves to be knocked down a peg or two."

I laughed, glancing at her. Dee gave me a tentative smile, and that hope was springing back. "Okay." I took a deep breath. "I'll go to prom—only because I don't want this conversation to get awkward."

Daemon tweaked my nose. "I'll take what I can get for as long as I can get it."

A cloud passed over the sun and seemed to halt. The temperature dropped significantly.

My smile started to falter as a chill snaked down my spine. This was a happy moment—a good moment. There was hope for Dee's and my relationship. And prom was a big deal. Daemon in a tux and all would be a pretty awesome sight. We were going to be normal teenagers for the night, but the shadow over us had somehow slipped inside me.

"What is it?" Daemon asked, concerned.

"Nothing," I said, but it was something. I just didn't know what.

30

One of the first things I did the next day was invite Lesa. I was thrilled when she perked up and agreed. It made me feel a lot better about my decision to go. Like Carissa's best friend approved and that went a long way.

Like me, she was a tad wary of going shopping with Ash, and a glimmer of her old personality shone through when she started making cracks.

"I bet she'll get something ridiculously tight and short and make the rest of us feel like unattractive Oompa Loompas." She sighed pitifully. "No. Scratch that. She'll probably just go to the dress store and parade in front of the mirror naked."

I laughed. "No doubt, but I'm happy Dee invited us."

"Me, too," she said seriously. "I miss her, especially after . . . Yeah, I just miss her."

My smile was a bit wobbly. Whenever Carissa came up in conversation, I never knew how to handle it. Luckily, for today, we were interrupted by Daemon, who decided to tug on my ponytail like a six-year-old.

He sat behind me and then poked me in the back with his trusty pen.

I rolled my eyes at Lesa and then turned around. "You and that damn pen."

"You love it." He leaned over his desk, tapping it off my chin. "Anyway, I thought I could catch a ride home with you after school. That *thing* we've got to do later was delayed for about an hour. And your mom's already at Winchester by then, right?"

A low hum of excitement thrummed through my veins. I knew where he was going with this. No Mom. An hour or so of time alone and without interruption—hopefully.

I couldn't stop my dreamy sigh. "That would be perfect."

"Thought so." He took his pen and sat back, eyeing me. "Can't wait."

Oxygen fled my brain while blood rushed everywhere. Feeling a bit out of it, I nodded and turned around. The look on Lesa's face told me she so overheard the conversation.

Her eyebrows waggled suggestively, and I felt my face burn. Oh, dear God . . .

After trig, the rest of the morning crept by in a slow procession. The cosmos were against me. Like they knew I was bouncing with energy and excitement. A little part of me was nervous. Who wouldn't be? If we actually had time alone and we weren't interrupted and stuff fell into place . . .

Stuff fell into place?

I smothered a giggle.

Blake looked up from his bio text and frowned. "What?"

"Nothing." I grinned. "Nothing."

He arched a brow. "Did Daemon tell you that Matthew has some after-school meeting with a kid's parents?"

I giggled again, earning a weird look from him. "Yeah, he did."

Blake stared at me a second and then placed his pen down. Without any warning, he reached over and picked a piece of lint out of my hair. I jerked back at the same time he pulled his arm away, which put my nose right at the perfect angle to get a sniff of his wrist.

The clean, citrusy scent sparked a muggy, uncomfortable feeling inside me. Like when you've done something stupid and you were about to face public humiliation. Pins and needles spread across my flesh.

A memory was wiggling loose. That smell . . . I'd smelled it before.

"You okay?" he asked.

I tilted my head to the side, like that helped my smelling abilities. Where did I know that scent? Obviously I'd smelled it on Blake before. No doubt it was one of those expensive colognes, but it was more than that.

Like when you hear an actor's voice but don't see his face. The answer was on the tip of my tongue and I couldn't shake the nagging feeling.

Why did that scent feel achingly familiar? Daemon's face popped in my head, but that wasn't right. He smelled earthy, like the outdoors and the wind. And his scent lingered long after he was gone, on my clothes, the pillow . . .

The pillow . . .

My heart stuttered and then skipped a beat. It sunk in and threatened to pull me through the seat. Shock washed over me, quickly followed by a bolt of anger so fierce I jerked forward.

I couldn't sit here. I couldn't breathe.

Static crackled under my shirt. Tiny hairs rose over my body. Burned ozone filled the air. At the front of the class, Matthew looked up. His gaze went to Dawson first, because hey, if anyone were going to lose it, it would be him. But Dawson was also glancing around the room, searching for the source of the increased friction and static in the air.

It was coming from me.

I was going to blow.

Snapping into action, I shut my book and shoved it into my messenger bag. Wasting no time, I stood on shaky legs. My skin felt like it was humming. And maybe it was at a low frequency. Violent energy rolled through me. Only once before had I felt this way and that was when Blake . . .

I headed past Matthew, unable to answer his look of concern, and ignored the curious stares. Hurrying from the room, I dragged in several deep breaths to try to calm down. Gray lockers blurred around me. Conversations were muted and sounded so very far away.

Where was I going? What was I going to do? Going to Daemon was out of the question, because right now, on top of everything, it was the last thing we needed.

I started forward, my fingers clenched tightly around my bag's strap. I felt . . . I felt like I was going to hurl. Anger and nausea roiled. I headed toward the girls' restroom at the end of the hall.

"Katy! Are you okay? Wait up?"

The floor dropped out from underneath me, but I kept walking.

Blake caught up with me, catching my arm. "Katy—"

"Don't touch me!" I wrenched my arm free, horrified . . . just horrified. "Don't ever touch me."

He stared at me, anger tightening the lines of his face. "What is your problem?"

A terrible, ugly feeling clawed its way through my insides. "I know, Blake. I *know*."

"Know what?" He looked confounded. "Katy, your eyes are starting to glow. You've got to chill out."

I stepped forward but forced myself to stop. I was so close to losing it. "You—you are a freak."

His brows shot up. "All right, you're going to have to give me a better explanation than that, because I have no idea what I've done to tick you off."

The hallway was empty for now, but this was no place to get into this kind of conversation. I turned, heading to the stairwell. Blake followed and once the door swung shut behind us, I whirled on him.

It wasn't my fist that hit him.

A blast of energy, probably what felt like a hit from a Taser, smacked him in the chest. Blake stumbled back into the door, mouth dropping open as his legs and arms twitched.

"What," he gasped. "What was that for?"

Static crackled over my fingers. I wanted to do it again. "You've been sleeping in my bed."

Blake straightened, rubbing a hand over his chest. The faint light coming from the window in the landing danced over his face. "Katy, I—"

"Don't lie about it. I know you've been. I smelled your cologne. It's been on my pillows." Bile filled the back of my throat and the urge to lash out hit me hard. "How could you? How could you do something so revolting and creepy?"

Something flickered in his eyes. Hurt? Anger? I didn't know or care. What he did was so wrong on so many levels that re-straining orders were usually issued in response.

Blake thrust his fingers through his hair. "It's not what you think."

"It's not." I barked out a short laugh. "I don't know what else it could be. You came into my house and my bedroom uninvited and you . . . you got into bed with me, you sick son of a—"

"It's not what you think!" he practically shouted and the Source inside me perked even more, responding to the out-burst. I expected teachers to rush the stairwell, but they didn't. "I've been keeping an eye on everything at night because of Daedalus. I patrol the area just like Daemon and the other Luxen do."

I scoffed. "They don't climb into my bed, Blake."

He stared back at me so blatantly I wanted to smack him.

"I know. Like I said, that . . . was never my intention. It was an accident."

My mouth dropped open. "Did you slip and fall on my bed? Because I don't understand how you've accidentally ended up there."

Red stained the tips of his cheeks. "I check the outside, and then I check the inside just to be sure. Hybrids can get into your house, Katy, as you already know. So could Daedalus if they wanted."

What would he have done if Daemon had been there? Then it struck me and I felt sick all over again. "How long do you watch at night?"

He shrugged. "A couple of hours."

So he'd have known if Daemon had come over most of the time, and the rest was just sheer dumb luck. Part of me wished he'd tried it just once when Daemon was there. He wouldn't be walking right for months.

There was a good chance he may leave this stairwell with a limp.

Blake seemed to sense where my mind went. "After I checked inside your house, I . . . I don't know what happened. You have bad dreams."

I wondered why. I had perverts sleeping in the bed with me.

"I just wanted to comfort you. That's all." He leaned against the wall, below the window, closing his eyes. "I guess I fell asleep."

"This wasn't a onetime thing. Not that once would be okay. Do you understand that?"

"I do." His eyes opened into thin slits. "Are you going to tell Daemon?"

I shook my head. I could handle this. I *would* handle this. "He would kill you on the spot and then we'd end up in Daedalus's hands."

Relief loosened his body. "Katy, I'm sorry. It's not as creepy as it—"

"Not as creepy? Are you serious? No, don't answer. I don't care." I stepped forward, my voice shaking. "I don't care if you were just worried and keeping an eye on me. I don't care if my house is on fire. You do not come in there again. And you sure as hell don't sleep in my bed again. You kissed . . ." I sucked in a sharp breath. The raw, ugly black feeling was back, crawling up my throat. "I don't care. I don't want to be near you any more than I have to be. Okay? I want you to stay away from me. No more watching or anything."

Hurt flashed in his churning eyes, and he looked like he'd protest for a long moment. "Okay."

I turned back to the door, my entire body shaking. I stopped and faced him. He stood under the opaque windows, his head lowered. He ran a hand through his spiky hair, clasping the back of his neck.

"If you do again what you've been doing, I will hurt you." Emotion clogged my throat. "I don't care what happens. I will hurt you."

Shaking off my discovery was hard to do. I alternated between wanting to take a scalding hot shower and anger so potent I could taste it the rest of the day. Luckily, I was able to convince Matthew that Blake had just ticked me off because he was Blake, which was believable and explained why Blake would follow me. I convinced Lesa I wasn't feeling well and that was why I rushed out of class, which she pointed out would put a damper on my afternoon plans.

Those had already been tainted.

I had no intention of bringing this up with Daemon. He would lose his ever-loving mind and as much as I hated it, we needed Blake. We had come too far to end up being captured by them because of whatever letter he had hanging over our heads. I also wasn't willing to risk not rescuing Beth.

Whenever I thought about it throughout the day, my skin crawled. I'd thought it had either been Daemon all of those times or a dream, but I should've known. Not once did I feel the warmth that our connection gave as warning whenever Daemon was near.

I should've known that Blake was a bigger freak than I could ever imagine.

On the way home, I swung by the post office. Daemon hopped out of the car and followed me in. Three steps from the door, he caught me around the waist from behind and lifted me up. He spun me around so fast my legs were like little windmills.

A woman and her child came out of the post office, narrowly avoiding being taken out by my legs. She laughed and I was sure it had something to do with the smile I knew Daemon was sporting.

When he placed me on my feet and let go, I swayed unsteadily through the door. He laughed. "You look a little drunk."

"No thanks to you."

He dropped an arm over my shoulder, apparently in a playful mood. We stopped at my mom's PO box and dug out the packages. A few were media mail and the rest a bunch of junk mail.

Daemon snatched the yellow packages from my hands. "Oh! Books! You have books!"

I laughed as several people waiting in line looked over their shoulders. "Hand them over."

He clutched them to his chest, making moony eyes. "My life is now complete."

"My life would be complete if I could actually post a review on something other than the school library computers."

I did that about twice a week since my latest laptop went to the big computer heaven in the sky. Daemon always went with me. In his words, he was there to "proof" my posts. In other words, he served as a huge distraction.

Taking the rest of the mail from me, he kissed my cheek. "Wouldn't that be nice? But I think you've exhausted your mom's allowance for laptops."

"Neither was my fault." I'd been hiding my recently destroyed laptop from her. She'd go postal if she found it.

"True." He held open the door for a little old lady and then let me shimmy past. "But I bet you go to bed every night dreaming and thinking about a shiny new laptop."

A warm breeze blew a strand of hair across my face as I stopped at my car. "Besides dreaming about you?"

"In between dreaming about me," he corrected, placing my mail on the backseat. "What's the first thing you'd do if you got a new laptop?"

Letting him take the keys from me, I went to the passenger side and thought about it. "I don't know. I'd probably hug it and promise it that I'd never let anything bad happen to it."

He laughed again, eyes twinkling. "Okay, other than that?"

"Make a vlog thanking the laptop gods for bestowing one upon me." I sighed then, because that would be the only way I'd get one. "I need to get a job."

"What you need to do is apply for college."

"You haven't," I pointed out.

He cast me a sidelong glance. "I've been waiting on you."

"Colorado," I said, and when he nodded, my mom's horrified expression loomed in my head. "Mom would freak."

"I think she'd be happy with the fact that you're going to college."

He had a point, but the whole college thing seemed up in the air at this point. I had no idea what next week would hold for us, let alone a few months down the road. But I had good grades and I had looked into scholarships for next year's spring enrollment.

In Colorado . . . and I knew Daemon had seen the pamphlet from the university. The prospect of going away to college with Daemon like normal teenagers was appealing. The problem was that getting my hopes up and not being able to do something like that would suck too much.

My house was silent and a little warm. I opened a window in the living room while Daemon helped himself to a glass of milk. When I walked into the kitchen, he was running the back of his hand over his mouth, his hair a mess of waves and eyes as green as spring grass. The movement pulled his shirt taut over his biceps and chest.

I bit back a sigh. Milk did a body good.

His smile was just as wicked. Putting the glass on the counter, he moved so fast I didn't see him until he was standing in front of me, taking my cheeks in his hands. I loved that he was able to be real around me. I used to think the freaky alien speed thing was to annoy me, but it was just his natural state. Slowing down to human speed actually caused him to use more energy.

But then he kissed me, and he tasted of milk and something richer, lush and smooth. I didn't realize he was guiding me backward and that we were at the bottom of the stairs until he lifted me up without breaking the kiss.

I thought the whole thing with Blake would ruin this afternoon, but I had underestimated the magnetism of Daemon and his kisses. I wrapped my legs around his waist, reveling in the feel of his muscles under my hands.

He didn't stop at the top of the stairs but kept going and kissing and my heart was pounding. Turning, he gently kicked my door open and then my heart was doing the skipping thing, because we were in my bedroom and there was no one around to interrupt us. Nervous excitement enveloped me.

Daemon lifted his head. A lopsided grin appeared on his lips and I slid down, breathing fast. I watched in a daze as he moved back and sat on the edge of my bed, his fingers slowly letting go of mine, trailing across my palm. I felt the tingles all the way up my arm.

Then he looked at my desk.

My gaze followed his and I blinked, thinking a mirage had appeared in my bedroom, because I couldn't be seeing what I was.

Resting on my desk was a MacBook Air in a cherry red sleeve.

"I . . ." I didn't know what to say. My brain emptied. Were we in the right house? I took in the familiar surroundings and decided that we were.

I took a step toward the desk and stopped. "Is that for me?"

A slow, beautiful smile crept across his face, filling his eyes. "Well, it is on your desk, so . . ."

My heart stuttered. "But I don't understand."

"See, there's this place called an Apple Store and I went there, picked one out. They didn't have any stock." He paused as if to make sure I was following him, and all I could do was stare. "So I ordered one. Meanwhile, I ordered a sleeve. I did take some liberties, since I prefer red."

"But why?"

He laughed softly. "Man, I wish you could see your face."

I clasped my hands over my cheeks. "Why?"

"You didn't have one and I know how much blogging and that stuff means to you. Using the school computer isn't doing it for you." He shrugged. "And we really didn't do the Valentine's thing. So . . . here we are."

It hit me then that he'd been planning this all day. "When did you put it here?"

"This morning, after you left for school."

I took a deep breath. I was about five seconds from full

fan-girl mode. "And you got this for me? A MacBook Air? Those things cost a lot of money."

"Thank the taxpayers. Their money funds the DOD who then turns over the money to us." He laughed at my expression. "And I save money. I have a small fortune stashed."

"Daemon, it's too much."

"It's yours."

My gaze was drawn back to the Mac like it was my own personal mecca. How many times since I could spell *laptop* had I dreamt of a MacBook?

I wanted to laugh and cry at the same time. "I can't believe you did this."

He shrugged again. "You deserve it."

Something deep inside me snapped. I tackled Daemon, and he laughed, sweeping his arms around my waist. "Thank you. Thank you," I said over and over again, in between raining quick kisses all over his face.

He tipped his head back on the comforter, laughing. "Wow. You're pretty strong when you're excited."

I sat up, grinning down at him. His face blurred a little. "I can't believe you did this."

Smugness filled his expression. "You had no idea, did you?"

"No, but that's why you kept bringing up the blog stuff." I smacked his chest playfully. "You are . . ."

He folded his arms under his head. "I'm what?"

"Amazing." I leaned forward, kissing him. "You're amazing."

"That's what I've been saying for years."

I laughed against his mouth. "Seriously, though, you shouldn't have."

"I wanted to."

I didn't know what to say, other than scream from the top of my lungs. Getting a MacBook was like Christmas and Halloween rolled into one.

He lowered his lashes. "It's okay. I know what you want to do. Go play."

"You sure?" My fingers itched to explore.

"Yes."

Squealing, I kissed him again and then rolled off, diving for the laptop. Carrying the super-lightweight book to my bed, I sat beside Daemon and placed it in my lap. Over the next hour, I familiarized myself with the programs and went through several phases of feeling extraordinarily cool and smart for having a MacBook Air.

Daemon leaned over my shoulder, pointing out certain features. "There's the webcam."

I squeaked and then grinned when our faces appeared on the screen. "You should do your first vlog right now," he said.

Giddy, I hit record and shrieked, "I have a MacBook Air!"

Daemon laughed as he buried his head in my hair. "You dork."

I hit the stop button and noticed the time. Powering down the laptop, I placed it beside us and threw my arms around him once more. "Thank you."

He pulled me down and reached up, tucking the hair behind my ear. His hand lingered. "I like it when you're happy, and if I can do something small, then I will."

"Something small?" Shock heightened my tone. "That's not something small. That had to have cost—"

"It doesn't matter. You're happy. I'm happy."

My chest swelled. "I love you. You know that, right?"

A cocky grin appeared. "I know."

I waited. Nothing. Rolling my eyes, I sat up on the other side of him and kicked off my shoes. Glancing out the bedroom window, I saw nothing but beautiful blue skies. It was nice enough for flip-flops. Flip-flops!

"You're never going to say it, are you?"

"Say what?" The bed shifted as he sat up, placing his hands on my hips.

I looked over my shoulder. Thick lashes shielded his eyes. "You know what."

"Hmm?" He slid his hands up my sides, distracting as usual.

It might bother some girls that their boyfriends never said the four-letter word. With any other guy, it might've bothered me, too, to be honest, but with Daemon, well, those words would never be easy for him to say, even though he had no problem showing it.

And I was okay with it. Didn't mean I wouldn't tease him about it, though.

He pressed a kiss to my cheek and slid off the bed. "I'm glad you like it."

"I *love* it."

Daemon raised an eyebrow.

"Seriously, I do love it. I can't thank you enough."

Now he waggled that brow. "I'm sure you can."

I stood and pushed him lightly as I scanned my bedroom floor for my flip-flops. I hadn't really looked for anything since the night Carissa had been here. I was still finding stuff they'd put away in odd places. Dipping down, I lifted up the edge of my polka-dotted comforter and peered into the no-man's-land under my bed.

Several loose sheets of notebook paper cluttered the floor. Rolled socks were everywhere. One sneaker was near the top, next to a couple of magazines. The other sneaker was nowhere to be found and appeared to have run off with half the socks, since none of them looked like a match.

The flip-flops were halfway in the middle. I lay down and stretched, smacking at the floor.

"What are you doing?" Daemon asked.

"Trying to get my flip-flops."

"Is it really that hard?"

Ignoring him, I concentrated on the shoes and willed them toward me. A second later, one hit my hand and when the second pair hit, something warm and smooth-feeling bounced off my palm.

"What the . . . ?"

Tossing the flip-flops aside, I felt around until my hand landed on the object. I wiggled out from under the bed and sat up, opening my palm.

"Oh my God," I said.

"What?" Daemon knelt beside me and sucked in a sharp breath. "Is that what I think it is?"

Resting in my palm was a shiny black stone with red streaked through the center, like a vibrant red flame. It must've been Carissa's and although the bracelet portion wasn't attached and must've been destroyed along with her body, this survived.

I was holding a piece of opal.

31

We sort of stared at each other like two doofuses, and then we both sprang into action. Taking the stone that was a little bigger than a nickel, we went downstairs. Our heart rates picked up.

I handed him the stone. "Try something—like that reflection thing."

Daemon, who'd probably been jonesing for a piece of opal since he learned what they could do, didn't refuse. He wrapped his palm around it, and concentration tightened the line of his mouth.

At first nothing happened, and then a faint shimmer surrounded the outline of his body. Like when Dee got excited and her arm would glimmer and fade, but then the shine spread over his body and he disappeared.

Completely disappeared.

"Daemon?" A soft chuckle came from the vicinity of the couch. My eyes narrowed. "I can't see you at all."

"Not at all?"

I shook my head. Weird. He was here, but I couldn't see him. Stepping back, I forced myself to focus on the couch. Then I noticed the difference. In front of the middle cushion and behind the coffee table, the space was distorted. Sort of wavy, like looking at water through glass, and I knew he had to be standing there, blending in like a chameleon.

"Oh my God, you're totally like the *Predator*."

There was a pause and then, "This is so cool." Moments later he reappeared, grinning like a kid who just got his first video game. "God, I am so going to sneak into your bathroom like the Invisible Man."

I rolled my eyes. "Give me the opal."

Laughing, he handed it over. The stone was body temperature, which I thought was weird. "Want to hear something crazier than me being completely invisible? It barely took any energy away. I feel fine."

"Wow." I turned the stone over. "We need to test this out."

Taking the stone, Daemon and I headed to the lake. We had about fifteen minutes before anyone else showed.

"You try it," Daemon said.

Holding the opal in my palm, I wasn't sure what to try. The hardest thing and the one that took the most strength was using the Source as a weapon. So I decided to go with that. I concentrated on the rush and it felt different this time—potent and consuming. Tapping into it came faster, easier, and within seconds, a ball of whitish-red light appeared over my free hand.

"Wow," I said, smiling. "This is . . . different."

Daemon nodded. "Do you feel tired or anything?"

"No." And usually this wiped me out pretty darn quickly, so the opal really did have an impact. Then I got an idea. Letting the Source fizzle out, I searched the ground and found a small branch.

Taking it to the bank of the lake, I squeezed the opal in one hand. "I could never do the heat-to-fire thing. Burned my fingers pretty badly the last time I tried it."

"Should you be trying it now, then?"

Ah, good point. "But you're here to heal me."

Daemon frowned. "Worst logic ever, Kitten."

I grinned as I focused on the branch. The Source flared once again, traveling along the slender, crooked twig of a branch, encasing it whole. A second later, the stick collapsed into an ash replica, and as the whitish-red light receded, the branch fell apart.

"Uh," I said.

"That wasn't fire, but it was pretty damn close."

I'd never done anything like that before. Had to be the opal-enhanced alien coolness, because I just turned a stick into Pompeii.

"Let me have it," Daemon said. "I want to see if it has any effect on the onyx."

Handing it over, I followed him to the pile of onyx, wiping the ash off my fingers. Holding the opal in one hand, he uncovered the stones and, jaw clenching, he picked one up.

Nothing happened. All of us had grown a tolerance to the rocks, but there was usually a gasp or flinch of pain.

"What's happening?" I asked.

Daemon lifted his chin. "Nothing—I don't feel anything."

"Let me try." We switched off and he was right. The bite of onyx wasn't there. We stared at each other. "Holy crap."

Footsteps and voices carried into the clearing. Daemon swiped the opal, sliding it in his pocket. "I don't think we should let Blake see this."

"No doubt," I agreed.

We turned as Matthew, Dawson, and Blake appeared at the edge of the woods. It would be interesting to see if the opal had any affect in Daemon's pocket or if we had to be physically touching it.

"I talked to Luc," Blake announced while we were all standing around the onyx. "He's good for this Sunday, and I think we'll be ready by then."

"You think?" Dawson said.

He nodded. "It's either going to work or not."

Failure wasn't an option. "So the Sunday after prom?"

"You guys are going to prom?" Blake asked, scowling.

"Why not?" I said defensively.

Blake's eyes darkened. "Just seems like a stupid thing to do the night before. We should be spending Saturday training."

"No one asked for your opinion," Daemon said, hands curving into fists.

Dawson shifted closer to his brother. "One night isn't going to hurt anything."

"And I have prom duty," Matthew said, sounding absolutely disgusted with the idea.

Outnumbered, Blake let out a disgruntled mumble. "Fine. Whatever."

We got started then, and I kept my eyes trained on Daemon when it came to his turn. When he touched the onyx, he immediately flinched but held on. Unless he was faking it, the opal had to be touching flesh. Good to know.

Over the next couple of hours, we did our rounds with the onyx. I was seriously beginning to think my fingers and muscle control would never be the same again. Blake kept the required ten feet distance and didn't try to talk to me. I liked to think my come-to-Jesus discussion had gotten through to him.

If not . . . then, well, I doubted I'd be able to control myself.

As we broke apart for the night, I lingered back with Daemon. "It didn't work in your pocket, did it?"

"No." He dug the thing out. "I'm going to hide this somewhere. Right now, I don't think we need anyone fighting over it or it getting into the wrong hands."

I agreed. "Do you think we're ready for this Sunday?" My stomach dropped thinking about it, no matter how long I'd known that this day was coming.

Daemon slipped the opal back into his pocket and then gathered me in his arms. Anytime he held me, it always felt unbelievably right and I wondered how I could've denied it for so long.

"We're going to be as ready as we ever will be." He brushed his cheek along mine and I shivered, closing my eyes. "And I don't think we can keep Dawson off much longer."

I nodded and wrapped my arms around him. Now or never. Oddly, in that moment, I felt like we didn't have enough time, even though we'd been practicing for months. Maybe it wasn't that.

Maybe I just felt we didn't have enough time together.

O n Saturday, Lesa and I piled into the back of Dee's Jetta. Windows rolled down, we enjoyed the seasonally warm temps. Dee seemed different today, too. It wasn't the pretty pink summer dress she'd worn, paired with a black cardigan and strappy sandals. Her hair was pulled up in a loose ponytail and her thick hair cascaded down her back, revealing a perfectly symmetrical face that bore an easy grin—not the one I was so familiar with and missed painfully, but *almost*. She was lighter somehow, her shoulders less tense.

Right now, she hummed along to a rock song on the radio, speeding around cars like a Nascar driver.

Today was a turning point.

Lesa grasped the back of Ash's seat, face pale. "Uh, Dee, you do realize this is a no passing zone, right?"

Dee grinned in the rearview mirror. "I think it's a suggestion, not a rule."

"I think it's a rule," Lesa advised.

Ash snorted. "Dee thinks yield signs are a suggestion, too."

I laughed, wondering how I could've forgotten Dee's terrifying driving. Normally I'd be clutching a seat or handle too, but today I couldn't care as long as she got us to the shop in one piece.

And she did.

And we only narrowly avoided wiping out a family of four plus a religious tour bus once.

The shop was downtown, occupying an old row house. Ash's pert little nose wrinkled as her heels touched the gravel we parked on. "I know it looks less than savory from the outside, but it's really not bad. They have cool dresses."

Lesa studied the old brick building, doubtful. "Are you sure?"

Sashaying past her, Ash cast a mischievous grin over her shoulder. "When it comes to clothing, I'll never steer you wrong." Then she frowned and reached out, flicking green-painted nails along Lesa's shirt. "We need to go shopping one day."

Lesa's mouth dropped open as Ash spun and headed toward the back door that bore an OPEN sign written in elegant calligraphy.

"I'm going to hit her," Lesa said under her breath. "You just watch. I'm gonna break that pretty nose of hers."

"I'd try to resist that urge if I were you."

She smirked. "I could take her."

Ah, no, she couldn't.

Finding dresses didn't take very long. Ash went with one that barely covered her ass, and I found a really great red dress I just knew Daemon would go gaga for. Afterward, we headed to Smoke Hole Diner.

Going out to eat with Lesa felt good, and Dee being there was like the proverbial icing on the cake. Ash? I wasn't so sure about that part.

I ordered a hamburger while Ash and Dee ordered practically everything on the menu. Lesa went with a grilled cheese sandwich and something I found entirely gross. "I don't know why you drink cold coffee. You can just get regular coffee and let it grow cold."

"So not the same," Dee answered as the waitress put our sodas down. "Tell them, Ash."

The blonde Luxen peered up from ridiculously long eyelashes. "Chilled coffee is more sophisticated."

I made a face. "I'll be uncivilized with my warm coffee."

"Why doesn't that surprise me?" Ash arched a brow and then turned her attention back to her cellphone.

Sticking my tongue at her, I smothered a giggle when Lesa elbowed me. "I still think I should've gotten the transparent wings for my dress."

Dee smiled. "They were cute."

I nodded, thinking Daemon would've loved them.

Lesa tugged her curls out of her face. "You guys are lucky you found dresses on this short notice."

Since her and Chad had made plans to go like ordinary people months ago, she had gotten her dress from some shop in Virginia. She had gone mostly along for the ride.

As conversation picked up and Dee started talking about her dress, I sat back against the booth. Sadness trickled through me, followed by bittersweet memories. I thought I'd known Carissa, but I really hadn't. Had she known a Luxen? Or had she been picked up by Daedalus and used? Months had passed and there had been no answers; the only reminder was the piece of opal I had discovered under my bed.

Some days I'd felt nothing but anger, but today, I let it slip off my shoulders with a deep breath. What had become of Carissa couldn't tarnish her memory forever.

Ash smiled. "I'm thinking my dress will be a hit."

Lesa sighed. "I don't know why you don't just go naked. That little black dress you found is little and nothing else."

"Don't tempt her," Dee said, grinning as our food was delivered to the table.

"Naked?" Ash scuffed. "These goods aren't showed off for free."

"Surprising," Lesa muttered under her breath.

It was my turn to elbow her.

"So, are you going to the prom with anyone?" Lesa asked, ignoring me as she waved her grilled cheese sandwich at Dee. "Or are you going solo?"

Dee shrugged one shoulder. "I wasn't going to go, you know, because of . . . Adam, but it's my last year, so . . . I wanted to go." There was a pause as she pushed her chicken tender around her basket. "I'm going with Andrew."

I almost choked on my bun. Lesa gaped. We stared at her.

Her brows rose. "What?"

"You're not . . . like, going out with Andrew, are you?" Lesa's cheeks flamed—*Lesa's*. "I mean, if you are, cool and what not."

Dee laughed. "No—God, no. That would be way too weird for the both of us. We're friends."

"Andrew's a douche," Lesa said what I was thinking.

Ash snorted. "Andrew has taste. Of course you would think he's a douche."

"Andrew has changed a lot. He was there for me and vice versa." And Dee was right. Andrew had simmered down a bit. Everyone had changed. "We're just going as friends."

Thank God, because even though I didn't want to judge, Dee hooking up with Adam's brother would be way too weird. And then Ash dropped the bomb of all bombs as I munched on a thick french fry. "I have a date," she said.

I think I might've developed a hearing problem. "With who?"

One delicate eyebrow arched. "No one you would know."

"Is he . . ." I caught myself. "Is he from around here?"

Dee bit down on her lip. "He's a freshman at Frostburg. She met him at the mall in Cumberland a few weeks back."

But that didn't answer the question burning to be asked. Was he human? Dee must've read what I was dying to know in my eyes, because she nodded and grinned.

I almost dropped my soda.

Holy country roads take me home, because this was an alternate reality if Ash was going to prom with a human—a subpar, ordinary old human.

Ash rolled cerulean eyes. "I don't know why you guys are

staring at me like you're on the wrong side of special." She popped another fry into her mouth. "I would never go to the prom alone. For example—"

"Ash," Dee said, eyes narrowing.

"I went with Daemon to the prom last year," she went on, and my stomach twisted into knots, which was made worse by the secretive smile that graced her full lips. "That was a night I'll never forget."

I wanted to punch her.

Taking a deep breath, I forced a smile. "Funny because Daemon hasn't mentioned that night."

Ash's eyes flashed in warning. "He isn't the kiss and tell type, dear."

My smile turned brittle. "*That* I know."

She got my message and that conversation was thankfully dropped and Dee started talking about some TV show she was watching, which somehow sparked another argument between Ash and Lesa over who was the hottest guy on the show. I'm pretty sure those two would argue over the color of the sky.

I took Lesa's side.

In the car ride back, Lesa turned to me. "So, are you and Daemon getting a hotel room or anything?"

"Uh, no. Do people really do that?"

Lesa leaned back and laughed. "Yes. Chad and I are getting one at Fort Hill."

In the front passenger seat, Ash snickered.

"What are you doing, Ash?" Lesa asked, her eyes sharpening. "Planning to stay at prom and beat up the prom queen?"

Ash laughed in her seat but said nothing.

"Anyway," Lesa drawled. "You and Daemon haven't done it yet, right? Prom—"

"Hey!" Dee shrieked, startling us. "I'm sitting here, remember? I don't want to hear about this."

"Neither do I," Ash muttered.

Oblivious to them, Lesa stared and waited. There was no way I was answering that question. If I lied and said yes, I'd scar Dee for life and if I told the truth, I was sure Ash would go into a detailed synopsis of their past sexual activities.

Finally Lesa dropped it, but it was all I thought about thanks to her. I sighed, staring out the window. It wasn't like we weren't ready. I guess. I mean, how do you know you're really ready? I don't think anyone seriously does. Sex wasn't something you could plan. It either happened or it didn't.

Getting a hotel room with the expectation of having sex? Hotels were so . . . so skeevy.

Part of me wondered if I'd been living in a cave or something, but I hadn't. At school, in-between classes, I'd heard other girls talking about the things they hoped and planned to happen after prom. I'd heard guys talking, too. But I had my mind on other things, I supposed.

And who was I to judge? A few days ago I'd really believed the reason Daemon wanted to come over to my house after-school was to . . . do it. But heck, at the rate we were going, we'd be fifty before anything like that happened.

Pushing the whole subject out of my mind by the time we got home, I said goodbye to Lesa and even Ash. I couldn't wait until I saw this human college boy.

Dee and I were left alone.

She started toward her house while I stood there like an idiot, unsure of what to say. But she stopped and then turned around. Her lashes were lowered as she fidgeted with the edges of her hair. "I had fun today. I'm glad you came."

"Me, too."

She shifted her weight. "Daemon's going to love that dress."

"You think?" I lifted up the garment bag.

"It *is* red." She smiled, taking a step back. "Maybe before prom we can get together and get ready . . . like with Homecoming?"

"I'd love that." My smile spread so fast I bet I looked a little crazy.

She nodded, and I wanted to run up and hug her, but I wasn't sure if we were there yet. With a little wave, she spun around and headed up her porch. For a moment, I stood there with my dress and let out a happy sigh.

This was progress. Maybe things would never be like they were, but this was really good.

Heading inside, I hugged my dress bag close and kicked the door shut. Mom had already left for work, so as I took my dress upstairs and hung it on my closet door. I wondered what I was going to make myself for dinner.

Pulling out my cell phone, I sent Daemon a quick text.

> What R U doing?

He responded a few moments later.

> With Andrew & Matthew, getting dinner.
> Want smthing?

I glanced at the bag, recalling how flirty the dress was. Feeling naughty, I texted him:

> You.

The response was lightning quick, and I laughed.

> Really?

And then,

> Of course, I alrdy knew that.

And before I could respond, my phone rang. It was Daemon. I answered, grinning like an idiot. "Hey."

"I wish I were home," he said, and a car honked. "I can be there in seconds."

Heading down the steps, I stopped and leaned against the wall. "No. You rarely get guy time. Stay with them."

"I don't need guy time. I need Kitten time."

My face flushed. "Well, you can get Kitten time when you come home."

He grumbled and then, "Did you get a dress?"

"Yes."

"Will I like it?"

I smiled and then rolled my eyes when I realized I was twirling my hair. "It's red, so I think so."

"Hot damn." Someone yelled his name—sounded like Andrew—and he sighed. "Okay. I'm going back in. Want me to pick you up anything? Andrew, Dawson, and I are going to Smoke Hole."

I thought about the hamburger I just ate. I'd be hungry later. "Do they have chicken fried steak?"

"Yes."

"With homemade gravy?" I inquired, starting back down the steps.

Daemon's laugh was husky. "The best gravy around."

"Perfect. I want that."

He promised to bring me home a hungry man's portion and then hung up. I went into the living room first and dropped my cell on the coffee table. Then I swiped up one of the books I'd gotten this past week for review and headed to the kitchen for something to drink.

Flipping over the book, I read the blurb and had to slow down because I almost walked into a wall. Laughing at myself, I stepped through the doorway and looked up.

Will sat at the kitchen table.

32

The book slipped from my lifeless fingers, falling to the floor. The *smack* reverberated inside me, all around me. I sucked in a breath but it got stuck around my heart pounding off my ribs.

My eyes had to be deceiving me. He couldn't be here. And he couldn't look the way he did. It was Will . . . It was but it *wasn't*. Something was dreadfully wrong with the man.

Will sat hunched over the table with his back to the fridge. The last time I'd seen him, his dark brown hair had been thick and wavy, with a hint of gray at the temples. Patches of his skull shone under a thin layer of mousy hair now.

Will . . . Will had been a handsome man, but this man who sat before me had aged dramatically. His skin was sallow and drawn tight across his face. No fat or form whatsoever, and he reminded me of the skeleton decorations used to scare children at Halloween. Some sort of rash affected his forehead, looking like a blotch of raspberries. His lips were incredibly thin, as were his arms and his shoulders.

Only his eyes were what I remembered. Pale blue, full of strength and determination, they fixed on mine. Something else sharpened them. Resolve? Hatred? I wasn't sure, but what shone deep in them was more frightening than staring down a horde of Arum.

Will let out a dry, painful-sounding laugh. "I'm a sight for sore eyes, aren't I?"

I didn't know what to do or say. As scary as hell as it was that he was here, he was in no shape to do a thing to me. That gave me a little confidence.

He sat back against the chair; the movement looked like it hurt and winded him.

"What happened to you?" I asked.

Will stared back a long moment before sliding a hand over the table. "You're smarter than that, Katy. It's obvious. The mutation didn't hold."

That I got, but it didn't explain why he looked like the crypt keeper.

"I did plan on coming back here after a few weeks. I knew the sickness would be rough—I knew I needed time to get control of it. Then I'd come and we'd be one big, happy family."

I choked. "There would be no way I'd let that happen."

"Your mother wanted that."

My hands curled into fists.

"It seemed to hold at first." A cough racked his frail body and I almost expected him to topple over. "Weeks went by and the things I could do . . ." A weak, brittle smile split his dry lips. "Moving objects with a wave of my hand, running miles without breaking a sweat . . . I felt better than I ever had. Everything had fallen into place just like I planned, just like I *paid* for."

My horrified gaze flickered over his sunken chest. "Then what happened to you?"

His left arm twitched. "The mutation didn't hold, but that doesn't mean it didn't change me on a cellular level. Something I'd wanted to prevent ended up being . . . propelled by the mutation. My cancer," he said, lip curling. "My cancer was in remission. The statistics of a complete recovery were high, but when the mutation faded, this . . ." He waved a weak hand around himself. "This happened."

I blinked, stunned. "Your cancer came back?"

"With a vengeance," he said, laughing that terrible, fragile laugh. "There's nothing that can be done. My blood is like a toxin. My organs are failing at an abnormal rate. Apparently, the whole theory of cancer being linked to DNA may have some basis to it."

Each word he spoke seemed to exhaust him and there was no doubt he was one step, maybe two, away from death. Reluctant sympathy flooded me. How crappy was it that everything he'd done to secure his health had ultimately led to his death?

I shook my head. Irony was such a witch. "If you had just left everything alone, you'd be fine."

His eyes met mine. "You want to rub that in?"

"No." And I really didn't. If anything, I was sickened by this. "It's just sad, really sad."

He stiffened. "I don't want your pity."

Okay. I crossed my arms. "Then what do you want?"

"I want revenge."

My brows shot up. "For what? You brought this on yourself."

"I did everything right!" He slammed his fist down on the table, rattling it and surprising me. Well, he was stronger than he looked. "I did everything right. It was him—Daemon. He didn't do what he was supposed to."

"He healed you like you wanted."

"Yes! He healed me! And that gave me a temporary mutation." Another fit of coughing stole his words. "He . . . he didn't mutate me. What he did . . . was he gave himself what he wanted and enough time for him to think he got away with it."

I stared at him. "The whole healing and mutation thing isn't an exact science."

"You're correct. The DOD has dedicated entire organizations to discovering how a successful hybrid is created." No big announcement there. "But Daemon is the strongest. There was no reason why it wouldn't have held."

"There's no way of knowing what would've happened."

"Don't pretend that you don't know," he spat. "That punk knew what he was doing. I saw it in his eyes. I just didn't know what it meant then."

I looked away and then faced him. "There has to be a true want behind the healing for it to work. Anything else won't do the job . . . or at least that's what we've learned."

"That's mystical BS."

"Is it?" My gaze drifted over him. Yeah, I was being a bitch, but he locked me in a cage, tortured me, and had slept with my mom to get what he wanted. I felt sympathy for the guy, but in a twisted way, he'd gotten what he deserved. "Sure doesn't seem that way."

"You're so cocky, Katy. The last I saw of you, you were screaming your head off." He smiled again, his head wobbling on his neck.

And there went my sympathy. "What do you want, Will?"

"I told you." He stood awkwardly, swaying to the left of the table. "I want revenge."

I arched a brow. "Not sure how you're going to pull that off."

He placed one hand on the counter, supporting himself. "This is your fault—Daemon's fault. I made a deal. I held up my end of the bargain."

"Dawson wasn't where you said he was."

"No. I had him released from the office building." His smug smile came off as a grimace. "I had to give myself more time to get away. I knew Daemon would come after me."

"No. He wouldn't have, because he really didn't know if it worked or not. If so . . ." I stopped.

"We'd be joined, and there'd be nothing he could do?" he supplied. "That's what I hoped."

I watched him place a hand on his bony hip, all at once grateful that Mom would never see him like this. Will would remind her of Dad. Part of me felt like I should help Will sit down or something.

He bared yellow teeth. "But you two are joined, right? One life split into two. One of you dies, so does the other."

I snapped to attention. My stomach lurched.

He caught my reaction. "If I had to pick what I'd want to accomplish here, it would be to make him suffer, to live on without the thing he cherishes most, but . . . he's not going to die instantaneously, right? He'll know—and those seconds of him knowing . . ."

His intentions sunk in slowly. A buzzing filled my ears and my mouth dried. He wanted to kill us. With what? His evil-eye power?

Will pulled a gun out from underneath his loose shirt.

Oh, yeah, that would do it.

"You can't be serious," I said, shaking my head.

"I'm as serious as they come." He took a breath, and his chest rattled a death sound. "And then I'm going to sit here and wait for your pretty mom to come home. She's going to see your dead body first and then she'll see the business end of my gun."

My heart tripped up. Ice water slipped over my skin. The buzzing roared now. Like a switch being thrown inside me, something else took over. It wasn't timid, gullible Katy who followed him into a car. It wasn't the one who stood in the kitchen seconds ago feeling sorry for him.

This was the girl who stood before Vaughn and watched the life seep out of him.

Maybe later I would be bothered by how quickly the change came over me. How easy it was for me to go from the girl who'd just bought her prom dress and flirted with her boyfriend to this stranger who now occupied my body, ready to do anything to protect those I loved.

But right now, I didn't care.

"You're not going to hurt Daemon. You're not going to hurt me," I said. "And you are sure as hell not going to hurt my mother."

Will lifted the gun. The metal looked too heavy for his feeble hand. "What are you going to do, Katy?"

"What do you think?" I took a bold step forward, my brain and mouth propelled by this stranger. "Come on, Will, you're smart enough to figure it out on your own."

"You don't have it in you."

Calmness settled over me, and I felt my lips spread into a smile. "You don't know what I'm capable of."

Up until then, I hadn't known what I was capable of, not truly, but seeing Will, staring down the barrel of that gun, I knew exactly what I *was* capable of. And as wrong as it may be, I was okay with what I was going to have to do.

Completely accepting of it.

There was a part of me that was scared of how easy that acceptance was and I wanted to cling to the old Katy, because she would've had a problem with this. She would've been sickened by this and the words I was saying.

"You do look a little ill, Will. You might want to get checked out. Oh, wait." I widened my eyes innocently. "You can't go to a regular doctor because even though the mutation *obviously* didn't stick, I'm sure it changed you and you can't go to the DOD, because that would be like suicide."

The hand around the gun trembled. "You think you're so smart and brave, don't you, little girl?"

I shrugged. "Perhaps, but I do know I'm completely healthy. What about you, Will?"

"Shut up," he hissed.

Stepping next to the kitchen table, I eyed the gun. If I could distract him, then I could take him out. I really didn't want to test the whole stopping-a-bullet theory.

"Just think of all that money you paid, and it didn't even work out in the end," I said. "And you've lost everything—your career, your money, my mom, and your health. Karma's a tool, isn't it?"

"You stupid bitch." Spittle flew from between his chapped lips. "I'm going to kill you, and you'll die knowing that your precious freak will be dead, too. And then I'm going to sit here and wait for your mother to come home."

My humanity clicked off. I was *so* done with this.

Will smiled. "Where's your smart mouth now?"

My gaze dropped to the gun, and I felt the Source soar over my skin. My fingers splayed, their tips already tingling. Drawing in the power, I focused on the gun. His hand shook again. The muzzle of the gun swayed to the left. The trigger finger twitched.

Will's throat spasmed as he swallowed. "What . . . What are you doing?"

I lifted my gaze, and I smiled.

His bloodshot eyes widened. "You—"

I waved my hand to the left and several things happened next. There was a popping sound, like a cork being pulled from a champagne bottle, but the sound and everything else was lost in the roar of electricity that flowed outward and then the gun flew from his hand.

It was like a bolt of lightning—pure and raw.

The stream of whitish-red light arced across the room, slamming into Will's chest. Maybe—maybe if he wasn't so ill, it wouldn't have done much, but the man was weak and I wasn't.

He flew backward, bouncing off the wall next to the fridge, his head flopping on his neck like a rag doll. He made no sound as he hit the floor in a boneless heap. That was it—it was over. No more wondering about Will or where he was, what he was doing. This part of our lives was closed.

My house is like the killing fields, I thought.

I exhaled and something—I don't know, something went wrong. Air was stuck in my throat, in my lungs, but when I dragged in a breath, there was this burning pain I hadn't noticed before. But as the Source receded back into me, the burning grew across my chest, spread over my stomach.

I looked down.

A red inkblot had formed on the pale blue shirt and it spread . . . larger and larger, an irregular circle that bled.

I pressed my hands against the circle—it was damp, warm, and sticky. Blood. It was blood—my blood. My head swam.

"Daemon," I whispered.

33

I don't remember falling, but I was staring at the ceiling, trying to keep my hands pressed to the gunshot wound, because I'd seen people do that on TV, but I couldn't feel my hands, so I wasn't sure if they were there or by my sides.

My face was wet.

I was going to die in minutes, maybe sooner, and I'd failed Daemon and my mom. Failed them, because Daemon would die, too, and my mom—oh, God, my mom would come home to find this. She wouldn't survive this, not after Dad.

A shudder rolled through my body and my chest labored for breath. I didn't want to die alone on the cold, hard floor. I didn't want to die at all. I blinked and when I reopened my eyes, the ceiling was fuzzy.

Nothing really hurt, though. Books got that right. There was a point where there was so much pain I couldn't process it or I was beyond it. Probably beyond it . . .

The front door opened and a familiar voice called out, "Katy? Where are you? Something's wrong with Daemon . . ."

My lips worked, but there was no sound. I tried again. "Dee?"

Footsteps crept closer and then, "Oh my God . . . oh my God."

Dee was suddenly in my line of sight, her face fuzzy around the edges. "Katy—holy crap, Katy . . . hold on." She moved my bloodstained hands away and placed hers over the wound as she looked up, seeing Will crumpled beside the fridge. "God . . ."

I worked to get out one word. "Daemon . . ."

She blinked rapidly, her form fading out for a second and then her face was in front of mine, her eyes glowing like diamonds, and I couldn't look away. Her eyes, her words, consumed me. "Andrew is bringing him over. He's okay. He's going to be okay, because you're going to be okay. Got that?"

I coughed out a response and something wet and warm covered my lips. It had to be bad—blood—because Dee's face paled even more as she placed both of her hands over the wound and closed her eyes.

My lids seemed way too heavy and the sudden warmth radiating from hers ebbed and flowed through me. Her shape faded out and she was in her true form—bright and lustrous like an angel—and I thought if I were to die, then at least I saw something as beautiful as this before the end.

But I had to hang on, because it wasn't just my life that hung in the balance. It was Daemon's. So I forced my eyes open, kept them trained on Dee, watching as her light flickered over the walls, bathing the room. If she healed me, would we be linked? The three of us? I couldn't wrap my head around that. And it wouldn't be fair to Dee.

And then there were voices. I recognized Andrew's and Dawson's. There was a *thud* beside my head and then *he* was there, his beautiful face pale and strained. I'd never seen him so pale, and if I concentrated, I could feel his heart laboring like mine. His hands were shaking as they touched my cheeks, smooth under my parted lips.

"Daemon . . ."

"Shh," he said, smiling. "Don't talk. It's okay. Everything is okay."

He turned to his sister, gently pulling her stained hands back. "You can stop now."

She must've responded directly to him, because Daemon shook his hand. "We can't risk you doing this. You have to stop."

Someone, it sounded like Andrew, said, "Man, you're too weak to do this." And then I realized it was him, and he was on my other side. I think he held my hand. I may've been hallucinating, though, because I saw two Daemons.

Wait. The second one was Dawson. He was holding Daemon, keeping him in an upright position. Daemon never needed help. He was the strongest—*is* the strongest. Panic blossomed.

"Let Dee do this," Andrew urged.

Daemon shook his head and after what seemed like forever, Dee pulled back and took on her human form. She scrambled out of the way, arms shaking.

"He's crazy," she said. "He's absolutely crazy."

When Daemon slipped into his true form and placed his hands on me, there was only him then. The rest of the room slipped away. I didn't want him to heal me if he was already weak, but I got why he didn't want Dee to do it. Too risky, not knowing how or if it would link the three of us together.

Heat flowed through me and then I wasn't really thinking. Daemon's voice was in my thoughts, murmuring reassurances over and over again. I felt light, airy, and complete.

Daemon . . . I said his name over and over again. I don't know why, but it was grounding to just hear his name.

And when I closed my eyes, they didn't reopen. The renewing warmth was in every cell, easing through my veins, settling into my muscles and bones. Heat and safety pulled me under and the last thing I heard was Daemon's voice.

You can let go now.

I did.

When I opened my eyes again, a candle somewhere in the room flickered and danced in the shadows. I couldn't move my arms and I didn't know where I was for a second, but as I dragged in a deep breath, an earthy scent surrounded me.

"Daemon?" My voice was hoarse, dry from panic.

The bed—I was in a bed—dipped and out of the darkness came Daemon. Half of his face was bathed in shadows. His eyes glowed like diamonds.

"I'm here," he said. "Right beside you."

I swallowed, keeping my gaze fixed on him. "I can't move my arms."

There was a deep, throaty chuckle and I thought it was terrible that he would laugh when my arms couldn't move. "Here, let me fix that for you."

Daemon's hands felt around me, finding the edges of the blankets. He loosened them. "There you go."

"Oh." I wiggled my fingers and then slipped my arms out. A second later, I realized I was nude—completely nude under the blankets. Fire swept over my face and down my neck. Did we . . . ? What the heck was I not remembering?

I clasped the edge of the blanket, wincing as skin pulled over my chest. "Why am I naked?"

Daemon stared back at me. One second passed and then two, three. "You don't remember?"

It took a moment or so for my brain to process everything

and when it did, I sat up and started to jerk the blanket away. Daemon stopped me with his hand. "You're fine. There's just a tiny mark—a scar, but it's really faint," he said, his large hand surrounding mine. "Honestly, I doubt anyone would notice it unless they were looking really close, and I'd be perturbed if anyone was looking that close."

My mouth worked without sound. Around us, the candle threw shadows along the wall. It was Daemon's bedroom, because my bed wasn't nearly as comfortable or as big as his.

Will had come back. He had shot me—*shot me* right in the chest and I . . . I couldn't finish that thought.

"Dee helped get you cleaned up. So did Ash." His eyes searched my face. "They put you in the bed. I didn't . . . help them."

Ash saw me naked? Stupidly, out of everything, that made me want to crawl back under the covers. Man, I needed to get my priorities straight.

"Are you sure you're okay?" He reached to touch me but stopped, his hand lingering an inch or so from my cheek.

I nodded. I'd been shot—shot in the chest. That thought was on repeat. I'd come close to death once before, when we'd fought Baruck, but to be shot was a whole different ballpark. It was going to take me a few moments to fully comprehend that, especially since it didn't seem real.

"I shouldn't be sitting up and talking to you," I said dumbly, peering through my lashes. "This is . . ."

"I know. It's a lot." He touched me then, placing the tips of his fingers on my lips reverently. He let out a shaky breath. "It's really a lot."

I closed my eyes for a moment, soaking in the low hum and warmth his touch brought. "How did you know?"

"I felt short of breath all of a sudden," he said, dropping his hand and inching closer. "And there was this red-hot feeling in my chest. My muscles wouldn't work right. I knew something had happened. Luckily, Andrew and Dawson were able to get me outside without causing a scene. Sorry, no chicken fried steak."

I didn't think I'd ever eat again.

A smile appeared on his lips. "I'd never been so scared in my life. I had Dawson call Dee to check on you. I . . . was too weak to get here myself."

I recalled how pale he'd looked and that Dawson had been supporting him. "How do you feel now?"

"Perfect." He tilted his head to the side. "You?"

"I feel fine." Only a dull soreness lingered, but it was nothing. "You saved my life—our lives."

"It was nothing."

I gaped. Only Daemon would think something like this was nothing. And then another new concern rose. Twisting on the bed, I searched out the bedside clock in the dark. Digital green lights showed that it was only a little past one in the morning. I'd slept for about six hours.

"I have to go home," I said, gathering the blanket around me. "There has to be blood and when my mom comes home in the morning, I don't—"

"It's all been taken care of." He stilled me. "They took care of Will and the house is fine. When your mom comes home, she won't know anything happened."

Relief was potent and I relaxed, but it didn't last long. An image surfaced of standing in the kitchen, smiling at Will and goading him, sending a shudder through me. Silence fell between us as I stared into the darkened room, replaying the evening over and over. I kept getting caught on how calm I had become, how cold I'd felt when that part of me decided I was going to have to . . . have to kill Will.

And I had.

A bitter taste filled the back of my throat. I had killed people and that was even counting the Arum. A life was a life,

Daemon had said. So how many had I killed? Three? So I'd killed four living creatures.

My breath rose and got stuck around the quickly rising lump in my throat. What was worse than the knowledge that I had taken lives was my acceptance of doing so. I'd had no qualms about what I did when it happened and that wasn't me—that couldn't be me.

"Kat," he said softly. "Kitten, what are you thinking?"

"I killed him." Tears welled up and spilled down my cheeks before I could stop them. "I killed him, and I didn't care at all."

He placed his hands on my bare shoulders. "You did what you had to do, Kat."

"No. You don't understand." My throat tightened and I struggled for breath. "I didn't *care*. And I should care about these kinds of things." I laughed hoarsely. "Oh, God . . ."

Pain flickered in his bright gaze. "Kat—"

"What's wrong with me? Something *is* wrong with me. I could've just disarmed him and stopped him. I didn't have to—"

"Kat, he tried to kill you. He shot you. You acted out of self-defense."

It all sounded reasonable to him. But had I? The man was weak and frail. Instead of goading him, I could've disarmed him and that was it. But I killed him . . .

My control slipped and broke. I felt twisted inside, balling up into so many knots I thought I'd never be straightened out again. This whole time I had been so convinced that I could do what was necessary, that I could easily kill and when it came down to it, I *had* killed, but Daemon had been right. Killing wasn't the hard part. It was what came afterward—the guilt. It was too much. All the ghosts of those who'd died by my own hand and those who had passed on who were tied to me appeared, surrounding me and choking me until the only sound I could make was a hoarse cry.

Daemon made a sound in the back of his throat and pulled me into his arms, blankets and all. The tears came, they kept coming, and he rocked me, holding me close. And it didn't seem right or fair that he'd comfort me. He didn't know how easy it had been for me to throw that switch, to become someone else. I wasn't the same girl. Not the Katy who had changed him and inspired him to be different.

I wasn't *her*.

I struggled to pull free, but he held on and I hated that—hated that he didn't see what I saw. "I'm a monster. I'm like Blake."

"What?" Disbelief thickened his tone. "You are nothing like him, Kat. How can you say that?"

Tears streaked down my cheeks. "But I am. Blake—he killed because he was desperate. How is what I did any different? It's not!"

He shook his head. "It's not the same."

I dragged in air by the lungful. "I'd do it again. I swear I would. If anyone threatened my mom or you, I would. And I knew that after everything that had happened with Blake and Adam. That's not how people react—it's not right."

"There's nothing wrong with protecting those you love," he argued. "Do you think I've enjoyed killing those I have? I haven't. But I wouldn't go back and change those things."

I wiped at my cheeks as my shoulders shook. "Daemon, it's different."

"How is it?" He grasped my face in his hands, forcing me to look at him through tear-soaked lashes. "Remember when I took out those two DOD officers at the warehouse? I hated that I did it, but I had no other choice. If they reported back that they'd seen us, it would all be over and I wasn't going to let them take you."

His fingers chased after the tears and he dipped his head, catching my gaze when I tried to look away. "And I hated what I have done—I hated every time I've taken a life, Arum or human, but sometimes, there is no other choice. You don't accept it. You don't become okay with it, but you do come to understand it."

I grasped his wrists. They were so thick that my fingers barely met. "But what . . . what if I was okay with it?"

"You're not okay with it, Kat." His belief in that statement, in me, rang true in his voice, and I couldn't understand that blind faith. "I know you're not."

"How can you be so sure?" I whispered.

Daemon smiled a little. Not a full breathtaking kind of smile, but it still reached down into me, wrapping around my heart. "I know you're good inside. You're warmth and light and everything I don't deserve, but you—you believe that I deserve you. Knowing all that I have done in my past to other people and to you, you still believe I deserve you."

"I—"

"And that's because you're good inside—you've always been and will be." His hands slipped down my throat, to curve around my shoulders. "There is nothing you can say or do that will change that. So grieve what you *had* to do. Mourn it, but never, ever blame yourself for things that are beyond your control."

I didn't know what to say.

His smile slipped into that smug half grin that infuriated and thrilled me. "Now get the rest of that crap out of your head, because you're so much better than that; you're more than that."

His words, well, they may not have washed away everything and they may not have changed the part in me that wasn't as perfect as he thought, but they wrapped around me like a soft down comforter. They were enough for that moment to . . . to understand what I had done and that was important, that was enough. There weren't any words for how much I appreciated what he said and what he had done. A thank-you wasn't enough.

Still shaking, my hands balled up into those tiny knots, I leaned forward and pressed my lips against his. His fingers tightened around my shoulders as his chest rose sharply. I tasted my own salty tears on his lips and as the kiss deepened, I tasted my own fear.

But there was more.

There was our love—there was our hope that we'd walk out of this with a future. There was our acceptance of each other—the good, the bad, and the downright ugly. There was so much pent-up longing. So much emotion that it packed a sucker punch straight to my soul and his, I knew it, because I could feel his heart rate picking up. Mine matched his—made for his. All of that was in a simple kiss and it was too much, not enough, and just perfect.

I pulled back, drawing in a sharp breath. Our eyes locked. A wealth of emotion shone in his brilliant green eyes. He cupped my cheek with one hand tenderly, and he spoke in his lovely language. It sounded like three lyrical words—a short, beautiful verse.

"What did you say?" I asked, my fingers loosening around the cover.

His smile was secretive and then his lips were on mine again and my eyes drifted shut. I let go of the blanket, felt it slip away, pool around my hips, and I felt Daemon stop breathing for a moment.

He guided me back, and I wrapped my arms around him. We kissed for what felt like an eternity and that wasn't long enough. I could keep going, never stop, because in that moment, we created a world where nothing else existed. We lost ourselves in each other for a while and time, it sped and crept by in the same instance. We kissed until I was breathless, pausing only to explore each other. We were warm and flushed, twisting against each other. My body arched against his and when I moaned, he stilled.

He lifted his head but said nothing. Stared for so long and so hard that every point in my body seemed stretched too far. My chest squeezed. I reached up, placing my trembling hand on his cheek.

His head dipped against my cheek, and his voice was rough and raw. "Tell me to stop and I will."

I wasn't going to. Not now. Not after everything. There was nothing to deny anymore, and my answer was to kiss him, and without words, he understood.

He settled over me, not touching, not quite. The electricity between us snapped and pulled. A wild feeling pulsed through me. I lifted my hands, sinking them into his hair, pulling him closer. I swept my lips over his, and his body trembled. His fiery eyes drifted shut as my thumb moved on his bottom lip. My hands were on the move, slipping over the thick cords in his neck and back, around his chest and down. Lower, over the hard planes of his stomach. He sucked in a sharp breath.

The edges of his body started to glow, casting the room in a soft light. Heat rolled off his body. Daemon's eyes snapped open and he sat up, pulling me into his lap. His eyes were no longer green, just orbs of pure light. My heart tripped over itself. A fire started in my stomach, spreading through me like a wave of lava.

His hands trembled on my hips and the sudden onslaught of fresh, unbridled power washed over me. It was like touching fire or being hit by a thousand volts of electricity. It was exhilarating.

I'd never been more excited, more ready.

When his lips met mine, a thousand emotions erupted in me. His taste was delicious and addictive. I pressed against him, our kisses deepening until I was swimming in heady sensations that beat against every pore in my body. Everywhere we touched my skin came alive. His lips trailed a fiery path from mine to the column of my throat. All around us, his light flickered, like a thousand stars lining the walls, fading in and out.

Our hands were everywhere. His fingers were on my stomach, moving up, between my ribs. There seemed to be something slower about this. Each touch was measured and precise. Breathing became difficult as our explorations grew. This was definitely not his first time at any of this, but he didn't rush and he shook as much as I did.

His jeans ended up somewhere on his floor and our bodies were flush. Hands delving lower and lower. Daemon took his time even when I was pushing him to go faster. He slowed it down, made it last for what felt like forever . . . until neither of us could wait any longer. I remembered what Dee had said about her first time. There was no awkwardness here. Most things were expected. Daemon had protection and there was *discomfort* . . . at first. Okay. It hurt, but Daemon . . . He made it *better*. And then we were moving against each other.

Being this way with him was like tapping into the Source but more powerful. The roller-coaster feeling was there, but different and deeper, and he was right there with me. It was more than perfect and beautiful.

After what felt like hours later and honestly could've been, Daemon kissed me softly, deeply. "Are you okay?"

My bones felt like mush in a totally good way. "I'm perfect." And then I yawned, right in his face. How romantic.

Daemon busted into laughter, and I turned my cheek into the pillow, trying to hide. He didn't let me, though. As if I expected anything less. He rolled onto his side, pulling me against him, tilting my head toward his.

His eyes searched mine. "Thank you."

"For what?" I loved the feel of his arms around me and how I fit against him, hard against soft.

He trailed his fingers over my arm, and I was amazed by how he could make me shiver. "For everything," he said.

Elation swelled inside my chest, and as we lay in each other's arms, our breaths coming out ragged, our bodies tangled together, we still couldn't get enough of each other. We kissed. We talked. We *lived*.

34

When I left Daemon's house early Sunday morning, he stayed with me until he heard my mom's car pull up the driveway. Then he did that freaky, super speed alien thing and got out without being seen. But while he'd lay there in bed beside me, apparent that he didn't want to leave me alone after what happened with Will, I never felt safer in my life. Sex had nothing to do with that, but when he came back in the afternoon and we left to get lunch for us and my mom, every small look and brush of our skin meant something infinitely more—a tender and knowing quality that had been there before, but was emphasized.

I didn't look any different. Part of me thought it would be posted on my forehead or something and I was half afraid that my mom would somehow guess and then we'd have that mortifying birds and the bees' conversation again, but she didn't.

Life went on and for a little while. It was the same . . . a little better in some areas, but over the next week, Daemon and I had very little time together. No one talked about Will with the exception of asking if I was okay. Even Andrew had asked and sounded genuine. Other than that, it was like that event never happened. There was a really good chance that Daemon had something to do with that.

Our practices had increased with Dawson, Matthew, and Blake, and they also included the rest of our crew. Everyone knew their plan. Everyone also knew that we wouldn't get another chance after Sunday if we failed.

We were already pushing our luck.

Blake stood apart from the group. He'd been that way since I'd confronted him about his creepy, stalkerish behavior . . . Thank God. "The time frame is still the same. We have fifteen minutes to get in and get out with them."

"And if anything goes wrong?" Dee asked, nervously twirling her hair around her faded fingers.

Daemon picked up a piece of Onyx. All of us at this point could handle it for about a minute and twenty seconds. And with the tiny piece of opal, it didn't even bother Daemon and I.

"We'll be fine with the onyx shields." He tossed the rock back into the pile. "Each of us can withstand it long enough."

"But it's not being sprayed in your faces," Dee protested, eyes wide. "You're just handling it."

Blake inched closer. "It was never sprayed in my face. All I did was handle it over and over again. It's the only logical explanation."

"No. It's not." She let go of her hair and faced her brothers. "Handling onyx and having a tolerance is one thing. Having it sprayed in your face is totally different."

Dee had a point, but it was all we could do.

Dawson smiled for her and it was always strange to me when he did smile, because it was so rare to see a real one, and it transformed his face. "We're going to be okay, Dee. I promise."

"And the lasers—you have the lasers to watch out for," Andrew threw in, grimacing.

"No doubt," Blake said. "But they shouldn't be an issue. The emergency doors are activated only when the alarm goes off and if everything goes smoothly, we'll be fine."

"That's a big if," Dee muttered.

Heck ya, it was a huge if, but we were in this to the end. Just looking at Dawson reaffirmed why we were about to put our lives on the line again. Because I knew beyond a doubt, if it were Daemon locked in Mount Weather, I'd take as many risks as there were to free him.

Part of Dawson was missing and the other half was Beth. None of us could expect him to walk away from this. And all of us would go to the end of the earth for the ones we loved.

After another grueling session with the onyx, we called it a night and gimped back to the houses. Matthew and the Thompsons left, as did Blake. Dee went inside while the three of us lingered and finally Dawson disappeared somewhere around the side of the house.

Daemon took my hand and sat on the third step up, pulling me down between his legs, so that my back was against his chest. "You feeling okay?"

"Yes," I said. It was the same question he asked every, single time after practice. And yeah, I sort of loved him for that. "You?"

"You don't need to worry about me."

I rolled my eyes, but leaned back, liking the feel of his chest and the way his arms circled me. He dipped his head, pressing his lips against my pulse. I could tell where his mind was going and I was on board that train.

Dawson reappeared, the fading sun casting a halo around him. That train came to a crashing halt. He shoved his hands into his jeans and rocked back on heels, not saying a word.

Daemon sighed and straightened. "What is it?"

"Nothing," he said, eyes squinting at the rapidly darkening sky. "I was just thinking."

We waited quietly, because we both knew that Dawson couldn't be rushed. He'd say whatever it was he wanted to say when he was ready. Again, I found myself wondering what he was like before all this terrible stuff had happened to him.

Finally, Dawson said, "You guys don't need to do this on Sunday."

Daemon's arms fell away. "What?"

"You guys shouldn't have to do this. Dee's right. It's too much of a risk. We don't know if we really are going to be able to walk past those onyx shields. Who knows what Blake's deal is really? This doesn't involve you all."

Dawson looked at us then, expression full of sincerity. "You shouldn't be doing this. Let Blake and I go in. It's our risks to take."

Daemon fell silent for several moments. "You're my brother, Dawson, so whatever risk is yours, it is mine."

I smiled, tipping my head back. "And whatever risk is Daemon's, is mine."

"*That* I don't agree with, but you get what we're saying?" Daemon placed his hands on my shoulders. "We're in this together, for the good and the downright crappy."

Dawson's lashes lowered. "I don't want to see either of you two get hurt. I don't think I could live with that."

"We're not going to get hurt," Daemon said, so strongly that there was no doubt in my mind that he believed this to be true. His hands landed on my shoulders, gently rubbing the tensed muscles. "All of us are going to walk out of there, along with Beth and Chris."

Pulling his hands out of his pocket, Dawson thrust them through his hair. "Thank you." His lips twitched as he lowered his hands. "You know, I'm going . . . I'm going to have to leave afterward? Maybe . . . I can finish out the semester, but Beth and I will have to leave."

Daemon's hands stilled and I felt his heart trip over itself, but then his hands started up again. "I know, brother. We'll make sure that Beth is hidden until you're ready to leave. It's going to suck, but . . . but I know what you have to do."

His brother nodded. "We'll stay in touch."

"Of course," Daemon said.

Lowering my gaze, I bit my lip. Man, I sort of wanted to start balling. Their family shouldn't be split up again. All of this because of what they were and none of them brought this on themselves. It wasn't fair.

Worst of all, it didn't seem like there was anything we could do about it.

Thursday evening, after another skin-numbing training session, Daemon and I caved to our mad sugar need by hitting up the local fast-food joint—sweet tea for the win. Instead of going in, he lowered the latch on the back of his SUV and we chilled out.

The skies were clear and the glimmering stars started to fill up the heavens. Whenever I looked at the stars, I thought of Daemon and his kind.

He elbowed me playfully. "What are you thinking?"

I grinned around the straw. "Sometimes I forget what you are, but then I see those stars, and I remember."

"Do you forget what you are?"

Laughing, I lowered my cup. "Yeah, I guess I do."

"Nice."

I swung my feet back and forth. "But seriously, I really do. I think that if the public knew about you guys, they'd get used to the Luxen."

"Really?" He sounded shocked.

I shrugged. "You guys really aren't any different."

"Besides the whole glowworm thing," he teased.

"Yeah, besides that."

He chuckled and leaned in, rubbing his chin along my shoulder like a big cat. Thinking he'd like the idea of him being compared to a lion or something, I grinned. "I want you to carry the opal on you on Sunday," he said.

"What?" I pulled away and twisted toward him. "Why? You're the stronger one out of all of us."

A cocky grin appeared. "And that's why I don't need the opal."

"Daemon." I sighed, handing over the rest of the tea. He took it. "Your logic fails. Because you are stronger, the opal will do more for you than any of us."

He sipped the tea, his eyes practically twinkling. "I want you to wear the opal in case anything goes wrong. I'm not arguing with you."

"Whatever." I crossed my arms.

"And if you don't agree, I'll tie you up—and not in the fun way—and lock you in your bedroom."

My mouth dropped open.

"Okay, maybe in the fun way. Like later, after everything is done, I'll come back and—"

I cut him off. "I'd like to see you try to tie me up."

His eyebrow arched. "I bet you would."

"Shut up," I growled. "I'm being serious."

"So am I. You're wearing the opal."

I scowled. "This makes no sense."

"It makes perfect sense." He kissed my cheek. "Because I'm perfect."

"Oh, dear God." I elbowed him, and he laughed. I turned my gaze back to the starry sky and then it hit me like a cement truck. How could we have not thought about this before? "I have an idea!"

"Does it involve getting naked?"

I elbowed Daemon. "God. No. You're such a perv. It involves the opal. What if we can break it up into pieces and share it between us?"

His brows furrowed in concentration. "It could work, but it's a huge risk. What if we shatter the rock? I doubt it would work in powder form. And even if we did manage to break it into pieces, will it still be effective?"

All good questions. "I don't know, but can't we try? Then everyone is protected, at least some."

He didn't say anything for a long moment. "It's so much of a risk. I'd rather know that you're protected instead of hoping that you are. And I know that makes me sound selfish, but I am. I am *incredibly* selfish when it comes to you."

"But Dawson . . . ?"

Daemon looked at me. "Like I said, I'm incredibly selfish when it comes to you."

I honestly didn't know what to say.

He sighed as he rubbed his palm along his jaw. "If we ended up destroying the piece of opal, then you go in there with nothing backing you up. Matthew, Dawson, and I are Luxen. We are going to be stronger than you. We won't tire as easily. We don't need the piece of opal, not like you do."

"But—"

"I'm not willing to risk it. If breaking up the opal weakens it, then how does it really help you out?" He shook his head. "We don't need the extra boost. You do."

My shoulders slumped at the finality in his words. Frustration swelled inside me. It wasn't that I didn't get what he was saying, we just didn't agree.

Later on, Daemon retrieved the opal from wherever his hidey-hole was and pressed it into my palm, wrapping his hand around mine as we stood on my porch. Night birds sung out around us, a canopy of chirps and calls. The spring roses

I'd planted after school a week before filled the air with a clean, fresh scent.

It would be romantic if I didn't want to punch him in the face.

"I know you're mad." His eyes met mine. "But this makes me feel better about everything. Okay?"

"A few days ago you told Dawson that nothing was going to go wrong."

"I did, but just in case . . . I want you to be able to get out no matter what."

My heart stuttered. "What . . . what are you saying?"

He smiled, but it was forced and I hated it. "If something goes wrong, I want you to get out of there. If you have to leave this damn town or state, do it. And if for whatever reason I can't get out of there, you don't stop. Do you understand?"

Air rushed out of my lungs painfully. "You want me to leave you?"

Daemon's eyes were brilliant as he nodded. "Yes."

"No," I cried out, wrenching away. "I will never leave you behind, Daemon."

He clasped my cheeks, holding me still. "I know—"

"No you don't!" I grasped his wrists, my fingers biting into his skin. "Would you leave me behind if something happened to me?"

"No." His face twisted into a fierce scowl. "I would never do that."

"Then how can you ask me to do the same?" I was close to tears, mainly because I couldn't bear the idea of Daemon being captured, suffering what his brother had. "You can't."

"I'm sorry." The lines of his face softened and he bent his head, quickly kissing me. "You're right. I shouldn't have asked you to do that."

I blinked furiously. "How could you even consider asking me to do something like that?" Now I really wanted to sock him, because my heart was racing and terrible, horrific images were in my head. But then . . . then I realized something.

"You caved pretty easily," I whispered, distrustful.

He laughed, sliding his arms around my shoulders, pulling me against him. "I just understand what you mean."

Uh, yeah, this was odd. I tipped my head back, searching his face for a telltale sign. But all I saw was tenderness and a bit of the smug self-assurance that was always there. I didn't bother asking him if he was hiding anything, because I doubted he'd 'fess up, and I wanted to believe that he'd seen the error of his ways.

But I wasn't stupid.

35

On the afternoon before prom, Dee stood in my bedroom, twisting my hair around a medium-barrel curling iron. While the conversation started off a bit awkward, it eased up about halfway through the styling process. The conversation was light and easy by the time she'd pinned my hair up in an intricate design that showed off all her hard work.

I was applying my own eye makeup when she sat on the edge of my bed, her hands clasped in her lap. She'd gone with a simple twist—a ponytail with her hair wrapped around it in a thick bun, a classic look that showed off her angular face perfectly.

Rubbing my pinkie under my eye, I blended the brown eyeliner. "Are you excited about tonight?"

She shrugged. "I just want to do it, because, you know, it's our last year. It's probably going to be our last year together—all of us—and I want to experience it. I know Adam would want me to go and have fun."

I placed the eyeliner in my bag and rooted around for my mascara. "He would," I said, glancing back into the bedroom. "He seemed like the kind of guy who would want the best for you, no matter what it meant for him."

A smile flickered and faded. "He was."

With a sense of sadness, I turned back to the mirror and my gaze dropped to the golden tube. She should be with Adam tonight. "Dee, I'm—"

"I know." One second she was on the bed and the next she was standing in the doorway. Her lower half faded out and wow, was that weird to see. "I know you're sorry. I know you never intended for Adam to die."

I turned toward her, twisting the piece of obsidian between my fingers. "I would change everything if I could."

Her gaze flickered away from me, settling over my shoulder. "Are you scared about tomorrow night?"

Facing the mirror once more, I blinked back tears. For a moment, it had felt like we'd come so far, but then the door had been slammed in my face. Okay, maybe we had come somewhere, but not as far as I wanted to.

So, stop being a wussy, I ordered myself. *That's a lot of makeup to waste.*

"Katy?"

"I'm scared," I admitted with a little laugh. "Who wouldn't be? But I'm trying not to think about it. That's what I did last time, and I was so freaked out."

"I would be freaked out no matter what—I *am* freaked out, actually, and all I'm doing is waiting by the car." She disappeared from the doorway in a flash and reappeared by the closet. She lovingly unwrapped my prom dress. "Just be careful and keep my brothers safe. Okay?"

My heart tripped and I didn't hesitate. "Okay."

Switching places, she finished with her makeup, and I slipped on my dress. Mom appeared in my bedroom, camera in hand, and here we went again. She snapped pictures of Dee and me, got all teary eyed, talking about how I used to play dress-up in her shoes and run around the house naked, and that was all before Dee left and Daemon arrived.

It could only get worse from there.

But when Daemon stepped into the living room where I waited, fiddling with a small clutch Mom had given me, I was struck speechless.

Daemon looked good in just about anything—jeans, sweats, a lumberjack outfit—but in a black tux tailored to his broad shoulders and narrow hips, he was absolutely amazing.

Dark waves fell across his forehead, swept to the right. He held a pretty corsage in one hand. As he straightened his tie, his gaze started at the tips of my shoes and made the slow perusal up, lingering in a few spots I hoped my mom didn't notice. His fingers stilled around the tie, and I flushed, feeling the intensity in his gaze and his approval.

Daemon did like the color red.

My cheeks had to match my dress by then.

He walked up to me with that rock-star swagger and stopped a foot before me, bent his head, and whispered, "You look beautiful."

A deep flutter started in my stomach and spread. "Thank you. You don't look so bad yourself."

Mom fluttered around like an erratic little bird, taking pictures and fussing over us. Whenever she looked at Daemon, she got the doe-eyed look on her face. She was totally smitten with him.

She took a lot of pictures of him taking the corsage out and tying it to my wrist. The corsage was a simple rose in full bloom surrounded by green leaves and baby's breath. Beautiful. We posed for Mom's pictures and the whole process was natural, nothing like Simon and homecoming. My thoughts wandered to Simon as we did a couple more pictures and Daemon swapped out the camera so we could do some of the mother-and-daughter bit.

Was Simon alive? Blake had sworn that the last he'd seen Simon, the boy had been alive as the DOD carted him away. Whatever happened to Simon was because he had seen me lose control of the Source. Another possible death linked to me, and Simon *had* to be dead, because what would the DOD or Daedalus want with him alive? He was just human . . .

I thought of Carissa.

Daemon placed his hand on my lower back. "Where are you at?"

I blinked, drawn back into the present. "I'm here, right with you."

"I hope so."

Mom came up, pulling me into a hug. "Baby, you look so beautiful—you two look so beautiful together."

Daemon stepped away, grinning at me over her shoulder.

"I just can't believe this is it. Your senior prom," she said, sniffling as she backed up, facing Daemon. "It was just yesterday when she was running through our house, tearing off her diapers—"

"Mom," I snapped, finally jumping into the conversation. Her telling any baby Katy stories was bad enough. Anyone hearing them was mortifying. But with Daemon it was about a thousand times more horrifying.

Daemon's eyes lit up with interest. "Do you have pictures? *Please* tell me you have pictures."

Her face broke out in a wide smile. "Actually, I do!" She spun toward a bookcase in the corner, stock full of humiliating pictures. "I chronicled every—"

"Oh, look at the time." I grabbed Daemon's arm and pulled. He didn't budge. "We really need to go."

"There's always tomorrow," he said to my mom, winking. "Right?"

"I don't go to work until five." She grinned.

That was so not happening. On the way out, she stopped and gave me another hug. "You do look beautiful, baby. I mean it."

"Thank you." I squeezed her back.

She held on like she was never going to let go and I didn't mind, because after tomorrow night, there was a chance that I may not come back. So I needed my mommy's hug and I wasn't too proud to admit that.

"I'm happy for you," she whispered. "He's a good boy."

I gave a watery smile. "I know."

"Good." She pulled back, patting my arms with both hands. "Curfew?"

"I—"

"You have none tonight." To my shock, she smiled. "Just behave and don't do anything you'll regret in the morning." Her gaze drifted over my shoulder, and she muttered, "Wouldn't be much."

"Mom!"

Laughing, she gave me a light shove. "I'm old, not dead. Now get going and have fun."

I left as fast as I could. "You didn't hear that last part, right?"

Daemon grinned.

"Oh, God . . ."

Tipping his head back, he laughed as he took my hand. "Come, milady, your chariot awaits."

I laughed as I climbed into Dolly and once he was inside, we argued over the radio until we were halfway to the school and Daemon sent me a sideways glance. "You really do look beautiful, Kitten. I mean it."

I smiled, running my fingers over the beads on my clutch. "Thank you."

There was a pause. "I thought you looked beautiful homecoming night, too."

My head snapped toward him, clutch forgotten. "Really?"

"Hells yeah. I hated that you were with someone else." He laughed at my expression and then refocused on the dark road. The easy grin tugged at my heart. "When I saw you with

Simon? I wanted to beat the ever-loving crap out of him and snatch you away."

I laughed. Sometimes I forgot that during those tumultuous first months of knowing each other, a teeny tiny part of him may have liked me.

"So, yeah, I thought you were beautiful then."

I bit my lip and then hoped I hadn't smeared my lip gloss. "I always thought you were . . ." *Beautiful* wasn't exactly a manly descriptor, so I went with, "Very handsome."

"What you mean is that you always thought I was incredibly hot and you couldn't take your eyes off me."

"We really need to work on your modesty." The woods blurred outside the windows, and I could see my grin in the reflection. "But God, did you ever tick me off."

"It's a part of my charm."

I snorted.

The prom was held the same place homecoming was—the high school gymnasium. Real fancy here. The parking lot was packed and because we were running a little late, we had to leave Dolly in the nosebleed section.

Daemon took my hand as we strolled up to the school. The air was warm with just a hint of coolness. The nights were still pretty cold here in May, but I didn't need a shawl or anything, not with Daemon beside me. He always blew off an incredible amount of heat.

At homecoming, the gymnasium had been transformed by all the fall festive decorations, but for prom, white lights had been strung along the ceiling and down the closed bleachers, forming a dazzling waterfall effect. Large, leafy potted plants had been brought in, surrounding the white-linen-covered tables sitting at the edge of the matted dance floor.

Music was loud, and I could barely hear what Daemon was saying to me as he tugged me forward. Lesa appeared out of nowhere, taking my hand and pulling me toward the floor. She looked awesome in a deep blue trumpet dress that flattered her hourglass curves. Out on the floor other girls surrounded us. Laughter mingled with the beat and I thought of the club in Martinsburg and the cages.

Totally different worlds.

Daemon reappeared, stealing me away from the girls. It was a slow dance and his arm fit perfectly around my waist. I rested my cheek on his shoulder, glad that he and Dee had convinced me into doing the prom thing. Getting out and doing this felt great, like a seven-ton weight was lifted from my shoulders.

Daemon hummed along with the song, his chin brushing my cheek every so often. I liked the way his chest thrummed against mine, reminding me of the natural way his body felt.

Toward the end of the song, I opened my eyes and they locked with Blake's.

I sucked in a sharp breath. Hadn't expected him to be here, so seeing Blake caused quite a bit of shock to shoot through me. Was he with someone? No girl was near him, but that didn't mean anything. Something about the way he stood there watching us was above the acceptable creep factor for my taste.

A couple moved in, laughing as the boy pawed at her hips. When they passed on, Blake was gone, but a weird, icky feeling had popped up in my stomach. The feeling I got whenever I saw Blake, which meant I tried not to think about him at all.

Seeing him made me think of someone else, though. I lifted my head. "Dawson didn't come?"

Daemon shook his head. "Nah, I think he'd feel like he was betraying Beth if he did."

"Wow," I whispered, unsure of what to think of that. His dedication to Beth was more than admirable—it was sort of awe-inspiring. Maybe it was the alien DNA.

Daemon's arm tightened and the tux pulled taut across his shoulders.

Yes, definitely the alien DNA at work on many, many aspects.

After the slow dance, Andrew and Dee joined us. She looked as divine as I thought she would in her dress and fresh, clean look. I noted that Dee and Andrew kept a discreet distance between each other. To me, it was clear they were just friends—more only because they shared something they lost.

When Daemon left to find something to drink, I was blindsided by Ash and her human date . . . and her little black dress.

Ash grinned like a cat that ate an entire family of canaries. "David, this is Katy. Don't worry about remembering her name. You'll probably forget."

I ignored her and offered a hand. "Nice to meet you."

David was handsome—very handsome—and could easily hold his own with the Luxen. He had curly brown hair and his warm whiskey-colored eyes were friendly, too.

He gave a good handshake. "My pleasure."

And polite. What was he doing with Ash?

"I have certain talents," she whispered in my ear, as if she read my thoughts, and I frowned at her. "Ask Daemon. He can tell you all about them." Straightening, she laughed.

Instead of hitting her, which was something I really wanted to do—and I could feel the Source begging me to be used—I smiled sweetly as I brushed past her and placed my hand on the exposed length of her slender back. A high-charged electric surge passed from my hand to her skin.

Letting out a low shriek, Ash jumped and spun around. "You . . ."

Beside her, David looked confused, but behind him, Dee busted out laughing. I kept smiling, giving Ash a little wink before turning around. Daemon stood there with two cups, one eyebrow arched.

"Bad little Kitten," he murmured.

Grinning, I stretched up and kissed him. It was an innocent one—or maybe it was on my end, but Daemon totally took it *there*. When we parted, I was breathless.

Leaving the group behind, we danced again, so closely that I kept waiting for a teacher to come around and break us apart. Several times I danced with Lesa and even Dee joined in once. We all looked ridiculous, flailing around and having fun.

By the time I was back in Daemon's arms, we'd been at the prom for about two hours. Some of the kids were already leaving, heading out to the notorious field parties held on farms.

"You ready to leave yet?" he said.

"Do you have something planned?" Oh gosh, did my mind go wild then.

"I do." He smiled mischievously. "I have a surprise."

And my mind went far, far south at that point. Daemon and the word *surprise* in the same sentence usually was an entertaining adventure.

"All right," I said, hoping I sounded adult and cool while my heart was doing the stupid happy-girl dance.

Finding Lesa, I told her we were leaving and gave her a hug. "Did you guys get a hotel room?" she asked, eyes glittering in the white lights.

I slapped her arm. "No. God. Well . . . I don't think so. He says he has a surprise for me."

"Totally the hotel room," she yelled. "Oh my God, you guys are going to have, you know, the three-letter word."

I smiled.

Lesa's eyes narrowed and then flew open. "Wait. Did you guys—"

"I've got to go." I started to pull away, but she followed.

"You have to tell me! I need to know." Behind her, Chad watched on curiously.

Getting away, I shook my head. "I really need to go. I'll talk to you later. Have fun."

"Oh, we'd better talk later. I demand it."

Promising to call her, I then looked for Dee but all I found was Ash, and after I zapped her earlier, she was looking like she wanted payback. I veered in the other direction, scanning the floor for the willowy raven-haired girl.

I gave up when I saw Daemon again. "Have you seen Dee?"

He nodded. "I think she left with Andrew. They decided to go to the diner or something and eat."

I stared.

Daemon shrugged.

Now I was unsure about my earlier conviction when it came to their relationship. Adam and Dee were notorious for doing things like that. Then again, Luxen liked to eat . . . all the time. "You don't think they're . . . ?"

"I don't even want to know."

Me neither, I decided. Taking his offered hand, we headed back out of the steamy gymnasium and down the streamer-laden hallway. The temps had dropped outside, but the cold air felt good against my flushed skin.

"Are you going to tell me about the surprise?"

"If I did, then it won't be a surprise," he replied.

I pouted. "But it's a surprise now."

"Nice try." He laughed, opening the door for me. "Get in and behave yourself."

"Whatever." But I climbed in, primly crossing my legs. Daemon laughed again as he loped around the front of his car and got in.

Casting me a glance, he shook his head. "You're dying to know, aren't you?"

"Yes. You should tell me."

He said nothing and remained quiet the whole way home, much to my surprise. Nervous excitement built inside me.

There'd only been a few minutes here and there of being alone together since that fateful Saturday night.

Strange how something so terrible and so beautiful could happen in one night—the best and the worst day of my life, I realized.

I didn't want to think of Will.

Daemon parked the car in his driveway. The living room light was on in his house. "Stay in the car, okay?"

When I nodded, he got out and disappeared—gone in a flash. Curious, I twisted around in the seat, but I didn't see him or anyone. What could he be up to?

Suddenly, my car door opened and Daemon extended his hand. "Ready?"

A little knocked off-kilter by his reappearance, I gave him my hand and let him swoop me out of the SUV. "So my surprise . . . ?"

"You'll see."

Hand in hand, we started walking. I thought he was going to lead me to his house, but he didn't, and when we passed mine and made our way down the road, I had no idea what he had planned. That was, until I saw that we were heading to the main road and when we stopped there, I was taken back several months to the first time I learned about Daemon's kind.

I'd walked out in front of a truck.

Yeah, idiotic move, but I'd been upset and hadn't been thinking. Douche-version of Daemon had been to blame.

Crossing the road, I got a general idea of where we were heading. The lake. Squeezing Daemon's hand, I fought back a stupid grin.

"Do you think you can walk in those heels?" he asked, frowning as if he'd just thought of it.

Doubtful, but I didn't want to ruin any of this for him. "Yeah, I'll be fine."

He took it slowly anyway, making sure I didn't fall flat on

my face or break my neck. Incredibly sweet, actually, as he made sure to get all the low-hanging branches out of the way and at one point, he even let a part of his true form take hold. White light surrounded his hand, casting over the uneven ground.

Who needed a flashlight when you had Daemon?

It took a little longer than normal to get to the lake, but I enjoyed the walk and his company. And when we stepped out of the last stand of trees and the scene before me unfolded, I couldn't believe what I was seeing.

Moonlight reflected off the calm waters and several feet away from the bank, next to the white wildflowers that had started to bloom, were several blankets spread out and piled atop one another, creating a comfy-looking sitting area. There were a few pillows and a large cooler. A fire crackled closer to the lake, surrounded by large stones.

There were no words.

The whole setup was exceptionally romantic, sweet, awesome, and so, so perfect that I wondered if I were dreaming. I knew Daemon was capable of surprising me—he always did, but this . . . ? My heart swelled so quickly I was sure I would float away.

"Surprise," he said, stepping ahead, his back to the fire. "I thought this would be better than a party or whatever. And you like the lake. So do I."

I blinked back tears. God, I needed to stop crying all the time, especially tonight, because I had loaded my lashes with mascara. "It's perfect, Daemon. Oh my God, it's wonderful."

"Really?" A bit of vulnerability crept into his voice. "You really like it?"

I couldn't believe he had to ask. "I love it." And then I started to laugh, which was better than crying. "I really love this."

Daemon smiled.

I launched myself at him, wrapping my arms and legs around him like a demented monkey-girl.

Laughing, he caught me and didn't stumble. "You really love it," he said, walking backward. "I'm glad."

So many emotions were running through me that I couldn't settle on one thing, but they were all good. When he put me down, I kicked off my shoes and moved to the blankets. They were soft under my toes, luxurious.

Sitting down, I tucked my legs under me. "What's in the cooler?"

"Ah, the good stuff." He flashed out and appeared beside the cooler, kneeling down. He cracked it open, pulled out a bottle of wine and two glasses. "Wine cooler—strawberry. Your favorite."

I laughed. "Oh my God."

He popped the cork with some kind of weird alien-mind-Source-Jedi power and poured each of us a glass. I took it and sipped the fizzy liquid. I liked the wine cooler because it didn't taste like alcohol and I was really a lightweight.

"What else?" I asked, leaning over.

Out came a canister and he carefully peeled the lid off and tilted it toward me. Chocolate-covered strawberries rolled temptingly.

My mouth watered. "Did you make them?"

"Ha. No."

"Uh . . . did Dee make them?"

That got a laugh. "I ordered them from the candy shop in town. Try one?"

I did and I think my mouth died and went to heaven. I may've even drooled on myself. "They are so good."

"There's more." He pulled out a plastic container full of sliced cheese and crackers. "Also pre-made from the store, be-cause *I* am not a cook or whatever."

Who cared how he got the stuff? He did this—this was all him.

There were also cucumber sandwiches and a veggie pizza. Perfect munchie food, and we dug in, laughing and eating while the fire slowly died off.

"When did you do all of this?" I asked, reaching for my fifth or so slice of veggie pizza.

He picked up a strawberry, inspecting it with narrowed eyes. "I had the stuff in the cooler down here and the blankets wrapped in canvas. All I did when we got back was come down here real quick, spread the stuff out, and start the fire."

I finished off my slice. "You're amazing."

"I know it didn't take you this long to realize that."

"No. I've always known it." I watched him root around for another strawberry. "Maybe not in the beginning . . ."

He peeked up. "My awesomeness is all about the stealth."

"Is it?" The temp had dropped and I huddled closer to Daemon and the dying fire, shivering but not anywhere near ready to head back.

"Uh-huh." He grinned, closing the bowl and placing the rest of the food back in the cooler. Tossing me a soda, he cleaned everything up. We'd moved on past the wine coolers a while ago. "I can't show all my dynamic sides at once."

"Of course not. Where's the mystery in that?"

He picked up a throw blanket. "There is none." Draping it over my shoulders, he then settled back down next to me.

"Thank you." I pulled the soft material close. "I think the general public would be shocked to know how deep your sweetness runs."

Daemon stretched out, resting on his side. "They can never know."

Grinning, I leaned forward and kissed his lips. "I'll take the secret to my grave."

"Good." He patted the spot next to him. "We can go back whenever you want."

"I don't want to leave."

"Then get your happy little hybrid butt over here."

Scooting over the remaining space, I laid down beside him. Daemon moved a pillow down so that it was under my head. Snuggled close to him, it would take an army of Arum to split us apart.

We talked about the dance, school, and even the university in Colorado. We talked well beyond midnight.

"Are you worried about tomorrow at all?" I asked, running the tips of my fingers along the curve of his jaw.

"I'm worried—but I'd be insane not to be." He kissed my finger when it drifted too close to his lips. "But not about what you think."

"What, then?" My hand drifted down his neck, over his shirt. He'd taken off the jacket a while ago. His skin was warm and hard underneath the thin material.

Daemon shifted closer. "I worry that Beth won't be like Dawson remembered."

"Me, too."

"I know he can handle it, though." He joined in, his hand sliding under the blanket, curving on my bare shoulder. "I just want the best for him. He deserves it."

"He does." I held my breath as his hand traveled south, over the dip in my waist then the flare of my hip. "I hope she's okay—that everyone is okay, even Chris."

He nodded and gently eased me onto my back. His hand smoothed over the skirt of my dress to my knee. I shivered. He smiled. "Something else is bothering you." When I thought about tomorrow and what the future might hold, a lot of things were bothering me. "I don't want anything to happen to you." My voice broke. "I don't want anything to happen to anyone."

"Shh." He kissed me gently. "Nothing will happen to me or anyone."

I balled my hands around his shirt, holding him, as if I could somehow stop the worst-case scenario from coming to fruition just by keeping him close. Silly, I knew, but holding him there kept the most horrific of fears at bay.

That I would walk out of Mount Weather, but Daemon wouldn't.

"What happens if we do succeed tomorrow night?"

"You mean *when* we do?" His leg brushed over mine, settling in between. "We go back to school on Monday—boring, I know. Then we hopefully pass our classes, which we will. Then we graduate. And then we have all summer . . ."

His weight did wicked things to my thoughts, but panic loomed too close. "Daedalus will come looking for Beth and Chris."

"And they won't find them." His lips pressed against my temple and then the curve of my brow. "That is, if they get close enough."

My stomach churned. "Daemon . . ."

"It'll be okay. Don't worry."

I wanted to believe. More like I needed to.

"Let's not think about tomorrow," he whispered, his lips grazing my cheek and then my jaw. "Let's not think about next week or the next night. It's just us right now and nothing else."

Heart racing, I tipped my head back and closed my eyes. It seemed impossible to forget all that was coming, but as his hand traveled over my knee and up under the hem of my dress, it really was only us and nothing else.

36

Like the last time we made our trip to Mount Weather, I spent the bulk of Sunday with my mom. We went to a late breakfast and I filled her in on all the prom details. She was misty-eyed when I told her about Daemon's surprise by the lake. Heck, I got misty-eyed and my chest fluttered as I told her.

Daemon and I had stayed out there until the stars had faded from the night and the sky had turned dark blue. It had been simply perfect and the things we'd done in those late hours still made my toes curl.

"You're in love," Mom said, chasing a piece of cantaloupe across her plate with her fork. "That's not a question. I can see it in your eyes."

Red swept across my cheeks. "Yeah, I am."

She smiled. "You grew up too fast, baby."

Didn't always feel that way, especially this morning when I couldn't find my other flip-flop and I'd been, like, two seconds from kicking a fit.

Then her voice lowered so that the packed church crowd couldn't hear. "You're being careful, right?"

Oddly, I wasn't embarrassed by the change in conversation. Maybe it had to do with the "naked baby Katy stripping off her diapers" comment yesterday. Either way, I was glad that she asked—that she cared enough. My mom may be busy working like most single parents, but she wasn't on the absentee list.

"Mom, I'd always be careful with that kind of stuff." I took a sip of my soda. "I don't want any baby Katys running around."

Her eyes widened with shock and then they watered again. Oh, dear . . . "You have grown up," she said, placing her hand over mine. "And I'm proud of you."

Hearing that felt good, because on the whole parent side of things, I wasn't sure what she could feel proud of. Sure, I went to school, stayed out of trouble—mostly—and got good grades. But I'd failed on the college thing so far, and I knew that bothered her. And everything else that I struggled and dealt with, she didn't know.

But she was still proud of me, and I didn't want to do anything to let her down.

When we arrived back home, Daemon stopped over for a little while and it took everything in me to keep Mom away from the photo albums before she went to grab a few hours of sleep, leaving Daemon and me to our own devices, which would sound like a really fun thing, but I was strung too tightly as the hours crept by.

Once I'd changed into the black sweats, Daemon asked for the opal. I handed it over.

"Don't look at me like that," he said, sitting across from me on my bed. He reached into his pocket and pulled out a thin, white string. "Instead of keeping it in your pocket, I thought I could make a necklace out of it."

"Oh. Good idea."

I watched him wrap the chord around the piece of opal, adjusting it so there was enough string left on either side to fit comfortably around my neck. I sat still while he tied it and slipped the stone under my shirt. It rested slightly above the piece of obsidian I wore.

"Thank you," I said, even though I still thought we should've risked shattering it.

He grinned. "I think we should skip out of lunch tomorrow and go to the movies."

"Huh?"

"Tomorrow—I think we should make it a half day."

Making plans to skip afternoon classes tomorrow wasn't on my priorities list and I was about to point that out when I realized what he was doing. Distracting me from the possibility there might not be a tomorrow that I wanted to see, keeping things normal and, in a way, hopeful.

I lifted my lashes and our eyes held. The green hue of his burned extraordinarily bright and then turned white as I rose to my knees, cupped his face, and kissed him—really kissed him like he was the very air I was thirsting for.

"What was that for?" he asked when I sat back. "Not that I'm complaining."

I shrugged. "Just because. And to answer your question, I think we should definitely skip and play truant for the day."

Daemon moved so fast that one second he was sitting and the next he was over me, his arms like bands of steel on either side of my head and I was on my back, staring up at him.

"Did I tell you I have a soft spot for bad girls?" he murmured. His form blurred at the edges, a soft white as if someone had taken a paintbrush and smudged an outline around him. A lock of hair fell forward, into those astonishing diamond-like eyes.

I couldn't find my breath. "Truancy does it for you?"

When he lowered his body, it thrummed with a low charge and where our bodies met, sparks flew. "*You* do it for me."

"Always?" I whispered.

His lips grazed mine. "Always."

Daemon left sometime later to meet up with Matthew and Dawson. The three of them wanted to run through things again, and Matthew, being the anal-retentive planner at heart, wanted to take a few more shots at the onyx.

I stayed back, hovering around my mom like a small child as she got ready. Feeling exceptionally needy, I even followed her outside and watched her back out of the driveway in her Prius.

Alone, my gaze went to the flowerbed skirting the porch. The faded mulch needed replacing and it could use a good weeding.

Stepping off the porch, I went to the small rose bushes and started pulling off the dead petals. I'd heard once that it could help the flowers bloom again. Wasn't sure if that was correct or not, but the monotony of carefully picking out the leaves eased my nerves.

Tomorrow, Daemon and I would skip out at lunch.

Next weekend, I would convince my mom I needed to do an overhaul on the flowerbed.

At the beginning of June, I would graduate.

Sometime that month, I would get serious about filling out the paperwork for University of Colorado and I would drop that bomb on my mom.

In July, I would spend every day with Daemon swimming in the lake and getting a Jersey Shore tan.

By the end of summer, things would be normal between Dee and me.

And come fall, I'd move on from all of this. Things wouldn't ever be mundane. I wasn't fully human anymore. My boyfriend—the guy I loved—was an alien. And there may become a point where, like Dawson and Blake, Daemon and I would have to disappear.

But there was going to be a tomorrow, a next week, month, summer, and fall.

"Only you would be out gardening right now."

I whipped around at the sound of Blake's voice. He leaned against my car, dressed in all black, ready for tonight.

This was the first time since our confrontation that Blake had come around me while I was alone, and the alien part of me responded. That roller-coaster feeling was swelling inside me. Static pricked along my skin.

I held my ground. "What do you want, Blake?"

He laughed softly as his gaze fell to the ground. "We're leaving soon, right? I'm just a little early."

And I was just a little bit of a book nerd. Yeah, right.

Brushing the dirt off my fingers, I watched him wryly. "How did you get here?"

"Parked at the end of the road at the empty house." He gestured with his chin. "The last time I parked here, I'm pretty sure someone melted the paint on the hood of my truck."

Sounded like Dee and her microwave hands. I crossed my arms. "Dee and Andrew are next door," I felt the need to point out.

"I know." He pulled a hand out, ran it through his spikey hair. "You looked really good at prom."

Unease unfurled in my belly. "Yeah, I saw you. Did you come alone?"

He nodded. "I was there only for a few minutes. Never did the high school dance thing. Kind of disappointing."

I said nothing.

Blake dropped his hand. "You worried about tonight?"

"Who wouldn't be?"

"Smart girl," he said, and smiled a little. It was more of a grimace than anything. "No one that I know of has infiltrated one of their facilities before or even gotten as far as we did last time. No Luxen or hybrid, and we can't be the first to attempt it. I bet there're a dozen Dawsons and Beths, Blakes and Chrises."

Muscles tightened in my neck and shoulders. "If this is supposed to be a pep talk, you completely fail at it." Blake laughed.

"I don't mean it that way. Just that if we do this, we're the strongest, you know. The best out of their hybrids and out of the Luxen."

Funny or maybe just ironic, I thought, that what Daedalus wanted so badly was the only ones who could go up against them.

I touched the chord around my neck, feeling the warm, smooth edges of the opal. "Then we're just awesome, I guess."

Another pained smile and then Blake said, "That's what I'm counting on."

We were all dressed like a ragtag group of reject ninjas. My skin sweated under the long-sleeved black thermal. The idea was that the less skin exposed, the less the onyx impacted us.

Didn't really pan out that way last time, but we weren't taking any chances tonight.

Driving to the mountains of Virginia was a quiet affair. This time around, even Blake was silent. Dawson was a ball of energy beside him. Once, luckily not when cars surrounded us, he slipped into his true form, nearly blinding all of us.

Blake's words lingered in my head. *That's what I'm counting on.* I was probably being paranoid, but they settled like sour milk. Of course he was counting on us to pull off the near impossible. He had just as much as us to gain.

And then I thought of Luc's warning: never trust those who have anything to gain or lose. But that meant we couldn't trust either him or our friends. All of us had something to gain or lose.

Daemon reached over the center console and squeezed my fidgeting hand.

Thinking these things right then wasn't the best route to travel. I was getting myself all worked up and spazzy.

I smiled at Daemon and decided to focus on our afternoon. We didn't really do anything. Just cuddled together, both of us wide awake, and somehow that was more intimate than anything else. Last night or early this morning had been a different story.

Daemon was a creative fellow.

My cheeks were stained red the rest of the trip.

The two SUVs arrived at the little farm at the bottom of the pitch-black access road with five minutes to spare. As we climbed out, Blake got his confirmation text from Luc.

Things were a go.

Instead of limbering up, we all stayed still, conserving our energy. Ash, Andrew, and Dee remained in their SUV. The rest of us moved to the edge of the overgrown field.

I hoped I didn't get infested with ticks.

With one last look at the Luxen in the vehicle, it was time to go. Letting the Source flow through my blood and bones and ripple over my skin, we took off into the darkness, without the light of the moon on the cloudy night. Like last time, Daemon stayed beside me. The last thing anyone needed was my tripping over something and rolling back down the hill.

Things were quiet and tense when we reached the edge of the woods, waited to see that only one guard manned the fence.

It was Daemon who took him out this time. Then we were at the fence, keying in the first code.

Icarus.

Taking off across the stretch of field, the five of us moved like ghosts. Visible in one's peripheral vision, but gone when looked at head-on.

At the set of three doors, Dawson entered in the second password.

Labyrinth.

And now it was do or die time. All these months had led up to this. Did our onyx training mean a damn thing? Daemon glanced at me.

I slipped my hand into around my neck, wrapping my fingers around the opal.

Going through the onyx spray would still hurt like the fiery bowels of hell for the others, but it should be manageable if Blake had been right.

The door slid open with an airlock sound and Daemon was the first through.

Air puffed and he flinched, but one leg moved in front of the other and then he was through, on the other side. He stopped, glancing over his shoulder, and smiled that half smile.

All of us let out a collective breath.

We filed through the onyx-shielded door. Each of the guys took the spray with a wince and grimace of pain. I barely felt a thing.

Inside Mount Weather for the first time, we fell behind Blake, who knew most of the way. The tunnel was shadowed, with small lamps placed every twenty feet or so on the orange walls. I searched for those murderous emergency doors but it was too dark to see them.

Tipping my head up, I noticed something terrifying about the ceiling. It was shiny—like it was wet or something, but it wasn't liquid.

"Onyx," Blake whispered. "The whole place is covered in onyx."

Unless they did a massive remodel recently, that couldn't be something new to Blake. Feeling the opal against my skin, I pulled on the Source and waited for the extreme rush of energy as we flew down the tunnel.

There was a tiny spark of extra energy, but nothing like it had been when Daemon and I had tested it out. My heart sunk as we neared the end of the long tunnel. It had to be all the onyx, somehow weakening the opal.

At the end of the tunnel, it split into a crossroad. Elevators were in the middle. Matthew edged toward the opening, checking the space first.

"Clear," he said, then faded out, moving so fast that when he hit the elevator button, my eyes couldn't track him until he was beside us again.

When the doors slid open, we moved at once, filling the steel elevator. Apparently the stairwells were under password and I wondered what the heck people did to get out in case of emergency.

I looked around the elevator, noting a few blackish-red shiny parts in the flickering overhead light. I half expected to be doused with onyx while we waited, but it didn't happen.

Daemon's hand brushed mine, and I looked up.

He winked.

Shaking my head, I shifted my weight restlessly. This seemed like the slowest-moving elevator in the world. I could figure out a trig formula faster.

Daemon squeezed my hand, as if he could sense my nervousness.

I stretched up on the tips of my toes and cupped Daemon's cheek, guiding his head down to mine. I kissed him deeply and without reservation.

"For good luck," I said after I pulled back, a bit breathless.

His emerald eyes glinted with a wealth of promises that sent a very different kind of chills over me. When we got home, we were so getting some one-on-one time.

Because we would get home, all of us. There could be no other outcome.

Finally, the elevator doors popped open, revealing a small waiting room. White walls. White ceilings. White floors.

We'd stepped into an insane asylum.

"Lovely decorative colors," Matthew said.

Daemon smirked.

His brother moved ahead, stopping at the door. There was no way, no idea of seeing what waited for us on the other side. With this code, we were going in blind.

But we'd come this far. Excitement hummed through me.

"Careful, brother," Daemon said. "We take this slow."

He nodded. "I've never been here. Blake?"

Blake moved to his side. "Should be another tunnel, shorter and wider, and there'll be doors on the right side. Cells, really, outfitted with a bed, a TV, and a bathroom. There'll be about twenty rooms. I don't know if the others are occupied or not."

Others? I hadn't thought about others. I looked at Daemon. "We can't just leave them."

Before he could answer, Blake intervened. "We don't have time, Katy. Taking too many will slow us down, and we don't know what kind of condition they are in."

"But—"

"For once, I agree with Blake." Daemon met my shocked stare. "We can't, Kitten. Not now."

I wasn't okay with this, but I couldn't run down the hall, letting people free. We didn't plan for that and we only had a set amount of time. It sucked—sucked worse than people who pirated books, sucked more than waiting a year for the next book in a beloved series, and sucked more than a brutal cliffhanger ending. Leaving here, knowing we could possibly be leaving innocent people behind, would haunt me forever.

Blake took a deep breath and keyed in the last code.

Daedalus.

The sound of several locks sucking back into place broke

the silence and a light at the top of the door, on the right, flashed green.

As Blake inched the door open, Daemon moved to stand in front of me. Matthew was suddenly behind me and I was shielded. What the . . . ?

"We're clear," Blake said, sounding relieved.

We went through the door, discovering another onyx shield. Now we had two more to get the others through. This wasn't going to be easy.

The tunnel was like the one above, but all white and like Blake had informed us, it was shorter and wider. Everyone was moving but me. We'd made it—we were here. My stomach lurched and my skin tingled.

I almost couldn't believe it.

Happy and anxious all at once, I felt the rush of responding Source, but it peaked and then quickly sputtered out. The amount of onyx in this building was insane.

"The third cell is hers," Blake said, rushing down the hall, toward the last cluster of doors.

Spinning back around, I held my breath as Dawson reached for the onyx-coated door handle and turned. It met no resistance.

Dawson stepped into the room, his legs shaking, his entire body trembling, and his voice cracked when he spoke. "Beth?"

That one word, that one sound was pulled from the depths of Dawson and we all stopped, our breaths holding again.

Over his shoulder, I saw a slender form on a narrow bed sit up. As she came into view, I almost cheered—I wanted to, because it was her, it was Beth . . . but she looked nothing like she had when I'd last seen her.

Her brown hair wasn't stringy or greasy but pulled back in a smooth ponytail. A few strands had slipped free, framing a pale but elfin face. A huge part of me feared that she wouldn't recognize Dawson, that she'd be that cracked shell of a girl

I'd met. I'd been planning for the worse. That she might even attack Dawson.

But when I saw Beth's dark eyes, they weren't empty like they'd been at Vaughn's house. They also looked nothing like Carissa's frighteningly blank stare.

Recognition flared in Beth's eyes.

Time stopped for those two and then sped up. Dawson stumbled forward, and I thought he was going to drop to his knees. His hands opened and closed at his sides as if he had no control over them.

All he could say was, "Beth."

The girl scrambled off the bed, her eyes bouncing over us and then they settled and stayed on him. "Dawson? Is that . . . I don't understand."

They both moved as one, rushing forward, crossing the distance at the same moment. Their arms went around each other and Dawson lifted her up, burying his face in her neck. Words were traded, but their voices were thick with emotion, too low and too fast for my ears to track. They were holding onto each other in a way I knew they were never going to let go.

Dawson lifted his head and said something in his language and it sounded just as beautiful as it did when Daemon spoke it. Then he kissed her, and I felt like an interloper watching them, but I couldn't look away. There was so much beauty in their reunion, in the way he showered her upturned face with tiny kisses and the wetness that gathered on her cheeks.

Tears crept up my throat, burning the back of my eyes. Happy tears blurred my vision. I felt Matthew place his hand on my shoulder and squeeze. Sniffling, I nodded.

"Dawson." Urgency filled Daemon's tone, reminding all of us that we were running out of time.

Pulling apart, Dawson grabbed her hand and turned around as a whole boatload of questions came streaming out of Beth's mouth.

"What are you guys doing? How did you all get in here? Do they know?" And on and on she went as Dawson, who was grinning like an idiot, tried to keep her quieted down.

"Later," he said. "But we have to go through two doors and it's going to hurt—"

"Onyx shields, I know," she said.

Well, that solved that problem.

I turned as Blake came back, carrying the prone body of a dark-haired Luxen boy. A reddish stain bloomed across the teenager's jaw. "Is he okay?"

Blake nodded. The skin around his lips was drawn tight and pale. "I . . . He didn't recognize me. I had to keep him quiet."

A tiny crack fissured my heart. The look in Blake's eyes was so hopeless and bleak, especially when they flickered toward Dawson and Beth. Everything he had done: lied, cheated, and murdered had all been for the guy in his arms. Someone he considered a brother. Again, I hated that I felt sympathy for Blake.

But I did.

Beth looked up and her onslaught of questions faded off. "You can't—"

"We need to go." Blake cut her off and stalked past us. "We're almost out of time."

And we were. The reminder whipped through me and I gave the other girl what I hoped was a reassuring smile. "We have to leave. Now. Everything else can wait."

Beth was shaking her head vigorously. "But—"

"We need to go, Beth. We know." And she nodded at Dawson's words, but panic was building in her eyes.

Urgency kicked adrenaline into high gear and without any more delay, the five of us took off down the hall. Daemon punched the code into panel on the wall, and the door opened.

The all-white waiting room wasn't empty.

Simon Cutters stood there—missing, presumed dead Simon Cutters—as big and burly as ever. All of us were caught off guard. Daemon took a step back. Matthew came to a halt. I couldn't wrap my head around how he was alive, why he was standing there, as if he were *waiting* for us.

The tiny hairs on my arms started to rise.

"Oh shit," Daemon said.

Simon smiled. "Missed me? I missed you guys."

Then he raised an arm. Light reflected off a metal cuff he wore. A piece of opal glittered, nearly identical to the one I wore around my neck. Everything happened so fast. Simon opened his hand, and it was like being hit with gale force winds. I was lifted off my feet and thrown back through the air. I crashed into the nearest door, my hip hitting the metal door handle. Pain exploded, knocking the air out of my lungs as I hit the floor.

Oh, my God . . . Simon was . . .

My brain raced to keep up with what was happening. If Simon had a piece of opal, then that meant he had to have been mutated. He probably wouldn't have gotten us if we hadn't been so unprepared to see him. It was like with Carissa. He was the last person I expected.

Daemon was picking himself up several feet back down the hall, as was Matthew. Dawson had Beth pressed back against the wall. Blake was closer, using his body to shield Chris's.

I pushed myself up, wincing as pain arced down my leg. I tried to stand, but my leg gave out. Blake was there, catching me before I hit the floor for the second time.

Simon stepped into the room and smiled.

Daemon staggered to his feet. "Oh, you are so dead."

"Ah, I think that's my line," Simon responded. A burst of energy flew from his hand, and I yelled Daemon's name. He narrowly avoided a direct hit.

Daemon's pupils were starting to glow white. He reared

back. Energy arced across the room, a whitish-red light. Simon dodged it, laughing.

"You're going to wear yourself out, Luxen." Simon sneered.

"Not before you."

Simon winked and then spun toward us, throwing his hand out again. Blake and I skidded back. I started to fall and Blake grabbed me. Somehow his arm ended up around my neck. There was a tugging feeling and then Daemon was beside me, shoving me behind him.

"This is so not good," Blake said, edging closer to Simon. "We're running out of time."

"No shit," Daemon spat.

Dawson shot toward Simon, but he threw him back, laughing. He was like a hybrid suped up on steroids. Another blast of energy flew at Blake and then toward Matthew. Both of them dive-bombed the floor to avoid taking a hit. Simon kept advancing, still smiling. I looked up and our eyes locked. His were devoid of all human emotion. Unreal. Inhuman.

And they were so very cold.

How had he been mutated? How was it successful? And how had it turned him into this unfeeling monster. There were so many questions, and none of them mattered right now. The breath-stealing pain made it difficult to concentrate, to even keep standing.

Simon's smile spread, and a shudder rolled through me as I pulled on the Source, feeling it spark deep inside me. Before I could release it, he opened his mouth. "Want to play, Kitty Kat?"

"Oh, screw this," Daemon growled.

Daemon was just so much faster than me. He shot past Blake and Matthew, beyond Dawson and Beth. Moving so fast had to have affected him with all the onyx, but he was like lightning. Half a heartbeat later, he was in front of Simon, his hands on either side of Simon's head.

A sickening crack echoed down the hall.

Simon hit the floor.

Daemon stepped back, breathing deeply. "I never liked that punk in the first place."

I stumbled to the side, heart racing as the Source stirred restlessly inside of me. Eyes wide, I swallowed hard. "He's . . . He was . . ."

"We don't have time." Dawson pulled Beth down the hall, into the waiting room. "They have to know we're here."

Blake scooped Chris up, casting a look at Simon as he passed the prone body. He said nothing, but what was there to say?

My stomach dipped as panic threatened to take hold. Forcing myself forward, I ignored the jagged pain racing up and down my leg.

"Are you okay?" Daemon asked, his fingers threading through mine. "You took a nasty hit."

"I'm okay." I was alive and I could walk, so that had to mean I was okay. "You?"

He nodded as we entered the waiting room. Taking the elevator filled me with so much dread I thought I'd hurl, but there were no doors to stairwells. Nothing. We had no other choice.

"Come on." Matthew slipped into the elevator, his face pale. "We need to prepare for anything once these doors are open."

Daemon nodded. "How is everyone?"

"Not feeling very good," Dawson answered, his free hand open and closing. "It's the damn onyx. I don't know how much is left in me."

"What the hell was up with Simon?" Daemon turned on Blake as the elevator pitched into motion. "He barely seemed affected by the onyx."

Blake shook his head. "I don't know, man. I don't know."

Beth was babbling on about something, but I couldn't pay attention. The ball of dread was building in my stomach, spreading into my limbs. How could Blake not know? I felt Daemon shift beside me, and then his lips brushed my forehead.

"It's going to be okay. We're almost out of here. We got this," Daemon whispered into my ear, and more tension seeped out of him, out of me. Then he smiled. It was a real one, so wide and beautiful that my own lips curved to meet his. "I promise, Kitten."

I closed my eyes briefly, soaking in his words and hanging onto them. I needed to believe in them because I was seconds away from freaking out. I had to hold it together. We were a tunnel away from freedom.

"Time?" Blake asked.

Matthew checked his watch. "Two minutes."

The doors released with a suction-cup sound and the long narrow tunnel appeared, thankfully, beautifully empty and devoid of anymore freak-me-out surprises. Blake and his bundle were the first out, his strides long and quick. Daemon and I took up the flank with Matthew in front of Dawson and Beth, just in case something happened.

"Stay behind me," Daemon said.

Nodding, I kept my eyes peeled. The tunnel was a blur, we were moving that fast. The pain in my leg increased with each step. As Blake reached the middle door, he shifted Chris to over his shoulder and entered in the key. The door rattled and then slid open.

Blake stood there, swathed in the darkness of the encroaching night. In his arms, the motionless Luxen was pale and seemed barely alive, but he'd be free in seconds. Blake had finally gotten what he wanted. Our eyes met from across the distance. There was something churning in those green flecks.

A great sense of foreboding took root and spread rapidly. Immediately, I reached for the opal around my neck and all I felt was the chain the piece of obsidian hung from.

Blake's lips slowly curved up at the corners.

My heart stuttered and then my stomach fell so fast I thought I'd be sick. That smile . . . That smile felt like a big *gotcha*. A surge of unbridled terror turned my skin icy cold. But it couldn't be. *No. No. No. It couldn't be . . .*

Blake cocked his head to the side as he stepped back. He opened his free hand. The thin, white string unraveled, slipping through his fingers. The piece of opal dangled there, in his grasp. "Sorry," he said, and he truly sounded sorry. It was unbelievable. "It had to be this way."

"Son of a bitch!" roared Daemon, breaking free from me. He launched forward, going after Blake in a way I knew would end in bloody violence.

Heat flared between my breasts, unexpected and just as terrifying as an army of DOD soldiers. I reached down, yanking the obsidian from my shirt. It glowed red.

Daemon drew up short, snarling.

The darkness behind Blake thickened and stretched out, creeping into the entrance of the tunnel. The blackness seeped over the walls. Lamps sparked and went out. The shadows dropped onto the floor, rising up all around Blake. Not touching him. Not stopping him. The smoke formed pillars at first and then human forms. Their skin was like midnight oil, slick and shiny.

Arum formed all around Blake—seven of them. All dressed the same. Dark pants. Dark shirts. Eyes shielded behind sunglasses. One by one, they smiled.

They ignored Blake.

They *let* him go.

Blake disappeared into the night as the Arum flew forward.

Daemon met the first one head on, his human form flickering out as he slammed the Arum back into the wall. Dawson shoved Beth to the side as he closed line on an advancing Arum, taking him down.

Reaching down, Matthew grabbed a slender shard of Obsidian, sharpened into a fine point. He spun around, slamming it deep into the belly of the nearest Arum.

The Arum drew up, losing its human form as it rose to the low ceiling. It hung there for a second and then shattered as if it were made of nothing more than frail bone.

I snapped out of it.

Knowing that none of them, including me, would be able to rely on the Source for very long, this would be a hand to hand kind of combat. I yanked the obsidian around my neck and the chain snapped just as one of the Arums reached me. I saw my pale face in its dark sunglasses and searched for the Source inside me.

He reached forward, and whitish-red light erupted from me, throwing the Arum back and knocking it flat on its ass. The energy rushed out like an overflowing stream. The onyx had lessened the blow, and the Arum was on his feet as Daemon took out the one he was fighting. Another explosion of black smoke rocked the corridor.

The Arum I knocked down was in front of me, sunglasses gone. His eyes were the palest blue, the color of the winter sky. They were just as cold as Simon's, if not more.

I took a step back, my hand clenching the piece of obsidian.

The Arum smiled, and then he twisted to the side, swinging his leg out and catching my bad one. I yelped as my leg caved. I started to go down, but he caught me around the neck, lifted me off my feet and into the air. Beyond him, I saw Daemon spin, saw the anger building in him, saw the Arum rising up behind him.

"Daemon!" I shouted as I slammed the piece of obsidian into the chest of the Arum holding me.

The Arum dropped me as Daemon whirled, dodging the other one. I hit the cement floor for the umpteenth time as the

Arum broke apart with such force it blew my hair back from my face.

Daemon grabbed ahold of the enemy closest to him by the shoulders, tossing it several feet behind me as I stood on shaky legs. My hand trembled around the heated obsidian.

"Go! We need to go!" Dawson grabbed Beth and started for the door, dodging an Arum. "Now!"

I didn't need to be told twice. This was a battle we wouldn't win. Not when we had no time left and there were four Arum still standing, obviously unaffected by the onyx.

Pushing past the pain, I started forward, taking a few steps before my leg was snatched from behind. I went down fast and hard, dropping the obsidian to save my face from smashing into the cement. The coldness of the Arum's touch soaked through my sweats, traveling up my legs as its grip on my ankle tightened.

I twisted onto my side and kicked out with my good leg, catching the Arum in the face. There was a satisfying wet crunching, sound and the Arum let go. I scrambled to my feet, gritting my teeth from the pain in my leg as I headed for Daemon. He'd turned and was coming back for me as a low hum rumbled through the building, gaining and gaining until it was all that we could hear. All of us stopped. Light flooded the tunnel and down the hall, automatic locks slamming into place. The *thump-thump-thump* went on in an endless succession.

"No," Matthew said, his eyes darting down from where we came. "*No.*"

Daemon's gaze shot behind me. I turned, seeing light flaring in the tunnel, crackling and forming a wall of shimmering blue light. One after another, every ten feet or so, over and over . . .

The blue light came down on one of the Arum not too far behind me. It caught it, and the light flared. There was a loud cracking sound, like a fly caught in one of those traps.

"Oh my God," I whispered.

The Arum was gone—simply just gone.

Don't go near the blue light, Blake had said. *They're lasers. Rip you right apart.*

Daemon lurched forward, his hands reaching for me, but it was too late. Before he could reach me, and not even a foot from my face, a sheet of blue light appeared and heat blew off it, blowing my hair back. Daemon let out a startled scream, and I jerked back.

I couldn't believe it. Not possible. I *refused* to believe it. Daemon was on the other side of the light, closer to the exit, and I . . . I was on the other side, the wrong side.

Daemon's eyes met mine and the look in them, the horror in his extraordinary green eyes cracked my heart into a million useless pieces. He understood—oh, God, he understood what was happening. I was trapped with the remaining Arum.

Shouts sounded. Booted feet pounded on the floors. They sounded like they were coming from everywhere. In front of us, from behind, and all corners. I couldn't turn, though, couldn't look behind me or away from Daemon.

"Kat," he whispered, pleaded, really.

Sirens blasted shrilly.

Daemon reacted so fast, but for once in his entire life, he wasn't fast enough. He couldn't be. Emergency doors started to slide from the top and bottom, and Daemon shot to the side, slamming his palm on a tiny control panel. Nothing was working. The doors kept sliding together. The blue light was like a stream of destruction separating us. Daemon whipped toward me. He launched toward the blue shield, and I let out a startled gasp. He'd be destroyed if he hit the lasers!

Pulling from the Source as much as I could, I held out my hand, ignoring the heat as I pushed at Daemon with the last of my strength and will, holding his straining body back from the blue lights until Matthew sprang into action, grabbing

Daemon around his waist. I slid to the floor, my knees barely catching me. Daemon went wild, throwing punches and dragging Matthew as he struggled to move forward, but Matthew got him back from the light, managing to bring Daemon down to his knees.

It was too late.

"No! Please! No!" he roared, his voice cracking in a way I'd never heard before. "Kat!"

The voices and sounds of pounding feet were drawing closer, and so was the bone-chilling coldness of the Arum. I felt them along my back, but I couldn't look away from Daemon.

Our eyes locked, and I would never, ever forget the terror in his, the look of pure helplessness. Everything felt surreal on my end, like I really wasn't here. I tried to smile for him, but I'm not sure I managed one.

"It'll be okay," I whispered as tears filled my eyes. The doors were coming out of the ceiling and the floor. "It'll be all right."

Daemon's green eyes held a glassy sheen. His arm reached out, fingers splayed. They never reached the laser or the door. "I love you, Katy. Always have. Always will," he said, voice thick and hoarse with panic. "I will come back for you. I will—"

The emergency doors sealed shut with a soft *thud*. "I love you," I said, but Daemon . . . Daemon was gone. Gone on the other side of the doors and I was trapped—with the Arum and Daedalus. For a moment I couldn't think, couldn't breathe. I opened my mouth to scream, but terror poured into me, cutting off the sound.

I turned around slowly, lifting my head as a tear rolled down my cheek. An Arum stood there, head tilted to the side. I couldn't see his eyes behind the sunglasses, and I was glad I couldn't.

He knelt, and beyond him and the other Arums, I could see men in black uniforms. The Arum reached out, trailing an icy finger down my cheek, chasing the tear, and I recoiled away, pressing against the emergency doors.

"This is going to hurt," the Arum said. He leaned in, his face inches from mine and his breath cold against my mouth.

"Oh God," I whispered.

A burst of pain encompassed every cell in my body, and the air flew out of my lungs. Suspended there, I couldn't move away. My arms didn't work. Someone grabbed me from the side, but I couldn't feel. It felt like I was still screaming, but there was no sound.

There was no Daemon.

ACKNOWLEDGMENTS

Thank you to the wonderful team at Entangled Teen—Liz Pelletier, Stacy Abrams, Stacey O'Neale, and Rebecca Mancini. And to my agent, Kevan Lyon, you rock as always. If it weren't for my friends and family, I'm sure I'd be a hermit living in a writing cave by now, so thank you for putting up with me when I go on a writing binge. A special thanks to Pepe Toth and Sztella Tziotziosz for being awesome cover models and joining us on our Daemon Invasion tours.

None of this would be possible if it weren't for the readers. I love you guys. I wish I could hug every one of you, but I suck at hugs, and it would just be all kinds of awkward. So trust me, this thank you is better than a hug. I promise.

ORIGIN

A Lux Novel

BOOK FOUR

JENNIFER L. ARMENTROUT

Entangled Publishing, LLC
2614 South Timberline Road
Suite 109
Fort Collins, CO 80525
Visit our website at www.entangledpublishing.com.

Edited by Liz Pelletier and Karen Grove
Text design by E. J. Strongin, Neuwirth & Associates, Inc.

Print ISBN 978-1-62266-075-9
Ebook ISBN 978-1-62266-076-6

Manufactured in the United States of America

First Edition September 2013

For my mother, who was my biggest fan and supporter.
You will be missed but never forgotten.

1

{ Katy }

I was on fire again. Worse than when I got sick from the mutation or when onyx was sprayed in my face. The mutated cells in my body bounced around as if they were trying to claw their way through my skin. Maybe they were. It felt like I was splayed wide open. There was a wetness gathering on my cheeks.

They were tears, I realized slowly.

Tears of pain and anger—a fury so potent it tasted like blood in the back of my throat. Or maybe it really was blood. Maybe I was drowning in my own blood.

My memories after the doors had sealed shut were hazy. Daemon's parting words haunted every waking moment. *I love you, Kat. Always have. Always will.* There had been a hissing sound as the doors closed, and I'd been left alone with the Arum.

I think they tried to eat me.

Everything had gone black, and I'd woken up in this world where it hurt to breathe. Remembering his voice, his words, soothed some of the torment. But then I remembered Blake's parting smile as he held the opal necklace—my opal necklace; the one Daemon had given me just before the sirens went off and the doors started coming down—and my anger flared. I'd been captured, and I didn't know if Daemon had made it out along with the rest of them.

I didn't know anything.

Forcing my eyes open, I blinked at the harsh lights shining down on me. For a moment, I couldn't see around their bright glow. Everything had an aura. But finally it cleared, and I saw a white ceiling behind the lights.

"Good. You're awake."

In spite of the pulsating burning, my body locked up at the sound of the unfamiliar male voice. I tried to look toward the source, but pain shot down my body, curling my toes. I couldn't move my neck, my arms, or my legs.

Icy horror drenched my veins. Onyx bands were around my neck, my wrists, my ankles, holding me down. Panic erupted, seizing the air in my lungs. I thought about the bruises Dawson had seen around Beth's neck. A shudder of revulsion and fear rocked through me.

The sound of footsteps neared, and a face, cocked sideways, came into view, blocking the light. It was an older man, maybe in his late forties, with dark hair sprinkled with gray buzzed close to the scalp. He wore a military uniform in dark green. There were three rows of colorful buttons above the left breast and a winged eagle on the right. Even in my pain-clouded mind and confusion, I knew this guy was important.

"How are you feeling?" he asked in a level voice.

I blinked slowly, wondering if this man was being serious. "Everything . . . everything hurts," I croaked.

"It's the bands, but I think you know that." He motioned to something or someone behind him. "We had to take certain precautions when we transported you."

Transported me? My heart rate kicked up as I stared at him. Where in the hell was I? Was I still at Mount Weather?

"My name is Sergeant Jason Dasher. I'm going to release you so we can talk and you can be looked over. Do you see the dark dots in the ceiling?" he asked. My gaze followed his, and then I saw the almost invisible blotches. "It's a blend of onyx and diamond. You know what the onyx does, and if you fight us, this room will fill up with it. Whatever resistance you've built won't help you here."

The whole room? At Mount Weather, it had just been a puff in the face. Not an endless stream of it.

"Did you know diamonds have the highest index of light refraction? While it does not have the same painful effects of onyx, in large enough quantities, and when onyx is in use, it has the ability to drain Luxen, leaving them unable to draw from the Source. It will have the same effect on you."

Good to know.

"The room is outfitted with onyx as a security precaution," he continued, his dark brown eyes focused on mine again. "In case you somehow are able to tap into the Source or attack any member of my staff. With hybrids, we never know the extent of your abilities."

Right now I didn't think I'd be able to sit up without assistance, let alone go ninja on anyone.

"Do you understand?" His chin lifted as he waited. "We don't want to hurt you, but we will neutralize you if you pose a threat. Do you understand, Katy?"

I didn't want to answer, but I also wanted out of the damn onyx bands. "Yes."

"Good." He smiled, but it was practiced and not very friendly. "We don't want you to be in pain. That is not what Daedalus is about. And it is far from what we are. You may not believe that right now, but we hope you will come to understand what we are about. The truth behind who we are and who the Luxen are."

"Kind of hard to . . . believe right now."

Sergeant Dasher seemed to take that for what it was worth, and then he reached down somewhere under the cold table. There was a loud *click*, and the bands lifted on their own, sliding off my neck and ankles.

Letting out a shaky breath, I slowly lifted my trembling arm. Entire parts of my body felt either numb or hypersensitive.

He placed a hand on my arm, and I flinched. "I'm not going to hurt you," he said. "I'm just going to help you sit up."

Given that I didn't have much control over my shaking limbs, I wasn't in any condition to protest. The sergeant had me upright in a few seconds. I clutched the edges of the table to keep myself steady as I took in several breaths. My head hung from my neck like a wet noodle, and my hair slid over my shoulders, shielding the room for a moment.

"You'll probably be a little dizzy. That should pass."

When I lifted my head, I saw a short, balding man dressed in a white lab coat standing by a door that was such a shiny black it reflected the room. He held a paper cup in his hand and what looked like a manual pressure cuff in the other.

Slowly, my eyes traveled over the room. It reminded me of a weird doctor's office, outfitted with tiny tables with instruments on them, cabinets, and black hoses hooked to the wall.

When motioned forward by the sergeant, the man in the lab coat approached the table and carefully held the cup to my mouth. I drank greedily. The coolness soothed the rawness in my throat, but I drank too fast and ended up with a coughing fit that was both loud and painful.

"I'm Dr. Roth, one of the physicians at the base." He put the cup aside and reached into his jacket, pulling out a stethoscope. "I'm just going to listen to your heart, okay? And then I'm going to take your blood pressure."

I jumped a little when he pressed the cold chest piece against my skin.

He then placed it on my back. "Take a nice deep breath." When I did, he repeated his instructions. "Good. Extend your arm out."

I did and immediately noticed the red welt circling my wrist. There was another above my other hand. Swallowing hard, I looked away, seconds from slipping into full freak-out mode, especially when my eyes met the sergeant's. They weren't hostile, but the eyes belonged to a stranger. I was utterly alone—with strangers who knew what I was and had captured me for a purpose.

My blood pressure had to be through the roof, because my pulse was pounding, and the tightening in my chest couldn't be a good thing. As the pressure cuff squeezed down, I inhaled several deep breaths, then asked, "Where am I?"

Sergeant Dasher clasped his hands behind his back. "You're in Nevada."

I stared at him, and the walls—all white with the exception of those shiny black dots—crowded in. "Nevada? That's . . . that's clear across the country. A different time zone."

Silence.

Then it struck me. A strangled laugh escaped. "Area 51?"

There was more silence, as if they couldn't confirm the existence of such a place. Area mother-freaking 51. I didn't know if I should laugh or cry.

Dr. Roth released the cuff. "Her blood pressure is a little high, but that's expected. I would like to do a more intensive examination."

Visions of probes and all kinds of nasty things lit up my brain. I slid off the table quickly, backing away from the men, on legs that barely held my weight. "No. You can't do this. You can't—"

"We can," Sergeant Dasher interrupted. "Under the Patriot Act, we are able to apprehend, relocate, and detain anyone, human or nonhuman, who poses a risk to the Nation's security."

"What?" My back hit the wall. "I'm not a terrorist."

"But you are a risk," he responded. "We hope to change that, but as you can see, your right to freedom was relinquished the moment you were mutated."

Legs giving out, I slid down the wall and sat down hard. "I can't . . ." My brain didn't want to process any of this. "My mom . . ."

The sergeant said nothing.

My mom . . . oh my God, my mom had to be going insane. She would be panicked and devastated. She would never get over this.

Pressing my palms against my forehead, I squeezed my eyes shut. "This isn't right."

"What did you think would happen?" Dasher asked.

I opened my eyes, my breath coming out in short bursts.

"When you infiltrated a government facility, did you think you would just walk out and everything would be fine? That there'd be no consequences for such actions?" He bent down in front of me. "Or that a group of kids, alien or hybrid, would be able to get as far as you did without us allowing it?"

Coldness radiated over my body. Good question. What *had* we thought? We had suspected it could be a trap. I had practically prepared myself for it, but we couldn't walk away and let Beth rot in there. None of us could've done that.

I stared up at the man. "What happened to . . . to the others?"

"They've escaped."

Relief coursed through me. At least Daemon wasn't locked up somewhere. That gave me some sort of comfort.

"We only needed to catch one of you, to be honest. Either you or the one who mutated you. Having one of you will draw the other out." He paused. "Right now, Daemon Black has disappeared off our radar, but we imagine it won't stay that way for long. We have learned through our studies that the bond between a Luxen and the one he or she mutates is quite intense, especially between a male and female. And from our observations, you two are extremely . . . close."

Yeah, my relief crashed and burned in fiery glory, and fear seized me. There was no point in pretending I had no idea what he was talking about, but I would never confirm it was Daemon. *Never*.

"I know you're afraid and angry."

"Yeah, I'm feeling both of those things strongly."

"That is understandable. We are not as bad as you think we are, Katy. We had every right to use lethal methods when we caught you. We could've taken out your friends. We didn't." He stood, clasping his hands again. "You will see we are not the enemy here."

Not the enemy? They *were* the enemy—a greater threat than a whole flock of Arum—because they had the *entire government* behind them. Because they could just snap up people and take them away from everything—their family, their friends, their entire life—and get away with it.

I was so screwed.

As the situation really sank in, my tenacious grip on keeping it together slipped, and then completely fell away. Stark terror whipped through me, turning into panic, creating an ugly mess of emotions powered by adrenaline. Instinct took over—the kind I hadn't been born with but had been shaped by what I'd become when Daemon had healed me.

I sprang to my feet. Aching muscles screamed in protest, and my head swam from the sudden movement, but I remained standing. The doctor moved to the side, his face paling as he reached for the wall. The sergeant didn't so much as blink an eye. He was not afraid of my badassery.

Calling upon the Source should've been easy, considering all the violent emotions rolling within me, but there wasn't a rush—like the kind you get when you're poised atop a high roller coaster—or even a building of static over my skin.

There was nothing.

Through the fog of horror and panic clouding my thoughts, a bit of reality seeped in, and I remembered I couldn't use the Source in here.

"Doctor?" said the sergeant.

In need of a weapon, I darted around him, heading for the table with the tiny instruments. I didn't know what I would do if I managed to get out of this room. The door could've been locked. I wasn't thinking beyond that very second. I just needed to get out of there. Now.

Before I could reach the tray, the doctor slapped his hand against the wall. A horrific, familiar sound of air releasing in a series of small puffs followed. There was no other warning. No smell. No change in the consistency of the air.

But those little dots in the ceiling and walls had released weaponized onyx, and there was no escaping it. Horror drowned me. The breath I took cut off as red-hot pain started at my scalp and coursed down my body. Like I was being doused with gasoline and set ablaze, a fire swept over my skin. My legs gave out, and my knees cracked off the tile floor. The onyx-filled air scratched my throat and scorched my lungs.

I curled into a ball, fingers clawing at the floor as my mouth opened in a silent scream. My body spasmed uncontrollably as the onyx invaded every cell. There was no end. No hope that the fire would be extinguished by Daemon's quick thinking, and I silently called out his name, over and over again, but there was no answer.

There was and would be nothing but pain.

***

{ Daemon }

Thirty-one hours, forty-two minutes, and twenty seconds had passed since the doors had closed, separating Kat from me. Thirty-one hours, forty-two minutes, and ten seconds since I last saw her. For thirty-one hours and forty-one minutes Kat had been in the hands of Daedalus.

Each second, every minute and hour that ticked by had driven me fucking insane.

They had locked me up in a one-room cabin, which was really a cell decked out in everything that would piss off a Luxen, but it hadn't stopped me. I'd blown that door and the Luxen guarding me into another damn galaxy. Bitter anger surged through me, coating my insides with acid as I picked up speed, flying past the row of cabins, avoiding the cluster of homes, and heading straight for the trees surrounding the Luxen community hidden under the shadows of Seneca Rocks. Not even halfway there, I saw a blur of white streaking straight for me.

They were going to try to stop me? Yeah, not going to happen.

I skidded to a halt, and the light zoomed past and then whirled around. Shaped like a human, it stood directly in front of me, so bright that the Luxen lit up the dark trees behind him.

We are only trying to protect you, Daemon.

Just like Dawson and Matthew had thought knocking me out at Mount Weather and then locking me up would protect me. Oh, I had a nuclear-size bone to pick with those two.

We don't want to hurt you.

"That's a shame." I cracked my neck. Behind me, several more were gathering. "I have no problem hurting you."

The Luxen in front of me extended his arms. *It doesn't have to be this way.*

There was no other way. Letting my human form fade was like shedding too-tight clothing. A reddish tint spread over the grass like blood. *Let's get this over with.*

None of them hesitated.

Neither did I.

The Luxen shot forward, a blur of brilliant limbs. I dipped under his arms, springing up behind him. Catching his arms, I slammed my foot into his bowed back. No sooner had that Luxen gone down than another took his place.

Launching to the side, I clotheslined the one racing at me and then dipped, narrowly missing a foot with my name on it. I welcomed this—the physicality of fighting. I poured every bit of fury and frustration into each punch and kick, tearing through three more of them.

A pulse of light cut through the shadows, aiming straight for me. Bending down, I slammed a fist into the ground. Soil flew into the sky as a shockwave rippled outward, catching the Luxen and tossing him into the air. I sprang up, grabbing him as intense, bright light blew off me, turning night into day for the briefest moment.

I spun, tossing him like a disk.

He smacked into a tree and hit the ground, but he quickly shot to his feet. Charging forward, white light tinged in blue trailed behind him like a tail on a comet. Lobbing at me what amounted to a nuclear power–strength ball of energy, he let out an inhuman battle roar.

Oh, so he wanted to play that way?

I leaned to the side; the bolt fizzled out as it zoomed past. Pulling on the Source, I reared back, letting the power soar. I slammed my foot down, creating a crater and another ripple, knocking the Luxen off balance. Throwing my arm out, I let the Source go. It flew from my hand like a bullet, hitting him squarely in the chest.

He went down, alive but all kinds of twitchy.

"What do you think you're doing, Daemon?"

At the sound of Ethan Smith's level voice, I turned. The Elder, in his human form, stood several yards back among the fallen. My body shook with unspent power. *They shouldn't have tried to stop me. None of you should have tried to stop me.*

Ethan clasped his hands in front of him. "You shouldn't be willing to risk your community for a human girl."

There was a good chance I was going to zap him into next week. *She is not something I'm ever going to discuss with you.*

"We are your kind, Daemon." He took a step forward. "You need to stay with us. Going after this human will only—"

I threw my hand out, grabbing by the neck the Luxen who was sneaking up on me. Turning to him, we both slipped into human form. His eyes filled with terror. "For real?" I growled.

"Crap," he muttered.

Lifting him into the air, I choke-slammed the stupid SOB into the ground. Soil and rock flew into the air as I straightened, returning my gaze to Ethan.

The Elder paled. "You're fighting your own kind, Daemon. That is unforgiveable."

"I'm not asking for your forgiveness. I'm not asking for shit."

"You'll be cast out," he threatened.

"Guess what?" I backed away, keeping an eye on the Luxen on the ground who had started to stir. "I don't care."

Anger rolled off Ethan, and the calm, almost docile expression vanished. "You think I don't know what you did to that girl? What your brother did to the other one? Both of you have brought this onto yourselves. This is why we don't mix with them. Humans bring nothing but trouble. You are going to cause trouble, cause them to look too closely at us. We don't need that, Daemon. You're risking a lot for a human."

"This is their planet," I said, surprising myself with that statement, but it was true. Kat had said it before, and I repeated her words. "We are the guests here, buddy."

Ethan's eyes narrowed. "For now."

My head cocked to the side at those two words. Didn't take a genius to figure out that was a warning, but right now, it wasn't my priority. Kat was. "Don't follow me."

"Daemon—"

"I mean it, Ethan. If you or anyone else comes after me, I won't go easy like I just did."

The Elder sneered. "Is she truly worth this?"

A cold wind moved down my spine. Without the support of the Luxen community, I'd be on my own, not welcomed in any of their colonies. Word traveled fast; Ethan would make sure of it. But there wasn't a moment of hesitation.

"Yes," I said. "She is worth *everything*."

Ethan sucked in a sharp breath. "You're done here."

"So be it."

Pivoting, I took off through the trees, racing toward my house. My brain was churning. I didn't have much of a plan. Nothing concrete, but I knew I was going to need a few things. Money was one of them. A car. Running the whole way to Mount Weather wasn't an option. Going back to the house was going to be difficult, because I knew Dee and Dawson would be there—and they would try to stop me.

At this point, I'd like to see them try.

But as I crested the rocky hill and picked up speed, what Ethan had said overshadowed my plotting. *Both of you have brought this onto yourselves.* Had we? The answer was simple and right in my face. Both Dawson and I had put the girls in danger simply by being interested in them. Neither of us had planned on them getting hurt, or that healing them would mutate them into something not quite human or Luxen, but we knew the risks.

I especially knew the risks.

It was why I had pushed Katy away in the beginning, had

gone to extremes to keep her away from Dee and me. Partly due to what had happened to Dawson, but also because there were so many risks. And yet I had brought Kat deep into this world. Held her hand and practically escorted her right into it. Look at what that got her.

It wasn't supposed to happen this way.

If anyone was to be caught, if things went down badly in Mount Weather, it should've been me. Not Kat. Never her.

Cursing under my breath, I hit a patch of ground lit by silvery moonlight seconds before breaking clear of the forest and slowed down without intending to.

My eyes went straight to Kat's house, and pressure clamped down on my chest.

The house was dark and still, as if it had been the years before she had moved in. No life, an empty, dark shell of a home.

I stopped beside her mother's car and let out a ragged breath that did nothing to relieve the pressure building in my chest. In the darkness, I knew I wasn't seen, and if the DOD or Daedalus were watching for me, they could take me in. It would make it easier for me.

If I closed my eyes, I could see Kat coming out the front door, wearing that damn shirt that said My Blog Is Better Than Your Vlog, and those shorts . . . those legs . . .

Man, I had been such an ass to her, but she hadn't backed down from me. Not for one second.

A light flipped on in my house. A second later, the front door opened, and Dawson stood there. The breeze carried his soft curse.

I had to say Dawson looked a thousand times better since I'd last seen him. The dark shadows that had been under his eyes were mostly gone. Some of the weight had returned. Like before the DOD and Daedalus had captured him, it would be nearly impossible to tell us apart with the exception of his longer, shaggier hair. Yeah, he looked like a million bucks. He had Bethany back.

I knew I sounded bitter, but I didn't care.

The moment my feet touched the stairs, a shockwave erupted from me, cracking the cement of the steps and rattling the floorboards.

Blood drained from my brother's face as he took a step back. A sick sense of satisfaction swelled in me. "Weren't expecting me so soon?"

"Daemon." Dawson's back hit the front door. "I know you're pissed."

Another burst of energy left me, hitting the ceiling of the roof. Wood cracked. A fissure appeared, splitting down the center. My vision tinted as the Source filled me, turning the world white. "You have no idea, brother."

"We wanted to keep you safe until we knew what to do— how to get Kat back. That's all."

I took a deep breath as I stepped up to Dawson, going eye to eye with him. "Did you think that locking me up in the community was the best answer?"

"We—"

"Did you think you could stop me?" Power shot from me, smacking into the door behind Dawson, blowing it off the hinges and into the house. "I'll burn the world down to save her."

2

{ Katy }

Soaking wet and chilled to the bone, I pulled myself off the floor. I had no idea how much time had passed since the first dose of onyx had been released and the last blast of icy water had knocked me flat on my back.

Giving in and letting them do what they wanted hadn't seemed like an option in the beginning. At first the pain was worth it, because I'd be damned if I was going to make this easy for them. Once the onyx had been washed from my skin and I could move again, I rushed the door. I wasn't making any progress, and by the fourth cycle of being doused with onyx and then drowned, I was done.

I was really, truly done.

Once I was able to stand without collapsing, I shuffled toward the cold table in slow, achy steps. I was pretty sure the table had a very thin layer of diamonds over the surface. The kind of money it must've taken to outfit a room, let alone a whole building, in diamonds had to be astronomical—and further explained the nation's debt problem. And really, out of everything to be thinking about, that shouldn't even make the list, but I think the onyx had shorted out my brain.

Sergeant Dasher had come and gone during the whole process, replaced by men in army fatigues. The berets they wore hid most of their faces, but from what I could see, they didn't seem much older than me, maybe in their early twenties.

Two of them were in the room now, both with pistols strapped to their thighs. Part of me was surprised they hadn't broken out the tranqs, but the onyx served its purpose. The one wearing a dark green beret stood near the controls, watching me, one hand on his pistol and the other on the button of pain. The other, face hidden by a khaki beret, guarded the door.

I placed my hands on the table. Through the wet ropes of my soaked hair, my fingers looked too white and pasty. I was cold and shivering so badly I wondered if I was actually experiencing a seizure. "I'm . . . I'm done," I rasped out.

A muscle popped on Khaki Beret's face.

I tried to lift myself onto the table, because I knew if I didn't sit, I was going to fall, but the deep tremor in my muscles caused me to wobble to the side. The room whirled for a second. There just might be some permanent damage. I almost laughed, because what good would I be to Daedalus if they broke me?

Dr. Roth had remained the whole time, sitting in the corner of the room, looking weary, but now he stood, pressure cuff in hand. "Help her onto the table."

Khaki Beret came toward me, determination locking his jaw. I backpedaled in a feeble attempt to put some distance between us. My heart pounded insanely fast. I didn't want him touching me. I didn't want any of them touching me.

Legs shaking, I took another step back, and my muscles just stopped working. I hit the floor hard on my butt, but I was so numb, the pain really didn't register.

Khaki Beret stared down at me, and from my vantage point, I could see his entire face. He had the most startling blue eyes, and while he looked like he was so over this routine, there seemed to be some level of compassion to his stare.

Without saying a word, he bent down and scooped me up. He smelled of fresh detergent, the same kind my mom used, and tears welled in my eyes. Before I could put up a fight, which would've been pointless, he deposited me on the table. When he backed away, I gripped the edges of the table, feeling like I'd been here before.

And I had.

Another cup of water was given to me, which I accepted. The doctor sighed loudly. "Is fighting this out of your system now?"

I dropped the paper cup on the table and forced my tongue to move. It felt swollen and difficult to control. "I don't want to be here."

"Of course you don't." He placed the chest piece under my shirt, like he had done before. "No one in this room, or even in this building, expects that from you, but fighting us, before you even know what we're about, is only going to hurt you in the end. Now breathe in deeply."

I breathed in, but the air got stuck. The line of white cabinets across the room blurred. I would not cry. I would not cry.

The doctor went through the motions, checking my breathing and blood pressure before he spoke again. "Katy—may I call you Katy?"

A short, hoarse laugh escaped me. So polite. "Sure."

He smiled as he placed the pressure cuff on the table and then stepped back, folding his arms. "I need to do a full exam, Katy. I promise it will not hurt. It will be like any other physical exam you've had before."

Fear balled in my core. I folded my arms around my waist, shivering. "I don't want that."

"We can postpone it for a little bit, but it must be done." Turning, he walked over to one of the cabinets and retrieved a dark brown blanket. Returning to the table, he draped it over my bent shoulders. "Once you regain your strength, we're going to move you to your quarters. There you will be able to wash up and get into fresh, clean clothes. There's also a TV if you want to watch, or you can rest. It's pretty late, and you have a big day tomorrow."

I held the blanket close, shaking. He made it sound like I was at a hotel. "Big day tomorrow?"

He nodded. "There is a lot we need to show you. Hopefully, then you'll understand what Daedalus is truly about."

I fought the urge to laugh again. "I know what you guys are about. I know what—"

"You know *only* what you've been told," the doctor interrupted. "And what you do know is only half true." He cocked his head to the side. "I know you're thinking of Dawson and Bethany. You don't know the whole story behind them."

My eyes narrowed, and the answering rush of anger warmed my insides. How dare he put what Daedalus did to Bethany and Dawson back on them? "I know enough."

Dr. Roth glanced at Green Beret by the controls, and then he nodded. Green Beret quietly exited the room, leaving the doctor and Khaki Beret behind. "Katy—"

"I know you basically tortured them," I cut in, growing more furious by the second. "I know you brought people in here and forced Dawson to heal them, and when that didn't work, those humans died. I know you kept them away from each other and used Beth to get Dawson to do what you wanted. You're worse than evil."

"You don't know the whole story," he repeated evenly, completely unfazed by my accusations. He looked at Khaki Beret. "Archer, you were here when Bethany and Dawson were brought in?"

I turned to Archer, and he nodded. "When the subjects were

brought in, both were understandably difficult to deal with, but after the female had gone through the mutation, she was even more violent. They were allowed to stay together until it became obvious there was a safety issue. That was why they were separated and eventually moved to different locations."

I shook my head as I pulled the blanket closer. I wanted to yell at them at the top of my lungs. "I'm not stupid."

"I don't think you are," the doctor answered. "Hybrids are notoriously unbalanced, even the ones who have mutated successfully. Beth was and is unstable."

Knots formed in my belly. I could easily remember how crazy Beth had been at Vaughn's house. She had seemed fine when we found her at Mount Weather, but she hadn't always been that way. Were Dawson and everyone in danger? Could I even believe anything these people were telling me?

"That's why I need to do a full exam, Katy."

I looked at the doctor. "Are you saying I'm unstable?"

He didn't respond immediately, and it felt like the table had dropped out from underneath me.

"There is a chance," he said. "Even with successful mutations, there is an instability issue that arises when the hybrid uses the Source."

Clenching the blanket until the feeling came back in my knuckles, I willed my heart to slow down. It wasn't working. "I don't believe you. I don't believe anything you're saying. Dawson was—"

"Dawson was a sad case," he said, cutting me off. "And you will come to understand that. What happened with Dawson was unintentional. He would've been released eventually, once we were sure he could assimilate again. And Beth—"

"Just stop," I snarled, and my own voice surprised me. "I don't want to hear any more of your lies."

"You have no idea, Miss Swartz, how dangerous the Luxen are and the threat those who have been mutated by them pose."

"The Luxen aren't dangerous! And the hybrids wouldn't be, either, if you left us alone. We haven't done anything to you. We wouldn't have. We weren't doing anything until you—"

"Do you know why the Luxen came to Earth?" he asked.

"Yes." My knuckles ached. "The Arum destroyed their planet."

"Do you know why their planet was destroyed? Or the origins of the Arum?"

"They were at war. The Arum were trying to take their abilities and kill them." I was totally up to date on my Alien 101. The Arum were the opposite of the Luxen, more shadow than light, and they *fed* off the Luxen. "And you're working with those monsters."

Dr. Roth shook his head. "Like with any great war, the Arum and Luxen have been fighting for so long that I doubt many of them even know what sparked the battle."

"So are you trying to say that the Arum and the Luxen are like the intergalactic Gaza Strip?"

Archer snorted at that.

"I don't even know why we're talking about this," I said, suddenly so tired I wasn't sure I could think straight. "None of that matters."

"It *does* matter," the doctor said. "It goes to show how very little you truly know about any of this."

"Well, I guess you're going to educate me?"

He smiled, and I wanted to knock the condescending look off his face. Too bad that would require my letting go of the blanket and mustering up the energy to do so. "During their prime, the Luxen were the most powerful and intelligent life-form in the entire universe. Just like in any set of species, evolution evolved in response, creating a natural predator—the Arum."

I stared at the man. "What are you saying?"

He met my gaze. "The Luxen weren't the victims in their war. They were the cause of it."

{ Daemon }

"How did you get out?" Dawson asked.

It had taken everything for me not to slam my fist into his face. I had calmed down enough that bringing the house down on its foundation was unlikely to occur. Still a possibility, though.

"Better question is how many did I lay out to get here?" I tensed, waiting. Dawson blocked the doorway. "Don't fight me on any of this, brother. You won't be able to stop me, and you know it."

He held my gaze for a moment, then swore as he stepped aside. I slid past him, my eyes going to the staircase.

"Dee's asleep," he said, running a hand through his hair. "Daemon—"

"Where's Beth?"

"Here," came a soft voice from the dining room.

I turned around and, hell, it was like the girl materialized out of smoke and shadows. I'd forgotten how much of a tiny thing she was. Slim and elfin, with lots of brown hair and a pointy, stubborn little chin. She was a lot paler than I remembered.

"Hey there." My beef wasn't with her. I glanced back at my brother. "You think it's wise to have her here?"

He went to her side, draping his arm over her shoulders. "We planned on leaving. Matthew was going to set us up in Pennsylvania, near South Mountain."

I nodded. The mountain was rocking a decent amount of quartzite but no Luxen community that we knew of.

"But we didn't want to leave right now," Beth added quietly, her eyes darting around the room, not settling on anything in particular. She was dressed in one of Dawson's T-shirts and a pair of Dee's sweats. Both swallowed her whole. "It didn't seem right. Someone should be here with Dee."

"But it's not really safe for you two," I pointed out. "Matthew could stay with Dee."

"We're fine." Dawson bent his head, pressing a kiss against Beth's forehead before pinning me with a serious look. "You shouldn't be out of the colony. We had you there to keep you safe. If the police see you or the—"

"The police aren't going to see me." That concern made sense. Since Kat and I were both presumed missing, or that we'd run away, my reappearance would raise a lot of questions. "Neither will Kat's mom."

He didn't look convinced. "You're not worried about the DOD?"

I said nothing.

He shook his head. "Shit."

Beside him, Beth shifted her slight weight from one foot to the next. "You're going after her, aren't you?"

"The hell he is," my brother cut in, and when I said nothing, he strung together so many curse words I was actually impressed. "Dammit, Daemon, out of everyone, I know what you're feeling, but what you're doing is insane. And seriously, how did you get out of the cabin?"

Striding forward, I brushed past him and headed for the kitchen. It was strange being back in here. Everything was the same—gray granite countertops, white appliances, the god-awful country decorations Dee had thrown up on the walls, and the heavy oak kitchen table.

I stared at the table. Like a mirage, Kat appeared, sitting on the edge. Deep pain sliced across my chest. God, I missed her, and it killed me not knowing what was really happening to her or what they were doing.

Then again, I had a good idea. I knew enough from what they'd done to Dawson and Beth, and that made me physically ill.

"Daemon?" He had followed me.

I turned from the table. "We don't need to have this conversation, and I'm not in the mood to state the obvious. You know what I'm doing. It's why you put me in the colony."

"I don't even understand how you got out. There was onyx all over that place."

Each colony had cabins meant to keep Luxen who'd become dangerous to our kind or to humans and that the Elders didn't want to take them to the human police.

"If there's a will, there's a way." I smiled when his eyes narrowed.

"Daemon . . ."

"I'm here to get a few things, and then I'm gone." I opened up the fridge and grabbed a bottle of water. Taking a swig, I faced him. We were the same height, so we met eye to eye. "I mean it. Don't push me on this."

He flinched, but his green eyes met mine. "There's nothing I can say that's going to change your mind?"

"Nope."

He stepped back, rubbing his hand down his jaw. Behind him, Beth sat in the chair, her arms wrapped around her waist, her gaze going everywhere except toward us.

Dawson leaned against the counter. "You going to make me beat you into submission?"

Beth's head jerked up, and I laughed. "I'd like to see you try, little brother."

"Little brother," he scoffed, but a faint smile pulled at his lips. Relief was evident on Beth's face. "By how many seconds?" he asked.

"Enough." I tossed the water bottle in the garbage.

Several moments passed, and then he said, "I'll help you."

"Hell no." I folded my arms. "I don't want your help. I don't want any of you taking part in this."

Determination set his jaw. "Bull. You helped us. It's too dangerous to do it on your own. So if you're going to be stubborn and ignore the fact that you kept me on a leash, which you are, I'm not going to let you do this by yourself."

"I'm sorry I held you back. Now, knowing exactly how you felt, I would've stormed that damn place the very same night you came home. But I'm not going to let you help. Look at what happened when we were in this all together. I can't be worried about you guys. I want you and Dee as far away as possible from this."

"But—"

"I'm not going to argue with you." I placed my hands on his shoulders and squeezed. "I know you want to help. I appreciate that. But if you really want to help, don't try to stop me."

Dawson closed his eyes, his features pinching as his chest rose sharply. "Letting you do this by yourself isn't right. You wouldn't let me."

"I know. I'm going to be okay. I'm always okay." I leaned in, resting my forehead against his. As I clasped the sides of his face, I kept my voice low. "You just got Beth back, and running off with me isn't right. She needs you. You need her, and I need . . ."

"You need Katy." He opened his eyes, and for the first time since the shit went down at Mount Weather, there was understanding in his gaze. "I get that. I do."

"She needs you, too," Beth whispered.

Dawson and I broke apart. He turned to her. She was still

sitting at the table, her hands opening and closing in her lap in quick, repetitive movements.

"What did you say, babe?" he asked.

"Kat needs him." Her lashes lifted, and although her gaze was fixed on us, she wasn't looking at us, not really. "They'll tell her things at first. They'll trick her, but the things they'll do . . ."

It felt like all the oxygen was sucked out of the room.

Dawson was by her side immediately, kneeling so that she had to look at him. He took her hand in his and brought it to his lips. "It's okay, Beth."

She followed his movements almost obsessively, but there was a strange sheen gathering in her eyes, as if she were slipping further away. The hair on the back of my neck rose, and I stepped forward.

"She won't be at Mount Weather," Beth said, her stare drifting over Dawson's shoulder. "They'll take her far away and make her do things."

"Do what?" The words were out of my mouth before I could stop them.

Dawson shot me a look over his shoulder, but I ignored it. "You don't have to talk about this, babe. All right?"

A long moment passed before she said anything. "When I saw him with you, I knew, but you all seemed like you knew, too. He's bad news. He was there, too, with me."

My hands curled into fists as I remembered Beth's reaction to seeing him, but we had shut her up. "Blake?"

She nodded slowly. "All of them are bad. They don't mean to be." Her focus drifted to Dawson, and she whispered, "I don't mean to be."

"Oh, baby, you're not bad." He placed a hand on her cheek. "You're not bad at all."

Her lower lip trembled. "I've done terrible things. You have no idea. I've ki—"

"It doesn't matter." He went down on his knees. "None of that matters."

A shudder rolled through her, and then she looked up, her eyes locking on mine. "Don't let them do those things to Katy. They'll change her."

I couldn't move or breathe.

Her face crumpled. "They've changed me. I close my eyes, and I see their faces—all of them. I can't get them out no matter what I do. They're *inside* of me."

Good God . . .

"Look at me, Beth." Dawson guided her face back to his. "You're here with me. You're not there anymore. You know that, right? Keep looking at me. Nothing's inside of you."

She shook her head vigorously. "No. You don't understand. You—"

Backing off, I let my brother handle this. He talked to her in low, soothing tones, but when she quieted, she stared forward, shaking her head side-to-side slowly, her eyes wide and mouth open. She didn't blink, didn't even seem to acknowledge him or me.

Nobody's home, I realized.

As Dawson talked her through whatever was afflicting her, horror—real, true horror—turned my insides cold. The pain that was in my brother's eyes as he smoothed her hair back from her pale face ate me up. At that moment, he looked like he wanted nothing more than to trade places with her.

I gripped the counter behind me, unable to look away.

I could easily see myself doing the same thing. Except it wouldn't be Beth I'd be holding in my arms and coaxing back to reality—it would be Kat.

I was only in my bedroom long enough to change into fresh clothing. Being in there was a blessing and a curse. For some reason it made me feel closer to Kat. Maybe it was because of what we'd shared in my bed and all the moments before then. It also tore me up, because she wasn't in my arms and she wasn't safe.

I didn't know if she'd ever truly be safe again.

As I pulled the clean shirt over my head, I sensed my sister before she spoke. Blowing out a low breath, I turned and found her standing in my doorway, dressed in bubblegum pink pajamas I'd given her for Christmas last year.

She looked as shitty as I felt. "Daemon—"

"If you're going to start in on how I need to wait and think this through, you can save it." I sat down on the bed, dragging a hand through my hair. "It's not going to change what I want."

"I know what you want, and I don't blame you." She cautiously stepped into my room. "No one wants to see you get hurt . . . or worse."

"Worse is what Kat is going through right this moment. She's your friend. Or was. And you're okay with waiting? Knowing what they could be doing to her?"

She flinched, and her eyes shone like emeralds in the low light. "That's not fair," she whispered.

Maybe not, and any other time I would've felt like an ass for the low blow, but I couldn't muster the empathy.

"We can't lose you," she said after a few moments of awkward-as-hell silence. "You have to understand that we did what we did because we love you."

"But I love her," I said without hesitation.

Her eyes widened, probably since it was the first time she'd heard me say it out loud—well, about anyone other than my family. I wished I had said it more often, especially to Kat. Funny how that kind of shit always turns out in the end. While you're deep in something, you never say or do what you need to. It's always after the fact, when it's too late, that you realize what you should've said or done.

It couldn't be too late. The fact that I was still alive was testament to that.

Tears filled my sister's eyes as she said in a quiet voice, "She loves you, too."

The burn in my chest expanded and crawled up my throat.

"You know, I always knew she liked you before she admitted it to me or herself."

I smiled slightly. "Yeah, same here."

Dee twisted the length of her hair in her hands. "I knew she'd be . . . she'd be perfect for you. She'd never put up with your crap." Dee sighed. "I know Kat and I had our problems over . . . Adam, but I love Kat, too."

I couldn't do this—sit here and talk about her like we were at some kind of wake or memorial. This shit was too much.

She took a little breath, a sure sign she was about to unload. "I wish I hadn't been so hard on her. I mean, she totally needed to know that she should've trusted me and all of that, but if I could've let go of it sooner, then . . . well, you know what I mean. It would've been better for everyone. I hate the idea that I might never—" She cut herself off quickly, but I knew what she was getting at. She might never see Kat again. "Anyway, I had asked her before prom if she was scared about going back to Mount Weather."

My chest seized like someone had grabbed me in a bear hug. "What did she say?"

Dee let go of her hair. "She said she was, but, Daemon, she was so brave. She even laughed, and I told her . . ." She stared at her hands, her expression pinched. "I told her to be careful and to keep you and Dawson safe. And you know, she said she would, and she did, in a way."

Christ.

I rubbed my palm over my chest where it felt like a fist-sized hole had opened up.

"But before I had asked her that, she had been trying to talk to me about Adam and everything, and I had cut her off with that question. She kept trying to make amends, and I kept pushing her back. She probably hated me—"

"That's not the case." I looked Dee dead-on. "She didn't hate you. Kat understood. She knew you needed time, and she . . ." I stood, suddenly needing to get out of this room and this house and onto the road.

"We haven't run out of time," she said quietly, almost like she was begging . . . and damn if that didn't hurt. "We *haven't*."

Anger flashed through me, and it took everything for me not to lash out. Because keeping me in that damn cabin had been nothing but a waste of time. Taking several deep breaths, I asked a question I wasn't sure I wanted an answer to. "Have you seen her mom?"

Her lower lip trembled. "I have."

I caught my sister's stare and held it. "Tell me."

Her expression said that was the last thing she wanted to do. "The police were at her house all day after . . . we got back. I talked to them, and then to her mom. The police think you two ran away. Or at least that's what they told her mom, but I think one of them is an implant. He was way too adamant about it."

"Of course," I muttered.

"Her mom doesn't believe it, though. She knows Katy. And Dawson has been keeping a low profile with Beth and all. It would seem suspicious to anyone with two brain cells." She plopped back down, arms falling in her lap. "It was really hard. Her mom was so upset. I could tell she thinks the worst, especially after Will and Carissa 'disappearing,'" Dee said, using air quotes. "She's really bad off."

Guilt exploded like buckshot, leaving dozens of holes in me. Kat's mom shouldn't be going through this—worrying about her daughter, missing her, and fearing the worst.

"Daemon? Don't leave us. We'll find a way to get her, but please don't leave us. Please."

I stared at her in silence. I couldn't make a promise I had no intention of keeping and she already knew that. "I have to go. You know that. I have to get her back."

Her lower lip trembled. "But what if you don't get her back? What if you are put in there with her?"

"Then at least I'm with her. I'm there for her." I walked up to my sister and clasped her cheeks. Tears rolled down, pooling along my fingers. I hated to see her cry, but I hated what was happening to Kat more. "Don't worry, Dee. This is me we're talking about. You know damn well I can get myself out of any situation. And you know I will get her out of there."

And nothing in this world would stop me.

3

I was amazed that with all the reeling my brain was doing, I'd be able to do something normal like change into fresh clothes—a pair of black jogging pants and a gray cotton shirt. The clothing fit on a disturbing level, even the undergarments.

Like they knew I'd be coming.

Like they had snooped around in my undie drawer and got my size.

I wanted to hurl.

Instead of dwelling on that, which would most definitely lead to me flipping out and getting a face full of onyx and icy water again, I focused on my cell. Oh, excuse me. My *quarters*, as Dr. Roth reminded me.

It was about the size of a hotel room, a good three hundred square feet or so. Tile covered the floors, cold under my bare feet. I had no idea where my shoes were. There was a double bed tucked up against the wall, a tiny end table beside it, a dresser, and a TV mounted on the wall at the foot of the bed. In the ceiling were the fearsome black dots of pain, but there were no water hoses in the room.

And there was a door across from the bed.

Padding to it, I placed the tips of my fingers on the door and cautiously pushed it open, half expecting a net made of onyx to drop on me.

It didn't.

Inside was a small bathroom with another door at the end. That one was locked.

I wheeled around and went back into the bedroom.

The trip to my cell hadn't been scenic. We'd walked straight out of the room I'd woken up in and into an elevator that had opened straight across from where I was now. I hadn't really even gotten a chance to look down the hallway to see how many rooms there were like the one I was in now.

I bet there were a lot.

Having no idea what time it was, if it were night or day, I shuffled over to the bed and pulled down the brown blanket. I sat and pressed my back against the wall, tucking my legs against my chest. I tugged the blanket to my chin and sat facing the door.

I was tired—weary to my very core. My eyes were heavy, and my body ached from the effort to sit up, but the idea of falling asleep scared the ever-loving crap out of me. What if someone came into the room while I slept? That was a very real concern. The door locked from the outside, meaning I was completely at their whim.

To keep myself from dozing off, I focused on the one thousand questions circling in my head. Dr. Roth had made that cloak-and-dagger statement about the Luxen being behind the war that had started God knew how long ago. Even if they had been, did it matter now? I didn't think it did. Not when this generation of Luxen was so far removed from what their ancestors might've plotted. I honestly didn't even understand why he had brought it up. To show how little I knew? Or was there something more? And what about Bethany? Was she really dangerous?

I shook my head. Even if the Luxen started a war hundreds, if not thousands, of years ago, that didn't mean they were evil. And if Bethany was dangerous, it probably had something to do with what they had done to her. I wasn't going to let them pull me into their lies, but I had to admit, what they had said unnerved me.

My brain mulled over more questions. How long were they planning to keep me here? What about school? My mom? I thought of Carissa. Had she been brought to a place like this? I still had no idea how she'd ended up mutated, or why. Luc, the ridiculously intelligent and even a bit scary teen hybrid, had helped us get into Mount Weather and had warned that I may never know what happened to Carissa. I wasn't sure I could live with that. Never knowing why she ended up in my bedroom and self-destructed wasn't right. And if I ended up like her, or like the countless other hybrids the government kidnapped, what would happen to my mom?

With no answers to any of those questions, I finally let my mind go where it wanted, where I'd been desperately trying to prevent it from going.

Daemon.

My eyes fell shut as I exhaled. I didn't even have to try to see him. His face pieced together perfectly.

His broad cheekbones, lips that were full and almost always expressive, and those eyes—those beautiful green eyes that were like two polished emeralds, abnormally bright. I knew my memory really didn't do him justice. He had this masculine beauty I'd never seen before in real life, had only read about in the books I loved.

Man, I missed books already.

In his true form, Daemon was extraordinary. All of the Luxen were breathtakingly beautiful; being made of pure light, they were mesmerizing to look upon, like seeing a star up close.

Daemon Black could be as prickly as a hedgehog having a really bad day, but underneath all that spindly armor, he was sweet, protective, and incredibly selfless. He'd dedicated most of his life to keeping his family and his kind safe, continually facing danger with little thought to his own safety. I was in constant awe of him. Though it hadn't always been like that.

A tear dripped down my cheek unbidden.

Resting my chin against my knees, I swiped at the wetness. I prayed that he was okay—as okay as he could be. That Matthew, Dawson, and Andrew were keeping a tight leash on him. That they wouldn't let him do what I knew he wanted to: the same thing I'd do if the situation were flipped.

Although I wanted him—needed him—to hold me, this was the last place I wanted him to be. The very last place.

Heart aching, I tried thinking about the good things—better things—but the memories weren't enough. There was a strong chance I might never see him again.

The tears slipped out of my tightly squeezed eyes.

Crying solved nothing, but it was hard to hold it in when exhaustion dogged me. I kept my eyes closed, slowly counting until the knot of messy, raw emotions climbed back down my throat.

The next thing I knew, I jolted awake, my heart pounding and mouth dry. I hadn't remembered falling asleep, but I must've. A weird tingle moved over my skin as I dragged in a deep breath. Did I have a nightmare? I couldn't remember, but something felt off. Disoriented, I threw the blanket back and looked around the dark cell.

Every muscle in my body seized as my eyes picked out a darker, thicker shadow in the corner by the door. Tiny hairs on my body rose. Air halted in my lungs, and fear sunk its icy claws into my stomach, freezing me in place.

I wasn't alone.

The shadow pulled away from the wall, moving forward quickly. My first instinct screamed Arum, and I reached blindly for the opal necklace, realizing too late I didn't have it anymore.

"You're still having nightmares," the shadow said.

At the sound of the familiar voice, fear gave way to rage so potent that it tasted like battery acid. I was on my feet before I knew it.

"Blake," I spat.

4

{ Katy }

My brain clicked off and something a hell of a lot more primitive and aggressive took over. I felt the horrible, sinking sense of betrayal. Swinging out, my fist connected with what felt like Blake's cheekbone. It wasn't a girlie hit, either. Every bit of anger and pent-up hatred I felt toward him was packed into that punch.

He let out a startled groan as white-hot pain danced across my hand. "Katy—"

"You bastard!" I swung again, my knuckles slamming into his jaw this time.

He let out another grunt of pain as he staggered back. "Jesus."

I spun, grabbing for a tiny lamp beside the bed, and without warning, the overhead light came on. I wasn't sure how it did. If my abilities didn't work in here, then Blake's shouldn't, either. The sudden glare caught me off guard, and Blake took advantage.

He sprang forward, forcing me to back away from the lamp. "I wouldn't do that if I were you," he warned.

"Go screw yourself." I swung at him again.

He caught my fist and twisted. Sharp pain shot up my arm, and I let out a surprised gasp. He spun me around, and I kicked out. Letting go of my arm, he narrowly avoided the thrust of my knee. "This is ridiculous," he said, hazel eyes narrowed. Anger churned the green flecks.

"You betrayed us."

Blake sort of shrugged, and, well, I sort of lost my shit again.

I launched myself at him like some kind of ninja—a really lame ninja, because he easily dodged my attack. My left leg banged into the bed, and the very next second, he slammed into my back. Air punched out of my lungs as I toppled forward, hitting the bed on my side, bouncing it against the wall.

His knees went down on the mattress as he grabbed hold of my shoulders, rolling me onto my back. I slapped at his arms, and he let out a curse. Rearing up, I swung at him once more.

"Stop it," he growled, grabbing my wrist. The next moment he had hold of my other one. Stretching my arms above my head, he leaned over me, bringing his face within inches of mine, and spoke low. "Stop it, Katy. There are cameras everywhere. You can't see them, but they are there. They are watching right now. How do you think the lights just came on? It's not magic, and they *will* flood this whole room with onyx. I don't know about you, but I don't find that very appealing."

I struggled to push him off, and he shifted his weight so that his knees pressed into my legs, trapping them. Panic was a slow crawl inside me, causing my pulse to jump. I didn't like his weight on me. It reminded me of how he had snuck into my house at night and slept beside me. How he'd watched me sleep. Nausea rose swiftly, and the panic grew. "Get off me!"

"I don't know. You're likely to hit me again."

"I will!" I bucked my hips, but he didn't move, and my heart was racing so fast, I was sure I was going to have a heart attack.

Blake gave me a little shake. "You need to calm down. I'm not going to hurt you. Okay? You can trust me."

Eyes wide, I let out a strangled laugh. "Trust you? Are you insane?"

"You really don't have a choice." Bronze-colored hair fell over his forehead. Usually it was styled in that artfully messy way, but it looked like he'd run out of hair gel today.

I wanted to hit him again, and I strained against his hold, getting nowhere. "I'm going to break your face!"

"Understandable." He pushed down, eyes narrowing. "I know we don't have the most stable relationship—"

"We don't have *any* relationship. We have nothing!" Breathing heavily, I willed my muscles to stop trembling. Several moments passed as he stared down at me, nostrils flared and mouth set in a hard, grim line. I wanted to look away, but to do so was a weakness, and that was the worst thing I could show. "I hate you." It seemed pointless to say that, but it made me feel better.

He flinched, and when he spoke, his voice was barely above a whisper. "I hated lying to you, but I had no choice. Whatever I would've told you, you would've told Daemon and the other Luxen. And I couldn't let that happen. Neither could Daedalus. But we aren't the bad guys here."

I shook my head, dumbfounded and pissed beyond belief. "You *are* the bad guys! You set us up! From the very beginning. It was all leading to this. And you helped them. How could you?"

"We needed to."

"This is *my* life." Tears of anger swelled in my eyes because I had no control over my life now, partly thanks to him, and I struggled to keep my voice level. "Was any of it true? Chris? You wanting to get him out of here?"

Blake didn't say anything for a long moment. "They would've let Chris go at any time. The story of them holding him against his will was just that—a story to make you sympathize with me."

"Son. Of. A. Bitch," I hissed.

"I *was* sent to make sure the mutation held. They didn't know what my uncle and Dr. Michaels were planning, but once they knew that the mutation had held, they needed to know who mutated you and how strong it was. That's why I came back after the night . . . the night you and Daemon let me go."

Our compassion that night had been the final nail in our coffins. It was so ironically sad. I wanted to claw his eyes out.

He let out a ragged breath. "We needed to make sure you were powerful enough for this. They knew Dawson would come back for Beth, but they wanted to see how far you'd get."

"This?" I whispered. "What is *this*?"

"The truth, Katy, the real truth."

"Like you're capable of telling the truth." I rolled my body, trying to throw him off. Muttering another curse, he lifted up, still holding my wrists, and hauled me off the bed. My bare feet slid over the tile as he dragged me toward the bathroom. "What are you doing?"

"I think you need to cool off," he replied, jaw set.

Digging in, all I managed to do was rub the bottoms of my feet raw. Once inside the bathroom, I threw my weight to the side, and he slammed into the sink. Before I could start whaling on him again, he thrust me backward.

Arms spinning like wheels, I toppled over the short rim of the shower stall and landed inside on my butt. A sharp slice of pain shot up my spine.

Blake bolted forward, one hand clamping down on my shoulder, the other reaching blindly to the side. An instant later, freezing water surged out of the showerhead.

Shrieking, I clamored to stand up, but his other hand landed on my shoulder, holding me still as the icy water drenched me. I sputtered, arms flailing against the cold. "Let me out of here!"

"Not until you're ready to listen to me."

"There's nothing you can say!" Soaked clothing clung to my skin. The steady stream of water plastered my hair to my face. Fearing he was trying to drown me, I went for his face, but he smacked my hands away.

"Listen to me." He grasped my chin, his fingers digging into my cheeks, forcing me to meet his eyes. "Blame me all you want, but do you think you wouldn't be here even if you never met me? If so, you're insane. The moment Daemon mutated you, your fate was sealed. If you want to get pissed at anyone, you need to get pissed at him. *He* put you in this situation."

Blake had stunned me into immobility. "You're freaking nuts. You're blaming Daemon for this? He saved my life. I would've—"

"He mutated you, knowing that he was being watched. He's not stupid. He had to know that the DOD would find out."

Actually, he and his family hadn't known about hybrids until I turned into one. "It's so typical of you, Blake. Everything is everyone else's fault."

His eyes narrowed, and the green flecks deepened. "You don't get it."

"You're right." I knocked his hands off my face. "I'll *never* get it."

Backing off, he shook his head as I climbed out of the shower stall. He reached over, turned off the water, and grabbed a towel, tossing it toward me. "Don't try to hit me again."

"Don't tell me what to do." Using the towel, I tried to dry off as best I could.

He clenched his fists. "Look, I get it. You're pissed at me.

Great. Get over it, because there are more important things to focus on."

"Get over it?" I was going to choke him with this towel.

"Yes." He leaned against the closed door, eyeing me warily. "You really have no idea what's going on, Kat."

"Don't call me that." I dabbed at my clothing angrily and uselessly.

"Are you calmed down enough? I need to talk, and you need to listen. Things are not what you think. And I wish I could've told you the truth earlier. I couldn't, but I am now."

A strangled laugh escaped me as I shook my head in disbelief.

His eyes narrowed, and he stepped forward. My back straightened in warning, and he didn't come any closer. "Let's get one thing clear. If Daemon was locked up somewhere, you would've thrown everyone and baby Jesus under the bus to free him. That's what you think I did. So don't act like you're better than me."

Would I? Yes, I would, but the difference between us was that Blake was looking for acceptance and forgiveness after he told more lies than truths. And to me, that was bat-shit crazy.

"You think you can justify this? Well, you're wrong. You can't. You're a monster, Blake. A real living and breathing monster. Nothing, no matter what your intentions are or what the real truth is, will ever change that."

A tiny flicker of unrest shone in his steady gaze.

It took everything in me not to rip the towel rod off the wall and shove it through his eye. I tossed the towel aside, shaking more from anger than the wet coldness seeping through my clothes.

He pushed off the door, and I took a step back, on guard. He frowned. "Daedalus aren't the bad guys here." Opening the bathroom door, he headed out. "That's reality."

I followed him. "How can you even say that with a straight face?"

He sat on my bed. "I know what you're thinking. You want to fight them. I get that. I do. And I know I've lied to you about almost everything, but you wouldn't believe the truth without seeing it. And once you do, things will be different."

There was nothing in this world that they could show me that would change my mind, but I also recognized the futility of fighting him on this. "I need to get dry clothes on."

"I'll wait."

I stared at him. "You're not staying in here while I get dressed."

He glared in annoyance. "Get changed in the bathroom. Close the door. Your virtue is safe from me." And then he winked. "Unless you want that to change, and I'm so down for that. It does get boring around here."

My palm itched to wrap around a very unladylike place and twist. The words that came out of my mouth were my own. I felt them. I *believed* them.

"I'm going to kill you one day," I promised.

A wry smile appeared on his face as he met my stare. "You've killed, Katy. You know how it feels to take a life, but you aren't a murderer. You aren't a killer." He caught my sharp inhale with a knowing look. "Not yet, at least."

I turned away, curling my hands into fists.

"Like I said, we aren't the bad guys. The Luxen are, and you will see that I'm not lying. We are here to stop them from taking over."

5

{ Katy }

The moment Blake and I stepped out of my cell, two military guys surrounded us. One of them was Archer. Seeing his familiar face didn't bring the warm fuzzies. He and the other guy were heavily armed.

They ushered Blake and me toward the elevator, and I craned my neck, trying to see around them to get a grasp on my surroundings. There were several doors like mine, and it looked just like the corridor at Mount Weather. A heavy hand landed on the small of my back, startling me.

It was Archer.

He sent me a look I couldn't decipher, and then I was in the elevator, squeezed between him and Blake. I couldn't even lift my hand to brush away the damp, cold hair that clung to the back of my neck without knocking into them.

Archer leaned forward, pushing a button I couldn't see because of his mammoth body. I frowned, realizing I didn't even know how many floors this place had.

As if he were reading my mind, Blake looked down at me. "We're underground right now. Most of the base is, with the exception of the two upper levels. You're on the seventh floor. Floor seven and six are housing for . . . well, visitors."

I wondered why he was even telling me this. The layout had to be important information. It was like . . . like he trusted me with the knowledge, like I was already one of *them*. I shook the ridiculous notion out of my head. "You mean the prisoners?"

Archer stiffened beside me.

Blake ignored that. "The fifth floor houses Luxen who are being assimilated."

Since the last of the Luxen arrived when Daemon and his family did, more than eighteen years ago, I couldn't imagine how they were still assimilating any of them. My educated guess was that these were Luxen who they believed didn't "fit" with the humans for one reason or another. I shuddered.

And underground? I hated the idea of being underground. It was too much like being dead and buried.

I wiggled my way out from between them, stepping back as I dragged in a deep breath. Blake eyed me curiously, but it was Archer who planted a hand on my shoulder, guiding me forward so I wasn't behind them, like I was going to ninja-stab them in their backs with my invisible knife.

The elevator came to a stop, and the doors slid open. Immediately I caught the scent of food—fresh bread and cooked meat. My stomach roared to life, grumbling like a troll.

Archer's brow went up.

Blake laughed.

My cheeks flamed. Good to know my sense of pride and embarrassment was still intact.

"When was the last time you ate?" Archer asked. It was the first time he'd spoken since I'd been with him and Dr. Roth.

I hesitated. "I . . . I don't know."

He frowned, and I looked away as we stepped out into the wide, brightly lit hallway. I honestly had no idea what day it was or how many days I had been out of it. Up until when I smelled food, I hadn't even been hungry.

"You're meeting with Dr. Roth," Blake said, starting toward the left.

The hand on my shoulder tightened, and even though I wanted to shove it off, I became very still. Archer looked like he knew how to break a neck in six seconds flat. Blake's gaze went from Archer's hand to the man's face.

"She's going to get something to eat first," Archer said.

Blake protested. "The doctor is waiting. So is—"

"They can wait a couple more minutes so the girl can eat something."

"Whatever." Blake lifted his hand in a way that said, *It's your problem, not mine*. "I'll let him know."

Archer steered me toward the right. Only then did I realize the other military guy had gone with Blake. For a second, everything spun as we started forward. He walked liked Daemon, taking long, quick strides. I struggled to keep up while trying to absorb every detail of where I was. Which wasn't much. Everything was white and lit by bright track lighting. Identical doors lined both sides of the endless hallway. The low hum of conversation behind closed doors was barely discernible.

The scent of food grew stronger, and then we came upon double glass doors. He opened them with his free hand. I felt like I was being escorted into the principal's office instead of into the rather normal-looking cafeteria.

Clean square tables were spaced in three rows. Most of the ones up front were occupied. Archer led me to the first vacant table and pushed me down into a seat. Not a big fan of being manhandled, I shot him a glare.

"Stay here," he said, then spun on his heel.

Where in the hell did he think I would go? I watched him walk toward the front where a short line of people was waiting.

I could still make a run for it and take the risk of not knowing where to go, but my stomach tumbled at the prospect. I knew how many floors were above. I scanned the room, and my heart sank. Little black dots of doom were everywhere, and the cameras weren't so hidden. Someone was probably watching me right now.

Men and women in lab coats and fatigues milled around, none of them giving me more than a cursory glance as they passed by. I sat uncomfortably straight, wondering how commonplace it was for them to see a kidnapped teenager scared out of her mind.

Probably more than I cared to know.

We are here to stop them.

Blake's words came back to me, and I sucked in a breath. Stop who? How could the Luxen be the bad guys? My mind raced, caught between wanting to figure out what he meant and not trusting anything he said.

Archer returned with a plate of eggs and bacon in one hand and a little carton of milk in the other. He sat them down in front of me wordlessly, then produced a plastic fork.

I stared at the plate as he sat across from me. A lump formed in my throat as I reached out slowly, my hand hovering over the fork. I suddenly thought of what Blake had said about his stay here—about how everything had been covered in onyx. Had that been true? The fork was obviously harmless, and I had no idea what to believe anymore.

"It's okay," Archer said.

My fingers wrapped around the plastic fork, and when nothing hurt, I breathed a sigh of relief. "Thank you."

He watched me, his expression telling me he had no idea what I was thanking him for, and I kind of wondered, too. I was surprised by his kindness. Or at least I saw this as kindness. He could've been like Blake and the other guy and not given a damn about my starving.

I ate my food quickly. The whole thing was awkward on a painful level. He didn't speak, and he didn't take his eyes off me once, like he was on alert for shenanigans. I wasn't sure what he expected me to do with a plastic plate and fork. Once, his gaze seemed drawn to my left cheek, and I wasn't sure what he was staring at. I hadn't looked in the mirror when I got ready.

The food tasted like sawdust in my mouth, and my jaw ached from the chewing, but I cleared the plate, figuring I needed the energy.

When I finished, the plate and utensil were left behind on the table. Archer's hand was on my shoulder again. Our trip back was silent and the hall a bit more crowded. We stopped outside a closed room. Without knocking, he opened the door.

Another medical room.

White walls. Cabinets. Trays with medical instruments. A table with . . . *stirrups*.

I backpedaled, shaking my head. My heart pounded crazy fast as my gaze bounced from Dr. Roth to Blake, who was sitting in a plastic chair. The other guy who'd gone with Blake earlier was nowhere to be found.

Archer's hand tightened, and before I could get completely out the door, he stopped me. "Don't," he said softly, loud enough for only me to hear. "No one wants a repeat of yesterday."

My head jerked toward him, and my eyes locked with his blue ones. "I don't want to do this."

He didn't blink. "You don't have a choice."

Tears rushed my eyes as his words sunk in. I glanced at the doctor, then at Blake. The latter looked away, a muscle popping in his jaw. The hopelessness of it all hit me. Up until that moment, I don't know what I was really thinking. That I still had some say in what was going to happen around me and *to* me.

Dr. Roth cleared his throat. "How are you feeling today, Katy?"

I wanted to laugh, but my voice came out a croak. "What do you think?"

"It'll get easier." He stepped to the side, motioning me toward the table. "Especially once we get this done."

Pressure clamped down on my chest, and my hands opened and closed at my sides. I'd never had a panic attack before, but I was pretty sure I was seconds away from one. "I don't want them in the room." The words came out quick and raspy.

Blake glanced around and then stood, rolling his eyes. "I'll wait outside."

I wanted to kick him as he strolled by, but Archer was still there. I turned to him, my eyes feeling like they were bulging out of my head.

"No," he said, moving to stand in front of the door. He clasped his hands. "I'm not leaving."

I wanted to cry. There would be no fighting back. The room, like the hallway and cafeteria, had shiny walls. No doubt it was the mixture of onyx and diamond.

The doctor handed me one of those god-awful hospital gowns, then pointed toward a curtain. "You can get changed behind there."

In a numb haze, I headed behind the curtain. My fingers fumbled over my clothing and then the gown. Stepping out from behind the curtain, my body was hot and cold, legs weak as I walked forward. Everything was too bright, and my arms shook as I hoisted myself onto the padded table. I clutched the little ties on the gown, unable to look up.

"I'm going to take some blood first," the doctor said.

Everything that happened next I was either hyperaware of or completely detached from. The sharpness of the needle as it slid into my vein, I felt all the way to my toes, then the slight tug of a tube being replaced atop the needle. The doctor was talking to me, but I didn't really hear him.

When it was all done, and I was in my clothes again, I sat on the table, staring down at the white sneakers he had given me. They were my size—a perfect match. My chest rose and fell in deep, slow breaths.

I was numb.

Dr. Roth explained that blood work would be done. Something about checking out the level of mutation, a workup of my DNA so it could be studied. He told me I wasn't pregnant, which was something I already knew; I almost laughed at that but felt too sick, really, to do anything other than breathe.

After that was all said and done, Archer stepped forward and led me out of the room. He'd said nothing the entire time. When he placed his hand on my shoulder, I shrugged it off, not wanting to be touched by anyone. He didn't place his hand on my shoulder again.

Blake was leaning against the wall outside the office, his eyes sliding open when the door shut behind us. "Finally. We're running late."

I kept my lips sealed, because if I opened my mouth to say anything, I was going to cry. And I didn't want to cry. Not in front of Blake or Archer or any of them.

"Okay." Blake drew the word out as we started down the hall. "This should be fun."

"Don't talk," Archer said.

Blake made a face but remained quiet until we stopped in front of closed double doors like the kind you see in hospitals. He smacked a black button on the wall, and the doors opened, revealing Sergeant Dasher.

He was dressed as he had been before, in full military uniform. "Glad you could finally join us."

That nervous, crazy-sounding laugh bubbled up my throat again. "Sorry." A giggle escaped.

All three guys sent me a look, Blake's the most curious, but I shook my head and took another deep breath. I knew I needed to keep it together. I had to pay attention and keep my wits about me. I was way beyond enemy lines. Freaking out and getting pummeled with onyx wasn't going to help me. Neither was breaking down in hysterics and finding a corner to rock in.

It was hard—probably the hardest thing I'd ever done—but I pulled it together.

Sergeant Dasher pivoted on his heel. "There's something I would like to show you, Katy. I hope this will make things easier for you."

Doubtful, but I followed him. The corridor split into two halls, and we headed down the right one. This place had to be massive—a massive maze of halls and rooms.

The sergeant stopped in front of a door. There was a control panel on the wall with a blinking red light at eye level. He stepped in front of it. The light went green, there was a soft sucking noise, and the door opened, revealing a large square room full of doctors. It was a lab and waiting room in one. I stepped through, immediately wincing at the smell of antiseptic. The sight and smell brought a wave of memories back.

I recognized rooms like this—I'd been in rooms like this before.

With my dad when he was sick. He'd spent time in a room very much like this one when he was receiving treatment for cancer. It paralyzed me.

There were several U-shaped stations in the middle of the space; each one displayed ten recliners that I knew would be comfy. Many were occupied with people—humans—in every stage of sickness. From the optimistic, bright-eyed newly diagnosed to the frail, barely even aware of where they were, and all of them were hooked up to fluid bags and something that looked nothing like chemo. It was clear liquid, but it shimmered under the light, like Dee used to when she faded in and out.

Doctors roamed, checking bags and chatting with the patients. Toward the back were several long tables where people peered into microscopes and measured out medicine. Some were at computers, their white lab coats billowing around the chairs.

Sergeant Dasher stopped beside me. "This is familiar to you, isn't it?"

I looked at him sharply, only vaguely aware that Archer was glued to my other side and Blake had stepped back. Obviously he wasn't as talkative around the sergeant. "Yes. How do you know?"

A small smile appeared. "We've done our research. What kind of cancer did your father have?"

I flinched. The words *cancer* and *father* still carried a powerful punch. "He had brain cancer."

Sergeant Dasher's gaze moved toward the station nearest us. "I would like you to meet someone."

Before I could say anything, he stepped forward, stopping at one of the recliners that had its back to us. Archer nodded, and I reluctantly shifted so that I could see what the sergeant was looking at.

It was a kid. Maybe nine or ten, and with the sallow skin tone and bald head, I couldn't tell if it was a boy or girl, but the child's eyes were a bright blue.

"This is Lori. She's a patient of ours." He winked at the young girl. "Lori, this is Katy."

Lori turned those big, friendly eyes on me as she extended a small, terribly pale hand. "Hi, Katy."

I took her cold hand and shook it, not sure what else to do. "Hi."

Her smile spread. "Are you sick, too?"

I didn't know what to say at first. "No."

"Katy's here to help us," Sergeant Dasher said as the little girl pulled her hand back, tucking it under the pale gray blanket. "Lori has grade four, primary CNS lymphoma."

I wanted to look away, because I was a coward and I *knew*. That was the same kind of cancer my father had. Most likely terminal. It didn't seem fair. Lori was way too young for something like this.

He smiled at the girl. "It's an aggressive disease, but Lori is very strong."

She nodded fervently. "I'm stronger than most girls my age!"

I forced a smile I didn't feel as he stepped to the side, allowing a doctor to check the bags. Her bright baby blues bounced among the three of us. "They're giving me medicine that'll make me get better," she said, biting down on her lower lip. "And this medicine doesn't make me feel as bad."

I didn't know what to say, and I couldn't speak until we stepped back from the girl and moved to a corner where we weren't in anyone's way. "Why are you showing this to me?" I asked.

"You understand the severity of disease," he said, turning his gaze to the floor of the lab. "How cancer, autoimmune diseases, staph infections, and so many more things can rob a person of his or her life, sometimes before it really gets started. Decades have been spent on finding the cure to cancer or to Alzheimer's to no avail. Every year, a new disease arises, capable of destroying life."

All of that was true.

"But here," he said, spreading his arms wide, "we take a stand against disease with your help. Your DNA is invaluable to us, just like the Luxen chemical makeup is. We could inject you with the AIDS virus, and you wouldn't get sick. We've tried. Whatever is in the Luxen DNA, it makes both them and the hybrids resilient to all known human diseases. It is the same for the Arum."

A shudder rolled down my spine. "You're really injecting hybrids and Luxen with diseases?"

He nodded. "We have. It enables us to study how the hybrid's, or the Luxen's, body fights off the disease. We hope to be able to replicate it, and in some cases we have had success, especially with LH-11."

"LH-11?" I asked, watching Blake now. He was talking to another young kid—a boy who was having fluid administered. They were laughing. It seemed . . . normal.

"Gene replication," the sergeant explained. "It slows the growth of inoperable tumors. Lori has responded well to it. LH-11 is a product of years of research. We are hoping it's the answer."

I didn't know what to say as my gaze moved across the room. "The cure to cancer?"

"And many, many more diseases, Katy. This is what Daedalus is about, and you can help make this possible."

Leaning against the wall, I flattened my palms. Part of me wanted to believe what I was hearing and seeing—that Daedalus was only trying to find the cure for diseases—but I knew better. Believing that was like believing in Santa. "And that's all? You're just trying to make the world a better place?"

"Yes. But there are different ways, outside of the scope of medicine, to make the world a better place. Ways that *you* can help make the world a better place."

I felt like I was getting a sales pitch, but even in the position I was in, I could recognize how powerful a cure for such deadly diseases could be, how much it would change the world for the better. Closing my eyes, I drew in a deep breath. "How so?"

"Come." Dasher cupped my elbow, not giving me much of a choice. He led me to the opposite end of the lab, where a section of the wall appeared to be a shuttered window. He knocked on the wall. The shutters rolled up, making a series of mechanical *click*s. "What do you see?"

The air went out of my lungs. "Luxen," I whispered.

There was no doubt in my mind that the people sitting in matching recliners on the other side of the window, letting doctors take their blood, were not from around here. Their beauty was a dead giveaway. So was the fact that a lot of them were in their true form. Their soft glow filled the room.

"Do any of them look like they don't want to be here?" he asked quietly.

Placing my hands on the window, I leaned in. The ones who didn't look like a human lightbulb were smiling and laughing. Some were snacking on food, and others were chatting. Most of them were older, in their twenties or thirties, I guessed.

None of them looked like hostages.

"Do they, Katy?" he prodded.

I shook my head, thoroughly confused. Were they here of their own volition? I couldn't understand how.

"They want to help. No one is forcing them."

"But you're forcing me," I told him, aware that Archer was now behind us. "You forced Bethany and Dawson."

Sergeant Dasher cocked his head to the side. "It doesn't have to be that way."

"So you don't deny it?"

"There are three kinds of Luxen, Miss Swartz. There are those who are like the ones on the other side of this window, Luxen who understand how their biology can greatly improve our lives. Then there are those who have assimilated into society and who pose little to no risk."

"And the third group?"

He was silent for a moment. "The third group is the one that generations before us had feared upon the arrival of the Luxen. There are those who wish to take control of Earth and subjugate mankind."

My head swung toward him. "What the what?"

His eyes met mine. "How many Luxen do you think there are, Miss Swartz?"

I shook my head. "I don't know." Daemon had once mentioned how many he thought were here, but I couldn't recall the amount. "Thousands?"

Dasher spoke with authority. "There are roughly forty-five thousand inhabiting Earth."

Whoa, that was a lot.

"About seventy percent of that forty-five thousand have been assimilated. Another ten percent can be trusted completely, like those in the other room. And the last twenty percent? There are nine thousand Luxen who want to see mankind under their thumbs—nine thousand beings who can wield as much destruction as a small warhead. We barely keep them under control as it is, and all it would take for a complete upheaval of our society is for them to sway more Luxen to their side. But want to know another startling number?"

Staring at him, I had no idea what to say.

"Let me ask you a question, Ms. Swartz. Where exactly do you think Daemon Black, his family, and his friends fall?"

"They aren't interested in subjugating a house fly!" I barked out a harsh laugh. "Insinuating that is just ridiculous."

"Is it?" He paused. "You can never really, truly know someone. And I am sure when you first met Daemon and his family, you never would've assumed what they are, correct?"

He had me there.

"You have to admit that if they were so good at hiding

the fact they weren't even human, how good they must be at hiding something as invisible as their allegiance," he said. "You forget that they are not human, and they are not, I can assure you, a part of the ten percent that we trust."

I opened my mouth, but no words came out. I didn't—couldn't—believe what he said, but he had said all of this without an ounce of scorn. As if he were just stating facts, like a doctor would when telling a patient he had terminal cancer.

He turned back to the window, lifting his chin. "It is speculated that there are hundreds of thousands of Luxen out there, in space, who traveled to other points in the universe. What do you think would happen if they came here? Remember, these are Luxen who have had little to no contact with mankind."

"I . . ." A shiver of unease traveled up my spine and across my shoulders. Turning my attention to the window, I watched a Luxen flicker into his true form. When I spoke, I didn't recognize my own voice. "I don't know."

"They would obliterate us."

I sucked in a sharp breath, still not wanting to believe what he was saying. "That sounds a little extreme."

"Does it?" He paused, sounding curious. "Look at our own history. One stronger nation takes over another. The Luxen's and even the Arum's mentalities are no different from ours. Basic Darwinism."

"Survival of the fittest," I murmured, and for a moment I could almost see it. An invasion of Hollywood proportions, and I knew enough about the Luxen to know that if that many came here, and they wanted to take over, they would.

Closing my eyes, I shook my head again. He was mind-screwing me. There wasn't an army of Luxen about to invade. "What does any of this have to do with me?"

"Besides the fact that you are strong, as is the Luxen who mutated you, and your blood could possibly help us come one step closer to a successful batch of LH-11? We would love to study the connection between you and the one who mutated you. Very few have been able to do it successfully, and it would be a great achievement to have another Luxen who could successfully mutate other humans and create hybrids who are stable."

I thought of all those humans Dawson had been forced to mutate and watch die. I couldn't bear it if Daemon had to go through that, creating humans that would only . . .

I took a deep breath. "Is that what happened to Carissa?"

"Who?"

"You know who," I said tiredly. "She was mutated, but she was unstable. She came after me and self-destructed. She was a . . ." Good person. But I stopped, because I realized that if the sergeant knew anything about Carissa, he either wasn't talking or he simply didn't care.

A few moments passed before he continued. "But that's not the only thing Daedalus is concerned with. Having the Luxen here who mutated you would be great, but that's not what we're focused on."

I looked at him sharply, and my heart rate picked up. Surprise shuttled through me. They weren't focused on luring Daemon in?

"We wanted you," Sergeant Dasher said.

It felt like the floor moved under my feet. "What?"

His expression was neither cold nor warm. "See, Miss Swartz, there're those nine thousand Luxen we need help dealing with. And when the rest of the Luxen come to Earth—and they will—we will need everything in our arsenal to save mankind. That means hybrids like you, and hopefully many more, who can fight."

What the . . . ? I was sure I'd slipped into an alternate universe. My brain pretty much imploded.

Dasher regarded me closely. "So, the question is, will you be with us, or will you stand against your own kind? Because you will have to make a choice, Miss Swartz. Between your own people or those of the one who mutated you."

6

After saying good-bye to Dawson and Bethany, I left the house just as dawn broke. What had happened with Beth haunted my every step. She seemed a little better, but I didn't know. I had no doubt that Dawson would take care of her, though.

I looked back at the house. A cold, distant part of me acknowledged that I might not see this place, or my brother and sister, ever again. That knowledge didn't lessen my resolve.

I headed in the opposite direction of the colony, picking up speed. Although I stayed in my human form, I moved faster than I could be tracked.

Dawson had told me earlier that my car had been stowed away at Matthew's, which helped detour local law enforcement that weren't bought out by the DOD and were actually concerned about another set of missing teenagers.

It took me less than five minutes to make the trek to Matthew's cabin in the middle of nowhere. I slowed as I reached his driveway, spying his SUV.

I smirked.

I needed to get out of state, at least into Virginia. I could travel the entire way in my true form. Hell, it probably would even be quicker, but I'd wear myself out, and I was pretty sure the little meet and greet I was going to do at Mount Weather would be exhausting.

Considering how ticked off I was at Matthew right at the moment, I was going to enjoy "borrowing" his car, since mine would draw attention from those I didn't have time to deal with. I slid into the driver's seat, reached down, and yanked on the manifold hiding the wires.

When Dawson and I were little, we used to hotwire cars with our fingers for shits and giggles at the mall in Cumberland. Took us a couple of tries until we discovered the exact charge needed to do a jump-start and not fry the computers or the whole wiring system. We'd then move them into different parking spots and watch the owners come out, dumbfounded by how their cars had moved.

We'd bored easily as kids.

I wrapped my fingers around the wires and sent a little charge through them. The car sputtered, and the engine turned over.

Still had the magic touch.

Not wasting any time, I got the hell out of Matthew's driveway and headed for the highway. There was no way he'd be as understanding as Dawson, at least not at the moment.

My brother was set to take care of a few things for me. He'd move enough money to get Kat and me by for a couple of years to an account I'd meticulously kept off the radar just in case shit went downhill one day.

And shit definitely had gone downhill.

Dawson and Dee also had strategically hidden "oh-crap" accounts, just as the Thompsons did. Matthew had gotten us doing that. I used to think it was paranoia, but, damn, he'd been smart. There was no way I could come back, and neither could Kat. We'd have to find a way for her to see her mom, but neither of us could stay here when I got her out of there. It would be too dangerous.

But before I headed to Mount Weather, I had a little visit to make.

Blake couldn't have been the only one to screw us.

There was a teen hybrid who had a lot of explaining to do.

A little bit after noon, I stashed Matthew's car behind the rundown gas station on the same road as Luc's club. Not that the potholed dirt pathway was really a road. The last thing I wanted was for them to know I was coming. Something about Luc was off, and in a big way. The fact that he was barely a teenager and running a club was a big clue. And he was out here, with other Luxen, and unprotected from the Arum?

Yeah, something was off about the kid.

Staying in my human form, I took off through the weeds and into the wooded area behind the gas station. Bright sunlight filtered through the branches, and warm May air rushed me as I flew over the uneven ground. Seconds later, I cleared the stand of trees and hit the overgrown field.

Last time I'd been here with Kat, the field was nothing more than a frozen patch of grass. Now the reeds whipped at my jeans and dandelions carpeted the grass. Kat had a thing for dandelions. She couldn't keep her fingers off them when we'd been training with the onyx. From the moment those yellow weeds started poking through the ground, she'd snap them up and pop their heads off.

A wry grin tugged at my lips as I skidded to a stop in front of the windowless door. *Demented Kitten.*

I placed my hands on the steel door, sliding them down the center, feeling for gaps or locks to manipulate. There was no way this door was unlocking anytime soon.

Backing up, I scanned the front of the building. Squat and no windows, more like a warehouse than a club. I stalked around the side, knocking empty cardboard boxes out of the way. In the back was a loading dock.

Score.

Pressing my hands on the thin gap between the doors, I heard the wonderful sound of locks unclicking. I quickly eased the door open and stepped into a dark storage area. Slipping through the shadows, I hugged the wall, my gaze flitting over white containers and piles of papers. There was a distinct smell of alcohol in the air. Another door loomed ahead, and I opened it. The minute I stepped into the narrow corridor lined with dry erase boards with stick figures—*what the hell?*—drawn all over them, the hair on the back of my neck rose, and a cold shiver snaked its way down my spine.

Arum.

I barreled out of the corridor, seconds from flipping into my true form. Instead I ground to a halt, face-to-face with the business end of a sawed-off shotgun.

That would sting.

The proud owner of the redneck killer was Big Boy the Bouncer, still rocking overalls. "Hands up, and don't even think about going Lite-Brite on my ass, pretty boy."

Jaw clenched tightly, I raised my hands. "There's an Arum here."

"No shit," the bouncer said.

I cocked a brow. "So Luc is working with Arum, too?"

"Luc ain't workin' for no one." The bouncer stepped forward, eyes narrowed. "Where's that girl who's normally with ya? She be sneakin' around here, too?"

He glanced behind me, and I took advantage of the momentary distraction. My hand shot out faster than he could react. I snatched the shotgun from his grip and flipped it around.

"How does it feel to have this pointed at your head?" I asked.

Big Boy's nostrils flared. "Ain't feelin' real good."

"Didn't think so." My finger itched on the trigger. "I'd like to keep my pretty face intact."

The bouncer chortled. "And you do have a pretty face."

Banjos started playing in my head.

"Oh, look," said a new voice. "A love connection is made."

"Not quite," I said, wrapping my free hand around the barrel.

"Did you think I didn't know you were here?"

Without taking my eyes off Big Boy, I smirked. "Does it matter?"

"Yeah, if you were trying to sneak up on me, I guess it does." Luc ambled out of the shadows and into my line of sight. He was dressed in black running pants and a T-shirt that read, Zombies Need Love, Too. Nice. "You can put the gun down, Daemon."

Smiling coldly, I let heat encompass my hand. Warmth flared, and the smell of burning metal wafted into the air. When the barrel was made useless, I handed it back to Big Boy.

The bouncer looked down at the gun and sighed. "I hate when this happens."

I watched Luc hop up on the bar and swing his legs like a petulant child. Under the dim bar lighting, the ring around his oddly colored eyes seemed to be blurred. "You and I need to—"

Whipping around, I let out a roar as my human form faded. I shot across the empty dance floor, heading straight for the mass of shadows forming under the cage.

The Arum turned, and the second before we slammed into each other like two boulders rolling down a hill, I saw him in his true form—dark as midnight oil and shiny as glass. The impact shook the walls and rattled the cages hanging from the ceilings.

"Oh, jeez," Luc said. "Can't we all just get along?"

The Arum swept his arms around my waist as I threw him back into the wall. Plaster cracked and plumed into the air. He didn't let go. The SOB was strong.

Spinning around, he broke my hold and his smoky arm snaked out, aiming for my chest. I darted to the side, throwing up my arm to blast the annoying bastard into next year.

"Boys. *Boys!* No fighting in my club," Luc called, sounding irritated.

We ignored him.

Energy crackled over my palms, spitting white fire into the air.

You don't know who you're messsing with, the Arum hissed, sending his words straight into my skull, which just pissed me off. I let go of the ball of energy.

It smacked into his shoulder.

He jerked away and then turned his head back to me, cocking it to the side. His form became more solid.

Static crackled down my arms. Light pulsed throughout the room. This guy was really starting to get on my nerves.

"I wouldn't do that if I were you," Luc said. "Hunter is very, very hungry."

I was about to show Luc just what I thought about his advice when a form stepped out of the hallway leading to his office. It was a woman—a pretty, blond-haired woman who was oh-so human. Her eyes were wide. "Hunter?"

What. The. Hell.

Distracted, the Arum glanced back at the woman around the same time the Source fizzled out of me. He must've communicated with her, because she frowned and said, "But he's one of *them*."

Hunter's head swung back to me, and his chest rose as he took a step back. A second later, a man stood before me, coming in at my height. Dark brown hair and those damn pale Arum eyes were fixed on me.

"Serena," he said. "Go back to Luc's office."

The woman's frown grew into a scowl, reminding me so much of Kat that my chest ached. "Excuse me?"

His head snapped toward her, eyes narrowing. An instant later, Big Boy strode across the dance floor, wrapping an arm around the woman's shoulders. "This really ain't where ya need to be right now."

"But—"

"Come on, I got some stuff to show ya," Big Boy said.

Hunter glared. "What stuff?"

Big Boy winked over his shoulder. "Stuff."

As they disappeared down the hallway, the Arum's lip curled. "I do not like this."

Luc chuckled. "She's not his type."

Wait—what in the hell was going on? An Arum with a human?

"You want to tone down the light?" the asshole said. "You're blinding me."

Power rippled through me, and I wanted to slam my fist through his face, but he wasn't attacking, which was strange. And he was with a human woman he appeared to be *really* with, which was even more bizarre.

I took my human form. "I don't like your tone."

He smirked.

My eyes narrowed.

"You two should play nice." Luc clapped his hands together. "You never know when you'll need such an unlikely ally."

Hunter and I looked at each other. Both of us snorted. Doubtful.

The boy shrugged. "Okay. So, this is a very exciting day for me. I have Hunter, who needs no last name and only shows up when he wants something or someone to feed off, and I have Daemon Black, who looks like he wants to do me physical harm."

"That's about right," I snarled.

"Care to tell me why?" he asked.

My hands curled into fists. "Like you don't know."

He shook his head. "I really don't, but I'll hazard a guess. I don't see Katy, and I don't feel her. So I'm assuming your little break-in at Mount Weather didn't go smoothly."

I took a step forward, rage swirling inside me.

"You broke into Mount Weather?" Hunter choked out a laugh. "Are you insane?"

"Shut up," I said, keeping my eyes on Luc.

Hunter made a deep noise. "Our little mutual white flag of friendship is going to come to a halt if you tell me to shut up again."

I spared him a brief glance. "Shut. Up."

Dark shadows drifted over the Arum's shoulder, and I faced him fully. "What?" I said, throwing my hands up in a universal come-get-some gesture. "I have a lot of pent-up violence I'd love to take out on someone."

"Guys." Luc sighed, sliding off the bar. "Seriously? Can't you two bromance it out?"

Hunter ignored him, taking a step forward. "You think you can take me?"

"Think?" I scoffed, going toe-to-toe with the alien. "I know."

The Arum laughed as he took one long finger and poked me in the chest—*poked me in the chest*! "Well, let's find out."

I grabbed his wrist, my fingers circling his cool skin. "Man, you really are—"

"Enough!" Luc shouted.

The next second I was pinned against one side of the club, and Hunter was on the other, several feet off the ground. The Arum's expression most likely mirrored mine. Both of us struggled against the invisible hold, but neither of us could do a damn thing to get down.

Luc moved to the center of the floor. "I don't have all day, guys. I have things to do. A nap I want to take this afternoon. There's a new movie out on Netflix I want to watch, and a god-damn coupon for a free Whopper Jr. that's calling my name."

"Uh . . ." I said.

"Look." Luc turned to me, his expression clouded. In that moment, he looked way older than I knew he was. "I'm guessing you think I was somehow a part of Katy being captured. You're wrong."

I sneered. "And I should believe you?"

"Do I look like I give a flying rainbow if you believe me? You broke into Mount Weather, a government stronghold. It takes no stretch of imagination to guess that something went wrong. I did what I promised."

"Blake betrayed us. Daedalus has Kat."

"And I told you to not trust anyone who had something to gain or lose." Luc exhaled roughly. "Blake is . . . well, he's Blake. But before you cast judgment, ask yourself how many people you'd crucify to get Katy back?"

The hold on me let go, and I slid down the wall, hitting my feet. As I stared at the teen, I believed him. "I have to get her back."

"If Daedalus has your girl, you can kiss her good-bye," Hunter said from across the room. "They are some fuc—"

"And you?" Luc cut in. "I told you to stay in my office. Not listening to me is not how to get something from me."

Hunter gave an awkward shrug, and a second later, he was standing on the floor, looking as cuddly as a pit bull.

Luc cast both of us dark looks. "I get that you two have problems—big problems—but guess what? You're not the only aliens out there who are butt sore. There are bigger problems than what you guys have. Yeah, I know, hard to believe."

I glanced over at Hunter, who shrugged again and said, "Someone didn't get his warm milk this morning."

I snickered.

Luc's head swung toward him, and damn if I couldn't believe I was standing in a room with an Arum and not killing him—but he was also not trying to kill me. "You need to be glad that I like you," Luc said in a low voice. "Look, I need to talk to Daemon. Can you go do something? If not, then maybe you can be helpful?"

The Arum rolled his eyes. "Yeah, I have my own problems." He started back toward the hall and then stopped, glancing at me. "See you on the flip side."

I gave him the middle finger good-bye.

When he disappeared down the corridor, Luc turned toward me and folded his arms. "What happened?"

Seeing that I had nothing to lose, I told him what went down at Mount Weather. Luc gave a low whistle and shook his head. "Man, I'm sorry. Truly I am. If Daedalus has her, then I don't—"

"Don't say it," I growled. "She's not lost to me. We got Bethany out. *You* got out."

Luc blinked. "Yeah, you got Bethany out, but Katy got caught in the process. And I'm . . . I'm not like Katy."

I didn't know what the hell that meant. Turning from him, I thrust my fingers through my hair. "Did you know that Blake would betray us?"

There was a pause. "And if I did, what would you do?"

A bitter laugh snuck out. "I'd kill you."

"Understandable," he replied evenly. "Let me ask you a question. Would you have still helped your brother rescue Bethany if you knew Blake would betray you?"

Facing Luc, I slowly shook my head as the truth hit me square in the chest. If I'd known that Kat wouldn't be coming home, I don't think I could say yes, and I couldn't put to words the fact that I would choose her over my brother.

He tipped his head to the side. "I didn't know. That doesn't mean I trusted Blake. I don't trust anyone."

"Anyone?"

He ignored the question. "What do you want from me, since you obviously aren't going to try to kill me? Do you want me to take down the security again? I can do that. It'll be a freebie for you, but it'll also be a suicide mission. They'll be expecting you."

"I don't want you to take anything down."

He looked at me, confused. "But you're going after her?"

"Yes."

"You'll get caught."

"I know."

Luc stared at me so long I thought the kid might've had a seizure. "So you really were coming here to kick my ass?"

My lips twitched. "Yeah, I was."

The kid shook his head. "Do you have any idea what you're getting yourself into?"

"I know." I folded my arms. "And I know once they have me, they are going to want me to make hybrids."

"Have you ever had to watch people die, over and over again? No? Ask your brother."

I didn't hesitate. "She's worth whatever I have to go through."

"There are worse things," he said quietly. "If you and Hunter could put away your differences for two seconds, he'd probably tell you himself. There are things that they are doing there that will blow your mind."

"Even more reason for me to get Kat out."

"And what's your plan? How are you going to get her out?" he asked, curious.

Good question. "I haven't gotten that far yet."

Luc watched me a moment, then busted into laughter. "Good plan. I like it. Only a few things could go wrong with that."

"How did you get out, Luc?"

He tilted his head to the side. "You don't want to know what I did. And you won't do what I did."

A cold shiver crawled over my skin. I believed the kid.

Luc stepped back. "I got to take care of this other issue, so . . ."

My gaze slid to the hallway. "Working with Arum, huh?"

His mouth twitched. "Arum and Luxen aren't that different. They're just as screwed as you guys are."

Funny. I didn't see it that way.

Luc tipped his chin down and swore. Looking up at me, he said, "Daedalus's biggest weakness is their arrogance. Their need to create what should never be created. Their need to control what can never be controlled. They're tinkering with evolution, my friend. That never ends well in the movies, does it?"

"No. It doesn't." I started to turn away.

"Wait," he called out, stopping me. "I can help you."

I faced him, head tilted to the side. "What do you mean?"

Luc's amethyst eyes, so like Ethan's that it was disturbing, latched onto mine. There was something a little off about his, though, with the line around the pupils. "Their biggest defense is that the world doesn't know they exist. They don't know *we* exist."

I couldn't look away, and I decided that this Luc kid was kind of creepy.

He smiled then. "They have something that I want, and I bet it's where they're keeping Katy."

My eyes narrowed. Tit for tat never sat well with me. "What do you want?"

"They have something called LH-11. I want that."

"LH-11?" I frowned. "What the hell is that?"

"The beginning of everything and the end of the beginning,"

he said mysteriously, and a strange gleam filled his purplish eyes. "You'll know it when you see it. Get it for me, and I'll make sure you get out of wherever it is you're at."

I stared at him. "I don't doubt your awesomeness, but how can you get Kat and me out of a place if you don't even know where it is?"

He arched a brow. "You must doubt my awesomeness if you're asking, and you shouldn't. I have people everywhere, Daemon. I'll check around with them, and they'll let me know when you show up."

Laughing softly, I shook my head. "Why should I trust you?"

"I've never asked you to trust me. You also have no other choice." He paused, and hell if he didn't have a point. "Get me the LH-11, and I'll make sure you and your *Kitten* get out of whatever hellhole they have you in. It's a promise."

7

{ Katy }

It felt like forever since I was given a lunch of mashed pota- toes and Salisbury steak. I was too amped up to check out the TV. Waiting in the silence drove me to pace the length of my cell. My nerves were stretched to the point that every time I heard footsteps outside the room, my heart leapt into my throat and I moved back from the door.

I was skittish, reacting to every sound. Having no concept of the amount of time that was passing or even what day it was, I felt like I was trapped in an airless bubble.

Making my hundredth pass in front of the bed, I mulled over what I did know. There were people here who wanted to be here—humans and Luxen, probably even a few hybrids. They were testing LH-11 on cancer patients, and God knew what LH-11 really was. A part of me could get behind that—if the Luxen really were here because they wanted to help. Find- ing the cure to deadly diseases was important. If Daedalus had simply asked me and hadn't wanted to keep me in a cell, I would've gladly given up my blood.

I couldn't shake what Sergeant Dasher had told me. Were there really nine thousand or so Luxen out there plotting against humans? Hundreds of thousands who could come to Earth at any time? Daemon had mentioned others before, but never once had he said anything about his kind, even a small enclave, wanting to take over.

What if that were true?

It couldn't be.

The Luxen weren't the bad guys here. The Arum and Daedalus were. The organization might have pretty packaging, but it was rotten inside.

Footsteps sounded outside the room, and I jumped a good couple of inches into the air. The door opened. It was Archer.

"What's going on?" I asked, immediately wary.

The beret that seemed permanently attached to his head hid his eyes, but his jaw was tight. "I'm to take you to the training rooms."

He did the hand-on-the-shoulder thing, and I wondered if he really thought I'd try to run. I wanted to, but I wasn't that stupid. Yet. "What goes on in the training rooms?" I asked when we were in the elevator.

He didn't answer, which wasn't very reassuring, and it ticked me off. The least these people could do was tell me what was going on. I tried to shrug off his hand, but it was glued to my shoulder the whole way.

Archer was a man of few words, and that made me even more nervous and jumpy, but it was more than that. There seemed to be something different about him. I couldn't put my fingers on it, but it was there.

By the time we hit the training floor, my stomach was churning. The hallway was identical to the medical floor, except there were a lot of double doors. We stopped at one and, when he keyed in a code, the doors slid open.

Blake and Sergeant Dasher were in the room. Dasher turned to us, smiling tightly. There was something different in his expression. A hint of desperation in his dark brown eyes unnerved me. I couldn't help but think of those blood work results.

"Hello, Miss Swartz," he said. "I hope you took the time to rest up."

Well, that didn't sound good.

Two men in lab coats sat in front of an array of monitors. The rooms on the screen looked padded to me. My fingers felt numb from clenching them so hard.

"We're ready," one of the men said.

"What's going on?" I asked, hating how my voice broke halfway through the question.

Blake's expression was blank, while Archer took up his position as sentry by the door.

"We need to see the extent of your abilities," Sergeant Dasher explained, moving to stand behind the two men. "Inside of this controlled room, you'll be able to use the Source. We know from our previous investigations that you do have some control, but what we don't know is the extent of your abilities. Hybrids who have successfully mutated can react just as quickly as a Luxen. They can control the Source just as well."

My heart skipped. "What purpose does this serve? Why do you need to know? I'm obviously a successful mutation."

"We don't truly know that, Katy."

I frowned. "I don't get it. Earlier you said I was strong—"

"You *are* strong, but you've never consistently used your abilities or done so without the hybrid who mutated you. It's possible that you've been feeding off his ability. And a hybrid may appear to have successfully mutated, but we've discovered that the more one taps into the Source, the more evident the instability in his or her mutation becomes. We need to test for any type of unpredict-ability in your mutation."

As his words sank in and made sense, I wanted to run from the room, but I was rooted to the floor. "So you want to see if I basically self-destruct like . . ." Like Carissa, but I couldn't say her name out loud. When he neither confirmed nor denied it, I took a step back. A whole new horror rose to the surface. "What happens if I do? I mean, I know what happens to me, but what about . . . ?"

"The one who mutated you?" he asked, and I nodded. "You can say it, Miss Swartz. We know it was Daemon Black. There is no need to try to protect him."

I still wouldn't say his name. "What happens?"

"We know that the Luxen and the human he mutates are joined on a biological level if the mutation holds. It's not something we understand completely." He paused, clearing his throat. "But for those who turn unstable, the connection is voided out."

"Voided out?"

He nodded. "The biological link between the two is broken. Possibly due to the fact that, in those cases, the mutation wasn't as strong as suspected. We really just don't know ev-erything yet."

A shudder of relief rolled through me. It wasn't like I didn't have a sense of self-preservation, but at least I knew if I blew up, Daemon would still be alive. But I stalled, not wanting to go into that room. "Is that the only thing that breaks the link?"

The sergeant didn't respond.

My eyes narrowed. "Don't you think I have a right to know?"

"All in good time," he replied. "Now is just not the time."

"I think it's a damn good time."

His eyebrows shot up in surprise, further angering me.

"What?" I said, throwing up my hands. Archer stepped closer to me, but I ignored him. "I think I have a right to know everything."

His surprise faded, replaced with a cool expression. "This is not the time."

I held my ground, hands curling into fists. "I don't see there being any better time."

"Katy . . ." Archer's soft warning was ignored, and he moved closer, his chest almost against my back.

"No. I want to know what else can break the link. Obviously something can. I also want to know how long you really think you can keep me here." Once the lid came off my mouth, there was no shutting it. "What about school? You want an uneducated hybrid running amuck? What about my mom? My friends? What about my life? My blog?" Okay, my blog was seriously the least of my worries, but dammit, it was important to me. "You've stolen my life and think that I should just stand here and take it? That I shouldn't demand answers? You know what? You can kiss my ass."

Whatever warmth had been in Sergeant Dasher's expression seeped away. He stared back at me, and in that moment, I realized I probably should've kept my mouth shut. I had needed to say those words, but the hard look he gave me was frightening.

"I don't tolerate foul language. And I don't tolerate smart-mouthed little girls who don't understand what is going on. We have tried to make this as comfortable as we can for you, but we all have limits, Miss Swartz. You will not question me or any of my staff. We will let you know things when we feel it's the appropriate time and not before. Do you understand?"

I could feel every breath Archer took, and it seemed like he stopped, waiting for me. "Yes," I spat. "I understand."

Archer took a breath.

"Good," the sergeant said. "Since that's now settled, let's move on."

One of the men at the monitors pressed a button and a small door opened to the training room. Archer didn't let me go until I was inside the room. Then he did.

I spun around as he backed toward the door, my eyes going wide. I started to ask him not to leave me, but he looked away quickly. And then he was gone, closing the door behind him.

Heart pounding, I darted my eyes around the room. It was about twenty feet by twenty, with a cement floor and another door on the opposite side, and the walls weren't padded. Nope. I wouldn't get that lucky. The walls were white with scuffs of red. Was that . . . dried blood?

Oh God.

But that fear trickled away as awareness kicked in. The rush of power was tiny at first, a rush that felt like tips of fingers were trailing down my arms, but it grew quickly, spreading to my core.

It was like taking a breath of fresh air for the first time. Numbness and exhaustion eked away, replaced with a low buzz of energy that was in the back of my skull, thrumming through my veins and filling the coldness in my soul.

My eyes fluttered shut, and I saw Daemon in my head. Not because I could *really* see him, but because feeling this reminded me of him. As the Source wrapped its way around me, I imagined being in Daemon's embrace.

An intercom clicked on overhead, and Sergeant Dasher's voice filled the room, causing my head to jerk up. "We need to test your ability, Katy."

I didn't want to talk to the ass-hat, but I wanted to get this over with more. "Okay. So you want me to call on the Source or what?"

"You will do that, but we need your ability tested under stress."

"Under stress?" I whispered, glancing around the room. Unease unfurled in my belly, spreading like a noxious weed, threatening to choke me. "I'm feeling pretty stressed right now."

The intercom clicked on again. "That's not the kind of stress we're talking about."

Before his words had a chance to sink in, there was a loud thumping noise that reverberated through the small room. I whipped around.

Across from me, the other door was sliding open, inch by inch. The first thing I noticed was a pair of black sweatpants like the pair I had on, and then a white shirt covering narrow hips. My gaze crawled up, and I let out a surprised gasp.

Standing before me was a girl I had met before. It felt like a lifetime ago, but I recognized her immediately. Her blond hair was pulled back in a neat ponytail, revealing a pretty face offset by bruises and scratches.

"Mo," I said, taking a step forward.

The girl who had been in the cage next to mine when Will had held me captive stared back at me. I'd wondered many times what had happened to her, and I guessed now I knew. A heartbeat passed, I said her name again, and then it hit me with startling clarity. She was showing the same vast emptiness that Carissa had when she'd been in my bedroom.

My heart sank. I doubted there was anything I could do that would remind the girl of me.

She stepped into the room and waited. A moment later, the intercom buzzed and Sergeant Dasher's voice came through. "Mo will assist in the first round of the stress tests."

First round? There was more than one? "What is she—?"

Mo flung her hand out, and the Source crackled over her knuckles. Shock held me immobile until the last possible moment. I darted to the side, but the blast of whitish light tinged in blue smacked into my shoulder. Pain burst and rushed down my arm. The impact spun me around, and I barely kept my balance.

Confusion swirled as I clutched my shoulder, not surprised to find the material singed. "What the hell?" I demanded. "Why—?"

Another blast sent me dropping to my knees as it whizzed by right where I'd been standing. It hit the wall behind me, fizzling out. In the blink of an eye, Mo was right in front of me. I started to stand, but her knee came up, catching me in the chin and snapping my head back. Starbursts blinded me as I fell back on my butt, stunned.

Reaching down, Mo grabbed ahold of my ponytail and lifted me to my feet with surprising ease. Her hand swung out, the blow catching me right below the eye. That burst of pain caused my ears to ring, and it did something else.

It knocked the stupor right out of me.

Suddenly I understood this stress test, and it sickened and horrified me. I had to believe that if Daedalus knew everything, then they had to have known that I'd met Mo. That seeing her here, in better physical shape than she had been in that cage, would not only knock me off guard but would confirm the futility of fighting against them.

But they did want me to fight—they wanted me to fight Mo, using the Source. Because what else, other than getting your ass handed to you on a silver platter, would cause such major stress?

Another punch caught me right under the eye. She put a hell of a lot of *oomph* behind it. A metallic taste sprang into my mouth as I called on the Source, just like the sergeant wanted.

But Mo . . . she was so much faster than me, so much better.

As the ass-kicking of a lifetime picked up, I held on to the small sliver of hope I had: Daemon wouldn't be subjected to this.

{ Daemon }

Stashing Matthew's SUV several miles from the access road leading to Mount Weather, I hoped whoever found his car got it back to him in one piece. It was a pretty sweet ride. Not as good as Dolly, but not many cars were.

I traveled the last couple of miles in my true form, rushing through the heavy thicket. I reached the access road within minutes, and seconds later I was at the cusp of the forest, staring at the all-too-familiar fence that surrounded the grounds.

There were definitely more guards on duty—at least three of them by the gate, and I bet there were more inside. Cameras and security systems weren't going to go down this time. I didn't want them to.

I wanted to get caught.

Dawson probably thought I hadn't given this much consideration. A lot was on the line—not only my future but my family's and Kat's. Once the DOD realized I was here, things were going to get rough. Getting in wouldn't be the problem, and if I got whatever it was that Luc wanted, he would get us out—if he wasn't lying. And if he was, I would find another way.

Part of me hoped that Kat was still here, that Daedalus hadn't moved her to another location. Probably foolish to hope for that, because I had a feeling a big ol' dose of disappointment was heading my way.

So, yeah, I wanted to get caught, but I wasn't going to make this easy for them.

Stepping out from under the cover of the trees, I let my human form take hold under a strong beam of sunlight. The guards were oblivious to my presence at first, and as I took another step forward, the conversation I had with Kat the night she finally admitted her feelings for me came to mind.

I'd told her that we made the good kind of crazy together, and I hadn't known how true that really was until this very moment, because what I was about to do was really, truly, 100 percent certifiable.

The first guard, who was pulling something—a cell phone?—out of his black cargo pants, turned, his eyes drifting through the trees. His gaze moved over me and then darted back. The cell phone fell from his fingers, and he shouted, one hand going for the gun on his thigh and the other for the microphone on his shoulder. The two guards behind him whipped around, drawing their weapons.

Time to get this show on the road.

Summoning the Source, I stayed in my human form, but I knew the moment they became sure of what I was. It was probably my eyes. The world was tinted in a brilliant sheen.

A series of popping sounds followed, telling me that the guards weren't messing around.

I raised my hand, and the bullets appeared to hit an invisible wall. In reality, it was the energy reflecting the bullets. I could've sent them back at the guards, but all I did was stop them. They fell to the ground harmlessly.

"I wouldn't suggest you try that again," I said, lowering my hand.

Of course they didn't listen. Why? That would be too easy.

The guard in the front unloaded his weapon, and I repelled all the bullets. After a few seconds, I was so done with this. Turning around, I extended an arm back toward the trees. They began to tremble. Branches shook, sending a waterfall of green needles whirling into the air. Pulling them forward, I spun around.

Thousands of needles shot through the air, speeding forward. They split around me, heading straight for the dumbstruck guards.

The needles slammed into the men, turning them into human pincushions. Not killing them, but if their grunts of pain and surprise were any indication, it had to sting like a bitch. The guards were on their knees, guns forgotten on the ground beside them. Waving my hand, I sent their weapons flying into the woods, never to be seen again.

I prowled forward, passing them with a smirk. Summoning the Source once more, I let the energy crackle down my arm. A bolt of light hit the gate on the electric fence. A burst of white exploded, dancing across the chain-link, frying out the power to the fence and leaving a nice, comfy hole to walk right through.

Stalking over the neatly trimmed landscape that we had previously run across, I took a deep breath as the doors to Mount Weather slid open.

A freaking army of officers emptied out, dressed like they were ready for Armageddon or a guest spot on a SWAT team. Their faces were covered with shields, like that would help them. Going down on one knee, they leveled a dozen or so semiautomatic rifles on me. Stopping so many bullets would prove tricky.

People were going to die.

That sucked, but it wouldn't stop me.

Then a tall, slender form came into view, walking out of the dimly lit tunnel. The men donned in black uniforms parted, never taking their rifles off me while allowing the primly dressed woman to easily navigate her way to the front.

"Nancy Husher," I snarled, my hands curling into fists. I'd known the woman for years. Never liked her, which was compounded by the fact that I knew she worked within Daedalus and had known what really happened to Dawson.

Her mouth spread into the tight-lipped smile she was famous for, the one that said she was about to shove a wicked dagger into your back while kissing your cheek. She was just who I was hoping to find.

"Daemon Black," she said, clasping her hands together. "We've been expecting you."

8

{ Katy }

After the disastrous training session, I knew the taste of true fear each time someone neared my door. My heart hammered painfully until the sound of footsteps faded, and when the door finally opened, revealing Archer with my evening meal, I almost vomited.

I had no appetite.

I couldn't sleep that night.

Every time I closed my eyes, all I could picture was Mo standing before me, more than ready to kick my ass every which way from Sunday. The vast emptiness that had clouded her eyes had quickly blossomed into determination. My beating may not have been as severe if I had fought back, but I hadn't. Fighting her would have been wrong.

When the door opened the following morning, I was only running on a few hours of sleep. It was Archer, and in his quiet way, he motioned me to follow him.

Sick to my stomach, I had no other choice but to go wherever he was leading me. The nausea grew as we rode the elevator to the floor that housed the training rooms. It took everything in me to step off the elevator and not grab onto one of the bars for dear life.

But he led me behind the room we'd gone to before, through double doors, and then farther down a hall, where we passed through another set of doors.

"Where are we going?"

He didn't respond until we stopped outside a steel door that glinted from an overabundance of onyx and diamonds. "There is something Sergeant Dasher wants you to see."

I could only imagine what rested beyond the door.

He placed his forefinger against the security pad, and the light flipped from red to green. Mechanical *clicks* followed. I held my breath as he opened the door.

The room inside was lit only by one dim bulb in the ceiling. There were no chairs or tables. To the right was a large mirror that ran the length of the wall.

"What is this?" I asked.

"Something you must see," Sergeant Dasher said from behind us, causing me to jump and spin around. Where in the hell had he come from? "Something I hope will ensure that we won't have a repeat of our last training session."

I crossed my arms and lifted my chin. "There's nothing you can show me that will change that. I am not going to fight other hybrids."

Dasher's expression remained the same. "As I explained, we must make sure you are stable. That is the purpose of these training sessions. And the reason why we must make sure you are strong and able to harness the Source lies beyond this mirror."

Confused, I glanced back at Archer. He stood near the door, face shadowed by the beret. "What's on the other side?"

"The truth," responded Dasher.

I coughed out a laugh that caused the scraped skin on my face to sting. "Then you have a room full of delusional military officers on the other side?"

His look was as dry as sand as he reached over, flipping a switch along the wall.

Sudden light exploded, but it came from behind the mirror. It was a one-way mirror, like in police stations, and the room was not empty.

My heart kicked in my chest as I stepped forward. "What . . . ?"

There was a man on the other side sitting in a chair, and not willingly. Onyx bands covered his wrists and ankles, locking him down. A shock of white-blond hair covered his forehead, but he slowly lifted his head.

He was a Luxen.

The angular beauty gave him away, and so did the vibrant green eyes—eyes that reminded me so much of Daemon that an ache pierced my chest and sent a ball of emotion straight into my throat.

"Can . . . can he see us?" I asked. It seemed that way. The Luxen's eyes were fixed on where I stood.

"No." Dasher moved forward, leaning against the mirror. A small intercom box was within arm's reach.

Pain etched the man's beautiful face. Veins bulged along his neck as his chest rose on a ragged breath. "I know you're there."

I looked at Dasher sharply. "You sure he can't see us?"

He nodded.

Reluctantly I returned my attention to the other room. The Luxen was sweating and trembling. "He's . . . he's in pain. This is so wrong. It's a complete—"

"You do not know who sits on the other side of this glass, Miss Swartz." He flicked a button on the intercom. "Hello, Shawn."

The Luxen's lips twisted up on one side. "My name is not Shawn."

"That has been your given name for many years." Dasher shook his head. "He prefers to go by his true name. As you know, that is something we cannot speak."

"Who are you talking to?" Shawn demanded, his gaze unnervingly landing on where I stood. "Another human? Or even better? An abomination—a fucking hybrid?"

I gasped before I could stop myself. It wasn't what he said but the distaste and hatred that bled into each word.

"Shawn is what you would call a terrorist," the sergeant said, and the Luxen in the other room sneered. "He belonged to a cell that we'd been monitoring for a couple of years. They planned to take out the Golden Gate Bridge during rush hour. Hundreds of lives—"

"Thousands of lives," Shawn interrupted, his green eyes glowing luminous. "We would've killed *thousands*. And then we would've—"

"But you didn't." Dasher smiled then, and my stomach dropped. It was probably the first real smile I'd seen from the man. "We stopped you." He glanced over his shoulder at me. "He was the only one we could bring in alive."

Shawn laughed harshly. "You might have stopped me, but you haven't accomplished anything, you simpleminded *ape*. We are superior. Mankind is *nothing* compared to us. You will see. You have dug your own graves, and you cannot stop what is coming. All of you will—"

Dasher flipped off the intercom, bringing the tirade to a halt. "I have heard this many times over." He turned to me, head tilted to the side. "This is what we are dealing with. The Luxen in that room wants to kill humans. There are many like him. That is why we are doing what we are doing."

Wordless, I stared at the Luxen as my brain slowly turned

over what I had just witnessed. The intercom was off, but the man's mouth was still moving, raw hatred seeping from his lips. The kind of blind animosity shown by all terrorists, no matter who or *what* they were, was carved into his face.

"Do you understand?" the sergeant asked, drawing my attention.

Wrapping my arms around my waist, I shook my head slowly. "You can't judge an entire race based on a few individuals." The words sounded empty to me.

"True," Dasher agreed quietly. "But that would only be the case if we were dealing with humans. We cannot hold these beings to the same moral standard. And believe me when I tell you, they do not hold us to theirs."

Hours turned into days. Days possibly into weeks, but I really couldn't be sure. I understood now how Dawson couldn't keep track of time. Everything blended here, and I couldn't remember the last time I'd seen the sun or the night sky. I wasn't served breakfast like I had the first day I'd been awake, which threw off the time of day for me, and the only way I knew when a full forty-eight hours had passed was when I was taken to Dr. Roth for blood work. I'd seen him around five times, maybe more.

I'd lost count.

I'd lost a lot of things. Or it felt that way. Weight. The ability to smile or laugh. Tears. The only thing I retained was anger, and each time I squared off with Mo or another hybrid I didn't know—didn't even care to get to know because of what we had to do—my anger and frustration went up a notch. It surprised me that I could still feel so much.

But I hadn't given in yet. I hadn't fought back during any of the stress tests. It was my only means of control.

I refused to fight them—to beat up on them or potentially

kill them if things got out of hand. It was like being in a real, albeit messed-up, version of *The Hunger Games*.

The Hunger Games for alien hybrids.

I started to grin but winced as the motion pulled my torn lip. I might have refused to go all *Terminator* on them, but the other hybrids were *so* on board. So much so that some of them talked while they kicked my ass. They told me that I needed to fight, that I needed to prepare for the day the other Luxen came and for those who were already here. It was obvious they sincerely believed that the true villains were the Luxen. They may have been drinking the Kool-Aid, but I was not. Even so, there was a tiny part of me that wondered how Daedalus could control so many if there wasn't some truth in what they were saying?

And then there was Shawn, the Luxen who wanted to kill thousands of humans. If I were to believe Dasher, there were a hell of lot more like him out there—just waiting to take over Earth. But to even think that Daemon or Dee, or even Ash, was a part of something like that . . . I couldn't even consider it.

Forcing my eyes open, I saw the same thing I always saw after being hauled out of the training rooms and deposited—mostly unconscious—in my cell. The white ceiling with little black dots—a mixture of onyx and diamond.

God, I hated those dots.

I took a deep breath and cried out, immediately wishing I hadn't. Sharp pain radiated across my ribs from a Mo-size kick. My entire body throbbed. There wasn't one part of me that didn't ache.

Movement from the farthest corner of my cell, by the door, drew my attention. Slowly and quite painfully, I turned my head.

Archer stood there, bundling a cloth in his hand. "I was beginning to worry."

I cleared my throat and then opened my jaw, wincing. "Why?"

He came forward, the beret forever hiding his eyes. "You were out for a while this time, the longest yet."

I turned my head back to the ceiling. I hadn't realized that he was keeping track of my ass-kickings. He hadn't been here other times when I awoke. Neither had Blake. I hadn't seen that ass-hat in a while, and I wasn't sure he was even here anymore.

I drew in a slower, longer breath. As sad as it was, when I was awake, I missed the moments of oblivion. It wasn't always just a black, vast nothingness. Sometimes I dreamed of Daemon, and when I was awake I clung to those faint images that seemed to blur and fade the minute I opened my eyes.

Archer sat on the edge of the bed, and my eyes snapped open. The aching muscles tensed. Although he proved to be not so bad, all things considered, I trusted no one.

He held up the bundle. "It's just ice. Looks like you could use it."

I watched him warily. "I don't . . . I don't know what it looks like."

"*It* being your face?" he asked, palming the bundle. "It doesn't look pretty."

It didn't feel pretty. Ignoring the throbbing in my shoulder, I tried to pull my arm out from under the blanket. "I can do it."

"You don't look like you can lift a finger. Just stay still. And don't talk."

I wasn't sure if I should be offended by the whole *don't talk* part, but then he pressed the icy bundle against my cheek, causing me to suck in a sharp breath.

"They could have gotten one of the Luxen to heal you, but your refusing to fight back isn't going to make it easy on you." He pressed the ice bag down, and I drew back. "Try to keep that in mind when you go to the training room next time."

I started to scowl, but it hurt. "Oh. Like this is my fault."

He shook his head. "I didn't say that."

"Fighting them is wrong," I said after a few seconds. "I'm not going to self-destruct." Or at least I hoped I wasn't. "Making them do that is . . . is inhumane. And I won't—"

"You will," he said simply. "You're no different than them."

"No different." I started to sit up, but he pinned me with a look that had me settling back down. "Mo doesn't even seem human anymore. None of them do. They're like robots."

"They're trained."

"T-Trained?" I sputtered as he moved the ice to my chin. "They're mindless—"

"It doesn't matter what they are. You keep doing this? Not fighting back, not giving Sergeant Dasher what he wants, you're going to keep being a human punching bag. And what does that solve? One of these days, one of the hybrids will kill you." He lowered his voice, so low that I wondered if the microphones could even pick it up. "And what happens to the one who mutated you? He will die, Katy."

Pressure clamped down on my chest and a whole different kind of pain surfaced. At once, I saw Daemon in my head—that ever-present, infuriating smirk on his expressive face—and I missed him so badly a burning crawled up my throat. My hands curled under the blanket as a hole opened up in my chest.

Several minutes passed in silence, and while I lay there, staring at his brown-and-white-camouflaged shoulder, I searched for something to say, anything to drive the emptiness out of me, and I finally came up with something.

"Can I ask you a question?"

"You probably shouldn't talk anymore." He switched the bag of ice to his other hand.

I ignored that, because I was pretty sure I'd go crazy if I kept silent. "Are there really Luxen out there who want to take over? Others like Shawn?"

He didn't respond.

Closing my eyes, I let out a weary sigh. "Will it kill you to just answer the question?"

Another moment passed. "The fact that you're even asking is answer enough."

Was it?

"Are there good humans and bad humans, Katy?"

I thought it was weird how he said *humans*. "Yes, but that's different."

"Is it?"

When the icy bundle landed on my cheek again, it didn't feel so bad. "I think so."

"Because humans are weaker? Keep in mind that humans have access to weapons of mass destruction, just like the Luxen do. And do you really think that the Luxen don't know what happens here?" he asked quietly, and I stilled. "That there are some who, for their own reasons, support what Daedalus does, while others fear losing what life they have built here? Do you really want an answer to that question?"

"Yes," I whispered, but I was lying. A part of me didn't want to know.

Archer moved the bag of ice again. "There are Luxen who want to take over, Katy. There is a threat, and if that day comes when the Luxen have to choose sides, which side will they stand on? Where will you stand?"

{ Daemon }

I was about ten seconds from snapping someone's neck.

Who knew how many days had passed since Nancy did the little meet and greet at Mount Weather? A couple? A week or more? Hell if I knew. I had no idea what time of day it was or how much time had passed. Once they had escorted me inside, Nancy had disappeared, and a whole slew of stupid shit proceeded to take place—an exam, blood work, physical, and the lamest interrogation this side of the Blue Ridge Mountains. I went along with everything to just speed up the process, but then absolutely freaking nothing happened.

I was stashed in a room—probably the same kind of room Dawson's ass had been held in once upon a time—growing more furious by the second. I couldn't tap into the Source. I could, however, take my true form, but the only good that did was lighting up the room when it was dark. Not exactly helpful.

Pacing the length of the cell, I couldn't help but wonder for the thousandth time if Kat was doing the same thing some other place. I didn't feel her, but the weird link between us only seemed to work if we were nearby. There was still a chance, a small sliver of hope, that she was at Mount Weather.

Who knew what time it was when the door to my room opened and three G.I. Joe wannabes motioned me out. I brushed past them, grinning when the one I knocked shoulders with muttered a curse.

"What?" I challenged, facing the guard, ready for a fight. "You got a problem?"

The guy sneered. "Move it along."

One of them, a very brave soul, prodded me in the shoulder. I turned my glare on him, and he wilted back. "Yeah, I didn't think so."

And with that, the three commandos guided me down the hallway that was nearly identical to the one that led to the room we'd found Beth in. Once in the elevator, we descended a couple of floors, and then walked out and into another corridor populated with various military personnel, some of them in uniform and others in suits. All of them gave our little happy group a wide berth.

My already nonexistent patience was stretched thin by the

time we stopped in front of two dark, shiny double doors. My spidey senses were telling me the thing was rigged with onyx.

The commandos did some secret squirrel shit with the control panel, and the doors slid open, revealing a long rectangular table. The room wasn't empty. Oh no. Inside was my favorite person.

Nancy Husher sat at the head of the table, hands folded in front of her and hair pulled back in a tight ponytail. "Hello, Daemon."

I so wasn't in the mood for bullshit. "Oh. You're still around after all this time? Here I thought you just dumped me."

"I'd never dump you, Daemon. You're too valuable."

"*That* I know." I sat down without being told and leaned back, folding my arms. The soldiers shut the doors and took up guard in front of them. I shot them a dismissive glance before turning to Nancy. "What? No blood tests or exams today? No endless stream of stupid questions?"

Nancy was clearly struggling to maintain her cool facade. I hoped to whatever God was out there that I pushed every button the woman had. "No. There's no need for any more of that. We've gotten what we need."

"And what is that?"

One of her fingers moved up and then stilled. "You think you know what Daedalus is trying to do. Or at least you have your assumptions."

"I honestly don't give two shits what your little freak group is doing."

"You don't?" One thin brow rose.

"Nope," I said.

Her smile spread. "You know what I think, Daemon? You're a whole lot of bluster. A smart mouth with the muscles to back it up, but in reality you have no control in this situation, and deep down you know that. So keep running your mouth. I find it amusing."

My jaw clenched. "I live to entertain you."

"Well, that's good to know, and since that is now cleared up, may we move on?" When I nodded, her shrewd gaze sharpened. "First I want to make it clear that if at any time you pose a threat to me or to anyone else, we have weapons here that I would loathe to use on you but will."

"I'm sure you would loathe to do that."

"I would. There are PEP weapons, Daemon. Do you know what that stands for? Pulse Energy Projectile. It disrupts electronic and light wavelengths on a catastrophic level. One shot and it is fatal to your kind. I would hate to lose you. Or Katy. Get what I'm saying?"

My hand closed into a fist. "I get it."

"I know you have your assumptions when it comes to Daedalus, but we hope to change that during the course of your stay with us."

"Hmm, my assumptions? Oh, are you referencing that time when you and your minions led me to believe that my brother was dead?"

Nancy didn't even blink. "Your brother and his girlfriend were held by Daedalus because of what Dawson did to Bethany—for their safety. I know you don't believe that, and that isn't a concern of mine. There is a reason why Luxen are forbidden to heal humans. The consequences of such actions are vast, and in most cases result in unstable DNA changes within the human body, especially outside of controlled environments."

I cocked my head at that, remembering what happened to Carissa. "What is that supposed to mean?"

"Even if humans survive the mutation with our help, there is still a chance that the mutations are unstable."

"With your help?" I laughed coldly. "Shooting people up with God knows what is helping them?"

She nodded. "It was that or let Katy die. That is what would have happened."

I stilled, but my heart rate picked up.

"Sometimes the mutations fade. Sometimes they kill them. Sometimes they hold, and then people combust under stress. And sometimes they hold perfectly. We have to determine that, because we cannot allow unstable hybrids into society."

Anger whirled through me like a freight train. "You make it sound like you're doing the world a favor."

"We are." She leaned back, sliding her hands off the table. "We are studying Luxen and hybrids, trying to cure disease. We are stopping potentially dangerous hybrids from hurting innocent people."

"Kat's not dangerous," I ground out.

Nancy tilted her head to the side. "That's yet to be seen. The truth is she's never been tested, and that's what we're doing now."

I leaned forward very slowly, and the room started to carry a white sheen to it. "And what does that mean?"

Nancy held up her hand, warding off the three stooges by the door. "Kat has proven to show signs of extreme anger, a hallmark of instability in a hybrid."

"Really? Kat's angry? Could it be because you're holding her captive?" The words tasted like acid.

"She attacked several members of my team."

A smile spread across my face. *That's my girl.* "So sorry to hear that."

"So was I. We have so much hope when it comes to you two. The way you've worked together? It's a perfect symbiotic relationship. Very few Luxen and humans have reached that. Mostly the mutation acts as a parasite to the human." She folded her arms, stretching the drab brown of her suit jacket. "You could mean so much to what we're trying to accomplish."

"Which is curing disease and saving innocent people?" I snorted. "And that's it? Really, do you think I'm stupid?"

"No. I think you're very much the opposite of stupid." Nancy exhaled through her nose as she leaned forward, placing her hands on the dark gray table. "Daedalus's goal is to change the landscape of human evolution. Doing so requires drastic methods at times, but the end results are worth every fleck of blood, trickle of sweat, and teardrop."

"As long as it's not your blood, sweat, and tears?"

"Oh, I have given this everything, Daemon." She beamed. "What if I could tell you that we could not only eradicate some of the most virulent diseases, but we could stop wars before they even started?"

And there it was, I realized. "How would you do that?"

"Do you think any country would want to fight an army of hybrids?" She cocked her head. "Knowing what a successfully mutated one is capable of?"

Part of me was disgusted at the implications. The other half was just plain old pissed off. "Creating hybrids so they can fight stupid wars and die? You tortured my brother for this?"

"You say tortured; I say motivated."

All right, this was one of the moments in my life when I really wanted to knock someone through a wall. And I think she knew that.

"Let's get to the point, Daemon. We need your help—your willingness. If things go smoothly for us, they will go smoothly for you. What will it take to come to an agreement?"

Nothing in this world should have made me consider this. It went against nature; that was how wrong this was. But I was a bartering man, and when it came down to it, no matter what Daedalus wanted, what Luc wanted, there was one thing that mattered. "There's only one thing I want."

"And that is?"

"I want to see Kat."

Nancy's smile didn't fade. "And what are you willing to do to accomplish that?"

"Anything," I said without hesitation, and I meant it. "I will do *anything*, but I want to see Kat first, and I want to see her now."

Calculating light filled her dark eyes. "Then I am sure we can work something out."

9

{ Katy }

My legs ached as I trailed behind Archer, limping our way to the training room. Who would I fight today? Mo? The guy with a Mohawk? Or would it be the girl with the really pretty red hair? It didn't matter. I'd be getting my butt kicked. The only thing I did know was that they wouldn't let any of the other hybrids kill me. I was too *valuable*.

Archer slowed his step, allowing me to gimp my way up to him. He hadn't said anything since he left my cell yesterday, but I was used to his silence. I couldn't figure him out, though. It didn't seem like he supported any of this, but he never said it outright. Maybe it was just a job to him.

We stopped in front of the doors I'd come to loathe. Taking a deep breath, I stepped through when they opened. No point in delaying the inevitable.

Sergeant Dasher waited inside, dressed in the same uniform he'd been wearing since the first time I saw him. I wondered if he had an endless supply of them. If not, he had to have one hell of a dry-cleaning bill.

These were the stupid things I thought of before I was pummeled into one giant bruise.

Dasher gave me a once-over. From the brief glimpse of my reflection in the foggy mirror in the bathroom, I knew I looked like a hot mess. On the right side of my face, my cheek and eye were an ugly shade of purple and swollen. My lower lip was split. The rest of my body looked like a smorgasbord of bruises.

He shook his head and stepped aside, allowing Dr. Roth to check me over. The doctor took my blood pressure, listened to me breathe, and then shined a light in my eyes.

"She looks a little worse for wear," he said, tucking his stethoscope under his lab coat. "But she can participate in the stress test."

"It would be nice if she actually participated," grumbled one of the guys at the control panels. "And not just stand there."

I shot him a glare, but before I could open my mouth, Sergeant Dasher cut in. "Today will be different," he said.

Folding my arms, I fixed my eyes on him. "No. It won't. I'm not fighting them."

His chin went up a notch. "Perhaps we've introduced you to the stress test incorrectly."

"Gee," I said, smiling inwardly at the way his eyes narrowed. "What part of this whole thing is incorrect?"

"We do not want you to fight to just fight, Katy. We want to make sure your mutation is viable. I can see that you are unwilling to hurt just another hybrid."

A tiny smidgen of hope flared inside me, like a fragile seedling poking through the ground. Maybe making a stand, accumulating all these bruises, had meant something. It was a small step that probably meant nothing to them but everything to me.

"But we must see your abilities under high stress." He motioned to the guys at the panels, and my hope crashed and burned. The door opened. "I think you will be more accepting of this test."

Oh God, I didn't want to walk through those doors, but I forced one foot in front of the other, refusing to show an ounce of weakness.

The door closed behind me, and I faced the other door, waiting while knots formed in my stomach. How in the world could they make this acceptable? There was nothing they could—

In that instant, the other door opened, and Blake stepped through.

I choked out a dry, bitter laugh as he swaggered into the room, barely paying heed to the door closing behind him. Suddenly Dasher's words about being more acceptable made sense.

Blake frowned as he stopped in front of me. "You look like crap."

The simmering anger sparked. "And you're surprised? You know what they're doing in here."

He thrust his fingers through his hair as his eyes moved over my face. "Katy, all you had to do was tap into the Source. You're making this harder on yourself."

"*I'm* making this—?" I cut myself off as the anger heated up in me. The Source stirred in my belly, and I felt the tiny hairs on my body rise. "You're insane."

"Look at yourself." He waved a hand at me. "All you had to do was do what they asked, and you could've avoided all of this."

I stepped forward, glaring at him. "If you hadn't betrayed us, I would've avoided all of this in the first place."

"No." A look of sadness crept across his face. "You would've ended up here no matter what."

"I don't agree."

"You don't want to agree."

I sucked in a deep breath, but the anger was getting the better of me. Blake moved to put his hand on my shoulder, but I knocked his arm away. "Don't touch me."

He stared at me a moment, and then his eyes narrowed. "Like I told you before, if you want to be mad at anyone, get mad at Daemon. He did this to you. Not me."

That did it.

All the pent-up anger and frustration whipped through me like a category-five hurricane. My brain clicked off, and I swung without thinking. My fist just grazed his jaw, but the Source had reared its head at the same time. A bolt of light shot from my hand and spun him around.

He caught himself on the wall, letting out a surprised laugh. "Damn, Katy. That hurt."

Energy crackled down my spine, fusing with my bones. "How dare you blame *him* for this? This isn't his fault!"

Blake turned around and leaned against the wall. Blood trickled from his lip, and he wiped at it with the back of his hand. A strange gleam entered his eyes, and then he pushed off the wall. "This is completely his fault."

I flung my arm out and another bolt of energy shot forward, but he dodged it, laughing as he spun around, his arms out at his sides. "Is that the best you got?" he goaded me. "Come on. I promise I'll go easy on you, *Kitten*."

At the use of the pet name—Daemon's pet name—I lost it. Blake was on me in a second. I darted to the side, ignoring the painful protest of my muscles. His arm came out in a wide sweep, and whitish-red light crackled. I spun at the last second, narrowly avoiding taking a direct hit.

Letting the rush of energy swell through me once more, I sent another blast arcing across the room, hitting him in the shoulder.

He stumbled back, hands dropping to his knees as he doubled over. "I think you can do better than that, *Kitten*."

Fiery hot rage slipped over my eyes like a veil. Launching myself forward, I tackled him like an NFL linebacker on speed. We went down in a mess of tangled legs and arms. I landed on top of him, swinging my arm back and bringing it down repeatedly. I wasn't really seeing where I was hitting, only feeling the flare of pain across my knuckles as they connected with flesh.

Blake shoved his arms between mine and swept them out, knocking me off balance. I teetered for a second, and then he raised his hips and rolled. I slammed onto my back, knocking the air out of my lungs. I aimed for his face, hell-bent on clawing his eyes out.

He caught my wrists and pinned them above my head as he leaned down. A cut had opened under his left eye, and his cheek was starting to swell. A vicious amount of satisfaction rushed through me.

"Can I ask you a question?" Blake grinned, turning the flecks of green in his eyes brighter. "Did you ever tell Daemon that you kissed me? I bet you haven't."

Each breath I took I felt in every part of my body. My skin became hypersensitive to his weight and proximity. The power built inside, and the room seemed to be tinted in a brilliant sheen of white. Fury consumed me, riding every breath and latching onto every cell.

His grin spread. "Just like you never told him how we liked to cuddle—"

The power burst from me, and suddenly I was off the floor—*we* were off the floor—levitating several feet in the air. My hair streamed down behind me, and his hair fell forward into his eyes.

"Shit," Blake whispered.

Flipping upward, I tore my wrists free from his grip and slammed my hands into his chest. Shock rippled across his pale face a second before he flew backward, crashing into the wall. The cement cracked, and a fissure spread out like a wicked spiderweb. The whole room seemed to shake with the impact as Blake's head snapped back, and then he slumped forward. Part of me expected him to catch himself before he smacked into the floor, but he didn't. He hit with a fleshy splat that knocked the anger right out of me.

As if I'd been held up by invisible strings that had now been cut, I landed on the balls of my feet and rocked forward a step.

"Blake?" I croaked out.

He didn't move.

Oh no . . .

Arms shaking, I started to kneel down, but something dark and thick spread out from under his body. My gaze flicked up to the wall. A Blake-size imprint was clearly visible, a form reaching through at least three feet of cement.

Oh God, no . . .

Slowly, I looked down. Blood pooled out from under his motionless body and seeped across the gray cement floor, stretching toward my sneakers.

Stumbling back, I opened my mouth, but there was no sound. Blake didn't move. He didn't roll over with a groan. He didn't move at all. And the visible skin on his hands and forearms was paling already, turning a ghastly shade of white that stood out with such stark contrast against the deep red of the blood.

Blake was dead.

Oh my God.

Time slowed and then sped up. If he was dead, then that meant the Luxen who had mutated him was, too, because that was how it worked. They were joined together, like Daemon and I, and if one died . . . the other died, too.

Blake had it coming in more ways than one. I'd even promised to kill him, but words . . . words were one thing. Actions were a totally different ballpark. And Blake, even with all the terrible things he'd done, was a product of circumstance. He was only goading me. He'd killed not really meaning to. He'd betrayed to save another.

Just like I did—and would.

My hand shook as I pressed it against my mouth. Everything I'd said to him came back in a rush. And in that tiny second when I'd caved to the fury—nothing in a span of millions—I had changed, become something I wasn't sure I could ever come back from. My chest rose rapidly at the same time my lungs compressed painfully.

The intercom clicked on, the initial buzz startling me in the dead silence. Sergeant Dasher's voice filled the room, but I couldn't take my eyes off Blake's lifeless form. "Perfect," he said. "You've passed this stress test."

It was too much—ending up here, so far away from my mom and Daemon and everything that I knew, then the exam and the subsequent showdowns with the hybrids. And now this? It was too much.

Letting my head fall back, I opened my mouth to scream, but there was no sound. Nothing as Archer entered and gently placed his hand on my shoulder, steering me out of the room. Dasher said something, sounding very much like an approving father, and then I was taken out of the training room and into an office, where Dr. Roth waited to take more blood. They brought in a female Luxen to heal me. Minutes turned into hours, and still, I said nothing and felt nothing.

{ Daemon }

Being handcuffed with metal coated in onyx, blindfolded for five hours, and then put on some flight wasn't my idea of a fun time. I guess they were afraid that I'd bring the plane down, which was stupid. It was getting me to where I wanted to go. I didn't know the location, but I knew it had to be where they were keeping Kat.

And if she wasn't there, I was going to go postal.

Once the plane landed, I was hustled to a waiting car. From underneath the blindfold, I could make out bright light, and the smell was really dry and acidic, vaguely familiar. The desert? It hit me during the two-hour drive that I was going back to the place I'd last been to damn near thirteen years ago.

Area 51.

I smirked. Keeping me blindfolded was pointless. I knew where we were. All Luxen, once discovered, were processed through the remote detachment of Edwards Air Force Base. I'd been young, but I'd never forget the dryness to the air or the remote, barren landscape of Groom Lake.

When the vehicle rolled to a stop, I sighed and waited for the door beside me to be opened. Hands landed on my shoulders, and I was dragged out of the car, thinking whoever had their hands on me was real lucky that mine were handcuffed behind my back, or someone was going to be leaving work today with a broken jaw.

The dry heat of the Nevada desert beat down as I was led several yards, and then a wave of cool air hit me, raising the strands of hair off my forehead. We were in an elevator before the blindfold was removed.

Nancy Husher smiled up at me. "Sorry for that, but we must take precaution."

I met her eyes. "I know where we are. I've been here before."

A single thin brow went up. "Many things have changed since you were a child, Daemon."

"Can I get these off yet?" I wiggled my fingers.

She glanced at one of the soldiers in camouflage. He was young from what I could tell, but the khaki-colored beret hid most of his upper face. "Unlock the handcuffs. He's not going to give us any trouble." She looked back at me. "I do believe Daemon knows this place is outfitted with an onyx defense system."

The guard stepped forward, fishing out a key. The set of his jaw said he wasn't too sure if he should believe her, but he unlocked the cuffs. They scraped along the raw skin of my wrists as they slipped off. I shook my shoulders out, relieving the cramped muscles. Red marks circled my wrists, but it wasn't too bad.

"I'll behave," I said, cracking my neck. "But I want to see Kat now."

The elevator slid to a stop and the doors opened. Nancy stepped out, and the soldier motioned me forward. "There's something you need to see first."

I ground to a halt. "That's not a part of the deal, Nancy. You want me to go along with this, I want to see Kat now."

She glanced over her shoulder. "What I'm about to show you has to do with Katy. Then you will see her."

"I want—" I whipped around, eyeballing the guard breathing down my neck. "Seriously, dude, you need to back the hell up."

The guy was half a head shorter than me and nowhere in my league of extraordinary ass-kicking abilities, but he didn't back down. "Keep. Walking."

I stiffened. "And if I don't?"

"Daemon," Nancy called, her voice laced with impatience. "All you're doing is delaying what you want."

As much as I hated to admit it, she had a point. Sending the punk one last promising look, I turned and followed the woman down the hall. Everything was white with the exception of the black dots in the wall and ceilings.

I didn't recall much about the inside of the buildings from when I'd been here as a kid, but I did remember there were very few places we'd been able to go. Most of the time we'd been kept to a community floor until we had assimilated and been set free.

Being back here didn't sit well with me for a multitude of reasons.

Nancy stepped in front of a door and leaned down. A red light clicked on and shone in her right eye. The light on the panel turned green and the door unlocked. That was going to prove tricky, and I wondered whether, if I took on Nancy's form, the systems had been prepped to recognize that. Then again, I felt as drained as the desert floor from whatever this building was outfitted with, so I wasn't sure what I could actually pull off.

Inside the small circular room, there were several monitors manned by men in uniform. Each of the screens showed a different room, hall, or floor.

"Leave us," she announced.

The men stood up from their stations and hastily exited the room, leaving Nancy and me with the tool who had come in with us.

"What did you want to show me?" I asked. "EuroCup?"

Her lips pursed. "This is one of many security control rooms stationed throughout the buildings. From here, we can monitor everything in Paradise Ranch."

"Paradise Ranch?" I laughed bitterly. "Is that what you're calling it now?"

She shrugged and then turned to one of the stations, her fingers flying over the keyboard. "All of the rooms are recorded. That helps us monitor activity for various reasons."

I ran a hand over the scruff growing on my cheek. "Okay."

"One of our concerns whenever we bring in new hybrids is to make sure they are not a danger to themselves or others," she began, folding her arms. "It's a process we take very seriously, and we go through several rounds of testing to ensure that they are viable."

I really did not like where this was heading if it had anything to do with Kat.

"Katy has proven to have some issues and can become very dangerous."

I ground down on my teeth so hard I was surprised they didn't crack. "If she's done anything, it's because she was provoked."

"Really?" Nancy punched a button on the keyboard, and the screen above her to the left flickered on.

Kat.

All the air went out of my lungs. My heart stopped and then sped up.

Kat was on the screen, sitting down with her back pressed against a wall. The image was grainy, but it was her—*it was her*. She was in the clothes she'd worn the night she was captured at Mount Weather, and that had to be weeks ago. Confusion rose swiftly. When was this taken? It couldn't be a live feed.

Her hair hung down on the sides, shielding her beautiful face. I started to tell her to look up but realized at the last minute that would make me look like an imbecile.

"As you can see, no one is near her," Nancy said. "That is Sergeant Dasher in the room with her. He is doing the initial interview."

Suddenly, Kat's chin jerked up, and she sprang to her feet, racing around a tall man in a military uniform. The next second, she hit the floor. I stared in open horror as Kat withered, and then one of the men unhooked a water hose from the wall.

Nancy flicked a button, and there was a different image. It took me a second to recover from the last scene and get what was going on now, but when I did, pure, red-hot rage lit me up.

On the screen were Kat and freaking Blake, squaring off. She whirled, grabbing for a lamp, but he darted in front, blocking her. When she swung on him, pride swelled in me. That was *my* Kitten, claws and all.

But the next thing had me searching for a way out of the room. Blake had intercepted her punch, twisted her arm, and swung her around. Pain registered on Kat's face, and then he had her down on her back, pinned to the bed.

I saw red.

"This isn't happening now," Nancy said calmly. "This was a while ago, when she first arrived. It's muted."

Breathing heavily, I turned back to the TV. They were struggling, and Blake had obviously overpowered her. She was still fighting, though, her back bowing and her body twisting under his. Violence rose in me, powered by potent rage and a level of helplessness I'd never felt before, and it tasted like Blake's blood. My hands formed fists, and I wanted to smash them in the monitor, since his face wasn't in front of me.

When he had pulled her off the bed, and I saw him dragging her across the floor and off the screen, I spun toward Nancy. "What happened? Where did he take her?"

"Into the bathroom, where there are no cameras. We do believe in some sort of privacy." She clicked something and the video fast-forwarded a couple of minutes, and Blake entered from the right. He sat on the bed—*her* bed—and Kat appeared a few seconds later, absolutely soaked.

I stepped forward, exhaling out of my nose. Words were exchanged between them, and then Kat whirled, opened a dresser, and grabbed clothes. She disappeared back into the bathroom.

Blake dropped his head into his hands.

"I'm going to fucking kill him," I promised to no one in

particular, but it was one I was going to keep. He would pay for this—all of this—one way or another.

The soldier cleared his throat. "Blake isn't an issue anymore."

I faced him, breathing raggedly. "Care to tell me why?"

He pressed his lips together. "Blake's dead."

"What?"

"He's dead," the guy repeated. "Katy killed him two days ago."

The floor felt like it dropped out from underneath me. My first response was to deny it, because I didn't want to believe that Kat would have had to do something like that—that she had to go through it.

The monitor was turned off, and Nancy watched me. "The reason I'm showing you this isn't to upset you or to make you mad. You need to see with your own eyes that Katy has proven to be dangerous."

"I have no doubt in my mind that if Kat really did do that, she had a reason." My heart thudded in my chest. I *needed* to see her. If she had done this . . . I couldn't bear to think about what she had to be going through. "And I would've done it, too, if I were in her shoes."

Nancy *tsk*ed softly, and I added her to my Going to Die Painfully list. "I hate to think of you as being unstable, too," she said.

"Kat isn't unstable. All these videos show is her defending herself, or that she was scared."

Nancy made a sound of disagreement. "Hybrids can be so unpredictable."

I met her gaze and held it. "So can Luxen."

10

{ Daemon }

They let me clean up in an empty communal area. At first I didn't want to waste the time. I needed to get to Kat, but they weren't giving me much of a choice, which turned out to be a good thing because I looked like something straight out of the mountains. The growth on my face was out of control. After a shave and a quick shower, I put on the black sweats and white shirt that had been left behind. Same standard uniform they had used years ago. Nothing like dressing everyone the same to make them feel like a nameless face in a crowd of nameless faces.

It was all about control and keeping everyone in line when I'd been here before. To me it looked like Daedalus was no different.

I almost laughed when realization kicked in. It probably had always been Daedalus running the show, even when I'd been assimilated here so many years ago.

When the guard returned, it was the tool from earlier, and the first thing he did was check the plastic razor for the blade.

I cocked an eyebrow at him. "I'm not that stupid."

"Good to know," was the reply. "Ready?"

"Been."

He stepped aside, allowing me back into the hallway. As we headed to another elevator, he was glued to my hip. "As close as you're riding me, man, I feel like I need to take you out to dinner or something. At least I should get your name."

He punched in a floor. "People call me Archer."

My eyes narrowed. There was something about him that reminded me of Luc, and hell if that boded well. "Is that your name?"

"That's what I was born with."

The dude was as charming as . . . well, as me on a bad day. Flipping my gaze to the red number on the elevator, I watched it steadily go down. My gut twisted. If Nancy was screwing with me and Kat wasn't here, I was about to find out.

I didn't know what I'd do if she wasn't. Probably go insane.

I couldn't stop what came out of my mouth next. "Have you seen her—Kat?"

A muscle flexed in Archer's jaw, and my imagination ran wild until he answered. "Yes. I've been assigned to her. I'm sure that pleases you to no end."

"Is she okay?" I asked, ignoring the jab.

He turned to me, and surprise crossed his features. Trading insults and barbs wasn't on my to-do list right now. "She can . . . she can be as expected."

I didn't like the way that sounded. Taking a deep breath, I ran a hand through my damp hair. The image of Beth freaking out popped into my head. A tremor ran down the muscles in my arm. There was no doubt in my mind that no matter what condition Kat was in, I could handle it. I would help her get better. Nothing in this world could stop that, but I didn't want her to have experienced anything that would've damaged her.

Like killing Blake surely would have.

"She was asleep the last time I checked in," he said as the elevator came to a stop. "She hasn't been sleeping well since they brought her in, but she seems to be making up for it today."

I nodded slowly and followed him out into the hallway. It struck me then how brave they were in only giving me one guard, but then again, they knew what I wanted, and I knew what was at risk if I acted a fool.

My heart was tripping out, my hands opening and closing sporadically at my sides. Anxious energy rolled through me, and as we neared the middle of the wide hall, I felt something I hadn't felt in way too long.

A warm tingle shimmied along the back of my neck.

"She's here." My voice sounded hoarse.

He glanced back at me. "Yes. She's here."

I didn't need to tell him that I'd had my doubts, that a part of me had held on to the cold possibility that they'd played to my weakness. It must've been written all over my face, and I didn't care to even hide it.

Kat was *here*.

Archer stopped before a door and punched in a code after doing the eye-reading bit. There was a soft sound of locks clicking out of place. He glanced at me, hand on the doorknob. "I'm not sure how long they'll give you."

Then he opened the door.

Like walking through quicksand or in a dream, I moved forward without feeling the floor beneath me. The air seemed to thicken, slowing my progress, but in reality I was rushing that damn door and still not moving quickly enough.

Senses on high alert, I stepped into the cell, vaguely aware of the door closing behind me. My gaze shot right to the bed pressed up against the wall.

My heart stopped. My entire world came to a halt.

I walked forward, and my step faltered. Only at the last possible second, I caught myself from hitting the floor on my knees. The back of my throat and eyes burned.

Kat was curled on her side, facing the door, appearing terribly small on the bed. The chocolate-colored length of her hair fell across her cheek, covering the sleeve of her exposed arm. She was asleep, but her features pinched as if even in rest she wasn't wholly comfortable. Her small hands were tucked under her rounded chin, lips slightly parted.

Her beauty struck me hard, like a bolt of lightning right in the chest. I froze there, for how long I don't know, unable to take my eyes off her, and then I took two long strides that brought me to the edge of the bed.

Peering down at her, I opened my mouth to say something, but there were no words. I was struck speechless, and I swear Kat was the only one who could do this to me.

I sat beside her, my heart pounding as she stirred but didn't wake. Part of me hated the idea of waking her. Up close, I could see the dark shadows blooming under her thick lashes like faint ink smudges. And honestly, I was happy—no, *thrilled*—to just be in her presence, even if it meant that I wasted the entire time soaking her up.

But I couldn't stop myself from touching her.

Slowly, I reached out and carefully brushed the silky strands of hair back from her cheek, fanning the long length over the stark white pillow. Now I could see the faint bruises across her cheekbone, a faded shade of yellow. There was a thin cut on her lower lip, too. Anger punched its way through me. I inhaled deeply, letting my breath eke its way out.

Placing one hand on the other side of her, I lowered my head and pressed a soft kiss to the cut on her lip, silently promising that I'd make whoever was responsible for the bruises and pain she'd faced pay dearly. Instinctively, I let the healing warmth flow from me to her, erasing the bruises from sight.

A soft, warm sigh blew across my mouth, and I lifted my gaze, unwilling to pull too far away. Kat's lashes fluttered and her shoulders hitched as she dragged in a deeper breath. I waited with my heart in my throat.

She slowly opened her eyes, and her gray stare was unfocused as it moved over my face. "Daemon?"

The sound of her voice, husky with sleep, was like coming home. The burning turned into a ball in my throat. Leaning back, I placed the tips of my fingers on her chin. "Hey, Kitten," I said, my own voice hoarse as hell.

She stared at me as the cloudiness in her gaze cleared. "Am I dreaming?"

My laugh came out strangled. "No, Kitten, you're not dreaming. I'm really here."

A heartbeat passed, and then she rose up on her elbows. A single strand of hair fell across her face. I straightened, giving her more room. My heart rate kicked into supersonic speed, matching hers. Then she was sitting up fully, her hands on my face. My eyes closed as I felt the gentle touch all the way to my soul.

Kat slid her hands over my cheeks, as if she were trying to convince herself that I was real. I placed mine over her hands and opened my eyes. Hers were wide and wet, shining with tears. "It's okay," I told her. "Everything's going to be okay, Kitten."

"How . . . how are you here?" She swallowed. "I don't understand."

"You're going to be mad." I pressed a kiss to her open palm. I reveled in the shudder that rolled through her. "I turned myself in."

She jerked back, but I held onto her hands, not letting her get away. And yeah, I was selfish. I wasn't ready to go without her touch. "Daemon, what . . . ? What were you thinking? You shouldn't—"

"I wasn't going to let you go through this by yourself." I slid my hands down her arms, cupping her elbows. "There was no way I could do that. I know that's not what you wanted, but *this* wasn't want I wanted."

She gave a little shake of her head, and her voice was barely a whisper. "But your family, Daemon? Your—"

"You're more important." The moment those words came out of my mouth, I knew they were true. Family had always come first for me, and Kat was a part of my family—a bigger part. She was my future.

"But the things they're going to make you do . . ." The wetness in her eyes swelled, and a single tear escaped, racing down her cheek. "I don't want you to go through—"

I caught the tear with a kiss. "And I'm not going to let you do this by yourself. You're my—you're my everything, Kat." At the sound of her soft inhale, I smiled again. "Come on, Kitten, did you really expect anything less from me? I love you."

Her hands fell to my shoulders, flexing until her fingers dug through the cotton of my shirt, and she stared at me for so long I started to worry. Then she sprang forward, wrapping her arms around my neck and practically tackling me.

Laughing against the top of her head, I caught myself before I toppled over. One second she was beside me, and then she was in my lap, wrapping her arms and legs around me. This— *this* was the Kat I knew.

"You're crazy," she whispered against my neck. "You're absolutely crazy, but I love you. I love you so much. I don't want you here, but I love you."

I slid my hand down her spine, curling my fingers against her lower back. "I'll never grow tired of hearing you say that."

She pressed against me, her fingers burying in the hair at the nape of my neck. "I missed you so much, Daemon."

"You have no idea . . ." I ran out of words at that point. Her being this close after so long was the sweetest kind of torture. Each breath she took, I felt in *every* part of my body, in some areas more than others. Really inappropriate, but she always had a powerful hold over me. Common sense jumped out the window.

She pulled back, her eyes searching mine, and then she reclaimed the distance, and, damn, the kiss was half innocent, half desperate, and wholly perfect. My grip on her back tightened as she tilted her head, and even though the kiss started out as something sweet, I totally took it there. I deepened the kiss, throwing every fear into it, every minute that had passed that we'd been separated, and everything I felt for her. Her breathy moan shook me, and when she wiggled it nearly undid me.

I gripped her hips and pushed her back. It was the last thing I wanted to do. "Cameras, remember?"

Color crawled up her neck and splashed across her cheeks. "Oh, yeah, everywhere except—"

"The bathroom," I supplied, catching the flash of surprise across her face. "They've filled me in."

"Everything?" When I nodded, the rosy color in her cheeks disappeared, and she quickly scuttled out of my lap. She settled beside me, her gaze straight ahead. Several moments passed, and she took a deep breath. "I'm . . . glad you're here, but I wish you weren't."

"I know." I didn't take offense to that statement.

She tucked her hair back. "Daemon, I . . ."

I placed two fingers under her chin and tilted her face back to mine. "*I know,*" I said again, searching her eyes. "I saw some of the stuff, and they told me about—"

"I don't want to talk about that," she said quickly, sliding her hands over her bent knees.

Concern rose inside me, but I forced a smile. "Okay. That's okay." I slid my arm back around her shoulders, tugging her closer. There was no resistance. She melted into my side, curling her fingers into my shirt. I kissed her forehead. I kept my voice low. "I'm going to get us out of this."

Her hand balled around my shirt as she lifted her head. "How?" she whispered.

I leaned over, pressing close to her ear. "Trust me. I'm sure they're watching us, and I don't want to give them any reason to separate us right now."

She nodded in understanding, but her mouth grew tense. "Have you seen what they've been doing here?"

I shook my head, and she took a deep breath. In hushed tones, she told me about the sick humans they were treating, the Luxen and the hybrids. As we talked, we stretched out on the bed, facing each other. I could tell she was skating over a lot of stuff. For one thing, she didn't talk about anything she'd been doing or how she got those bruises. I figured it had to do with Blake and that was why she was mum on the topic, but she did mention a little girl named Lori who was dying from cancer. A pinched look appeared when she talked about her. Kat hadn't smiled once. The knowledge nagged at me, threatening to ruin the reunion.

"They said that there are bad Luxen out there," she said. "That it's why they have me here, to learn how to fight against them."

"What?"

She tensed. "They said that there were thousands of Luxen who wanted to harm humans and that more would be coming. I'm guessing they didn't say anything like that to you?"

"No." I almost laughed, but then I remembered what Ethan had said. There was no way that could've had anything to do with what she was saying. Or could it? "They told me they want more hybrids." A troubled look crossed her face, and

I wished I hadn't said that. "What kind of cancer does Lori have?" I asked, running my hand up her arm. I hadn't stopped touching her. Not once since I'd entered the room.

The tips of her fingers were resting on my chin, and we were as close as we could be that would seem appropriate, considering we had eyes on us. "Same kind of cancer my dad had."

I squeezed her hand. "I'm sorry."

Her fingers followed the curve of my jaw. "I only saw her once, but she's not doing too well. They're giving her some kind of treatment they're getting from the Luxen and hybrids. They call it LH-11."

"LH-11?"

She nodded and then frowned. "What?"

Holy crap, that was what Luc wanted. Which begged the question, what the hell did Luc want with a serum that Daedalus was using on sick humans? Her frown deepened, and I bridged the insignificant space between us, keeping my voice low. "I'll tell you later."

Understanding flared, and she brought her leg up a little so it rested against mine. My breath caught, and a different kind of awareness crept into Kat's eyes. She bit down on her lower lip, and I fought back a groan.

That pretty color edged into her cheeks again, so not helping the situation. I brought my hand up her arm, senses flaring as she shivered. "You know what I'd give for some privacy right about now?"

Her lashes lowered. "You're terrible."

"I am."

Her expression clouded over. "I feel like there's a big clock hanging over us right now, like we're running out of time."

We probably were. "Don't think about it."

"It's kind of hard not to."

There was a pause, and I cupped her cheek, smoothing my thumb over the delicate bone. Several moments passed.

"Did you see my mom at all?"

"No." I wanted to tell her why, and tell her more, but divulging any information at this point was a risk. I had an idea, though. I could take my true form and talk to her that way, but I doubted the powers that be would appreciate that. I wasn't willing to risk it at this moment. "But Dee has been keeping an eye on her."

Kat kept her eyes closed. "I miss my mom," she whispered, and my heart cracked. "I really miss her."

I didn't know what to say, and what could I say? *I'm sorry* wouldn't cut it. So as I searched for a distraction, I let myself get reacquainted with the angles of her face, the graceful column of her neck, and the slope of her shoulders. "Tell me something I don't know."

Several moments passed before she spoke. "I've always wanted a Mogwai."

"What?"

Kat's lashes still fanned her cheeks, but she was finally smiling, and some of the pressure eased off my chest. "You've seen *Gremlins*, right? Remember Gizmo?" When I nodded, she laughed. The sound was hoarse, as if she hadn't laughed in a while. Which I figured she hadn't. "Mom let me watch it when I was a kid, and I was obsessed with Gizmo. I wanted one more than I wanted anything in the world. I even promised Mom that I wouldn't feed it after midnight or get it wet."

I rested my chin atop her head and grinned at the image of the little brown and white furball-sprouting pods. "I don't know."

"What?" She burrowed closer, tucking her fingers against the collar of my shirt.

Throwing my arm around her waist, I took what felt like

the first real breath in weeks. "If I had a Mogwai, I'd totally feed it after midnight. That Mohawk gremlin was a badass."

She laughed again, the sound tinkling inside me, and I felt about a thousand pounds lighter. "Why doesn't that surprise me?" she said. "You'd totally bond with the gremlin."

"What can I say? It's my sparkling personality."

11

{ Katy }

Part of me still believed I was dreaming. I would wake up and Daemon would be gone. I'd be alone with my thoughts, haunted by what I had done. Fear and shame kept me from telling him about Blake. Killing Will had been one thing. An act of self-defense, and the bastard had still managed to shoot me, but Blake? That had been an act of anger and nothing else.

How could Daemon look at me the same, knowing I was a murderer? Because that was what I had done—I had murdered Blake.

"You with me?" he asked.

"Yes." Pushing away the troubling thoughts, I touched him. Honestly, I kept touching him, reminding myself that he was really there. I thought he was doing the same thing, but he had always been the touchy type, something I loved about him. I wanted more. There was a desperate urge to lose myself in him, in a way I'd only ever been able to do with Daemon.

I traced his lower lip with the pad of my finger. A muscle flexed in his jaw, and his eyes brightened. My heart did a funny little cartwheel, and he closed those beautiful eyes, face tensing. I started to pull my hand back.

He caught my wrist. "Don't."

"I'm sorry. It's just that you . . ." I trailed off, not sure of how to explain it.

A lopsided grin appeared on his face. "I can deal. Can you?"

"Yes." *Not really*, I admitted to myself. I wanted to climb into him. I wanted nothing between us. I wanted *him*. But shenanigans of the fun and naughty kind weren't appropriate given the situation, and exhibitionism wasn't something I wanted to indulge in. So I settled for the next best thing. I threaded my fingers through his. "I feel bad that I'm happy you're here."

"Don't be." His eyes opened, and the pupils shone like diamonds. "I honestly don't want to be anyplace else."

I snorted. "Really?"

"Really." He kissed me softly and quickly pulled back. "Sounds crazy but it's true."

I wanted to ask him how he planned on getting us out of here. There had to be a plan. Hopefully. I couldn't imagine that he busted up in Daedalus and hadn't thought about a way out. It wasn't like I hadn't been thinking about how to escape. There was just no foreseeable escape route. I licked my lips. Daemon's eyes flared.

"What if . . . ?" I swallowed, keeping my voice low. "What if this is our future?"

"No." The arm around my waist drew me forward, and an instant later I was pressed against his front. His mouth moved against the sensitive spot under my ear as he spoke in a low whisper. "This isn't our future, Kitten. I promise you."

I sucked in a sharp breath. Memories of being this close to him hadn't done the real thing any justice. The hardness of his chest against mine scrambled my thoughts, but it was his words that flooded my body with warmth. Daemon never promised something he didn't hold to.

Fitting my head in the space between his neck and shoulder, I inhaled the smell of soap and the outdoorsy scent that was uniquely his. "Say it," I whispered.

His hand slid up my spine, leaving a wake of shivers. "Say what, Kitten?"

"You know."

He rubbed his chin in my hair. "I love . . . my car, Dolly."

My lips cracked into a tiny grimace. "That's not it."

"Oh." His voice dripped innocence. "I know. I love *Ghost Investigators*."

"You're such a douche."

He laughed softly. "But you love me."

"I do." I pressed a kiss against his shoulder.

There was a pause, and I felt his heart rate kick up. Mine quickly matched his. "I love you," he said, voice gruff. "I love you more than anything."

I let myself rest against him, probably relaxing for the first time since I'd gotten there. It wasn't that I felt stronger because he was there, though in a way I was. But it was because I now had someone on my side, someone who had my back. I wasn't alone in this, and if it had been the other way around, I would've done the same thing he'd done. I doubted—

The door to the cell opened suddenly, and Daemon stiffened just like I did. Over his shoulder I saw Sergeant Dasher and Nancy Husher. Behind the incredibly douchetastic duo was Archer and another guard.

"Are we interrupting?" Nancy asked.

Daemon snorted. "No. We were just saying how sad we were that you guys weren't visiting us."

Nancy clasped her hands. In her black pantsuit, she looked

like a walking ad for women who hate color. "For some reason I doubt that."

My grip on the front of Daemon's shirt tightened as my eyes bounced to the sergeant. His gaze wasn't outright hostile, but then again, that didn't tell me much.

The sergeant cleared his throat. "We have work to do."

Insanely fast, Daemon was sitting up, and somehow he'd maneuvered his body so that I was behind him. "Work on what?" he asked, threading his fingers together between his knees. "And I don't believe I've had the honor of meeting you."

"That's Sergeant Dasher," I explained, trying to move so I wasn't behind him. He shifted, blocking me once more.

"Is that so?" Daemon's voice became low and dangerous, and my stomach sank. "I think I've seen you before."

"I don't think you have," Dasher responded evenly.

"Oh, he has." Nancy gestured at me. "I showed him the video of the first day Katy was here and your meeting with her."

I closed my eyes and muttered a curse. Daemon was so gonna kill him.

"Yeah, I've seen that." Each word was punctuated with what I knew was a death glare. I pried an eye open. Dasher didn't look completely unfazed. The lines around his mouth were tense. "I've tucked those images away in a very special place," Daemon finished.

I placed a hand on his back. "What work do we have to do?"

"We need to run some joint tests, and then we'll go from there," answered Dasher.

My muscles locked up, an action duly noted by Daemon. More stress tests? I couldn't foresee that going well with Daemon involved.

"It's nothing too complicated or intensive." Nancy stepped aside, motioning to the door. "Please. The sooner we get started, the quicker it is over."

Daemon didn't move.

Nancy eyed us calmly. "Do I need to remind you of what you promised, Daemon?"

I shot him a sharp look. "Promised what?"

Before he could respond, Nancy did. "He promised to do whatever we asked *without* causing trouble if we brought him to you."

"What?" I stared at him. When he didn't say anything, I almost wanted to hit him. God only knew what they'd make him do. Taking a deep breath, I scooted around him and stood. A second later, he was on his feet and in front of me. Tucking my hair back, I slid my sneakers on.

We didn't say anything as we stepped out into the hall. I glanced at Archer, but he was closely watching Daemon. I must not have been the DEFCON threat anymore. When we stopped in front of the elevator, I felt Daemon's hand wrap around mine, and a little of the tautness eased out of my shoulders. How many times had I stepped into these elevators? I'd lost count, but this time was different.

Daemon was here.

They led us to the med floor and took us into a room that accommodated two patients. Dr. Roth was waiting for us, his expression eager as he hooked both of us up to a blood pressure meter.

"I've been waiting a long time to run tests on someone like you," he said to Daemon, voice high-pitched.

Daemon arched a brow. "Another fanboy. I have them everywhere."

I muttered, "Only you would see that as a good thing."

He shot me a grin.

Color heightened the doctor's cheeks. "It's not often we get a powerful Luxen like you. We had thought that Dawson would be the one, but . . ."

Daemon's face turned dark. "You *worked* with my brother?"

Uh oh.

Eyes widening, Dr. Roth glanced at where Nancy and Sergeant Dasher stood. He cleared his throat as he unwrapped the cuffs. "Their blood pressure is identical. Perfect. One-twenty over eighty."

Nancy scribbled it down on a clipboard that I swore just appeared in her hands. I shifted in the chair, bringing my focus back to Daemon. He was eyeballing the doctor like he wanted to beat information out of him.

Dr. Roth checked our pulses next. Resting pulse was in the fifties, which was apparently a good thing, because Roth was practically humming. "Katy's rate was in the high sixties each time before, blood pressure well into the high levels. It appears that with his presence, her rates are optimizing, matching his. This is good."

"Why is it good?" I asked.

He pulled out a stethoscope. "It's a good indication that the mutation is on a perfect, cellular level."

"Or an indication that I'm pretty damn awesome," Daemon suggested coolly.

That earned a small smile from the doctor, and my anxiety notched up. One would think that Daemon being his normal cocky, arrogant self was a good thing, but I'd learned that his smartass responses could mean he was seconds from exploding.

"Hearts beating in perfect sync. Very good," Roth murmured, turning to Dasher. "She passed the stress test, correct? No outward signs of destabilization?"

"She did perfectly, as we'd hoped."

I sucked in a sharp breath, pressing my hand to my stomach. I'd done as they expected? Did that mean they expected me to kill Blake? I couldn't even consider that.

Daemon glanced at me. His eyes narrowed. "What exactly are these stress tests?"

My mouth opened, but I didn't know what to say. I didn't want him to know what had happened—what I'd done. I turned to Dasher, and his expression was guarded. I prayed that the man had common sense. If he told Daemon about the fighting, it was likely that Daemon would go postal.

"The stress testing is run of the mill," he explained. "I'm sure Katy can tell you that."

Yeah, totally run of the mill, if getting your ass kicked and murder were ordinary things; but in a twisted way, I appreciated the lie. "Yeah, completely run of the mill."

Doubt crossed Daemon's features as he turned back to the doctor. "Were these stress tests the same kind of things Dawson did?"

No one answered, which was answer enough. Daemon was very still, but his stare was sharp, and his mouth pressed into a hard line. He then reached over and took my hand in his, the gentle grasp so at odds with his demeanor.

"So we can move on to the more important phase of our work today." Dr. Roth walked over to a cart full of utensils. "One of the most remarkable things about our extraterrestrial friends is their ability to heal not only themselves but others. We believe that unlocking that ability will provide us with the necessary information to replicate the function to heal others suffering from various diseases."

The doctor picked up something, but his hand hid it as he turned back to us. "The whole purpose of this next exercise, Daemon, is to see how fast you can heal. We need to be able to see this before we can move on."

The anxiety that had been riding me exploded like a cannonball. This could only be leading to one thing.

"Do tell?" Daemon asked in a low voice.

Roth visibly swallowed as he approached us, and I noticed that Archer and another guard were also closing ranks. "We need you to heal Katy," he said.

The hand around mine tightened, and Daemon leaned forward. "Heal her from what exactly? Because I'm a little confused. I've already taken care of those bruises—which, by the way, I would *love* to know how she got them."

My pulse kicked up as I took in my surroundings. The black dots were everywhere, and I had a feeling we were about to get reacquainted with the loving embrace of onyx.

"It won't be anything serious," the doctor explained gently. "Just a minor scratch that she will barely feel. Then I'm going to do some blood work and monitor your vitals. That is all."

Suddenly all I could think about was Dawson and Bethany, of all the things they had done to Bethany to force Dawson to heal others. Nausea rolled, and I felt dizzy. Dasher hadn't acted like getting Daemon here was a priority, but now that he was, we were going to see all the sides of Daedalus. And how could they start rolling in other people to heal until they knew the true extent of his abilities?

"No." Daemon was seething. "You're not going to hurt her."

"You promised," Nancy said. "Do I need to continuously remind you of that?"

"I didn't agree to you hurting her," he replied, the pupils of his eyes starting to glow.

Archer moved in closer. The other guard moved to the wall, near a very unfriendly looking button. Stuff was about to hit the fan, and when Dr. Roth showed what was in his hand, Daemon shot to his feet, letting go of mine and moving in front of me.

"Not going to happen, buddy," he said, hands closing into fists.

Light glinted off the steel scalpel Roth held. The good doctor took a wise step back. "I promise she will barely feel it. I'm a doctor. I know how to make a clean cut."

The muscles in Daemon's back locked up. "No."

Nancy made a sound of impatience as she lowered the clipboard. "This can be easy or this can become very difficult."

His head swung in her direction. "Difficult for you or me?"

"For you and for Katy." She took a step forward, either very brave or very stupid. "We could always restrain you. Or we could do this and get it over with. The choice is yours."

Daemon looked like he was going to call their bluff, and I knew that they would go through with it. If he or I put up a fight, they'd fill this room with onyx, restrain him until they did whatever they wanted to me, and then release him. Either way, this was going to happen. The decision was ours—to go the clean or messy route.

I stood on legs that felt weak. "Daemon."

He looked over his shoulder at me. *"No."*

Forcing a smile that felt weird, I shrugged. "It's going to happen either way. Trust me." Pain flickered across his face at the last two words. "If we do this, then it's over. You agreed to this."

"I did *not* agree to this."

"I know . . . but you're here, and . . ." And this was why I didn't want him here. Turning to the doctor, I held out my hand. "He's not going to let anyone do this. I'm going to have to do it myself."

Daemon stared at me incredulously. The doctor turned to Nancy, who nodded. It was obvious that her position, whatever it was, usurped the sergeant's.

"Go ahead," Nancy said. "I trust that Katy knows what will happen if she decides to use that knife in a very bad manner."

I shot the woman a hateful look as the cool instrument landed in my palm. Mustering up my courage, I turned to Daemon. He was still staring at me like I was insane. "Ready?"

"No." His chest rose in a deep breath, and a very rare thing happened. Helplessness had crept into his eyes, turning them a mossy shade of green. "Kat . . ."

"We have to."

Our eyes locked, and then he extended his hand. "I'll do it."

I stiffened. "No way."

"Give it to me, Kat."

There were several reasons why I wasn't giving him the scalpel. Mainly because I didn't want him to feel guilty about it, and I was also afraid he'd turn it into a projectile. I shifted slightly, opening my left hand. I'd never cut myself before, at least on purpose. My heart was pounding crazy fast and my stomach was jumping. The edge of the scalpel was wicked sharp, so I assumed it wouldn't take much pressure to do the deed.

I poised it over my open palm, squeezing my eyes shut.

"Wait!" Daemon shouted, causing me to jerk. When I looked up, his pupils were completely white. "I need to be in my true form."

Now I was staring at him like he was nuts. There had been many times when he did quick patch-up work in his human form. He only turned into a glow stick when things were serious. I had no idea what he was up to.

He turned to Nancy and the sergeant, who wore mirror looks of suspicion. "I want to make sure I do this quick and fast. I don't want her to be in pain, and I don't want it to scar."

They seemed to believe that, because Nancy nodded her approval. Daemon took a deep breath, and then his body started to shimmer. He was changing. The outline of his form began to fade out, clothes and all. For a second, I forgot that we were in this room, that I was holding a scalpel about to slice open my own flesh, and that we were basically prisoners of Daedalus.

Watching him take on his true form was nothing short of awe-inspiring.

Just before he'd completely faded out, he started to take shape again. Arms. Legs. Torso. Head. For a brief second, I could see him, *really* see him. The skin was translucent, like a jellyfish, and the network of veins was filled with a pearlescent glow. The features were Daemon, but sharper and more defined, and then he was shining as bright as the sun. A human-shaped light tinged in red that was so beautiful to look upon that tears filled my eyes.

I really don't want you to do this.

Like always, hearing his voice in my head came as a shock. I didn't think I'd ever get used to it. I started to respond vocally but caught myself. *You shouldn't have come here, Daemon. This is what they want.*

The luminous head cocked to the side. *Coming here for you was the only thing I could do. Doesn't mean I have to be okay with everything. Now do this before I change my mind and see if I really can't tap into the Source and kill someone.*

My gaze fell to the scalpel, and I cringed. Getting a good grip on the handle, I could feel several eyes on me. Being the coward that I am, I squeezed my eyes shut, brought the blade down on my palm, and sliced.

I hissed at the flare of pain and dropped the scalpel, watching the thin cut immediately bubble with blood. It was like a paper cut times a million.

Jesus H. Mary mother of Christ in crutches, came Daemon's voice.

I'm not sure that's how it goes, I told him, squeezing my palm shut against the burn.

I was vaguely aware of the doctor stooping down and grabbing the blade as I looked up. The light from Daemon surrounded me as his hand outstretched, fingers becoming more visible as they circled my injured hand.

Open up, he said.

I shook my head, and his phantom sigh bounced around my head. He gently pried my hand open, his touch as warm as clothes freshly removed from the dryer. *Man, that hurt more than I thought.*

There was a low growl that replaced the sigh. *Did you really think it wasn't going to hurt, Kitten?*

Whatever. I let him guide me over to the chair, and I sat, watching as he knelt before me, his head bowed. Heat flared over my palm as he started to do his thing.

"Amazing," Dr. Roth whispered.

My eyes were trained on Daemon's glowing, bent head. The warmth that blew off him filled the room. I reached out and placed my uninjured hand on his shoulder. His light pulsed, and the red at the edges bled inward an inch or so. Interesting.

You know how I like it when you touch me in this form. His voice sent a shiver down my spine.

Why do you have to make everything sound so dirty? But I didn't pull my hand back.

His chuckle rolled through me, and by then, the pain in my palm had stopped. *I'm not the one with the dirty mind, Kitten.*

I rolled my eyes.

Both of his hands circled mine, and I was sure at that point my hand was already healed. *Now stop distracting me.*

I snorted. *Me? You're such a douche canoe.*

"Fascinating," Dr. Roth murmured. "They're communicating. It never fails to amaze me when I see it."

Daemon ignored him. *I took this form to tell you that I spoke with Luc before I went to Mount Weather.*

I sat up straight, all ears. *Did he have anything to do with this? No. And I believe him. He's going to help us get out. I need—*

"Show us your hand, Katy." Nancy's voice intruded.

I wanted to ignore her, but when I glanced up, I saw the other guard moving closer to Daemon with what looked like a stun gun in his hand. I jerked my hand from Daemon's and showed them. "Happy?"

"Daemon, take your human form," Nancy ordered, voice clipped.

A heartbeat passed, and then Daemon stood. In his true form, he seemed taller and was a hell of a lot more intimidating. His light pulsed once, more red than white, and then it dimmed out.

He stood there, minus the glowworm thing. Only his eyes burned with white light. "I don't know if you've realized this or not, but I don't like to be ordered to do things."

Nancy cocked her head to the side. "I don't know if you've realized this or not, but I'm used to people taking my orders."

A smirk graced his face. "Ever hear of the saying you catch more lions with honey than vinegar?"

"I think it's 'catch more bees' and not lions," I mumbled.

"Whatever."

Dr. Roth examined my hand. "Remarkable. Only a faint pink line. It will probably be completely gone within the hour." He turned to Nancy and Dasher, practically thrumming with excitement. "Other Luxen have healed in this amount of time, but not to where the cut is completely sealed."

Like Daemon needed help feeling special.

The doctor shook his head as he stared up at him. "Truly amazing."

I wondered if the good doctor was going to kiss him.

Before he could start drooling on Daemon, the door burst open and an out-of-breath officer appeared, cheeks ruddy with the color of his buzzed hair. "We have a problem," he announced, taking several deep breaths.

Nancy gave him an arch look, and I couldn't help but think the guy in the doorway would probably get yelled at later for barging in here.

Dasher cleared his throat. "What is the problem, Collins?"

The officer's eyes bounced across the room, moving over Daemon and me before darting back to us and then finally settling on the sergeant. "It's a problem in building B, sir, from the *ninth* floor. It requires your immediate attention."

12

Building B? I vaguely remembered hearing someone mention another building attached to this one underground but had no idea what or who was housed there. I was 100 percent ready to find out, though. Whatever it was, it appeared dire, because Sergeant Dasher left the room without further word.

Nancy was right on his heels. "Take them back to their rooms. Doctor?" She paused. "You will probably want to join us." And then they were gone.

I turned to Archer. "What's going on?"

He gave me a look that said I was dumb for asking. I scowled. "What's in building B?"

The other soldier stepped forward. "You ask too many questions and need to learn when to shut up."

I blinked. That was all it took, and Daemon had the stocky guard by the neck and pinned to the wall. My eyes popped.

"And you need to learn to speak to the ladies with a little bit of manners," he snarled.

"Daemon!" I screeched, preparing myself for the onyx.

But it never came.

Daemon pried his fingers off the gasping soldier's throat, one by one, and stepped back. The soldier slumped against the wall. Archer had done nothing.

"You let him do that?" the guard accused, pointing at Archer. "What the hell, man?"

Archer shrugged. "He had a point. You need to learn manners."

I squelched the urge to laugh because Daemon was eyeballing the soldier like he wanted to snap his neck. Hurrying to Daemon's side, I wrapped my hand around his and squeezed.

He looked down, not seeing me at first. Then he lowered his head, brushing his lips across my forehead. My shoulders slumped in relief. I doubted Archer would've allowed a round two.

"Whatever," the man spat, then spun on his heel, exiting the room and leaving Archer to fend for himself with the two of us.

He didn't look concerned.

The trip back to our cells was uneventful up until the moment Archer said, "Nope. You two are not going in one of them together."

I whirled on him. "Why not?"

"My orders are to put you two in your rooms—plural." He punched in the code. "Don't make this hard. If you do, all they're going to do is keep you apart longer."

I started to protest, but the hard set to his mouth told me that he wouldn't be convinced. I took a ragged breath. "Will you at least tell us what's in building B?"

Archer looked at Daemon and then me. Finally he muttered a curse and stepped forward, chin lowered. Beside me Daemon stiffened, and Archer shot him a warning glare. Voice low, he said, "I'm sure they'll show you eventually, and you'll probably wish they hadn't. Origins are kept in that building."

"Origins?" Daemon repeated, brows furrowing. "What the hell is that?"

Archer shrugged. "That's all I can tell you. Now please, Katy, go into your room."

Daemon's hand tightened around mine, and then he swooped down, catching my chin in his other hand and tilting my head back. His mouth was on mine, and the kiss . . . the kiss was fierce, hard and branding, curling my toes inside my sneakers and stealing my breath. My free hand fell to his chest as the touch of our mouths rearranged my insides. In spite of the audience, luscious heat rose as he angled the kiss, pulling me hard against him.

Archer exhaled loudly.

Lifting his head, Daemon winked at me. "It'll be okay."

I nodded and barely remembered walking into my room, but there I was, staring at the bed Daemon had been sitting on earlier, as the door closed and locked behind me.

I smacked my hands over my face, stunned for a minute or two. When I'd fallen asleep the day before, I had been physically exhausted from using the Source and emotionally devastated from what I'd done. As I'd lain on that damn bed, staring at the ceiling, hopelessness had crept in, and even now it still had a hold on me.

But things were different. I had to keep telling myself that, to stop the bleakness from taking complete control. Pushing down what I'd done probably wasn't something therapists across the nation would suggest as a healthy practice, but I had to. Those hours before I'd fallen asleep . . .

I shook my head.

Things *were* different now. Daemon was here. Speaking of which, I had this feeling that he was still nearby. The tingling had died off, but I just knew that he was still close; I felt it on a cellular level.

I turned, eyeing the wall. Then I remembered the door in

the bathroom. Spinning around, I hurried into the bathroom and tried the knob on the door. Locked. Hoping my suspicions were correct, I knocked. "Daemon?"

Nothing.

I pressed my cheek against the cool wood, closing my eyes as I flattened my palms on the door. Did I really believe that they'd put us in two cells joined by a bathroom? Then again, they had kept Dawson and Bethany together in the beginning—hadn't that been what Dawson had said? But my luck wasn't that—

The door opened, and I tumbled forward. Strong arms and a hard chest caught me before I toppled right over.

"Whoa, Kitten . . ."

I looked up, heart pounding. "We share a bathroom!"

"I see." A small grin appeared, his eyes sparkling.

Grabbing fistfuls of his shirt, I rocked back on the heels of my sneakers. "I can't believe it. You're in the cell beside me! All we—"

Daemon's hands landed on my hips, his grip tight and sure, and then his mouth was on mine, picking up that soul-shattering kiss we'd started in the hallway. He was moving me backward at the same time. Somehow, and I really didn't know how other than that he had skills, he managed to shut the door behind us without taking his hands off me.

Those lips of his . . . they moved over mine, tantalizingly slow and deep, as if we were kissing for the very first time. His hands slid around, and when my back hit the sink, he lifted me so that I perched on the edge, and he kept pressing forward, pushing my knees apart with his hips. The smoldering heat was back, a flame that burned brighter at the slow, thorough kiss.

My chest rose and fell rapidly as I clutched his shoulders, almost completely lost in him. I'd read enough romance novels in my day to know that a bathroom and Daemon were things fantasies were made of, but . . .

I managed to break contact—though not much. Our lips brushed when I spoke. "Wait. We need to—"

"I know," he cut in.

"Good." I placed my trembling hands on his chest. "We're on the same page—"

Daemon kissed me again, spinning my senses. He was leisurely in his exploration of the kiss, pulling back and nipping at my lip until a breathy moan that would've embarrassed me any other time escaped me.

"Daemon—"

He caught whatever else I was going to say with his mouth. His hands slid up my waist, stopping when the tips of his fingers brushed the underside of my chest. My whole body jerked, and I knew right then that if I didn't stop this, we were going to waste very valuable time.

I pulled back, dragging in air that tasted of Daemon. "We really should be talking."

"I know." That half grin appeared. "That's what I've been trying to tell you."

My mouth dropped open. "What? You haven't been talking! You've been—"

"Kissing you senseless?" he asked innocently. "Sorry. It's all I want to do while you're here. Well, not *all* I want to do, but pretty close to everything else I—"

"I get it." I groaned, wanting to fan my face. Leaning back against the plastic mirror, I dropped my hands into my lap. Touching him wasn't helping, either. Neither was that smug half grin of his. "Wow."

With his hands exactly where they stopped under my chest, he leaned in and pressed his forehead against mine. In a low voice he said, "I want to make sure your hand is okay."

I frowned. "It is."

"I need to make sure." He leaned back a little, his eyes meeting mine meaningfully, and then I got it. When he saw the understanding cross my face, he grinned. A second later, he was in his true form—so bright in the small room, I had to close my eyes. *They say there are no cameras in here, but I know the room has to be bugged,* he said. *Besides, I also don't trust the fact that they're letting us have access to each other. They have to know we'll do this, so there's probably a reason.*

I shuddered. *I know, but they did let Dawson and Bethany stay together until . . .* I forced that thought out of my head. We were wasting time. *What did Luc tell you?*

He said he can help us get out of here, but he really didn't go into detail. He apparently has people on the payroll here and said they'd find me once I get something for him—something you've mentioned. LH-11.

Shock rippled through me. *Why would he want that?*

Don't know. Daemon's hands moved back to my hips, and then he tugged me off the sink. Moving too fast for me to comprehend, he sat on the closed lid of the toilet and settled me in his lap. His hand came up my back, pressing down on the nape of my neck until my cheek rested against his shoulder. The heat from him in his true form wasn't overwhelming like it had been the first time. *And it doesn't really matter, right?*

I savored his embrace. *Does it? That stuff is being given to humans who are sick. Why would Luc want that?*

Honestly, it can't be any worse than what Daedalus is doing with it, no matter how many good things they claim to be using it for.

Very true. I sighed. I didn't dare be hopeful about this. If Luc really was on our side and he could help us, there were still a lot of obstacles in our way. Almost impossible ones. *I've seen it before. Maybe we'll be close to it again.*

We need to be. A couple of moments passed, and then he said,

We can't stay in here forever. I have a feeling they are allowing this, and if we abuse it, then they'll separate us.

I nodded. What I didn't understand was why they would allow this unsupervised visit? Something that we could do whenever we wanted. Were they trying to show us that they weren't going to keep us apart? After all, they'd claimed they weren't the enemies here, but there was so much about Daedalus I didn't understand, like with Blake . . .

Shuddering, I turned my head in to his shoulder and breathed deeply. I wanted to force the memory of Blake out of my head, make as if he never existed.

"Kat?"

Lifting my head, I opened my eyes and realized he was no longer in his true form. "Daemon?"

His eyes drifted over my face. "What have they been doing to you in here?"

I froze, our gazes locking for an instant, and then I pushed off him, retreating a couple of steps. "Nothing really. Just tests."

He dropped his hands to his bent knees and softly said, "I know it's more than that, Kat. How did you get those bruises on your face?"

I glanced at the mirror. My complexion was pale, but there wasn't a trace left from the fights. "We shouldn't talk about this."

"I don't think they care that we're talking about this. The bruises are gone now, from when I healed you, but they were there before—faint but there." He stood, though he didn't come any closer. "You can talk to me. You should know that by now."

My eyes swung back to him. God, I did know that. I'd learned the hard way over the past winter. If I had trusted him with my secrets, Adam would still be alive and neither of us would probably be in this situation.

Guilt soured my stomach, but this was different. Telling him about the exams and the stress tests would only upset him, and he'd act upon it. Plus, admitting that I had killed Blake—and not so much in self-defense—was horrifying to even consider. I didn't want to think about it, let alone talk about it.

Daemon sighed. "Don't you trust me?"

"I do." My eyes went wide. "I trust you with my life, but I just . . . There's nothing to say about what has been going on in here."

"I think there's a lot to say."

I shook my head. "I don't want to argue about this."

"We're not arguing." He crossed the distance, placing his hands on my shoulders. "You're just being stubborn as hell, as usual."

"Look who's talking."

"Great movie," he replied. "I watched a lot of old movies in my spare time."

I rolled my eyes but cracked a grin.

He cupped my cheek as he lowered his chin, peering at me through thick lashes. "I'm worried about you, Kitten."

Pressure clamped down on my chest. Rarely did he admit to being worried about anything, and that was the last thing I wanted him to be doing. "I'm okay. I promise."

He continued to stare, as if he could see right through me, right through my lies.

{ Daemon }

Hours had passed since Kat and I parted ways and some poor excuse for dinner had been brought to my room. I tried to watch TV and even tried to sleep, but it was damn hard when I knew she was right next door, or when I heard her moving around in the bathroom. Once, in what might have been the middle of the night, I'd heard her footsteps at the door, and I knew she had been standing there, fighting the same need I was. But we had to be careful. Whatever reason they had for putting us in a space we could share couldn't be a good thing, and I didn't want to risk them relocating us, forcing us apart.

But I was worried about her. I knew she was hiding stuff, keeping whatever had gone on there before I arrived to herself. So like an idiot with no self-control whatsoever, I had gotten up and opened the bathroom door.

It had been dark and quiet, but I'd been correct. Kat was standing there, arms at her sides and so incredibly still. Seeing her like that punched a hole in my chest. She couldn't stand or sit still for longer than twenty seconds, but now . . .

I'd kissed her gently and had said, "Go to sleep, Kitten. So we both can rest."

She nodded and then said those three little words that never failed to bring me to my knees. "I love you."

And then she was back in her room, and I was in mine. Finally, I did sleep.

When morning came, so did Nancy. Nothing like seeing her prim face and plastic smile first thing to start the day off right.

I'd expected to be reunited with Kat, but I was taken to the med floor for more blood tests and then shown the hospital room Kat had spoken of.

"Where is the little girl?" I asked, scanning the chairs for the small child Kat had mentioned but not seeing one. "I think her name was Lori or something."

Nancy's expression remained blank. "Unfortunately, she didn't respond as we'd hoped. She passed a few days ago."

Shit. I hoped Kat didn't learn that. "You guys were giving her the LH-11?"

"Yes."

"And it didn't work?"

Her gaze sharpened. "You're asking a lot of questions, Daemon."

"Hey, you have me here, most likely using my DNA for this. Don't you think I'm going to be a little curious about it?"

She held my stare for a moment and then turned back to one of the patients who was having a fluid bag changed out. "You think too much, and you know what they say about curiosity."

"That it's possibly the most cliché and stupid saying ever?"

One side of her lips tipped up. "I like you, Daemon. You're a pain in the ass and a smart-mouth, but I like you."

I smiled tightly. "No one can deny my charm."

"I'm sure that's true." She paused as the sergeant entered the room, conversing quietly with one of the doctors. "Lori was given LH-11, but her reaction was not favorable."

"What?" he asked. "It didn't heal the cancer?"

Nancy didn't respond, and that was that. Somehow I figured the unfavorable reaction was due to more than the cancer not healing. "You know what I think?" I said.

She tipped her head to the side. "I can only imagine."

"Messing with human, hybrid, and alien DNA is probably asking for a world of trouble. You guys really don't know what you have."

"But we're learning."

"And making mistakes?" I asked.

She smiled. "There are no such things as mistakes, Daemon."

I wasn't so sure about that, but then my attention shifted to the window at the end of the room. My eyes narrowed. I could see other Luxen in there. Many of them looked as happy as a kid at Disneyland.

"Ah." Nancy smiled, nodding at the window. "I see you've noticed. They are here because they want to help. If only you'd be that accommodating."

I snorted. Who knew why the other Luxen were here,

happy as clams, and I really didn't care. I got that there were parts of Daedalus that were actually attempting to do something good, but I also knew what they did to my brother in the process.

All around me, doctors and lab technicians milled about. Some of the bags hooked up to the patients had a strange glittering liquid in them that vaguely resembled what we bled in our true form. "Is that LH-11?" I asked, gesturing at one of the bags.

Nancy nodded. "One of the versions—the newest—but that really isn't a concern of yours. We have—"

A siren sounded, cutting off her words with an ear-piercing shrill. Lights on the ceilings flashed red. Patients and doctors looked around in alarm. Sergeant Dasher stormed out of the room.

Nancy cursed under her breath as she spun toward the door. "Washington, escort Mr. Black back to his room immediately." She pointed at another guard. "Williamson, shut this room down. No one goes in or out."

"What's going on?" I asked.

She shot me a look before stomping past. Like hell I wanted to go back to my room when things were obviously just getting fun. Out in the hall, lighting was dim and the blinking red light caused an annoying strobe effect.

The Guard of the Moment took one step, and chaos stormed into the corridor.

Soldiers poured out of rooms, locking them down and taking up guard in front of them. Another came down the hall, clutching a walkie-talkie in a knuckle-white grip. "We have activity on elevator ten, coming out of building B. Lock it down now."

Huh, the infamous building B strikes again.

Farther down the hall, another door opened, and I saw Archer first and then Kat. She had a hand pressed over the fleshy part of her elbow. Behind her was Dr. Roth. My eyes narrowed when I saw a wicked-looking syringe in his hand. He brushed past Kat and Archer, heading straight for the guy on the walkie-talkie.

Kat turned, her gaze finding me. I started forward. No way was I not going to be beside her when the shit hit the fan, which apparently was happening.

"Where do you think you're going?" Washington demanded, hand going to the weapon on his thigh. "I have orders to take you back to your room."

I turned to him slowly, then back to the three elevators across from us. All of them were stopped on different floors, the lights red. "Exactly how are we supposed to get to my room?"

His eyes narrowed. "Stairwell?"

Tool had a point, but like I cared. I turned away, but his hand clamped down on my shoulder. "You stop me, and I will end you," I warned.

Whatever Washington saw in my face must've assured him that I wasn't fooling around, because he didn't interfere when I shrugged off his grip and went to Kat, dropping an arm around her shoulders. Her body was tense.

"You okay?" I asked, eyeing Archer. He also had his hand on his weapon, but he wasn't watching us. His eyes were on the middle elevator. He was hearing something in his earpiece and, by the look on his face, he wasn't happy.

She nodded, pushing a strand of hair that had escaped her ponytail out of her face. "Any idea what's going on?"

"Something about building B." Instinct suddenly told me that maybe being in our rooms would be a good thing. "This has never happened before?"

Kat shook her head. "No. Maybe it's a drill."

Double doors at the end of the hall suddenly burst open, and a swarm of officers in SWAT gear came through, armed to the teeth with rifles, faces shielded.

Reacting immediately, I swept an arm around Kat's waist and shoved her back against the wall, shielding her with my body. "I don't think this is a drill."

"It's not," Archer said, drawing his weapon.

The light above the middle elevator blinked from floor seven to floor six and then floor five.

"I thought the elevators were locked down?" someone demanded.

The men dressed in black shuffled forward, going down on their knees in front of the elevator. Someone else said, "Locking down the elevators ain't going to stop it. You know that."

"I don't care," the man yelled into the radio. "Shut down the damn elevator before it reaches the top level. Drop cement down the shaft if you need to. Stop the damn elevator!"

"Stop what?" I glanced at Archer.

The red light blinked on the fourth floor.

"Origin," he said, a muscle popping in his chin. "There's a stairway to the right, all the way down the hall. I'd suggest getting there now."

My gaze swung back to the elevator. Part of me wanted to stay to see what the hell an origin was and why they were acting like the *Cloverfield* monster was going to come out of the elevator shaft, but Kat was here, and obviously whatever was about to rain down on us wasn't a friendly.

"What the hell is up with them recently?" one of the men in black gear muttered. "They've been acting up nonstop."

I started to turn, but Kat smacked me. "No," she said, her gray eyes wide. "I want to see this."

My muscles clenched. "Absolutely not."

A *ding* ricocheted through the floor, signaling that the elevator had arrived. I was seconds from just picking Kat up and throwing her over my shoulder. She saw it, too, and her look became challenging.

But then her gaze shot over my shoulder, and I turned my head. The elevator doors slid open slowly. Guns were clicked, safeties going off.

"Don't shoot!" Dr. Roth ordered, waving the syringe around like a white flag. "I can take care of this. Whatever you do, don't shoot. Don't—"

A small shadow fell out of the elevator, and then one leg appeared, covered in black sweats, and then a torso and tiny shoulders.

My mouth dropped open.

It was a kid—*a kid*. Probably no older than five, and he stepped out in front of all the grown men with *really* big guns trained on him.

The kid smiled.

And then the proverbial poo hit the fan.

13

{ Daemon }

"Uh . . ." I muttered.

The kid's eyes were purple—like two amethyst jewels with those weird lines around the pupils, just like Luc's. And they were cold and flat as they scanned the officers in front of him.

Dr. Roth stepped forward. "Micah, what are you doing? You know you're not supposed to be in this building. Where is your—?"

Several things happened so fast and, seriously, I wouldn't have believed it if I hadn't seen it with my own eyes.

The kid lifted a hand, and there was a succession of several pops—of bullets leaving the chambers of the rifles. Kat's horrified gasp said she was thinking the same thing I was. Were they really going to shoot a kid?

But the bullets stopped, as if the kid were a Luxen or hybrid, but he wasn't one of my kind. I would've felt that. Maybe he was a hybrid, because those bullets hit a shimmery blue wall around him. The blue light expanded, swallowing the bullets—dozens of them—lighting them up like blue fireflies. They hung in the air for a second and then popped out of existence. The kid curled his fingers inward, like he was motioning them to come play with him, and in a total Magneto way, the guns flew from the officers' hands, zinging toward the kid. They, too, stopped in midair and lit up in vibrant shades of blue. A second later the guns were dust.

Kat's hands dug into my back. "Holy . . ."

"Shit," I finished.

Dr. Roth was trying to push past the soldiers. "Micah, you can't—"

"I don't want to go back to that building," the kid said in a voice that was oddly high and flat at the same time.

Washington the Tool moved in, holding a pistol. Dr. Roth shouted, and Micah's head whipped around. The guard's face paled, and Micah closed his fist. Washington hit the floor on his knees, grasping his head as he doubled over. Mouth open in a silent scream, blood poured from the guy's eyes.

"Micah!" Dr. Roth shoved an officer out of the way. "That is bad! Bad, Micah!"

Bad—that was *bad*? I could come up with dozens of words better suited than *bad*.

"Holy smokes," Kat whispered. "The kid's like Damien from *The Omen*."

I would've laughed, because with the bowl-cut brown hair and slight, mischievous grin, he did look like the little Antichrist. Except it wasn't funny because Washington was facefirst on the floor, and the freaky kid was now staring at me with those purple eyes.

Man, I did not like freaky kids.

"He was gonna hurt me," said Micah, never taking his eyes off me. "And you all are going to make me go back to my room. I don't wanna go back to my room."

Several of the officers shuttled backward as Micah took a step forward, but Dr. Roth remained, hiding the syringe behind his back. "Why don't you want to go back to your room, Micah?"

"A better question is why is he staring at you?" Kat whispered.

True.

Micah cautiously made his way around the officers, who were now giving him a wide berth. His steps were light and extremely catlike. "The other ones don't want to play with me."

There were more of him? Dear God . . .

The doctor turned, smiling at the boy. "Is it because you're not sharing your toys?"

Kat choked on what sounded like a near-hysterical laugh.

Micah's eyes slid to the doctor. "Sharing is not how you assert dominance."

What. The. Holy. Hell.

"Sharing doesn't always mean you're giving up control, Micah. We've taught you that."

The little boy shrugged as he turned his gaze back to me. "Will you play with me?"

"Uh . . ." I had no idea what to say.

Micah cocked his head to the side and smiled. Two dimples appeared in his round cheeks. "Can he play with me, Dr. Roth?"

If that doctor said yes, I was going to have a serious issue with this.

Dr. Roth nodded. "I'm sure he can later, Micah, but right now we need you to go back to your room."

The little boy's lower lip stuck out. "I don't wanna go back to my room!"

I half expected the kid's head to start spinning, and maybe it would have, but the doctor shot forward, syringe in hand.

Micah spun and shouted as he balled up his tiny hands. Dr. Roth dropped the syringe and went down on one knee. "Micah," he gasped, pressing his hands to his temples. "You need to stop."

Micah stomped a foot. "I don't wanna—"

Out of freaking nowhere, a dart slammed into the kid's neck. His eyes widened, and then his legs gave out. Before he fell face-first, I shot forward and caught the tyke in my arms. Kid was freaky as hell, but still, he was a kid.

I looked up and saw Sergeant Dasher standing to the right. "Good shot, Archer," the sergeant said.

Archer slid the gun back into his holster with a curt nod.

I turned back to Micah. His eyes were open, and they locked onto mine. He wasn't moving at all, but the kid was in there, fully functional. "What the hell?" I whispered.

"Someone get Washington to the med room and make sure his brains aren't completely scrambled." Dasher was giving out orders. "Roth, get the kid into an exam room immediately and find out how he was able to get out of building B, and where in the hell is his tracker?"

Roth stumbled to his feet, rubbing his temple. "Yes . . . yes, sir."

Dasher stepped up to him, eyes glinting and his voice low. "If he does it again, he will be terminated. Do you understand?"

Terminated? Jesus. Someone appeared at my side and grabbed for the kid. I almost didn't want to let him go, but that became a nonissue. Micah's hand caught the front of my shirt and held on as the officer picked him up.

Those strange eyes were even more bizarre up close. The circle around the pupils was irregular, as if the black had bled at the edges.

They don't know we exist.

Stunned, I jerked back, breaking the grip on my shirt. The kid's voice was in my head. Impossible, but it had happened. I watched in disbelief as the officer had him now and was turning away. Stranger yet, it was the exact same thing Luc had said.

That kid wasn't like Kat or me. That kid was something completely different.

{ Katy }

Holy crap on a cracker . . .

A kid had just disarmed about fifteen men and probably would've done a hell of a lot more if Archer hadn't tranq'd the kid. To be honest, I didn't even know what I just saw or what the kid was, but Daemon looked substantially more freaked than I felt. Fear pinged inside me. Did the kid do something to him?

Pushing off the wall, I hurried to Daemon. "Are you okay?"

He ran a hand through his hair as he nodded.

"Someone needs to get these two back to their rooms," Sergeant Dasher said, taking a deep breath and then barking out more orders. Archer moved toward us.

"Wait." I wrapped an arm around Daemon's, refusing to budge. "What was *that*?"

"I don't have time for this." Dasher's eyes narrowed. "Take them back to their rooms, Archer."

Anger rose inside me, bitter and powerful. "Make time for this."

Dasher's head snapped toward me, and I glared back at him. Daemon was tuning in to the conversation, fixing his attention on the sergeant. The muscles under my hand flexed. "That kid wasn't a Luxen or a hybrid," he said. "I think you guys owe us a straight-up answer."

"He is what we call an origin," Nancy answered, coming up behind the sergeant. "As in a new beginning: the origin of the perfect species."

I opened my mouth, then clamped it shut. The origin of the perfect species? I felt like I'd fallen headfirst into a really bad science-fiction movie, except this was all real.

"Go ahead, Sergeant. I have time for them." She tipped up her chin, meeting Dasher's incredulous stare. "And I want a complete write-up on how and why there have been two incidences with the origins in the matter of twenty-four hours."

Dasher exhaled loudly out his nose. "Yes, ma'am."

I was sort of stunned when he snapped his heels together and pivoted, but my suspicion about Nancy being the one who ran the show was confirmed.

She extended an arm toward one of the closed doors. "Let's sit."

Keeping an arm around Daemon's, I followed Nancy into a small room with just a round table and five chairs. Archer joined us, forever our shadow, but remained by the door while the three of us sat.

Daemon dropped an elbow on the table and a hand on my knee as he leaned in, his bright eyes fixed on Nancy. "Okay. So this kid is an origin. Or whatever. What does that mean exactly?"

Nancy leaned back in her chair, crossing one leg over the other. "We weren't ready to share this with you yet, but considering what you witnessed, we really don't have a choice. Sometimes things don't go as planned, so we must adapt."

"Sure," I said, placing my hand over Daemon's. He flipped his up, his fingers threading mine, and our joined hands rested on my knee.

"The Origin Project is Daedalus's greatest achievement," Nancy started, her gaze unwavering. "Ironically, it started as an accident more than forty years ago. It began with one and has grown to more than a hundred as of now. As I said before, sometimes what we plan for doesn't happen. So we must adapt."

I glanced at Daemon, and he looked as bewildered and as impatient as I felt, but I had this sickening, sinking feeling. On some level I knew that whatever we were about to hear was going to blow our minds.

"Forty years ago we had a Luxen male and a female hybrid who he had mutated. They, very much like you two, were young and in love." Her upper lip curled in dismissive mirth. "They were allowed to see each other, and at some point during their stay with us, the female became pregnant."

Oh, jeez.

"At first we weren't aware, not until she started to show. You see, back then, we didn't test for hormones related to pregnancy. From what we've gathered, it is very difficult for a Luxen to conceive with another, so it didn't cross our minds that one would be able to conceive with a human, hybrid or not."

"Is that true?" I asked Daemon. Baby making wasn't something we talked about. "That it's hard for Luxen to conceive?"

Daemon's jaw worked. "Yes, but we can't conceive with humans, as far as I know. It's like a dog and cat getting together."

Ew. I made a face. "Nice comparison."

Daemon smirked.

"You're right," Nancy said. "Luxen cannot conceive with humans, and for the most part, they cannot conceive with a hybrid, but when the mutation is perfect, complete on a cellular level, and if there appears to be a true *want*, they can."

For some reason, heat crawled up my neck. Talking about babies with Nancy was worse than having the sex talk with my mom, and that had been bad enough to make me want to punch myself in the stomach.

"When it was discovered that the hybrid was pregnant, the team was split on whether or not the pregnancy should be terminated. That may sound harsh," she said in response to the way Daemon stiffened, "but you must understand we had no idea what this pregnancy could do or what a child of a Luxen and hybrid would be like. We had no idea what we were dealing with, but thankfully termination was vetoed, and we were given the opportunity to study this occurrence."

"So . . . so they had a baby?" I asked.

Nancy nodded. "The length of pregnancy was normal by human standards—between eight and nine months. Our hybrid was a little early."

"Luxen take about a year," Daemon said, and I winced, thinking that was a hell of a long time to be stuck carrying triplets. "But like I said, it's hard."

"When the baby was born, there was nothing remarkable in appearance, with the exception of the child's eyes. They were purplish in color, which is an extremely rare human coloring, with a wavy dark circle around the iris. Blood work showed that the baby had adopted both human and Luxen DNA, which was different from the mutated DNA of a hybrid. It wasn't until the child started to grow that we realized what that meant."

I had no idea what that meant.

A smile graced Nancy's face—a genuine one, like a kid's on Christmas morning. "Growth rate was normal, like any human child, but the child showed signs of significant intelligence from onset, learning to speak well before a normal child, and early intelligence tests put the child over two hundred in the IQ department, which is rare. Only a half of one percent of the population has an IQ over one hundred and forty. And there was more."

I remember Daemon telling me before that Luxen matured faster than humans, not in physical appearance but in intellect and social skills, which seemed doubtful considering how he acted sometimes.

He slid me a long look, as if he knew what I was thinking. I squeezed his hand. "What do you mean by more?" he asked, turning back to Nancy.

"Well, really, it's been limitless and still a learning experience. Each child—each generation—appears to have different abilities." A certain light filled her eyes as she spoke. "The first one was able to do something that no hybrid has been able to do. He could heal."

I sat back, blinking rapidly. "But . . . I thought only Luxen could do that?"

"We believed the same thing until Ro came along. We named him after the first documented Egyptian Pharaoh, who was believed to be a myth."

"Wait. You named him? What about his parents?" I asked.

She shrugged one shoulder, and that was all the answer we got. "Ro's ability to heal others and himself ran parallel to Luxen ability, obviously inherited from his father. Over the course of his childhood, we were able to learn that he could speak telepathically with not just Luxen and hybrids but humans, also. Onyx and diamond mixtures had no effect on him. He had the speed and strength of a Luxen but was faster and stronger. And like the Luxen, he could tap into the Source just as easily. His ability to problem solve and strategize at such a young age was off the charts. The only thing that he and any of the other origins have not been able to do is change their appearance. Ro was the perfect specimen."

It took a few moments for all of this to sink in, and when it did, one thing stood out among everything she had said. It was a small word but so powerful. "Where is Ro now?"

A little of the light went out of her eyes. "Ro is no longer with us."

Which explained the use of past tense. "What happened to him?"

"He died, simply put. But he was not the last. Several more were born, and we were able to learn how the conception was possible." Excited, her speech sped up. "The most interesting factor was that conception could happen between any Luxen male and female hybrid who had been successfully mutated."

Daemon slipped his hand free as he leaned back in the chair. His brows furrowed in awareness. "So Daedalus just happened to have a bunch of horny Luxen and hybrids who were willing to do it while they were here? Because that seems odd to me. This place isn't really the most romantic. Doesn't really set the mood."

My stomach roiled at where his questions were heading, and the air turned stagnant in the room. There was a reason Nancy was being so open with us. After all, Daemon and I were the "perfect specimens," according to Dr. Roth, mutated on a cellular level.

Nancy's gaze turned cool. "You'd be surprised what people in love do when they have a few moments of privacy. And really, it only takes a few moments."

And suddenly, the fact that we were able to share a bathroom also made sense. Was Nancy hoping that Daemon and I would cave to our wild-monkey lust and bring little Daemon babies into the world?

God, I thought I was going to hurl when she confirmed it.

"After all, we haven't stopped you from spending a few moments here and there alone, have we?" Her smile officially creeped me out. "And you two are young and so very much in love. I'm sure you'll make use of your free time sooner or later."

Sergeant Dasher hadn't mentioned any of this during his sales pitch about protecting the world against an alien invasion or curing diseases. Then again, there were many sides to Daedalus. He had said that.

Daemon opened his mouth, no doubt to say something I'd kick him for, but I cut him off. "I have a hard time believing you've had that many people who just . . . well, you know."

"Well, in some cases, the pregnancies were purely accidental. In other instances, we assisted the process."

Air came into my body but got stuck in my lungs. "Assisted?"

"It's not what you think." She laughed; the sound was shrill and nerve-racking. "There have been volunteers over the years, Luxen and hybrids who understand what Daedalus is truly about. In other cases, we did in vitro fertilization."

The knots moved up my throat like bile, which was a bad thing because my mouth was hanging open. Nothing there to stop it from spewing out.

A muscle in Daemon's jaw was working overtime, thumping away. "What? Is Daedalus moonlighting as Match.com for Luxen and hybrids?"

Nancy sent him a dry look, and I couldn't stop the shudder of revulsion. In vitro meant there had to be a female hybrid to carry the baby. No matter what she said, I doubted all of them were willing.

The pupils of Daemon's eyes had started to glow. "How many of them do you have?"

"Hundreds," she repeated. "The younger ones are kept here, and as they grow older, they are moved to different locations."

"How are you controlling them? From what it looked like, you barely had any control over Micah."

Her lips thinned. "We use trackers that usually keep them where they are supposed to be. However, from time to time, they find ways around them. The ones who aren't controllable are dealt with."

"Dealt with?" I whispered, horrified at where my imagination took that.

"The origins are superior in almost every way. They are remarkable, but they can become very dangerous. If they have not assimilated, then they have to be dealt with accordingly."

My imagination had been dead-on. "Oh my God . . ."

Daemon slammed his hand down on the table, causing Archer to move forward, hand going to his weapon. "You're basically creating a race of test-tube babies, and if they're not acceptable, you kill them?"

"I don't expect you to understand," Nancy replied evenly as she stood and moved behind her chair. She gripped the back. "The origins are the perfect species, but like with any race of being or creature, there are . . . duds. It happens. The positives and potential outweigh the nastier side."

I shook my head. "What exactly is so positive about this?"

"Many of our origins have grown up and have assimilated into society. We have trained them so that they will reach the height of success. Each of them has been tailored from birth to assume a certain role. They will become doctors of unequaled abilities, researchers who will unlock the unknown, senators and politicians who are able to see the bigger picture and will bring about social change." She paused and turned toward where Archer stood. "And some will become soldiers of unprecedented talent, joining the ranks of hybrids and humans, creating an army that will be unstoppable."

Tiny hairs on the back of my neck rose as I slowly twisted in my chair. My eyes met Archer's. His expression was emotionless. "Are you . . . ?"

"Archer?" Nancy said, smiling.

Taking his hand off the handle of his gun, he reached up to his left eye with two fingers. He made a pinching motion and a colored contact lens popped out, revealing an iris that was shiny like an amethyst jewel.

I sucked in a sharp breath. "Holy crapola . . ."

Daemon swore under his breath, and now it made sense why it was only Archer who guarded Daemon and me. If he was anything like Micah, he could handle whatever we threw at him.

"Well, aren't you just a special snowflake," Daemon murmured.

"That I am." Archer's lips quirked into a half grin. "It's a secret. We wouldn't want the other officers or soldiers to be uncomfortable around me."

Which explained why he hadn't gone all superhuman on Micah and had shot him with a tranq gun instead. A thousand questions rushed to the tip of my tongue, but I was struck silent by the implications of what and who he was.

Daemon folded his arms as he focused on Nancy again. "Interesting reveal and all, but I have a bigger question to ask you."

She spread her arms wide in a welcoming way. "Go ahead."

"How do you determine who brings the babies into the world?"

Oh God, my stomach tensed even more, and I bent over, clutching the end of the table.

"It's simple, actually. Besides the in vitro, we look for Luxen and hybrids like you two."

14

We had to get out of there. Sooner, not later. That was all I could think about.

When we were escorted back to our rooms, I looked at Archer a little more differently and a hell of lot more closely. The soldier had always seemed different, but I would've never guessed that he was something other than human. I had sensed nothing unusual from him, not a damn thing other than this off vibe, but I did notice that Kat seemed comfortable around him. Other than a few smartass responses, which I of all people couldn't hold against him, he seemed like a pretty okay guy.

And frankly, I didn't care what the hell he was. Knowing that he was something different only meant I needed to watch him more carefully. What *did* matter was the fact that they were breeding children here.

That disturbed the hell out of me, and it also angered me.

The moment the door was shut behind me, I headed for the bathroom. Kat had the same idea. A second later, her door opened, and she walked in, quietly shutting the door behind her.

Her face was pale. "I want to vomit."

"Well, let me get out of the way, then."

Her brows pinched. "Daemon, they . . ." She shook her head, eyes wide. "There are no words for this. It's beyond anything I could've imagined."

"Same here." I leaned against the sink as she sat on the edge of the closed lid. "Dawson never mentioned anything like that to you, did he?"

She shook her head. Dawson rarely spoke about his time with Daedalus, and when he did, he usually told Kat. "No, but he said some of the things were insane. He was probably talking about this."

Before I said any more, I shifted without warning to my true form. *Sorry*, I said when she winced. *Luc had warned me that the things here would blow my mind. Speaking of which, notice anything about Archer's and Micah's eyes—and who has the same kind? Luc's got the weird, blurred line effect going on, too. Hell, I should've known that kid wasn't a normal hybrid. He's an origin.*

Kat ran her palms over her thighs. When she was nervous, she was always fidgeting. Normally I found it cute, but I hated the why behind it now. *This is beyond us*, she said. *How many kids do you think they have? How many people are out there in the world, masquerading as normal humans?*

Well, that's no different than us pretending to be normal.

We're not superhumans who can drop a person on the ground by curling our fists.

I was kind of envious of that ability. *Yeah, too bad, because that would come in handy when someone is getting on your nerves.*

Her hand shot out, smacking my leg. *And what the heck was that? She—that evil woman in a pantsuit—didn't mention anything about that.*

Pretty much all women who wear pantsuits are evil.

Kat's head tipped to the side. *Okay. I do have to agree with that, but can we focus?*

We can now that you agree. I reached over and tweaked her

nose, which earned me a dirty look. *We need to get the hell out of here and quick.*

I agree. She knocked my hand away when I went for her nose again. *No offense, but I have no desire to be making any weird babies with you right now.*

I choked on my laugh. *You'd be blessed to have a child of mine. Admit it.*

Her eyes rolled. *Seriously, your ego knows no limit, no matter the situation.*

Hey. I like to be consistent.

That you are, she said, voice dry in my thoughts.

As much as I love the idea of the whole process involved in making a baby with you, it's not ever going to happen under these circumstances.

A pretty flush covered her cheeks. *Glad we're on the same page, buddy.*

I laughed.

We need to get the LH-11 and somehow get in contact with Luc. That sounds impossible to me. Kat's gaze wandered to the closed door. *We don't even know where it's kept.*

Nothing is truly impossible, I reminded her. *But I think we do need another plan.*

Any ideas? She tugged the elastic band out of her hair and untangled the mass of waves. *Maybe we could set the origins loose in the compound. I bet that would cause enough of a distraction. Or maybe you could take on the form of one of the staff here . . .*

They were good ideas, but there were problems: I bet Daedalus had defenses in place in case a Luxen morphed into someone else, and how would we get to the other building to let out a bunch of miniature super-soldiers?

Kat turned to me, biting on her lower lip as she reached out. Her fingers snaked through the light and touched my arm. My entire body jerked. In my true form, I was hypersensitive. *They weren't really good ideas, were they?*

They were great ideas, but . . .

Not easily done. She slid her hand up my arm, her head tilting to the side as her gaze wandered over me. My light reflected off her cheeks, giving her a rosy glow. She was beautiful, and I was so, so desperately in love with her.

Her chin jerked up, and she sucked in a breath, eyes widening.

Okay, I may have actually thought that last bit at her.

You did. A small smile split her lips. *I liked hearing it. A lot.*

Kneeling down so I was eye level with her, I cupped her cheek. *I promise you that this isn't going to be our future, Kitten. I will give that to you—a normal life.*

Her eyes glistened. *I don't expect a normal life. I just expect a life with you.*

Yeah, that did crazy things to my heart. Like it stopped beating for a moment, and I was dead in front of her for a second. *Sometimes I don't think I . . .*

What?

I gave a shake of my head. Never mind. I lowered my hand and backed up, breaking contact. *Luc said he'd know once I got ahold of LH-11. Obviously who he has in here has to be close to us. Anyone you can think of who might be a friendly?*

I don't know. The only ones I've really been around are the doctor, the sergeant, and Archer. She paused, her nose wrinkling. It did that whenever she was concentrating. *You know, I always thought Archer might be on Team Not Insane, but knowing that he's one of them—an origin—I don't know what to think of him.*

I thought about that for a moment. *He's been good to you, hasn't he?*

Some of the color leeched from her cheeks. *Yeah, he has been.*

Counting to ten before I continued, I said, *And the other ones really haven't been?*

She didn't answer immediately. *Talking about that stuff isn't going to help us get out of here.*

Most likely not, but—

"Daemon," she said out loud, eyes narrowing. *We need a plan to get out of here. That's what I need. Not a therapy session.*

I rose to my feet. *I don't know. Therapy might help that temper of yours, Kitten.*

Whatever. She folded her arms, lips pursed. *So, back to other options? Sounds like everything will be a Hail Mary. And anything we attempt, if we're busted, we're totally, irrevocably screwed.*

Holding my breath, I slipped back into my human form, then shook my shoulders out. "Sounds about right," I agreed.

{ Katy }

Days passed, and while there weren't any more origins running amuck through the compound, and no one was trying to coerce Daemon and me into making babies like there was no tomorrow, a general sense of unease had settled over me.

My stress tests had picked back up, but they didn't involve any other hybrids. For some reason, I was kept away from the others, though I knew they were still there. During my tests, I was forced to use the Source for a really messed-up version of target practice.

Minus the guns and bullets.

It still blew my mind that they were actually training me, like I had been drafted into the army. A day or so ago, while we were in the bathroom, I had asked Daemon again about the other Luxen.

A look of surprise had flickered over his face. "What?"

Having a conversation while knowing that we were most likely being listened to was difficult. Very quickly and quietly, I had told him about Shawn and what Dasher had said.

"That's insane." He'd shaken his head. "I mean, I'm sure

there are Luxen out there who hate humans, but an invasion? Thousands of Luxen turning on mankind? I don't believe that."

And I could see that he didn't. I wanted to believe that, too. I didn't think he had reason to lie to me, but Daedalus had so many sides to them. One of them had to be the truth.

All of this was so much bigger than Daemon and me. We wanted out of here, to have a future where we weren't a freak science experiment or controlled by a secret organization, but what Daedalus was doing with the origins had far-reaching implications that went beyond what either of us could understand.

I kept thinking of the *Terminator* movies, about how the computers became self-aware and then nuked the hell out of the world. Take out the computers and replace them with origins. Heck, replace them with Luxen, Arum, or hybrids, and we had an apocalyptical event on our hands. Stuff like this never ended well in the movies or books. Why would real life be any different?

We hadn't gotten any further in our escape plans, either. We sort of sucked at that, and I wanted to be mad at Daemon for exposing himself to this with no clear plan, but I couldn't, because he had done it for me.

It was sometime after lunch had been brought that Archer showed up and escorted me to the med room. I expected to see Daemon, but they had gotten him earlier. I hated not knowing what was going on with him.

"What are we doing today?" I asked, sitting on the table. We were alone in the room.

"We're waiting on the doctor."

"That much I figured." I glanced at Archer and took a deep breath. "What does it feel like? Being an origin?"

He folded his arms. "What does it feel like being a hybrid?"

"I don't know." I shrugged. "I guess I feel like I've always felt."

"Exactly," he replied. "We aren't that different."

He was completely different from anything I'd ever seen. "Do you know your parents?"

"No."

"And that doesn't bother you?"

There was a pause. "Well, it's not something I've dwelled on. I can't change the past. There's very little I can change about anything."

I hated the bland tone, as if none of this affected him at all. "So you are what you are? And that's it?"

"Yes. That is it, Katy."

Pulling my legs up, I sat cross-legged. "Were you raised here?"

"Yes. I grew up here."

"Did you ever live anyplace else?"

"I did for a short period of time. Once I got older we were moved to a different location for our training." He paused. "You're asking a lot of questions."

"So?" I popped my chin onto my fist. "I'm curious. Have you ever lived on your own, in the outside world?"

His jaw flexed, and then he shook his head.

"Have you ever wanted to?"

He opened his mouth and then closed it. He didn't answer.

"You have." I knew I was right. I couldn't see his eyes under the beret, and his expression hadn't changed, but I knew it. "But they won't let you, will they? So you've never been to a regular school? Gone to an Applebee's?"

"I've been to an Applebee's," he responded drily. "And an Outback, too."

"Well, congrats. You've seen everything."

His mouth twitched. "Your sarcasm is not needed."

"Have you ever been to a mall? Gone to a normal library? Have you fallen in love?" I shot off questions left and right, knowing I was probably getting on his nerves. "Have you dressed up for Halloween and gone trick-or-treating? Do you celebrate Christmas? Ever eaten an overcooked turkey and pretended it tasted good?"

"I'm assuming you've done all those things." When I nodded, he took a step forward, and then suddenly he was in my face, leaning down so low that the beret touched my forehead. It shocked me, because I hadn't seen him move, but I refused to back away. A small smile appeared on his lips. "I'm also assuming there's a point to these questions. That maybe you want to somehow prove to me that I haven't lived, that I haven't experienced life, all the mundane things that actually give a person reason for living. Is that what you're trying to do?"

Unable to look away from him, I swallowed. "Yes."

"You don't have to prove that or point it out to me," he said, then straightened. Without speaking out loud, I heard his next words in my thoughts. *I already know I haven't truly lived a single day, Katy. All of us know that.*

I gasped at the intrusion of his voice and at the bleak hopelessness of his words. "All of you?" I whispered.

He nodded as he took a step back. "All of us."

The door opened, silencing us. Dr. Roth came in, followed by the sergeant, Nancy, and another guard. Our conversation immediately dropped out of my thoughts. Seeing the sergeant and Nancy together didn't bring good tidings.

Roth went straight to the tray and started messing with the instruments there. Ice drenched my veins when he picked up a scalpel. "What's going on?"

Nancy sat down in a chair placed in the corner, trusty clipboard in hand. "We have more testing to complete, and we need to move forward."

Remembering the last test that involved a scalpel, I blanched. "Details?"

"Since you have proven to have undergone a stable mutation, we can now focus on the more important aspect of the Luxen abilities," Nancy explained, but I wasn't really watching her. My eyes were trained on Dr. Roth. "Daemon has proven to have remarkable control over the Source, as expected. He has passed all of his testing, and that last healing he did on you was successful, but we need to make sure he can heal more severe injuries before we can bring in subjects."

My stomach dropped, and my hands shook as I clenched the edge of the table. "What do you mean?"

"Before we can bring in humans, we must make sure he can heal a severe injury. There's no reason to subject a human to it if he cannot do it."

Oh God . . .

"He can heal serious injuries," I blurted out, shrinking back when the doctor stood in front of me. "How do you think I got mutated in the first place?"

"Sometimes that is a fluke, Katy." Sergeant Dasher moved to the other side of the table.

I dragged in air, but my lungs seemed to have stopped working. Daedalus could barely replicate the mutation and had subjected Beth and Dawson to horrific things, trying to get Dawson to mutate other humans. What Daedalus didn't know was that there had to be a true want, a need behind the healing. A need and want like love. That was why it was so hard to replicate.

I almost told them that to save my own skin, but then I realized it probably wouldn't make a difference. Will hadn't believed me when I told him. There was no science behind that. It made the whole healing thing almost magical.

"We've learned from the last time that having Daemon in the room during the procedure isn't a good idea. He will be brought in after we are done," Dasher continued. "Lay down on your stomach, Katy."

A little relief eked through me when I realized it would be way too hard to slit my throat with me lying on my stomach, but I still delayed. "What if he can't heal me? What if it was a fluke?"

"Then this whole experiment is over," Nancy said from her corner. "But I think you and I both know that won't be the case."

"If you know it won't be the case, then why do you need to do this?" It wasn't just the pain I was trying to avoid. I didn't want them to bring Daemon in here and make him go through this. I'd seen what that had done to Dawson, what that would do to *anyone*.

"We have to do trials," Dr. Roth said, his look sympathetic. "We would sedate you, but we have no way of knowing how that would affect the process."

My eyes swung toward Archer, but he looked away. No help there. There was no help anywhere in this room. This was going to happen, and this was going to suck donkey butt.

"Get on your stomach, Katy. The quicker you do this, the quicker it will be over." Sergeant Dasher placed his hands on the table. "Or we will put you on your stomach."

I looked up, my gaze locking with his, and my shoulders squared. Did he really think I was just going to do this willingly and make it easy for all of them? He so had another thing coming.

"Then you're going to have to put me on my stomach," I told him.

He put me on my stomach pretty quickly. It was rather embarrassing how fast he got me flipped over with the help of the other guard who had come in with them. Dasher had hold of my feet, and the guard had my palms pinned down next to my head. I flopped around like a fish for a few seconds before realizing it was doing no good.

All I could lift was my head, which put me at eye level with the guard's chest. "There's a special place in hell for you people."

No one responded—not out loud, that is.

Archer's voice filled my head. *Close your eyes, and take a deep breath when I tell you.*

Too panicked to even pay attention to what he was saying or give much thought to why he was trying to help me, I gasped for a breath.

The back of my shirt was lifted and chilly air rushed over my skin, sending a wave of goose bumps from my spine to my shoulders.

Oh God. Oh God. Oh God. My brain was shutting down, fear taking hold with razor-sharp claws.

Katy.

The cold edge of the scalpel came down on my skin, right below my shoulder blade.

Katy, take a deep breath!

I opened my mouth.

There was a quick jerk of the doctor's arm and fire lit my back, an intensely deep, burning pain that split my skin and muscle.

I didn't take a deep breath. I couldn't.

I screamed.

15

I didn't feel too spiffy.

About four minutes ago, my heart had started pounding like crazy. I felt sick to my stomach and could barely concentrate on putting one stupid foot in front of the other.

The feeling was vaguely familiar. So was the shortness of breath. I'd experienced this own brand of hell when Kat had been shot, but that didn't make any sense. Relatively speaking, she was sort of safe here, at least from random psychos with guns, and there was no reason anyone would hurt her. Not at this moment, that was, but I knew they had done stuff to Beth to force my brother to mutate humans.

A warm tingle exploded along the back of my neck as the guard and I headed down the hall on the med floor. Kat was nearby. Good.

But the sick feeling, the general sense of dread and pressure building in my chest only worsened the closer I got to her.

This wasn't good. Not good at all.

I stumbled, almost losing my balance, and that brought a

big ol' dose of what-the-hell. I *never* stumbled. I had wonderful poise. Or balance. Whatever.

The Rambo wannabe stopped in front of one of the many windowless doors and did the eyeball thing. There was a clicking sound, and the door opened. Air punched out of my lungs the moment I got a good eyeful of the room.

My worst nightmare had come true, springing to life in horrifying clarity and detail.

No one was standing near her, but there were people in the room, even though I really didn't see them. All I saw was Kat. She was lying on her stomach, head turned to the side. Her face was ungodly pale and strained, eyes barely open. A fine sheen of sweat covered her forehead.

Dear God, there was so much blood—seeping off Kat's back, pooling on the gurney table she was lying on, and dripping into the pans below the table.

Her back . . . her back was a mangled mess. Muscle cut and bone exposed. It looked like Freddy Krueger had gotten hold of her. I was pretty sure her spine was . . . I couldn't even finish the thought.

Maybe a second had passed from when I entered the room and lurched forward, knocking the dumbass guard out of the way. I faltered when I reached her side and threw my hands out to catch myself. They landed in blood—her blood.

"Jesus," I whispered. "Kat . . . oh God, Kat . . ."

Her lashes didn't move. Nothing. A strand of hair clung to her sweat-soaked, pale cheek.

My heart was pounding erratically, struggling to keep up, and I knew it wasn't mine that was faltering. It was Kat's. I didn't know how this happened. Not that I didn't care, because I did want to know, but it wasn't what was important now.

"I got this," I told her, not paying heed to anyone in the room. "I'm going to fix this."

Still nothing, and I cursed as I turned, preparing to shed my human skin, because this . . . this would require everything in me to fix.

My gaze met Nancy's for a second. "You bitch."

She tapped her pen on her clipboard and made a soft *tsk*ing sound. "We need to make sure you can heal again on what is considered a catastrophic level. Those wounds were made precisely to be fatal, but to take time, unlike a stomach wound or inflictions to other various parts of the body. You will need to heal her."

I was so going to kill that lady one day.

Rage spiked, fueling me, and I shifted into my true form; the roar rose from the depths of my soul. The table shook. Utensils clamored and toppled off the tray. Cabinet doors opened.

"Jesus," someone muttered.

I placed my hands on Kat. *Kitten, I'm here. I'm here, baby. I'm going to make this go away. All of this.*

There was no answer, and the tangy taste of fear coated me. Warmth radiated out from my hands, and the white light tinged with red swallowed Kat. Vaguely I heard Nancy saying, "It's time to move on to the mutation phase."

Healing Kat had exhausted me. That made everyone in that room very lucky because I was sure I could've taken out at least two of them before they got hold of me, if I could move my legs.

They had tried to remove me from the room after I'd healed Kat. Like hell I'd leave them alone with her. Nancy and Dasher had left some time ago, but the doctor hung out, checking Kat's vitals. They were fine, he'd said. She was perfectly healed.

I wanted to murder him.

And I think he knew because he stayed far from my reach.

The doctor eventually left. Only Archer remained. He didn't

speak, which was freaking fine by me. What little respect I'd gained for the man was lost the second I realized that he'd been in this room the entire time they did . . . did this to her. All to prove that I was strong enough to bring her back from the brink of death.

I knew what was coming next: an endless stream of half-dead humans.

Pushing that reality out of my head, I focused on Kat. I sat by the bed, on the stupid rolling chair Nancy had been in, holding her limp hand, smoothing my thumb in circles, hoping that it reached her somehow. She hadn't woken yet, and I hoped she had been passed out through the whole process.

At some point, a female nurse had come in to clean her up. I didn't want anyone near her, but I also didn't want Kat to wake up covered in her own blood. I wanted her to wake up and have no memory of this—of any of this.

"I got it," I said, standing.

The nurse shook her head. "But I—"

I took a step toward her. "I will do this."

"Let him do it," Archer said, shoulders stiff. "Leave."

The nurse looked like she would argue, but finally she left. Archer turned his head as I stripped away the blood-soaked clothing and began cleaning her back. And her back . . . there were scars—vicious, angry-looking red marks below her shoulder blades—reminding me of one of those books she had at home about a fallen angel whose wings had been ripped away.

I don't know why she scarred this time. The bullet had left a faint mark on her chest, but nothing like this. Maybe it was because of how long it took me to heal her. Maybe it was because the bullet hole was so small and this . . . this wasn't.

A low, inhuman sound crawled up my throat, startling Archer. I mustered whatever energy I had left and finished changing her. Then I settled back down and picked up her small hand. The silence was as thick as fog in the room until Archer broke it.

"We can take her back to her room."

I pressed my lips to her knuckles. "I'm not leaving her."

"I wasn't suggesting that." There was a pause. "They didn't give me any specific orders. You can stay with her."

A bed would be better for her, I imagined. Pushing myself up, I clenched my jaw as I slid my arms under her.

"Wait." Archer was beside us, and I turned, curling my lip in a snarl. He backed away, holding his hands up. "I was only going to suggest that I could carry her. You don't look like you're capable of walking right now."

"You're not touching her."

"I'm—"

"No," I growled, hoisting Kat's slight weight off the table. "Not happening."

Archer shook his head, but he turned, heading for the door. Satisfied, I turned Kat as gently as I could in my arms, worried that her back would cause her pain. When I was sure she was okay like this, I took a step forward and then another.

The trip back to the room was as easy as walking barefoot over a floor of razors. My energy level was in the pits. Laying her down on her side and crawling in the bed beside her soaked up whatever strength I had left. I wanted to pull the blanket up so she wouldn't be cold, but my arm was like stone between us.

Any other time I would've rather taken Nancy out to a romantic dinner than accept Archer's help, but I said nothing when he lifted the blanket and draped it over us.

He left the room, and finally Kat and I were alone.

I watched her until I could no longer keep my eyes open. I then counted each breath she took until I could no longer remember what the last number was. And when that happened,

I repeated her name, over and over again, until it was the last thing I thought before I slipped into oblivion.

{ Katy }

I woke with a start, gasping in air and expecting it to burn me from the inside out, for the pain to still be there, ravaging every ounce of my being.

But I felt okay. Aching and sore, but otherwise okay, considering what had happened. Oddly, I felt detached from what the doctor did, but as I lay there, I could still feel the ghost hands on my wrists and ankles, holding me down.

An ugly feeling, a mess of emotions ranging from anger to helplessness, rattled my stomach. What they had done to prove that Daemon could heal fatal injuries was horrendous, and that word felt too light, not severe or heavy enough.

Feeling icky and uncomfortable in my own skin, I forced my eyes open.

Daemon lay beside me in a deep sleep. Dark shadows fanned his cheeks. Bruised shadows were under his eyes, a purplish tint of exhaustion. His cheeks were pale and lips parted. Several locks of wavy dark brown hair tumbled over his forehead. I'd never seen him look so worn out before. His chest rose steadily and evenly, but fear trickled through my veins.

I rose up on my elbow and leaned over, placing my hand on his chest. His heart beat under my palm, slightly accelerated due to mine.

As I watched him sleep, that ugly mess of emotion took on a new form. Hatred encased it, crystallizing into a hardened shell of bitterness and rage. My hand curled into a fist against his chest.

What they had done to me was reprehensible, but what they had forced Daemon to do was beyond that. And it would only get worse from this point on. They'd start bringing in humans, and when he failed to mutate them successfully, they would hurt me to get at Daemon.

I would become Bethany, and he'd become Dawson.

Squeezing my eyes shut, I exhaled a long breath. No. I couldn't let this happen. *We* couldn't let this happen. But in reality, it was already happening. Pieces of me had gone dark by what I'd done and what had been forced upon me. And if these ugly things kept piling up—which they would—how could we be any different? How could we not turn into Bethany and Dawson?

It struck me then.

I opened my eyes, my gaze traveling over Daemon's broad cheekbones. It wasn't that I had to be stronger than Beth, because I was sure she had been strong and still was. It wasn't that Daemon had to be better than Dawson. We had to be stronger and better than *them*—Daedalus.

Lowering my head, I placed a soft kiss to Daemon's lips and swore in that moment, we would walk out of this. It wasn't just Daemon promising me. It wouldn't just be in his hands to fix.

It would be us—together.

His arm suddenly snaked around my waist, and he tugged me against him. One startling green eye opened. "Hey there," he murmured.

"I didn't mean to wake you."

The corner of his mouth tipped up. "You didn't."

"You've been awake a while?" When his smile spread, I shook my head. "So you just laid there and let me stare at you like a creeper?"

"Pretty much, Kitten. I figured I'd let you get your fill, but then you kissed me and, well, I like to be a bit more involved in that." Both eyes opened, and as always, staring into them had an exhilarating quality to it. "How are you feeling?"

"I'm okay. I feel great, actually." Settling down beside him, I wiggled my head onto his arm, and his hand curled back, tangling in my hair. "How about you? I know that had to have taken a lot out of you."

"You shouldn't be worried about me. What they—"

"I know what they did. I know why they did it." I tipped my chin down as I slid a hand between us. He stiffened as the back of my knuckles brushed over his stomach. "I'm not going to lie. It hurt like hell. When they were doing it, I wanted . . . You don't even want to know what I wanted, but I'm okay because of you. But I hate what they made you do."

His breath grazed my forehead, and there was a long stretch of silence. "You amaze me," was all he said.

"What?" I looked up. "Daemon, I am not amazing. You are. The things you can do? What you have done for me? You—"

He placed a finger on my lips, silencing me. "After what you went through, you're more concerned about me? Yeah, you amaze me, Kitten, you really do."

I felt a grin pulling at my lips, and it kind of felt strange to want to smile after everything. "Well, how about this? We're both amazing."

"I like that." He lowered his mouth to mine, and the kiss was sweet and tender, just as consuming as the other ones because it offered a promise—a promise of more, of a future. "You know, I haven't told you this enough, and I should tell you every chance I get, but I love you."

I sucked in a sharp gasp. Hearing him say those words never failed to affect me deeply. "I know you do, even if you don't say it all the time." I reached up and ran the tips of my fingers over the curve of his cheek. "I love you."

Daemon's eyes drifted shut, and his body tensed. He seemed to draw those words into him.

"How tired are you?" I asked after a couple of moments of staring at him like a goober.

His arm tightened around me. "Pretty tired."

"Would it help to go into your true form?"

He gave a lopsided shrug. "Probably."

"Then do it."

"Aren't you bossy?"

"Shut up and take your true form so you feel better. How about that for bossy?"

He laughed softly. "I love it."

I started to point out that he was getting mighty comfortable with that L-word, but he shifted ever so slightly and brought his lips to mine once more. This kiss was deeper, starved and urgent. Eyes closed, I could still see the white light as he started to change. I gasped in surprise, getting lost in the warmth and the intimacy of the moment. When he pulled back, I could barely open my eyes, he was so bright.

"Better?" I asked out loud, voice thick with emotion.

His hand found mine. It was strange seeing those light-encased fingers thread through mine, curling around them. *I was better the moment you woke up.*

16

{ Daemon }

Daedalus wasted no time once they were confident I had mad healing skills. As soon as they thought I was rested, they brought me into a room on the med floor. There was nothing in the white-walled space except two plastic chairs facing each other.

I turned to Nancy, brows raised. "Nice decorating you got going on here."

She ignored it. "Sit."

"What if I prefer to stand?"

"I really don't care." She turned to where a camera was perched in the corner and nodded. Then she faced me. "You know what is expected of you. We're starting out with one of our new recruits. He's twenty-one and in otherwise good health."

"Except for the fatal injury you're about to inflict on him?"

Nancy shot me a bland look.

"And he signed up for this?"

"That he did. You'd be surprised by how many people are willing to risk their lives to become something great."

I was more surprised by the level of stupidity of some people. To sign up for a mutation that had a success rate of less than one percent didn't seem very bright to me, but what did I know?

She handed over a wide cuff. "This is a piece of opal. I'm sure you're well aware of what it does. It will enhance in the healing and ensure that you're not going to be exhausted."

I took the silver cuff and stared at the black stone with the red marking in the center. "You're literally handing me a piece of opal, knowing it counteracts the onyx."

She gave me a pointed look. "You also know that we have soldiers armed with those nasty little weapons I told you about. That outweighs you having opal."

Slipping it around my wrist, I welcomed the jolt of energy. I glanced up at Nancy, finding her watching me like I was her prized bull. I had a feeling that even if I ran from room to room, zapping people to death, she wouldn't bring the big guns out. Not unless I did something crazy insane.

I was just too special.

And I was pissed off, too. She could've given me the piece of opal when I had needed to heal Kat. One of these days I was going to do serious harm to this woman.

The bright-eyed, bushy-tailed soldier marched into the room, and without further instructions copped a squat on one of the chairs. The kid looked on the young side of twenty-one, and while I tried to have no feelings about any of this, a niggle of guilt rose.

Not because I planned on screwing this up or anything. Why would I? If I didn't successfully bring a hybrid into this world, then eventually they'd turn their evil, sadistic eyes on Kat.

So, yeah, I was rocking the whole "there needs to be a 'true want' to heal the person," but I still had no idea if it would work. If it didn't, homeboy here would either live out the rest of his life as a boring old human being or would self-destruct in a few days.

For his sake and Kat's, I hoped he was welcomed into the world of happy hybrids.

"How are we doing this?" I asked Nancy.

She motioned for one of the two guards who'd come into the room with Patient Zero. One of them stepped forward, brandishing a nasty-looking knife, the kind that Michael Myers would run around with in *Halloween*.

"Oh jeez," I muttered, folding my arms. This was going to get messy.

Patient Too Stupid to Live handled the knife with confidence. Before he could do anything with it, the door opened and Kat walked in, Archer right on her heels.

My arms fell to my sides as unease exploded into alarm. "What is she doing here?"

Nancy smiled tightly. "We thought you could use the motivation."

Understanding lit me up like a firecracker. Their kind of motivation was a warning. They knew damn well that we were aware of what happened to Bethany when Dawson failed. I watched Kat shake off Archer's hand and stomp over to the corner. She stayed there.

I focused on Nancy, staring her down until she finally, after several moments, broke eye contact. "Get on with it, then," I said.

She nodded at Patient Most Likely to Die, who, without saying a damn word, took a deep breath and slammed that serial-killer knife right into his stomach with a wheezy grunt. He then yanked the knife out, letting it fall from his grasp. A guard shot forward, grabbing it.

"Holy shit," I said, eyes going wide. Patient Zero had balls.

Kat winced and looked away as blood spilled from the fresh wound. "That . . . that was disturbing."

He probably had less than two minutes to live if blood kept pounding out of his rapidly paling body like that. He was clutching his stomach, doubled over. A metallic scent filled the air.

"Do it," Nancy said, shifting her weight as eagerness filled her gaze.

Shaking my head in macabre fascination, I knelt by the guy and placed my hands on his stomach. Blood immediately covered my hands. I didn't have a light stomach, but, damn, I could see the dude's intestines. What kind of magic Kool-Aid was this kid drinking to willingly do this to himself? Christ.

I let my human form fade out, and whitish-red light swallowed the guy and most of the room. Concentrating on the wound, I pictured the jagged edges healing shut, stopping the blood loss. I honestly didn't have a freaking clue when it came to healing. It was something that sort of happened on its own. I pictured the wound, and sometimes snapshots of the energies would flicker through my head with no thought of my own. What I did focus on was the light filtering through the veins . . . and Kat.

I glanced up as I took a breath. An expression of rapture had settled on Nancy's face, that of a mother who caught her first glimpse of her child. I sought out Kat, and there she was. She had a look of awe on her beautiful face as she stared back at me.

My heart skipped, and I turned back to the guy I was healing. *I'm doing this for her*, I told him. *You better hope it was enough, for your sake.*

The guy's head jerked up. Color had already returned to his cheeks.

With the opal, I didn't feel a bit drained like I normally would after such a massive healing.

I let go and stood, drifting back a step. Staying in my true form long enough for the man to stand on shaky legs, I glanced over at Kat once more. One hand was pressed to her chin. Beside her, Archer looked a bit unnerved by the whole thing. Something occurred to me then.

Slipping back into my human form, I turned to Nancy, who was staring at Patient Zero with so much awe and hope it was actually sickening. "Why can't they make hybrids?" I asked. "The origins can heal. Why can't they?"

Nancy barely looked at me as she motioned at the camera. "They can heal just about any wound, but they cannot cure disease or mutate. We do not know why, but it is their only limitation." Guiding the guy back into the seat, she handled him with surprising gentleness. "How are you feeling, Largent?"

After taking several deep breaths, Largent cleared his throat. "A little sore, but otherwise I feel good—great." He smiled as he glanced between Nancy and me. "Did it work?"

"Well, you're alive," I said drily. "That's a good start."

The door opened, and Dr. Roth rushed in, stethoscope thumping over his chest. He spared me a glance. "Amazing. I was watching through the monitors. Truly remarkable."

"Yeah. Yeah." I started toward Kat, but Nancy's sharp voice rang out, like claws on a chalkboard.

"Stay there, Daemon."

I turned my head slowly, aware that the other guards had moved between Kat and me. "Why? I did what you wanted."

"We haven't seen anything yet other than the fact you healed him." Nancy moved around the chair, watching the doctor and Largent. "How are his vitals?"

"Perfect," the doctor said, standing as he wrapped the stethoscope around his neck. He reached inside his lab coat and pulled out a small black case. "We can start Prometheus."

"What is that?" I asked, watching as the doctor pulled out a syringe full of shimmery blue liquid. Out of the corner of my eye, I saw Archer cock his head to the side as he stared at the needle.

"Prometheus is Greek," Kat said. "Well, he was a Titan. In mythology, he created man."

A flash of amusement flickered in my eyes.

She shrugged. "It was in a paranormal book I read once."

I couldn't hold back a small grin. Her and her nerdy reading habits. Made me want to kiss her and do other stuff. And she picked up on it, too, because a flush stained her cheeks. Alas, wasn't going to happen.

Dr. Roth rolled up Largent's sleeve. "Prometheus should act faster, without the need to wait for the fever. It will speed up the mutation process."

Hell, I wondered if Largent really was okay with being the first guinea pig. But it didn't matter. They shot him up with the blue gunk. He slumped over—not a good sign—and Roth went into doctor mode. Vitals were through the roof. People were starting to look a tad bit nervous. No one was really paying attention to me, so I started inching toward Kat. I was halfway there when Largent shot up from the chair, knocking the doctor on his ass.

I put myself between Kat and the general area of where Largent was standing. He stumbled forward and then bent over, grasping his knees. Sweat poured off the guy's forehead, dripping onto the floor. A sickly sweet stench replaced the metallic.

"What is happening?" demanded Nancy.

The doctor started to unwind the stethoscope as he went to the soldier's side and placed a hand on his shoulder. "What are you feeling, Largent?"

The man's arms were trembling. "Cramping," he gasped. "My whole body is cramping. It feels like my insides are—" He jerked up, throwing his head back. Throat working, he opened his mouth and let out a scream.

A bluish, blackish substance spewed from his mouth, splattering the doctor's white lab coat. Largent wobbled to the side, his hoarse scream ending in a thick gurgle. The same liquid leaked from the corners of his eyes, streamed from his nose and ears.

"Oh boy," I said, backing up. "I don't think whatever you injected him with is working."

Nancy cut me a dark glare. "Largent, can you tell me what—?"

The soldier spun around and ran—and I mean he ran at full light speed—toward the door. Kat screamed and then clasped her hands over her mouth. I moved to block the grisly sight, but it was too late. Largent smacked into the door with a fleshy, wet *thud*, hitting it at the kind of speed jumping out of a fifty-story window would do.

Silence descended, and then Nancy said, "Well, that was disappointing."

{ Katy }

As long as I lived, I'd never be able to scrape from my mind the sight of the soldier going from relatively normal to something that looked like stage one of a zombie infection to going splat against the door.

We had to wait in that room until staff came and cleaned up enough of the mess that we could leave without stepping in the . . . uh, stuff. They wouldn't let Daemon or me get within an inch of each other as we waited, like it was his fault somehow. He'd healed the guy—he did his part. Whatever was in Prometheus had done this. The blood wasn't on Daemon's hands.

Out in the hallway, the soldiers took Daemon down one wing, and Archer took me down another. We were halfway toward the elevators when one of the elevator doors on the right opened, and two soldiers stepped out, escorting a child.

I skidded to a complete stop.

Not just any child. It was one of them—the origins. Tiny hairs on my body rose at the sight. The boy wasn't Micah, but he had the same dark hair cut in the same style. Maybe a little bit younger, but I was never good at judging ages.

"Keep walking," Archer said, placing a hand on my back.

Forcing my legs to move, I didn't know what it was about those kids that freaked me out. Okay. There were probably a lot of things about those kids that could freak me out. The main thing was the abnormal intelligence gleaming in their oddly colored eyes and the small childlike smile that seemed to mock the adults around them.

God, Daemon and I needed to get out of this place for a whole truckload of reasons.

As we crossed paths with them, the little boy lifted his head and looked straight at me. The moment our gazes collided, a sharp tingle of awareness traveled up my spine and exploded along the back of my skull. Dizziness swept through me, and I stopped again, feeling strange. I wondered if the kid was doing some kind of weird Jedi mind trick on me.

The kid's eyes widened.

My fingers started to tingle.

Help us, and we'll help you.

My mouth dropped open. I didn't—I couldn't. My brain stopped working, and the words repeated themselves. The kid broke contact, and then they were behind us, and I was standing there, quaking with adrenaline and confusion.

Archer's face came into view, eyes narrowed. "He said something to you."

I snapped out of it and immediately went on guard. "Why would you think that?"

"Because you have a freaked-out look on your face." Dropping his hand on my shoulder, he spun me around and gave a little push toward the elevator. As the doors slid shut, he hit the stop button. "There are no cameras in the elevators, Katy.

Besides the bathrooms, it's the only area in the building free from watchful eyes."

Having no idea where he was going with that and still mind-blown from everything, I took a step back, hitting the wall. "Okay."

"The origins are able to pick up thoughts. It's one thing that Nancy didn't tell you. They can read thoughts. So you better be very careful what you're thinking when you're around one of them."

I gaped. "They can read minds? Wait, that means you can do it, too!"

He gave a noncommittal shrug. "I try not to. Hearing other people's thoughts is really annoying more than anything else, but when you're young, you really don't think about it. You just do it. And they do it all the time."

"I . . . This is insane. They can read minds, too? What else can they do?" I felt like I'd fallen through a rabbit hole and woken up in an X-Men comic. And all of the things I've thought about around Archer? I was sure at some point I had thought about escaping here and—

"I've never told anyone anything I've picked up from you," he said.

"Oh my God . . . you're doing it right now." My heart pounded. "And why should I trust that?"

"Probably because I've never asked you to trust me."

I blinked. Hadn't Luc said something like that? "Why wouldn't you tell Nancy?"

He shrugged again. "That doesn't matter."

"Yes. It totally—"

"No. It doesn't. Not right now. Look, we don't have a lot of time. Be careful when you're around the origins. I picked up on what he said to you. Have you seen the movie *Jurassic Park*?"

"Uh, yeah." What an odd question.

A wry smile appeared. "Remember the raptors? Letting the origins out would be like unlocking the gates on the raptor cages. You get what I'm saying? These origins, the newest batch, are nothing like what Daedalus has had in the past. They're evolving and adapting in ways no one can control. They can do things I cannot even think of. Daedalus already has problems keeping them in line."

I struggled to process all of this. Strangely, common sense kept spewing out denials, when in reality I knew anything was possible. I was an alien/human hybrid, after all. "Why are these origins different?"

"They were given Prometheus to help accelerate their learning and abilities." Archer snorted. "Like they needed it. But unlike poor Largent, it worked with them."

Largent's mangled body flashed before me, and I winced. "What is the Prometheus serum?"

He looked at me skeptically. "You know what Prometheus was in Greek mythology. I can't believe you haven't figured it out yet."

Gee, way to make me feel stupid.

He laughed.

I glared at him. "You're reading my thoughts, aren't you?"

"Sorry." He didn't look sorry at all. "You said it yourself. Prometheus was credited with creating mankind. Think about it. What is Daedalus doing?"

"Trying to create the perfect species, but that really doesn't tell me anything."

He shook his head as he reached over and tapped a finger along the fleshy part of my elbow. "When you first mutated, you were given a serum. It was the first serum that Daedalus created, but they want something better, something faster. Prometheus is what's being tested now, and not just on humans healed by Luxen."

"I . . ." I didn't get it at first, and then I thought about those bags in the room where the sick patients were receiving Daedalus's own breed of medication. "They're giving it to humans who are sick, aren't they?"

He nodded.

"Then that means Prometheus is LH-11?" When he nodded again, I forced myself not to go any further with the realization, lest Archer was being nosy. "Why are you telling me this?"

He pivoted slightly and restarted the elevator. Casting me a long look, he simply said, "We have a mutual friend, Katy."

17

I could barely contain myself waiting for a few moments alone with Daemon. We hadn't been abusing the bathroom privileges, knowing that's what they wanted us to do. It took forever before I felt the familiar tingle along my neck. Holding off a couple of minutes, I then bum-rushed the bathroom and knocked softly on the door to his cell.

He was there within a second. "Miss me?"

"Do your Lite-Brite thing." I moved from one foot to the other. "Come on."

He looked at me strangely, but a second later he was a glowing comet. *What's up?*

In a rush, I told him everything about the creepy kid in the hallway, what Archer had said about them, what Prometheus really was, and what Archer had said about us sharing a mutual friend. *I don't trust any of this, but either Archer hasn't told anyone what he's picked up from you or me or he has, and for some reason we haven't been called out on it.*

Daemon's light pulsed. *Jesus, this just keeps getting more and more bizarre.*

You're telling me. I leaned against the sink. *If they decide to shoot someone up with it again . . .* I shuddered. *Maybe they'll just wait until the mutation takes hold this time.*

That, or I have a feeling they're going to have a really hefty cleanup bill.

Ew. That was really . . .

One light-encased arm stretched out. Warm fingers brushed my cheek. *I'm sorry you had to see that.*

I'm sorry you had to be a part of that. I took a deep breath. *But you know what happened to Largent isn't on your conscience, right?*

Yes. I know. Trust me, Kitten, I'm not going to take on any unnecessary guilt. His sigh shuttled through me. *So, about Archer . . .*

We talked a couple more minutes about Archer. Both of us agreed that there was a good chance he was Luc's inside guy, but it didn't make sense. Archer obviously had access to the LH-11 and could've gotten it for Luc. We couldn't trust him—we weren't going to make the mistake of trusting anyone again.

But I did have an idea. One that Daemon was also interested in. Once we got our hands on the LH-11, we had only one chance to escape. And if the origins really were like raptors, then they could become the perfect distraction, allowing us a small shot to bust out of there.

No matter what we did, it would be risky, with about a 99 percent fail rate. But both Daemon and I felt more confident relying on each other than just Luc—and possibly Archer. We'd been burned way too many times before.

Daemon took his human form and kissed me quickly before we went back into our rooms. This was always the hardest—forcing ourselves to go to our own beds—but the last thing we needed was to risk getting caught up in the moment . . . in each other. Because that always seemed to happen when we were together. And we also didn't fully trust that they'd allow us to come and go from each other's rooms—everything felt like a test.

I headed back to my bed. Sitting down, I pulled my knees up to my chest and rested my chin on them. Those quiet moments of doing nothing were the worst. In no time, things I didn't want to think about crept in and pushed away the stuff I needed to focus on.

I really wanted Daemon to see that I was holding it together, that none of this was messing with my head. I didn't want him to worry about me.

Closing my eyes, I shifted until my forehead was against my knees. I told myself the cheesiest thing possible: there was a light at the end of this dark tunnel. I followed that up with the ever faithful: every dark cloud had a silver lining.

I wondered how long I could keep telling myself that.

{ Daemon }

The wondrous team behind Daedalus actually waited until the mutation took hold this time around. It was another recruit who apparently had been all kinds of gung ho. This one stabbed himself in the chest, right below the heart instead of the gut. Still messy. Kat had been there to witness it again. I had healed the idiot. Overall it was a relative success, except I couldn't get near the LH-11. A damn shame, because there had been serum left over in the syringe.

Kat and I weren't relying on Luc, but if we could get the LH-11, and if it turned out that someone, whether it was Archer or not, could help us get out, I was going to take it. Kat's plan of letting the kids loose was the best we had, but the technicalities of how we could do that remained to be seen. Not to mention we had no idea what we'd actually be unleashing. As much as I hated to admit it, there were innocent people in these buildings.

In the three days while we waited for the second guinea

pig to show signs of mutation, I was asked to heal three more soldiers and one who had to be a civilian—a female who looked too nervous to have signed up for this without coercion. She didn't stab herself but was injected with a lethal dose of something.

And I hadn't been able to heal her, like, at all. I didn't know what it was, and it had been terrible. She'd started foaming at the mouth, convulsing, and I tried, but there had been nothing I could do. I couldn't *see* the injury in my head, and it just didn't work.

The woman had died right there, under Kat's horrified gaze.

Nancy hadn't been happy when they carted off the woman's motionless body. Her mood was compounded on the fourth day, when Prometheus, otherwise known as LH-11, was given to the second soldier I had healed. Later that day, he ended up face-planting a wall. I didn't know what it was with them and running into walls, but that was number two.

On the fifth day, the third subject was given LH-11. He lasted an additional twenty-four hours before bleeding out through every orifice, including the belly button. Or that was what I was told.

The deaths, well, they did stack up, one after another. Kind of hard not to take them personally. Did I blame myself? Hell to the no. Did it piss me off and make me want to douse the entire compound in gasoline and start throwing matches? Hell yes.

They kept me away from Kat most of the days, only allowing us to be in the same room when I did the healing thing, and we had a few minutes here and there in our bathroom of secrets. It wasn't enough. Kat looked as exhausted as I felt, which I'd thought would've given my hormones a rest, but oh no. Every time I heard the shower click on, I had to call upon every ounce of self-control. The bathrooms didn't have cameras, and I could be quiet, which was perfect for a little freaky deaky, but there was no way in hell I was risking the chance of baby Daemons in this hellhole.

Was I totally against the idea of having kids with Kat one day? Other than breaking out in hives at the thought of that, the idea wasn't too horrible. Of course, I wanted the white picket fence bullshit . . . if it occurred a good ten years from now, and the kids didn't have weird bowl haircuts and couldn't Jedi mind-screw people.

I didn't think that was asking too much.

On the sixth day, when the third soldier was given LH-11, he made it through the rest of the day and well into the seventh day. He immediately began showing signs of a successful mutation. He passed the stress test with flying colors.

Nancy was so thrilled, I thought she was going to kiss me—and I thought I was actually going to have to hit a chick.

"You deserve a reward," she said, and I thought I deserved to put my foot up her ass. "You may spend the night with Kat. No one will stop you from doing so."

I said nothing. While I wasn't going to turn that down, it was rather creepy hearing Nancy tell me I could spend the night with Kat while they watched us on video. I thought of those kids on the lower floors. Yeah, not going to happen.

Kat had been up to something, inching closer to the tray. She had stopped when Nancy made her announcement. Her nose wrinkled, and I was a bit insulted, although she was probably thinking the same thing I was.

They brought in another subject, this one another soldier, but I was distracted by whatever Kat was doing. She was way too close to the trays, practically standing in front of them.

A stabbing motion later, and I had blood on my hands and a very happy Nancy bouncing around the room.

Dr. Roth had placed the spent needle next to the unused ones. I saw Kat make grabby fingers, but something occurred to me.

"Does this mean I'm joined to them?" I asked, wiping my hands on a towel that had been all but thrown at me. "The ones who don't face-plant a wall? If I die, they die?"

Nancy laughed.

My brows rose. "I don't see how that's a funny question."

"It's a very good, self-serving question." She clasped her hands together, dark eyes glimmering. "No. The Prometheus serum that is given to the mutated subject breaks the bond."

That was a relief. I didn't like the idea of several Achilles' heels running around. "How is that possible?"

A guard opened the door as Nancy crossed the room. "We've had many years to narrow down the interworking of the mutation and the consequences, Daemon. Just as we know that there needs to be a true want behind the mutation." She turned to me, head tilted to the side. "Yes. We've known that. It's not a magical or spiritual thing, but a mixture of ability, strength, and determination."

Well, shit . . .

"Your brother was almost there." Nancy's voice lowered, and my body tensed. "It wasn't lack of determination or ability. And trust me, he was motivated. We made sure of that. But he simply was not strong enough."

I locked my jaw down. Anger slithered through my veins like venom.

"We don't need him. Bethany, on the other hand, well, that's yet to be seen. But you?" She placed a hand on my chest. "You're a keeper, Daemon."

18

{ Katy }

Y*ou're a keeper, Daemon.*

Oh my God, I almost stabbed the needle through Nancy's eye. Good thing I didn't, because that would defeat the whole purpose of what I'd done.

Crossing my arms, I folded my hands around the syringe and kept it hidden under my arm. I dutifully followed Daemon and Archer out, half expecting someone to tackle me from behind.

No one did.

In the excitement of a potentially successful mutation, no one was paying attention to me. No one besides Daemon ever did during these things, except Archer, and if he was peeping into my thoughts, he sure as hell hadn't said anything.

I hadn't really thought any of this through when I grabbed the serum, but as I held it in my hand, I knew that if I did get caught, I was probably going to regret it. So would Daemon. If Archer was peeking in my thoughts right now, and he wasn't working with Luc, we were so screwed.

We went to the elevator, Nancy and the newly mutated hybrid

heading in the other direction. We were alone—just the three of us—as the elevator doors slid shut. I almost couldn't believe our luck. My heart was pounding with excitement and fear, like a drummer doing a solo.

Nudging Daemon in the arm, I got his attention. He glanced at me, and I looked down at my hand, carefully opening my fingers. Just the tip of the top of the syringe was visible. His eyes flicked up and widened, meeting mine.

In that instant, both of us knew what this meant. With the LH-11 in hand, we had no time. Someone would eventually realize it was missing, or they might've even caught me on the security tapes. Either way, it was do or die time.

The elevator doors slid shut, and Archer turned to us. Daemon shifted forward, but Archer's hand shot out. My breath caught in my throat as his hand hit the control panel. The elevator didn't move.

Archer's gaze dropped to my hand, and his head tilted to the side. "You have the LH-11? Jesus. You two are . . . I didn't think you'd do it. Luc said you would." His eyes flicked to Daemon. "But I really didn't think either of you would pull it off."

My heart was pounding so fast my fingers tingled around the needle. "What are you going to do about it?"

"I know what you're thinking." Archer's attention was on Daemon. "Why didn't I get the serum for Luc? That's not what I was here for, and we don't have time to explain it. They're going to know it's missing very soon." There was a quick pause, and he was back to me. "And the plan in your head is crazy."

I had been thinking about the origins, but now I was thinking about Rainbow Brite doing the Electric Slide. Anything to keep Archer out of my head.

He made a face. "Seriously, guys?" he said, taking off his beret. He shoved it in his back pocket. "What exactly do you two hope to accomplish? Your plan has a hundred percent fail rate."

"You're a smart-ass," Daemon said, shoulders stiffening. "And I don't like you."

"And I don't care." Archer turned to me. "Give me the LH-11."

My fingers tightened around it. "Hell no."

His eyes narrowed. "Okay. I know what you guys are about to do. Even though I warned you not to do it, you're planning on letting the freak show out, and then what? Making a run for it? Besides the fact you don't know how to get to that building, you're going to need your hands, and you don't want to stick yourself with that needle. Trust me."

Indecision flooded me. "You don't understand. Every time we've trusted someone, we've been burned. Handing this over . . ."

"Luc's never betrayed you, has he?" When I shook my head, Archer grimaced. "And I would never betray Luc. Even I'm a bit scared of that little shit."

I glanced at Daemon. "What do you think?"

There was a moment of silence, and then he said, "If you screw us over, I will not think twice about killing you in front of God and everyone. You got that?"

"But we need to get the LH-11 out of the compound," I said.

"I'm going with you guys, like it or not." Archer winked. "I hear the Olive Garden is a good restaurant to try out."

I remembered our conversation about him having a normal life, and for some reason that made what I was about to do a little easier. I didn't understand why he was helping us or Luc, or why he hadn't gotten this before, but like he said, we were already in too deep. Swallowing hard, I handed over the syringe and felt like I was handing over my life, which in a way I was. He took it, grabbed his beret, and wrapped it around the syringe, then shoved the bundle in his front cargo pocket.

"Let's get this show on the road," Daemon said, eyeing Archer as he reached down and squeezed my hand briefly.

"You're wearing a piece of opal?" Archer asked.

"Yes." He flashed a daring grin. "Nancy's crush on me is useful, huh?" He waved his wrist around, and the red inside the opal seemed to flicker. "Time to be awesome."

"Turn into Nancy." Archer hit the floor button. "Quickly."

Daemon's form flickered and morphed, shortening several inches. His waves straightened into thin, dark hair pulled into a ponytail. His features blurred completely. Boobs appeared. That's about when I knew where he was going with this. A drab woman's pantsuit later, Nancy Husher stood beside me.

But it wasn't Nancy.

"That's so freaky," I murmured, eyeing him/her/whatever for a telltale sign that it was really Daemon.

She smirked.

Yep. It was still Daemon.

"Do you think this is going to work?" I asked him.

"I'm going to say the glass is half full on that."

I tucked loose strands of hair behind my ear. "That's reassuring."

"We're going to let the kids loose, and then we're going to get back on this elevator and head to ground level." He eyed Archer with every ounce of authority Nancy carried. "I'm going to give her the opal when we get outside." He glanced at me. "Don't argue with me about that. You're going to need it because we are going to run, and we'll run faster than we've ever run before. Can you do that?"

This plan did not sound good to me. There was nothing but a desert wasteland outside, probably for a hundred miles, but I nodded. "Well, we know they won't kill you. You're too awesome."

"You betcha. Ready?"

I wanted to say no, but I said yes, and then Archer hit the

button for the ninth floor. As the elevator jerked into movement, my heart pounded.

It stopped on the fifth floor.

Crap. We had not planned on that.

"It's okay," Archer said. "This is how you access building B."

Terror pooled in my stomach as we stepped out into the wide hallway. All of this could be a trap or another setup, but there was no going back.

Archer placed his hand on my shoulder, like he normally would when he was escorting me around. If that made Daemon unhappy, he didn't show it. His expression remained in the cool disdain that was all Nancy.

There were people in the hall, but no one really paid any attention to us. We made it to the end of the hall and got in a wider elevator. Archer hit a button marked B, and the elevator kicked into gear. Once it stopped, we entered another hall and went straight across to yet another elevator, and then he chose the ninth floor.

Nine floors underground. Ugh.

It seemed like a long way to travel for the little origins to get out, but then again, they were like baby Einsteins on crack.

Mouth dry, I willed my heart to slow down before I had a panic attack. Within seconds, the elevator stopped, and the doors opened. Archer stepped aside, letting Daemon and me walk out first. Out of the corner of my eye, I saw him hit the stop button.

The elevator had opened into a small, windowless lobby. Two soldiers were posted in front of double doors. They straightened immediately when they saw us.

"Ms. Husher. Officer Archer," the one on the right said, nodding. "May I ask why you're bringing her down here?"

Daemon stepped forward, clasping his hands together in total Nancy fashion. "I thought it would be a good idea for her to see our greatest achievements in their own environment. Perhaps it will give her a better understanding of things here."

I had to clamp my mouth shut, because the words that came out of his mouth were so like Nancy that I wanted to laugh. Not a normal laugh, either, but that crazy, hysterical giggling kind.

The guards exchanged looks. Mr. Talkative stepped forward. "I'm not sure if that's a good idea."

"Are you questioning me?" said Daemon, in the snootiest Nancy voice ever.

I bit down on my lower lip.

"No, ma'am, but this area is closed to all personnel that don't have clearance and . . . and to guests." Mr. Talkative glanced at me and then Archer. "That was the order you gave."

"Then I should be able to bring who I want down here, don't you think?"

With each heartbeat, I knew we were running out of time. The hand on my shoulder tightened, and I knew even Archer was thinking that.

"Y-Yes, but this goes against protocol," Mr. Talkative stuttered. "We can't—"

"You know what?" Daemon took a step forward, glancing up. I didn't see any cameras, but that didn't mean they weren't there. "Protocol this."

Daemon/Nancy threw out his hand and a bolt of light erupted from his palm. The arc of energy split in two, one smacking into the chest of Mr. Talkative and the other into the silent guard. They went down, smoke wafting up from their bodies. The smell of burned clothing and flesh hit my nose.

"Well, that's one way of doing it," Archer said drily. "No turning back now."

Daemon/Nancy cast him a look. "Can you open these doors?"

Archer stepped forward and bent. The red light on the panel flipped green. The airtight seal popped, and the doors slid open.

Half expecting someone to jump out and point a gun at our faces as we walked into an open area of the ninth floor, I held my breath. No one stopped us, but we did get a couple of weird looks from the staff milling about.

The floor was a different layout than the ones I'd seen, shaped like a circle with several doors and long windows. In the middle was something that reminded me of a nursing station.

Archer dropped his hand, and I felt something cool pressed into mine. I looked down, startled to find I was holding a gun. "No safety, Katy." Then he stepped up beside Daemon. In a low voice, he said, "We've got to do this fast. See the double doors there? That's where they should be at this time of day." He paused. "They already know we're here."

A chill snaked down my spine. The gun felt way too heavy in my hand.

"Well, that isn't creepy or anything." Daemon glanced at me. "Stay close."

I nodded, and then we started around the station toward the double doors with two tiny windows. Archer was right behind us.

A man stepped out. "Ms. Husher—"

Daemon threw his arm out, hitting the guy in the chest with a broad swipe. The man went up in the air, white lab coat flapping like the wings of a dove before he smashed into the window of the center station. The glass splintered but did not break as the man slid down.

Someone screamed; the sound was jarring. Another man in a lab coat rushed toward the opening to the station. Archer spun around, catching him around the neck. A second later, a blur of white shot past my face and smacked into the opposite wall.

Chaos erupted.

Archer blocked the entrance to the station, which must've had stuff we didn't want them to get access to, sending one person flying after another until the remaining staff had huddled against the door—the door we needed to get into.

Daemon stepped before them, the pupils of his eyes turning white. "If I were you guys, I would move out of the way."

Most of them ran like rats. Two stayed. "We can't let you do this. You don't understand what they're capable of—"

I raised the gun. "Move."

They moved.

Which was a good thing because I had never shot a gun before. Not like I didn't know how to use one, but pulling the trigger seemed harder than moving a finger. "Thank you," I said, and then felt stupid for saying that.

Daemon hurried to the door, still in Nancy form. I saw a panel and realized we'd need Archer. I started to turn to him, but the sound of locks turning echoed like thunder. I whipped around, my breath stalling in my chest as the doors receded into the walls.

Daemon took a step back. So did I. Neither of us had been prepared for this.

Micah met us at the door of the classroom. All the chairs were filled with little boys of different ages. Same haircuts. Same black pants. Same white shirts. All had a look of disturbingly keen intelligence, and they were turned in their seats, staring at us. At the front of the classroom, a woman lay on the floor, facedown.

"Thank you." Micah smiled, stepping out. He stopped in front of Archer and lifted his arm. A thin black bracelet circled his wrist.

Silently, Archer moved his fingers over the bracelet, and there was a soft *click*. It slipped from Micah's arm and clattered to the floor. I had no idea what that was, but I figured it was important.

Micah turned to where the remaining staff huddled together. His head tilted to the side. "All we want to do is play. None of you let us play."

That's when the screams started.

The staff started dropping like hot potatoes, hitting the floor on their knees, clutching their heads. Micah kept smiling.

"Come on," Archer said, wheeling a chair toward the door. He shoved it in place, keeping the door open.

Glancing back at the classroom, I saw that the boys were on their feet, moving toward the door. Yeah, it was definitely time to go.

The men were still unconscious in the hallway, and we hit the elevator on the right. Once inside, Archer pressed the button for the ground level.

Daemon glanced down at my hand. "You sure you're okay with that?"

I forced a smile. "This is all I have until I get out of this stupid building."

He nodded. "Just don't shoot yourself . . . or me."

"Or me," added Archer.

I rolled my eyes. "What faith you guys have in me."

Daemon lowered his head toward mine. "Oh, I have faith in you. There's other—"

"Don't even think about saying something dirty or trying to kiss me while you're still in Nancy's body." I put a hand on his chest, holding him back.

Daemon chuckled. "You're no fun."

"You two need to focus on the task at hand—"

A siren went off somewhere in the building. The elevator

jerked to a stop on the third floor. Lights dimmed, and then a red light flicked on in the ceiling.

"Now it's really going to get fun," Archer said as the elevator door opened.

In the hall, soldiers and staff rushed about, calling out orders. Archer took out the first soldier who looked our way and shouted. Daemon did the same. A soldier pulled a gun, and I lifted mine, squeezing off a round. The kickback startled me. The bullet hit the guy in the leg.

Daemon lost his hold on Nancy's form, slipping into his own. His eyes were wide as he stared at me.

"What?" I asked. "You didn't think I'd do it?"

"Stairwell," Archer shouted.

"Didn't realize you shooting a gun would be so sexy." Daemon took my free hand. "Let's go."

We raced down the hallway a few feet behind Archer. Overhead lights went out, replaced by flashing red and yellow domes. Archer and Daemon were throwing blasts of energy balls like it was going out of style, causing most of the soldiers to stay back. We passed a set of elevators. Two of them opened and a handful of origins stepped out. We kept going, but I had to look back—I had to see what they were going to do. I had to *know*.

They were the perfect diversion.

Everyone's attention was on them. One of the little boys had stopped in the middle of the hallway. He bent and picked up a fallen handgun, and I saw that his wrist was bare of the bracelet. The gun smoked and then melted, re-forming into the shape of a small ball.

The little boy giggled.

And then he spun, throwing the twisted wreck of a gun right at a soldier creeping up on him. The gun went straight through the man's stomach.

My step faltered. Holy crap.

Had we done the right thing letting them loose? What would happen if they got out—out into the real world? The kind of damage they could render was astronomical.

Daemon's grip on my hand tightened, pulling me back to the task at hand. I'd have time to worry about them later. Hopefully.

We rounded the corner at full speed, and I was suddenly forehead-level with a pistol, so close that I could see the finger on the trigger, see the tiny spark of it firing. A scream got stuck in my throat. Daemon roared, the sound final as it bounced around my skull.

The bullet stopped, its tip singeing my forehead. It didn't go any farther. Just stopped. Air leaked out of my lungs.

Daemon snatched the bullet away, then yanked me to his chest as we spun, and there was Micah several feet behind us, one hand raised.

"That wasn't very nice," he said in that monotone child voice. "I like them."

The soldier blanched, and then he was on the floor face-first— not screaming or clutching his head—and blood pooled out from under him.

Another origin appeared behind Micah, and then another and another and another. The soldiers blocking the stairwell hit the floors. *Thump. Thump. Thump.* A path was cleared.

"Come on," Archer urged.

Turning back to Micah, my gaze locked with the child's. "Thank you."

Micah nodded.

With one last look, I turned and darted around the bodies. The thin soles of my shoes slipped on the wet floors—floors slippery with blood. It was already seeping through the bottom of my shoes. I couldn't think about that now.

Archer pushed open the stairwell door, and as it swung shut behind us, Daemon spun on me, his hands suddenly gripping my upper arms. He roughly pulled me against him and up on the tips of my toes.

"I almost lost you. Again." His lips brushed over the hot spot on my forehead, and then he kissed me, a deep and forceful kiss that tasted of residual fear, desperation, and anger. The kiss was dizzying in its intensity, and when he pulled back I felt stripped bare.

"No time for swooning," he said with a wink.

Then we were tearing up the stairs, hand in hand. Archer caught a soldier on the landing. With a brutal throw, he tossed him over the railing. A series of sickening cracks caused my stomach to lurch violently.

Soldiers spilled out onto the second-floor landing. In their hands weren't normal pistols but what looked like stun guns.

Using the railing, Daemon let go of my hand and vaulted up a level. A soldier blew past me, landing two levels down on his side. Archer was right behind Daemon. He ripped a stun gun away and tossed it down to me. Switching the pistol to my left hand, I hurried up the rest of the stairs and squeezed on the first soldier I was near.

Like I suspected, it was some kind of Taser. Two wires shot out, smacking the soldier in the neck. The man started twitching like he was having a seizure and went down. The clip disengaged, allowing me to hit the one swinging on Archer.

Once the landing was clear, Daemon dragged two of the unconscious men to the door, stacking them atop each other.

"Come on," Archer urged as he rounded the landing, shedding the long-sleeve camo top. He reached to his neck, tucking dog tags under his white shirt.

With all the onyx and diamond in the building, I was pretty useless without my gun and Taser. The muscles in my legs were starting to burn, but I ignored them and pushed on.

When we reached ground level, Archer looked over his shoulder at us. He didn't speak out loud, and the message was directed at both of us. *We don't try to take any vehicles from the hangar. Once outside, we'll be faster than anything they have. We head south toward Vegas, on Great Basin Highway. If we get separated, we meet at Ash Springs. That's about eighty miles from here.*

Eighty miles?

There's a hotel called The Springs. It's used to having weird people show up. While I wondered what kind of weird people, and realized that was a stupid thing to even be thinking about, Archer reached into his back pocket and pulled out a wallet. He shoved cash in Daemon's hand. *This should be enough.*

Daemon nodded curtly, and then Archer looked at me. "Ready?"

"Yes," I croaked, my fingers tightening around the guns.

With fear so thick I could taste its bitter tang, I took a deep breath and nodded again, mostly for my own benefit.

The door opened, and for the first time in what had to be months, I breathed in fresh air from the outside. Dry but clean air, not manufactured. Hope bubbled up, giving me the strength to power forward. I could see a slice of sky beyond the vehicles, the color of dusk, pale blue and orange-red. It was the most beautiful thing I'd ever seen. Freedom was right *there*.

But between us and freedom was a small army of soldiers. Not as many as I'd expected, but I assumed that a lot were still underground, dealing with the origins.

Daemon and Archer wasted no time engaging. Bursts of white light lit up the hangar, ricocheting off tan Humvees, tearing through canvas. Sparks flew. Punches were thrown in close combat. I did my part—Tasing anyone I could get close to.

As I darted around the fallen bodies, I spied an artillery load in the back of a flatbed truck. "Daemon!"

He twisted around and saw what I was pointing at. I took off, narrowly avoiding being tackled. I turned, squeezing off another round. Metal prongs dug into the back of the soldier. Bright white light tinged in red crackled over Daemon's shoulders, wrapping around his right arm. Energy pulsed, arcing over the space between him and the truck.

Seeing what he was about to do, several soldiers ran, taking cover behind the large Humvees. I did the same, heading for a row of vehicles as Daemon hit the back of the truck, and it went up like the Fourth of July. The explosion rocked through the hangar, a powerful wave that shook my insides and knocked me flat on my butt. Thick gray smoke billowed through the enclosure. In an instant, I lost sight of Daemon and Archer. Over the popping explosions, I thought I heard Sergeant Dasher.

I was stunned into immobility for a second, blinking out the acrid stench of burning metal and gunpowder. A second was all it took.

Out of the heavy smoke, a soldier appeared. I sat up, whipping the stun gun around.

"Oh, no you don't," he said, catching my arm in both hands, above my elbow and below, and twisting.

Pain shot up my arm and burst along my shoulders. I held on, rolling my body so that I broke the brutal hold. The soldier was trained, and even with all the work Daedalus had put into training me, I was no match. He caught my arm again, the pain sharper and more intense. I dropped the stun gun, and the soldier landed a stinging blow across my cheek.

I don't know what happened next. The other gun was in my left hand. My ears were ringing. Smoke burned my eyes. My brain had clicked into survival mode. I fired the gun. Warm liquid sprayed me across the face.

With the gun being in my left hand, my aim was slightly off. I hit him in the left side of his chest. I wasn't even sure what part of him I was aiming at, but I hit him. There was a gurgling sound that I found so strange, because I could hear it over the yelling, over the screaming, and over the shells still going off. Nausea rolled up my stomach.

A hand landed on my shoulder.

Screaming, I whirled and came within two seconds of offing Daemon. My heart almost stopped. "Dammit. You scared the crap out of me."

"You were supposed to stay with me, Kitten. That wasn't staying with me."

Sending him a look, I edged around the back of a Humvee. The encroaching night sky beckoned us like a siren. Archer was a few Humvees down. He caught sight of us, looked at the opening, and nodded.

"Wait," Daemon said.

Dasher appeared out one of the doors, surrounded by guards. His usually neat hair was a mess. His uniform was wrinkled. He was scanning the strewn debris, issuing orders I couldn't make sense of.

Daemon looked up, his gaze tracking the floodlights. A half grin appeared, and he caught my stare, winking. "Follow me."

We backtracked, creeping along the side of the Humvee. Peering out around the scorched canvas, I saw the coast was clear. Hurrying down the row of vehicles, Daemon stopped in front of a metal pole that rose to the ceiling.

When he placed his hands on the beam, the Source flared from his fingertips. A wave of light rolled up the pole and spread out across the ceiling. Lightbulbs blew, one after another, stretching the length of the hangar, plunging the room into near darkness.

"Nice," I uttered.

Daemon chuckled and grabbed my hand. We started running again, meeting up with Archer. Panicked voices rose, creating a diversion for the three of us to head toward the lower opening, in the opposite direction from Dasher's crew. But the moment we stepped out from behind the row of Humvees, the dim glow from outside cast enough light.

Dasher spotted us immediately. "Stop!" he screeched. "This

isn't going to work. You can't leave!" He pushed past the guards, literally shoving them out of the way. He was absolutely frazzled, probably knowing that Nancy's golden boy was within steps of freedom. "You won't get away!"

Daemon whipped around. "You have no idea how badly I've wanted to do this."

Dasher opened his mouth, and Daemon threw his arm out. The unseen push of the Source lifted Dasher off his feet and sent him flying into the air like a rag doll. He cracked into the wall of the hangar and fell forward. Daemon started toward him.

"No!" yelled Archer. "We don't have time for this."

He was right. As much as I wanted to see Dasher taken out, one more second and we'd be overrun. Tugging on Daemon, I pulled him toward the darkening opening of the hangar. "Daemon," I pleaded. "We need to go!"

"That man's been touched by God, I swear." Daemon turned, a muscle jumping in his jaw.

The sound of boots pounding on pavement echoed like thunder around us as Archer moved to the front. "Get down."

Daemon's arms went around my waist as we bent down, and he curled his body over mine in a near-crushing embrace. Through the thin slit between his arms, I saw Archer place his hands on the back of a Humvee. I didn't know how he did it, but the six-thousand-pound vehicle lifted into the air and was thrown like a Frisbee.

"Good God," I said.

The Humvee crashed into the others. Like a hulking domino, it created a rolling chain reaction, destroying nearly the entire fleet and sending soldiers fleeing.

Daemon sprang up, bringing me with him. He tore the silver cuff off his wrist and slid it onto mine. Almost immediately, a jolt of energy went through me. Layers of exhaustion lifted off, my lungs expanded, and my muscles flexed. It was like taking several shots of pure caffeine. The Source roared to life, a warm spring bubbling through my veins.

"Don't shoot!" screamed Nancy, barreling out from the side hangar. "Don't shoot to kill! We need them alive!"

Daemon's hand tightened on mine, and then we were running with Archer. Each step took us closer to the outside. My speed picked up, as did theirs.

And then we were outside, under the deep blue sky. I looked up for a second and saw stars poking through, glimmering like a thousand diamonds, and I wanted to cry, because we were out.

We were out.

19

{ Daemon }

We were out.

But we weren't free yet.

Not all the vehicles were out of order. They were after us, on land and in the sky. We were moving fast, though. Wearing the opal, Kat could almost pick up my kind of speed, but with the chopping of helicopter blades quickly approaching about ten miles out, Archer broke apart from us, heading to the west.

I'll create a diversion, he said. *Remember. Ash Springs.*

Then he was off, a blur that disappeared into the horizon. There wasn't an opportunity to ask what he was doing or to stop him. A few seconds later, there was a pulse of light, and then another spaced out a mile apart. I didn't look back to see if the spotlights from the helicopter had veered off our course, taking the bait. I didn't think about what would happen to him if he were caught. I couldn't afford to think or worry about anything other than getting Kat somewhere safe, even if it was just for the night.

We raced across the desert, our feet stirring up the scent of sage. There was nothing for miles, and then we came across a herd of free-roaming cattle. Then nothing again as we kept close to the highway.

The farther and longer we went, concern piled on top of itself. Even with the opal, I knew Kat couldn't keep up for much longer, not for eighty miles. Hybrids tired quickly, even with the enhancer. Unlike us, where it actually took more energy to slow down, she was going to crash. Hell, eighty miles would wear me out, but Kat . . . For her I'd run a million miles. And I knew she'd do the same for me, but she couldn't. It wasn't in her DNA.

There was no time to stop and ask her how she was doing, but her heart rate was through the roof, and each ragged breath she took expelled immediately.

The trickle of fear that had been in my veins grew with each step and each rapid beat of my heart. This could kill her, or at the least do some serious damage.

I spared a brief glance at the night sky. Nothing but stars, and no lights in the distance. We still had another thirty or so miles to go, and it would be too much of a risk for me to take my true form and speed up the process. Light streaking across the desert at night would be way too obvious and give all those UFO enthusiasts something to talk about.

Slowing down unexpectedly, I had to slip an arm around Kat's waist to keep her from falling. She was breathing heavily as she looked up at me, the skin around her mouth pale and pinched.

"Why . . . why are we stopping?"

"You can't go on much longer, Kitten."

She shook her head, but her hair stayed plastered to her cheeks. "I can—I can do this."

"I know you want to, but this is too much. I'll take the opal and carry you."

"No. No way—"

"Kat. Please." My voice broke on the last word, and her eyes widened. "Please let me do this."

Her hands shook as she brushed the sweat-soaked hair away from her face. That stubborn little chin raised a notch, but she took off the opal cuff. "I hate . . . the idea of being carried."

She handed over the cuff, and I slipped it on, getting a little zap from it. I also took the gun from her, slipping it in the waistband of my pants. "How about you get on my back? So in a way you're not being carried—you're riding me." I paused and then winked.

Kat stared.

"What?" I laughed, and her eyes immediately narrowed. "You should see yourself right now. Like a kitten—that's what I keep telling you. Your hackles are raised."

Her eyes rolled as she shuffled behind me. "You should conserve your energy and stop talking."

"Ouch."

"You'll get over it." She placed her hands on my shoulders. "Besides, you could be knocked down a peg or two."

I crouched, hooking my arms under the backs of her knees. With a little hop, she slid her arms around my neck and wrapped her legs to my sides. "Baby, I'm so far up the ladder there aren't any pegs under me to be knocked down."

"Wow," she said. "That's a new one."

"You loved it." Tightening my grip on her, I let the Source tap into the opal and blend with it. "Hold on, Kitten. I'm going to start to glow just a little, and we're going to go fast."

"I like when you glow. It's like having my own personal flashlight."

I grinned. "Glad I can be of assistance."

She patted my chest. "Giddy up."

Feeling much better about this, I kicked off the ground and picked up the kind of speed I couldn't while running alongside

Kat. Her weight was nothing, which was concerning all by itself. I needed to get the girl some steak and burgers stat.

When I saw we were approaching city lights, I veered closer to the highway, searching out a sign, and there it was. Ash Springs—ten miles out.

"Almost there, Kitten."

I had slowed down enough that she was able to wiggle free. "I can run the rest of the way."

Wanting to argue but knowing that if I did, it would only delay getting somewhere to hunker down, I kept my mouth shut. I also knew it was more than that. Kat wanted to prove, not just to me but to herself, that she was an asset not a hindrance. That need to show she could stand on equal ground with me and the other Luxen had been what drove her to trust Blake. I took off the opal and handed it back to her. "Let's do this, then."

She nodded. "Thank you."

I took her smaller hand in mine, and we ran the rest of the way to Ash Springs. The whole trip took us about twenty or so minutes, but those minutes felt like a lifetime. Depending on how Daedalus was searching for us, we had a good two-hour lead on them, more if they followed Archer.

Once we hit the outskirts of Ash Springs, we slowed to a walk, keeping off the sidewalks and away from the lampposts. The town was small—Petersburg small. Signs everywhere pointed to one of the many natural hot springs.

"I bet I smell like day-old funk." Kat stared longingly at a sign for one of the hot springs. "I'd love a bath right about now."

Both of us were covered in a fine layer of dust from the desert. "You do smell kind of ripe."

She shot me a dirty look. "Thanks."

Chuckling under my breath, I squeezed her hand. "You smell like a ripe blossom about to bloom."

"Oh, whatever. Now you're just being dumb."

I led her around a hedge shaped like . . . hell, I had no idea what it was supposed to be. An elephant crossed with a giraffe? "What things would you do for a bath?" I turned, lifting her over a fallen branch. "Nasty, bad things?"

"I have a feeling you're going to turn this into a perverted conversation."

"What? I would never do such a thing. You have such a twisted brain, Kitten. I'm aghast at your suggestion."

She shook her head. "I'm sorry that I've tainted your innocence and virtue."

I cracked a grin as we stopped at an intersection. Up ahead were several glowing signs for hotels. The streets were empty, and I wondered what time it was. Not a single motorist had gone by.

"I think I'd shank someone for a shower," Kat said as we crossed the street. "Including you."

I let out a surprised laugh. "You couldn't take me."

"Do not doubt my need to get this funk off me— Hey." She stopped, pointing down a side road. "Is that it?"

There was a sign in the distance. The *S* was a dim red, which made it look like The prings Motel. "I think so. Let's check it out."

Hurrying down the narrow side road and past dark storefronts, we hit the parking lot. It was definitely off the beaten track and . . .

"Oh boy," Kat said, slipping her hand free. "I think this is one of those motels that charge by the hour, and people come to overdose in them."

She had a point. It was ranch-style, one level, and shaped like a *U* with the lobby in the middle and a wooden deck wrapping around the entrances to the motel rooms. Lighting was dim in and around the building, and the parking lot had a few cars in it—the kind of cars that were a day away from hitting the junkyard.

"Well, now we know what kind of places Archer likes to visit," I said, eyes narrowing on the yellow light seeping out onto the wooden planks in front of the lobby.

"He hasn't been to many places." She shifted from one foot to the other. "He hasn't even eaten at Olive Garden, so I doubt he's a connoisseur of hotels."

"No Olive Garden?"

She shook her head.

"Man, we've got to get that boy some endless breadsticks and salad. Travesty," I murmured. "You talked a lot to him?"

"He was the only one who really was . . . nice to me. Well, in his own way. He's not really a warm and fuzzy guy." She paused, tilting her head back as she gazed at the star-strewn sky. "We didn't talk a lot, but he was always there with me. I never thought he'd be the one to help us in the beginning. I guess first impressions really don't mean jack."

"I guess not." A sudden wariness had etched across her face as she lowered her chin. I could see the weight of everything settling on her. Almost the same look I'd seen on Beth's face the morning I left, before she'd freaked out.

I didn't know what to say as we headed across the parking lot. There really were no words that fit how far Kat's life had been derailed. Nothing I could say would make it better, and trying to seemed to undervalue everything she'd gone through. Like telling someone who'd lost a loved one that the deceased was in a better place. No one wanted to hear that. It didn't change anything, make the grief go away, or shine any light on why it happened.

Sometimes words were cheap. They could be powerful, but in those rare occasions like now, words meant nothing.

We stopped under a faint lamp along the side of the hotel

that faced several benches and picnic tables. Soot covered Kat's face. Dried blood dotted her cheeks. My stomach lurched. "You were bleeding?"

She shook her head, casting her eyes back to the sky. "It's not mine. It was a soldier's. I . . . shot him."

What little relief I felt was overshadowed by what she'd had to do and would still have to do if push came to shove. I handed her the gun. "Okay. All right." I cupped her cheeks. "Stay here. I'm going to take a different form and get the keys. If anything looks fishy, you shoot first and ask questions later. Okay? Don't use the Source unless you have to. They can track that stuff."

She nodded. I noticed that her hands were fidgety. Adrenaline was still pumping through her, keeping her on her feet. She'd need a sugar overdose real soon. "I'm not going anywhere," she said.

"Good." I kissed her, wanting to linger so as not to leave her out there alone. But there was no way I could take her into the lobby like this. Sketchy people checking in or not, she was bound to draw attention. "I'll be right back."

"I know."

I still didn't move. My eyes searched her weary ones, and my heart rate kicked up. Kissing her once more, I forced myself to let go and then turned, heading back around to the front. I called up the image of one the guards and took his form. Memory supplied jeans and a T-shirt. All of it was a facade, like a mirror throwing off a reflection. Except the image I reflected was fake, and if you looked too long and too hard, you started to see cracks in the disguise.

A bell gave a jovial little *ding* as I entered the lobby. The air smelled of clove-scented cigars. There was a gift shop to the right, several old chairs positioned in front of vending machines, and to the left was the check-in desk.

An older man waited behind the counter. His eyes were

bug-like behind thick glasses. He was rocking plaid suspenders. Awesome attire.

"Howdy," said the man. "Need a room?"

I approached the counter. "Yes. Got any available?"

"Sure do. Looking for a few hours or the night?"

I almost laughed because of what Kat had said outside. "For the night, maybe two."

"Well, we'll start out with just one night and go from there." He turned to the register. "That will be seventy-nine. We only take cash here. Nothing for you to sign and no ID required."

No big surprise there. I dug into my pocket and opened up the wad of cash. Holy shit, what was Archer doing carrying several hundred dollars with him all the time? Then again, it wasn't like he'd be easy to mug.

I handed over a hundred. "Mind if I take a look at the shop?"

"Go ahead. I ain't got much to do." He nodded at the TV on the counter. "Reception is always spotty around here in the middle of the night. The same with the TV in your room—room fourteen, by the way."

Nodding, I took my change and the key to the room and headed over to the gift area. There was a stack of unisex shirts with the words Route 375: Extraterrestrial Highway emblazoned in a bold green across the front. I grabbed a large one for myself and a small for Kat. There was a pair of jogging pants that would be a little big on her but would do. I picked a pair for myself and then turned, scanning for food.

My eyes landed on a stuffed green doll with an oval head and large black eyes. I picked it up, frowning. Why in the world did humans think aliens looked like a whacked-out Gumby?

The motel manager chuckled. "If you're into the alien stuff, then you're in the right place."

I grinned.

"You know you're about eighty or so miles from Area 51. We get a lot of visitors here on their way to do some UFO watching." His glasses had slid down his nose. "Of course, they don't get into Area 51, but people like to get as close as possible."

I put the doll back and turned toward the food aisle. "You believe in aliens?"

"I've lived here my whole life, son, and I've seen some crazy unexplainable things in the sky. Either it's aliens or the government, and I'm not a big fan of the idea of it being either."

"Me neither," I replied, grabbing up as much sugar as I could find. I added a They R Among Us tote bag, one of those crappy pay-as-you-go phones, and a few other things that caught my attention. Before I headed back to the counter, I wheeled around and grabbed the stupid alien doll.

As I checked out, I kept an eye on the parking lot. Nothing had moved, but I was itching to get back to Kat.

"There's an icebox outside if you need it." He handed over the bag. "And if you need another night, just come on by."

"Thank you." I turned, spying a clock above the counter. It was a little after eleven. Sure felt a hell of a lot later than that. And it was damn strange that the town was so dead this early in the night.

Back outside, I pulled the key out of my pocket and waited until I was around the corner before I slipped back into the Daemon she was familiar with.

Kat was waiting where I'd left her, leaning against the wall, which put her back in the shadows. Smart girl. She turned, smoothing her hands through her hair. "How'd it go?"

"Great." I reached inside the bag. "Got you something."

She tilted her head to the side as I stopped in front of her. "A portable bath?"

"Better." I pulled out the alien doll. "Made me think of you."

A short, hoarse laugh bubbled out of her as she took the doll, and my chest did a funny spasm. I couldn't remember the last time I heard her laugh or anything that remotely sounded like one. "It looks just like you," she said. "I'm going to name it DB."

"Perfect choice." I dropped my arm over her shoulders. "Come on, we're on the right side for our room. Your shower awaits."

She held DB close to her chest, sighing. "I cannot wait."

The room wasn't as bad as I thought it would be. Recently cleaned, and the smells of Lysol and fresh linen were decidedly welcomed scents. Bed was a double, sheets turned down. A bureau across from the bed featured a TV that looked like it would have reception problems any time of the day. A small desk butted up to it.

I sat the goodies on the table and checked out the bathroom. There were towels, soaps, and the essentials, which was good because my dumb ass forgot about that. I returned to the room, finding Kat standing there, still clutching DB. It was ridiculous and weird and a thousand other things how cute I thought she looked, covered in dirt, sweat, and blood.

"You okay with me taking the first shower?" she asked. "Because I was joking. I wouldn't shank you."

I laughed outright. "Yeah, get in the shower before I throw your dirty behind in there."

She wrinkled her nose at me and then placed DB on the bed so the alien doll looked like it was about to watch some bad TV. She then sat the gun on the nightstand. "I'll be quick."

"Take your time."

She hesitated a moment, looking like she wanted to say something, and then changed her mind. With one last long look at me, she turned and disappeared into the bathroom. The hiss of the shower was so immediate it brought a smile to my face.

Heading to the bag, I dug out the disposable phone and opened the package. It was already preloaded with a hundred minutes. I wanted to call my sister and brother, but doing so this soon was too much of a risk. I set it aside and moved to the window. It faced the road and parking lot, which was perfect.

Peering out from behind the thick burgundy curtains, I wondered how long it would take for Archer to find us or if he even would. Might make me a cold-hearted bastard, but the outcome of Archer didn't matter to me. It wasn't that I didn't appreciate what he'd done for us and what he'd risked, but there wasn't enough room in me to worry about others. We were out. And we were never going back. I'd take out an army, burn down an entire city, and throw the world into chaos if I had to in order to keep Kat out of that place.

20

{ Katy }

The near-scalding, steady stream of water had washed away the grime and whatever else was stuck to my skin. I turned a few times and finally stopped, pressing shaky hands to my face. I'd already used the tiny bottle of shampoo—twice—and I needed to get out of there, but being in the stall with rust stains near the drain and uneven pressure was so different from the bathrooms in the compound that I didn't want to leave. It was like being in a bubble, safe from reality.

Water coursed over my body, cascading off the jagged scars along my back, pooling around my feet. Lowering my hands, I looked down. The water wasn't draining fast, causing it to gather in the bottom of the tub. The water had a pink tint to it.

I swallowed hard and turned off the faucets. Stepping out of the tub and into the steam-filled bathroom, I grabbed a towel and wrapped it around me, securing it at the top. I did my best to get the excess water out of my hair, going about it methodically. Wrap. Squeeze. Wrap. Squeeze. When that was done, I realized I had no other reason to hide in the bathroom.

And that was what I was doing. Hiding. I didn't know why, except it felt like my insides were bruised and frayed, too exposed. We were out—we were free for now. That alone was reason to celebrate, but we were far from in the clear. There was the unknown fate of Archer, where we would go from here, and an entire life I'd left behind in Petersburg—my mom, my school, my books . . .

I needed to leave the bathroom before Daemon thought I passed out or something.

Clutching the top of the towel, I went into the room. Daemon was at the window, his back straight like a sentry. He turned at the waist, his gaze moving from the top of my head to my feet. The light was on beside the bed, and it was dim, but when he looked at me like that, it felt like a spotlight had been turned on me. My toes curled into the carpet.

"Feel better?" he asked, not moving from the window.

I nodded. "Much better. There may be some hot water left."

One side of his lips curved up. "Know what date it is?" I shook my head, and he gestured at the desk. "There's one of the day calendars on it, the kind where you tear off the pages each day. If it's up to date, it's August eighteenth."

"My God," I whispered, deeply unsettled. "I've been gone . . . we've been gone for practically four months."

He said nothing.

"I knew it had been awhile, but time was so strange there. I just didn't think it was that long. Four months . . ."

"Feels like forever ago, huh?"

"Yes, it does." I inched closer to the bed. "Four months. Mom probably thinks I'm dead."

He turned back to the window, his shoulders tensed. Several moments passed before he spoke. "I got you some clean clothes. They're in the bag. I think you'll appreciate the shirt."

"Thank you."

"It's no biggie, Kitten."

I bit down on my lip. "Daemon . . . ?" He turned to me, his eyes unnaturally bright. Two beautiful green eyes. "Thank you for everything. I wouldn't be out of there if it—"

He was suddenly in front of me, clasping my cheeks. I sucked in a startled breath as he lowered his forehead to mine. "You do not need to thank me for any of this. You would've never been in this situation if it weren't for me. And you don't need to thank me for something I wanted and needed to do."

"This wasn't your fault," I told him, meaning it. "You know that, right?"

He pressed a kiss to my forehead. "I'm going to clean up. There's food in the bag, too, if you're hungry. If not, you should try to get some rest."

"Daemon—"

"I know, Kitten. I know." He dropped his hands and gave me that cocky smile of his. "If anyone shows up while I'm in the shower, even Archer, you don't let him in, okay?"

"I doubt a door would stop him."

"That's what the gun is for. I don't think he's going to screw us, but I'd rather be safe than sorry."

He had a good point, but as I watched him grab a pair of sweats and then disappear into the fogged-over bathroom, I loathed the idea of picking up that gun again. I would if I had to. I just hoped I'd never have to again, which was silly because, more than likely, the violence of my recent everyday life was nowhere near over.

Picking up the bag, I brought it over to the bed. I sat down and started rummaging through it as the water kicked on in the bathroom. I looked up, my gaze falling to the closed door. A warm flush crept over my cheeks. Daemon was in the shower. Completely naked. I was in a towel. We were alone, for the first time in four months, in a shady motel room.

My stomach dipped.

The flush heated up, and I groaned in exasperation.

What was I doing even thinking about that kind of stuff right now? Over the course of the last couple of months, I'd heard Daemon in the shower a million times over. This wasn't a romantic getaway at the Ritz, unless running for your lives counted as foreplay.

Shaking my head, I refocused on the bag. Inside I found a wide selection of sugary goodness, which caused me to blink back tears because I knew he'd bought that for me. God, he was considerate when I didn't even know he was trying, when it mattered.

I pulled out the bottles of soda and got up, placing them with the chips and sugar on the desk. The tote bag brought a smile to my face. The shirt made the smile stretch in a way that felt unfamiliar, like it would crack my skin.

I glanced at the alien doll. "DB . . ."

Going back to the bed, I found flip-flops in the bag. Perfect. I never wanted to see those bloody shoes again. I reached the bottom of the bag, and my fingers brushed over a square box. I pulled out the last item.

Heat swept my face, and my eyes popped out. "Oh . . . oh, wow."

The water shut off, and a second later Daemon came out with the sweats hanging low on his hips, and his skin was dewy, glistening. My eyes were fixated on his stomach and the drops of water running over the dips, disappearing under the band of the sweats. I was still only in a towel.

And I was holding a box of condoms in my hand.

My face was red as a ladybug.

One dark eyebrow went up.

My gaze fell to the box and then went back to him. "Confident, aren't you?"

"I'd like to call it being prepared for any occasion." He sauntered over to the bed in a way only Daemon could without looking like a complete douche. "Although, I am disappointed they don't have little alien faces on them like everything else."

I choked on my next breath. "What kind of motel sells condoms?"

"My favorite kind of motel?" He took the box from my boneless fingers. "You've spent this entire time looking at this instead of eating something, haven't you?"

A laugh burst from me—a real, normal laugh.

Daemon's eyes widened, and the hue flared. The box fell from his fingers, landing with a soft *thud* against the carpet. "Do that again," he said, his voice gruff.

The sound sent a shiver down my spine. "Do what?"

"Laugh." He bent over me, the tips of his fingers grazing my cheeks. "I want to hear you laugh again."

I wanted to laugh again for him, but all the humor had dried up under the raw intensity of his stare. Emotion swelled inside me like a balloon tethered by a fine string. I opened my mouth, but I didn't know what to say. Muscles tensed throughout my body. My belly felt like a nest of butterflies was about to take flight. I raised a hand, placing it on his cheek. The slight stubble tickled my palm and caused my heart to jump. I slid my hand over the curve of his jaw and then down the cords of his neck to his shoulder. He jerked under my touch, and his chest rose sharply.

"Kat." He breathed my name; he took it into himself, said it like it was some kind of prayer.

I couldn't look away, and for a moment I was frozen, then I stretched up, placing my mouth against his. The slight touch sent a shock through my system. I moved my lips, familiarizing myself with the feel of him. Strange, but it was like we were kissing for the first time. My pulse was pounding, and my thoughts were in a heady, dizzy swirl.

He slipped a hand through my hair, his fingers curling along the back of my skull. The kiss deepened until his taste was everywhere, and there was nothing but us—only us. The rest of the world fell away. None of our problems vanished, but they were put on hold as my mouth opened for him. We kissed like we were famished for each other, and we were. Those kisses intoxicated me, and his fingers moved over my jaw and down my throat, delicately tracing a path. But my hands were greedy and rushed as they slipped over his chest, and I followed the lines of his hard stomach. The way my touch affected him was marveling to me. He made a throaty sound, and I melted.

He eased me back, positioning his body over mine and supporting his weight on one arm, but only our mouths touched in the sweetest torture. We'd been intimate before, twice, but right now it felt like the first time. Excited nervousness hummed through me while my blood heated up.

Daemon lifted his head. Between the narrowed slits of his eyes, his pupils were like polished diamonds following the movement of his hand. My insides tightened as his fingers moved dangerously close to the edge of the towel. Each slow pass along the fabric had my pulse pounding. My gaze traced over his broad cheekbones and then got hung up on the perfection of his lips.

His hand stilled around the knot I had made in the towel, his eyes flicking up to mine. "We don't have to," he said.

"I know."

"I really didn't buy the condoms thinking that we'd do this tonight."

I slipped into a grin. "So . . . you weren't overly confident?"

"I'm always overly confident." He swooped down, kissing me softly. "But I don't know if this is too much right now. I don't want—"

I silenced him by slipping my hands to the band of his pants, hooking my fingers under it. "You're perfect. I want this—with you. It's not too much."

A breath shuddered through him. "God, I was hoping you'd say that. Does that make me a terrible person?"

A little laugh came out. "No. It just makes you a dude."

"Oh? Is that it?" He captured my mouth again, then pulled back with a slight nip. "Just makes me a dude?"

"Yes." I gasped. My back arched as he moved his hand down my front and then back up to the knot. "Okay. You're more than just a dude."

He chuckled deep in his throat. "Thought so."

His breath was warm against my swollen lips, scorching hot as it trailed down my neck. He pressed a kiss to where my pulse pounded in my throat. I closed my eyes, happily swept away in the rush of sensations. I needed this—we needed this. A moment of normalcy, of just him and me, together like we were supposed to be.

He kissed me as his fingers worked the knot loose, distracting me as he parted the towel. Goose bumps followed the cool air rushing over my body. He murmured something in that lyrical language of his, a language I wished I could understand because his words sounded beautiful.

As he lifted up, his gaze chased away the tiny bumps, searing me from the inside out. The edges of his body blurred into a faint whitish light. "You're beautiful."

I thought about my back.

"Every part," he said, as if he read my mind.

Maybe he had, because when I tugged him closer by the band of his pants, he obliged, fitting his body to mine. Bare chest to bare chest. I tangled my hands in his hair as I wrapped a leg around his hips.

He took a sharp breath. "You drive me insane."

"Feeling's mutual," I rasped out, tilting my hips up against his.

The muscles in his arms bulged as he made a sound deep in his throat. The set to his jaw was hard, the lines of his mouth tense as he slipped a hand between us. Those clever fingers went from soothing to breath-stealing in a second, and I felt the coiling deep—

A bright yellow light suddenly flooded the room, shattering the moment.

Daemon was off me so quickly, he stirred the hair around my temples as he shot toward the window and peeled back a small section of the curtain. I scrambled up, smacking the mattress until I found the towel, covering myself as I darted off the bed, grabbing the pistol.

Terror climbed up my throat. Had they found us already? I twisted to where he stood, as I still clutched the towel around me. My hand shook so badly the pistol rattled.

Daemon let out a long breath. "It's just headlights—some ass with his high beams on pulling out of the parking lot." Letting the curtain fall back into place, he turned. "That's all."

My hand tightened around the gun. "Headlights?"

His gaze dropped to what I held. "Yeah, that's all, Annie Oakley."

The gun felt glued to my hand. My heart was still pumping fast with residual terror, and that horror was slow to drain from my veins. It hit me then, in startling clarity, that this was what our lives had been reduced to. Flying into defense and panic mode every time headlights came through a window or someone knocked on our door or a stranger approached us.

This was it.

My first reaction to headlights would be to grab a gun, to get ready to shoot—to shoot to kill if necessary.

"Kat . . . ?"

I shook my head. A fire crawled through my stomach, up my throat. Tears burned my eyes. So many thoughts raced through my mind. Pressure clamped down on my chest, tightening around my lungs with icy fingers. A shudder rolled down my spine. Four months of tears I didn't let fall built inside me.

Daemon was in front of me in an instant, gently and carefully peeling my fingers away from the gun. He placed it on the bedside table. "Hey," he said, cupping my cheeks with both his hands. "Hey, it's okay. Everything is okay. No one is here but us. We're okay."

I *knew* that, but it was more than headlights in the night. It was *everything*—an accumulation of four months of no control over any aspect of my life or my body. *Everything* piled up on me—the tangy fear that never eased, the dread I had woken up with every day, the exams, and the stress tests. The pain of the scalpel and the horror of watching the mutated humans die. It all cut through me. The harrowing escape where I shot people—real, live people who had families and lives of their own—and I knew I'd killed at least one of them. His blood had been splattered all across my face.

And then there was Blake . . .

"Talk to me," Daemon pleaded. His emerald eyes were full of concern. "Come on, Kitten, tell me what's going on."

Turning my head, I closed my eyes. I wanted to be strong. I'd told myself over and over again that I had to be strong, but I couldn't get past *everything*.

"Hey," he said softly. "Look at me."

I kept my eyes squeezed shut, knowing that if I looked at him, the balloon that had been so full and tethered so delicately would burst. I was wrecked inside, and I didn't want him to see that.

But then he turned my face to his and dropped a kiss on the lids of my closed eyes and said, "It's okay. Whatever you're feeling right now is okay. I got you, Kat. I'm here for you, only you. It's *okay*."

That balloon burst, and I lost it.

(Daemon)

My heart cracked as the first tear rolled down her cheek and broke with a hoarse sob, making its way out of her lips.

I pulled her against me, wrapping my arms around her as she shook with the force of her grief, her pain. I didn't know what to do. She wasn't talking. There was no room around the tears for that.

"It's okay," I kept telling her. "Let it out. Just let it out." And I felt stupid for saying that. The words were so lacking.

Her tears streamed down my chest; each one cut like a knife. Helpless, I picked her up and brought her to the bed. I gathered her close, yanking up the blanket that seemed too coarse for her skin and wrapping it around her.

She burrowed into me, her fingers clutching the strands of hair at the nape of my neck. The tears . . . they kept coming, and my heart was shattering at the raw sound of each of her breaths. Never in my life had I felt more useless. I wanted to fix this, to make her better, but I didn't know how.

She had been so strong through all of this, and if I had thought for one instant that she hadn't been deeply affected, then I was an idiot. I *had* known. I'd just hoped—no, I'd *prayed*—that the scars and wounds would just be physical. Because I could fix them—I could heal them. I couldn't fix what bled and festered underneath, but I would try. I would do anything to take this pain away from her.

I don't know how much time passed before she settled

down, until the tears seemed to dry up and her ragged breathing evened out, and she'd exhausted herself into sleep. Minutes? Hours? I didn't know.

I got her under the covers, and I stretched out beside her, tucking her warm body close. She didn't stir once through the whole thing. With her cheek against my chest, I kept running my hands through her hair, hoping that the motion could reach her in her sleep and would soothe some of her troubles. I knew she liked it when I played with her hair. It seemed like such an insignificant thing, but it was all I had at that moment.

At some point, I drifted off to sleep. I hadn't wanted to, but the last six or so hours had taken their toll. I had to have slept for a couple of hours, because when I opened my eyes, daylight streamed in through the gap in the curtains, but it only felt like minutes.

And Kat wasn't beside me.

I blinked quickly, rising up on my elbows. She was sitting on the edge of the bed, dressed in the shirt and pants I'd found last night. Her hair fell down the middle of her back; the waves shifted as she turned toward me, bringing a leg up on the bed.

"I didn't wake you, did I?"

"No." I cleared my throat, glancing around the room, slightly disoriented. "How long have you been awake?"

She shrugged. "Not too long. It's a little past ten in the morning."

"Wow. That late?" I rubbed my brow with the heel of my hand as I sat up.

She looked away, studying the strap on her flip-flops. Her cheeks were red. "Sorry about last night. I didn't mean to cry all over you."

"Hey." I scooted over, sliding an arm around her waist, and tugged her closer. "I needed the second shower. It was better than the first."

She laughed hoarsely. "That was a huge mood killer, right?"

"Nothing kills my mood when it comes to you, Kitten." I brushed her hair back, tucking it behind her ear. "How are you feeling now?"

"Better," she said, lifting her gaze. Her eyes were red and swollen. "I think . . . I think I needed to do that."

"Want to talk about it?"

She wetted her lips nervously as she fidgeted with the ends of her hair. I was happy to see the opal bracelet still on her slim wrist. "I . . . A lot happened."

I held my breath, not daring to move, because I knew it took a lot for her to get the words out sometimes. She internalized a ton of crap, kept it in. Finally, she gave a wobbly little smile.

"I was so scared," she whispered, and my chest spasmed. "When I saw the headlights? I thought it was them, and I just freaked out, you know? I've been in that place for four months. I know that's nothing compared to Dawson and Beth, but . . . I don't know how they did it."

I exhaled slowly. I didn't know how they did it, either, how Dawson and Beth weren't more messed up than they already were. I kept my mouth shut as I ran my hand up her back and then down, up again.

Her gaze focused on the bathroom door, and she was quiet for what felt like forever. Then, very slowly, the words tumbled out of her. The onyx sprays. The *thorough* exams. The stress tests with the hybrids and how she'd refused to participate, and what that had meant for her until they had paired her up with Blake. How he'd goaded her into fighting him and tapping into the Source. The guilt that she carried for his death was evident in her voice. She told me everything, and through it all, I had to check myself about a million times. Rage like I'd never known coated my insides.

"I'm sorry," she said, shaking her head. "I'm rambling. It's just that . . . I needed to get it out."

"Don't apologize, Kat." I wanted to punch a hole in the

wall. Instead I slid over so I was sitting beside her, thigh to thigh. "You know what happened with Blake isn't your fault, right?"

She twisted a section of hair around two fingers. "I killed him, Daemon."

"But you were defending yourself."

"No." She let go of the hair and looked at me. Her eyes were glassy. "I wasn't defending myself, not really. He goaded me, and I lost control."

"Kat, you have to look at the entire situation. You were getting beat up . . ." Saying that out loud made me want to go back to the compound and burn it down. "You were going through *a lot* of stress. And Blake . . . whatever his reasons were for doing what he did, he repeatedly put you and so many other people in danger."

"You think he had it coming?"

A real sadistic part of me wanted to say yes, because yeah, some days I thought that. "I don't know, but what I do know is that he went into the room to goad you into fighting him. You did. I know you didn't want to kill him or anyone else, but it happened. You're not a bad person. You're not a monster."

Her brows pinched, and she opened her mouth.

"And no, you're not like Blake. So don't even go there. You could never be like him. You're good inside, Kitten. You bring out the best in people—even me." I nudged her with my arm, and she cracked a grin. "That alone should earn you the Nobel Peace Prize."

She laughed softly, and then she rose onto her knees. Wrapping her arms around my shoulders, she leaned down and placed the softest kiss, the kind I'd treasure forever, against my lips.

"What was that for?" I circled my arms around her waist.

"A thank-you," she said, resting her forehead against mine.

"Most guys would've probably left in the middle of the night and run far away from the hysterics."

"I'm not most guys." I tugged her over so she was sitting in my lap. "Haven't you figured that out yet?"

She dropped her hands to my shoulders. "I'm a little slow sometimes."

I laughed, and she responded with a smile. "Good thing I don't like you for your brains."

Her mouth dropped open, and she smacked me on the arm. "That's so ignorant."

"What?" I wiggled my brows suggestively. "I'm just being honest."

"Shut up." She brushed her lips against mine.

I nipped at her lower lip, and a rosy flush appeared on her cheeks. "Hmm, you know how I like it when you get all mouthy with me."

"You're mental."

My hands flattened against the small of her back, and I pulled her close. "I have something really corny to say. Get ready for it."

She traced the line of my jaw. "I'm ready."

"I'm mental for you."

She busted into laughter. "Oh my God, that *is* corny."

"Told you." I caught her chin and brought her lips to mine. "I love the sound of your laugh. Is that too corny?"

"No." She kissed me. "Not at all."

"Good." I slid my hands up her waist, the tips of my fingers stopping below her chest. "Because I've got—" A sensation crawled through my veins, spreading all over my body.

Kat stilled, sucking in a sharp breath. "What is it?"

I gripped her hips and deposited her on the bed beside me. Swiping the gun off the table, I handed it to her, and she took it with wide eyes. "There's a Luxen here."

21

I stood quickly, palming the gun. "Are you sure?" I winced. "Okay. That was a stupid question."

"I don't—"

A knock rattled the motel door, jarring me to the point that I almost dropped the pistol. Daemon shot me a concerned look, and I flushed. I really needed to pull it together. Taking a deep breath, I nodded.

He prowled to the door silently, with the grace of a lethal predator, and there I was, stumbling around like a colt. Inching closer, I told myself I was ready to use this gun. Using the Source, which was just as dangerous, would be too risky. Shooting a gun would draw attention, but hopefully only the local kind.

Daemon leaned in, peering out the peephole. "What the hell?"

"What?" My heart skipped a beat.

He looked over his shoulder at me. "It's Paris—the Luxen who was with Luc."

It took me a moment to remember who he was—the really pretty blond Luxen who had been with Luc at his club. "He's a friendly?"

"We'll see." Daemon squared his shoulders and cracked the door open. I couldn't see anything beyond his bare back, which, if I had to be stuck staring at something, at least it was that. "Surprised to see you all the way out here," he said.

"Should you be?" came the response.

"You tell me. Why are you here? And why shouldn't I blast you into next week?"

My palm was sweaty around the gun. Daemon really wouldn't blast Paris. Wait. Yes he would, risky or not.

"Because that would draw way too much attention," Paris replied in his smooth voice. "And besides, I'm not alone."

Daemon must have seen someone else, because his shoulders relaxed a fraction of an inch, and he stepped aside. "Well, come in."

Paris stepped through the door, his strides long and sure. He took one look at me holding the gun. "Nice shirt."

I glanced down, forgetting I was wearing the extraterrestrial highway shirt. "Thanks."

Then Archer popped in, looking fresh and clean. Not at all like someone who'd spent the night running around the desert. Suspicion bloomed like a noxious weed. He looked at Daemon. "Were we interrupting?"

Daemon's eyes narrowed as he closed the door. "What's going on?"

Archer reached into his jeans and pulled out a glass case. He handed it over to Daemon. "Here is the LH-11. I thought I'd let you do the honors." He looked at me. "Are you going to shoot me, Katy?"

"Maybe," I mumbled, but I lowered the gun and sat on the edge of the bed. "Where have you been?"

Archer frowned as Paris milled about, casting a distasteful sneer at the room. "Well, I did have a busy night keeping half the military off your tracks. Then when I was heading back to meet you, I ran into our friend here."

"I wouldn't consider him a friend," Daemon said as he came to stand beside where I sat.

Paris placed a hand against his chest. "You wound me."

Daemon rolled his eyes, and then in a lower voice, he said. "You can put the gun down, Kitten."

"Oh." I flushed. Stretching over, I placed it on the table. Then I addressed Archer. "We owe you a thank-you for . . . for everything." I waited for Daemon to chime in. When he didn't, I kicked his leg.

"Thank you," Daemon muttered.

Archer's mouth curved in amusement, and I think it was the first time I saw him really smile. I was blown away by how young it made him look. "You have no idea how gleeful that makes me feel to hear you say that, Daemon."

"I can imagine."

"Seriously," I cut in. "We do thank you. We would've never made it here if it wasn't for you."

He nodded. "It wasn't just for you two."

"Explain?" Daemon said.

Paris huffed as he hopped up on the desk. Thank God the thing didn't give out on him and wrinkle his pressed pants. "Do you guys really think that Archer enjoyed being Daedalus's perfect little example of how an origin should be?"

"I guess not." Daemon sat beside me. "And I guess Luc didn't, either."

Paris raised a slender shoulder. "And I guess you didn't enjoy being their perfect, little mutant-maker?"

"Oh, yeah, and Nancy was totally loving you." Archer folded his arms. "You were her all-star Luxen. How many humans did you mutate in the short period of time there? More than any other Luxen has."

Daemon stiffened. "That really has nothing to do with this. Why are you helping us, and why are you with Paris?"

"And where is Luc?" I piped in, figuring he couldn't be too far.

Paris smiled. "He's around."

"We don't have a lot of time for questions, but I can give you the short and dirty version," Archer said. "I owed Luc a favor, and Paris is right. *You* were right, Katy. Being in Daedalus means not having a life. They controlled every aspect. It doesn't matter how I came into creation." He spread his arms out, palms up. "What matters, always matters, is *living*."

"Why now?" Daemon asked, a hard edge of distrust to his tone.

"And that's the question of the year, huh?" Paris chimed in, grinning like he ingested some happy pills or something. "Why would Archer pick right now to risk everything—his life, what little life he had?"

Archer sent the other Luxen a dark look. "Thanks, Paris, for adding that. Escaping Daedalus is not easy. Besides Luc and a handful of others, no one has ever succeeded. Yeah, I could've run a hundred times over, but they would've found me. I also needed a diversion."

It hit me then. "You used us as a diversion."

He nodded. "Nancy and Sergeant Dasher are going to be more concerned about finding Daemon and you. I'm not going to be at the top of their priority list."

Some of the tension eked out of Daemon's frame. "Nancy had said that there were other origins out in the world pretending to be normal humans."

"There are some," Archer confirmed. "I doubt they'll be a problem right now. They have high-profile lives, so they won't come within ten miles of any of us."

There was still something I didn't understand. "Why didn't Luc just have you get him the LH-11? He could've hidden you."

Paris laughed softly. "Do you think there's a method to Luc's madness?"

"I hoped there would be," Daemon muttered, running a hand through his hair.

"Actually, there is a method. Besides the fact that I could play spy to keep Luc . . . and a few others up to date on what Daedalus was doing, I knew that they changed the LH-11 strain, and that's what Luc wanted, the new version—Prometheus. I was never around the new drug. No one was. Not until they brought you in," Archer said to Daemon. "It was sort of the perfect storm for everyone. But I don't know why Luc wants the drug."

"And I wouldn't ask him," Paris said ominously.

I shivered at his tone, but then I thought of what Archer had told me. "What about the Luxen—the ones Sergeant Dasher claimed wanted to take over? Was that true?"

Archer slid a look at Daemon. "It's true, and your boy toy over here seems to know one of them."

Daemon's eyes narrowed. "Stay out of my head."

I turned to him. "What is he talking about?"

"It's just something Ethan White said. Remember him?" he asked, and I nodded. I'd met the Elder Luxen briefly. "When I left the colony to come looking for you, he said something about Earth not belonging to the humans forever, but I really didn't give it much thought, because come on . . . I'm sure there are Luxen out there who want to be in control, but it would never happen."

Archer didn't look convinced, and neither was I, but then the origin cocked his head to the side. "Speaking of the devil . . ."

A moment later, the hotel door opened. Daemon shot to his

feet, eyes turning all white as I started for the gun, my heart leaping into my throat.

Luc strolled in, holding a plastic bag and a pink box. His hair was pulled back into a short ponytail, a big grin plastered across that angelic face. "Hey, guys!" he said cheerfully. "I brought doughnuts."

I blinked slowly as I settled back down. "Good God, you almost gave me a heart attack."

"I'm pretty sure I locked that door," Daemon growled.

Luc set the box of doughnuts down, and I eyed them like they held the answer to life. "And I'm pretty sure I let myself in. Hey, Katy!"

I jumped at my name. "Hey, Luc . . ."

"Look at what I got." He dug into his bag and pulled out an extraterrestrial highway shirt. "We can be soul twins now."

"That's . . . um, really nice."

Paris's lip curled. "Are you actually going to wear that shirt?"

"Yeah, I am. Every day of my life. I think it's ironic." Luc's amethyst gaze circled the room, landing back on me. "Now, I think you two have something for me?"

Daemon let out a low breath and picked up the glass case. He tossed it over to Luc, who snatched it out of the air. "There you go."

The kid popped open the small and narrow case, exhaling slowly. He closed it reverently and slid it into the back pocket of his jeans. "Thank you."

I had a feeling that, like Daemon, he didn't say thank you a lot. "So . . . what do we do from here?" I asked.

"Well . . ." Luc drawled out the word. "Shit's about to get real. Daedalus will spare no expense or life to get their grubby little hands on you, Daemon. They are going to tear this town apart. They already are. And they will use every means possible to drag you back in."

Daemon stiffened. "They're going to go after my family, aren't they?"

"Most likely," he replied. "Actually, you can count on that. Anyway!" Luc spun on Archer so fast that the older origin took a step back. "I got us some new wheels."

"Really," Archer replied.

"And it's roomy enough for the five of us." Luc turned back to Daemon and me with an impish grin that spelled no good. "I have a surprise for you guys. But first, I'd suggest putting on some clothes." He reached in his bag, pulled out a shirt, and tossed it at Daemon. It was a plain white T-shirt. "Me and Katy look adorkable in extraterrestrial highway shirts. You would just look stupid. You can thank me later."

I wondered how in the world Luc knew that Daemon also had one of those shirts.

"And eat some damn doughnuts. In either order will do."

Daemon scowled, while I was just happy to start eating doughnuts. I peeked inside the box. Glazed. My favorite.

"What kind of surprise?" Daemon asked, holding the shirt and making no attempt to put it on.

"Now if I told you, it wouldn't be a surprise. But we need to get on the road soon. So eat and pack up. We've got places to go."

Daemon exhaled through his nose and then glanced at me. I could tell he didn't take too kindly to being bossed around by Luc, but my mouth was full of glazy goodness, so I really didn't have anything to add at the moment.

Finally, he nodded. "All right, but if you—"

"I know. If I'm screwing with you guys, you're going to find a way to make my death slow and painful. Got it." Luc winked. "I consider myself warned."

"By the way," Archer said as Daemon leaned over my shoulder and started poking around the doughnuts. "Don't forget the box of condoms on the floor."

My focus shot to the floor. There they were, right where Daemon had dropped them last night. My face burned like holy hell, and I almost choked on the doughnut, the sound of Daemon's laughter ringing in my ears.

{ Daemon }

I so didn't forget the condoms when I packed what little stuff we had into our alien tote. Kat still looked a little red in the face, and it took everything in me not to tease her mercilessly about it. I went easy on her because she looked so damn cute standing there in that stupid T-shirt and those cheap plastic flip-flops, clutching the alien doll to her chest.

I dropped my arm over her shoulders as we headed out into the bright glare of the August desert sun.

Archer brushed past us, his gaze falling to what I carried. "Nice bag."

"Shut up," I replied.

He snorted.

We rounded the corner of the motel, and I got my first look at our ride. "Whoa! That's your wheels?"

Luc threw his new T-shirt over his shoulder as he patted the rear bumper of a black Hummer. "It suits me, I like to think."

Kat shifted the doll to her other arm as she took in the monster. "Did you drive this small village crusher all the way from West Virginia?"

He laughed. "No. I borrowed this."

Yeah, I had a feeling that Luc's "borrowing" was the same way I had "borrowed" Matthew's car. Heading around the driver's side, I opened the back door for Kat. "Think you can climb up in this thing all by yourself?"

She shot me a look over her shoulder, and I grinned. Shaking her head, she grabbed the bar and hoisted herself up. Of course, being the helpful guy that I am, I assisted with a well-placed push.

Kat's head whipped around, her cheeks flushed. "You're such a dog sometimes."

I chuckled as I hopped in beside her. "Remember what I said about petting me."

"Yeah, I remember."

"Keep that in mind for later." I reached around her, grabbing the seat belt before she could.

She sighed as she lifted her arms out of the way. "You know, I am totally capable of buckling myself in."

"How cute," Archer said from the other open door. He climbed in on the other side of Kat.

"There's a reason why I'm doing this." I ignored him, sliding the waist strap over her lap. She sucked in a soft gasp as my hands slid along her lower stomach. I gave her a wicked grin as I buckled her in. "Understand now?"

"Like I said: such a dog," she murmured back, but her eyes had turned a soft heather gray.

Leaning over, I pressed my lips to her temple and then lifted my arm. There was enough give in the seat belt for her to snuggle up against my side. "So, is this car my surprise? I can get down with that."

From the front passenger seat, Luc laughed. "Hell no. I think I might keep this one."

"Just sit back and enjoy the ride," Paris said, starting the Hummer. "Actually, it's a pretty boring ride. Besides the funny alien signs on the highway and maybe a cow or two, there's nothing to look at."

"Fun." As I readjusted my legs, I glanced at Archer. He was tapping his fingers over his denim-clad knees, eyes narrowed on the back of the seat. I didn't really trust any of them in this car, not 100 percent. They could be leading us right back to Area 51.

Archer turned his head to me. *We're not going to betray you or Katy.*

My eyes narrowed. *For the last time, get out of my head.*

It's hard not to. You have such a big head. One side of his lips curved up as he returned to staring at the seat in front of him. *Besides, how could I bring you back? You saw what I did to get us out of there.*

He had a point. *Could just be a setup, like it was with Blake. He did the same thing.*

I'm not Blake. I want to get away from them just as badly as you do.

I didn't respond to that. Turning my gaze to the window, I watched the small houses and the signs for the hot springs blur and then finally fade into the flat open highway of nothing but small brush and tan soil. It wasn't until I saw the sign that I relaxed a little.

"Las Vegas? Are we're going to gamble and take in a Flamingo show?"

Luc shook his head. "Not unless that's your thing."

Not knowing where we were going or why didn't settle well with me. I kept on guard, my eyes peeled to the road, looking for any suspicious vehicles that got a little too close. About seven miles into the almost two-hour trip, Kat dozed off. I grabbed the doll before it hit the floorboards and held onto it. I was relieved that she was getting more rest. She needed it.

Every time we came near a police car, I would tense, ready for them to pull us over for a multitude of reasons, varying from a stolen car to taking out military personnel. But no one stopped us. Not a damn thing happened the entire drive, except for Luc and Paris arguing over the radio like an old married couple. I couldn't figure the two out. Then again, I couldn't figure out myself.

I thought about the craziest shit on that drive to Vegas. And I mean some really far-out-there stuff, and I don't know if it had to do with the fact that there were two people in the car who could potentially be peeking inside my head that made me think of things I really didn't want other people to be privy to.

It all started when I looked away from the window and my attention fell to my leg. Kat's left hand was curled up against my thigh. For several minutes, I couldn't look away. What was it about the left hand? It was just a hand, and Kat had a really great hand and all, but it wasn't that.

It was what typically went on the left hand, on the ring finger.

God, thinking about rings and the left hand made me want to get out of this vehicle and do about a hundred laps, but being married to Kat—*married?* My brain tripped up over that word, but it wouldn't be terrible. Nah, it would be far from that. It would be sort of . . . perfect.

Spending the rest of my life with Kat was something I planned on. There was no question or doubt when it came to that. I saw her—*only* her—in my future. Making a decision like that didn't send me into a cold sweat. Maybe it was because my kind mated young, usually right out of high school, and our version of marriage was really no different than what the humans did.

But we were young. Wet behind the ears, or at least that's what Matthew would say.

Why in the hell was I even thinking about that right now, when our lives were a complete mess? Maybe it was because when everything was chaotic and tomorrow might not come, it made you think about these things? Made you want to seal the deal, so to speak? I hated thinking it, but there might not be a couple of years down the road to get married.

Shaking the thoughts out of my head, I tightened my arm around Kat and focused on the road. When the skyscrapers started to come into view, I gently roused her. "Hey, sleepy-head, take a look."

She lifted her head from my shoulder and rubbed her eyes. Blinking a couple of times, she bent a little and stared out the front window. Her eyes widened. "Wow . . . I've never been to Vegas before."

Luc twisted in his seat, grinning. "It's better to see at night, with all the buildings lit up on the Strip."

Eagerness filled her gaze, but she settled back, shoulders slumping. As much as I would love to take her out, there would be no sightseeing for us. It would be too risky.

I leaned over, pressing my lips to her ear, and said, "Next time. I promise."

She turned slightly, eyes closing. "I'll hold you to that."

Kissing her cheek, I ignored the speculative look Archer gave me. As we entered Vegas, Kat was straining over me to see everything. The palm trees lining the Strip were probably familiar to her, but the pirate ship in front of Treasure Island wasn't something you saw every day.

It took forever to get through the packed traffic, and normally that would have had me clawing at my eyeballs with impatience, but it wasn't too bad. Not with Kat practically bouncing halfway in my lap, pointing out well-known hotspots like the Bellagio, Caesar's Palace, and the Eiffel Tower at Paris.

I was sort of in heaven.

Unfortunately, this version of heaven had an audience. Dammit.

As we reached the outskirts of Vegas, I started getting weary of this whole surprise bullshit, especially when Paris turned off the main avenue, following another road around a country club and huge golf course. We kept heading farther down the road, farther away from the teeming city. There was nothing out there but a few sprawling mansions, and then a twenty-foot security wall came out of nowhere, a glittering sandstone structure.

I leaned forward, dropping my hand on the back of Paris's seat. "Is that quartzite in the stone?"

"You better believe it."

Kat glanced at me, her eyes widening with realization as Paris slowed in front of a wrought-iron gate that had tiny specks of the quartz in it. I'd never seen anything like it.

An intercom popped on and Paris said, "Knock. Knock."

Static and then a woman's voice said, "Who's there?"

Kat raised a brow at me, and I shrugged.

"The interrupting cow," Paris said, glancing at Luc, who shook his head.

From the intercom, "The inter—?"

"Moooooo!" Paris said, snickering.

Kat giggled.

Archer rolled his eyes and shook his head.

There was an audible huff from the intercom. "That was stupid. The gate is opening. Give it a sec."

"That was pretty lame," I said.

Paris chuckled. "I saw it on the Internet. Made me laugh. I got more. Want to hear them?"

"No." My rebuttal was joined by Archer's. Something we agreed on. Huh. Go figure.

"Too bad." Paris eased forward as the gates split, spreading wide. "That wasn't even my best one."

"It was pretty good," Kat said, grinning when I shot her a look. "It made me laugh."

"You're easy to impress," I told her.

She went to smack my arm, but I caught her hand. Threading my fingers through hers, I winked. She shook her head. "You do not impress me."

I would've believed her if she and I both didn't know better.

It took me a few seconds to realize the road also had large quantities of quartz embedded into the asphalt. The first house we came upon, a modest structure, looked like someone puked quartz all over it—on the roof, the shutters, the front door.

Holy crap.

Since there were no natural formations of quartz nearby, they had brought it in, protecting the Luxen community.

"You didn't know about this?" Surprise colored Luc's voice.

"No. I mean, never seemed impossible, using the quartz like this, but it had to cost a pretty penny, and I didn't even know there was a community out here."

"Interesting," Luc murmured, his jaw setting in a hard line.

Paris glanced at him, and I didn't understand the look they exchanged.

"Neither does Daedalus," Archer said. "It's right under their noses. Perfect hiding spot."

"This is insane." I shook my head as we passed more houses decked out in quartz, each home getting larger. "How did I not know about this? Do you know someone in here, Luc?"

He shook his head. "Not really. I have some . . . friends in Arizona, but we need to make a pit stop here first. Let it die down for a few days so the highway won't be such a danger traveling."

"So we're going to Arizona next?" Kat asked, glancing between Luc and me.

Luc shrugged. "It's an offer on the table. That's where Archer is heading to hide out for a while, but it's up to you guys. You can take my offer of hospitality or shove it up my rear."

Kat frowned.

"Makes no difference to me," he added.

She shook her head a little. "I don't get why you all would risk so much to keep helping us."

Good question.

Luc looked over his shoulder. "We have the same enemy, and we're stronger in numbers. Just like in the horror movies."

I started picking up on other Luxen who had to be in the houses or behind the tall walls circling most of the backyards. I really couldn't believe this—an entire community supposedly unseen by Daedalus and protected from Arum by man-made quartz deposits.

Huh. Mind blown.

We'd finally reached another wall and the gate opened before us. The house, if you could call the monstrous thing a house, loomed ahead like a mirage.

"This is where we're going?" Kat asked. A look of awe crossed her expression. "It's a palace."

That brought a smile to my face.

The place really was absurd. Had to be way more than seven thousand square feet, maybe more, rising three stories, with a sky dome over the middle section and a wing flanking each side. Like the rest of the houses, it was white sandstone with quartz embedded deep into the structure. It, too, had a tall wall blocking whatever existed behind the home.

Paris followed the driveway, stopping halfway through the circle in front of the wide steps. In the middle of the circle was a marble statue. Of a dolphin. Weird.

"All right, kids, we're here!" Luc threw open the passenger door and bounded up the steps. On the porch, he turned back to the Hummer. "I'm not getting any younger here."

Taking a deep breath, I grabbed Kat's hand. "You ready?"

"Yes." She gave me a little smile. "I want to see what it looks like inside."

I laughed. "Absurd opulence is what I'm betting on."

"Same here," Archer muttered, stepping out.

We climbed down and walked around the Hummer. She took the tote this time, sticking the alien doll in it so its head popped out of the top. Giving her hand a squeeze, I headed up the steps while I prepared myself for God knows what. The way Luc was smiling had me wary. He looked like he—

The feeling that swept down my spine was warming and familiar but totally impossible. So was the startling jump in energy that caused me to drop Kat's hand. No way.

I took a step back from the door.

Kat turned, concern pinching her face. "What is it? What's going on?"

Words failed me as I stared at the door. All I could do was shake my head once. Part of me was elated, while the other half was horrified by what I was sensing—and I hoped it was my imagination.

Moving to my side, Kat placed her hands on my upper arm. "What's—?"

The red-painted door opened, and, as a figure stepped out of the shadowy recesses, my suspicions were confirmed.

"We came all this way to rush in and save your ass, but then you end up saving your own ass before we could do anything." Dee popped her hands on her hips, and her chin was tipped up stubbornly. "Way to steal our thunder and glory, Daemon."

Luc clapped his hands together. "Surprise!"

22

{ Katy }

Daemon was absolutely dumbfounded into silence. So was I. The only two people who weren't gawking at Dee were Luc and Paris. Even Archer had the open-mouth thing going on, but I think that had less to do with what their appearance meant to Daemon than it did with how beautiful she was.

And Dee was out of this world, extraordinarily beautiful. With her glossy black curls cascading around her exotic face and with those emerald eyes, she was stunning. A more delicate, feminine version of Daemon and Dawson. She stopped humans, aliens, hybrids, and apparently origins in their tracks.

Archer looked like he just saw baby Jesus in a manger or something.

Dee dashed out the door, tears streaming down her rosy cheeks. I stepped back in the nick of time. She launched herself at Daemon from several feet away. He caught her as she wrapped her arms around his neck.

"Jesus," he said, his words muffled by all of her hair. "What are you doing here?"

"What do you think?" she responded, voice thick. "We had to do something. You just beat us to it as usual, you punk."

I clasped my hands over my chest, close to tears, as another form appeared in the doorway and drifted out. Sucking in a soft breath, I couldn't believe how . . . how different Dawson looked. Filled out and his hair trimmed up, with the gaunt pull to his face gone and the dark shadows under his eyes erased, he was the spitting image of his brother.

Daemon lifted his head, as if he sensed the arrival. His mouth worked, but there weren't any words. None of us could've expected to see them here. Like me, Daemon probably figured he might never see his siblings again.

Dawson crossed the porch and dropped his arms around his sister and brother. Their three heads were bent together. Daemon had one hand fisted around the back of Dee's shirt and the other around Dawson's.

"It's true," Dawson said, grinning. "What the hell, brother? Always got to one-up me, huh?"

Daemon grabbed the back of his brother's neck and pressed his forehead against his. "You idiot," he said, letting out a choked laugh. "You should know better. I've always got things covered."

"Yeah, and wait—I'm pissed at you!" Dee pulled back and hit Daemon in the chest hard. "You could've gotten yourself killed doing what you did! You jerk-face, douchebag, imbecile." She hit him again.

Archer winced and muttered, "Damn, that girl . . . that girl can hit."

"Hey!" Laughing, Daemon grabbed her hand. "Knock it off. I obviously didn't get myself killed."

"I worried, you ass!" Dee pushed her curls out of her face and inhaled deeply. "But I forgive you, because you're in one piece and apparently no worse for wear, and you're here, but if you ever do anything that—"

"Okay," Dawson said, dropping an arm around his sister's neck, spinning her. "I think he gets the point. We've *all* got the point."

Dee broke free as her eyes skipped over Paris and Luc. She didn't pay them much attention, but her gaze bounced over Archer, then went right back before moving on. I had stayed out of the reunion, remaining by one of the pillars. I didn't think Dee even noticed me until that moment.

In the blink of an eye, she practically knocked me over. I'd forgotten what her hugs were like. For someone who had a ballet dancer's body, she was ridiculously strong. And her hugs . . . well, it had been so long since I'd been on the receiving end of one of her bear squeezes.

I was slow to respond, more taken off guard than anything else, but then I dropped the tote and threw my arms around her. Tears welled up, and I squeezed my eyes shut. The part of my being that had felt achy over what happened with Dee warmed, and that warmth spilled over.

"I'm so sorry," she said, tears clogging her voice. "I'm so, so sorry."

"For what?"

She still hadn't let go, and I didn't mind. "For everything— for not seeing your side of things, for being so caught up in my grief and anger that I totally abandoned you. For never telling you that I missed you before . . ."

Before it was too late was what she was going to say.

Blinking back tears, I smiled against her shoulder. "You have nothing to apologize for, Dee. I mean it. None of that . . ." Well, it did matter. Adam's death mattered. "It's okay now."

She held me tighter and whispered, "Is it? Because I've been so worried about you and Daemon and what could've . . ."

My body roiled into nervous knots, and I willed the sudden rise of dread to go away. It wasn't welcome here, not in this happy moment. "It's okay."

"I've missed you."

A few tears snuck out. "I've missed you, too."

"Okay. Okay. I think you're starting to cut off her air supply." Dawson tugged on Dee's arm. "And I think Daemon is starting to get jealous."

"*Pfft*. It's my turn with Katy," she replied, but she let go.

And then Dawson replaced his sister. He hugged me, nothing as fierce as Dee's but still powerful. "Thank you," he said quietly, and I knew those two words encompassed so much. "I hope you know how thankful I am for everything you've done."

Unsure if I could speak, I nodded.

"Okay. Now I *am* getting jealous," Daemon said, and Paris laughed.

Dawson gave me a quick squeeze. "I'm forever in your debt."

I wanted to tell him that wasn't necessary. Helping him get Bethany was something I'd do all over again, even knowing that Blake had set us up. After being in Daedalus's grips, now more than ever I understood how important it had been to get her out. The only thing I would've changed was where I was standing in that damn tunnel in Mount Weather.

He stepped aside as his brother swooped in, picking up the tote and circling his arm around my waist. Dawson cocked his head to the side. "What is up with the alien doll?"

"Daemon thought it would remind me of him," I told Dawson.

"Tell him what you named it," Daemon said, and then he dropped a kiss atop my head.

My heart jumped, and my cheeks flushed. "I named it DB."

Dee peered at the alien toy over Dawson's shoulder. "It kind of does look like you, Daemon."

"Ha. Ha." I tugged the doll out of the bag and held it close. For some reason, I loved the stupid thing.

"Everyone want to head in?" Luc rocked back on the heels of his Converse sneakers. "I'm starving."

Dee spun around so that she was on my other side as we headed in. She stole a peek at Archer, who walked in behind us. If I noticed that, so did Daemon. And whatever Dee was thinking right now, most likely Archer was eavesdropping in on.

I so needed to give her a heads-up on that.

Plus the fact that Archer was, well, he was really different from all of us.

The temperature was a good thirty degrees cooler inside the brightly lit foyer, even with the glass sky dome allowing the sunlight inside. Quartz was embedded in the tile floor, making everything so *sparkly*. There were large, leafy plants positioned at the corners, which made my fingers itchy to dig into soil.

Sinking my fingers into soil . . . wow, how long had it been since I'd done that? The day we'd left for Mount Weather? Too long.

"You doing okay?"

"Huh?" I glanced up at Daemon, and I realized that I must've stopped walking, because everyone else was already in the hall beyond the foyer. "Yeah, I was just thinking about gardens."

An emotion crossed his face. Before I could decipher what it was, he looked away. I reached over and tugged on the hem of his shirt. "How about you? Seeing Dawson and Dee?"

He thrust his fingers through his hair. "I don't know what to think." He kept his voice low. "I'm happy to see them, but . . . dammit."

I nodded in understanding. "You don't want them any-where near this?"

"No. Not at all."

I wanted to somehow lessen his concern, but I knew there

was nothing I could say that would do so. I stretched up and kissed his cheek. That was the best I had.

He grinned down at me once I settled back on my feet. He opened his mouth to say something, but Dee popped back into the foyer.

Expression exasperated, she put her hands on her hips. "All right, you two, come in a little farther. There are people here in the great room who would like to say hi. Whatever a 'great room' is I really have no idea, but it is pretty great."

God, I missed her so much.

Daemon lifted his head, smiling at his sister. "Yeah, I think I know who's waiting."

The people waiting to say hello were none other than Matthew, plus Ash and Andrew Thompson. I shouldn't have been surprised to see them. All of them—Matthew, the Thompsons—were like a family. They converged on Daemon at once, and they swallowed him, Dawson and Dee included.

I hung back again, because this was his reunion—a well-deserved one. And the room was rather distracting. Oriental carpet. More statues of dolphins. Quartz-trimmed furniture. A couch big enough for the Duggar family.

Luc plopped down on a chaise longue and started texting away on his cell phone. Paris hung near him, like a grinning shadow. Archer was like me, on the outskirts, probably unsure of what to do as Dee started crying again.

Even Ash was crying.

I expected to feel the hot wave of jealousy when Daemon hugged her, but I didn't. Other than the fact Ash still managed to make crying look glamorous, I was so over that useless emotion. If there was one thing I knew and understood in this world, it was that Daemon loved me.

Matthew stepped forward, grabbing Daemon's shoulders. "It's good . . . it's good to see you."

"You, too." Daemon clasped his arms. "Sorry about your car."

I wondered what happened to Matthew's car, but that question was lost in the lump that was slithering up my throat. Watching them embrace each other, I was reminded of how important Matthew was to all of them. He'd been the only father any of them remembered.

"It's hard, isn't it?" Archer asked quietly.

Looking at him, I frowned. "Are you in my head again?"

"No. Your emotions are all over your face."

"Oh." I blew out a breath as I glanced back at the huddle. "I miss my mom, and I don't know . . ." I shook my head, not wanting to finish.

When the group broke apart, Matthew was the first to approach me. The hug was a bit stiff, but I appreciated it. Ash and Andrew both appeared in front of me, and I was immediately wary of the two. They had never been big fans of mine.

Ash's vibrant blue eyes were red-rimmed when she gazed at me, no doubt taking one look at my outfit and writing me off as a giant fashion fail. "I can't say I'm overly thrilled to see you, but I'm happy you're alive, or whatever."

I choked on my laugh. "Uh, thanks?"

Andrew scratched his chin, face scrunched. "Yeah, I second that statement."

I nodded, having no idea what to say. I raised my hands and gave a little shrug. "Well, I'm happy to see you guys, too."

Ash laughed, the sound throaty. "No you're not, but it's cool. Seriously, our rampant dislike of you really isn't at the top of the priority list right now."

Archer blew out a low whistle and studiously looked away, which gained Ash's catlike interest. As beautiful as she was, I doubted most could resist her.

I was saved from more awkward hellos by the newest entrance. The woman was around Matthew's age, early thirties, tall and slender, wearing a strapless white sundress that swished around her ankles. She was model beautiful with long blond hair.

Obviously an alien.

She smiled warmly as she clasped her hands together. Brown bamboo bangles on her wrists thudded off one another. "I'm glad to see everyone made it here. My name is Lyla Marie. Welcome to my home."

I murmured a hello as Daemon crossed the room and shook the Luxen's hand. He was surprisingly much better at this than I was. Who knew? But seeing everyone here, being surrounded by people I once thought I'd never see again, was a little on the overwhelming side. I was happy, and I was confused, and this terrible coating of foreboding was like sweat on my skin.

Here we were, all of us, a couple of hundred miles from Area 51.

Trying to push those thoughts out of my head as Daemon introduced Archer, I sat on the edge of the couch, holding DB in my lap. Dee sat beside me, her cheeks flushed with emotion. I knew she was going to start crying again.

Dawson made his way over to Lyla's side. "Is Bethany lying down?"

Bethany? My ears perked up. Of course she'd be here with Dawson. In the wave of faces, I just hadn't thought of her. Was she sick?

Lyla patted Dawson on the back. "She's okay. Just needs to rest a little bit. It was a lot of traveling."

He nodded but didn't look relieved as he turned to Daemon. "I'll be right back. I just want to check on her."

"Go," Daemon said as he sat on the other side of me. Leaning against the cushion, he draped his arm along the back of the couch. "So . . . how is all of this possible? How did you guys know to come here?"

"Your lovely sister and brother showed up at my club and threatened to burn it down if I didn't tell them where you were," Luc said, glancing up from his phone. "True story."

Dee wiggled under Daemon's glare. "What? We knew you'd go there and that he'd probably know where you were."

"Wait," Daemon said, leaning around me to look at Dee. "Did you graduate? You better have graduated, Dee. I'm freaking serious."

"Hey! Look who's talking, Mr. I Have No High School Degree. Yes. I did graduate. Dawson did, too. Bethany . . . didn't go back."

That made sense. No way could they explain Bethany's presence.

"We graduated, too, you know." Ash paused, picking at her purple fingernail polish. "Just want to throw that out there."

Running a hand through his blond hair, Andrew made a face at his sister but said nothing. Archer looked like he was fighting a grin—either that or he was grimacing at the crystal dolphin beside him.

"And what about this?" Daemon asked, gesturing at the house.

Lyla leaned against the arm of the couch. "Well, I've known Matthew since we were teenagers. We've kept in touch over the years, so when he called and asked if I knew of any places to stay, I extended him an invite."

Daemon dropped his arms between his knees as his gaze met Matthew's. "You never mentioned anything like this."

There wasn't any accusation in Daemon's tone, mostly confusion. Matthew sighed. "It's not something I felt comfortable telling anyone, nor did I think I'd ever have to. It just never came up."

Daemon didn't say anything for a moment; he seemed to

ingest that and then rubbed both hands down his face. "You guys really shouldn't be here."

Beside me, Dee groaned. "I so knew you were going to start in with this. Yes. Being here is dangerous, we get that. But we weren't going to let this happen to you and Katy. What the hell would that have said about us?"

"You don't think before you act?" Daemon suggested gamely.

I smacked his knee. "I think what he's trying to say is that he doesn't want you guys to be in danger."

Andrew huffed. "We can handle anything they throw at us."

"Actually, no you can't." Luc swung his feet onto the floor and sat up, slipping his phone into his pocket. "But here's the thing. They were already in danger, Daemon. Deep down, you acknowledge that. Daedalus would've gone right after them. Make no mistake about that. Nancy would've shown up at their door."

Daemon's muscles locked up in his arm. "I get that, but this is like going from the frying pan into the damn volcano."

"Not really," Dawson said from the doorway. He carried two black billfolds in his hand as he walked them over to Daemon and me. He handed one to each of us. "We stay here for a day or so. Figure out our next move and where everyone is going to go, and then we all disappear. That's what's in your hands. Say hello to your new identities."

23

Reading my new name for a third time, I still couldn't believe it. Something about this name was familiar. "Anna Whitt?"

Dee bounced a little. "I picked the names."

Things started to click into place. "What's yours, Daemon?"

He flipped his billfold open and snickered. "Kaidan Rowe. Hmm. That has a nice ring to it."

My mouth dropped open as I twisted toward Dee. "You picked names from a book!"

She giggled. "I thought you'd like that. Besides, *Sweet Evil* is one of my favorites, and you made me read it, so . . ."

I couldn't help it. I laughed as I stared down at my picture ID. It was an identical copy of my real driver's license, except it was a different state and address. Underneath it was my actual ID—Katy Swartz—and a few other sheets of folded paper.

Gosh, I missed my books. I wanted to hug them, love them, squeeze them.

"I found that in your bedroom," Dee explained, tapping a finger off it. "I snuck in and got you some clothes and this before we left."

"Thank you," I said, sliding my new ID over my old one. Staring at both was going to give me an identity crisis.

"So, wait, my new name is from one of those books?" Daemon frowned. He also had his real ID, but there was a bank card underneath, set to Kaiden's name. "I'm afraid to even ask what it's about. I better not be named after any kind of magician or something lame like that."

"No. It's about angels, demons, and nephilim, and . . ." I stalled, acutely aware that everyone was staring at me like I'd grown a third eye. "Kaiden's like the embodiment of lust."

His eyes sparkled in interest. "Well, now that couldn't be any more fitting." He elbowed me, and I rolled my eyes. "Huh? Perfect, right?"

"Ew," Dee said.

"Anyway," Dawson said, sitting down on the arm of the couch, "I had your accounts switched over to the new names. You'll also find high school transcripts, so even though both of you are dropouts"—he flashed a grin—"no one will be the wiser. We're all rocking new identities."

"How did you guys take care of all this?" I asked, completely out of the loop when it came to making IDs and faking records.

Luc smirked. "Among my various and extensive talents, making fake IDs and forging documents is one of them."

I stared at the kid, wondering if there was anything he couldn't do.

"Nope." Luc winked at me.

My eyes narrowed.

Daemon thumbed through his papers. "Guys, really, thank you. This is a start." He looked up, his jade eyes bright. "This is something."

I nodded, trying not to focus on everything that I was losing by starting over. Like my mom. Somehow, I'd have to find a way to see her. "Yes."

We stayed in the room for a little while, mainly catching up. No one talked about plans, because I really didn't think anyone knew exactly where to go from there. Lyla gave me a tour of her beautiful home when I asked to use the restroom, which, by the way, was the size of a bedroom and had interior, glass walls.

The house had more rooms downstairs than any living person could find use for. And it seemed like Lyla didn't have a significant other, so it was just her in this sprawling home. Dee tagged along, wrapping an arm around mine as Lyla led me through an open kitchen and sunroom.

"You're going to love this," Dee said. "Just wait."

Lyla tossed a smile over her tan shoulder. "I think Dee's spent the last week out here, trying to come up with a way to free you guys, but . . . we really didn't have a plan that Matthew and I could allow them to carry out that didn't end with them being captured."

Filled with curiosity, I let them lead me outside, back into what I expected to be breath-stealing temperatures, but I ended up stepping into an oasis.

"Oh my God . . ." I breathed.

Dee rocked back on her heels. "Told you that you were going to love this. Beautiful, isn't it?"

All I could do was nod. Numerous medium-size palms lined a quartz-embedded privacy wall, creating the perfect shaded area. The space was rectangular, with a large patio with a grill, fire pit, and various lounge chairs. Brightly colored flowers lined the paver walkway, as did bushes I'd seen in the desert but couldn't name. The scent of jasmine and sage was strong in the air. Toward the end of the property was a pool with a natural stone deck.

It was the kind of garden you saw on TV.

"When Dee told me that you loved to garden, I knew we'd

have something in common." Lyla ran her fingers along a red and yellow croton. "I think your love of gardening has rubbed off on Dee. She's been helping me."

"It helped." Dee shrugged. "You know, not to think about so many things."

That's what I'd loved about gardening. It was the great mind-emptier. After investigating everything from the mulch to the neutral-colored pebbles, I followed Dee upstairs to the second floor. Daemon was with Dawson, Matthew, and the Thompson siblings. He needed to spend time with them. Besides, hanging out with Dee was bringing me a world of warm fuzzies.

One of the bedroom doors was closed, and I figured that was where Beth was. "How is Beth doing?" I asked.

Dee slowed down, falling in step with me. Her voice was low. "She's okay, I guess. She doesn't talk much."

"Is she . . . ?" Wow. How did I ask this question without sounding insensitive?

"Sane?" suggested Dee, but she did so without scorn. "Some days are better than others, but she's been really tired lately, sleeping a lot."

I stepped around a giant urn packed with snake plants. "Well, she can't be coming down with something. We don't get sick."

"I know." Dee stopped at a bedroom at the end of the hall. "I just think the traveling has her stressed out. She wanted to help, don't get me wrong, but she's scared."

"She has a right to be." I brushed a few strands of hair out of my face and focused on the room. The bed was big enough for five people and had a mountain of pillows stacked against the headboard. "So this is our bedroom?"

"Huh?" Dee was staring at me, and then she shook her head. "Sorry. Yes. For you and my brother." A giggle escaped.

"Wow. A year ago, Katy . . ."

A smile tugged at my lips. "I would've rather stabbed myself repeatedly in the eye with a spork than sleep in the same *house* as Daemon."

"A spork?" Dee laughed as she went over to the closet. "That's serious."

"It is." I sat on the bed and immediately fell in love with the firmness. "Sporks are only used in the most dire situations."

Tugging her hair up into a ponytail, she stepped inside. I could see a few of my outfits in there. "I grabbed a couple of everything—jeans, shirts, dresses, underoos."

"Thank you. I mean it. This," I said, gesturing at myself, "is all I have. It will be nice to change into something that's mine after . . ." I trailed off, not seeing the point in going there. Scanning the room for a distraction, I spotted another door. "Do we have our own bathroom?"

"Yep. Every room does. This house is sick." She blinked out in front of the closet and reappeared on the bed beside me. "It makes it kind of hard to leave this place."

I'd only been here a few hours, and I wanted to adopt the house. "So, where are you going after this? With us?"

She shrugged. "I honestly don't know. I'm not thinking about it yet, because I don't know how possible it's going to be for all of us to stay together. Going home is out of the question for a ton of reasons." She paused, looking at me. "Everyone at school was so . . . different after you and Daemon disappeared. With all the police and the journalists back again, people really started to get paranoid. Lesa was beside herself, especially after what happened to Carissa. It's good she has her boyfriend. She thinks Dawson and I left town to visit family. Kind of true."

Worrying the hem of my shirt, I steeled myself. "Can I ask you a question?"

"Sure. Anything."

"My mom—how is she?"

Dee took a moment to respond. "You want the truth, or do you want me to make you feel better?"

"It's bad, isn't it?" Tears welled up in my eyes so fast I had to look away.

"You know the answer to that." She found my hand and squeezed. "Your mom is upset. She took a lot of time off work—her jobs were okay with that. Very understanding from what I heard. She doesn't believe you and Daemon ran away. That's what the police finally decided when they could find no evidence of why you, Daemon, and Blake disappeared, but I also think some of the officers were in on it. They jumped to the runaway conclusion way too fast."

I shook my head. "Why doesn't that surprise me? Daedalus has people everywhere."

"Your mom found the laptop Daemon bought you. I had to tell her that he got it for you. Anyway, she knew you'd never run away without a laptop."

I gave a short laugh. "That sounds about right."

She squeezed my hand again. "Your mom is doing okay, though, all things considered. She's really strong, Katy."

"I know." I looked at her then. "But she doesn't deserve this. I can't stand the idea of her not knowing what happened to me."

She nodded. "I've spent a lot of time with her, just hanging out and helping with the house until we left. I even kept your garden weeded. I thought that could somehow make up for everything we dragged you into."

"Thank you." I moved so I was facing her. "I mean that. Thank you for spending time with her and helping her out, but you guys didn't drag me into anything. Okay? None of this is your fault or Daemon's."

Her eyes glistened, and she said in a small voice, "You

really mean that?"

"Of course!" Shock rippled through me. "Dee, you guys didn't do anything wrong. This is all on Daedalus. That's who I blame. They are responsible. No one else."

"I've just been so upset. I'm happy to know that you don't feel that way. Ash said you probably hated me—hated us."

"Ash is a douche."

Dee laughed outright. "She can be sometimes."

I sighed. "I just wish there was something we could do other than just run."

"Yeah, me, too." Her knee bounced as she let go of my hand and tugged her ponytail down. "Can I ask you a question?"

"Sure."

She bit down on her lower lip. "How bad was it?"

I tensed. The one question I didn't want to be asked, but Dee waited, her expression so earnest that I had to say something. "Some days were better than others."

"I can imagine," she said softly. "Beth talked about it once. She said they would hurt her."

Thinking about my back, I pressed my lips together. "They do that. They did and said a lot of things."

She paled and several moments passed. "While we were heading here, Luc said that you . . . that Blake is dead. Is that true?"

I sucked in a sharp breath. Archer must've told him. "Blake's dead." I stood, tugging my hair back. "This isn't something I want to talk about—not any of the stuff that happened there. I'm sorry. I know you're just concerned. But it's not something I want to think about. It screws with my head."

"Okay. But if you ever do, you know I'm here for you, right?" I nodded, and Dee fixed a bright smile across her face. "So let's move on to better stuff. Like that fine-looking specimen of a man who came in with you—the one with the military cut?"

"Archer?"

"Yes. He's hot. And I'd spell that H-A-W-T."

I busted out laughing, and once I did I couldn't stop. Tears tracked down my face while she watched, perplexed. "What?" she demanded.

"I'm sorry." I wiped at my face with my fingers and plopped back down beside her. "It's just that I'm positive Daemon would stroke out if he heard that."

She scowled. "Daemon would stroke out if I showed interest in any kind."

"Well, Archer is different," I started slowly.

"Why? Because he's older? He can't be that much older, and besides, he's obviously a good guy. He risked his life to help you guys. But there is something different that I'm picking up on from him. Probably it's the whole military vibe."

I figured it was time to drop the bomb. "Archer isn't human, Dee."

Her frown deepened. "So he's a hybrid? Makes sense."

"Uh, no. He's, well, he's something different. He's what they call an origin—he's a kid of a Luxen and a hybrid."

After that sunk in, she shrugged. "So? I'm an alien. I'm not judgmental."

I smiled at that, glad she was showing interest in a guy after Adam. "Well, there's one more thing. I'd be careful of what you think around him."

"Why?"

"The origins have some freaky abilities," I explained, watching her eyes widen into saucers. "He can read your mind without you even knowing."

Dee's face went from pale to bright cherry. "Oh God."

"What?"

She smacked her hands over her face. "Well, the whole time we were downstairs, I was *so* picturing him naked."

After changing into an old terry-cloth tube dress that passed the show-no-scars test, I joined Dee and everyone downstairs. A massive dinner of extravagant levels followed, consisting of juicy fruits I didn't even know existed, tangy and sweet meats, and a salad that filled the biggest bowl I'd ever seen. I ate more than I'd thought humanly possible, even some of the grilled meat off Daemon's plate. Bethany had joined us, and she had hugged me the moment we crossed paths. Other than looking utterly worn out, she seemed fine, and her appetite rivaled my own.

Daemon nudged his plate over to me with his finger. "You're going to eat Lyla out of house and home."

Shrugging, I picked up another cube from his shish kebab and popped it into my mouth. "It's been so long since I had food that wasn't bland and served on a plastic tray."

He winced, and I immediately regretted saying that. "I—"

"Eat as much as you want," he said, glancing away. A muscle began to pulse in his jaw.

Then he piled more skewers on my plate, plus a handful of grapes and roasted pork loin, so much food that if I ate all of it, they'd have to roll me out of there. My gaze flicked away, meeting Dawson's. He looked . . . he just looked sad.

I reached under the table and placed my hand on Daemon's knee, giving it a squeeze. His head swiveled toward me, a deep brown curl falling across his forehead. I smiled for him, and it seemed to go a long way, because he relaxed once more.

And I ate as much food as I could stomach, knowing that it did something for Daemon. What it did exactly, I wasn't sure, but by the end of the dinner, he was being his usual charming and douchey self.

Our group moved outside after dinner. Daemon stretched out his happy ass on one of the white-cushioned lounge chairs, and I sat by his legs. The talk was light, what everyone needed. Luc and Paris joined us, as did Archer. Even Ash and Andrew weren't their normal antisocial selves.

Well, they really didn't talk to me, but they chimed in whenever Daemon or Dawson or Matthew made a comment. I didn't say much, mainly because I was busy paying attention to Bethany and Dawson.

They were just too adorable.

Sharing a chair, Beth sat in Dawson's lap, her cheek nestled under his chin. He continuously moved his hand up and down her back. Every so often, he'd murmur something in her ear, and she'd smile or laugh quietly.

When I wasn't watching them, I was keeping track of Dee.

Throughout the evening, she crept closer . . . and closer to where Archer sat chatting with Lyla. I was counting the minutes until Daemon noticed.

It took twenty.

"Dee," he called out. "Why don't you go get me a drink?"

His sister froze halfway between the patio table and the fire pit. Her luminous eyes narrowed. "What?"

"I'm thirsty. I think you should be a nice sister and get a drink for your poor brother."

Twisting at my waist, I shot Daemon a dirty look. He raised his brows at me and folded his hands behind his head. I turned back to Dee. "Don't you dare get him a drink."

"Wasn't planning on it," she replied. "He's got two legs."

Daemon wasn't deterred. "Then why don't you come over here and spend time with me?"

I rolled my eyes.

"I don't think there's room for me on that lounge." She folded her arms. "And as I much as I love you two, I don't want to get *that* close."

By that point, Daemon had successfully captured everyone's attention. "I'll make room for my sister," he cajoled.

"Uh huh." She spun around and stalked over to the patio.

Pulling out a chair, she plopped down next to Archer and shoved out her hand. "I don't think we've been officially introduced."

Archer glanced down at her slender hand, then at Daemon for the tiniest second, and then he took her hand. "We haven't."

Six feet and a lot of inches of alien stiffened behind me. Oh dear.

"I'm Dee Black. I'm the sister of the douchebag known as Daemon." She smiled brightly. "But you probably already know that."

"That he's a douchebag or that he's your brother?" Archer asked innocently. "The answer is yes to both."

I choked on my laugh.

Heat rolled off Daemon. "Am I also the brother who's going to kick your ass if you don't let go of my sister's hand? The answer is yes to that, too."

Dawson snickered from his chair.

I found myself smiling. Some things never changed. The overprotective side of Daemon was still an overbearing ass.

"Ignore him," Dee said. "He has poor social skills."

"I can vouch for that," I threw out.

Daemon knocked his foot off my hip, and I glanced back at him. He winked and said in a low voice, "*That* is so not happening."

Archer still hadn't let go of Dee's hand as he talked with her, and I wondered if he was doing that to goad Daemon or if he just wanted to hold her hand. Daemon opened his mouth to say something jerkish.

I grabbed his ankle. "Leave them alone."

"No can do."

Sliding my fingers under the hem of his jeans, I met his stare. "Please?"

His eyes narrowed into incandescent green slits.

"Pretty please?"

"Is there sugar on top?"

"Maybe."

"There has to be, and there better be a lot of sugar." He sat up fluidly and moved so that his knees were on either side of my hips. He wrapped his arms around my waist, resting his chin on my shoulder. I turned my cheek toward his. A shiver skated over my skin as his lips brushed my chin. "I needs lots of sugar," he added. "What say you?"

"Leave them alone and maybe," I replied, more than a little breathless at the prospect.

"Hmm . . ." He tugged me back into the *V* of his legs. "You drive a hard bargain."

Something really dirty popped into my head, and I flushed.

Daemon leaned back, head tilting to the side. "What are you thinking, Kitten?"

"Nothing," I said, biting my lip.

He didn't look convinced. "Are you having impure thoughts about *me*? Gasp."

"*Impure* thoughts?" I giggled. "I wouldn't go that far."

Daemon's lips brushed the lobe of my ear, and another shiver made its way down my spine. "I'd go that far and then some."

Shaking my head, I realized Daemon was thoroughly distracted from who Dee was talking to. She owed me. Not that being in Daemon's arms and feeling the length of him was a chore or anything. Not when his fingers started toying with the hem of my dress, the back of his hand lazily brushing my thighs.

Dawson and Beth were the first ones to call it a night. They shuffled past us, Beth sending me a smile and a soft "good night." Matthew and Lyla were next, though they seemed to go in different directions. I couldn't let myself entertain any other idea there. That would just be gross, because Matthew *had* been my teacher.

Night broke and everyone else headed inside, including Archer and Dee. As they entered the sunroom, Daemon craned his neck so far I thought his head would fall off, which was pointless because they both were going upstairs.

I decided to keep that observation to myself lest he go tearing after them.

Only Daemon and I remained in the courtyard, staring up at the star-ridden sky. As soon as we were alone, I crawled into his lap, tucking my head under his chin. Every so often he placed a kiss against my forehead, my cheek . . . my nose, and every time he did, he erased another minute of the time spent with Daedalus. His kisses really did have the power to change lives. Not that I'd admit that. His ego was ginormous as it was.

We weren't talking, because I think there was so much to say and, at the same time, there was nothing to be said. We were out of Area 51, and for that very second we were safe, but our future was unknown. Daedalus was searching for us, and we couldn't stay there forever. It was too close to Area 51, and with this kind of sizeable population there were too many prying eyes from people who would begin to ask questions. Luc had the LH-11, and we had no idea what it was truly capable of or why Luc wanted something so volatile. There were the hybrids and Luxen back at the facility and those kids . . . those freaky kids.

I had no idea what was going to happen from here on out, and even thinking about it scared the ever-loving crap out of me. Tomorrow wasn't guaranteed. Neither were the next couple of hours. My breath caught with that realization, and I stiffened. The next minute was unknown to us, and it might not even come.

Daemon's arms tightened around me. "What are you thinking, Kitten?"

I considered lying, but at that moment, I didn't want to be

strong. I didn't want to pretend like we had everything under control, because we didn't. "I'm scared."

He tugged me back against his chest and pressed his cheek against mine. The stubble tickled and, in spite of everything, I grinned. "You'd be insane not to be scared."

I closed my eyes, sliding my cheek against his. I was probably going to end up with carpet burn, but it would be worth it. "Are you scared?"

Daemon chuckled softly. "Me, seriously? No."

"You're too awesome for that?"

He kissed the sensitive spot under my ear, sending a wake of shivers through me. "You're learning. I'm proud of you."

I laughed.

Daemon stilled, like he seemed to do whenever I laughed, and then he squeezed me until I squeaked. "Sorry," he murmured, rubbing his nose against my neck as he loosened his hold. "I lied."

"About what? You being proud of me?" I teased.

"No. I'm always in awe of you, Kitten."

My heart did a little trippy-trip dance as I opened my eyes.

He let out a shuddering breath. "I was terrified the whole time they had you and I didn't know where you were. I was scared out of my mind that I would never see you again or get to hold you. And when I did see you? I was afraid I'd never hear you laugh again or see your beautiful smile. So, yeah, I lied. I was terrified. I'm still lying."

"Daemon . . ."

"I'm scared shitless that I'll never be able to make this up to you. That I'll never be able to give you back your life and—"

"Stop," I whispered, blinking back tears.

"I've taken everything from you—your mom, your blog, *your life*. So much so that you found *enjoyment* in eating something just because it wasn't on a plastic tray. And your back . . ." His jaw locked down, and he gave his head a little shake. "And I have no idea how I'm going to fix all of that, but I will. I will keep you safe. I will make sure that we have a future to hold on to and look forward to." He took a breath at the same time I did. "I promise you."

"Daemon, this isn't—"

"I'm sorry," he said, voice cracking. "This—all of this—is my fault. If I—"

"Don't say that." I turned in his lap, my dress riding up as I placed my hands on either side of his face. I stared into his brilliant eyes. "This isn't your fault, Daemon. None of this is."

"Really?" he said in a low voice. "I think the whole mutating-you thing was my fault."

"It was either that or let me die. So you saved my life. You didn't ruin it."

He shook his head, sending the short, dark waves across his forehead. "I should've kept you away since the beginning. I should've kept you safe so you never ended up getting hurt in the first place."

My heart ached at his words. "Listen to me, Daemon. This isn't your fault. I wouldn't change a damn thing. Okay? Yes, things have sucked, but I'd go through it all again if I had to. There are things I would want to change, but not you—never you. I love you. That's never going to change."

His lips parted on a sharp inhale. "Say it again."

I smoothed the pad of my finger over his lower lip. "I love you."

He nipped at my finger. "The other words, too."

Leaning down, I pressed a kiss to the tip of his nose. "I love you. That's never going to change."

He slid his hands up my back, one stopping just below my shoulder blade and the other cupping the nape of my neck as his eyes searched mine. "I want you to be happy, Kitten."

"I am happy," I said, tracing my fingers over the curve of his cheek. "*You* make me happy."

His chin lowered, and he pressed his lips to the tips of each of my fingers. Under and all around me, his muscles tensed, and then he placed his mouth to my ear and whispered in a deep voice, "I want to make you *really* happy."

My heart fluttered. "Really happy?"

He dropped his hands to my outer thighs, his long fingers slipping under the material. "Exceedingly, insanely happy."

I was breathless. "There you go again with the adverbs."

His hands inched up, causing heat to flood my body. "You love it when I whip out the adverbs."

"Maybe."

He trailed his lips in a hot line down my throat. "Let me make you exceedingly, insanely happy, Kat."

"Now?" My voice came out an embarrassing squawk.

"Now," he growled.

I thought about all the people inside the house, but then his lips were on mine, and it felt like forever since he'd kissed me. His hand moved into my hair as the kiss deepened, our breaths mingling. He dropped his arm around my waist, and then he was standing, and my legs were wrapped around his hips.

"I love you, Kitten." Another deep, scorching kiss lit up my insides. "And I'm going to show you just how much I love you."

24

My arms tightened around her as I waited for her answer. Not that I really believed she'd turn me down. It wasn't about that. I wanted to make sure she was ready after everything. Last time, she hadn't been ready, and it hadn't just been the headlights. If she wasn't, it'd be okay. Holding her all night would be just as amazing.

But I'd need a cold and really long shower.

Because having her in my lap, with the softest part of her pressed against the hardest part of me, was testing my self-control and had me turned on like no one in and beyond this world could.

Kat lifted her chin, her eyes locking with mine. Everything I needed to see, needed to believe in was in her eyes. "Yes."

I wasted no time after hearing that one little word. Doing this, being with her in every way that I could, wouldn't replace all the terrible things that had happened, but it was a start.

"Hold on," I told her, and then I captured her breathy response with a kiss.

She circled her arms around my neck as I gripped her hips. As I stood, her legs clamped down on me, and I bit back a groan. Surprised by the fact that I was even attempting to make it to a bed, I never took my mouth off hers. Kissing her. Drinking her in. It wasn't enough, could never be enough.

I carried her into the house and through the many useless rooms that would never, ever end, it seemed. She giggled against my mouth when I bumped into something that probably cost a small fortune. I found the stairs, climbed them without breaking both our necks, and found the bedroom I'd deposited our stuff in earlier.

Kat reached out, slapping at the air until she found the edge of the door and closed it behind us, just as I caught her lower lip with my teeth. A little nip, and the sound she made boiled my blood. I was going to combust before anything got started.

I turned us toward the bed, lifting my mouth from her warm lips. I wanted to strip the sheets and comforter and find richer, suppler coverings that were worthy of Kat.

She pressed a hot little kiss against my pounding pulse.

Screw finding better sheets.

I placed her down on the bed, moving slower than my body demanded. She sent me a tiny smile, and my heart turned over in my chest as I knelt on my knees before her. Our eyes locked.

My pulse pounded fast, feeling it in every part of my body. "I don't deserve you." The words came out before I could stop them. They were the truth. Kat deserved the world and then some.

Leaning forward, she placed her hand on my cheek, and I felt the touch through every cell in my body. "You deserve everything," she said.

I turned my head, kissing her palm. So many words came to the tip of my tongue, but when she stood and reached down, hooking her fingers under the hem of her dress, my heart stopped, and the words died in the silence between us.

Kat lifted the dress over her head and dropped it onto the floor beside me.

I couldn't move. I couldn't even get my lungs to function. Thinking became almost impossible as I stared up at her. She consumed me. Wearing nothing but a thin scrap of cloth, her hair tumbling down her shoulders and over her breasts, she stood there, looking like some kind of goddess.

"You . . . you are so beautiful." I stood slowly, my eyes following the slight flush down her neck. I grinned. "You're really beautiful when you blush."

She ducked her head, but I caught her chin, forcing her eyes back to mine. "Seriously," I told her. "Absolutely beautiful."

The tender, almost shy smile appeared again. "Flattery will totally get you everywhere right now."

I chuckled. "Good to know, because I'm planning on going everywhere—and taking the scenic route."

That flush deepened, but she grabbed at my shirt. I beat her to it. Tugging it over my head, I let it fall wherever her dress landed. For a moment, we stood there, separated by only a few inches. Neither of us spoke. A current of electricity filled the air, raising the hair along my arms. The pupils of Kat's eyes started to dilate.

Sliding a hand around the nape of her neck, I gently pulled her toward me. Then we were chest to chest, and the shudder that rolled through her short-circuited my senses. Her lips parted the moment they touched mine; her fingers found the button on my jeans, and my fingers discovered the delicate string resting on her hips.

I guided her to the bed, and her hair fanned out around her like a dark halo. Her eyes were heavily hooded as she watched me, but I could see the dim white glow radiating from them.

Her stare burned me from the inside. I wanted to worship her. I needed to. Every inch. Starting at the tips of her toes, I worked my way up. Slowly. Some areas held my attention a lot longer. Like the graceful arch of her foot and the sensitive skin behind her knees. The curves of her thighs enticed me, and the valleys above beckoned me. The way her back arched, her rapid breaths, soft sounds, and how her fingers dug into my skin rattled my world. When finally I climbed my way up to her, I placed my hands on either side of her head.

Staring down at Kat, I fell for her all over again. Lost my heart when she smiled. Found a whole new purpose when she reached between us and touched me. I broke away long enough to grab protection. And the moment there was nothing between us, there was no more waiting, any intentions of selflessness vanished. My hands were greedy. I was greedy, and my hands were everywhere, my lips following their path. Our bodies moved together like there had been no time separating us. And as I stared down at her, my gaze traveling over her flushed cheeks and swollen lips, I knew right then that there'd never be a more beautiful, more perfect moment in my life than this.

I was drunk on her taste, on her touch. There was only the sound of our pounding hearts, until she called out my name, and I broke apart. The room was awash in flickering white light; I wasn't sure if it was coming from her or me, and I didn't care.

For the longest time, I couldn't move. Hell, I didn't want to move. Not with her hands sliding down my back, her breathing ragged in my ears. But my weight had to be crushing her even if she wasn't complaining.

Lifting up, I rolled onto my side. My hand trailed over her rib cage, across her hip, and she turned in to me, wiggling so close that once again there wasn't an inch between us.

"That was perfect," she murmured sleepily.

I still wasn't capable of speech. God only knew what would come out of my mouth at that moment, so I placed a kiss against her damp forehead. She let out a contented sigh, and then she dozed off in my arms. I had been wrong before.

There was not a more perfect, more beautiful moment than *this*. And I wanted a lifetime of them.

{ Katy }

In the morning, our legs and arms were tangled together, and the sheet twisted around my hips. It took some ninja-stealth moves to wiggle free from Daemon. Stretching my arms above my head, I expelled a happy sigh. My body was one big pleasant ache.

"Mmm, that's sexy."

My eyes snapped open. Startled and exposed, I grabbed for the sheet, but Daemon's hand shot out, catching mine. Fire swept across my face as my gaze collided with his forest-green one.

"What?" he murmured lazily. "You're modest now? Don't really see the point."

Heat swept down my throat, and my skin prickled. Daemon kind of made sense. Modesty hadn't been anywhere last night, but still. Early morning sunlight streamed in from the window. I tugged the sheet from his grip and covered myself.

He pouted, and it was ridiculous that he could do it and still manage to look sexy.

"I'm trying to keep the mystery alive," I told him.

He chuckled, and the deep sound rolled through me. Shifting closer, he kissed the tip of my nose. "Mystery is overrated. I want to get to know every freckle and every curve on a personal level."

"I think you did that last night."

"Nah." He shook his head. "That was just a meet and greet. I want to know their hopes and dreams."

I laughed. "That's ridiculous."

"It's the truth." He rolled then, throwing the sheet off him and swinging his feet to the floor.

My eyes widened.

Naked as the day he was born, he stood fluidly, totally uncaring that every inch of him was displayed. He raised his arms high above his head as he stretched. His back bowed, muscles popped and rippled. The indents by his hips tensed, drawing my attention for far too long to be decent.

Finally, I forced my gaze up. Our eyes met. "You know, there's this thing called pants. You should try it out."

He cast me a cheeky grin as he turned. "You'd be devastated. Just think, you get to see this every day from here on out."

My heart did a trippy dance. "Your naked ass? Gee. Sign me up for that."

He laughed again and then disappeared into the bathroom. Feeling way too warm, I closed my eyes. Every day? Like, forever? That had my tummy fluttering in all kinds of pleasant loops that had nothing to do with his current state of undress. Waking up next to Daemon, going to sleep beside him?

I opened my eyes when I heard the door reopen. He was rubbing his eyes, and I was staring at him again, like really staring at him in completely inappropriate places. It was like knowing you shouldn't look at something, so your eyes automatically just want to go there.

He lowered his arm. "I think you're drooling a little."

"What? I am not." But I might have been. So I tugged the sheet up over my face. "A gentleman would never point out something so unseemly."

"I'm not a gentleman." He shot forward, snatching the sheet from me. I held on, the playful struggle not lasting very long. "There's no hiding. I caught you."

"You suck."

"At least I don't drool on myself." He tossed the sheet to the other side of the massive bed. His slow perusal caused my toes to curl. "Okay. I think *I* might be drooling right now."

My face was going to burn off before breakfast. "Stop it."

"I can't help it." He planted a hand on the other side of my hips and leaned in, brushing his fingers over my chin. "Got the drool."

Laughing, I pushed at his rock-solid chest. "You have an overinflated sense of self-worth."

"Uh huh." He pressed down until our bodies were flush and his thigh was between mine. He supported his weight on his arms as he bent his head, brushing his lips against mine. "Kiss?"

I gripped his upper arms and gave him a quick peck. "There you go."

He lifted his head, scowling. "That was the kind of kiss you give your grandma."

"What? You want a better one?" Craning my neck, I put a little more *oomph* behind the kiss. "How about that?"

"Sucked."

"That's not very nice."

"Try it again," he said, eyes narrowing into lazy slits.

My breath hitched in my throat. "I don't know if you deserve a better kiss after telling me the last one sucked."

He did something truly remarkable with his hips, causing me to gasp. "Yeah," he said smugly. "I deserve another kiss."

Yes—yes he did. I kissed him again but settled back before the kiss could turn into something deeper. Daemon's scowl went up a notch, and I grinned. "That's all you deserve."

"I strongly disagree with that." The tips of his fingers drifted down my arm and across my rib cage. The featherlight touch continued over my stomach and farther south. The whole time his gaze was held to mine. "Try again."

When I didn't move, he did something clever with his

fingers that caused my heart to pound against my ribs. I lifted my head, feeling dizzy and light. Brushing my mouth against his, I kissed him again, paying special attention to his lower lip. As I started to pull away, he wrapped his hand around the back of my neck.

"No." His voice was low. "That was barely better. Maybe I just need to show you."

I shivered at the heat in his stare. My entire body tightened. "Maybe you do."

And he did—oh God, did he ever. Last night had been sweet and slow and mind-blowingly perfect, but this was something entirely different and just as heart-stopping. There was a razor edge of desperation to each kiss, to each touch. A rawness had built between us, increasing with every breath we took. Daemon moved over me and then inside me, turning the slow fire into a tempest that burned out of control. My hands grasped at him as the tension inside me unfurled, and the edges of his body blurred as whatever restraint he had snapped.

Neither of us moved for what felt like ages. Our hips still pressed tightly together. My arms locked around his neck. One of his hands lay against my cheek, the other curved around my waist. Even when he rolled onto his side, he brought me with him. He didn't have much of a choice. I wasn't letting him go. I didn't want to. I wanted to press stop on everything and stay there, right there with him. Because I knew the moment we left this bed, left this room, an unknown reality waited. Serious stuff needed to be decided. Decisions that none of us could go back on had to be made.

But I thought about the every-morning thing—the forever. No matter what we faced, we would face it together. That made me ready.

"What are you thinking about, Kitten?" he asked, brushing the hair off my cheek.

I opened my eyes and smiled. "I was just thinking about the things we need to decide on."

"Me, too." He kissed me. "But I think we need to be showered and changed before we go down that road."

I laughed. "True."

"Have I told you that I love the sound of your laugh? Doesn't matter. I'm going to tell you again. I love the sound of your laugh."

"And I love you." I pressed my lips to his and then sat up, taking the sheet with me. "I call dibs on the shower."

Daemon rose up on his elbow. "We can always do it together."

"Yeah, we'd end up needing a shower after taking a shower." Wrapping the sheet around me, I scooted off the bed. "I'll be back."

He winked. "I'll be waiting."

{ Daemon }

If I'd had any doubts about Kat being the perfect female before, all doubts would've been cleared up right then. She took a shower in less than five minutes. Remarkable. I hadn't even thought that was humanly possible. Dee's idea of a quick shower was fifteen minutes.

And then she came out, a towel secured under her arms, as she dabbed at her soaked hair. When she looked over at the bed, a pretty flush crawled across her cheeks.

Guess I could've put some clothes on, but then I'd miss that blush of hers.

Throwing my legs off the bed, I strolled over. As I passed her, I tweaked her pink cheek. Her face flamed even brighter, and I laughed as she muttered something very unladylike under her breath.

The bathroom was nice and steamy. As I stood under the showerhead, letting the water beat down on my face, I thought about last night, about this morning. My thoughts spun further back, to the first time I'd seen Kat walking out her front door, heading over to my house to ask directions. Even if I hadn't wanted to admit it in that moment, she had sunk her claws into me, and I didn't want them out.

At that point, my brain pretty much unloaded a bunch of crap on me. Bringing up memories I'd almost forgotten—of Kat arguing with me over the flower bed and refusing to go to the lake with me the day Dee had hid my keys. Like I had needed my keys to go somewhere. Even then I'd been looking for a reason to spend time with her. There were so many moments. Like when she went ninja on the Arum after homecoming. She had risked her life for me, even when I'd been nothing but a giant tool to her. And Halloween night? She would've died for Dee and me.

I would've died for her.

Where would we go from there? Not just where would we end up living or any of that crap, but both of us had and would sacrifice just about anything for each other. There was a next step involved. I thought about the car ride there, when I'd been staring at her left hand.

My heart did a funny thing in my chest, something between a panicked squeeze and an excited jump. I dipped my head back under the stream. Something was building in my chest, piling up until there was no denying what I wanted. My hands curled into fists against the tile.

Shit.

Was I really thinking this? Yes. Did I really want this? Hell yes. Was it probably the craziest thing I'd ever considered? Most definitely. Was it going to stop me? Nah. Did I feel like I was going to pass out? Only a little.

I'd been in the shower for more than fifteen minutes.

I was such a girl.

That panicked/excited feeling was increasing as I turned to the faucets, shutting the water off. My hand trembled a little, and my eyes narrowed.

I should really think about this.

Then again, who was I kidding? When I set my mind to something, I did it. And my mind was set. No pussyfooting around it. No point in waiting. It was right. It *felt* right. And that's what mattered—the only thing that mattered.

I was in love with her. I would always be.

Wrapping a towel around my hips, I entered the bedroom. Kat sat on the bed, cross-legged in jeans and wearing her My Blog Is Better than Your Vlog shirt. Yep, that pretty much sealed the deal for me.

"So I was thinking," I said, my mouth moving before my brain really caught up with it. "There're eighty-six thousand, four hundred seconds in a day, right? There're one thousand, four hundred and forty minutes in a day."

Her brow knitted. "Okay. I'll take your word for it."

"I'm right." I tapped my finger against my head. "A lot of useless knowledge up here. Anyway, are you following me? There're one hundred and sixty-eight hours in a week. Around eighty-seven hundred and then some hours in a year, and you know what?"

She smiled. "What?"

"I want to spend every second, every minute, every hour with you." Part of me couldn't believe something that cheesy had come out of my mouth, but it was also so beautifully true. "I want a year's worth of seconds and minutes with you. I want a decade's worth of hours, so many that I can't add them up."

Her chest rose sharply as she stared at me, eyes widening.

I took one more step and then went down on one knee in front of her, in a towel. Probably should have put some pants on. "Do you want that?" I asked.

Kat's eyes met mine, and the answer was immediate. "Yes. I want that. You know I want that."

"Good." My lips curved up. "So let's get married."

25

Time stopped. My heart skipped a beat and then took several leaps. My stomach felt like I was hurdling mountains. I stared at him so long that one single dark brow rose.

"Kitten . . . ?" He tipped his head to the side. Strands of wet hair fell across his forehead. "Are you breathing?"

Was I? I wasn't sure. All I could do was stare at him. He couldn't have said what I thought he had. *Let's get married.* The statement, because I was pretty sure it wasn't a question, came so far out of left field that I was stunned.

A lopsided grin appeared on his face. "Okay. Your silence is stretching out further than I'd thought it would."

I blinked. "Sorry. It's just . . . what did you ask me?"

He chuckled deeply and reached over, threading his fingers through mine. "I said: let's get married."

Sucking in another deep breath, I squeezed his hand as my heart did another flip. "Are you serious?"

"Serious as I'll ever be," he replied.

"Did you hit your head in the bathroom? Because you were in there a long time."

Daemon barked out a laugh. "No. Should I be offended by that question?"

I flushed. "No. It's just . . . you want to marry me? Like, really get married?"

"Is there more than one kind of marriage, Kitten?" His lips were tilting up again. "It wouldn't be legal, because we'd have to use our new IDs, so in a way, it wouldn't be real, but it would be real to me—to *us*. I want to do this. Right now. I don't have a ring, but I promise I'll get you one worthy of you when things . . . things die down. We're in Vegas. No better place. I want to marry you, Kat. Today."

"Today?" My voice came out a squeak. I thought I might faint.

"Yes. Today."

"But we're . . ." We were young, but really, was there such a thing as too young for us? I was eighteen, months shy from turning nineteen. I had always pictured being at least in my mid-twenties before I tied the knot, but our future was so unknown to us. And it wasn't the common world that people faced every day, not knowing how short their lives may very well be. We were on the sucky statistic side of things not working in our favor. If we didn't manage to make it into hiding and were captured again, I doubted Daedalus would be so keen on allowing us to be together. That is, if we survived any of this. We didn't have the guarantee of years to figure out our relationship.

"But what?" he asked softly.

I wasn't sure we needed those years to determine if we wanted to be together. I knew right that second that I wanted to spend the rest of my life with Daemon, but it wasn't that simple. Something else could be driving this decision of his.

He squeezed my hand. "Kat?"

My heart was going crazy fast. I felt like I was on top of a roller coaster. "Are you wanting to do this because tomorrow may never come? Is that why you want to marry me? Because there might not be a later to do this?"

He leaned back. "Can I say that doesn't play some role in wanting to do this now? No. It does. But it's not the sole reason or even the major reason why I want to marry you. It's more like the catalyst."

"The catalyst," I whispered.

He nodded. "I'm going to do everything in my power to make sure nothing bad happens. I will do anything to make sure we have the time for *everything* that we want, but I'm not stupid enough to disregard the fact that something may happen that I can't control. And, dammit, I don't want to look back and see that I didn't seize the chance to make you mine, to really prove that I want to spend the rest of my life with you. That I lost that opportunity."

Air hitched around the sudden lump in my throat. Tears burned my eyes.

"I want to marry you because I'm *in love* with you, Kat. I will *always* be in love with you. That's not going to change today or two weeks from now. I will be just as in love with you in twenty years as I am today." He let go of my hand and rose slightly, cupping my cheek. "That's why I want to marry you."

The tears welled up, and a few snuck out. He caught each one with his thumb. "Are the tears a good or a bad thing?"

"It's just . . . that was such a beautiful thing to say." I wiped at my face, feeling like an overemotional fool on the verge of having a stroke. "So you really want to get married today?"

"Yes, Kat, I really want to get married."

"In a towel?"

His head tipped back, and he let out a deep laugh. "Maybe I'll put some clothes on."

My thoughts raced. "But where?"

"There are tons of places in Vegas."

"Is it safe to go out there?"

He nodded. "I think so, if we're quick about this."

A quickie marriage in Vegas? I almost laughed because we would be just one in a million who came to Vegas and got married. Some of the numbness faded with the acknowledgment of how . . . common it was to do this.

To get married.

My heart did a backflip.

"If you're not ready, that's okay. We don't need to do this," he said, his eyes meeting mine. "I'm not going to be upset if you don't feel it's the right time, but I am going to ask one more time. You don't even have to say no. Just don't say anything. Okay?" He took a little breath. "Will you make me the luckiest bastard on Earth and marry me, Katy Swartz?"

My breath shuddered. Tension rolled through my entire body. I'd imagined a proposal being very different than this. It never involved a towel, and I'd have a long engagement, plan a wedding, and have family and friends witness the moment, but . . .

But I was in love with Daemon. And like he'd said, I'd be in love with him tomorrow and twenty years from now. That was never going to change. The emotions were complex, but the answer was simple.

I took a breath, and it felt like the first breath I'd ever taken. "Yes."

He stared at me in wonder. "Yes?"

I nodded vigorously, like a seal. "Yes. I will marry you. Today. Tomorrow. Whenever."

In the blink of an eye, he was standing, and I was captured in his strong embrace. His arms were tight around me, my feet several inches off the floor, and his mouth was on mine. That kiss was more a stake of claim than any marriage certificate could be.

I came up for air, clutching his shoulders. He'd started to

glow a beautiful soft white as he stared back at me with a look of awe in his expression. I smiled. "Well, let's get this show on the road."

{ Daemon }

I wouldn't let Kat change her shirt. I had a fondness for it. After all, it was the first shirt I'd seen her in, and I thought it was fitting.

Feeling like I might have just climbed Mount Everest in a second, I quickly changed into a pair of jeans and a shirt. Okay. Maybe not quickly. I kept getting distracted with Kat's lips, because those lips had said yes, which made them suddenly something I couldn't stop touching.

They were swollen by the time we made it downstairs. Still early, only Lyla was up. I had no qualms about asking her to borrow a car, because I didn't want Kat to hoof it into Vegas. Lyla easily gave up her keys to a Jag, which I traded in for a Volkswagen I saw in the garage, along with two more cars she owned. My fingers itched to get behind the wheel of a Jag, but that would draw way too much attention.

I honestly didn't think we'd run into any problems. The last place Daedalus would be looking for us would be at a place we could get married, but I took the same appearance of the guy I'd used in the motel, and we found a floppy sun hat and glasses for Katy.

"I look like a fake celebrity," she said, staring at herself in the side mirror. She twisted toward me. "And you're kind of hot."

I snorted. "I'm not sure if I should be bothered by that."

She giggled. "You know, Dee is going to kill us."

We'd decided not to tell anyone. Mainly because Matthew would probably object, Dee would freak out, and, honestly, we wanted to do this alone. It was our moment. Our little slice of pie that we weren't sharing.

"She'll get over it," I said, knowing that was doubtful. Dee would probably kill me for not being able to take part. Coasting the VW out of the driveway and down the access road, I reached over and patted Kat's thigh. "Serious moment, okay? When all of this crap is settled, if you want the big wedding and all that jazz, I'll make it work. You just need to tell me."

She took off her oversize sunglasses. "Big weddings cost a lot of money."

"And I have a lot of money stashed away. Enough to make sure we have nothing to worry about until we figure out what we're doing, so more than enough to cover a wedding."

She shook her head. "I don't want the big wedding. I just want you."

I almost stopped the VW right there and crawled all over her. "Just keep it in mind for later if you change your mind." I wanted to give her everything—the ring that weighed her finger down and the wedding to end all weddings. Neither was feasible right now—and, I had to admit, I was turned on by the fact she didn't seem to care about either of those things.

Okay. I was almost always turned on by her, but that was beside the point.

"You know where I want to get married? Married. Wow. I can't believe I just said that. Anyway," Kat said, her eyes lighting up under the brim of her hat. "I want to do the little church—the one everyone goes to Vegas to get married at."

It took me a moment. "You mean The Little White Wedding Chapel? The one in *The Hangover*?"

Kat laughed. "It's sad that's how you know the church, but yes. I think there are a couple of them in Vegas. And it should be perfect. I doubt they require much but the fee and an ID."

I shot her a grin. "If that's what you want, you got it."

It didn't take us long to get into Vegas and to stop at one of the tourist vendors. Kat hopped out and grabbed a handful of brochures. One of them was about the chapel. Apparently impromptu weddings were a big theme. Duh.

We had to get a marriage license.

She frowned. "I don't want to do it under our fake names."

"Neither do I." I pulled up in front of the courthouse, letting the engine run. "But it's too risky to use our real names. Besides, we'll need the marriage license under our useable ID. You and I will always know the difference."

She nodded and grabbed the door handle, but her fingers slipped off. "You're right. Well, let's do this."

"Hey." I stopped her. "You're sure, right? You want this?"

She faced me. "I'm positive. I want this. I'm just nervous." Leaning in, she tipped her head to the side and kissed me. The edge of her hat brushed my cheek. "I love you. This . . . this feels right."

Air punched from my lungs. "It does."

Sixty dollars later, we had a marriage license in hand, and we were en route to the chapel on the Boulevard. Since our fake IDs were under the images of our real selves, I'd have to change back over once we pulled into the parking lot.

The whole drive, I kept an eye out for anyone suspicious. The problem with that was that everyone looked suspicious to me at the moment. Even as early as it was, the streets were teeming with tourists and people heading to work. I knew there could be implants anywhere, but I doubted there'd be one dressed as Elvis or hidden in a chapel.

Kat squeezed my arm when the sign for the chapel came into view. The heart on the side was a nice, gaudy touch. "The Little White Wedding Chapel isn't so little," she said as I turned into the parking lot.

I parked the car, and as I pulled the keys out of the ignition, I slid back into the form Kat was accustomed to.

An amused smile lit her face. "Better."

"I thought the other guy was hot?"

"Not as hot as you." She patted my knee, then pulled back. "I've got the license."

Turning to the window, I almost couldn't believe that we were here. Not that I was having second thoughts or anything, but I couldn't believe we were actually doing this, that in an hour or so, we'd be man and wife.

Or Luxen and hybrid.

We hurried inside and met with the "wedding planner." Handing over our license, IDs, and the fee, we got the ball rolling. The bleach-blonde behind the counter tried selling us every package they had, including the ones where we could rent a tux and gown.

Kat shook her head. She'd taken off the hat and sunglasses. "We just need someone to marry us. That's all."

The blonde flashed an ultra-white smile as she leaned against the counter. "You two lovebirds in a hurry?"

I dropped an arm over Kat's shoulders. "You could say that."

"If you just want something quick, no bells and whistles or a witness, then we have Minister Lincoln. He's not included in the fee, so we do ask for a donation."

"Sounds good." I bent down, brushing my lips along Kat's temple. "You want anything else? If so, we'll do it. Whatever it is."

Kat shook her head. "I just want you. That's all we need."

I smiled and glanced at the blonde. "Well, there you go."

The woman stood. "You two are adorable. Follow me."

Kat bumped me with her hip as we trailed behind the blonde entering the "Tunnel of Love"—and boy did I have a ton of nasty comments building up in me about the name of that. I'd save them for later.

Minister Lincoln was an older man who looked more like a grandfather than some guy who married people on a whim in Vegas. We chatted with him for a few minutes, and then we had to wait for another twenty while he finished up a few things. The delays were starting to make me paranoid, and I expected an army to storm the chapel any second. I needed a distraction.

I pulled Kat onto my lap and circled my arms around her waist. While we waited, I told her about the ceremonies my kind did, which were very much like a human wedding with the exception of rings.

"Is there anything you do in its place?" she asked.

Tucking her hair back behind her ear, I smiled a little. "You'll think it's gross."

"I want to know."

My hand lingered along the curve of her neck. "It's kind of like a blood oath. We're in our true form." I kept my voice low, just in case anyone was listening, though I was sure stranger things were heard in the Tunnel of Love. "Our fingers are pricked and pressed together. That's about it."

She lightly stroked my hand. "That's not too gross. I was expecting you to say something like you have to run around naked or consummate the relationship in front of everyone."

I dropped my head to her shoulder and laughed. "You have such a dirty mind, Kitten. That's why I love you."

"That's all?" She wiggled down so that her cheek was beside mine.

My grip tightened. "You know better than that."

"Can we do it—what your kind does—later?" she asked, tapping her finger on my chest. "When things die down?"

"If that's what you want."

"It is. I think that would make it more real, you know?"

"Miss Whitt? Mr. Rowe?" The blonde appeared at the opened doors. I was sure the tan chick had a name but couldn't recall it for the life of me. "We're ready when you are."

Hoisting Kat to her feet, I took her hand. The chapel portion was actually pretty nice. Enough room if you wanted people to be there. White roses were everywhere—on the ends of the pews, bouquets of them in the corners and hanging from the ceiling and placed upon the pedestals at the front. Minister Lincoln stood between the pedestals, holding a bible in his hand. He smiled when he saw us.

Our steps made no sound on the red carpet. Actually, we could've been stomping our feet and I wouldn't have heard it over the pounding of my heart. We stopped in front of the minister. He said something. I nodded. God only knew what it was. We were told to face each other, and we did, our hands joined.

Minister Lincoln kept talking, but it was like Charlie Brown's teacher, because I didn't understand a single word of it. My gaze was locked on Kat's face, my attention focused on the feel of her hands in mine and the warmth of her body next to me. At some point I heard the important words.

"I now pronounce you husband and wife. You may kiss the bride."

I think my heart exploded. Kat was staring up at me, her gray eyes wide and misty. For a moment, I couldn't move. Like I was frozen for a precious few seconds, and then I was moving, cupping her cheeks and tilting her head back. I kissed her. I'd kissed her at least a thousand times before this, but this one—oh, yeah—this one was different. The touch and taste of her reached down into me and branded my soul.

"I love you," I said, kissing her. "I love you so very much."

She gripped my sides. "And I love you."

Before I knew it, I was smiling, and then I was laughing like an idiot, but I didn't care. I pulled her into my arms, cradling her head against my chest. Our hearts were racing, beating in tandem—*we* were in tandem. And in that moment, it seemed like everything we'd been through, everything we'd lost and had to give up, was worth it. This was what mattered—would always matter the most.

26

Feeling like one of those cartoon characters that daintily raised a leg when she was kissed by Prince Charming, I was dizzy with happiness and absolutely swept off my feet in a way I never believed possible. It was just a piece of paper I clenched in my hand. A certificate of marriage between two names that weren't even real.

But it meant the world.

It meant everything.

I couldn't stop smiling, nor could I get the emotional lump out of my throat. Since we'd exchanged vows, I'd been in a constant state of almost crying. Daemon probably thought I was insane.

On the way out, the blonde from the front stopped us. She handed me a photo. "On me," she said, smiling. "You two are a beautiful couple. It would be a shame if you didn't have something to capture the moment."

Daemon peered over my shoulder. The photo was of our kiss—our first kiss as a married couple. "Good Lord," I said, feeling my cheeks burn. "I'm pretty sure we're eating each other's faces."

He laughed.

The blonde smiled as she stepped aside. "I think that's the kind of passion that lasts a lifetime. You're lucky."

"I know." And in that instant, I did know how lucky I was, all things considered. I looked up at my . . . *my husband*. Deep down, I knew the marriage wasn't legal, but it felt real to me. My eyes wanted to start with the waterworks again. "I do know how lucky I am."

Daemon rewarded me with a scorching kiss that lifted me clear off the floor. Any other time I would've been embarrassed by that, since we were in public, but I didn't care. Not at all.

We totally cornballed it up on the way back to the house, holding hands and making googly eyes. It took us a couple of minutes to get out of the car. The moment he turned off the engine, we were all over each other. Greedy—we both were so greedy. The kissing wasn't enough. I crawled over the gearshift, straddling his lap. My hands were under his shirt, against the ridges of his stomach. He slid his hands up my back, tracing the line of my spine until his fingers tangled in my hair.

I was breathing heavily when he pulled back, pressing his head against the seat. "Okay," he said. "If we don't stop, we're going to do something very naughty in this car."

I giggled. "That's one hell of a way to pay her back for letting us borrow it."

"No doubt." He reached over and opened the driver's door. Cool air washed over us. "You better get going before I change my mind."

I wasn't sure if I wanted him to change his mind, but I forced myself to climb out of the car. Daemon was right behind me, his hands on my hips as we entered the house through the door that led into a small pantry.

Matthew was in front of us the moment we stepped into the

kitchen, blue eyes flashing with anger. "Where in the hell have you two been?"

"Out," replied Daemon. He stepped around, blocking most of Matthew.

"Out?" Matthew sounded flabbergasted.

I peeked around Daemon, holding the license close to my chest. "I wanted to see a few things."

Matthew's mouth dropped open.

"I really don't think that was a good idea," Archer said, appearing in the open archway. "To go sightseeing when you have half the government gunning for your ass."

Daemon stiffened. "It's all good. No one saw us. Now if you would excuse us . . ."

Archer's eyes narrowed. "I can't believe you two . . ."

The whole time he was talking, I was singing "Don't Cha" in my head, desperately trying not to think about the marriage, but one of us must've failed, because Archer's mouth snapped shut, and he looked floored. Like someone just explained to him that you can have an endless salad bowl at Olive Garden.

Please don't say anything. Please. I kept thinking the words over and over, hoping he was peeping in my head at the moment.

Matthew glanced back at Archer, brows furrowed. "You okay, bud?"

Shaking his head, Archer pivoted on his heel and muttered, "Whatever."

"I know you're butt sore about this, Matthew. We're sorry. We'll never do it again." Daemon reached back, finding my hand. He started forward. "And you can yell at us all you want in about . . . five or so hours."

Matthew folded his arms. "What are you up to?"

Sliding past him, Daemon cast him a cheeky grin. "It's not

what. More like who." I smacked his back, which was ignored. "So can your epic lecture hold off for a little while?"

Matthew really wasn't given a chance to say any more. We breezed out of the kitchen and through a purposeless room with lots of statues and a table in the middle. Dee's and Ash's voices echoed from another room.

"We'd better hurry," Daemon said, "or we'll never get away."

Though I was eager to spend some quality time with Dee, I knew why we were hurrying. Halfway up the stairs, Daemon turned and wrapped his arm under my knees, picking me up.

Biting back on the giggles, I looped my arms around his neck. "That's not necessary."

"Totally is," he said, and then made like an alien. Within seconds, he was placing my feet on the floor of the bedroom and closing the door behind us.

Clothing didn't stay on very long. Things were fast and tumultuous at first. He spun around, backing me up until I hit the door, his large body crowding mine. There was something different about what was happening. It seemed truer in its nature, as if that funny piece of paper that was now lying on the floor changed everything, and maybe it did. My legs were wrapped around his hips, and everything moved at a fevered pitch. I told him that I loved him. I showed him that I loved him. And he did the same. We finally made it to the bed, and things were sweet and tender then.

Hours passed, probably a little more than the five that Daemon had promised Matthew. No one had interrupted us, which was surprising. I was mighty comfortable in his arms, my cheek resting against his chest. I know it might sound stupid, but I loved listening to his heartbeat.

Daemon played with my hair, twisting strands around his fingers while we talked about anything and everything that had nothing to do with the immediate future and everything to do with the one we hoped for—the one where we were in college, we had jobs.

We had a life.

It was good, like cleansing the soul in a way.

Then my stomach grumbled like Godzilla.

Daemon chuckled. "Okay. We've got to get some food in there before you start gnawing on me."

"Too late," I said, nipping at his lower lip. He made that sexy sound in his throat, the kind that led to things that would take up another couple of hours. I forced myself to put some distance between us. "We need to go downstairs."

"So you can eat?" He sat up, running a hand through his hair. He looked adorably disheveled.

"Yeah, but we also need to find out what everyone is doing." Reality was a bit sobering. "We need to figure out what *we're* doing."

"I know." He bent over the edge of the bed and picked up my shirt. He tossed it to me. "But there better be food involved."

Thank God there was. Dee was in the kitchen making a late lunch—or was it an early dinner?—consisting of cold cuts. Daemon headed off toward the sound of his brother's voice, and I sidled up to Dee.

"Can I help?" I asked, rocking back.

She glanced at me. "I'm almost done. What kind do you want? Ham? Turkey?"

"Ham, pretty please." I grinned. "Daemon probably wants ham, too. And I can make them if you haven't."

"Daemon wants anything he can consume." She reached up, grabbing a paper plate. I thought it was kind of funny that this house even had paper plates in it. As she slapped two ham sandwiches on it, a burst of loud, male laughter caused her to glance over her shoulder. She looked relieved.

"What?" I asked, glancing back to the hall Daemon had disappeared down.

"I don't know." A small smile appeared. "I'm just surprised. Archer is in that room. I figured there'd be yelling instead of laughter."

"Daemon is just . . . you know, a bit overprotective when it comes to you."

His sister laughed. "A bit?"

"Okay. A lot. It's not against Archer. He's actually a really good guy. He helped me—helped us—while we were with Daedalus, but he's older, he's different, and he—"

"Has a penis?" Dee supplied. "Because I think that's Daemon's main problem."

Giggling, I grabbed two cans of soda. "Yeah, you're probably right. So have you been talking to him?"

She shrugged. "Not much. He's not very talkative."

"He's a guy of few words." I leaned my hip against the counter. "And he hasn't been exposed to a lot. So he's probably just taking all of this in."

She gave a little shake of her head. "It's just insane and horrible what they're doing to people. And there's more, right? I wish there was something we could do."

I thought about the hybrids I'd seen and the origins we let loose. Could some of them have escaped? Setting the cans aside, I sighed. "There's so much wrong with so much."

"That is true."

There was another explosion of laughter that I recognized as Daemon's. I was smiling like a goofball before I even realized it.

"Look at you. Aren't you chipper today." Dee elbowed me. "What's going on?"

I shrugged. "Just a really good day. I'll have to tell you about it soon."

She handed me a cold cut. "If it's what you two have been doing in that room upstairs all afternoon, I don't even want to know."

I laughed. "I'm not talking about that."

"Thank God." Ash slinked between us, grabbing the jar of mayo. "Because no one wants to hear about that."

Unless it involved Ash's past with Daemon, then she was all kinds of talkative, but whatever. I smiled at her, which earned me a strange look.

Ash grabbed a spoon, scooped up some mayo, and popped it in her mouth. My stomach turned. "The fact that you're so damn skinny and you eat mayo by the spoonful is universally messed up."

She winked a catlike eye. "Be jealous."

The funny thing was, I wasn't.

"Then again, maybe I'm the one who should be jealous, *Kitten*."

Dee smacked Ash's arm. "Don't start."

She grinned as she tossed the spoon in the sink. "I didn't say I wanted to be his Kitten, but if I did, well . . . this story may have a different ending."

A couple of months ago, she would've gotten a rise out of me. Now I just smiled.

She stared at me a moment, and then her blue eyes rolled. "Whatever."

I watched her leave the kitchen. "I think I'm growing on her," I said to Dee.

She giggled as she put the last sandwich on the platter. There were more than a dozen. "Actually, I think the biggest problem is that Ash *wants* to dislike you."

"She does a good job at it."

"But I don't think that's how she really feels." Dee picked up the platter, cocking her head to the side. "She really did care for Daemon. I don't think it was ever love, but I think she always believed that they'd be together. That's a lot to get over."

I sort of felt guilty. "I know."

"But she will. Besides, she'll find someone who can tolerate her bitchiness, and all will be right in the world."

"And you?"

She giggled and winked. "I just want everything to be right in the world for *one* night—if you know what I mean."

I choked on my laugh. "Good God, do not let Daemon or Dawson hear that."

"No kidding."

Everyone was in the rec room—bodies draped over couches, settees, and lounges. The biggest TV I'd ever seen hung on the wall, damn near the size of a theater screen.

Daemon patted the spot beside him on the couch, and I sat down, handing him his plate and soda. "Thank you."

"Your sister made them. I just carried ours."

Dee placed the platter on the coffee table and glanced over to where Archer sat with Luc and Paris. Then she took two sandwiches and retreated to the burgundy settee. Two pink spots bloomed on her cheeks, and I hoped she was having nice, clean thoughts.

One glance at Archer, who was now staring at Dee, had me assuming that she wasn't.

On the other side of me, Dawson leaned forward and grabbed two of the subs, one for him and the other for Beth. The girl was bundled up in a quilt, looking half asleep. Our eyes met, and a tentative smile brightened her face.

"How are you feeling?" I asked.

"Great." She picked at the bread, pulling off little brown patches. "I'm just tired."

Again, I wondered what could possibly be wrong with her, because something was. She didn't look just tired; she looked absolutely exhausted.

"It's been a lot of traveling," Dawson elaborated. "It's kind of worn me out, too."

He didn't look worn out. If anything, he looked like he was

bursting at the seams. His green eyes were particularly bright, especially every time he looked at Beth.

Which was all the time.

"Eat," he said quietly to her. "You need to eat at least two of these."

She laughed softly. "I don't know about two."

We stayed there for a while, long after the food was gone, and I think everyone was delaying the inevitable—the big talk. So much so that Matthew left the room, telling us he'd be back in a few moments.

Daemon leaned forward, dropping his hands to his knees. "Time to get down to business."

"True dat," Luc said. "We need to get on the road soon. Tomorrow would be best."

"I think that's assumed," Andrew said. "But where exactly on the road are we heading to?"

Luc opened his mouth, but Archer held up a hand, silencing him. "Hold that thought."

The younger origin's eyes narrowed, but then he sat back, his jaw clenched. Archer stood and strode out of the room, hands closing into fists.

"What's going on?" Daemon asked.

Unease snaked down my spine. I glanced over at Dawson, who also was suddenly on alert. "Luc," I said, feeling my heart trip up.

Luc stood, his chest rising sharply. One second he was standing in front of the settee and the next he was across the room, a hand around Lyla's throat. "How long?" he demanded.

"Holy shit." Andrew jumped to his feet, moving in front of his sister and Dee.

"How long?" Luc demanded again, his fingers tightening on her throat.

Blood drained from the female Luxen's face. "I-I don't know what you m-mean."

Daemon stood slowly and stepped forward. His brother was behind him. "What's going on?"

Luc ignored him, lifting the frightened Luxen off the floor. "I'm going to give you five seconds to answer the question. One. Four—"

"I didn't have a choice," she gasped out, clutching the boy's wrist.

My blood chilled.

Understanding rippled across the room, followed by horror. I moved closer to Beth, who was struggling to unwrap herself from the blanket.

"Wrong answer," Luc said, voice low as he dropped Lyla. "You always have a choice. It's the one thing that no one can strip from us."

Luc moved so quickly that I doubted even Daemon could fully track what he did. His arm shot out. White swirled down his arm, exploding from his hand. A wave of heat and power flowed through the room, blowing the hair back from my face.

The energy smacked into Lyla's chest, throwing her backward into the oil painting of the Vegas Strip. A look of shock crossed her face, and then there was nothing. Her eyes were blank as she slid down the wall, her legs tucking under her.

Oh my God . . . I stepped back, clamping my hand over my mouth.

There was a hole in Lyla's chest. Smoke wafted out of it.

A second later, she blurred like bad reception, and then she was in her true form, the luminous glow fading until it revealed the translucent skin and network of dull veins.

"Care to explain why you just killed our host?" Daemon asked in a dangerously even voice.

Archer reappeared in the wide opening of the room, one hand clamped on the back of Matthew's neck and a crushed phone in the other. Blood trickled out from Matthew's nose, a deeper red with a blue tint to it.

Daemon and Dawson shot forward. "What the hell?" Daemon's voice thundered through the house. "You have two seconds to answer that question before I tear this room apart with your ass."

"Your friend here was making a phone call." Archer's tone was flat, so calm that a shudder worked its way through my muscles. "Tell them, Matthew, tell them who you were calling."

There was no response from Matthew. He just stared at Daemon and Dawson.

Archer's grip tightened, jerking Matthew's head back. "The bastard was on the phone with Daedalus. He screwed us. Bad."

27

Daemon stepped back, actually physically recoiling from the accusation. "No." His voice was hoarse. "No way."

"I'm sorry," Matthew said. "I couldn't let this happen."

"Let what happen?" Dee said. Her face was pale as her hands clenched at her sides.

Matthew didn't take his eyes off Daemon. His voice, his entire being pleaded with Daemon to understand the unthinkable. "I can't keep losing you all—you're my family, and Adam is dead. He's dead because of what Daedalus wants. You have to understand. It's the last thing I wanted to go through again."

A cold sensation raced through my veins. "Again?"

Matthew's vibrant blue eyes slid toward me, and it was like the shutters were off. For the first time, I saw the distrust and the loathing in his stare. So potent and powerful, it reached across the room and latched onto me. "*This* is why we don't mix with humans. Accidents happen, and it's in our nature to save the ones we love. That's why we don't love humans. It leads to this! The moment one of us gets involved with a human, Daedalus is only a few steps behind."

"Oh my God." Dee clasped her hands over her mouth.

Paris *tsk*ed softly. "That is a terrible reason to betray those you consider family."

"You wouldn't understand!" Matthew struggled free from Archer's grip. "If I have to sacrifice one to save everyone else, I will. I *have* done it. It has been for the best."

I was dumbfounded. Struck absolutely stupid for a few seconds, but then I thought of that night Daemon and I had gone to Matthew after we saw the Arum go into the house with Nancy—the same night Matthew had confirmed that if Beth was alive, Dawson had to be.

There had been so much that Matthew had known that we never questioned. And the fact that he knew about this place and never mentioned it before? Horror rose in me as I stared at him.

Luc cocked his head to the side. "What did they offer you? Everyone would go free if you turned over just one of them? An equal exchange. A life for a handful of others?"

I was going to be sick.

"They wanted Daemon and Kat," he said, his gaze sliding back to Daemon. "They promised that everyone else would walk away from this."

"Are you insane?" shrieked Dee. "How is that helping anyone?"

"It will!" Matthew roared. "Why do you think they left Daemon and you alone? You two knew about Dawson's relationship and that Bethany knew the truth about us. All of you were at risk. I had to do something."

"No." Beth's quiet voice shook the room. "My uncle was the one who turned us—"

"Your uncle confirmed what was suspected," Matthew spat. "When they came to me about you two, they gave me an option. If I told the truth about the extent of your relationship and what you knew, everyone else would be left alone."

"You son of a bitch." The edges of Daemon's body started to blur. "You turned over Dawson to them? My brother?" Venom dripped from his words.

Matthew shook his head. "You know what they do to Luxen who break the rules. They are never heard from again. They threatened to take you all in." He spun toward Ash and Andrew. "Even you. I had no choice."

Energy crackled through the room.

"Yeah, they end up in Daedalus," Archer said, his hands flexing. "Right to the same place you just sent Daemon and Katy."

"You told them about Beth and me?" Dawson's voice broke halfway through.

Matthew nodded his head again. "I'm sorry, but you exposed everyone to them."

Daemon looked stricken, as if he'd been sucker punched, but the sudden heat rising in the room wasn't coming from him. It was from Dawson. A fine current of energy rolled out from him.

"It's the same now." Matthew pressed his hands together, as if he were about to pray. "All they want is Daemon and Katy. Everyone else, including you and Beth, will walk away from this. I had to do it. I have to protect—"

Dawson reacted so quickly that if anyone in the room wanted to stop him, he or she didn't have a chance. Rearing back, he sent a blast of pure, unstable energy straight into Matthew. The bolt slammed into Matthew's chest, spinning him around.

I knew Matthew was dead before he hit the ground.

I knew it was Dee who screamed.

I knew it was Daemon who grabbed my arm and pulled me from the room.

I knew it was Archer's voice that rose above the chaos, joining Daemon's in issuing orders.

And I knew we had to get out of there. Fast.

But I never expected that Matthew would do something like this, or that Dawson would kill him without so much as blinking an eye.

"Stay with me, Kitten." Daemon's deep voice glided over my skin. We were passing the kitchen. "I need you to—"

"I'm fine," I cut in, watching Luc spin around to pull a thunderstruck Ash into the foyer. "They're coming. Now."

"You can bet your little behind on that," Archer said, reaching behind him. He pulled out a gun.

"I don't like you talking about Kat's behind, but besides that, where are we going?" Daemon asked, his grip on my hand tightening. "What's the plan? Run out of here like we're insane?"

"Sounds about right," Andrew said. "Unless we all want to get carted away."

"No." Luc kept a careful eye on Dawson and Beth. The Luxen was still sprouting some major rage face. "We head out of town, toward Arizona. I got a place those assholes won't find. But we have to get out of the city."

Daemon glanced at his brother. "Sound good to you?" When Dawson nodded, Daemon let go of my hand and stepped up to his brother, clasping him on the shoulder. "You did what you had to do."

Dawson placed a hand over Daemon's. "I'd do it again."

"All right, family bonding time aside, anyone who gets into one of these cars outside is in it for the long haul," Paris said, shaking a set of car keys. "If you even think you're not ready to put your life on the line for everyone here, then you stay behind. If you screw us out there, I will end you." He flashed a rather charming smile. "And I will probably enjoy it."

Daemon cut him a dark look but said, "I second that."

"I'm already in it this far," Andrew said, shrugging. "Might as well go all the way."

Everyone looked at Ash.

"What?" she said, tucking short strands of hair behind her ears. "Look. If I didn't want to take part in this craziness, I would've stayed home, but I'm here."

She had a point, but I wanted to ask why she or Andrew would risk everything when they weren't fans of Beth or me. Then it hit me. It wasn't about us. It was about Daemon and Dawson—it was about family.

I could get behind that.

We hurried toward the front door, but at the last second, I grabbed Daemon's arm. "Wait a minute! I need to go upstairs."

Archer whirled around. "Whatever it is, we can leave it. It's not important."

"*Daemon . . .*" My fingers dug in. I assumed everyone else had their IDs. I didn't know, but we *needed* our papers. We had to have them.

"Shit." He got what I was talking about. "Go ahead outside. I'll be faster."

Nodding, I darted around him and rejoined Archer. "Really?" he growled in a low voice. "Those *papers* are that important."

"Yes." We didn't have rings. We didn't have a certificate under our real names and, yeah, it wasn't *real*, but we had that license, our fake IDs, and right now those things meant everything. They were our future.

Dawson already had Beth loaded in the backseat of an SUV. Ash and Andrew were climbing in with them.

"Go with them," I told Archer, knowing he'd keep them safe. "We'll go with Paris and Luc."

Archer didn't hesitate. He intercepted Dawson and got behind the wheel. "You want me driving in case stuff goes down. Trust me."

Dawson didn't look convinced, and in that moment he was an exact replica of his brother, but he did something Daemon pretty much never did. He didn't argue. Just got in the passenger side and shut up.

A second later, Daemon appeared behind me. "They're in my back pocket."

"Thank you."

We climbed into the Hummer, Paris behind the wheel and Luc in the front. Luc twisted around as we slammed the doors shut. "Sorry about Matthew," he said to Daemon. "I know you were close. He was family. That sucked. But people do sucky things when they're desperate."

"And dumb," Paris muttered under his breath.

Daemon nodded as he settled back against the seat. He glanced at me and lifted the arm closest to me. I didn't hesitate. Heart aching something fierce, I scooted over and pressed against his side. His arm came around me, his fingers digging into my arm.

"I'm sorry," I whispered to him. "I'm so sorry."

"Shh," he murmured. "You have nothing to be sorry for."

There was a lot to be sorry for. Things I couldn't really even wrap my head around as we peeled out of the driveway. And the other things, like the fact that Daedalus was most likely en route right now? Yeah, I couldn't think about that. Panic was already simmering inside, wanting to sink its claws in me. I'd be useless freaking out.

The gate up ahead wasn't opening. Daemon held on tight as Paris didn't break. He plowed through the metal gate.

"Good thing we're in a Hummer," Luc said.

Daemon reached for the seat belt. "You really should be wearing this."

"What about you?" I let him buckle me in the middle seat.

"I'm harder to kill."

"Actually . . ." Luc drawled the word out. "I'm probably the hardest thing to kill."

"Special snowflake syndrome strikes again," Daemon muttered.

Luc snorted as Paris hit breakneck speed on the narrow road, Archer close behind us. "Did Daedalus ever show you their neatest weapon?"

"They showed us a lot of things," I said, lurching sideways as Paris hit a curve.

"How about that special gun of theirs?" Luc put a foot up on the dashboard, and I hoped the airbag didn't deploy anytime soon. "The one that can take out a Luxen with one shot—the PEP? Pure Energy Projectile."

"What?" My stomach dipped as I glanced back and forth between Luc and Daemon. "What kind of weapon is that?"

"It's some kind of energy pulse that disrupts light waves—high tech. Kind of like onyx, but much worse." Daemon's brows lowered. "I didn't see it, but Nancy told me about it."

"It's an electromagnetic weapon," Luc explained. "And it's very dangerous to anything around it. If they break it out, they aren't messing around. The damn thing will disrupt signals and can even hurt humans since the brains, lungs, and heart are all controlled by low-voltage electricity. The Pulse Energy Projectile isn't fatal for humans in a low frequency, but it is catastrophic to our kind at any frequency."

Ice drenched me. "One shot?"

"One shot," Luc repeated gravely. "You two probably have nothing to worry about, since they want you alive, but you need to realize that if they bring out the big guns, people are going to die."

I froze, unable to drag in a breath. More people would die. "We can't let that happen." I twisted toward Daemon, going as far as the seat belt let me. "We can't let people die because—"

"I know." Daemon's jaw set with determination. "We can't go back, either. We just have to get out of here before we need to worry about anything like that."

My heart pounded in my chest as I glanced at Luc. He didn't look so convinced. I knew Daemon was trying to reassure me. I appreciated that, but guilt piled on top of the terror. If anyone died . . .

"Don't," Daemon said quietly. "I know what you're thinking. Don't."

"How can I not think about that?"

Daemon didn't have an answer. The creeping terror was like an endless hole, growing in size as we neared the teeming city at dusk. The red and blue neon lights of the billboards and flashing lights were harsh instead of welcoming.

Traffic had ground to a halt south of the Boulevard, an endless stream of vehicles that was more parking lot than road.

"Well, shoot." Paris smacked his hands on the steering wheel. "This is inconvenient."

"Inconvenient? Understatement of the year." Daemon gripped the back of his seat. "We need to get out of traffic. We're sitting ducks here."

Paris snorted. "Unless you have a hovercraft in your back pocket, I don't see how I'm supposed to get us out of here. There are side roads we can take, but they're farther down this road."

With shaky fingers, I unbuckled the seat belt and scooted forward until my knees pressed against the center console. A quick glance back confirmed that Archer was there. "Why isn't the traffic moving at all? Look." I pointed. The line of cars heading out of the city stretched all the way from the Caesar's Palace sign and down. "It's *completely* stopped."

"There's no need to panic yet," Paris said. A cheerful smile crossed his face. "It's probably just an accident or a naked person running through traffic. It happens. We're in Vegas, after all."

Someone outside laid on a horn. "Or the more likely scenario is that they have the traffic blocked at the interstate exit. I'm just saying," I said.

"I think he's trying to look on the bright and stupid side of things, Kitten. Who are we to bring a dose of reality into the mix?"

Running my sweaty palms over my thighs, I started to respond when a hushed sound caught my attention. Leaning back, I peered out the passenger window. "Oh, crap."

A black helicopter flew over the city, incredibly low. It looked like the whirling blades would clip a building at any second. It could be any helicopter, but I had a sinking feeling that it was Daedalus.

"I'm going to check this out," Luc said, reaching for the door. "Stay here. I'll be right back."

Luc was out of the Hummer and slinking around cars before any of us could respond. Irritation flashed across Daemon's face. "Do you think that was smart?"

Paris laughed. "No. But Luc does what Luc wants. He'll be back. He's good like that."

A soft knock on the back window caused me to jump out of my skin. It was only Dawson.

Daemon rolled the window down. "We got problems."

"Figured. Traffic not moving at all? Not good." Dawson leaned in. As always, seeing them together was a little disconcerting at first. "Luc up there?"

"Yeah," I said, pressing my hands between my knees.

Someone behind Dawson, in the other lane, whistled. He ignored it.

Luc returned. As he climbed into the Hummer, he tugged his loose hair into a stubby ponytail. "Guys, I have bad news and I have good news. What do you want first?"

Daemon's knuckles turned white from where he was gripping the seat. I knew he was about two seconds from smacking one of the guys up front. "I don't know. How about you start with the good?"

"Well, there is a barricade up the road about a mile in. That gives us some time to think of something."

My words came out hoarse. "That's the *good* news? What in the hell is the bad news?"

Luc grimaced. "The bad news is they got, like, a SWAT team moving up the line of cars, checking each one, so the time to make a decision is sort of limited."

I stared at him.

Daemon made a masterpiece out of F bombs. He pushed back from the seat, rocking the car. A muscle flexed in his jaw. "This is not how we're going to go down."

"I would like to think it's not," Luc replied. He looked out the front window, shaking his head slowly. "But even I'm thinking the best case is to ditch the cars and run."

"Run where?" Dawson asked, eyes narrowing. "There's nothing but desert on either side of Vegas, and Beth—" He pushed off the car, thrusting his fingers through his hair. "Beth can't run for miles. We need another plan."

"You got one?" Paris quipped. "Because we're all ears."

"I can't." Dawson dropped his hand to the window. "If you guys want to run, I understand, but Beth and I will have to hole up somewhere here. You leave—"

"We're not splitting up," Daemon cut in, his voice sharp with anger. "Not again. We all stay together, no matter what. I have to think of something. There has to be something . . ." He trailed off.

My heart skipped. "What?"

Daemon blinked slowly, and then he laughed. I frowned. "I have an idea," he said.

"Waiting." Luc snapped his fingers.

Daemon's eyes narrowed on the kid. "You snap your fingers at me and I'll—"

"Daemon!" I shouted. "Focus. What's your idea?"

He turned to me. "It's risky, and it's completely insane."

"Okay." I pulled my hands free. "Sounds like something you'd come up with."

Daemon smirked, and then his gaze focused on Luc. "It's something you said before. About their strength being in the fact that no one knows about them—no one knows about *us*. We change that, we get the upper hand. They're going to be too busy doing damage control to look for us."

My brain hardly digested that. "Are you suggesting that we expose ourselves?"

"Yes. We go out there, and we make the hugest scene possible. Get the humans wound up. Create a big enough scene to cause a diversion."

"Like at Area 51? Except this time . . ." This would be epic and completely uncontrollable.

Dawson smacked his hands down on the side of the Hummer, earning an outraged look from Luc. "Then let's do it."

"Wait," Paris said.

Ignoring him, Daemon reached for the door handle. There was a series of clicks, and Daemon got nowhere. He turned a stunned look on Paris. "Did you just hit the childproof locks on me?"

"I did." Paris threw his hands up. "You need to think about this first."

"We don't need to think about anything," Dawson said. "It's a good enough plan. We cause enough chaos, we should be able to slip out."

Luc leaned over his seat, on his knees. His amethyst eyes fixed on the brothers. "Once we do this, there's no going back. Daedalus will be even more pissed and gunning for us."

"But it will give us time to get away," Daemon argued. His pupils were starting to glow. "Or do you have a problem with cutting them off at the knees?"

"A problem?" Luc laughed. "I think it's brilliant. Honestly, I'd love to see the looks on their faces when there are Luxen walking around on the evening news."

"Then what's the problem?" Dawson demanded, giving a quick glance to the line of cars ahead. There wasn't any movement yet.

Luc smacked the back of the seat. "You all just need to be sure about what you're planning to unleash. It's not just Daedalus, but the entire Luxen community that is going to be upset. Me? I'm all about causing a rebellion—and this will be a rebellion."

"There are others," Paris added quickly. "They will use this for their own benefit, Daemon. They will take advantage of the chaos."

I swallowed hard, thinking of that nasty percentage of Luxen Dasher had mentioned. "We're stuck between a mountain and a volcano about to explode."

Daemon's eyes met mine. I already knew what he'd decided. When it came down to his family and the rest of the world, he would choose his family. He put his hand on the handle. "Open the door."

"You sure?" Luc said solemnly.

"Just make sure there aren't any humans hurt," I said.

A wide, wild smile broke out across Luc's face. "Well then, it's time to introduce the world to a little bit of extraterrestrial awesomeness."

28

{ Daemon }

This had to be one of the craziest stunts I'd ever pulled. Not only was I throwing everything in the face of Daedalus and the DOD, I was breaking every rule the Luxen lived by. This decision didn't affect just me, it affected everyone. Something this massive should make me hesitate at least a little bit. Make me rethink things, come up with another route.

But there wasn't time. Matthew . . . Matthew had betrayed us, and now we were here on the verge of being caught.

Like I said before, I'd burn down the world to keep Kat safe. The same went for my family. This would just be a different kind of fire.

People were already watching us, trying to figure out why we were abandoning our cars as we walked back toward where Archer waited behind the wheel. I knew the fact that Dawson and I were walking together was driving a lot of the attention.

"I already know." Archer killed the engine. "I think it's crazy, but it could work."

"What is crazy?" Dee asked from the front seat, which was duly noted. She must've been chomping at the bit to get her butt up there the moment Dawson got out.

"We're basically trapped in this line of cars," I told her, leaning in the window. "They have the road blocked up ahead, and there's a group of soldiers searching vehicles."

Beth sucked in a sharp breath. "Dawson?"

"It's okay." He was immediately at the back door, opening it. "Come here."

She slipped out of the SUV and planted herself to his side.

"We're going to cause a little bit of trouble to distract them," I said, eyes narrowing on the two. Something was definitely up, more than the overprotectiveness that might run in the family, but I didn't have time for that. "Hopefully we can get the roads cleared at the same time and get the hell out of here."

"Call me cynical, but how are we going to get this cluster-fuck cleared and get out without being stopped?" Andrew asked.

"Because it's not a little bit of trouble we're going to cause," Archer explained, opening the door and forcing me to take a step back. "We're going to light up the Vegas strip like they've never seen before."

Dee's eyes went wide. "We're going to show our true selves?"

"Yep."

Ash leaned forward. "Are you insane?"

"Quite possibly," I answered as I knocked a strand of hair out of my eyes.

Archer folded his arms. "Need I remind everyone that by getting in that car back at the house, you agreed that you'd be down for just about anything? This would be the part of 'anything' Paris had been talking about."

"Hey, you have no arguments from me." Andrew grinned, hopping out. "So we're exposing ourselves?"

Kat made a face, and I almost laughed. Andrew did seem way too excited about this.

He stopped at the front of the SUV. "You have no idea how badly I've wanted to freak out a few humans."

"I'm not sure if I should be offended by that or not," Kat mumbled.

He winked, and I felt a rumble move up my chest. "You're not too human anymore," Andrew pointed out and then grinned at me. "When do we do this?"

We were minutes away from nightfall. "Now. But—pay attention—we don't split up too far. We keep everyone in eyesight. Either I or . . ." The next words took a lot for me to say. Physically hurt my soul. "Or Archer will let everyone know when it's safe to get out of the city. If our wheels are gone—"

"God I hope not," Luc whined.

I shot him a look. "If our wheels are gone, we'll get the next best thing. Don't worry about it. Okay?"

There were a few nods. Ash still looked like we'd lost our damn minds, but Dawson tugged her out of the SUV. "I need you to do something big for me, okay? A huge favor," he said.

Ash nodded seriously. "What?"

"I need you to stay with Beth. Keep her out of the way and safe if anything starts to go wrong. Can you do that for me? She's my life. If anything happens to her, it happens to me. You understand?"

"Of course I can," Ash said, taking a deep breath. "I can keep her out of trouble while you guys run around glowing like a bunch of fireflies."

Beth scowled. "I can help, Dawson. I'm not—"

"I know you can help, baby." He placed his hands on her cheeks. "I don't think you're weak, but I need you to be careful."

She looked like she was about to argue, and I was starting to get antsy *and* feel bad for my brother. God knew I'd spent way too much time arguing with Kat about not running in front of a firing squad. Speaking of which . . .

"Don't even say it," Kat said without looking at me.

I chuckled. "You know me too well, Kitten."

Beth relented and was handed off to Ash. Thank God, because people were starting to follow our trend, getting out of their cars and milling around. Some guy opened a can of beer and plopped down on the hood of his car, watching dusk deepen into a dark blue. I could go for a beer right about now.

"Ready?" I said to Andrew.

Andrew cracked his neck. "This is going to be awesome."

"Please be careful," Ash pleaded.

He nodded. "I'm cool." Then he swaggered past where I stood. "Cause a scene? Got it."

Turning around, I felt the need to hold my breath. There was no going back. Out of the corner of my eye, I saw Ash usher Beth through the backed-up lane and to the median. They stopped under a cluster of palm trees.

"Stay close to me," I told Kat.

She nodded as she watched Andrew easily navigating the cars. "Not going anywhere." Pausing, she bit down on her lower lip. "I almost can't believe you guys are going to do this."

"Me neither."

Kat looked at me, and then she laughed. "Are you having second thoughts?"

I grinned wryly. "A little late for that."

And it was. Andrew stepped up on the sidewalk, heading toward a ginormous pirate ship. Dozens of people were behind him. Many of them had cameras hanging from around their necks. Perfect.

"What do you think he's going to do?" Kat asked, still nibbling on her lower lip.

I had to give it to her. She was trying so hard to be brave, but I could see her hands shaking and the way she kept glancing up toward the bend, where Daedalus would surely be making their way toward us. She was strong, and I was constantly in awe of her.

"How do you say it?" I said, drawing her attention. "He's going to go all Lite-Brite on us."

Her eyes lit up. "This should be fun."

Andrew hopped up on the retaining wall of the pool the boat was rigged over. I tensed as several of the humans turned to him. It seemed like time froze for a full minute, and then, with that shit-eating grin on his face, Andrew spread out his arms.

The edges of his body blurred.

I heard Kat's sharp inhale.

No one noticed the minute difference at first, but then the haze shifted over Andrew's white shirt and down the rest of his body.

A low murmur rose from the crowd.

Then Andrew faded out. Gone. Poof.

Shouts of surprise were a crescendo, a symphony of excited squeals and sounds of confusion. Motorists gawked from inside their cars. People stopped mid-step on the crowded sidewalk, creating a domino effect.

Andrew reappeared in his true form. Nearly six and a half feet, his body shone brighter than any star in the sky or light on the Strip. A pure white light with edges tinged in blue. His light was like a beacon, forcing everyone and anyone on the street to look at him.

Silence.

Man, it was so quiet you could hear a grasshopper karate chop a fly.

And then thunderous applause drowned out my expletive.

Andrew was up there, standing in front of a damn pirate ship, glowing like someone shoved a nuclear weapon up his ass, and people were cheering?

Paris chuckled as he stepped up beside me. "Guess they've seen weirder stuff on the streets of Vegas."

Huh. He had a good point.

Soft flashes of light from cameras flickered all through the crowd. Andrew, who apparently was a showman at heart, bowed and then straightened. He did a little jig.

I rolled my eyes. Seriously?

"Wow," Kat said, her arms falling to her sides. "He didn't just do that."

"Time for me to join the fun," Paris said, striding forward. He made it to the car in the next lane, a red BMW driven by a middle-age man, and then slipped into his true form.

The man jumped out of his car, shuffling backward. "What the . . . ?" he said, staring at Paris. "What the hell is going on?"

In his true form, Paris drifted among the cars, heading toward the crowd gathered in front of the pirate ship and Andrew. He stopped just short, and his light pulsed once, bright and intense. A wave of heat blew off him, forcing several of the gawkers to take a hurried step back.

Dee hopped up on one of the cars several feet back and stood tall and straight, the slight breeze picking up her long hair, tossing it around her face. Within seconds, she was in her true form.

The couple in the car darted out and rushed to the sidewalk, where they spun around and stared openmouthed at Dee.

Dawson was next. He stayed near Beth and Ash, on the other side of the congested road. When he took his true form, several people let out startled shrieks.

"I mean it, Kitten, stay close to me."

She nodded again.

Off in the distance, I could hear the helicopter. No doubt it was circling back to make another run at the Boulevard. It was about to get all kinds of real.

Unease grew among the humans, becoming as thick as the heat-clogged air. It seeped into me, making me itchy as I let my human form slip away.

Like someone pressed a universal pause button, the humans around us seemed frozen. Their hands clenched on cameras and cell phones. The awe in their expressions changing from surprise to confusion, and then fear slowly crept in. Many were exchanging glances. Some were starting to move away from Andrew, but they couldn't get far on the congested sidewalks.

We need to turn this up a notch. Dawson's voice filtered through my thoughts. *See the Treasure Island sign? I'm going to take it out.*

Make sure no one is hurt, I said.

Dawson floated a step back. Raising an arm, he looked like he was reaching up into the sky to grab a star. Energy crackled in the air, charging it with static. The Source flared, wrapping down his arm like a snake. The burst of light shot from his palm, shooting high into the sky and racing across the four lanes. It arched over the pirate ship, striking the white bulkhead.

Light exploded in a flash, turning night into day for a brief second. The energy rolled across the sign and then shot down, flaring out the eye sockets of the giant skull under the sign in a shower of sparks.

Andrew had spied the Venetian tower and all the pretty golden lights at the top. He turned to me. Twisting at the waist, I summoned the Source. It really was like taking a nice deep breath after being underwater for several minutes. Light arced from my hand, smacking into the tower, taking out the lights in a shower of fireworks.

That's about when people realized that this wasn't some kind of show, an optical illusion or something to stand around and point at. They might not have understood what they were seeing, but whatever instinct humans possessed that triggered that flight response kicked in.

It became all about survival—about getting away from the big, bad unknown—while trying to snap pictures of the spectacle at the same time.

Got to love the near-innate human response to capture everything on film.

People scurried like ants, running in every direction, abandoning their cars in their rush. They streamed out of the streets, a flood of different shapes and sizes, pushing into one another, falling over their own feet. Some guy knocked into Kat, forcing her away from the SUV. For an instant, I lost sight of her in the pandemonium.

I rushed forward, parting humans like the Red Sea. Their excited screams were already an annoying buzz in my ears.

Kat!

Her answer was both in my head and out loud. "I'm here!"

She stumbled around a woman who had frozen in front of me. The look of shock on the lady's pale face roused a bit of guilt in me, but then Kat was in front of me, her eyes wide.

"I think we got a lot of people's attention," she said, dragging in air.

You think? I touched her arm, overly glad at the welcoming spark that traveled from her skin to mine.

Luc appeared beside us, along with Archer. "We should move some of the cars out of the way?"

Good idea. Keep Kat with you.

I centered my attention on the line of cars in front of us. Four lanes. All packed with vehicles ranging from ones on their last leg to luxury cars I was really sad about scratching.

Archer joined me. "I'll help."

He took one lane while I focused on the one in front of the Hummer. The ability to repel things away from us was easier than pulling it toward us. It was the release of energy, like a shockwave.

Stretching my arms out, I watched the car before me start to shake, its rims rattling and gears grinding. Then it shifted to the side. One after another, cars were sliding out of the way like an invisible giant had swiped its arm across the road. I went as far as I could see, then pulled back, knowing that Daedalus already had to be aware of what was going on.

Turning back to where Andrew stood, I saw him shooting off blasts of energy like there was no tomorrow. Hidden behind an empty tourist bus was a teenage guy, filming it all on his phone.

A bit of restlessness trickled through my veins. This would be all over YouTube in seconds. Off in the distance, I could hear sirens. With the way traffic was backed up behind us, I doubted they'd be here soon.

"Look!" Kat shouted and pointed to the sky.

Overhead, a helicopter circled the scene, shining floodlights over where Andrew stood. It wasn't the military. A KTNV 13 News emblem was emblazoned on the side. Damn. They'd gotten here before the police.

"This will be live," Kat said, stepping back. Her eyes were wide. "They'll be filming live—it'll be *everywhere*."

I don't know why it didn't sink in until that moment. Not like I didn't fully grasp what this would mean, but seeing the news copter circling the Boulevard struck home. The images were fed into the newsrooms, and from there it would be signaled out to the entire nation within *seconds*. The government could take down a few videos here and there, even a hundred of them, but this?

They couldn't stop *this*.

Right now people were most likely sitting in front of their TVs, watching this unfold and having no idea what they were really seeing, but knowing that what they were viewing was something serious.

"Something epic," Luc threw out, meaning he was being a peeping bastard. "You did it, man. They can't lock this down. The world will know humans aren't the only life-form chilling on this planet."

Yeah, it was going to be . . . epic.

My gaze crawled along the road. There were still a lot of people fixated on what Andrew and Dawson were doing. Both were zipping back and forth across the road, practically skipping over the cars behind us like an alien game of Frogger.

That was what people all across the world were seeing.

There was no way that could be explained away. Daedalus was going to freak.

"That's what you wanted, right?" Archer frowned as a man darted across the street. "Go public. You got—"

A dark helicopter flew in from between two large hotels—a large black bird. It didn't take a genius to realize *that* was a military copter. It flew overhead but didn't shine any lights down like the news copter was doing, tracking the movements of Dawson and Andrew.

It circled around Treasure Island, disappearing behind the wide hotel. The feeling of unease magnified. Reaching out, I wrapped my fingers around Kat's wrist and at the same time yelled for my brother.

He stopped on top of a red BMW, crouched in his true form. When he picked up what I was feeling, he shot off the car, grabbing Dee from the car behind him and bringing her down to road level.

Not a second too soon, either.

The black bird circled back around, rising high in the sky as it flew sideways, as if it were lining itself up . . .

"I have a real bad feeling about this," Luc said, walking backward. "Archer. You don't think—"

I saw it first—the tiny spark from the bottom of the military bird. It was nothing. Just a minimal flare of light and shouldn't have turned my insides cold or stopped me dead in my tracks. What came out of the copter moved too fast for human eyes to track. The stream of white smoke against the dark blue sky told me all I needed to know.

Whirling around, I pulled a stunned Kat against my chest and brought us both down to the warm pavement, curving my body over hers.

A loud *crack* caused her to jerk in my arms, and I tightened my hold.

Horror settled in my gut like stones. Anger was an acid in my veins. The news copter spun erratically as smoke billowed out of the tail. It whirled across the sky, its floodlights dipping and rising over the pirate ship and beyond. The copter kept spinning, falling out of the sky, heading straight for Treasure Island.

The explosion rocked the cars. Kat screamed as she twisted in my arms, trying to look up. But I didn't want her to see it. I held her down, pressing her face against my chest. I knew my touch was hot and had to be nearly unbearable this long, but I didn't want her to see this.

Oh my God . . . Someone's thoughts mirrored my own. Dawson? Dee? Archer? Luc? One of the Thompsons? I didn't know.

Flames shot out of the center of the hotel, an orange glow that quickly crawled up the trembling structure. Plumes of thick smoke rose, darkening the sky.

Archer was frozen beside the Hummer. "They did it. Holy . . . They shot it down—the military *shot* them down."

29

{ Daemon }

Panic erupted, the kind of which I'd never witnessed before. People streamed out of the hotel—the ones who'd been able to escape—and spilled into the pavilion and the streets.

Still in my true form, I pulled Kat off the street. She was saying something, but her words were lost in the screams. Christ. I never expected this—I never thought they'd go after humans, but I had underestimated the extent to which they'd go to keep us secret.

"But it's too late," Luc said, grabbing the arm of a woman who'd tripped and went down on her hands and knees. He pulled her up. The side of her face was a mess of raw tissue and burns. "There's no stopping what has already been seen. And look."

I twisted around, bringing Kat with me. She'd been staring at the woman's mangled face for too long. The man who'd been in the car Dee had jumped on was still filming everything—us—on his phone.

Shielding Kat, I turned back to Luc. He had his hand on the woman's forehead, and she stood as still as a statue. He was healing her.

"Go," Luc ordered when he finished. The woman stared back at him. She was in some kind of costume—leather bra and skirt. *"Go."*

She scrambled off.

Archer swung around. "They're coming."

They were.

Men dressed in SWAT gear edged along the sides of the street—not Vegas SWAT. Daedalus—military. And their guns were big.

PEP.

They shot first—a flare of red light aiming straight for Andrew.

Andrew avoided the hit, flying off the retaining wall and rearing back. A bolt of energy streaked out from him, slamming into the ground before the advancing men. The pavement cracked and rolled, knocking several of them off their feet. Guns fired. Red light flashed into the sky.

There were more—men in camo behind those in black.

"Shit," Archer groaned. "This is about to get bad."

Thanks for the update, Captain Dickhead. Shoving Kat behind me, I slammed my foot down, sending a fissure through the road. Raising my arms, I let the Source roll through me.

Placing my hands on the bumper of a Mercedes in front of me, I sent a shock of electricity dancing over the exterior. I lifted it up, tossing it like a Frisbee toward the advancing soldiers, who scattered like cockroaches. It flew through the air, rolling and rolling until it smacked into a palm tree, taking it out.

Red light pulsed, flying over our heads and between Archer and me, narrowly missing Luc. I turned slowly. *Oh no, no you did not.*

Energy burst from me in a tumultuous wave, smacking into four of the five soldiers, throwing them back into the tourist bus.

Another blast went off to our right, and I spun, grabbing Kat as I saw Paris dart in front of me. He slammed into Luc, knocking him out of the path of the PEP.

Paris took a direct hit.

He jerked to a stop, his body spasming as his form shifted from human to Luxen, back and forth. Electricity crawled across his body, blowing out at his elbows and kneecaps. He went still, his light dulling until he crumbled to the ground. Shimmering blue liquid pooled underneath him.

Dead.

Luc let out an inhuman sound, and a bright glow swallowed him. He rose several feet into the air, static and little fingers of light crackling out from under his body. His light flared once, as bright as the sun at noon, and then there were screams. The smell of burned flesh permeated the air.

Shots rang out, zinging past my head and smacking into the cars. The cavalry had arrived, it appeared, with good old-fashioned guns.

Dawson zipped up to my side, his fingers brushing the back of a sedan. It was flung at the bus, pinning the soldiers.

Stay behind me, I warned when I felt Kat inching around me.

I can help.

You can die. So stay behind me.

Anger radiated from her, but she gritted her teeth and stayed back. There were bigger problems. The grinding of heavy tires drew our attention. Clearing the road had worked against us. A fleet of Humvees came out of the smoke, and a— *Is that a tank?*

"You have got to be kidding me," Kat said. "What do they plan on doing with that?"

Its gun moved toward where we all stood, glowing like damn Hit Me Now, Please and Thank You signs.

"Crap," Archer said.

Racing across the cars, Andrew slammed his fist into the

hood of a truck. Flames erupted as he used the truck to Molotov the tank. Soldiers streamed out of the hull, scrambling away seconds before the thing blew. The M1 went up in the air like a firecracker, flinging across the Boulevard. Hitting the gardens in front of the Venetian, it rolled across the parking lot.

Heart pounding like a jackhammer, I willed the pieces of broken asphalt off the ground. I flung them toward the cops, forcing them back. Everything was happening fast. Soldiers were coming out of everywhere, and Luc was going after them, holding nothing back. Cops were coming down the Boulevard shooting at just about anything that breathed. People—innocent people—were hiding behind cars, screaming. Dee was trying to usher them off the road, out of harm's way, but they were all frozen in fear. After all, she was glowing like a damn disco ball.

Dee slipped into her human form in front of a man and woman clutching two children. "Get out of here!" she screamed. "Go! Go now!"

They hesitated a second, and then the couple picked up their kids and raced back toward the median where Ash still stood guard before Beth.

Red light streamed past my face, spinning me around. A bolt of white light arced, and I heard a body hit the ground behind me. I saw Kat before me, her pupils glowing. I turned slowly, finding a soldier on the ground, a PEP weapon by his lifeless hand.

"I can help," she said.

You saved my life. I turned back to her. *That is so hot.*

She shook her head and lifted her chin. "We need to get—Oh my God, Daemon. *Daemon.*"

My heart tripped in response to the fear in her voice. I started toward her, and then I *felt* it. I felt it deep and in every part of my being. I saw Dawson stop. I saw Andrew spin back.

Over the neon signs for Caesar's Palace and the Bellagio hotel, dark clouds moved incredibly fast, blocking out the stars. But they weren't clouds . . . or a swarm of bats.

They were Arum.

{ Katy }

Things went from bad to craptastic in a matter of seconds.

At no point from the second Daemon had announced his plan, up until the military took down the chopper full of innocent humans, had I believed that it would go down like this. All we'd wanted was to throw them off guard—to cause a little bit of chaos to make our escape.

We hadn't planned on starting a war.

Now Paris was dead and something worse than monsters under the bed was coming our way.

At no point did I doubt that the shadows racing across the sky were not here on accident. Yeah, there was a lot of Luxen mojo going on right now, but the likelihood of Arum just popping up and joining the fun? Not likely.

They were here because of Daedalus, because they worked with them.

The dark cloud broke apart, streaming across the sky like blotches of insidious oil. It dipped behind Caesar's Palace, disappearing for a second, and then exploded out of the side of the hotel. Shards of glass and debris flew into the air.

I opened my mouth to scream, but there was no sound.

An Arum came down the Boulevard, moving so fast I couldn't even say it took a second to get where it was going.

Flying over the back of the Hummer, it slammed into Andrew, lifting him several feet into the air. Ash's horror-filled scream ricocheted through me. The Arum took shape mid-flight, its skin black and shiny like obsidian. It threw Andrew like he was a rag doll and nothing more.

Another Arum shot down the strip, zipping in and around the cars. It rose, catching Andrew, and the two of them nose-dived into the Treasure Island pool.

Daemon leaped off the ground—a burst of bright light and then he was in the air—slamming into the other Arum, cutting him off from the pool. They collided, a mixture of darkness and light, rolling through the sky like a cannonball. Dawson raced forward, dodging the blasts of red light.

The Arum and Andrew resurfaced in the pool and, rear-ing back, the Arum slammed its hand into Andrew's chest. He jerked, his light flickering like a lightning bug.

I started forward, but arms circled my waist.

It wasn't a friendly hug.

Panic sliced through me as my feet were lifted off the ground just as I saw the Arum lift Andrew into the air. An-other pulse of light, and then Andrew . . . Oh God . . .

Ash's scream confirmed what I suspected. I saw her switch into her true form and then back out again, like she couldn't control it. A wave of energy rolled across the lanes.

A second later I was on my back, the air knocked from my lungs, and I was staring up into a shielded face. My breath faltered, and for a moment I had no idea what to do. I was frozen, caught between disbelief and terror. Paris was dead. Andrew was dead.

The muzzle of a strange-looking gun was pointed right at my face.

"Don't even think about moving," the muffled voice said.

My brain stopped processing things at a normal level and speed. As I stared up, my own wide eyes reflected in the tacti-cal helmet, the human part of me switched off. Rage boiled up in me, and it felt good. It wasn't fear or panic or grief. It was power.

The scream that had been building inside me, the kind of scream that left an imprint on its surroundings decades later, let loose. I don't know how I did it, but the soldier and his gun were no longer above me. All around me, vehicles rattled and slid forward, overturning. Glass cracked and then exploded, pelting the road and me with tiny shards. The little nicks of pain were nothing.

Who knew where the soldier went? He was simply gone, and that was all that mattered.

I pushed myself up, looking around. Fire poured out of Treasure Island and Caesar's Palace. The Mirage was smoking. Windows were knocked out of cars. Bodies were lying in the street. I'd never seen such destruction before, not in real life. I searched for Daemon and my friends, finding him first. He was battling an Arum, and they were nothing more than a blur of black and white. Archer was wrestling with the Arum from the pool, and Dee was pulling Andrew's lifeless body from its depths. Water streamed off her face and clung to her hair. She got him over the retaining wall and wrapped her arms around him. The scene . . . it made every part of me hurt.

I turned to where Ash was still guarding Beth. She was in her human form and looked torn between doing what she promised Dawson and going to her brother. That was something I *could* do. I could keep Beth safe, and Ash could go where she needed to be.

The military chopper circled back around, halting my progress. Archer appeared out of nowhere. The Source radiated over him like a wave of light, and he threw out his arms. A bolt of pure white light hit the belly of the chopper, sending it spinning back toward one of the casinos.

The impact was deafening, and the resulting fireball lit up the night sky.

I turned back to where he had been standing, but he was gone, like a ninja. Jesus.

Digging my toes into the cracked pavement, I eyed the path to Beth and Ash. Luc had the soldiers occupied. Or what was left of them. There was this god-awful smell that turned my stomach, and I remembered what the origins could do. Apparently, evil little fire-starters could be added to their list of freakish descriptors. I pushed out, running around an overturned truck.

Beth's head swung in my direction. Her arms were wrapped around her waist protectively. She looked terrified. I made it around a downed palm tree and was so close.

And then I was off my feet, flying backward.

I hit the side of a van; the impact rocked my body and snapped my head back. Darts of pain shot down my spine. My sight clouded as I slid to the road. Criminy. That hurt. I blinked slowly, trying to clear my vision.

Groaning, I rolled onto my side and placed my hands on the split asphalt. My arm shook as I attempted to push myself up. My insides felt rattled and rearranged. I needed to get—

Darkness crept along the edge of my vision. There was a second before I realized it wasn't because I was on the verge of passing out. Goose bumps rose along my arms. Something cold pressed along me.

Arum.

I flattened my body and wiggled under the van, seeking a few extra seconds to regain my strength and bearings. The smell of oil and fumes clogged my throat. I squeezed my eyes shut as I slid over the road, ignoring how the asphalt abraded my skin. I made it out on the other side and crawled around a sedan, gripping the bumper to lift myself.

The van started to shake, and then it slid out of the way.

The Arum stood in his human form, pale and eerily beautiful, a cold and apathetic beauty that stole my breath and repelled me. A slow, unnerving smile twisted his lips, and it was like being hit with frigid air.

He didn't speak as he raised his arms.

Air stirred around me as I stumbled backward. Behind me, the palms shook and metal groaned. Wind roared, and at the last second I ducked. The trees were uprooted, spinning toward the Arum. The car slipped out of my grasp as if he were sucking it in. A tourist brochure rack spun in the air. Pieces of the road rose up, hovered for a second, and then flew to him. There was a sharp scream that pierced my ears.

A woman was flung past me, disappearing behind the Arum. Another crumpled body joined those on the ground.

He was like his own personal black hole, sucking up everything around and drawing it to him. I was no exception. No matter how hard I dug in, my feet dragged over the ground.

His icy fingers wrapped around my throat, and he lowered his head to mine. I couldn't remember seeing an Arum's eyes before. They were the palest shade of blue, like all the color had been leeched from them.

"What do we have here?" The Arum spoke out loud. He inhaled deeply, closing his eyes as if he could taste me. "A hybrid. Tasty."

I was so not down with being an intergalactic late-night snack.

I threw my arm back, pulling on the Source, but the Arum's free hand clamped down on my wrist, his grip punishing. My heart leaped in my throat as his cold cheek pressed against mine. His lips moved near my ear, sending a shudder of revulsion through me.

"This might hurt. A little," he said, and then he laughed harshly. "Okay. It might hurt a lot."

He was going to feed.

And that little part of my brain that still functioned thought this was a hell of a way to go out. After everything—Daedalus, the guns, the bullets, and everything else—I was going to be sucked dry.

Everything tightened inside me, a mixture of fear and rage, disgust and panic. It unraveled like a compressed Slinky, lashing out from the inside.

Energy roared through me, heightened my senses. I felt the Arum against me. I felt him align his mouth with mine, a scant few inches apart. I felt the breath he took, the deep shudder of power opening up inside him. And I felt the chilling, sucking pull that reached deep inside me, digging in with tiny hooks.

I placed my hand on the Arum's chest, and that rush of energy left me like a sucker punch. There was no space between it and the Arum, nothing to lessen the effect. The Source exploded from me and immediately went into the Arum. The flare of light from me to him was intense. Energy *imploded*, throwing us apart.

The stars did cartwheels.

I hit the pavement on my side and rolled onto my back. The Arum was suspended in the air, his arms and legs spread wide. His body trembled once, then twice. A spot of light over his chest, the mark the Source had left behind, raced across his body in tiny fissures of white cracks, encompassing his entire body.

He burst into a thousand little pieces.

Holy alien babies . . .

As I staggered to my feet and twisted at the waist, my eyes met that of a young man. He looked like someone who was on autopilot, seeing everything but not really understanding what he was witnessing. I kind of sympathized with the dude. I was sure I'd had that same WTF look on my face when I saw Daemon stop the truck and realized I wasn't dealing with something human.

I probably had that WTF look on my face right now.

My gaze dipped.

In his white-knuckled grip was a smartphone. Everything—he had captured *everything* on his cell phone. Namely my face. Such a stupid thing to worry about in that moment, especially considering everything else he must've captured, but I thought of this video being loaded on the Internet, going viral like those damn Hey Girl memes.

This wasn't how I'd wanted my mom to discover that I was alive. Maybe not alive *and* well, but definitely kicking around.

But it was really too late.

I started toward the guy to get the phone, but he snapped out of it and took off. I could've run after him, but there were bigger problems to deal with.

The stench of smoke and death was everywhere. I staggered back to where I knew I had seen everyone last, using the red tourist bus as a destination, aching on a cellular level as I took in the damage. The guns—those PEP weapons—weren't harmless if they didn't hit a Luxen or hybrid. Lampposts were broken in two or melted, about to collapse. Pockets of fire lit up the entire Strip.

There were bodies littering the road.

I shuffled around them, grimacing at the melted and burned clothes, the ragged holes and scorched skin. It seemed unnecessary that there'd be so many innocent deaths. The Luxen were glowing like walking lightbulbs, and even we hybrids were pretty obvious. It was like the military didn't care how many were taken out in friendly fire. Were they insane?

And I knew how the government would spin this—that it was our fault, that the Luxen were to blame, even though they had made the first strike, taking innocent lives.

Looking at all the bodies turned my stomach, but I kept picking my way through them until I felt the warmth skittering over the nape of my neck. Lifting my head, I saw Daemon in his human form fighting hand to hand with a soldier. My heart leaped when the soldier got a right hook in, but Daemon rebounded, taking him out with one punch.

He looked over, his gaze locking onto mine. His hair was damp, clinging to his forehead and temples. His eyes glowed like diamonds. Relief shot across his face, and he shook his head, the emotion in his eyes unbearable.

There was a flare of red farther down the Strip, reminding me of how incredibly dangerous the streets still were. I took another step forward, seeing Ash and Beth rounding an overturned Humvee. I was happy to see them still standing, even though tears were flowing freely from Ash's eyes. Her brother . . .

I sucked in a breath. So much—

"Kat!" roared Daemon.

Strong arms circled me from behind. The instinct to fight and struggle kicked in, but I was pulled back an instant before a red pulse shot past right where I'd been standing. The PEP zoomed by, heading straight for Beth. I heard Dawson's enraged shout, and time slowed down until it was a near crawl. The arms around me loosened enough. Archer's voice was yelling in my ear. Daemon was running, leaping cars.

Ash spun toward Beth, moving incredibly fast, as fast as a bullet. Her arms went around the girl and she twisted, shoving Beth out of the way.

The shot hit Ash in the back.

Light exploded up her spine, following the network of veins. Her head snapped back and her knees folded under her. She fell forward, lacking the grace that always seemed natural to her.

She didn't move.

I broke free from Archer's hold, reaching her side the moment Daemon did. He grasped her shoulders, turning her over. Shimmery blue liquid spilled out of her mouth as her head flopped back over Daemon's arm.

Somewhere, a man's scream was cut short by a sickening crunch.

"Ash," Daemon said, giving her a little shake. *"Ash."*

Her eyes were fixed on the endless sky above. Part of me already knew it, but my brain refused to accept it. Ash and I would never be friends. We probably would never be upgraded to frenemy status, either, but she was incredibly strong, stubborn, and I honestly thought she'd be like a cockroach, outliving nuclear fallout.

But that beautiful human form—those painfully stunning features—faded in the soft glow that quickly dulled. There was nothing of Ash in Daemon's arms, just a shell of translucent skin and narrow veins.

"No," I whispered, staring at Daemon.

His body shuddered.

"Dammit," Dawson said. His arms were around a softly crying Beth. "She . . ."

Beth gulped. "She saved my life."

Standing beside Dawson, Dee pressed her hands to her mouth. She said nothing, but it was all etched upon her face.

"Guys, we really need to . . ." Luc appeared behind Daemon, pausing with a severe frown. "Damn."

I lifted my head, having no idea what to say. And it would be pointless if I had. A car or something exploded somewhere.

"I've got a big SUV about a block down the road—all of us will fit in it," Luc started. "We've got to go while the road is clear. They'll send more soldiers, and I won't be able to take them out again. Neither will all of you. We're running out of steam."

"We can't leave them here," Daemon argued fiercely.

Archer chimed in. "We don't have a choice. We stay here a second longer and we join them—Kat joins them."

A muscle flexed in Daemon's jaw, and my heart ached for him. They'd grown up with the Thompsons, and I knew a part of Daemon did love Ash. Not the same way he loved me, but no less important.

"I don't want to leave Paris here," Luc said, catching Daemon's eyes. "He doesn't deserve to be left behind, but we have *no* choice."

Something must've connected in Daemon's head, because he laid Ash down gently and stood. I followed his lead. "Where's the car?" he asked, his voice hard.

Luc gestured down the road.

I reached out to Daemon, and he took my hand. There had been ten of us however many minutes ago. Now only seven raced across the dark road strewn with burned-out cars, bodies, and debris. I kept my legs moving, refusing to allow myself to really think about things.

Luc had found a Dodge Journey and a truck, but we only needed one of them now. That realization sent a pang of grief through me. Archer got in the driver's seat of the Journey and Luc in the front.

"Hurry," Luc urged. "There's still some traffic up ahead, but it's moving, and the blockade is gone. People are fleeing the city. We should get lost among them."

Dawson helped Beth into one side while Daemon and I went to the other. We climbed into the very back, and Dee joined Dawson and Beth in the middle row. The doors weren't even shut before Archer peeled off.

Numbness settled into my body as I twisted in the seat, staring out the back window as we raced around cars and narrowly avoided panicked people in the streets. We were leaving the city behind—leaving Paris, Andrew, and Ash behind.

I kept staring out the back window, watching Vegas burn.

30

The ride was silent and tense. Besides the fact that all of us were looking over our shoulders, expecting the entire military to be on our tails, none of us knew what to say or if anything could be said.

Turning in Daemon's arms, I pressed my face into his chest and inhaled the rich, woodsy scent. The scent of death and destruction hadn't lingered on him, and I was grateful. If I closed my eyes and held my breath until I lost a few brain cells, I could almost imagine that we were just taking a ride in the desert.

He hadn't bothered with the buckling stuff. At some point, he had pulled me away from the back window and nestled me between his thighs. I didn't mind. More than anything, his embrace was grounding in the aftermath. And I think he needed it, too. I wished I could be inside his head, knowing what he was thinking right now.

I smoothed my thumb over the spot above his heart, mindlessly tracing odd shapes against his chest. I hoped guilt wasn't eating away at him. None of what happened— the deaths—had been his fault. I wanted to tell him that, but

I didn't want to break the silence, either. It seemed that everyone in the car was mourning someone.

I hadn't been close with Andrew and Ash, and I hadn't known Paris that well, but their deaths hurt nonetheless. Each of them had died saving someone else, and most people would never know their names or what they'd sacrificed. But we would. Their loss would leave a mark on all of us for a long time coming, if not for eternity.

Daemon's hand smoothed up my back and threaded through my messy hair until his fingers brushed the back of my neck. He shifted slightly, and I felt his lips on my forehead. My grip on his shirt constricted along with my chest.

I stretched up, my lips brushing against his ear. "I love you so very much."

His body tensed and then relaxed. "Thank you."

Unsure of what he was thanking me for, I curled against him, listening to his heart beat steadily. Every part of me ached, and I was tired, but sleep seemed impossible. Two hours in, Luc had said that heading to Arizona would be too risky and too close to Vegas. I hadn't even noticed in which direction we were heading. There was another place he had—in one of the largest towns in Idaho, something called Coeur d'Alene. Another fifteen hours from where we were.

Dee had spoken up then, asking how he had so many properties when he was barely pushing fifteen. I thought that was a very good question.

"There's a lot of money in the kind of club I run, and favors don't come cheap," he said. "So I like to keep my options open, own a couple of hidey holes around the States. You never know when you'll need them."

Dee seemed to accept the answer. And really, what choice did we have?

We stopped once to get gas somewhere in northern Utah the following morning. Dawson and Daemon went in to pick up some drinks and food, but not before changing their appearances. The rest of us stayed behind the tinted windows while Archer filled the tank, keeping his head low under a baseball cap that had been in the car.

Too anxious to sit still, I leaned forward and checked on Bethany.

"She's sleeping," Dee said quietly. "I don't know how she can sleep. I don't think I'll ever sleep again."

"I'm sorry." I placed my hand on the back of her seat. "I really am. I know you were close to them, and I wish . . . I wish a lot of things were different."

"Me, too," she said, placing her hand over mine. She laid her cheek on the seat and blinked several times. Her eyes were misty. "None of this seems real. Or is it just me?"

"It's not just you." I squeezed her hand. "I keep thinking I'm going to wake up."

"And it'll be months ago, right before prom, huh?"

I nodded, but that kind of wishful thinking was a one-way ticket to Downersville. Daemon and Dawson returned, their arms full of bags.

When Archer was once again behind the wheel, they started doling out drinks and snacks. Daemon handed me a small green bag of Funyuns. My breath was going to be kicking. "Thank you."

"Just don't try to kiss me for a while," he said.

I smiled, and it felt weird to do so, but his eyes glimmered when I did, and I knew the no-kissing rule wasn't going to last very long. Not when he had that look in his eyes.

"Did you hear anything interesting in the convenience store?" I asked, curious.

Daemon and Dawson exchanged a quick glance. I couldn't decipher it, but I was immediately suspicious when Daemon shook his head. "Nothing important."

My eyes narrowed.

He arched a brow at me.

"Daemon . . ."

He sighed. "There was a TV on behind the counter, airing live from Vegas. It was muted, though, so I couldn't hear what they were saying."

"Nothing else?"

There was a pause. "A few people checking out were talking about aliens and how they always suspected that the government was covering it up. Something stupid about a UFO crashing in Roswell back in the fifties. I honestly stopped listening."

I relaxed a little. That was good news. At least there was no mention of lynch mobs hunting down aliens. We drove most of the day, but the more miles we put between Vegas and ourselves didn't really ease the tension. It would be a long time before any of us was truly comfortable.

The first things I noticed about northern Idaho were the tall fir trees and the majestic slope of the mountain range in the distance. The town near the large, deep blue lake was small in comparison to Vegas but bustling. We passed an entrance to a resort, and I tried to pay attention to the directions Luc was giving Archer, but I sucked at directions. He lost me at "turn right at the intersection."

Another fifteen minutes or so and we were at the edge of the national forest. And if I thought Petersburg was in the middle of nowhere, I obviously hadn't seen anything yet.

The Dodge bumped along a narrow dirt road crowded with firs and other trees that looked perfect for hanging Christmas decorations.

"I think we might get eaten by a bear," Daemon commented as he stared out the window.

"Well, that might happen, but you won't have to worry about too many Arum." Luc twisted in his seat and flashed a tired grin. "This place has natural quartzite deposits but no Luxen that I'm aware of."

Daemon nodded. "Good stuff."

"The Arum . . . do you think they just happened to show up?" Dee asked.

"Not at all," Archer replied, looking in the rearview mirror for a second. He smiled a little, I think for Beth. "Daedalus has some Arum on the back burner, called out when Luxen . . . step out of line. There was this issue in Colorado, right before they caught up with you guys outside of Mount Weather. Some lady in a wrong place, wrong time situation, and an Arum was brought in."

"You met him," Luc said, glancing back at Daemon. "You know, the Arum at my club you wanted to go all He-Man on? Yeah, he was called in by the DOD to take care of one of the problems."

I looked at Daemon, who was sporting a major frownie face. "He didn't look like he was taking care of the problem."

Luc's smile turned part mysterious, part sad. "Depends on how you look at taking care of things." He paused, turning back around. "That's what Paris would say."

I settled back in the crook of Daemon's arm, planning on asking him about that later. The vehicle slowed down on a bend, and parts of a log cabin peeked out from the firs—a very large, very expensive log cabin that was two floors and the size of two houses.

Luc's bar must have been doing amazingly well.

The vehicle coasted to a stop before a garage door. Luc hopped out and loped around the front of the car. Stopping in front of the doors, he flipped open a keypad and entered a code with quick, nimble fingers. The door opened smoothly.

"Come on in," he called, ducking under the door.

I couldn't wait to get out of the vehicle as it rolled into the garage. My butt was numb and my legs a little shaky when I put my feet on the cement. Getting the blood moving again, I walked out of the garage and into the sunlight. It was significantly cooler for August, probably in the low seventies. Or was it September? I had no idea what month it was, let alone the day.

But it was beautiful here. The only noise was the chirping of birds and the rustling of small woodland creatures. The sky was a nice shade of blue. Yeah, it was pretty here and reminded me of . . . home.

Daemon came up behind me, wrapping his arms around my waist. He leaned into me, resting his chin atop my head. "Don't run off like that."

"I didn't run off. I just walked out of the garage," I said, placing my hands on his strong forearms.

His head slid down, and the stubble on his cheek tickled me. "Too far for right now."

Any other time I would've read him the riot act, complete with the diva crown, but after everything, I understood the why behind it.

I turned in his arms, forcing mine under his and around his waist. "Is everyone already investigating the house?"

"Yep. Luc was talking about one of us going back into town later and getting some food, before it gets too late. Looks like we're all going to be holed up here for a while."

I squeezed him hard. "I don't want you to go."

"I know." He reached up and smoothed my hair back off my face. "But only Dawson and I can change the way we look. And I'm not letting him go by himself or letting Dee go."

Inhaling deeply, I squared my shoulders. I wanted to rant and rave. "Okay."

"Okay? You're not going to give me evil Kitten eyes?"

I shook my head, focused on his chest. Sudden emotion crawled up, getting stuck in my throat.

"Hell must've frozen over." His fingers splayed across my cheek. "Hey . . ."

Pressing forward, I rested my head against him, and my fingers dug into his sides. One arm slipped to my waist, and he held me close. "I'm sorry," I said, swallowing hard.

"A lot has happened, Kat. There is no need to apologize. We all are doing the best we can right now."

Lifting my head, I blinked back tears. "And you? Are you doing okay?"

He stared down at me, silent.

"You don't blame yourself for what happened back in Vegas, do you? It wasn't your fault. None of it."

Daemon was silent for a very long time. "It was my idea."

My heart turned over heavily. "But we all got behind it."

"Maybe there was something different we could've done." He looked away, throat constricting. A taut pull appeared at the corners of his mouth. "The whole way here I kept thinking it over. What other options did we have?"

"We didn't have any." I wanted to crawl inside him and somehow make it better.

"Are we sure of that?" His voice was quiet. "We didn't have a lot of time to think it through."

"We didn't have *any* time."

Daemon nodded slowly, eyes narrowed and focused on the tree line. "Ash and Andrew and Paris—they didn't deserve that. I know they agreed to it and knew the risks, but I can't believe that they are . . ."

I stretched up, cupping his cheeks. The aching spread though my chest, becoming a physical pain. "I'm so sorry, Daemon. I wish there was something more I could say. I know they were like your family. And I know they meant the world to you. Their deaths aren't your fault, though. Please don't think that. I couldn't—"

He silenced me with a kiss—a sweet, tender kiss that

eclipsed all my words. "I need to tell you something," he said. "You might hate me afterward."

"What?" I pulled back, totally not expecting that comment. "I couldn't hate you."

He cocked his head to the side. "I gave you a lot of reasons to hate me in the beginning."

"Yeah, you did, but that was in the beginning. Not anymore."

"You haven't heard what I have to say."

"It doesn't matter." I sort of wanted to punch him in the face for even suggesting that.

"It does." He took a breath. "You know, when the shit started really going down back in Vegas, I had my doubts. When I saw Paris get taken out, then Andrew and Ash, I asked myself if I would've done this again, the same way, knowing the risks."

"Daemon . . ."

"The thing is, I knew the risks when I got out of the car. I *knew* people could die and that didn't stop me. And when I looked up and saw you standing there, alive and okay, I knew I would do it all over again." His bright emerald eyes settled on me. "I would do it, Kat. How incredibly selfish is that? How messed up? I think that makes me pretty worthy of your distaste."

"No," I said, and then I said it again. "I get what you're saying, Daemon. It doesn't make me hate you."

His jaw clamped down. "It should."

"Look, I don't know what to say. Is it a hundred percent right? Probably not. But I understand it. I understood why Matthew turned Dawson and Bethany over and then tried to turn us over. We'll all do crazy shit to protect the ones we love. It may not be right, but . . . but it is what it is."

He stared down at me.

"And you can't beat yourself up over this. Not when you told me I couldn't beat myself up over what happened with

Adam because of the decisions *I* made." My breath was shaky. I wanted to erase the pain in his eyes, the hurt. "I couldn't hate you. Ever. I love you no matter what. And it doesn't matter what happens in the future or what happened before this." Tears burned my eyes. "I will always love you. And we are in this together. That's never going to change. Do you understand?"

When he said nothing, my heart skipped. "Daemon?"

He moved so fast that he startled me. He kissed me again. It wasn't sweet and tender like the last one. It was fierce, intense, and powerful—a thank-you and a promise rolled into one. That kiss broke me down and then rebuilt me. His kiss . . . well, it made me.

He made me.

And because of that, I knew it went both ways. He made me. And I made him.

{ Daemon }

The trip into town with Dawson had been surprisingly uneventful. We were in and out of the market quickly. There was no avoiding the newspapers with pictures of glowing figures splashed all across them or overhearing the conversations while in line. Some of it was just plain crazy, but tension cloaked the people in the store, in a small town nestled against a lake, a world away from Vegas.

From what we could gather, the government hadn't made any official announcement with the exception of declaring a state of emergency for Nevada and labeling the "horrific actions" an act of terrorism.

Things were going to get bad. Not just from the human standpoint but from the Luxen. Many of them had no problems living in secrecy. We'd blown that right through the roof.

And then there were those who would take advantage of the chaos, like Luc had said. I couldn't help but think about Ethan White, and his warning.

It was late once we got back to the cabin, and Kat and Dee fixed spaghetti. It was mostly Kat cooking, since Dee tried to heat up everything with her hands, which usually had disastrous results. Beth had helped with the garlic bread, and it was good seeing her up and moving around. I almost couldn't remember what she'd been like before Daedalus. I did know she was a lot more talkative then.

And she had smiled more.

I helped Kat clean up afterward. She washed the dishes, and I dried them. The kitchen was outfitted with a dishwasher, something Luc had felt the need to point out, but I think the tedious task was calming. Neither of us spoke. There was something intimate about this, our elbows and hands brushing.

Somehow Kat got a cluster of frothy white bubbles on her nose. I wiped it off, and she grinned, and, damn, her smiles were like basking in the sun. They made me feel and think a lot of things, including some majorly cheesy stuff I would probably never say out loud.

She could barely keep her eyes open by the time we finished. I ushered her into the living room, and she plopped down on the couch. "Where are you going?" she asked.

"I'm going to finish up in the kitchen." I dropped an old patchwork quilt over her. "Get some rest. I'll be right back."

Heading through the rec room, I could hear Archer and Dee talking in one of the rooms. I was halfway there before I stopped myself. Closing my eyes, I cursed under my breath. Dee needed someone to talk to. I just wish it wasn't *him*.

I stood there in the dark hallway, staring at the gaudy wood paneling for God knew how long before I forced myself back into the kitchen.

Dee would not be taking him to Olive Garden. That was where I drew the line.

Grabbing the wet dishcloth, I slopped it on the table and cleaned up Luc's mess. The kid's eating habits and spaghetti didn't go together well. Finishing up, I glanced at the clock. It was almost midnight.

"You lied to Kat."

I turned at the sound of my brother's voice, already knowing what he was talking about. "You would've done the same thing."

"True, but she's going to find out sooner or later."

Picking up a bottle of water off the counter, I chose my next words carefully. "The last thing I want her to know right now is that her face is plastered all over national news. Instead of being concerned about what that means for her, she's going to worry about her mother and . . . there's nothing we can do about that right now."

Dawson leaned against the counter and folded his arms. He stared at me, and I stared back. Knowing what that look meant, the lowered brows and determined set of his jaw, I sighed. "What?" I demanded.

"I know what you're thinking."

I tapped my fingers on the water bottle "Do you?"

"It's why you're in here playing Suzy Homemaker. You're wondering what you've started."

I didn't answer for a long moment. "Yeah, I'm wondering that."

"It wasn't just you. It was all of us. We *all* did this." Dawson paused, staring out the window over the sink into the dark void that surrounded the cabin. "I would do it again."

"Would you? Knowing that Ash and Andrew would die?" Saying their names was a hot slice of pain.

He ran a hand through his hair. "I don't think you want me to answer that question."

I nodded. We'd answer that question the same way. What did that say about us?

Dawson exhaled heavily. "That's some shit, though. God, they were like family. It's not going to be the same without them. They didn't deserve to die like that."

I rubbed my jaw. "And Matthew . . ."

"Screw Matthew," he spat, eyes narrowing.

Setting the bottle aside, I watched my brother. "We sort of did the same thing, bro. We risked people's lives to keep Dee and the girls safe."

He shook his head. "That's different."

"Is it?"

Dawson didn't immediately respond. "Well, then screw us."

I let out a dry laugh. "Yeah, screw us."

His lips twitched as he looked at me. "Man, what the hell are we going to do?"

I opened my mouth, but I laughed again. "Who the hell knows? I guess we have to wait and see what the fallout will be. I need to figure out how to make Kat look like the innocent victim in this. She can't hide forever."

"None of us can," he said solemnly. Then he added, "I would pay good money to know what the Elders are thinking right now."

"Easy. They probably want our heads."

He shrugged, and a couple of moments passed before he spoke again. Whatever he was about to say, I knew he was unsure of it. His mouth worked on it for a while. "I know this isn't the best time to tell you this. Hell, I'm not sure there is a right moment for this, but it seems like after what happened to Ash and Andrew, I should just keep my mouth shut."

My muscles tensed. "Just spit it out, Dawson."

"Okay. Fine. I do need to tell you because, well, I think someone other than us needs to know." The tips of his cheekbones flushed, and I really had no idea where this conversation was going. "Especially as things start to progress and—"

"Dawson."

He took a deep breath and said two words that blew my mind. "Beth's pregnant."

My mouth opened, but there were no words. Truly no words at all.

Everything came out of Dawson in a rush. "Yeah, so she's pregnant. That's why she's been tired a lot and I didn't want her doing anything when we were in Vegas. It was too risky. And the traveling had really worn her out, but . . . but yeah, we're having a baby."

I stared at him. "Holy . . ."

"I know." His face cracked into a smile.

"Shit," I finished. Then I shook my head. "I mean—congratulations."

"Thank you." He shifted his weight.

I almost asked how Beth got pregnant but stopped myself before I asked that stupid question. "Wow. You're . . . you're having a baby?"

"Yeah."

I gripped the edges of the counter. I was struck stupid, and all I could think about were those kids in Daedalus—the origins. The children of a male Luxen and female hybrid, so rare that if Daedalus learned of this . . .

I couldn't finish the thought.

Dawson let out a shaky breath. "Okay. Say something else."

"Uh, how . . . how far along is she?" Is that what people asked under normal circumstances?

His shoulders relaxed. "She's around three months."

Damn. They must've had one hell of a reunion.

"You're mad, aren't you?" he asked.

"What? No. I'm not mad. I just don't know what to say."

And I kept thinking that in six months we were going to have a baby that could fry brain cells with a single thought if it didn't get its binky. "I just wasn't expecting this."

"Neither was I, or Beth. We didn't plan this. It just sort of . . . happened." His chest rose sharply. "It wasn't like I thought having a baby at this age was a smart thing, but it happened, and we're going to do our best. I . . . I already love him more than I've loved anything."

"Him?"

Dawson's smile was part awkward, part joyous. "The baby could be a girl, but I've been calling it a 'he.' Drives Beth crazy."

I forced a smile. He didn't seem to know about the origins. Was it possible that Beth didn't know, either? If so, they had no idea what they were about to bring into this world. I started to say something but cut myself off. Now wasn't the time.

"I know things are going to be hard," he went on. "We can't go to a normal doctor. I know that, and it scares the shit out of me."

"Hey." I pushed forward, clamping a hand on his shoulder. "It'll be okay. Beth and the . . . and the baby will be okay. We'll figure this out."

Dawson's smile of relief was evident.

I had no idea how we were going to figure this out, but women had been having babies since the beginning of time without doctors. Couldn't be that hard, right? I sort of wanted to punch myself in the face after that, though.

Childbirth scared the crap out of me.

We talked for a little while longer, and I promised to keep things quiet. They weren't ready to share the news with everyone, and I could understand that. Kat and I hadn't told anyone that we were sort of married.

Marriage.

Babies.

Aliens in Vegas.

The freaking world was coming to an end.

Still feeling a little shell-shocked, I headed into the living room. I stopped in front of the couch where Kat was curled up against the arm, the quilt bunched up under her chin. She was asleep.

Lowering myself, I carefully picked her up and placed her in my lap, her legs spread out between mine. She stirred, rolled onto her side, but remained asleep.

I stared out the window into the darkness for hours.

Now more than anything we had to do something. Not just run and hide. That was going to be damn near impossible as it was. The world knew about us now. Things would only get more dangerous from here on out.

And in a few months, we'd have a baby to worry about—a baby that could wreak all kinds of havoc.

We had to do something. We had to make a stand, change the future, or there'd be no future for any of us.

I smoothed my hand up Kat's spine, curving my fingers around the nape of her neck. Tipping my chin down, I pressed my lips to her forehead. She murmured my name sleepily, and my chest clenched with the degree of emotion I felt for her. I leaned back on the couch and stared through the window into the darkness.

The uncertainty of tomorrow loomed like a storm cloud, but there was one thing I was fairly confident of, something more ominous than the unknown waiting for all of us.

We would be hunted by the humans and the Luxen.

And if they thought exposing the truth to the world was the most extreme thing I could do to protect those I loved, they hadn't seen anything yet.

They had no idea what I was truly capable of.

31

{ Katy }

I'd been vaguely aware of Daemon coming to the couch and wrapping himself around me, but that wasn't what woke me several hours later. At some point during the night, his arms had tensed around me in a near chokehold.

And he was in his true form.

As beautiful as that was, it was also very hot and blinding.

Struggling to loosen his grip, I twisted in his embrace, squinting against the harsh glare. "Daemon, wake up. You're—"

He jerked awake, sitting up so fast I almost fell onto the floor. The light dimmed, and he was back in his human form, a bewildered expression on his face. "That hasn't happened since I was a kid—changing into my true form without realizing it."

I stroked his arm. "Stress?"

He shook his head, his gaze settling over my shoulder. His expression tensed. "I don't know. It . . ."

Footsteps pounded upstairs and within seconds, the whole crew was downstairs looking just as out of it as Daemon did. Untangling myself from his embrace, I shoved the quilt off and stood. "Something's going on, isn't it?"

Dee moved toward the window and pulled the thin curtain back. "I don't know, but I feel . . ."

"I woke up thinking someone was calling my name." Dawson wrapped an arm around Beth's shoulders. "And I was glowing."

"Same here," Daemon said, standing.

Luc ran a hand through his messy hair. In his pajamas, he finally looked his age. "I feel itchy."

"So do I," Archer commented quietly. He rubbed the side of his jaw, squinting into the darkness outside the cabin window.

I looked at Beth, and she shrugged. It seemed we were the only two who weren't feeling whatever it was that had the Luxen and origins in a tizzy.

All of a sudden, they stiffened—all of them except Beth and me. One by one, Daemon, Dawson, and Dee switched to their Luxen forms for a brief second and then resumed their human facades. It was so quick, so immediate, that it was like the sun was in the room for a moment or two.

"Something is happening," Luc said, spinning around. He headed for the front door. "Something big is happening."

He was out the door and everyone followed. I stepped out into the cool night air, sticking close to Daemon as he walked onto the gravel pathway in front of the porch and then into the grass. The cool blades were soft under my bare feet.

A strange fissure worked its way down my spine and then out through my nerve endings. A sense of awareness tightened the muscles in my neck as Luc walked farther across the patch of cleared land. The edges of the forest appeared dark and end-less, wholly uninhabitable in the darkest hours of night.

"I feel something," Beth said, her voice barely above a whisper. She glanced at me. "Do you?"

I nodded, unsure of exactly what I was feeling, but Daemon stiffened beside me, and then I felt his heart rate kicking up in his chest, jarring mine.

"No," he whispered.

A small burst of light lit up the sky far off in the distance. Air hitched in my throat as I watched that tiny speck of light travel down, a bright, smoky tail trailing behind it. The light disappeared as it zoomed behind the Rocky Mountains. Another appeared in the sky. Then another, over and over again, and they fell as far as the eye could see, like stars shooting down to Earth. The sky was lit with them, thousands and thousands of bursts of light as they entered our atmosphere and rained down. So many of them that I couldn't keep track of just how many there were, until their streaming tails blended together, until night turned into day.

Luc let out a strangled, hoarse laugh. "Oh shit. ET so phoned home, kids."

"And he's brought friends," Archer said, taking a step back as several of the speeding lights came close, disappearing among the tall elms and firs.

Daemon reached down, threading his fingers through mine. My heart jumped as they continued to fall before us. Tiny explosions rocked the trees, shook the ground. Light pulsed, lighting up the forest floor every couple of seconds until an intense light flared for several seconds and then faded out.

Then there was nothing. Silence fell around us. There were no crickets, no birds, no scurrying of small animals. There was nothing but our respective short breaths and my own pounding heart thundering in my veins.

A speck of light appeared farther back among the elms. One by one, they appeared, an endless succession of lights coming into existence. So many that I knew there had to be hundreds here just in the forest surrounding us.

"Should we be running right now?" I asked.

Daemon's hand tightened on mine, and he pulled me against his side. His arms wrapped around my body, holding me close, and when he spoke, his voice was hoarse. "There's no point, Kitten."

My heart stuttered a beat as pressure clamped down on my chest.

"We wouldn't outrun them," Archer said, his hands closing into fists. "Not all of them."

I could only stare as a bone-deep understanding settled in me. They neared the edge of the woods, taking shape. Like Daemon and every Luxen I'd seen, their forms were human-shaped and their arms and legs well defined. They were tall, each and every one of them. Their lights cast shimmery shadows as they stopped a few feet outside of the edge of the woods. One continued forward, its light brighter than the sun during summer, tinged in a deep, vibrant crimson, just like Daemon when he was in his true form.

Sergeant Dasher and Daedalus may have lied about a lot of things, but this—oh God—this had been the truth. They had come, just as Dasher had warned, and there had to be hundreds here, and hundreds of thousands elsewhere.

The light flared red again from the one in front. A pulse of energy rolled across the clearing, raising the tiny hairs along my body. I trembled, unsure of what was happening, but then something did.

Dee was the first to lose hold of her human form and then Dawson. I wasn't sure if it was confusion, fear, or something otherworldly, something in them that responded to the proximity of so many of their kind, but a heartbeat later, Daemon's arms shuddered around me, and he slipped into his true form as well.

His arms fell away from me, and it was suddenly unbearably cold without his warmth. I saw Dawson do the same and move toward his sister. The three of them stepped forward, separated from us.

"Daemon," I called out, but he didn't hear me.

He didn't respond.

Suddenly Archer was beside me and Luc was near Beth. We were backing up, but I didn't feel my feet moving or my muscles working. My eyes were trained on Daemon until the others of his kind swallowed his light.

Fear coated the inside of my mouth and turned the blood into slush in my veins. In that instant I couldn't help but think of what Dasher had said about what would happen when the Luxen came—and whether Daemon would stand with his own kind or with mine.

I wasn't sure Daemon even had a choice.

I wasn't sure I did, either.

ACKNOWLEDGMENTS

I have to give my family and friends major props for putting up with my nonstop writing and for being so understandable.

There are many people I'd like to thank who were an integral part in the creation of the Lux series and *Origin*. Major kudos to the team at Entangled: Karen Grove, Liz Pelletier, and Heather Riccio. Daryl Dixon from *The Walking Dead* also was a big help. Not sure why, but I think he and his cut-off shirt look good in my acknowledgments. Thank you to Kevan Lyon, the agent of awesome, for knowing when to go to bat for me and when to pat me on the head. Much appreciation to Stacey Morgan for listening to me ramble on about what Daemon and Kat are doing and insisting that there be more kissing. And cowbell. And country music. The last two things did not make it into the books. Cannot forget Marie Romero for helping shape *Origin* into something readable! I'm pretty sure I'd be nowhere without *Honey Boo Boo* and *Supernanny*. Another thing I'm not sure why, but why not? Thank you to Lesa Kidwiler for doing things I probably shouldn't ask her to do. Wink. Wink. Nudge. Nudge. Thank you to Wendy Higgins for allowing me to borrow from her wonderful books.

I also want to thank some people who have always been huge supporters of my writing and the Lux series: Stacey O'Neale, Valerie from Stuck in Books, the YA Sisterhood, Good Choice Reading, Mundie Moms, Vee Nguyen, the Luxen Army chicks, Amanda from Canada (because that's how I know you), Kayleigh from England (because that's how

I know you), Laura Kaye and Sophia Jordan (two awesome ladies I can talk to forever), Gaby, Books Complete Me ladies, Book Addict, Momo, and I am forgetting a ton of other people, so please don't stone me, but it's sort of late as I'm writing this, and my brain stops functioning around this time, and all I can think about is when is *The Walking Dead* coming back on?

The biggest and most important thank-you is to you—the person reading this right now. If it weren't for you, Daemon Black wouldn't be much of anything. You are the reason why I write these books, and I can never say thank you enough.

BONUS
CONTENT

Exclusive never-before-seen content from OPAL and ORIGIN . . .

SHE'S GONE

{ Daemon }

End of Opal

The proverbial shit just hit the fan inside Mount Weather. Simon Cutters? What in the hell was up with that? There was really no time to think about that, though. I could feel the dread pouring off Kat, and she was my number one concern. I needed her to keep it together.

"It's going to be okay. We're almost out of here. We got this." I smiled, and that damn organ in my chest actually squeezed when I saw her lips curve in response. "I promise, Kitten."

It was a promise I'd do anything to keep.

"Time?" Blake asked.

Matthew glanced at his wrist. "Two minutes."

Aw man, this shit was making me anxious. Two minutes. The doors slid open with a pop and thank God, the tunnel to our exit was empty.

Blake darted out first into the wide hallway, carrying Chris. Then Matthew, quickly followed by Dawson and Beth. As planned, Kat and I were the last to leave. "Stay behind me," I told her, keeping my hand wrapped firmly around hers.

She nodded as we raced forward, slowing only when Blake shifted the unconscious Luxen to his shoulder, and then banged in the code. The door opened and the darkness from the night beyond seeped in.

Blake stepped out of the tunnel and then paused. He looked

over his shoulder. Not at me. At Kat. My free hand formed a fist as I saw Kat reach with her other hand toward her nape. Awareness pricked at my skin, crawling up the back of my neck like an army of a thousand fire ants.

Then Blake smiled.

Shit.

He raised a hand and a white rope dangled from his fingers. At the end was the piece of Opal I'd given to Kat. "Sorry. It had to be this way."

Rage exploded inside me like a bottle rocket.

"Son of a bitch!" I shouted as I dropped Kat's hand and shot forward. That was it. I was going to kill him *dead*.

I'd made half the way when I felt the shiver of coldness skating over my skin. I skidded to a halt, snapping in fury.

Arum.

The shadows around that asshole deepened and spread out, slipping into the entrance and stretching over the walls and ceiling like a damn fungus straight from hell. The shadows dropped as lights exploded in a shower of sparks.

Seven of the bastards formed and then stepped past Blake and the Luxen he carried, walked right past him.

And then Blake was gone.

Fury burned inside me like a volcano erupting. This was not happening. This was not *fucking* happening.

I met the first Arum that charged forward. After shoving my hand into the Arum's chest, I slammed it back into the wall just as Dawson pushed Bethany to the side and took down the other Arum.

Fights broke out all around. Matthew shanked an Arum with a piece of obsidian and it went bye-bye in an explosion somewhere along the ceiling. Kat had tapped into the source, laying out another Arum. The asshole didn't stay down long and there was no way she could keep tapping into the source.

Turning back to the Arum I was facing, I simply ended

it—quickly. Brutally. I wheeled around, just in time to see another Arum touch her. If I thought I was pissed before, I'd been wrong, because I could taste it on my tongue.

"Daemon!" she shouted.

I spun around, catching an Arum creeping right up on me. Slamming my foot into it's chest, I knocked it back. I didn't have time for this shit. I heard the shout of the Arum Kat had tangled with and then it was up on the ceiling, doing its imploding thing. I grabbed the Arum in front of me, tossing it to the side.

We need to get out of here. Dawson sent the message to me, and I tossed a no shit look back in his direction.

I spun toward Matthew, who was picking himself off of the floor. Our gazes collided. Unease built in his eyes, and that bad taste spread in my mouth. *Remember the plan. Get Kat out of here.*

That message was sent directly at Matthew. He pushed forward, lips pressing into a firm, thin line as he nodded.

"Go! We need to go!" Dawson had a hold of Bethany and was practically carrying her out of here.

I turned, starting back to Kat, and I saw my mistake in painful detail. I'd told her to stay behind me like I was some kind of alien Hercules. She'd listened, for once in her life, she'd listened to me, and now there were too many feet between us. She was limping forward, her gaze on mine. One of the fallen Arums reached out, snapping her foot. Then she was down, catching herself with her hands as she hit the cement floor. Panic punched into my gut as she twisted onto her side, kicking the bastard right in the face.

Picking up speed, I was soon a body length from her when I heard it, when the hairs all over my body rose, and the panic spread in me like a damn virus.

Light drenched the tunnel. Locks slammed into place in an endless stream of we-were-so-screwed.

"No," Matthew cried, turning to where we'd come from. "*No.*"

Those words were on an endless repeat as I saw the movement behind Kat. Blue light flashed from the ceiling to the floor, every ten feet, over and over. One of the shields cut an Arum, slicing right into it and then it was gone in a poof of dirty dust.

Holy shit.

My heart leapt into my throat, right along with my stomach as I lurched forward, reaching for Kat as she scrambled toward me. The tips of my fingers were inches—*fucking* inches—from her and then blue stream of light smacked down right in front of my face.

Right in front of Kat.

"Shit," I gasped out as she jerked back, her hair blowing off her face from the impact of the lasers.

No. No. No.

I shook my head as I stared at her form through blue light. No. Hell no. Absolutely no.

Our eyes locked and horror poured into me, invading every cell, and the bitter twang of fear coated the inside of my mouth. I staggered to the side, searching for a way around, but there was none. She was on the other side and she wasn't alone. There were Arum and there were soldiers piling into the hall behind her. She was trapped.

She was trapped with them.

I couldn't breathe. "Kat . . ."

Sirens blasted.

No.

I shot forward, but I wasn't fast enough. It was too late. Emergency doors started to slide down from the top and the bottom. Pure panic fueled my actions. I stopped thinking as more and more of Kat disappeared behind the doors. I reached for her, determined to make it through the lasers in one piece, out of sheer will.

She threw out her hand, and I felt the source punch through the shield, smacking into my chest and pushing me back—away from the lasers. I fought the concentrated blast until arms clamped down on my waist, holding me back, pulling me away from her.

I lost my mind.

Twisting around, I slammed my fist into Matthew's jaw, but he held on, and after another punch, I gave up on him. Dragging him forward, I reached for Kat. I had to get to her, one way or another, I had to get to her.

Kat dropped to her knees, and I was a second behind her, hitting the ground as Matthew managed to bring me down. Her lower lip trembled as her chest rose sharply. Something cracked in my chest, fissured down my core. Terror I'd never known before exploded.

"No! Please! No!" My voice broke. "Kat!"

They were crowding in around her, but she never took her eyes off me. She held my gaze as I tried to shake off Matthew.

Then she smiled a little, and my chest imploded. It was weak and wobbly and frail, and a part of me died right there.

"It'll be okay," she said, her eyes welling with wetness. "It'll be all right."

The doors were almost closed as I reached out, my fingers spread. Matthew jerked me back and I braced myself with my other hand. My heart pounded as she was seconds from disappearing behind the door, seconds from being cut off from me.

My chest ripped right open and I said what I should've said days ago, weeks and months ago. "I love you, Katy. Always have. Always will. I will come back for you. I will—"

The doors sealed shut.

She was gone.

I stared at the doors, shaking my head again. "Kat? Kat!" I shouted.

"Come on." Matthew pulled me back, and struggled to his feet. "Daemon, we've got to go."

I didn't move. I was dead weight.

"Kat!" I screamed at the door, my voice breaking over the siren.

Dawson was suddenly there, grabbing my other arm, and I pulled free, swinging at him. But Matthew caught me from behind, wrapping his arms around mine, pinning them to my sides.

The look in Dawson's eyes was wild. "I'm sorry, but we've got—"

"This wasn't the plan!" I shouted in his face. "We were supposed to make sure she got out!" I twisted into Matthew's grip. "Let me the hell go. I need to get her."

"You can't," Matthew said. "We can't get to her now. Daemon, we've got to go."

The horror of reality soaked into me. "She's gone," I whispered, staring at my brother, and then I lost my shit all over again.

I broke free from Matthew and whirled toward the door. I pulled on the source, intent on blowing a hole right through it. I would get to her, one way or another I would get to her.

Matthew cursed.

Sudden pain exploded along the back of my head, and I took one step before my legs went out from underneath me. I crumbled like a damn paper bag, down for the count, seeing blackness instead of stars. My brother's face blurred into focus for a moment.

"She's gone," I repeated as my vision darkened. "Kat's gone."

And then there was nothing.

DAEMON AND KATY GO
HALLOWEEN COSTUME SHOPPING

Turning in his embrace, I cocked my head to the side. "Just the ears?"

The grin he wore now was half challenging and half sin. "Yeah. Just the ears. Absolutely nothing else. Okay. Maybe heels, 'cuz that would be sexy. It can be our own personal trick or treat. And I promise you, I'll have a big treat for you."

My mouth dropped opened.

So did the older lady who was holding a nun outfit behind him. She sucked in a huffy breath and muttered, "Well!"

Daemon glanced over his shoulder and then shrugged. "Or not."

My face flaming, I smacked him on his rock solid chest. "I can't take you anywhere."

His deep chuckle sent a shiver down my spine and he leaned in, kissing my cheek. I hurried around the rack before I turned into a total puddle of goo or we started making out in front of everyone and the baby Jesus costume.

Spotting a purple fedora and fluffy scarf, I yanked it off the rack and whirled around.

"How about this for you?"

Daemon's brows shot up. "A pimp outfit? Seriously?"

Giggling, I stuck in back in the rack and then pulled out another one. "What about this?"

"A priest outfit?"

"Well, you are so very modest."

"Ha. Ha" Daemon took the costume from my hand and put it back. "I don't think there is anything—whoa, look at that."

"What?" I turned, following his gaze. Up on the shelf was a mask with two flesh-colored plastic ears attached to a mask that was brown on one side and white on the other. I said I wasn't wearing ears or a tail, but this . . . Ooh no, this was so different. "Oh, sweet baby aliens, is that what I think it is?"

Daemon edged around me and reached up, yanking the full outfit down. Lean muscles of his back flexed under the black shirt, almost distracting me from what he held in his hands. I vhopped up to his side, clapping my hands together like a seal on crack. He was trying not to laugh. "Yep, I think it is. Or you have to pee. One or the other."

I ignored that, my eyes focused on the cute white dress with brown arms and a ring of brown fur along the bottom hem. It even came with white socks with brown trimmings.

"The official Gizmo costume," Daemon said, reading the tag. He cleared his throat. "Excuse me, the official sexy Gizmo costume. Well, that's kind of disturbing. Since when is Gizmo sexy?"

"I have to have it," I said, making grabbing fingers. "Gimme."

He handed it over, and I clutched it to my chest. I was about to make a mad dash to the cash register when I noticed pointy green ears, reptilian like, poking out from behind the rest of the Gizmo costumes.

My eyes bugged and I darted around Daemon, grabbing the costume. Whipping around, I shoved Spike, the Gremlin costume at Daemon. "You have to get this. We could be Gizmo and Spike. And you like Spike, remember? You said he was a badass."

"He is." Daemon frowned. "But this looks like pajamas."

"But it has a mohawk. Win."

"I see." Daemon shook his head, sighing. "I can't believe I'm considering this."

Considering this meant he was going to do it, probably with a lot of complaining and sulking, but he'd do it, because it was Daemon.

He'd do it for me.

Stretching up to the tips of my toes, I kissed his slightly parted lips. "Thank you."

His eyes flashed an intense shade of green as he lowered his head, pressing his forehead against mine. When he spoke, he lips brushed mine. "You're so going to owe me for this."

"You're right."

I grinned, taking a step back. Turning around, I picked up the furry black ears and faced him. "I'll buy the kitten ears too."

Daemon's lips parted. "And that's all?"

"That's all."

Turn the page for a sneak peek
at the first chapter of

Opposition

the fifth and final book in the LUX series,
releasing August 2014

OPPOSITION

(Fifth and Final Book in the Lux Series)

by Jennifer L. Armentrout

1

Katy

Back in the day, I had this plan for the off chance that I was around for the whole end-of-the-world business. It involved climbing up on my roof and blasting R.E.M.'s "It's the End of the World as We Know It (And I Feel Fine)," but real life never turns out that cool.

It was happening—everything about the world as we knew it was ending, and it sure as hell did not feel fine.

Opening my eyes, I inched back the flimsy white curtain. I peered outside, beyond the porch and the cleared yard, into the thick woods surrounding the cabin Luc had stashed in the forests of Coeur d'Alene, a city in Idaho I couldn't even begin to pronounce or spell.

The yard was empty. There was no flickering, brilliant white light shining through the trees. No one was out there. Correction. *Nothing* was out there. No birds were chirping or fluttering from leafy branch to branch. Not one sign of any woodland creatures scurrying anywhere. There wasn't even the low hum of insects. Everything was silent and still.

My gaze fixed on the woods, glued to the last place I'd seen Daemon. A deep, throbbing ache lit up my chest. The night we'd fallen asleep on the couch seemed like ages ago, but it had only been forty-eight hours or so since I'd woken up, overheated, and nearly been blinded by Daemon's true form. He hadn't been able to control it, although if we'd known what it signaled, it probably wouldn't have changed anything.

So many others of his kind, hundreds—if not thousands—of Luxen, had come to Earth, and Daemon . . . he was gone, along with his sister and brother, and we were still here, in this cabin.

Pressure clamped down on my chest as if someone were squeezing my heart and lungs with vise grips. Every so often, Sergeant Dasher's warning came back to haunt me. I'd seriously thought the man, that all of Daedalus really, was riding the crazy train into Insanity Land, but they had been right.

God, they had been so right.

The Luxen came like they'd warned, like they had prepared for, and Daemon . . . The ache pulsed, ripping the air right from my lungs, and I squeezed my eyes shut. I had no idea why he left with them or why I hadn't seen or heard from him or his family. The terror and confusion surrounding his disappearance were a constant shadow that haunted every waking moment and even the few minutes I'd been able to sleep.

What side would Daemon be standing on? Dasher had asked that of me once, while I'd been held at the very real Area 51, and I couldn't let myself believe that I had that answer now.

In the last two days, more Luxen had fallen from the sky. They'd kept coming and coming like an endless stream of falling stars and then there was—

"Nothing."

My eyes popped open and the curtain slipped from my fingers, softly falling back into place. "Get out of my head."

"I can't help it," Archer replied from where he sat behind me, on the couch. "You're broadcasting your thoughts so damn loudly I feel like I need to go sit in the corner and start rocking, whispering Daemon's name over and over again."

Irritation pricked at my skin, and no matter how much I tried to keep my thoughts, my worries and fears, to myself, it was useless to do so when there was not one, but two Origins in the house. Their nifty little ability to read thoughts got real annoying real fast.

I picked at the curtain again, watching the woods. "Still no sign of any Luxen?"

"Nope. Not a single glowing light crashing to Earth in the last five hours." Archer sounded as tired as I felt. He hadn't been sleeping much, either. While I'd been fixated on keeping an eye on the outside, he'd been focused on the TV. News all across the globe had been reporting the "phenomenon" nonstop. "Some of the news stations are trying to say it was a massive meteorite shower."

I snorted.

"Trying to cover up anything at this point is useless." Archer sighed wearily, and he was right.

What happened in Las Vegas—what we had done—had been videotaped and blasted all over the internet within hours. At some point during the day after the absolute obliteration of Las Vegas, all the videos had been pulled down, but the damage had already been done. From what the news copter had captured before Daedalus had shot it down, to those on the scene who recorded everything with their camera phones, there was no stopping the truth. The internet was a funny place, though. While some people were blogging that it was the end of times, others took a more creative approach to everything. Apparently, there was even a meme created already.

The incredibly photogenic glowing-alien meme.

Which had been Daemon phasing into his true form. His human features were blurred to unrecognizability, but I knew it had been him. If he'd been around to see that, he would've really gotten a kick out of it, but I didn't—

"Stop," Archer said gently. "We don't know what the hell Daemon, or any of them, are doing or why at this point. They will come back."

I turned from the window, finally facing Archer. His hair, a sandy brown color, was cut close to the scalp, typical military style. He was tall and broad-shouldered, someone who looked like he could throw down when it counted, and I knew he could.

Archer could be downright deadly.

When I'd first met him at Area 51, I had believed he was just a solider. It wasn't until Daemon had arrived that we discovered he was Luc's implant with Daedalus and also, like Luc, an Origin, a child of a Luxen male and mutated, hybrid female.

My fingers curled inward. "You really believe that?"

Amethyst eyes flicked from the TV to mine. "It's all I can believe at this point. It's all any of us can believe right now."

That wasn't really reassuring.

"Sorry," he replied, letting it be known he'd picked up on my thoughts yet again. He nodded at the TV before I could get ticked off once more. "Something's going on. Why would that many Luxen come to Earth and then just go silent?"

That was also the question of the year.

"I think it's kind of obvious," said a voice from the hall. I turned as Luc entered the living room. Tall and slender, he had his brown hair pulled back in a ponytail at the nape of his neck. Luc was younger than we were, around fourteen or fifteen, but he was like a little teen mafia leader and, at times, scarier than Archer. "And you know exactly what I'm talking about," he added, eyeing the older Origin.

As Archer and Luc locked eyes in a battle of the stare down, something they'd been doing a lot of during the last two days, I sat on the arm of a chair by the window. "Care to explain out loud?"

Luc had a certain boyish quality to his beautiful face, like he hadn't quite lost the roundness of childhood yet, but there was a wisdom in his purple eyes that went beyond a handful of years.

He leaned against the doorframe, crossing his arms. "They're planning. Strategizing. Waiting."

That didn't sound good, but I wasn't surprised. An ache formed between my temples. Archer said nothing as he went back to staring at the TV.

"Why else would they come here?" Luc continued as he tilted his head, gazing at the curtained window near me. "I'm sure it's not to shake hands and kiss babies' cheeks. They're here for a reason, and it's not good."

"Daedalus always believed they would invade." Archer sat back, clasping his hands over his knees. "The whole Origin initiative was in response to that concern. After all, the Luxen don't have a history of playing nice with other intelligent life-forms. But why now?"

Wincing, I rubbed my temples. I hadn't believed Dr. Roth when he'd told me how the Luxen were actually the cause of the war between them and the Arum—a war that had destroyed both of their planets. And I'd thought Sergeant Dasher and Nancy Husher, the head bitch in charge of Daedalus, were crazy freaks.

I'd been wrong.

So had Daemon.

Luc arched a brow as he coughed out a laugh. "Oh, I don't know, might have to do with the very public spectacle we put on in Vegas. We know there were implants here, Luxen who aren't that fond of humans. How they communicated with the Luxen not on this planet is beyond me, but is that really important now? This was the perfect moment to make an entrance."

My eyes narrowed. "You said it was a brilliant idea."

"I think lots of things are brilliant ideas. Like nuclear weapons, zero-calorie soft drinks, and blue jean vests," he replied. "That doesn't mean we should nuke people, or that diet drinks taste good, or that you should run out to the local WalMart and buy a jean vest. You people shouldn't always listen to me."

My eyes rolled so hard they almost fell out of the back of my head. "Well, what else were we supposed to do? If Daemon and the others hadn't exposed themselves, we would've been captured."

Neither of the guys replied, but the unspoken words hung between us. If we'd been captured, it would've sucked donkey butt and then some, but Paris, Ash, and Andrew would probably still be alive. So would the innocent humans who had lost their lives when everything went to crap.

But there was nothing we could do about that now. Time could be frozen for short periods, but no one could go back and change things. What was done was done, and Daemon had made that decision to protect all of us. I'd be damned if anyone threw him under the spaceship.

"You look exhausted," commented Archer, and it took a moment for me to realize he was talking to me.

Luc turned those unnerving eyes on me. "Actually, you look like crap."

Gee. Thanks.

Archer ignored him. "I think you should try to sleep. Just for a little while. If anything happens, we will get you."

"No." I shook my head just in case my verbal cue wasn't enough. "I'm fine." The truth was I was far from being fine. I was probably one step away from going to that dark corner in the room and rocking back and forth, but I couldn't break down, and I couldn't sleep. Not when Daemon was out there somewhere, and not when the whole world was on the verge of . . . hell, turning into a dystopia, like one of those novels I used to read.

Sigh. Books. I missed them.

Archer frowned, and it turned his handsome face a little scary, but before he could lay into me, Luc pushed off of the doorway and spoke. "I think she needs to go talk to Beth, actually."

Surprised, I glanced at the stairwell in the hall outside the room. The last I checked, the girl had been sleeping. That was all Beth seemed to do. I was almost envious of her ability to sleep all of this away.

"Why?" I asked. "Is she awake?"

Luc ambled into the living room. "I think you two need some girl-talk time."

My shoulders slumped as I sighed. "Luc, I really don't think this is the time for girl bonding."

"It isn't?" He dropped onto the couch beside Archer and kicked his feet up on the coffee table. "What else are you doing besides staring out the window and trying to sneak past us so you can go off into the woods, look for Daemon, and probably get eaten by a mountain lion?"

Anger punched through me as I flipped my long ponytail over my shoulder. "First off, I wouldn't get eaten by a mountain lion. Secondly, at least I'd be trying to do something other than sitting on my ass."

Archer sighed.

But Luc just smiled at me. "Are we going to have this argument again?" He glanced at a stone-faced Archer. "Because I like it when you two get into it. It's like watching a mom and dad have a marital disagreement. I feel like I need to go hide in a bedroom or something to make it more authentic. Maybe slam a door shut or—"

"Shut up, Luc," Archer growled, and then he turned his glare on me. "We've been down this road more times than I care to even think about. Going after them isn't smart. There will be too many of them and we don't know if—"

"Daemon is not one of them!" I shouted, jumping to my feet and breathing heavily. "He hasn't joined them. Neither would Dee or Dawson. I don't know what's going on." My voice cracked and a swell of emotion rose in my throat. "But they wouldn't do that. *He* wouldn't."

Archer leaned forward, eyes glittering. "You don't know that. We don't."

Clamping my lips together, I shook my head so fast my ponytail turned into a whip. I turned away, stalking toward the doorway before we did get knee-deep in this argument again.

"Where are you going?" asked Archer.

I resisted the urge to flip him off. "I'm going to have girl talk with Beth, apparently."

"Sounds like a plan," commented Luc.

Ignoring him, I rounded the stairs and all but stomped up them. I hated sitting around and doing nothing. I hated that every time I opened that front door, Luc or Archer was there to stop me. And what I hated most of all was the fact that they could stop me.

I might be a hybrid, mutated with all that special Luxen goodness, but they were Origins, and they could kick my butt from here to California if it came down to it.

The upstairs was quiet and dark, and I didn't like being up here. Wasn't sure why, but the tiny hairs on the back of my neck rose every time I came up here and walked down the long, narrow hall.

Beth and Dawson had commandeered the last bedroom on the right the first night here, and that's where Beth had holed herself up since he left. I didn't know the girl well, but I knew she'd been through a lot when she'd been under the control of Daedalus, and I also didn't believe that she was the most stable of all hybrids out there, but that wasn't her fault.

Stopping in front of the door, I rapped my knuckles on it instead of busting up into the room.

"Yes?" came the thin and reedy voice.

I winced as I pushed the door open. Beth sounded terrible, and when I got an eyeful of her, she looked just as bad. Sitting up against the headboard with a mountain of blankets piled around her, she had dark circles under her eyes. Her pale, waiflike features were sharp, and her hair was an unwashed, tangled mess. I tried not to breathe too deeply, because the room smelled of vomit and sweat.

I halted at the bed, shocked to my core. "Are you sick?"

Her unfocused gaze drifted away from me, landing on the door to the adjoined bathroom. It didn't make sense. Hybrids—we couldn't get sick. Not the common cold or the most dangerous cancer. Like the Luxen, we were immune to everything out there in terms of disease, but Beth? Yeah, she wasn't looking too good.

A great sense of unease blossomed in my belly, stiffening my muscles. "Beth?"

Her watery stare finally drifted to me. "Is Dawson back yet?"

My heart turned over heavily, almost painfully. The two of them had been through so much, more than Daemon and I had, and this . . . God, this wasn't fair. "No, he's not back yet, but you? You look sick."

She raised a slim, pale hand to her throat. "I'm not feeling very well."

I didn't know what level of bad this was, and I was almost afraid to find out. "What's wrong?"

One shoulder rose, and it looked like it had taken great effort. "You shouldn't be worried," she said, voice low as she picked at the hem of a blanket. "It's not a big deal. I'll be okay once Dawson comes back." Her gaze floated off again, and as she dropped the edge of the blanket, she reached down, put her hand over her blanket-covered belly, and said, "We'll be okay once Dawson comes back."

"We'll be . . . ?" I trailed off as my eyes widened. My jaw came unhinged and dropped as I gaped at her.

I stared at where her hand was and watched in dawning horror as she rubbed her belly in slow, steady circles.

Oh no. Oh, hell to the no to the tenth power.

I started forward and then stopped. "Beth, are you . . . are you pregnant?"

She tipped her head back against the wall and squeezed her eyes shut. "We should've been more careful."

My legs suddenly felt weak. The sleeping. The exhaustion. All of it made sense. Beth was pregnant, but at first, like a total idiot, I didn't understand how. Then common sense took over, and I wanted to scream, *Where were the condoms?* But I doubted that would help things at this point.

An image appeared in my head of Micah, the little boy who'd helped us escape Daedalus. Micah, the little kid who had snapped necks and destroyed brains with a mere thought.

Holy alien babies, she was carrying one of them? One of those creepy children—creepy, dangerous, and extremely deadly? Granted, Archer and Luc had probably both been one of those creepy kids at one time, but nothing about that thought was reassuring, because the newest batch of Origins that Daedalus had whipped up was different than the ones Luc and Archer had popped out of.

And Luc and Archer were still kind of creepy.

"You're staring at me like you're upset," she said softly.

I hadn't realized I was staring at her like that, so I forced a smile on my face. I knew it probably looked crazy. "No. I'm just surprised."

A faint smile appeared on her lips. "Yeah, we were, too. This is really bad timing, isn't it?"

Ha. Understatement of the lifetime.

As I watched her, the smile slowly slipped off her lips. I had no idea what to say to her. Congratulations? That didn't seem appropriate for some reason, but it also seemed wrong not to say it. Did they even know about the Origins, about all those kids Daedalus had?

And would this baby be like Micah?

My chest tightened, and I thought I might be having a panic attack. "How . . . how far along are you?"

"Three months," she said, swallowing hard.

I needed to sit down.

Hell, I needed an adult.

Visions of dirty diapers and angry, red little faces danced in my head. Would there be one baby or would there be three? That was something we never thought about when it came to the Origins, but the Luxen always came in threes.

Oh, holy llama drama, *three* babies?

Beth's eyes met mine again, and something in those eyes caused me to shudder. She leaned forward, her hand stilling over her belly. "They're not coming back the same, are they?"

"What?"

"Them," she said. "Dawson and Daemon and Dee. They're not going to come back the same, are they?"

About thirty minutes later, I walked downstairs in a daze. The guys were where I'd left them, sitting on the couch, watching the news. When I entered the room, Luc glanced at me, and Archer looked like someone had shoved a pole up some very uncomfortable place.

And I *knew*.

"Both of you knew about Beth?" I wanted to hit them when they stared blankly back at me. "And no one thought to tell me?"

Archer shrugged. "We were hoping it wouldn't become an issue."

"Oh my God." Not become an issue? Like being pregnant with an alien hybrid baby wasn't a big deal and would just, I don't know, go away? I dropped into the chair, placing my face in my hands. What next? Seriously. "She's going to have a baby."

"That's usually what happens when you have unprotected sex," Luc commented. "Glad you two talked, though, because I so did not want to be the bearer of that news."

"She's going to have one of those creepy kids," I went on, smoothing the tips of my fingers over my forehead. "She's going to have a baby and Dawson is not even here and the whole world is going to fall apart."

"She's only three months along." Archer cleared his throat. "Let's not panic."

"Panic?" I whispered. The headache was getting worse. "There are things she needs, like, I don't know, a doctor to make sure the pregnancy is going all right. She needs prenatal vitamins and food and probably saltine crackers and pickles and—"

"And we can get those things for her," Archer replied, and I lifted my head. "Everything except the doctor. If someone draws her blood, well, that would be problematic, especially given what's going on."

I stared at him. "Wait. My mom—"

"No." Luc's head whipped toward me. "You cannot contact your mom."

My spine stiffened. "She could help us. At least give us the general idea of how to take care of Beth." Once the idea popped into my head, I latched onto it. I was totally honest with myself.

Some of the reason why it seemed like such a great idea was because I wanted to talk to her. I *needed* to talk to her.

"We already know what she needs, and unless your mom has the down low on how to care for pregnant hybrids, there's not much more she can tell us that Google won't." Luc pulled his feet off the coffee table and they thumped on the floor. "And it will be dangerous to get in contact with your mom. Her phone could be monitored. It's too dangerous for us and her."

"Do you really think Daedalus gives two craps about us right now?"

"Is that something you want to risk?" Archer asked, meeting my gaze. "You willing to put all of us in danger, including Beth, all based on a hope they have their hands full? You willing to do that to your mom?"

My mouth screwed shut as I glared at him, but the fight leaked out of me like a balloon deflating. No. No, I wouldn't risk that. I wouldn't do that to us or to my mom. Tears pricked my eyes and I forced a deep breath.

"I'm working on something that will hopefully take care of the Nancy problem," Luc announced, but the only thing I'd seen him work on was the fine art of sitting on his butt.

"Okay," I said, voice hoarse as I willed the headache to go away and for the edges of bitter panic to recede. I had to keep it together, but that dark corner was looking better and better. "We need to get stuff for Beth."

Archer nodded. "We do."

Less than an hour later, Luc handed over a list of items he'd searched down on the internet. The whole situation made me feel like I was in some kind of twisted after-school special.

I wanted to laugh as I folded the piece of paper into the back pocket of my jeans, but then I probably wouldn't stop laughing.

Luc was staying behind with Beth in case . . . well, in case something even worse happened, and I was going to go with Archer. Mainly because I thought it would be a good idea to get out of the cabin. At least it felt like I was doing something and maybe—maybe going into town would give us some clues to where Daemon and his family had disappeared.

My hair was tucked up under a baseball cap that hid most of my face so the chances I'd be recognized were slim. I had no idea if anyone would, but I didn't want to take that risk.

It was late afternoon, and the air outside carried a chill that made me grateful I was wearing one of Daemon's bulky long-sleeve shirts. Even in the heavily pine-scented air, if I breathed in deeply, I could catch his unique scent, a mix of spice and the outdoors.

My lower lip trembled as I climbed into the passenger seat and buckled myself in with shaky hands. Archer passed me a quick glance, and I forced myself to stop thinking about Daemon, about anything I didn't want to share with him.

So I thought about belly dancing foxes wearing grass skirts.

Archer snorted. "You're weird."

"And you're rude." I leaned forward, peering out the window as we traveled down the driveway, straining to see among the trees, but there was nothing.

"I told you before. It's hard to not do it sometimes." He stopped at the end of the gravel road, checking both ways before he pulled out. "Trust me. There are times when I wish I couldn't do it."

"I imagine being stuck with me the last two days has been one of them."

"Honestly? You haven't been bad." He glanced at me when I raised my brows. "You've been holding it together."

I didn't know how to respond to that at first, because since the other Luxen had arrived, I felt like I was seconds from shattering apart. And I wasn't sure what exactly was keeping me together. A year ago, I would've freaked out and that corner would've been my best friend, but I wasn't the same girl who had knocked on Daemon's door.

I would probably never be that girl again.

I'd been through a lot, especially when I'd been in the hands of Daedalus. Things I'd experienced that I couldn't dwell on, but the time with Daemon, and those months with Daedalus, had made me stronger. Or at least I liked to think that it did.

"I have to keep it together," I said finally, folding my arms around me as I stared at the rapidly passing pines. "Because I know Daemon didn't lose it when I . . . when I was gone. So I can't, either."

"But—"

"Do you worry about Dee?" I cut him off, turning my attention fully on him.

A muscle thrummed along his jaw, but he didn't respond to that, and as we made the quiet trip into the largest city in Idaho, I couldn't help but think that this wasn't what I really needed to be doing. That instead, I needed to do what Daemon had done for me.

He had come for me when I'd been taken.

"That was different," Archer said, cutting into my thoughts as he turned toward the closest supermarket. "He knew what he was getting into. You don't."

"Did he?" I asked as he found a parking space close to the entrance. "He might have had an idea, but I don't think he really knew and he still did it. He was brave."

Archer cast me a long look as he pulled out the keys. "And you are brave, but you are not stupid." He opened the door. "Stay close to me."

I made a face at him but climbed out. The parking lot was pretty packed, and I wondered if everyone was stocking up for the upcoming apocalypse. On the news, there'd been rioting in a lot of the major cities after the "meteorites" fell. Local police and military had locked it down, but there was a TV show called *Doomsday Preppers* for a reason. For the most part, Coeur d'Alene appeared virtually untouched by what was happening, even though so many Luxen had landed in the nearby forests.

There were a lot of people in the store, though, their carts stacked high with canned goods and bottled water. I tried to keep my gaze down as I pulled out the list and Archer grabbed a basket, though I couldn't help but notice no one was grabbing toilet paper.

That would be the first thing I grabbed if I thought it was the end of the world.

I stuck close to Archer's side as we headed to the pharmacy section and started scanning the endless rows of brown bottles with yellow caps.

Sighing, I glanced down at the list. "Couldn't this crap be in alphabetical order?"

"That would be too easy." His arm blocked my vision as he picked up a bottle. "Iron on the list, right?"

"Yep." My fingers hovered over folic acid and I picked it up, having no idea what the hell that even was.

Archer knelt down. "And the answer is yes to your earlier question."

"Huh?"

He looked up through his lashes. "You asked if I was worried about Dee. I am."

My fingers tightened over the bottle as my breath caught. "You like her, don't you?"

"Yes." He turned his attention to the oversize bottles of prenatal vitamins. "In spite of the fact that her brother is Daemon."

As I stared down at him, my lips twitched into the first smile since the Luxen had—

The boom, like a sonic clap of thunder, came out of nowhere, shaking the rack of pills and startling me into taking a step back.

Archer stood fluidly, his shrewd gaze swinging around the crowded market. People stopped in the middle of the aisles, some hands tightening on their carts, others letting go, the wheels creaking as the carts slowly rolled away.

"What was that?" a woman asked a man who stood next to her. She turned, picking up a little girl who had to be no more than three. Holding the child close to her bosom, she spun around, her face pale. "What was that—?"

The clap of sound roared through the store again. Someone screamed. Bottles fell from the racks. Footsteps pounded across the linoleum floor. My heart jumped as I twisted toward the front of the store. Something flashed in the parking lot, like lightning striking the ground.

"Dammit," Archer growled.

The tiny hairs on my arms rose as I walked toward the end of the aisle, forgetting all pretense of keeping my head down.

And the sound came again and again, rattling the bones in my body as streaks of light lit up the parking lot, one after another after another. The glass window in front cracked, and the screams . . . the screams got louder, snapping with terror as the windows shattered, flinging glass at the checkout lanes.

The streaks of blinding light took form in the parking lot, stretching and taking on legs and arms. Their tall, lithe bodies tinged in red, like Daemon's, but deeper, more crimson.

"Oh God," I whispered, the bottle of pills slipping from my fingers, smacking off the floor.

They were everywhere, dozens of them. Luxen.

Check out more of Entangled Teen's hottest reads . . .

THE WARRIOR

A Dante Walker novel by Victoria Scott
May 2014

Dante is built for battle, Dante's girlfriend, Charlie, is fated to save the world, and Aspen, the girl who feels like a sister, is an ordained soldier. In order to help Charlie and Aspen fulfill their destiny and win the war, Dante must complete liberator training at the Hive, rescue Aspen from hell, and uncover a message hidden on an ancient scroll. The day of reckoning is fast approaching, and to stand victorious, Dante will have to embrace something inside himself he never has before—faith.

PERFECTED

by Kate Jarvik Birch
July 2014

Ever since the government passed legislation allowing people to be genetically engineered and raised as pets, the rich and powerful can own beautiful girls like sixteen-year-old Ella as companions. But when Ella moves in with her new masters and discovers the glamorous life she's been promised isn't at all what it seems, she's forced to choose between a pampered existence full of gorgeous gowns and veiled threats, or seizing her chance at freedom with the boy she's come to love, risking both of their lives in a daring escape no one will ever forget.

ANOMALY

by Tonya Kuper

November 2014

What if the world isn't what we think?
What if reality is only an illusion?
What if you were one of the few who could control it?

Yeah, Josie Harper didn't believe it, either, until strange things started happening. And when this hot guy tried to kidnap her . . . Well, that's when things got real. Now Josie's got it bad for a boy who weakens her every time he's near and a world of enemies want to control her gift. She's going to need more than just her wits if she hopes to survive much longer.

PSI ANOTHER DAY

by D.R. Rosensteel

May 2014

By day, I'm just another high school girl who likes lip gloss. But by night I'm a Psi Fighter—a secret guardian with a decade of training in the Mental Arts. And I go to your school. And I'm about to test those skills in my first battle against evil. Unfortunately, so do the bad guys. My parents' killer has sent his apprentice to infiltrate the school to find me. And everyone is a potential suspect, even irresistible new kid, Egon, and my old nemesis-turned-nice-guy, Mason. Fingers crossed I find the Knight before he finds me . . .

THE WINTER PEOPLE

by Rebekah L. Purdy
September 2014

Salome Montgomery is a key player in a world she's tried for years to avoid. At the center of it is the strange and beautiful Nevin. Cursed with dark secrets and knowledge of the creatures in the woods, his interactions with Salome take her life in a new direction. A direction where she'll have to decide between her longtime crush Colton, who could cure her fear of winter. Or Nevin who, along with an appointed bodyguard, Gareth, protects her from the darkness that swirls in the snowy backdrop. An evil that, given the chance, will kill her.

SCINTILLATE

by Tracy Clark
January 2014

Cora Sandoval's mother disappeared when she was five and they were living in Ireland. Since then, her dad has been more than overprotective, and Cora is beginning to chafe under his confines. But even more troubling is the colorful light she suddenly sees around people. Everyone, that is, except herself—instead, she glows a brilliant, sparkling silver. As she realizes the danger associated with these strange auras, Cora is inexplicably drawn to Finn, a gorgeous Irish exchange student who makes her feel safe. But then she meets another silver-haloed person and discovers the meaning of her newfound powers and their role in a conspiracy spanning centuries—one that could change mankind forever . . . and end her life.

About the Author

Kody Keplinger was born and raised in a small Kentucky town. During her senior year of high school, she wrote her debut young adult novel, which has since been adapted into a major motion picture. She is the author of many other books as well, including the middle-grade novel *The Swift Boys & Me*. Her books have landed on the *New York Times* bestseller list, the *USA Today* bestseller list, and the YALSA Top Ten Quick Picks for Reluctant Young Adult Readers list, and have been nominated for numerous awards. Kody lives in New York City, where she teaches writing workshops and continues to write books for kids and teens. You can find more about her and her books at kodykeplinger.com.